ARIANRHOD'S LINE

The Pirates' Web – Book Three

SANDI CAYLESS

www.sunskerrypress.com

www.sunskerrypress.com

CONTENTS

1: A WAKE-UP CALL

The captain of the *PSS Arianrhod* scanned the depths of the *Half Moon in a Puddle* from her viewpoint at the bar. Several ships of the PSS fleet were in the Web, that vast mercantile grid of docks that lit up the sky over Merkat Three like Armageddon, and she spotted two crews other than her own among the *Half Moon's* clientèle. She waved to her first mate, seated at a corner table with no-one at her back and a good view of the entry. The commander had company, and the captain groaned as she turned back to the bar and its hovering proprietor.

"Set me up a tab, Ally, and make my ale a large one," she said. "And another for Commander Apnis, I see she's drained her pot. How long have Fleetskup and Buntle been in?"

"A few minutes," Ally replied as he dealt the goods. "*Tallulah* came in two days ago. Captain Fleetskup's promoted his chief tactical officer to first mate, though he's only been lieutenant commander for less than a year, Mr Buntle said," he added. "Doesn't want a repeat of the last one, I guess. But *Tallulah's* still short-handed; with new trade ships coming online and the expansion of the charted galaxy to beyond zone Mu, competition for crews must be tough."

Captain Cinnabar Ahxenta accepted the news with a nod and made off to join her mate and the two from the *Tallulah*. Numerous pairs of beady eyes tracked her progress, two of which belonged to a brace of topers in a wall booth with one of the best views in the house.

"Wonder how long *Arianrhod's* stopping in, Malty," one of the two mused as he took a sip from his mug. "She was out by Alto Finglas last I heard, swopping insults with the ISP over unpaid bills."

"How did you hear that?" his friend enquired. "I've heard nothing and I spoke to her senior navigator only this morning."

"You don't ask any of *Arianrhod's* crew about their business," was the sibilant retort. "None of them will tell you, 'cos if they did, Captain Ahxenta would have their ears, and then she'd have yours. I got it from an ensign off the *Tallulah*, a new blood she picked up at Milkit Major. He was wet behind the ears and didn't know not to talk ship's business off-ship, even if you've had a few."

"He'll learn, Jurry my lad; or maybe he won't, given the *Tallulah's* his ride," Malty replied. "But how did *he* find out?"

"Tallulah Tommy's big mouth," said Jurry, squinting at the table where the privacy shield's glow and visible jammers implied that those seated discouraged intrusion. He quickly looked away when he caught Ahxenta's icy eyes on him. "Pinch of salt with anything Tommy Buntle says; another lesson *Tallulah's* crew has to learn," he slurred. "But I heard *Arianrhod* was in a dust-up with two Treskk heavy cruisers off Brown Amber not long ago and routed the pair of them. It was said to be payback for the trouble she caused a gang of Treskk shady dealers here, helping to put them and their slimy mates out of business. Some people never learn that you don't take on the *Arianrhod* and win."

The hollow tale of her clash with the finance wing of the Interstellar Systems Protectorate had reached Captain Ahxenta's ears and she was justly irritated. Her affairs she did not intend to share with any outside her own, and as subtle probing by Buntle alerted her to a likely source of the rumour, she was quick to quash it and to state in concise terms the fate of any she caught broadcasting it.

"You know how these things spread, Captain," Murmur Fleetskup said sonorously. "And trade's testing just now, with these Starfall ships beyond the mapped zones under the TA flag, *and* more coming in. It's hard times, with trade and crew shortages across the board. I still have posts to fill aboard *Tallulah*. You've had more dealings with the Starfall fleet than most: are they as fast and cut-rate as people say?"

"I'm not privy to their methods or their business strategy," was the coolly acid response.

"The expanding galaxy's big enough for us all, Murmur, don't you think?" Tallica Apnis cut in. "And there's plenty trade if you look for it. It's what you pay your supercargo and his team for. With rebuilding going on all over the mapped zones *and* all the mop-up after the war, large carriers like ours are always in demand."

A rising tide of noise among the crowd in the *Half Moon* despite the muting effect of the privacy shield caused the four to look round. The entry's holo veils had lifted to allow entry to two dark-clad individuals, who looked about stonily as they made for the bar.

"They still cause all the heads in the place to turn when they show up, Cap," Apnis remarked. "Maybe it's their natural charm makes them so easy to spot. *Kel'Moth* must be in, though I didn't notice her on the list of ships due. You think it's this meet with the Trades Alliance?"

"No, Thal wouldn't go out of his way for the TA. He's spotted us," Ahxenta said, returning the salute of the aloof Captain Vexin Thal with a nod and a mimed invitation to join them.

"Why are you asking him over?" Fleetskup demanded in alarm.

"Because he's an acquaintance and a fellow PSS commander. And he doesn't bite, most of the time," she added sardonically.

"Doesn't drink either, and knows a rogue when he sees one," Apnis added for Buntle's benefit. "That's his first mate, Marlin Seer," she edified the two from the *Tallulah*. "He drinks *and* he bites."

Fleetskup's appalled face gave her a moment's glee as the two hove up and sat. The *Kel'Moth* was on layover for two days to take on cargo, Thal replied to Ahxenta's enquiry. Buntle's query on the nature of the freight met with narrowed eyes and a retort that it was not his concern. Thal did say that he had come via Keystone Kell from his home port of Starfall, before which he had been at Telzilt. That name still made his lips twitch, Ahxenta noted, as Fleetskup's sedate tones broke in to ask Thal's opinion of the current state of trade and give his own.

"Here's trouble," Apnis warned minutes later as the muted hum beyond the privacy shield swelled. "Hope Ally's back-up is about."

Their table was the target of every eye, but no-one had been so rash as to intrude. The advancing trio were Treskk and no friends of hers, Ahxenta knew. They were well-oiled: when sober none of them would have had the guts to take on officers of the *Arianrhod* or the *Kel'Moth*.

"We want a word with you," was the garbled greeting to Ahxenta from the character in the van when they reached her.

"So talk. I can hear you."

"Your damn ship hit two of ours off the beacon at Brown Amber twelve days ago," the man accused.

"Really?"

"You left them flak. They belonged to my kin. I'm here to collect."

"Really?" Ahxenta repeated, undoing the phase rifle strapped in her leg sheath as two of her crewmen at nearby tables stood quietly.

"Break it up, people, and sit," a voice ordered at their backs.

The rearguard of the trio was swift despite his tipsy state, and spun round to aim a punch at the waitress. She was ready, grasping his raised arm and twisting it viciously to jerk him off his feet to the ground. She laid him out with a calculated kick to his temple. By that time the other two were down, for Ahxenta's fist had connected with one dribbling jaw and Apnis' phase rifle had stunned the second.

"Just once it would be nice to have a quiet drink without these high jinks," *Arianrhod's* first mate remarked. "Best get your hands under a steriliser, Cap, he looked to be a messy drinker. And if you need crew, Murmur, Ms Munnet there would make you a handy security officer."

"I'll call Merkat security," Wekki Munnet announced dryly, with a sidelong look at Apnis. "You want to press charges, Captain?"

"No," Ahxenta said as she made to heed her first mate's sage advice. "They've probably got enough against them already to lock them away for a while. I'm sure you'll see to it. I'll be back," she told the others.

"What was that about Brown Amber?" Fleetskup burbled to Apnis.

"Two Treskk war cruisers tried to waylay us off the Amber beacon. Their mistake," she told him as she re-sheathed her sidearm. "We sent an advisory over the Ultraviolet III and local nets in case there were more nearby looking for trouble. Didn't you get it?"

"Obviously, but I skimmed it. I'd other priorities," he said evasively as the crowd settled and two of Ally's guards rolled up to eye the scene.

"Put them in restraints," Apnis advised, pointing. "They'll do until Merkat security gets in."

It was fifteen minutes before order was restored and the three taken off, by which time Thal and Seer had left, with a word from the former to Ahxenta that he would contact her privately later. The two from the *Tallulah* proved harder to shift but they finally set off, after having told of meeting Captain Mikbeam of the *Urania* at Delta Iridium, his home port. His ship had been buzzed by two strange fighters off Delta's Iris Three outpost. Local authorities had been alerted, but as deep scanning had been the only incursion, he had not reported it widely.

"What does Thal want to say that he wouldn't mention in front of Fleetskup and Buntle?" the first mate asked once the coast was clear.

"No idea. But he's been trading at Telzilt, so beyond current zone edges. I expect his trade fleet is still spreading its wings. He *has* the nav-charts to do it," Ahxenta responded.

"As do we, thanks to Azular's precious shuttle," Apnis noted. "The great beyond *is* being charted by the ISP and others, and those charts will be linked to the ones the ISP can lever out of the new allies it's chatting up, Norvalla and Telzilt to name but two. The TA wants more of us out there, as it means bigger profits for it, *and* dibs on new tech. That's maybe what the meet tomorrow is about. You plan to go, Cap?"

"We'll both be going. Senior officers of all the Privates in port that fly the TA flag, the note said. But no other TA trading partners. And you may be right: the ISP and its chums are fixing to send out explorers with first contact mandates to sectors past Alpha, Theta and Iota zones as well as Mu. Telzilt and Norvalla are talking to the ISP, Coalition, Non-Treaty and United Independents coterie, because of alien trouble after the major hostilities of the war *and* the help given by certain ships of our acquaintance out that way."

"Major hostilities," Apnis repeated. "War's not over yet, not by a long way. We still hear stories of attacks that can't be pinned on raiders or scum like the Treskk. But how do you know the ISP's grand Alliance plans to send out explorers? Surely they wouldn't tell the likes of us? Anyhow, I'd have thought they'd all still be licking their wounds after the last big bust-up and would hardly have the ships or the credit."

"They'll be ISP ships already tasked with that remit. Azular heard it from Captain Kerrix, who'll have got it through her second mate. As an ex-ISP Intelligence agent, I bet Levettiza still has links to her old unit and is in some info loop. And Azular gets updated star charts far more often from Kerrix than we do from the TA or the ISP."

"Starfall will get them too, as the *Moonstone's* part of it. Kerrix runs a tight ship and is loyal to her own; but giving out data like that would *have* to be on Levettiza's say-so. Maybe I shouldn't have told Fleetskup to take on Munnet. Not that she'd go, but why is she still here?" Apnis whispered. "I'd have thought that with the breakup of local corruption rings and the shutdown of the hostile ops base here, she'd be sent off. ISP's Intelligence Division can't have so many agents that it can leave some in place. It would increase the risk of their cover being blown."

"That's not a topic for here, despite jammers," the captain warned. "And we'd better get aback aboard – Lindell and Perla Jute should have finished in marketing. It's almost the close of trading hours."

"Must be: Nat Holdspan, Sol Treskitt and their super have come in and I bet that's where they've been… what in hell's happened to Nat?"

The shock in her voice caused Ahxenta to turn. The captain of the *Nyx Warrior* had clearly met trouble: he was walking stiffly, had one arm strapped, and the heavy sheen of his uniform hid inbuilt support, Ahxenta was sure. She waved as he looked over and indicated her table, giving a negative to his mimed offer of more drinks.

"We won't get back aboard at this rate," Apnis murmured. "But what's happened? Nat's one of the savviest captains in the fleet for all he's young and he's got one of the best-equipped ships with the latest tech – almost up to our standard. He's attracting plenty eyes from the other PSS crews in, so they must be in the dark. Here he is. I'll alert Lindell that we'll be late and tell him to hang fire until I link again."

Captain Nathan Holdspan greeted the two calmly, the only sign of his hurts a grimace of pain as he sat in response to Ahxenta's invitation.

"What happened, Nat?" *Arianrhod's* captain asked with customary bluntness. "You've seen some action."

He smiled painfully, looked around and tapped the jammer on the table. "The *Warrior* did, twenty one days ago standard," he admitted in a low voice as he hauled out and set down his own jammer. "This isn't common knowledge, Captain, and the ISP has asked me to keep it that way until it releases the details, any time now," he said starkly. "Against my wishes, I have to say. I trust I can count on your discretion?"

"Of course," Ahxenta responded, with a warning nod to Apnis.

"We met a huge ISP battleship off Idledott beacon, on the way out of Silverglass Station. We'd dropped cargo," he told her, with another glance round. "She read as the dreadnought *ISPS Revenge*, and naturally we checked her credentials and her spec before we made contact. She was listed as currently under refit, but being ISP, we got no more. The ship off our bows was shielded, but we'd picked up a call-sign and a hint of weaponry. We sent a courtesy hail as we turned for the bypass but got no response. We tried again, still no answer: that rang alarm bells. My science officer's scans of her hull read off-beam: shifting readings that rang false. I ordered a probe in and called red alert – just as well. My tactical team caught a power build-up and more science scans read hull inclusions with trace zukivianite. That was enough for me and we set for battlestations."

"Zukivianite!" Apnis echoed as the *Warrior's* first mate Sol Treskitt and supercargo Ettis Book, turned up with drinks. Treskitt placed one for his captain and sat, glancing at the two jammers on the table.

"Yes," Holdspan continued once the privacy shield had reformed. "I remember the trouble the *Obsidian* had with self-directed drones that attached to her, destabilised her systems and breached her hull plates. That was at Barfit, close by Silverglass. You passed the details of the attacking ships to the fleet and the ISP, Captain; and *you* met similar at Brown Amber and at Merlin later, I think. And we had the data we got when both our ships took a hand in the clash that the *Tallulah* had with two similar blips by Silverglass. My science officer took the inclusions to be limpet drones. By then the *Revenge* had turned and was powering weapons. I ordered us in: we were too close to attempt a run and there were no other ships nearby. It's all right, Sol, this won't go any further," he added, aware of the uneasy expression on Treskitt's face.

"We sent a distress: she'd cut her external projection and now read hostile. She'd a huge net of detachable drones and more firepower than any ISP dreadnought ever had. We held our own but they let go a big cluster of drones. Five hit us before my gunners could stop them. And they weren't the same as those that got the *Obsidian*: they shot through my hull as if it was paper, so they'd been coded to breach on contact. And they were capable of more than destabilising our tech. They were pre-set for self-defence and could send out bolts that would take down an armoured defence bot," Holdspan said bitterly.

"We had two fatalities," Sol Treskitt put in quietly.

"My people held them off with everything we had – at least we *could* track their progress through the ship. And then two other ships reading ISP jumped in; these were the real articles and had massive firepower. I found out later they'd been tracking the hostile but it had got a start on them. The *ISPS Repulse* was the lead ship," he smiled mirthlessly.

"Myrtleberry," Ahxenta stated.

"She *was* in command," he agreed. "And her ship's been fitted with all the ISP can throw at it. Their mission was to capture the hostile, not destroy it. They did, very efficiently, which gave us time to track down and finish the last drones aboard the *Warrior*. Hence my injuries."

Ahxenta and Apnis traded glances. That was typical of Holdspan: he would take the lead in any danger that threatened his crew.

"My condolences on your losses," *Arianrhod's* captain said softly. "I heard zip on PSS channels. It's not like you to hold back on a report."

"No. Colonel Myrtleberry contacted me the instant they'd got the blip tied up. She said that the ISP was concerned that the ship wasn't a one-off and wanted to make sure that no word of its capture got into unfriendly ears until they found out more. The *Repulse* escorted us back to Silverglass. The colonel used her clout to have the *Warrior* repaired at ISP expense and my crew's injuries attended to, providing I held back on my report until ISP HQ released an official report."

"You argued the toss," Ahxenta guessed.

"I did, and Myrtleberry agreed to send out the official report as soon as possible. *And* she has influence. But my ship and my crew had taken a pasting and Silverglass was the only suitable place in the sector."

"Cleft stick," Apnis said gently. "Myrtleberry's an expert at getting her own way and tricksy to boot; she'd figure the best way to attack."

"Naturally we'll say nothing, even to our own, Nat," the captain of the *Arianrhod* told the troubled young commander. "There *is* one thing you should know, and it's something that it won't be wise to spread about, particularly near ISP ears: Colonel Ellin Myrtleberry is the ISP's version of an info-sent. We know but we can't prove it, and she sure as hell would deny it, but be aware if she crosses your path again. She's probably not the only one in ISP, but I bet she's the most challenging. If she *does* contact you and tries to provoke you, don't rise to the bait; keep your cool and stick to your guns."

"I *did* find her overbearing," he admitted.

"And as a favour Nat, I'd like the readings you got on the hostile and its attached tech. At your discretion of course," Ahxenta added.

"I'll make sure you get them, Captain. I'll set things in motion when

I get back to my ship. And thank you for your information."

"Any time, Nat. And now we have to go. I've more to do before the end of the day." Ahxenta squeezed his sound arm in sympathy as she rose. "See you again," she added to the other two officers.

"Wonder what that was about," Jurry whispered to his mate from their dark lair, where the two had been eyeing the action through the privacy shield's haze. "It looked serious and Holdspan's been through the mill. If we could get *that* story, it should be worth a jar or two."

"Don't even think of asking," his mate counselled. "You'd be worse hurt than Nat Holdspan once they'd finished with you. But we'll keep our noses to the ground. Something's bound to crop up in a day or so. We'll see a few of the *Warrior's* crew in, I'll be bound."

Ahxenta and Apnis were silent on their way to their shuttle, berthed in green twelve and several levels below the *Half Moon*. The first mate linked to tell their supercargo they were in transit and by the time they arrived, Lindell and his second, Ensign Perla Jute, were there.

Once aboard, Ahxenta made for the bridge. Everything was in trim, duty officer Lieutenant Mitt Snow stated as he released command. The captain sat and pulled her ops board over to confirm ship's status and the constantly updating summary of traffic in and out of the Web.

Apnis slid in alongside. "*Warrior* got here five hours ago," she noted quietly. "Nat was quick off the mark to get to marketing, then. Wants to keep things as normal as possible for his crew, I guess."

"How many will turn up for this Trades Alliance meet tomorrow, I wonder?" Ahxenta asked, with a sharp glance that warned Apnis to curb her tongue. "Thal's here still, but may give it a miss. Fleetskup will be there, with his new first mate, if Ally's news is accurate."

"Given that Tommy Buntle was the source, it may not be. But who *is* the *Tallulah's* chief tactical officer? I don't recall him."

"We'll find out. But *Green Comet*, *Hexameter*, *Firedrake* and *Nova Stella* are in as well as the *Nyx Warrior*, *Tallulah* and *Kel'Moth*. The *Pearl Shield's* gone, but I expect the TA vis-record will be sent round. I need to see Lindell about the deals he's agreed with our clients. And I want a word with Azular. You hang here until the next watch comes on. If anything comes in, let me know – especially that link from Captain Thal."

"Roger that, Cap," Apnis acknowledged.

Ahxenta's visit to the supercargo's office was dealt with rapidly, after which she tracked Azular to his lab. She wanted the latest that her Berzic senior science officer had on the exodus of a fleet of explorer ships as a joint venture between the ISP and its major allies. It seemed risky, with recent hostilities barely over and limited but deadly action still likely. Incursion from outside the historic limits of the charted galaxy was also a worry, despite the expansion of those margins and rumours of the merger by treaty of new sectors.

"Shouldn't you be on the bridge?" the captain greeted him.

"I'm monitoring my station from here, ma'am, and upgrading our nav-charts, which is a simpler process from this console," he replied equably. "I've set updating to continuous, to link in tactical and science data as our hull sensor arrays receive it."

"I thought you and Crizz Cottontail were working on the decoy's cloak. Talking of which, *Arianrhod's* cloak could use an overhaul; with all the new tech on line, it's too easy for other vessels to get past it."

"I'm aware of it, Captain, and Lieutenant Greffy's listing potential upgrade areas. And the chief's busy with main engine repairs, owing to our clash with the Treskk. She's had to realign all the sensors in fusion reactor two and she reckons the core's outer sheath is buckling."

"I got her report. And I saw from the comms log that a private link from Captain Kerrix came in for you five hours ago. Anything in it I should know about? Tallica and I have the TA meet at oh nine hundred and their reps haven't sent an agenda, which leads me to think they're up to something. Maybe about trade links, or opening bypass routes off charted edges to regular traffic: the node that Captain Thal's lot call Starfall Exit is a main entry to a bypass that runs clear from the Curtain Nebula to that beacon at K457:003, but Thal and his fleet have got it sewn up. I'm waiting for a link from Thal. It may concern that – he hasn't given me a clue. And then there's the snippet you gave me about ships with first contact directives to explore beyond Alpha, Theta and Iota? It strikes me that the ISP is stretching itself if it thinks it can equip the likes of those without help. If they're anything like Commander Levettiza's last ship, the *Advance*, they'll not be economy class."

Azular was nodding. "The *Moonstone's* heading in," he told her. "As is the *Kel'Beth*. Their command officers will attend the meeting."

"Aha! So the Starfall fleet will be there in force. Any idea why?"

"No ma'am. But the ISP's sent out two diplomatic missions with specific mandates: to boost ISP influence and build treaties with Telzilt and Norvalla; and to bring as many of *their* allies as possible into full ISP Council membership. Which means, as happens in our zones, that they'd have to provide an agreed level of military, emergency and law enforcement support in the form of ships, personnel, equipment and stations to the whole. And they'd have to fly the ISP flag and would be called on as and when necessary for joint operations."

"And be equipped with the best of Norvallan and similar tech this side of the galactic plane," Ahxenta added wryly. "That means an ISP sector beyond Mu, which'll be a helluva area if it stretches from Kirtish to Norvalla. And it'll give the ISP a toehold on what's between. How did Captain Kerrix come by the info? ISP politics are secret, and no way would Levettiza's old mates in Intelligence let her in on that."

Azular smiled. "Captain Heltakt of the Telzilt fleet has links to his planetary authority, and his government wants to know more than it's been told by couriers and despatches. Telzilt was almost brought to its knees by years of hostile annexation; it has no capacity to subsidise an external union, however useful. And as its present authority includes many who fought a rearguard action against the hostiles, it's got no inclination to tie itself into a new alliance."

"Reasonable, but I don't see why he called Kerrix to talk it over."

"He gave evidence at her court martial," Azular reminded her. "He kept in touch: the *Twin Star* with Xanna in command, and the *Kel'Moth* and her sister ships risked everything to come to Telzilt's defence. And the Starfall fleet has trading relations with the Telziltic."

"Gratitude for leaping in," Ahxenta said tartly. "Starfall base *is* very handy for a quick trip out that way. Thal knows the sector and part of the *Moonstone's* crew is Norvallan, and her captain *is* half-Telziltic. But if this *is* accurate and the ISP's trying for first dibs on the new sectors opening up, the Coalition will cry foul because it didn't think of it first and the NTA will accuse the ISP of pulling a fast one. It'll shake their grand Alliance, despite their fancy new central office at Alto Finglas."

"That was a joint project between those bodies and the zone Mu Independents, though the ISP bore the brunt of the expense."

"To let it call the shots," the captain put in, as comms called to say that Captain Thal was on the link for a private word.

"Put it through here, Bellfish. Azular, I'd like the use of your lab."

"Aye, ma'am. I'll be in my office. I'll set privacy on the way out."

Thal's dour face materialised in the view grid and Ahxenta sat back to listen. Ninety minutes passed before the science officer was told that he could have his lab back, and despite the late hour, Ahxenta called a senior staff briefing. She and Azular made their way up to the room, where Apnis, second mate Whisper Earbleat, chief engineer Cottontail and senior tactical officer Lieutenant Pollux Gliss were waiting.

"The doc and Bellfish are on the way," Apnis stated. "Goldwash is still in medbay. The only thing we've had from the TA is a request to know if we'd attend. I confirmed. I take it the urgent link for you after Thal's call was the ISP report you were expecting?" she added. "I saw that Nat Holdspan sent a short advisory across just after it arrived."

Ahxenta nodded as the entry opened on the final two. "That's us," she said. "I've left Lindell out of the loop as he's busy with contracts. I'll update him privately later. Sit down. I'll start with the ISP link…"

The Interstellar Systems Protectorate report did concern the attack on the *Nyx Warrior* near the ISP's Silverglass holding station. Tactically placed on the border between zones Epsilon and Zeta, it was a huge, costly and well-equipped supply centre that catered for the entire ISP fleet. That the hostile had posed as an ISP ship was serious, but that it could take on a ship as technically superior as the *Warrior* and hit her with such massive firepower was worse. The limpet drones coded to pierce hull plate had been confirmed as an advance on those met with before, which had seriously damaged the *Obsidian Sky*.

"The ISP, in the guise of our pal Myrtleberry, has the ship at a secret base and is taking it apart bolt by bolt," the captain told her team. "By what's in the report, it was poorly manned; but it's not clear who or what the crew are, though they *are* classed as hostile entities."

"Not much help," Apnis snorted.

"No, but the existence of one implies more. The ISP's combing the area; there *was* a hostile base at Zeta Dixt that was taken out, and I don't have to remind you that we hit trouble at Ochre Valley and *that* turned out to have a hidden base and a shipbuilding facility."

"The ISP figures it's missed something?" Earbleat asked.

"I'm not second-guessing the ISP," was the dry retort. "But it's sent data on the ship and its ops factors *and* on ways that may help in dealing with any like it. Nat Holdspan's sent me the data his teams got before it hit and during the assault, and on the tech used to cripple the *Warrior*. He'll send it out to the rest of the fleet. Gliss and Azular, add it to our tactical and science databanks and update our hull arrays. Nat's sent data on his crew's injuries and their treatment for you, Axellina. I don't know how many of his crew are still critical but as he'd two fatalities, I expect a few took bad hits. *He* was certainly a mess when we met him."

"What did Captain Thal have to say?" Apnis asked. "It seemed to take a while and he's not normally one for a cosy chat."

"The TA contacted him. Now that some of his fly the TA flag, it's started to push. Its central council's decided that the covert bypass that his people use should be on the usual TA trade routes list. The TA's figured that the ISP's using part of it in any case, from Starfall Exit out, as it had to get its ships in place to deal with hostiles coming in; and the ISP's now opened diplomatic relations with Norvalla and Telzilt. Thal's verified that the bypass runs from a dead system by his Twilight Station off the Curtain Nebula, clear across mostly uncharted space as far as the orange star system beyond Mu that the ISP tagged K457:003. It dips into the outer edges of Delta and Zeta zones. The only settled planets near its entry points are Pollens Sentry and Wemm. There are nodes close to both, *and* the bypass cuts across a strip of Mu."

"It has to link to other routes," Azular cut in. "At the peak of their activity, the aliens could direct fleets at opposite ends of the galaxy, so there must have been ways of reaching their bases by Mellifly and the Outer Reaches. We know there are nearby bypass routes close to K457 that lead to Telzilt, Norvalla and its colonies and beyond. Perhaps the ISP has suspicions of other such routes, hence its alleged plans to send ships to explore beyond Alpha, Theta *and* Iota zones."

"That's not verified and not our concern," Ahxenta reproved. "*We* suspected that the hostiles could jump into existing hyperspace routes off the bypass from the Curtain to K457, especially where it cuts into mapped space and particularly on the cut-through in Mu; now it looks like the TA's figuring it. Thal wouldn't confirm or deny and was peeved I mentioned it, but if that bypass *has* covert crossovers to existing trade or local routes, then it raises issues."

"You mean Starfall can access trade routes that the rest of us allied to the TA can't, thus it's not a level playing field," Apnis clarified.

The captain laughed shortly. "That's not what's vexing the TA. Part of what we pay in loads levies and subs goes for upkeep and security of named hyperspace trade routes through the sectors we travel in, and Starfall ships using them do the same; and we *have* to use the routes, as does most other traffic. But the TA creams a lot off local systems close to exit and entry nodes: it bolsters local trade, especially if the TA can set up a base and trade on its own account. When part of the PSS fleet uses non-TA-listed routes to trade, the TA can't use its influence on local systems, and so loses out."

"Tough," Crizz Cottontail snorted. "The TA's excuse for charging us is that they funded a good part of bypass route-building way back, and they update and expand current routes. They can't change the rules now that there are new kids on the block that do it their way. But why was Thal bending your ears over it, Cap?"

"He knows me better than any PSS captain outside his own and wanted my views. Jesse Inks advised he contact me, as he'd sounded *him* out. The TA wants to include his bypass on its list of regular trade routes, so it wants to know every link on and off it, *and* it wants the access codes. There's been a subtle threat of revoking the Starfall fleet's rights to the TA flag if Thal doesn't comply."

"But they've only just joined up!" Earbleat exclaimed.

"There are loads of other complications. That bypass *and* others like it were and maybe still are used by hostiles, and their influences persist. But Thal's people know them and their quirks, and know the systems in local space, hence the ISP and TA interest. But if any covert bypass links into a known trade route, there could be trouble. You seem preoccupied, Azular: what's up?"

"It *could* lead to serious trouble, as Captain Thal sees. He knows of many routes that are closed to most users in the charted zones, but I don't think the TA would withdraw its flag from the Starfall fleet, as it would lose too much revenue by it and it would look weak by removing rights it's so recently given. And would risk the creation of a rival trade network: the Starfall fleet has links into the unmapped sectors and the TA wants those links. But there are other problems. Opening up routes by listing will give groups outside the law such as raiders more scope, and cause trouble in areas that have so far been free of them. But I've been looking at possible routes from what we think is the end of the Starfall bypass, Twilight, to the next known ex-hostile base by Mellifly. We can assume *that's* now part of Thal's network, as the final ex-hostile base we know, off Theta and close enough to Fivepoint and Kanelian Juxta to be of concern, is called Nexus Station by his people."

"Yes, Nat Holdspan told me way back that a ship out of Nexus jumped in when the *Warrior* ran into trouble near Kanelian with a huge beat-up hostile warship that was trying to remove his cargo pods. The commander of the Starfall ship said she'd come from there," Ahxenta said. "The ship was called the *Kel'Lath*, or something like."

"Yes, ma'am; but there's another aspect. The hostiles we met in the war, that we'd believed had been holed up in their places of power for eons before they struck out from nowhere in such a short time to take on the known galaxy, could *not* have taken over raider bases as centres. Their ships looked like known raider designs, and that's how they were first spotted, but their posts must have existed for centuries, maybe on planets near hyperspace exits. We've heard of Thal's other bases but only seen Starfall: others may be planet-based. We'd assumed that alien dens were once raider bases because they took so many raiders, but the raiders used *known* bypass routes. And many raider packs are now back in business, and they surely can't operate from Thal's bases."

"Are we getting to a point?" the chief medic interrupted. "I've been on duty fifteen hours straight and I need my rations. This briefing was meant to be on the TA meet and what it may mean for us, not history."

"Sorry, doctor, but it comes to the same thing. The TA *wants* the routes and codes the hostiles used and reckons Thal know them, as his fleet includes offshoots of hostile fleets. And as far as we know, Starfall has taken over all their known bases, and ops including shipbuilding. And Thal's reluctant to give up the details, Captain?" Azular asked.

"It seemed so to me. I can see his point: why should he give the TA all the gen? It'll muscle in and set up its own trading posts and offices to badger local systems into signing on with it for trade, and then rake in the profits. But I bet the ISP has a finger in the pie, as it will want to know all it can about bypasses that may lead it to unknown systems that might be persuaded into signing on with it, or pose a threat to the stability of the current zones where it holds sway if they won't."

"That's not the main point of my doubts of the whole thing, ma'am. I can see a possible reason why Captain Thal would be loath to disclose the route of secret bypasses to the TA or others. It strikes me that eons ago, when we guess that these bypasses were built by the ancestors of those we call hostiles, the charted galaxy would *not* have had the zone and sector system we have now; *that* was set up over time by seeding habitable worlds with small groups, and bringing in treaties on self-government, trade and so on. If these hostile centres are as ancient as we think, the links between them would have been as direct as possible. I've mapped them out, given the situation of the four known ex-hostile bases on the edge of the present galactic zones, and the one called Twilight Station, which we didn't know of before we met Thal."

Azular turned his info-pad towards the captain. "This is a possible, almost direct course from Twilight to the base near Mellifly, and this is one from Mellifly to Nexus. And then there's Lartzeg Trine, which could use most of the current route from Kanelian Juxta to Fivepoint, Marridan, Selliden and Lonagan. Marridan *was* the first world known to have been targeted by the hostiles."

"Bloody hell!" Ahxenta exclaimed.

"And if this is close to accurate, it might provide an explanation as to why the hostiles had that holding area for their ships within the Ginseng Nebula," Azular went on relentlessly. "A plausible route from Twilight Station to the base beyond Mellifly passes straight through it."

"And damn close to a lot of other places as well!" Apnis breathed. "If that's anything like accurate, the TA will choke on itself and the ISP and its allies will totally freak."

2: TRADE WARS

Early next day found Ahxenta and Apnis in a secure conference room in main marketing, reserved by the Trades Alliance. A late TA memo the night before had notified those attending and others on the way in to the Web that the agenda would be issued at the session and that two ISP delegates would report. The captain nodded to her associates and headed to a rations station. She, Apnis and Azular had already had an early meeting with Thal and Seer of the *Kel'Moth*.

Captain Sarie Jikelleli of the *PSS Green Comet* was picking up a drink and asked about the clash with the Treskk and the later spat in the *Half Moon*. Ahxenta updated her briefly; she was more focused on what the TA and their ISP guests had under their hats. Jikelleli was equally wary that it would bode ill for ships flying the TA flag. The two were joined by Bee Lyvy Coxen of the *Hexameter* and her first mate, who were musing on similar. They looked around for others who had made it in. Ma'Lappis and Poppet of the *Firedrake*, the *Nova Stella's* Maris Fleete and her mate, and Holdspan and Treskitt of the *Nyx Warrior* were close by. Holdspan's injuries caused sharp intakes of breath.

"What in blazes happened?" Coxen queried. "Something to do with the ISP alert we got and the note from Holdspan? Anybody know?"

"That's maybe why the ISP's here; as for the rest, Nat can tell you," Ahxenta parried as Apnis hove to with Ace Periwinkle of the *Comet*. "And here's Fleetskup. That'll be his latest first mate. He gets through them. He'll no doubt get huffy when Jesse Inks shows."

"Inks?" Periwinkle echoed. "Another Starfall ship in? I checked out arrivals before we shuttled over and didn't see the *Moonstone* listed, but we *were* here early for a marketing meet."

"Captain Thal said the *Moonstone* and the *Kel'Beth* were both due in," Ahxenta told him. "I guess Fleetskup's here sharp to get a good seat."

"It'll be fun around *that* table," Apnis grunted. "It's big enough to host a fleet dinner and festooned with buttons. I suppose the great and the good from the TA and the ISP will sit at the high altar under the holo-grid that those ops are playing with, well away from us in case we throw spoons at them. Here are more of ours: Djassi and Tynissel of the *Equinox* and Strong of the *Pole Star* and his first mate."

The wordy captain of the *Tallulah* ambled over to present his mate, Commander Juke Spickle. He seemed awed, but saluted the group with admirable brevity. Before Fleetskup could launch into his usual trivial nothings, Apnis nudged her captain.

"Starfall's here in force," she said in an undertone. "But no sign of TA or ISP reps and it's gone nine hundred. And with no external links, this meet won't go out live to any of the PSS fleet in the vicinity."

The drop in chat was palpable as the six, led by Thal, strode in. The *Moonstone's* Captain Xanna Kerrix and Commander Jesse Inks were known to most; Captain Kismulin Ver and her first mate Kell Irissin of the *Kel'Beth* were not, although *Arianrhod* had dealt with Ver. Kerrix smiled at Ahxenta but the smile faded as she took in Holdspan. She made for him but had no time to chat, as three reps sporting TA logos filed in with two armed guards, to a ripple of cutting comment. They made for the raised dais at the far side of the hall.

The leading woman, wearing an info-pad under an arm and a formal look, stepped behind the lectern to face the throng. She waited until the other two sat, and then rang a bell as the guards fell in either side.

"I am Sigma Dishell, senior Trades Alliance executive for this sector of zone Alpha and head of the Merkat TA Office. These are senior TA Council members Jell Shanks and Rod Spokel. Mr Shanks heads trade route expansion; Mr Spokel is our membership liaison. Please sit. I'll begin when the Interstellar Systems Protectorate delegates arrive."

The attendees' table formed a huge semi-circular arc facing the dais, but Ahxenta noted that it was closed and a set of uniformed legs would not be visible. She found herself next to the two from the *Moonstone*.

"Do you know what this is about, Captain?" Ahxenta asked coolly: she and Kerrix had never been best friends, despite a mutual respect.

"No; though I gather Captain Thal spoke to you about what the TA wants from him, and you had an early meet with him and Commander Seer to which the other Starfall officers here were not invited."

"That's my concern. What's the ISP's part in this, apart from that report that turned up last night? I can't imagine they hot-shipped a pair of reps in here to repeat what it's already put out and to let us into the secrets of what its experts found."

"My second mate's not privy to the ISP's secrets; she's not part of it now," Kerrix retorted. "Apologies Captain, I didn't mean to sound uncivil," she added at an annoyed flicker on Ahxenta's face. "As the ISP's to be prating, something's up that concerns us. Vetta *did* find out that the ISP reps here had a closed sitting with their Coalition and NTA peers last night and there's been diplomatic bluster to bring in the outer systems for months. I don't know about Norvalla, but Telzilt's been pulled in and its council's irritated at ISP pressure to sign up."

"Sign up to what?"

"Full ISP membership and all it entails, as I'm sure Azular told you. But these ISP reps are late. I wonder if they're waiting for news before they say what they're up to. The TA reps are getting restive: Dishell's having a sharp talk to somebody in that comm booth."

Kerrix was right, as the TA exec cut the link, snapped shut her info-pad and stalked back to her post, a grim look on her face.

"Attention, please! The ISP delegates are delayed, but as I'm assured they'll be here soon, I'll begin for the Trades Alliance. Recorders set?" she asked a lackey as she poked a panel in front of her. "Security fields operative and keep your eyes and ears open," she ordered her guards.

"Is she expecting trouble or does she think what she's got to say will cause a riot?" Apnis asked her captain.

"I don't have all day, so she'd better hurry up and say it."

Dishell quickly set her agenda on the holo-grid. As it appeared on the table-top holos, she eyed her security and watched for reactions.

"Doesn't tell us much," Tallica Apnis observed derisively.

"They couldn't fill it in the way they wanted," Ahxenta replied, with a look at Thal further along the table.

"It's nothing but a blank shopping list!" an irate voice spat from a few seats down. "A string of bullet points that mean zip."

Dishell rapped for order, calling that those wanting to speak should signal their intent. The result was a constellation of lights. Tranquil, she waited until the noise subsided, launched into a lecture on the benefits of TA affiliation, and ended by saying that those who had signalled would be called in order, *if* time allowed, after the close of her report.

The star chart that she lit up on the wall resulted in virtual silence, as everyone sat back to digest the gist of the expanded areas marked as new trade sectors. They included a clear zone off Mu that brought in Norvalla and Telzilt. Both systems were said to have reacted positively to moves towards joint trade pacts. Dishell held up a hand when a testy voice enquired how in hell they would get there, as there were no listed bypasses out of Mu. Her response was to light up the newly-completed zone Mu double bypass. She indicated the end node at Wild, on the edge of the ISP sector of Kappa, from where the route cut across Mu to Kollaskin Ambit, the limit of currently-mapped space. The second arm of the track ran at a ninety-degree angle from Kollaskin through the major axis of Mu to Cassary, close to the Iota border. The United Independents, which acted for the treaty-aligned Mu systems, had agreed that TA members could access the bypass for an increase in fees, as the TA, with the ISP and its allies, had pledged support for the venture *and* its extension, as and when appropriate.

The rising hum around the hall and the flush of lights indicated that several attendees wanted to express their views, but Ahxenta was aware of Kerrix leaning forward on her elbows for a close look at the image.

"Here it comes," she whispered to her fellow captain. "So that's what the bastards were up to…"

"What?"

"Kollaskin Ambit: build a small extension to the bypass from there *beyond* Mu, and where will it lead?"

It was a rhetorical question, for the captain of the *Arianrhod* could see exactly where it would lead. "What do you know?" she asked.

"I'd heard a report that three ships were seen out at K457:003 about forty days ago: a huge ISP survey ship, a heavy constructor out of one of the zone Mu UI-aligned systems, and a Norvallan heavy cruiser."

"And?"

"That's all. It came from one of our ships out that way with supplies for Telzilt. The ships were off the bypass, at the node but not active."

"Thal didn't mention it earlier," Ahxenta remarked dryly. "But even if the TA now has an official route to Kollaskin, it's a jump in building technology to take it as far as K457, though the systems are relatively close in galactic terms."

"Unless there's another way through: how did the ISP initially chart K457? Explorer ships or not, I bet they didn't make a full run in normal space. There *are* known short bypasses and stable wormholes out there used by the Norvallans, and I bet the ISP has a few up its sleeve. There *were* Norvallan trial ships capable of sustained hyperlight flight that in effect made their own bypasses, but they didn't get far, rarely acted as predicted and were so costly that even the super-rich couldn't afford them. But *that* extension to the Mu bypass would obviate the TA's need to stake a claim in Starfall's hyperspace route out that way, so why *is* the TA Council so keen to gets its teeth into *our* bypass? What…"

She was interrupted by Apnis. "Here comes the ISP. Three of them. And you'll sure as hell recognise one, Cap."

"Myrtleberry! What's the ISP planning now and what does it have to do with *her*? And us," Ahxenta added grimly.

"At least it's shut Fleetskup up: you can hear *his* voice beyond the doors. And I bet Dishell won't answer questions from the floor."

It was obvious that one of the ISP band was a fleet colonel. Another bore a badge that Jesse Inks had called up on his info-console.

"Diplomatic Corps," he said to Kerrix. "An attaché. And that other is one step down from director. There'll be fireworks."

Fireworks there were. Dishell's speech ended sourly, with questions shelved and the news that after the ISP envoys had spoken on a current issue, there would a be a break before a second ISP report. *That* would be halted the instant notice came in of a live emergency bulletin by all Alliance members; it was to be broadcast on all nets to every zone, as it directly impacted every system. After that, and close of ISP matters, a session would cover changes in TA contract terms with the PSS fleet.

"Don't want us escaping at half time," Apnis muttered to Ahxenta. "Emergency bulletin about what? No journalists in here, and I bet they don't let us out the door to tell anyone. What's going on?"

Half the room was asking the same. Dishell had to buzz repeatedly for order before she could introduce ISP vice-director Ainya Sateen, diplomatic attaché Carr Shell and Colonel Ellin Myrtleberry. The latter gave the first ISP report. It dealt with the attack on the *PSS Nyx Warrior* at Idledott and the failure of ISP experts to develop a response to the new threat. Holdspan sat in cold anger, refusing to speculate.

The short and noisy recess had every officer linking their ship about the imminent bulletin. Ahxenta left Apnis to it and sought Thal out for his views. At their earlier talks she had faced him with Azular's theories on the routes through mapped space that hostiles, and later his fleet, used. He had not been drawn, but he *had* been aware of possible efforts to join the Mu bypass to the K457 node. The two were interrupted by Kerrix asking for privacy: she had news. As she was still wearing her earpiece, word had clearly just reached her. And she was angry.

Her wrath had a basis: the presence of three ships at the K457:003 system had had more than one purpose. The ancient bypass node had been re-energised and made safe, and using access codes taken from the wreck of the Norvallan *NFS Twin Star*, the controlling powers were planning to annex the bypass that ran from K457 to Starfall Exit.

"The ISP, UI and Norvallans plan to use it to cross Mu from Kirtish and past Canna. And we won't be able to block them at Starfall Exit — which is damn close to Starfall Base. The Norvallans get routes into a new, profitable and charted set of zones and sectors *without* Starfall as a passport; the ISP gets similar on the far side as part of the deal, with Mu's Independents in the middle. As the UI's a lately set-up club, it'll hardly be able to sort its own socks, so a big project beyond its borders will need help. And the UI's part of this Alliance that the ISP is taking the lead in. But there *must* be more to it. Before you ask, the info's from a Norvallan source. I won't say where, but take it as accurate."

At that point the two-minute recall rang, with the star chart set up earlier by Dishell again in view. Myrtleberry and attaché Shell stood by the lectern. The starfield that had included a marked area beyond zone Mu that took in Telziltic and Norvallan space had expanded again, and was now defined by a continuous line that marked a boundary.

"Here cometh the riot," Apnis predicted as seats were resumed.

The ISP vice-director joined the others and gazed around, her eyes resting on Dishell's guards. Silence restored, she flicked her console. The holo shifted and zone Mu lit up, its key systems shining like jewels. The label that had so recently been UI was now marked UI-ISP.

Sateen coolly reintroduced herself and stated that a majority of zone Mu's Independents had agreed to accept ISP backing. Negotiations to integrate the UI fully into the ISP were in the final stage, and as a token of support to its new systems, the ISP would fund an extension to the Mu double bypass. The split node at Kollaskin Ambit would now run three ways, the third arm reaching star system K457:003, as shown on the holo. The K457 node linked to trade routes beyond, meaning that her listeners would have trade prospects outside currently-navigable sectors. Certain of the PSS fleet already *had* those benefits, she added silkily, the barb clearly aimed at the Starfall fleet.

Sateen's light-cursor lanced across to circle an area including Telzilt, Norvalla and systems between and beyond, but before she could utter a word, a shrill alert heralded the emergency bulletin announced earlier.

* * *

The holo faded as the bulletin ended, as did the forms of ISP Director Armor and his equals from the Coalition, Non-Treaty Alliance, and the lately-allied UI, along with others new to almost everyone in the room. There was a stunned silence before every mouth opened. The language was fruity, but it diminished as Sateen brought up the updated map of the charted galaxy and its expansion into a newly-affiliated area beyond Mu's border. The area bore a new designation: zone Psi.

"The Council of the Interstellar Systems *Alliance* is consulting with the governments of Norvalla Three and Telzilt Three to formally align them and as many of *their* allies as possible to the ISA," Sateen declared. "Norvalla and Telzilt are on board with joint *trade* treaties. As you saw in the bulletin, both sent delegates to the ISA for negotiations. Added extensions into zone Psi must be negotiated with the sovereign powers there, many of which belong to a Union of Federated Systems, which extends beyond the new zone you see here."

The ISP vice-director, now possibly out of a job, continued blithely to describe the nature of nearby systems and their links to their stellar neighbours, to a restive stirring of her audience. Shell was next, his soft monotone a relief to the ears, but little else. Joint diplomatic missions set up by the three largest powers under their new legally-linked status were on the verge of departure to their latest allies, he told them.

"Waiting for ISA tags for their ships' hulls," Apnis snickered. "Bet the Coalition argued over the colour scheme. Hell, are we expected to listen to *her* now?" she snapped as the next speaker rose.

Myrtleberry deployed her light-cursor and sharp voice to point out places of recent attacks and where the joint ISA fleet would begin ops. Her eyes flashed at a loud interjection that this was politics, and little to do with the PSS fleet; though military, emergency, and other services might now be legally bound, ISP, Coalition, Non-Treaty and UI limits would still exist, with home fleets under current planetary system and colony controls. Recognising the gruff tones of Captain Pa Ma'Lappis, Ahxenta gave a wry smile. Pa had never minced words.

"The active cooperation of *all* shipping, including the PSS fleet, will be required in this major shake-up of the galactic system of authority. You'll hear more after the recess," the colonel promised harshly.

"They'll need a lot of paint to get ISAS on the hulls of all those ISP, Coalition, NTA and UI ships," Apnis remarked over an angry hubbub. "As well as call-sign integration into hull plates and other bits of kit. That'll be why the TA's in on it: rubbing its hands in anticipation of profit. But there's one advantage of the new name: hostiles pretending to be the *ISPS Revenge* will soon be outdated."

"Cynic," Ahxenta accused. "This active cooperation means a heap of trouble for us. But an extension to Mu's bypass from Kollaskin to K457 shouldn't affect Starfall. It has its own ways in and out of charted space, doesn't it, Captain?" she enquired of her neighbour.

Kerrix regarded her with a shrewd but grim smile. "Yes, we do."

"And as this Interstellar Systems Alliance, as I suppose we now call it, will be able to get to Starfall Exit using the bypass *from* K457:003, it rather reduces Captain Thal's bargaining power."

"What?" Apnis interjected.

"This ISA plans to annex the bypass from K457 to Starfall Exit," Ahxenta murmured. "*If* it does, it and its allies *could* change the access codes as they re-energise and make safe every node and jump point."

"Thal's trying to catch Myrtleberry to let her know what he knows, I suspect," Kerrix noted. "*His* leverage is that he'll make it very publicly known how the original access codes were got. And no, his bargaining power won't be cut, Captain. The ISP's been pressing on from mapped space into areas where there must be uncharted habited systems, and I don't think that now it's part of the ISA, with more ships to call on, it will ditch that. The ISP fleet's the largest and ISP ships will lead, but it'll have TA backing, given the sniff of profit. And it's a slow process unless you have a bypass system or worm-pockets. Ways in and ways out. How do you think my fleet gets from our Twilight Station off Lambda to our Gemstone Station off Beta near Mellifly?"

"A direct, hidden bypass from Twilight through Lambda, Gamma and Beta zones to your next base," Ahxenta said in a low, ironic voice, a mockingly-raised eyebrow daring Kerrix to comment.

A hiss escaped the *Moonstone's* captain as she stared back, thoughts chasing each other across her face. "Azular worked that out! *That's* why he was in the meet you had with Thal this morning, wasn't it?"

"No comment," Ahxenta returned.

"Have it your way. But though the *Moonstone's* only lately joined the Starfall fleet, I *am* party to a lot of nav-data. I have to be. And how do you think we get from Gemstone to Nexus Station off Theta?"

The question hung in the air for an instant. "You have a cut-through bypass. But if it's straight, it'll cross the Belts, where there's little but rocks and the mining outfits that get about using their own short links, and then a strip of zone Alpha. Much of *that's* filled by the Orriga Two asteroid field and the rest is already mapped," Ahxenta stated.

"I'm aware of that, Captain. And yes, the bypasses are straight – but don't cut through much of Alpha. If you'll excuse me, I have business."

"Bypasses," Ahxenta mused. "Now that's interesting."

"I see Thal *has* buttonholed Myrtleberry," Apnis noted. "But what in blazes was that about annexation and changing access codes?"

The captain clarified as the two made for comfort breaks before the next spell. The morning was gone and in Ahxenta's view the only news impacting the PSS fleet was the expansion into Psi, implying new trade routes, competitors, and very likely increased fees. Regional and local councils would still exist to squabble over territorial and other rights.

"Where's Myrtleberry gone?" Apnis asked Jesse Inks, whom she met on her way back to her chair. "Has Captain Thal scared her off?"

"Making a link from that booth by the high table, the one with the guard outside. She didn't look happy at what Captain Thal was saying."

"I'll bet. But what's the TA got up its sleeve for us? Even credit says it's upped fees and fewer benefits."

"I don't think it's as clear-cut. The TA does *that* as standard and wouldn't need the cover of the ISP's diplomatic and military arms."

"The ISA," Apnis amended. "A new uniform for Myrtleberry. And diplomacy as the job of this Council that Sateen was jawing about. But here's Dishell calling us to sit and have our ears bent for another hour."

The TA exec rang for order and called on her fellows. Shanks ran over trade route growth, patently ignoring a new line from K457 node, now dubbed Amity Beacon on the holo, to an unnamed system off Mu that was clearly Starfall Exit. Thal was livid but did not cut in as Spokel reminded everyone of the terms of TA affiliation *and* their obligations under the contract they had signed.

"It *is* about changing our contract!" Ahxenta hissed. "I might have known. By why the hoo-ha? What are they trying to dun us for now?"

She soon found out. Dishell, a holo of ISP Director Ayr Armor at her back, waited for hush before dropping the bombshell. The TA had drafted a new section to its contract with *all* its affiliated shipping lines. They would now be required to render aid in any capacity as and when decreed, in times of general unrest, as an adjunct to the new-born ISA fleet. No clause would make participation voluntary or limit it to tasks such as transport, as had been the previous case. The place erupted.

"They can draft us when they feel like it!" snarled Apnis. "And look what happened last time, when Myrtleberry and her cronies used some sub-section at the bottom of a paragraph to haul us into that bloody war! And though they said it was voluntary, the threat of removing our flag was the alternative. And now they think they can use us as cannon fodder by shoving us into any front line they choose!"

"That's what it looks like," Ahxenta said, dangerously calm. "But I want to see the precise text – and sub-text."

* * *

An hour had gone before the room was quiet, but not one PSS captain would agree even in principle to the terms. All had sent word to their supercargoes to dissect the revised contract and copy it to their legal reps. The news buzzed over the Ultraviolet III, as every ship in the PSS fleet had been notified via the TA net.

"Does this signal the imminent breakup of the Trades Alliance?" the wearying voice of Murmur Fleetskup said at Ahxenta's back.

"That'll be the day," was her dry reply. "It has too many systems in its back pocket and majority rights to too many trade routes and ports. Breakaway groups have never been successful before."

"Starfall fleet might be the first," Apnis put in. "Looks like it's done, as the TA's not taking questions. What about the wait in line and you'll get your say? Though I guess we'll all be saying stick your new contract where the sun don't shine. Myrtleberry vanished twenty minutes ago and the holo-Armor is shuffling his info-pad."

"I wonder where Azular's got to?" Ahxenta responded.

"*Half Moon*, if he's got sense. I vote we head there: half this lot will be trying to call their legal reps until night falls on Merkat Three; or trying to waylay that pack of bin rats up there. Here it comes."

His attempt at a closing speech being drowned out, Armor gave up, perhaps thankful he was not there in person. The delegates who *were* slid out of a back door as the lights dimmed and the holo-grid cut off.

"The dust will have settled by tomorrow," Kerrix said to her first mate. "We'll join Thal and Ver and hear what gives. I'll see you before the *Arianrhod* leaves, Captain?" she added to Ahxenta.

"We're for the *Half Moon*. I expect we'll get more sense there than we've heard in here over the whole morning."

"What's with telling her we're for the *Half Moon*, Cap? Hoping she'll head there to see Azular and tell him things she won't tell you?" Apnis asked once the two from the *Moonstone* were out of earshot.

"Covering bases," was the grim reply.

* * *

The *Half Moon in a Puddle* was busy as it was well into lunch time. The two from *Arianrhod* were not the first of the fleet in. They found Grey Bluejohn and his first mate Ginger Stone of the *PSS Obsidian Sky* with jars in their hands propping up the bar.

"Got into port too late for the start of the meet and the guards on the door wouldn't let us in," Bluejohn told them. "I'd business, so I dealt with that. We're here for lunch. My comms officer linked the TA news over. Marketing's in a spin, as the TA is one of its primary clients – mainly us and the bigger shipping lines. That emergency bulletin's all over the public nets and they've been harping on it on every channel. Mostly about zone Psi: people reckon it's an omen. Catch the Coalition giving up *any* sovereign rights to a third party, even for fancy new seats on the ISA Council, is the popular view. But what didn't we hear?"

As the four made for a far table and set privacy, a pair of inebriates peered out from the shelter of their booth to scrutinise the party.

"Must be expecting company, Jurry," Malty said. "That's a big table for a cosy chat for four. In fact, here's one more. It's Dr Azular. Ally's got to him and is bending his ear. *Moonstone's* in, so maybe it's about Captain Kerrix. *She* used to work here after all."

"Don't be a fool. There's more to it than dates in a bar. This merger of the ISP, Coalition and whoever into a huge interstellar protection racket will be on the news nets from now until doomsday. We saw the charts: it goes from Point Wrath in Theta to Brittle at Mu's end on one vector, and from the Skipper Nebula to the Seafoam along the other. *And* the new zone Psi will stretch Mu to infinity out that way."

"Interstellar Systems Alliance," Malty enunciated. "It's a mouthful: why not just *Alliance*? It's a bunch of systems that belong to one union or another making even more sure they don't get beaten up or invaded when the bad guys hit town, or some other big set-up gets over-bossy."

"The *ISA*," Jurry said. "It sounds scary if other groups out there try to muscle in; *and* it'll make renaming their fleet ships easier on the eye."

"How so?" Malty wanted to know.

"Else their joint ships would be titled the *Alliance Star Ship Scratch*, or whatever," his mate explained. "In other words, the *ASS Scratch*. That would look dandy on any hull, wouldn't it?"

"I see your point. I also see Dr Azular's escaped Ally's clutches and is heading this way. Eyes down and don't make any fast moves."

The science officer barely glanced at them as he made for the far table and sat. He listened as the others talked over the heated debates of earlier, with brief pauses as food was served and allowance made for its eating. At the end of their meals, Ahxenta turned to him.

"You've been quiet, Azular; did you pick up anything we should know about while you were checking out your usual haunts?"

He nodded. "Speculations, ma'am. It's thought that the ISP won't give up the advantage of being the main link to Norvalla and Telzilt. It's claiming more ISA Council seats than the other big agencies, *and* is blocking sending in any other than ISP or joint ships. It's also said that Telzilt has vetoed joining the ISA, though Norvalla, but none of its colonies thus far, has agreed in theory to membership. As for take-over of the bypass from K457 to Starfall Exit, Captain Thal's closed his borders around his base to any ship that's not his, including ISA and TA-affiliated ships. And he's set his face against any concessions to the ISA on the other routes his fleet use."

"How in hell did you get that so quickly?" Apnis demanded.

"I met Commander Levettiza and her supercargo in marketing. She was briefed in a link, from Captain Kerrix I assume, as she mentioned that I was with her. There was more, but she didn't share it. She left to join Captains Kerrix, Thal and Ver on the *Kel'Moth*, for a meeting. The *PSS Kel'Lath* is due and her commander will be there."

His brow creased in a fleeting frown and Ahxenta grinned wryly: he would miss a chance to meet Kerrix, then. "Anything else?"

"The refit of ISP fleet ships to carry ISA insignia and call-signs has started. The ISP dockyard at Alto Finglas is already adapting existing ships *and* building new. The strike on the *Nyx Warrior* by a blip posing as ISP is the catalyst for rushing output. As the attack rattled Coalition and other players, it set the seal on ratifying the ISA's creation, hence the closed session before the TA meet. And there *was* another hit, near Daff Six in Coalition space: a Coalition heavy cruiser. The alien was disguised as a Coalition Protector Class battleship, allegedly."

Apnis whistled. "Where did you get that, and did the ship survive?"

"I don't have anything on the ship, ma'am, but the story came from a zone Alpha news broadcast – Ally told me, half an hour ago."

"So, accurate," the first mate said scathingly. "But look who's here: Fleetskup, with his replacement for the nasty Ms Dyne-Bek. You won't know the shy Commander Juke Spickle, Grey?"

"But I do," Bluejohn grinned. "He was one of my tactical ops until he fell for the charms of a certain Primrose Toadflax, and deserted the *Obsidian* for the *Tallulah*. I let him go without debate. He won't light up the galaxy, but he's a skilful tactical officer and he'll make a good first mate, *if* he can find his voice and a stronger captain."

Apnis laughed. "Hell, Fleetskup knows how to pick them. Toadflax is now *Emerald's* first mate and Melly Goodsocks won't be picking Mr Spickle out of a line-up if she needs a new tactical op."

Bluejohn was quick to congratulate his ex-officer on his promotion when the two hove up, but Fleetskup was bursting with news of the exit of the Starfall officers, who had repulsed all his attempts at a chat, and the arrival of another of their ships in the Web.

"The *PSS Kel'Lath*, under Captain Olith Dun," Azular remarked, effectively stopping Fleetskup's mouth for a moment.

"Well, the Starfall fleet will no doubt tell the ISA and TA where to go, though it's no right to have private ways through hyperspace that we don't," the stiff-necked captain went on. "Don't you agree, Juke?"

"No sir, I don't," Spickle replied quietly. "I think the Starfall fleet has every right to argue the misuse of its bypass by others for profit. A move like that will leave the Starfall fleet open to a host of unknowns flying close to its home planet. It should at least be compensated."

The other officers traded glances: it seemed the new dog had teeth.

"What compensation would you suggest?" Azular asked politely.

Spickle shrugged. "Not knowing the facts, I can't be specific. Trade discounts, rights to set up local facilities, waiving of charges for hosting others' services? The ISA and TA both claim the bypass, and that ISP rep had a dig at Starfall in her talk. I don't know its base, but its home planet must be close as the fleet's so large; it looks to have more ships than most other lines, though they're not all cargoes. But almost every port you stop at these days has seen or heard tell of them."

"You know a great deal about Starfall, Captain Ahxenta," Fleetskup broke in pointedly, his eyes popping at the verbosity of his first mate.

"Perhaps you'll tell us about their base?"

"I do and I won't," was the reply. "I have business, so I need to go. How long are you in for, Grey? We've at least three more days as we're waiting for release of our next cargo and have other trade set up."

"And Maris Fleete and her first mate have shown," muttered Apnis as Bluejohn told them he planned to ship out the next day.

The three from *Arianrhod* swiftly said farewell. The talkative captain of the *Nova Stella* had spied them and Ahxenta had no wish for an hour of her chat. She settled her bar tab, nodding to Fleete in passing.

"Back aboard for us," she said. "We'll meet Lindell at the shuttle, and you can tell us what you didn't say in here on the way up, Azular."

The supercargo was waiting for them. "We'll leave your report and review of the revised contract for later," the captain told him as the four boarded. "When you're ready, Tallica," she said to her first mate, who was piloting. "Now Azular: what else have you got?"

"I've sourced the bits to update our cloak, ma'am. I'll run the details by Chief Cottontail and pass them to you for approval – they *are* pricy."

"Thanks for that," Ahxenta said curtly. "That's not what I meant and you know it. What else did you find out from Levettiza and who or what else did you see and hear that I should know about?"

"The ISP and Coalition are more forward in their plans than they're saying," he told her. "Coalition HQ is on Friskianx Four but its main shipyard's off Settle and it has half a fleet of explorer ships near ready. They're based on an advanced ISP survey ship design – like the *ISPS Advance*, Commander Levettiza's last ride."

"And Levettiza just upped and told you that, did she?"

"No ma'am, I got it first from a Berzic friend, the supercargo of the Vreskot ship *Marjenna*. We answered her distress at Triple Pinks, if you recall? The *ISPS Repulse* jumped in: she'd been tailing the hostiles on the *Marjenna*. Colonel Myrtleberry was in command of the *Repulse* and towed the surviving alien ship to an ISP base for detailed analysis."

"I remember; she demanded our science and tactical data and then left without an offer of help. We towed the *Marjenna* to Delta Iridium."

"The *Marjenna* had been hired to deliver gear to Settle. Her captain was amazed at the growth of the place, asked, and was told to back off. So my friend asked the reps he was dealing with; they were loath to say but he *was* told that they'd had new government contracts in place for a time but couldn't discuss them. The last time the *Marjenna* was there was more than a year ago, standard galactic."

"What was the *Marjenna's* cargo, do you know?"

Azular smiled. "High-spec comms array wafers for fitting into the advanced semi-complete ships sat in Settle's orbital bays. I *did* ask Ms Levettiza about it, and about the ships being built at Alto Finglas and Stinward. We know about the ISP comms array production unit at the Alto Finglas yard; and the Allied Central Office built to bring the main parties together after the war *is* at Alto Finglas. The new ships *are* state-of-the art, she said, and talks have been going on for months under ISP and Coalition leadership, but I don't know where she got that."

"She hasn't cut her ties to her old department," was Ahxenta's view. "Which helps Thal's fleet, though I bet she keeps a lot back. But if ISP Intelligence is now ISA Intelligence, she may find herself cut out of a few loops, especially as she's on a Starfall ship."

"True. But there's been a rise in building and sending out explorers. The ISP *has* historically had that mandate, as Coalition interests lie in trade, profit and power; but pushes into new systems will boost those. The Non-Treaty and Independent groups have always been too small and system-centric to have remote survey at the top of their agendas."

"That's politics," Apnis said from the pilot's seat. "What's in it that concerns us, apart from the firing lines we might be pulled into if we can't stop the TA in its tracks?"

"The TA seems to be cosying up to the ISA," he said mildly. "There may be other directives that the PSS and other TA-linked fleets may find themselves stuck with."

"Such as?" the first mate demanded.

"First contact, if a new civilisation is met in a poorly-charted sector of space: we *will* have the option of trading beyond zone Mu once the new bypass is built from Kollaskin Ambit."

"You're kidding, Doc?" Lindell broke in.

"He isn't," Ahxenta snapped. "And he's looking forward to it."

"It would be intriguing – but it isn't our directive."

"You're damn right it isn't. We're traders, not diplomats. Did your reading of the new contract pull anything like that up, Lindell?"

"I'll recheck the small print but there *is* a clause about other issues that the TA and its allies see as vital for the common good or galactic safety – galactic being the areas administered by the ISA *and its allies*."

"Define common good and allies."

"I can't, ma'am, and the TA doesn't," he replied. "Our legal rep has the full record and is going over it as a priority. And every other legal rep in the sector will be doing the same, but the text will be watertight."

"There's no such thing as watertight. Anything else, Azular?"

"Nothing vital, ma'am, but the *ISPS Repulse* is in an outer berth and Colonel Myrtleberry and another officer were seen to head to the green four shuttle bay after that meeting. As ISP, the *Repulse* has no need to produce a manifest, so there was nothing in Port Authority updates."

"Who saw her make for the shuttle bay?"

"I did, and others, including Ms Munnet from the *Half Moon*. She wasn't in her usual garb and was in the open area of marketing. I think she was recording. I'd been talking to Bix Holt of the *Nyx Warrior*. She waited for me when she realised I'd spotted her."

"I bet she didn't confirm or deny what she was up to."

"She didn't, nor would she say much else. She *did* warn me that PSS officers leaving the meet would be furious, so ISP Intelligence had to know what was to be discussed. I asked her why the colonel ran off so quickly, but she claimed not to know. The colonel *was* heading to her shuttle: after Ms Munnet left, I checked the outer berth Web vis-net. I recognised the *Repulse* and there *was* a high-spec shuttle heading in. It looked like that advanced military combat shuttle we shipped from Silverglass to Stinward for testing months ago. The one that held what we found was Colonel Myrtleberry's miniaturised cyber suite."

"The one that her pilot Horn broke your jaw over because you'd figured it's hiding place and what it was," Ahxenta said coldly.

"Aye, ma'am. The last I saw, in the *Half Moon*, the *Repulse* was still in port – and still bearing ISP insignia," he added with a grin.

"She'll be off to get her new call-sign integration and paint job done before everybody else," Apnis said. "But hold tight: we're nearly home and there's another ship heading into the berth next to ours."

There was, for an urgent link from *Arianrhod's* duty officer warned that a ship reading as an advanced cruiser was on approach and in line for the berth next to theirs and the shuttle would have to divert out of her way. She was listed as ISP but her name and class were restricted.

"Let's see who she is," Ahxenta growled, calling up a visual as Apnis checked her ops and set a heading to avoid the latest arrival. "Bring us up on her starboard so that we get a good view, Tallica," she said.

The captain paused, an ironic snort escaping her, as the visual swept around. "I've heard of that ship, though I've never seen her in the flesh before! That's Commander Levettiza's old ride, the *ISPS Advance*... what in hell is *she* doing out here?"

The last that *Arianrhod* had heard of the *ISPS Advance* was that she was beyond Mu, in what was now zone Psi. After helping tow the stricken *NFS Twin Star* to Norvalla, she had been sent to scout nearby sectors for hostiles that were aiming to cross into the charted zones, on top of her mandates of exploration and first contact. She had also been tasked with setting up diplomatic links to help the ISP forward its plans in the new area, but had been ordered back to Norvalla Three to keep tabs on Thal's ship, the *Kel'Moth*, there for repair and causing unease.

"Now she's here," Ahxenta said. "Levettiza told us at the time that a diplomatic ship was heading to Norvalla, but then Levettiza joins the *Moonstone* and we hear zip of the *Advance*. What's her remit now? She's not called in for the social ambience and the choice of bars."

"We could call Ms Levettiza up and ask?" Lindell remarked.

"Very funny. But why is she berthed next to us? She's big but there are plenty other berths available in the belts closer in."

"Our rep," Apnis said trenchantly, turning on final approach. "And the outer belts make for a quick escape, they're not over-stocked, *and* she's ISP military: she'll call the shots on where she berths."

"Maybe Colonel Myrtleberry is to be reassigned?" Azular suggested flippantly. "The *Repulse* is still here."

"Hell help the crew if she is," snorted the first mate. "But an info-sent as part of an explorer ship's crew makes sense, though she'd have to be in command: she'd not put up with less. But isn't she too useful to the ISP here, now that it's the ISA?"

"I don't give a damn where she's based, as long as she stays out of my hair," the captain growled. "I'll call a briefing once we're on board, after I've read that damn new contract, made some links and checked if our legal rep has come back with anything."

Once docked, Lindell headed to his office whilst Ahxenta, Apnis and Azular made for the bridge. No shuttle had left the *Advance* for the harbour office, the usual course on arrival, Earbleat reported.

"We didn't dare scan her, Cap," she said. "She'd have had our ears. But she's a beauty: she's got so much sensory, comms and other gear, *and* weapons, you can barely see the shade of her hide. And that faceted surface is chameleon. Chief Cottontail was trying to gauge her engines on the way in but got nothing."

* * *

The captain was in her chair studying the fine print of the TA contract yet again when Azular came over to ask leave to check up on his sci-shuttle, run diagnostics and take her out for a test ride.

"Why?" Ahxenta said dangerously, scenting a lot of trouble.

"I've carried out surface scans around the *Advance's* berth…"

"You've done *what*!?"

"None intrusive, Captain," he assured her. "But I'm certain she has Norvallan tech fused to her hull, and possibly internally. I've compared what I got to what's available in ISP military databases, and I've noted subtle variations to her class ship. My Norvallan scanner links into our scanning relays: it can connect to relevant data sources and self-update, if new data's been input. And it can connect to already-updated control units in range. Such units *are* standard aboard Norvallan fleet ships."

"And updates are sent from source to bases and ships," the captain recalled darkly. "You told me that systems can rove for new data, and if they find it, access the unit with it. You're way off-beam mister, if you think I'll let you off ship to buzz the *ISPS Advance*. Anyhow, she'd deny access to anything unknown; didn't you say that inbuilt security prevents unauthorised access? Which would damn well mean a PSS."

"Ma'am, the *Xanna* is a Norvallan sci-shuttle…"

"With *Arianrhod's* call-sign fused into her hull! And has it escaped you that a Norvallan shuttle in the Web will look a tad out of place?"

"She has a cloak, Captain, and naturally I'd not attempt to update any instrumentation aboard. I merely want to…"

"The answer's no. And if you attempt to scan *any* ship without my sanction again, you'll be in the brig for the duration. Do you get me?"

"Yes ma'am."

"My office, now!"

"Whew! He's done it this time," Box whispered to his mate at navi-helm as Azular trailed Ahxenta out. "What possessed him?"

Helmswoman Romanna Dox turned. "It's *more* than obvious."

The navigator's perplexed look gave way to a complacent smile. "He's missing Captain Kerrix."

"Shut up and keep your eyes on your boards, you fool!" she advised.

Fifteen minutes later a call came in from the captain's legal rep, and Bellfish patched it through to the office. Azular returned and made for his seat, smiling quietly. The link to the legal rep was long: Lindell was called in, and half an hour passed before it ended. A long-distance call followed, to whom no-one but the comms officer was privy.

Every head on the bridge turned fractionally and eyes swivelled as Ahxenta's door slid aside and she made her way to her command chair, settling in heavily beside the first mate with a gusty sigh.

"I take it the news on the TA contract isn't good, Cinnabar?"

"They've got us over a barrel. It's now down to any joint actions by the PSS fleet and other affiliated shipping lines. I'll give the news time to go round before I call our fleet ships here. Any more due?"

"No – though we've had another military beast show, a big one, a dreadnought," Apnis grinned widely. "The *ISAS Avenger*."

"You what!"

"Look: the new ISA colours and insignia. They've not wasted paint, it's similar to the ISP. We've pulled in what we can of her call-sign and spec so if we meet another we'll know what to look for. Azular checked the records using our sources and the data we got from Nat, and we put in a link to Levettiza. *That* ship's been totally refitted. Everything matched but the name and colours. She's been renamed and she's hot-shipped it here from Alto Finglas. She used to be the *ISPS Revenge*."

"You're not joking?"

"No way, Cap. Interesting turn of events don't you think?"

"It is. Anything new on what happened to the *Nyx Warrior*?"

"No. I thought we'd get more on what was found when they took the blip apart, but zip. Looks like the official report is it. Our Selliden cargo's passed muster; it'll be loaded into pods by late tomorrow, so we can ship it in the day after. Lindell got us any more business?"

"Yes, but until a new contract's agreed, there are questions over it," the captain told her. "We've got thirty days to finish current business under existing terms, but as most of our trade's long haul, it's tight."

"The fleet will end up signing. The TA has fingers in too many ports for it not to. And as there were ISP top guns at the meet, the ISA won't object," Apnis said. "Are they expecting trouble, that they're making sure we and other fleets can be drafted in as and when they shout?"

"The ISA will take on the ISP's exploratory role; the first ships out will be ex-ISP *and* they'll be pushing into uncharted sectors this end of the galaxy," Ahxenta pointed out. "The locals beyond Mu are friendly, but the ones at this end of mapped space may not be. As there *were* several hostile hidey holes outside Mu, how many more are there off Alpha and other zones that Thal and his fleet don't know about?"

"Plenty, I guess. But surely that makes Thal and his fleet too useful to piss off? They know more than most about what goes on outside current borders: they've got bases out there. When exploration really kicks off, there'll be an exodus of explorer ships in every direction."

"That had occurred to me. I've had zero on what the Starfall fleet's been up to, but the senior officers here may still be on the *Kel'Moth*."

"They are: Gliss kept an eye via Web nets and no shuttles have left. But what does the new contract mean for us on a daily basis, Cap?"

"You'll find out at the briefing, if nothing more comes in that needs me to jump," Ahxenta replied, pulling her boards across. "Everything's in order. We'll meet in half an hour in briefing room four and it'll be short: with all this in the air, we'd best be ready for action."

* * *

The briefing was put on hold, as the captain was called out by a comm, which she elected to take at once. She returned twenty minutes later.

"What did Zillah want, Cinnabar?" the first mate enquired.

"It was the reply to a link *I* sent, asking what the ISA deal would mean for Freskat, its one seat on the ISP Council, and the home fleet. They're away from the action at the end of Lambda, now everything's shifted towards Mu and our new allies out that way."

"Why are we bothering with politics?" Crizz Cottontail demanded gruffly. "Our business is trade."

"We fly the TA flag, and the TA's more political than the ISP and Coalition jointly when profit's the prize. Admiral Zillah's got no time for politics and runs her fleet her way. She won't want ISA meddling, for all that Freskat's obliged to fund two ISP warships. She was warned weeks ago about this *and* told she'd have a permanent ISA presence on her watch. Freskat's the main centre in the ISP-run sector of Lambda, with the Curtain Nebula off its edge, by Aoria Six."

"Thal's Twilight Station…" Apnis breathed.

"Exactly. The ISP knew about the bypass linking Starfall, Sunrise and Twilight. Levettiza told us it had probed Sunrise, after the *Twin Star* hove into the Web, as that Norvallan Admiral Posettix had spoken of it. It was a hub for Starfall's fleet at the last faceoff at Freskat, where Thal threw in his lot with the Alliance. *That's* what made TA affiliation easy for the ships that he'd registered as PSS. But the ISA's looking for a link between Twilight and the other two known ex-hostile bases, and figures that Thal and his lot have control of them – which they do."

"Have they found anything, Captain?" Azular asked anxiously.

"Not yet."

"Will you alert Captain Thal, ma'am?"

Ahxenta smiled sardonically. "I did. He and his are still mulling over the problems the TA and ISA have dealt him. As the ISA knows of the bypass his fleet uses, he's got little option but to allow access, because it's known to hostiles still out there and their hangers-on, they can get to it, and they're capable of spiking it. But he won't give access for free and he'll want safeguards, as the main nodes are near his active bases. And his people don't have a planet to call home. The only thing close was their base off sector sixteen, near the edges of Beta and Gamma. The aliens were tipped off by a mole and took out everything and everyone," she said, with a frown of pity that was mirrored by Azular.

"Thal was very bitter over it," Apnis recalled. "He'd never say why, but he's bitter and twisted anyhow, or it seems that way."

"He's got reason, but that isn't the point. Zillah's now in a difficult fix. She knows about the changes to our TA contract, but Freskat's treaty with the ISP will shift under the ISA. Freskat currently has a right to its own navy, and the admiral-in-chief has first call on it for home defence. But the ISA treaty has a clause that puts interstellar, not stellar, defence first. Zillah called the shots when she was ordered to the defence of Skyrtek: she refused to leave Freskat unprotected, with the alien threat so close. Just as well, or Freskat would have been lost."

"So as well as trade and other fleets, this ISA can call on members' own fleets as backup if things go belly-up, Cap?" Earbleat cut in.

"They always could. But now they can't refuse *if* they sign the treaty. Zillah says many are refusing. It'll be thrashed out at the next meeting of the ISP Council – the last, as it'll be the ISA Council after that. But it's the politicians that'll be arguing, and that's worrying Zillah. But we can do zip about it. Our immediate concern is this contract. I haven't heard from any other of our fleet captains, but it won't be long."

It was not: minutes after the briefing, Fleetskup called for Ahxenta's opinion on what the PSS response should be, as he was reluctant to commit until he had heard other views. He was followed by Bluejohn: his ship was due out and would be gone for fifteen days. The existing contract covered it this time, but two of his regular clients had called, concerned what the new terms would mean for them in the future.

* * *

The captain was having a quiet bite in the mess when she was accosted by her first mate, who sat down with a questioning look.

"What is it, Tallica? I know that face."

"Azular. Ever since he met Kerrix, he's not been the same. I don't see the appeal. She's smart, exotic I suppose, being Norvallan…"

"Half-Norvallan…"

"That also. Now she commands a unique PSS. And he owes her, or did: I expect they figure they're even. That aside, what did he think he was doing trying to scan the *Advance*? Whatever he says, that *is* what he wanted. You tore him off a strip and hauled him in for a chinwag, but he came out smiling. The bridge crew's wondering why."

"They can wonder," the captain said abruptly.

"Cinnabar!"

"He had a point; if the *Advance* has Norvallan tech, she can do a lot, including cloak. And *that* could take in a chameleon facility that could disguise her as something else."

"And the hostiles have similar if they're sending out fake ships that can almost fool someone as sharp as Nat Holdspan. So the *Advance* has been recalled, as her new tech could be used to develop a response to alien tech. But why doesn't the ISP part of the ISA call up its Norvallan chums and ask for it, or trade it for concessions in ISP space?"

"It doesn't want to show weakness by asking or admit that it doesn't have similar; it doesn't want to concede anything; or it's suspicious that that's where the hostiles got the gear in the first place. But the ISA's got that bogus ship now, so that's not why the *Advance* is here."

"All this doesn't explain Azular's face," interrupted the first mate.

"I've given him the go-ahead to contact Kerrix to see what he can find out, and meet up Web-side if she agrees. After all, when we first met Thal and the *Kel'Moth* and realised that he and it were more than they said on their wrappings, he admitted he had allies in salient places. He wouldn't say where, but he was hunting Lokterix and other moles that he said were still undermining him. It was after they'd taken out two of his ships and destroyed his base by sector sixteen. He must still have spies: how else can he run such a huge set-up and come out of it in one piece? And as Kerrix is Starfall, she might have a clue."

"She won't tell Azular, if I'm any judge."

"I agree; she has loyalties to Thal that we can only guess at. But we now know there *is* a covert bypass where Azular figured, and that's a huge piece of bargaining power. It was Azular who suggested I contact Zillah, by the way. I passed the stuff on the *Advance* to Thal, figuring that Levettiza will hear it. We give her info, she may reciprocate…"

"This is turning into a political spy epic, Cap; I don't like it."

"Neither do I, but our living depends on politics whether we agree or not. And I'd like to know, or rather Azular would, what the *Advance* is up to and why Myrtleberry's still here. The speed she raced back to her ship, I expected she'd be long gone. And now we have the *Avenger*. A survey ship and two battlecruisers: something's in the wind."

"And Azular being Azular, his nose is twitching."

"Exactly," Ahxenta said. "*And* he wants a good look-see around the *Moonstone*: he's only been aboard once, and he didn't see much then."

"There are a few who'd like a look-see around *that* ship, though I bet Azular's more interested in the inside of Captain Kerrix' quarters."

"Stow it. But as for those military ships: your friend Kit Biernop is a Dockers' Guild security liaison and keeps his nose to the ground. If they've had repair or other work done here, he'd know about it."

"That's not likely, Cap; the ISP has its yard at Alto Finglas and that huge one at Stinward. Its ships wouldn't drop in here for a tidy-up."

"Depends where they came in from; but check with him and see what you can dig up. I doubt you'll find anything that will help our case with the TA, but there may be something he's noticed."

"Will do. For now, I'll set up a shore leave rota, as we're here for a few days. And Box and Dox have personal things they want to discuss with you. Best get your dress uniform out and your stat pins polished."

"Very funny, Commander."

"Oh, come on, Captain, ma'am! We haven't had a wedding aboard *Arianrhod* yet. This'll be a first — and a first for you, as officiator."

"Back to work, Commander Apnis!"

∗ ∗ ∗

Little had been agreed amongst senior PSS officers in the aftermath of the TA-led meeting. Almost every legal agent had concluded that the altered contract allowed no give and take, and unless the TA agreed on concessions, the alternative was the withdrawal of its flag and thus the rights to insurance subsidies, and certain travel routes and port entries. And the majority of the PSS fleet could not afford that alternative.

The next morning saw the exit of the *Obsidian Sky* and the *Firedrake*. Two hours later, the *Advance*, *Repulse* and *Avenger* set off on the same line. Rumour was rife as to their endpoint and intent. Apnis picked up a clue during a chat with Biernop. He had heard nothing on the needs of the military ships or resupply, but in an earlier talk he had had with Nat Holdspan about repairs to a shuttle, the young captain had been interrupted by a link from his ship, to tell him that a senior ISP officer was online and pressing for a response on an urgent matter. Holdspan had made for a nearby comm station to deal with the issue in private and had then left Biernop with a short farewell.

"Even credit it was Myrtleberry," Apnis told Ahxenta at their later meet-up in marketing. "Nat seemed narked, Kit said. But how did your talks go? Any more deals on the cards for us?"

"Yes. I left Lindell to tackle it. After we drop the pods of lifting gear at Selliden Central, we've a pick-up there for Marridan, big industrial stuff. And then maybe Kanelian Juxta, if Lindell can sort it out: an arms cargo for the ISP shipyard at Alto Finglas. Or ISA yard, or what in hell it'll be called by the time we get there."

"If they need arms for their fancy new ships, why don't they get one of their own in?" Apnis asked. "There must be plenty troopships with empty holds and platoons of grunts to do the heavy work."

"Would you trust a bunch of ISP troopers to shift cargo?"

"I see your point. But let's head to the *Half Moon*. Nat may be there, unless he *is* aboard biting Myrtleberry's ears off long-distance. I've not seen or heard of Azular since he took off on his own this morning. What did he have planned?"

"No idea. And I didn't ask," the captain returned.

They did not find Holdspan or their errant science officer in the *Half Moon* but they did find the *Hexameter's* captain and first mate.

"Every head in the place turns when they see a PSS uniform come in," Captain Coxen greeted them. "I figure they've got bets running on what we're going to do about the TA."

"What are *you* going to do, if you don't mind me asking, Captain?" Ally asked Ahxenta as he filled two pots of ale and set them down.

She grinned. "Tell me what everyone here's saying we *should* do."

Ally cocked an eye at his clientèle. "Most of them reckon you'll tell it to go hang. But that won't happen, will it, ma'am? Captain Fleetskup, Commander Spickle and Mr Buntle were in and saying that you'd have to make the TA back down, but Mr Spickle thinks it won't work, as no PSS has any say in what the TA writes into its contracts."

"That man's got more nous than I gave him credit for," observed Apnis. "But will Fleetskup listen to him?"

"It's Buntle he'll have to convince," her captain informed her. "You and Rosee here for lunch, Bee, or just a drink?"

"Just the drink: we've meets in marketing, to get our next contracts in place before this thirty day grace period is up and we have to bite the bullet. But here are Nat Holdspan and Sol Treskitt. Maybe they'll keep you company: you don't want to sit with anybody else here."

"Roger that. See you on the flipside one of these days."

Two shrewd pairs of eyes had been watching the exchange from the safety of a booth in the far corner. "Reckon *Arianrhod* will still be trading after all these shenanigans have died down, Malty?"

"Course she will, Jurry lad. Nobody, even the TA, will get one over on *Arianrhod*. She'll see a way through. Maybe she'll join that Starfall fleet and they'll set up on their own."

"If that's a joke, Malty, it's not funny. And I wouldn't suggest it to Captain Ahxenta: she'll have your ears for lunch," Jurry told his mate. "The *Arianrhod* plays second fiddle to nobody, especially that Captain

Thal and his bunch of renegades."

"I wouldn't call Thal a renegade where any of his crew can hear you, or your face will meet the floor faster than Ahxenta's fist can fly when she's in a temper," Malty returned. "But these pots are empty; anybody in here we can persuade to fill them up for us?"

Holdspan and Treskitt made for Ally's counter, where the barman had two mugs of ale waiting for them, on Captain Ahxenta's tab.

"You look as if you need it, Nat," the *Arianrhod's* captain greeted him, gesturing to the drinks. "Had a hard morning?"

Holdspan nodded his thanks as he raised his glass. "I'll say. Sol and I have been arguing with marketing reps for two hours. But maybe we should speak in private: we're the target of every eye in the place."

Ally sighed in regret, having hoped for gossip. He turned to tune the holo that he kept linked to Web external channels and the berths of the outer belts that housed the huge ships that used the port.

"What in blazes is *that?*" he asked of the air in such an arresting tone that the four leaving the bar turned back.

"That," said a voice whose owner had just come in, "Is a Norvallan war cruiser, *Starpilot* class. Her markings say she's the *NFS Serenity* and she's a diplomatic ship, but what she's doing here is anyone's guess."

"Good to see you back, ma'am," Ally greeted Xanna Kerrix civilly. "And you, Dr Azular. What'll it be? It's on the house," he added.

"Can I use your office for a private call, Ally?" Kerrix asked politely.

"Yes, ma'am. You know the way. Here's my key, take all the time you need," Ally assured her, handing over his security token.

"Thank you. I'll be back," she said to Azular with a quick smile as she turned on her heel and made off behind the counter.

"Unexpected, then," remarked Apnis. "Maybe the *Serenity's* late, and had planned to link up with Myrtleberry and her chums for their jaunt to wherever? We'll maybe find out. Had a nice morning, Azular?"

"Informative, Commander," he returned placidly.

"We're eating here, and then Tallica and I are heading up, after we pick up my supercargo," Ahxenta said. "You having lunch, Nat?"

"We may as well," Holdspan replied, with a last look at the viewer. "She's big for a consular ship; and she's a war cruiser? Odd choice."

"The Norvallans tend to have grand ideas," Ahxenta told him as they made for a far table, most eyes in the place following them.

"You'd think we were the star attractions in a zoo!" Apnis spat as she sat. "The TA has a lot to answer for."

"Cool it, Tallica, and order your lunch," her captain advised. "Are you eating with us, Azular?"

"No ma'am; I have other plans."

Privacy set, Ahxenta asked after Holdspan's health. Improving, he told her, and then brought up their rights under the new TA rules. In his view, the PSS fleet would have to accept the changes if it wanted to continue trading in and beyond the known zones, but concessions would be worth fighting for. A restive Azular kept eyeing the bar, but it was fifteen minutes before Kerrix emerged, arriving as their meals did. The science officer stood to offer her the seat next to his.

"I can't stay long, I must get back to my ship," she announced, and then sat quietly until the waiter had left and the shield reformed.

"The *Serenity's* here at the invite of the ISP Council. She came in via Alto Finglas and will head back there. She brought in the Norvallans for that bulletin; the ambassador had heard of the Web and wanted to see it. As she's here to direct and firm up trade relations, it makes sense: this *is* the main trading centre this side of Psi. But there's more to it, if the Norvallans are slapping diplomatic plates onto war cruisers."

"How did you find out thus much?" Azular asked.

"My high-ranking chief medic has family aboard the *Serenity*. But he couldn't ask much – the link was monitored and the comm *did* raise a query. The ambassador's asked for a private talk with me, but I'll call from my office. I'll let you know if anything relevant crops up," she told the two captains.

"Do you know this ambassador, Captain?" Solmar Treskitt asked.

Kerrix shook her head. "We've never met, but Ambassador Merysta Lix Winavona Posettix, Lady of the Family Maryax of Norvalla Three, is Admiral Posettix' niece. If she's like her uncle, she'll be a force to be reckoned with. But I have to go. Are you coming, Dr Azular?"

His concerned frown vanished in the face of her mischievous look, to be replaced by an elated smile. "At your service, Captain."

Apnis had trouble hiding a grin as the two made their farewells and left. "Bet he thought he'd missed out on a tour of the *Moonstone*."

"He's going aboard the *Moonstone*?" Treskitt queried sharply.

"I guess so. I can't imagine that all Captain Kerrix wants is an escort to her shuttle. But she's been asked for a chat by an ambassador?"

"I'm sure she'll cope," Ahxenta stated. "On another note… what do you make of the joint exit of the *Advance*, *Repulse* and *Avenger*, Nat? The ISP alias the ISA is up to something big?"

That was sufficient for Holdspan to mention the call from a senior ISP officer. It *had* been Myrtleberry. On the basis of the repairs to his ship and the top-class care his crew had received after the attack by the bogus *Revenge*, she insisted on a copy of all that his tactical and science teams had got, from the second they logged the ship until her capture, details not part of the report he sent. She also wanted the data on and the remains of the tech that had breached his ship. He had refused, but heeding Ahxenta's warnings on her info-sent nature, he had been cool. She had no time to pursue it, as she was on a vital mission.

"They *are* up to something then, all three of them," Ahxenta mused. "They set off as one to the local bypass. Not that it should concern us. But now our problem: the TA and the barrel it's got us over."

"How likely are we to be called up?" Holdspan asked. "It was always a last resort in extreme emergency. But in the war, when it looked like the hostiles might win, the entire PSS fleet was mobilised. *Arianrhod* was at the battle for Skyrtek, Captain, as were several PSS vessels."

"That and more. *We'd* been in the fight for Freskat. And the ISP lost its HQ and key shipyard at Skyrtek. There was nothing left."

"But with the help of the renegade fleet that's now morphed into the Starfall fleet, we *did* more or less break the hostiles, though pockets of them have been plaguing us ever since," Apnis put in. "That could be the reason for this: the TA's been put up to it by parties in the ISP that don't want a repeat of the last war. It broke out so quickly and nearly overran the charted galaxy – which is now larger than it was."

"And with so many new friends," Ahxenta added. "But we've cargo to shift, Tallica, so back aboard. You said you're for marketing, Nat. We'll come with you that far. Our shuttle's on green four."

* * *

Three hours later, the captain was called to her office to take a private link from Azular, still aboard the *Moonstone*. She was surprised to see Commander Levettiza with him but not Captain Kerrix, who was aboard the *NFS Serenity* for a meeting with Ambassador Posettix.

Azular had been given a tour of the *Moonstone* by Levettiza. As both were Berzic telepaths, Ahxenta saw the logic. He wanted leave to stay aboard until the captain's return. Meanwhile, he would meet her senior science officer and chief engineer to discuss the ship's cloaking gear.

"You didn't call me to tell me about your social schedule for the rest of the day," Ahxenta remarked acidly. "What is it, Commander?"

Levettiza smiled at the tone. She had found out that the ISP had asked Norvalla to send envoys to the launch of the ISA. A war cruiser had been used to deter trouble. The *Serenity* had teamed up with the Telzilt cruiser carrying *her* ambassador, though the latter was still at Alto Finglas. The *Advance* had escorted both ships but had her own mandate. As a custom-built survey ship, she was set to explore beyond the edges of zone Alpha with the *ISPS Repulse*. Both were now making for Alto Finglas for rebranding. However, the ISA, with TA influence, was keen to locate and use any hyperspace routes in uncharted Alpha space, and one body liable to have such data was Starfall. Bypasses at the other end of ISA space, across Psi, had been mapped by Norvallan, Telziltic and other fleets and one reason that Ambassador Posettix was staying on was to broker their use with the TA, and thus support trade in zone Psi. Ambassador Jotakt of Telzilt had similar authority.

"What has that to do with my business, Commander?"

"Several Starfall ships are on the PSS registry *and* under the TA flag. Captain Thal's in a strong position if the TA wants codes and consents to use bypasses in regions beyond Alpha, and make profits, if there *are* worlds out there that can be brought into the ISA. He *will* compromise on the bypass from Starfall to K457 if concessions are made. The TA via the ISA was aiming to annex the bypass anyhow and he knows that with both of them on his back, they'll eventually carry the day. And they're sending in a solid argument: the *ISAS Avenger* is on a route that will take her across four zones to Zeta. A course change there will put her on a line to zone edge at Wester 287 and Starfall. We think she's being sent in to patrol the area and keep an eye on ISA interests."

"How did you find all this out and why are you telling me?"

"I served aboard the *Advance*, Captain; I have associates there I can call on; there *and* elsewhere," Levettiza said levelly. "Captain Thal also has contacts in various places. And he'll need PSS backing if he's going to argue with the TA on what it can and can't put in its contract with the PSS fleet. The *Arianrhod* is a major player in that fleet, and the voice of her captain will be listened to, whether you like it or not."

"I'm not a politician and I don't intend spending my time arguing," Ahxenta said firmly. "I've better things to do than sit around bandying words back and forth that ultimately will change zip. Nor will I put my name on a page with a bunch of disaffected others that are intent on causing upheaval in trading circles."

"I understand that, Captain, as does Thal," said Levettiza. "He's of a similar view. But he won't sell his people short, nor let Starfall Base become a bargaining chip in a trade war. That's why he's sending in an independent negotiator."

"An independent negotiator?" repeated Ahxenta.

"An independent negotiator: Admiral Pertik Posettix of Norvalla. You've met him, of course."

4: CASTAWAYS

Ahxenta sat in her command chair wrapped in thought, after checking the Selliden cargo manifest. The pods were being moved by grapples to the outer cargo bays, with her ops tracking each step. She called up the science and tactical data and sighed.

"What's biting you, Cinnabar?" Apnis asked softly. "We don't have much time if we plan to make Selliden ahead of schedule; and we can, as all meets are off due to the TA shake-up. It would help to head out, as Selliden Orbital's promised a bonus for early delivery."

"We'll rearrange our schedules and ship out," she said at last. "The crew still on leave will have to forego the rest of their time out. Where's Crizz? She should be here supervising loading."

"Gem Ferry's handling it. Crizz is in main engineering with Azular, running sims of the upgraded cloak. They've had to realign hull sensors to take the new data routines for the add-on units that Azular brought in from the *Moonstone*. They were tricky to install, and some are fixed to our hull plates. Crizz is in two minds as to whether they're worth it. And that doesn't answer my question: what's biting you?"

"I had link from Grey Bluejohn last night; two of his regulars are nervy about the terms they'd have to agree once the new TA contract's in place. One's threatening to cancel, as he's heard that any PSS not signing as soon as the contract is in force will lose its right to the TA flag. Grey's sent that to the fleet on the UV-III and asked TA Central why the fleet hadn't been told."

"I expect he'll have a long wait for an answer," was the acid reply.

* * *

The payload had been lifted aboard quickly and attached by locking bolts and magnetic grapples to the cargo decks. The fine-meshed safety shields protecting the bays from space were dropped, and by twelve hundred *Arianrhod* was ready to ship out. Clearances were in place and Cottontail and Azular had finished the primary upgrades to the ship's cloak. The stalemate over the new TA contract still stood.

All the ship's senior bridge officers were in post as the ship made to leave, as the captain preferred her most experienced people in place. With the *Nyx Warrior's* troubles close to Idledott beacon and rumours of other action out there, she needed no glitches on the first part of the trip. Their cargo was vital for the orbital engineering platform for which it was meant, as Selliden was increasing shipbuilding in response to the merger of the chief governing powers into the ISA. She gave the order to release docking struts and the great vessel slipped her traces. The routine farewell of Port Control echoed across the bridge as the ship slowly pulled out of her berth under the helmswoman's skilful hands, and slid into free space.

"Selliden Central via local bypass, Captain?" asked Navigator Box.

"Selliden Central, aye; best speed to the bypass, helm."

"Best speed, aye, ma'am," Dox called as she set her controls.

The first mate sighed gustily. "It's good to be out after the chaos of the past few days, Cap," she remarked as the glittering meshwork that was the Web vanished to a pinprick of light.

"Roger that. I expect there'll be a heap of hogwash jamming hyper-channels from now on. Bellfish is keeping his ears open for anything related to us or the fleet, and tactical and science are on long-distance scan. Every system's had a complete overhaul and we're fully-supplied, so we should be up to anyone that decides we might be worth picking."

"Unless we meet a bogus ISP battleship with our name on it."

"Azular's coded all we got from Nat Holdspan into our arrays, so we should spot anything that tries it on," the captain told her.

"Not if they've changed their tactics or tech since then, Cap. The aliens or whoever sent out the ship that almost got the *Warrior* sure as hell know it was captured, and if they have bigger and better at home, they might not be afraid to use them."

"Thanks for that ray of sunshine."

"Welcome. But on another note: Thal's choice of that Norvallan admiral as a negotiator. This morning's briefing was short and you had a chat to Captain Kerrix after it."

"She'd nothing else. Admiral Posettix *is* in command of the *Serenity* and his last ship was the *Twin Star*, also used for consular missions. He knows of the mischief round that ancient bypass node tagged K457 that links to Starfall Exit. The access codes *had* been got with Norvallan help from the wreck of the *Twin Star*, and he was pissed. Kerrix reckons he's dead straight and likely to be sympathetic to Thal's position."

"And the ambassador's his niece? Won't the TA and the ISA have something to say about conflict of interest?" Apnis asked.

"They wouldn't dare; they want firm links to Norvalla and its allies and riling high-ranking Norvallans isn't the way to get them. I don't know whose idea it was to get this admiral in, but he *was* the one that got Kerrix off court martial charges before she got her hands on the *Moonstone*, and he's well-versed in Norvallan law. Kerrix *had* a chat to that ambassador, so it may have sprung from there – she wouldn't say."

"She doesn't let out much," Apnis noted. "Didn't she contact you? And what's the *Moonstone* up to, or wouldn't she say? I saw a few of her crew in the *Half Moon*, but I didn't speak to them: they're a rum bunch."

"She's a PSS," the captain retorted. "She's for Mu in a day or so, via Keystone Kell. Kerrix wouldn't say why or where, though it *is* a trade trip. Much of Starfall's trade is out that way, as most places on the usual trade routes don't trust them. And what she specifically had to say I'm keeping to myself, for now," she grinned. "Let it be a surprise for later, as you're partly responsible for it."

The first mate had to be content with that, for inside the next few hours the *Arianrhod* had hit the bypass and was on her way to Selliden, on the Alpha-Epsilon border. The captain, on her rounds, had stopped off in medbay for a word with chief medic Axellina Flintlock when the loud voice of duty officer Mitt Snow rang out, calling her to the bridge. She set off, tabbing her comm to confirm and request the cause. The glow of an amber alert was already pulsing along the bulkheads.

"We're picking up a distress, ma'am; it's from the direction of Veil but it's weak," Snow reported. "No craft detected in the vicinity."

"Slow to jump-off speed and ready us to change course to head in. Do *not* respond but call all senior bridge officers in now," she ordered.

In the minutes it took her to reach the bridge, the source of the distress had been verified as the Veil system, about half way between Selliden and Lesser Kirrin.

"All stations report! Change course for Veil and cloak up, Ms Dox," Ahxenta directed. "Continue to monitor that signal but don't respond until we know the score – I won't risk giving away our presence."

"Let's hope whatever Azular, Greffy and Crizz did to the cloak, it'll keep us out of the sensors of anything out here," Apnis said as she sat down next to the captain and hauled her ops boards across.

Arianrhod slid off the bypass, every bridge station vigilant. Ahxenta had upped the alert to red and ordered the main holo-grid to full, with long-range scanners tied in. Tactical chief Pollux Gliss had refined the signal to pinpoint its source: the third and only habitable planet of the Veil system. It was listed as uninhabited by sentients and no authority claimed it, though it was oxygen-rich, capable of sustaining organic life and with a mix of flora and minor fauna. *Arianrhod's* sensor arrays were picking up no activity in local space but there was a risk that something might be hiding out of range. As the ship closed in, tactical and science data revealed surface details and isolated the locus of the distress.

"Signal hasn't changed but it's stronger, a repeated pattern," comms officer Lynxi Bellfish stated.

"Triangulating," Gliss called. "It's a small metallic structure sitting on a jutting ridge of a shallow rocky outcrop that's rising out of what looks like thick vegetative ground cover."

"It reads as a small vessel, Captain, but power emissions are low," Azular cut in. "The distress may be automated. I can't get lifesigns this far out, but I'll try to get size and shape. It's maybe an escape craft, as it's too small to be a long-distance ship of any kind."

"Get us into high orbit, Dox and we'll see what else we can pick up. And cut our cloak, it's using too much energy. Azular, send out three linked scanning probes to keep eyes on our blind spots – I want to see anything before it sees me."

A full orbit later and nothing else was logged in or near the system. Ahxenta thus ordered a response of *Arianrhod's* name and status, with a situation request. There was no reply. The call was repeated.

"What do we do? Call it in to Selliden or Lesser Kirrin and let them deal with it?" Apnis asked. "Or shuttle down to see what's going on?"

"Still no sign of life down there, Azular?"

"None, Captain. I'm still trying to get a profile. She's got active hull shields and surface jammers but I *can* read her hull structure: it's dense, complex and very strong. Hold on! Sending to grid! We've seen similar before, but a long while back and *very* far from here."

"What have you got?" the captain demanded, her eyes scanning the slowly forming shape in the grid. "I'll be… power down our weapons, Earbleat, in case she can read us. Gliss, keep tactical eyes and ears open. Maintain all channels online and repeat our hail. Azular, send a probe in to get clearer readings, but not too close in case this is a set-up. But get a positive ID on her insignia. I want to know what ship she's from."

"You and me both, Cinnabar," Apnis breathed.

Guided by Greffy, the probe launched into a decreasing orbit to the surface. By the time it made visual range, Azular had caught fine details of the stranded craft. It was a small, streamlined shuttle, her hull scored and pitted. She had seen severe action and was in no shape to launch, much less attempt orbit. Azular had also picked up four active lifesigns at distance from the ship that read humanoid. As he homed in on the ship's side, a distorted but legible image clarified.

"Comparison!" Ahxenta barked.

"Comparison, aye," Azular echoed. "There's a match! Structure *and* markings indicate that she's from the *SS Kel'Tarn*, taken out by hostiles off Axle Lexo, by the Astrella Nine asteroid field."

"But how could she have got all this way from Kappa?" Lieutenant Greffy asked the question that was on everyone's lips.

"I don't know," Azular told him frankly. "We'd have to ask, if those blips *are* her crew, or what's left of them. They're heading to the shuttle, Captain: they may have been too far off at first to catch our hail."

"They're in for one helluva surprise," Apnis remarked.

Ahxenta tabbed her link. "Engineering, prep the *Gadfly* for launch. Security, I need a landing party of three, protective suiting and heavy phase rifles. I'll need a medic," she added to Apnis. "Dr Oak, as he's the cyber expert and they may have implants if they *are* survivors off the *Kel'Tarn*. But we don't take it as read: Azular, you're with me."

"Cinnabar, you're not going down yourself? As your second…"

"You'll obey my orders," she was told. "And we talk before we go; they must be near enough to their boat to realise their distress has been heard. No wonder it's weak, if it's been going all this time."

"This smells fishy, Cap," the first mate persisted. "The last we heard of the *Kel'Tarn*, it was halfway across the mapped galaxy. No way could they have made it this far in that ship, even if it's super-strong and it's taken all the time since then. It must be near a galactic year ago."

"Based on the growth around her and the degree of settling into the substrate, she's been there a long time," Azular observed. "It looks like the area's been cleared. The ridge is light in foliage, but there's a void behind her that may be a cave. They've made the shuttle, ma'am."

Several minutes passed. The four had entered the small craft, where their lifesigns were masked by the shuttle's shielding.

"I read a power build-up, Captain!" Azular called. "Very small – I doubt they've much left to call on."

"Looking us over and wondering if we're here to do them damage," Apnis guessed.

"If we wanted to do them damage, we'd have done it by now," said Ahxenta. "They're making sure we are who we say we are. Not that they'll work *that* out, our surface jammers will see to that."

"We have a response to our hail!" the comms officer exclaimed. "I have audio. I'll try for visual – they're trying to up their signal."

"Let's see what you have, Mr Bellfish."

The rail-thin male stated warily that he was Lieutenant Kur Spree; he and his crew had escaped their ship when it had come under attack by hostiles, so long ago that they had almost given up. His three fellows crowded at his back, craning to see what evidently was a small viewer.

In reply to the captain's queries on his ship, her home port, his last heading and what had happened to bring them to where they were, he verified his ship as the *SS Kel'Tarn*. He was sharp enough not to give her origin, but told Ahxenta that three shuttles had got out. They had been attacked near Axle Lexo in zone Kappa. He paused: he clearly knew that he was a long way from there.

"Axle Lexo," she repeated, eyeing him and the others as the holo sharpened. "What was your business there and how came you here?"

"Why do you have to know? We can't do you any harm."

"If I'm bringing you aboard my ship, mister, I want to know all about you and yours," she informed him tersely. "And if I find any of it is fabricated, you'll be enjoying my brig until I can hand you over to the nearest law enforcement agency. Do you understand me?"

As Azular relocated his probe closer to the ship to pull in data from the surroundings, Bellfish refined the comm image to bring up a clearer visual. The garb of the four was rough and had seen wear, but a jacket worn by one of the three behind Spree was part of a dark, armoured uniform that the captain recognised.

Spree nodded wearily. "We were searching for one of our ships that had gone missing when we caught a distress. We answered, but it was a trap: there were two. We lit out for a local asteroid field – old mining ops had left debris we hoped would mask our signals. But they blew our main engines and came in after us. Our commander ordered us to the shuttles. She and a few volunteers stayed on board to put up a fight to distract them. Our shuttles took off on different headings through the asteroid field, in the hopes one of us at least would make it out."

"And?"

"I agreed to head to Iota, for a bypass node between Axle Lexo and Dice Gold – I knew I could make for Kell Lyne from there."

Ahxenta exchanged a glance with Azular, and could hear a hiss from Apnis. None of them had heard of such a node but if the route ended at or cut through near Kell Lyne, an isolated port on the Iota-Kappa border, it was thought-provoking. Azular was manipulating an auxiliary console at his station and soon pulled up a star chart.

"And?" the captain prompted. "Axle Lexo and Kell Lyne are a long way from here. You know where you *are*, I take it?"

Spree looked at her. "Yes, we do. We made the bypass and jumped on. We'd taken damage and the ride was rough but as far as we knew we hadn't been tracked. We'd been on for four days when we spotted a tail. It's a little-known bypass, so it was either one of ours… or a ship intent on taking us out. I took us off at the Sox system, near the Kappa border; I knew of a worm-pocket that came out near Hervesta Tertius.

It's risky in any ship; in a shuttle it could have been fatal, but I saw little option. We went in at hyper speed, hit it and rode the storm, expecting to jump out at Hervesta. But we didn't. Our nav-gear and sensors were out, our comms were down, we were spinning. Our auto systems had cut in, as we'd blacked out. I don't know how long we drifted until we got some gear back up and could navigate. We'd one dead at that point and were almost out of air. This was the nearest place that could sustain life. I got her down, just. And we've been here since. We lost another crewman shortly after. She'd been injured in the exit from the pocket."

After more questions and answers, Ahxenta directed the four to remain in the shuttle until hers had landed and prepare to be lifted off. She and Azular were reasonably sure that they had heard the truth. The distress had been set off soon after crashing, Spree told them, but its use had been impeded by the highly variable local climate and they had been wary in its use lest it drew in trouble, as initially they had had no idea where they were. He also verified Thal as his fleet commander and gave the names and ranks of his fellows. He agreed to a full scan of his shuttle and turned off the operative external shielding.

"Stand by," was the captain's final order. "We'll be with you shortly. You will not be armed, nor carry anything but the barest essentials; but you *will* extract the technical data you have on what happened to you after you left the *Kel'Tarn*, particularly the nav-data in relation to the worm-pocket you found yourselves in that brought you here. Clear?"

"Yes ma'am," Spree responded. "We'll be ready."

* * *

The *Gadfly* made a soft touchdown next to the battered shuttle. Azular probed with his Norvallan scanner before the team stepped out, led by the captain. The three males and one female had waited as ordered and alighted as soon as the *Gadfly* powered down.

They were a sorry sight but not starving, badly injured or sick. After introductions, Zaiklyn Oak began checks to capture their biosigns and ensure that they were disease-free whilst Azular set off to their shuttle.

Ahxenta looked round the site. A crude low barrier of boulders was set against a sheer rock wall at their backs, where a deep hollow in the rock face had been used as a shelter, with cut boughs for shade. Two cairns off to one side marked the final resting places of their two lost crewmen. Traces of a fire, with rough-and-ready cooking implements nearby, told how they had survived.

"There's a small spring close by with a source higher up that we use for water," Spree explained, noting her interest.

She could tell they were still unsure that she had their best interests at heart, but they were clearly desperate to be rescued.

"You'll be thankful to know that both your other shuttles made it," she told them, to their evident shock. "I'll contact Captain Thal once we're back aboard my ship. Let's go."

"*Captain* Thal?" queried Lieutenant Olanta, her jaw dropping.

"It's a long story."

The trip up to *Arianrhod* was largely silent. Ahxenta took the pilot's seat as she needed her crewmen to keep their eyes, ears and scanners on the castaways. She had taken the precaution of having armed guards meet the party in the shuttle bay, where she also found her CMO, who insisted on their direct transfer to medbay and vetoed any interviews until she had passed them as physically and mentally fit.

The captain left Greffy to locate the worm-pocket that Spree had given as his exit into local space; unknown, it was a hazard to travel. Azular was told to analyse the data that Spree had handed over, and to summarise it into a succinct report of the loss of the *Kel'Tarn*, and the shuttle's trip across five zones. That and the medical data she planned to pass to Thal, after he had verified the identities of the four. She also wanted more on the bypass that Spree had used, and the risky trip that had allegedly brought his small ship halfway across the mapped galaxy.

Back on the bridge, the captain examined the junior science officer's progress. Greffy had homed in on an area of high negative mass-energy density between Veil and Lesser Kirrin as a probability: there had been reports of missing ships and odd debris trails over the years.

"Keep checking and liaise with Dr Azular once he's finished what he's doing – he has the data from Spree's shuttle. Meanwhile, we can't hang about here, we have cargo to deliver."

She ordered a final sweep before retrieving their probes and setting for the bypass and directly to Selliden. The worm-pocket puzzle would have to wait. Azular had meanwhile completed his analyses of Spree's data shard and pulled out the details. Flintlock had found the four fit but malnourished, and she intended to keep them in medbay. Their biosigns she gave to the science officer to add to his data package.

Her pieces in place, and with the names and ranks of the four and their shuttle's spec ready to transmit, Ahxenta told Bellfish to raise the *Kel'Moth* to request an urgent talk to Thal. She figured that he may have left Merkat and zone Alpha, but she wanted her guests off ship quickly, and had no doubt that they would prefer to be with their own – who would be another surprise for them, Apnis commented.

It took twenty minutes to contact Thal, by which time the rescued crew were settled in a medical bay. The *Kel'Moth* had left the Web for

Alto Finglas when it went through. Her surprised captain was on duty, as grim as ever. Ahxenta came to the point at once.

"We answered a distress that took us to the third planet of the Veil system in zone Alpha. Its source was a crashed shuttle with the insignia of the *SS Kel'Tarn*. What was left of it matched the shuttle from the *Kel'Tarn* that we picked up near Tressic Minor, a year ago. You recall?"

"What?" Thal was incredulous. "A shuttle from the *Kel'Tarn*? In a system in zone Alpha? You're sure it *is* a shuttle from that ship?"

"We checked. The surviving crew claim it is, *and* claim you as their fleet commander. I have their names and the shuttle's spec, which I'll link across. Perhaps you'd confirm before I give you more details."

"Link received. Stand by."

As the holo-grid regained its typical setting of the external starfield stretched by hyperspace currents and the *Arianrhod's* course within it, the captain sighed. "I guess we made his day for him."

"He looked stunned," the first mate answered. "Those four *are* the real article and this isn't a hoax of massive proportions?"

"Can it. Flintlock's confirmed that they *have* inclusions that point to genetic and cybernetic alteration, and the removal of some by amateur means, but they *are* humanoid. And Azular's had the nous to check the faces against ones we hold of renegade ships' crews: the ship at Skyrtek, Kerrix' records of her capture at Starfall, when she logged the external, including the techs that were trying to break into her shuttle. And he's found a fit: one of the techs aboard the ship that caught Kerrix' shuttle matches Lieutenant Lymnik, the one who says he's a science officer."

"Trust Azular. And he's sure the shuttle *is* one off the *Kel'Tarn*?"

"He's sure. And here's Thal."

Thal verified the names on Ahxenta's list as crew from his lost ship and asked to talk to Spree. She had him linked in. Azular was back on the bridge and she wanted to hear his progress on the shuttle data and Greffy's input, as it was vital that news of an unknown worm-pocket in the busy zone Alpha was circulated. She was also curious as to why the wreck had not been spotted sooner. Azular could answer that: the distress had only recently been set up in continuous mode, as previous attempts had been thwarted by the recurrent violent storms that swept the planet. That was possibly the reason that it had never been settled permanently, despite its abundant wildlife.

Thal's talk took an hour, by which time the promised data had been sent to the *Kel'Moth* and a report prepared for the PSS fleet. Meanwhile, the *Kel'Moth's* first mate Marlin Seer had refused to discuss the Sox and Hervesta worm-pockets, despite their implications for travel, Hervesta being a production hub of top grade scientific and other kit.

"I don't get him," Apnis grumbled to the captain. "What's his beef against the galaxy? And how come Thal took him on as first mate?"

"He's maybe as bitter as Thal and for similar reasons," she replied quietly. "He *is* probably a very capable officer."

"Or maybe he needed the job and Thal was in a good mood the day he applied," the first mate said, stretching. "Hell, I'm tired. Once we're through with the *Kel'Moth*, we take a break. There can't be much more for the universe to throw at us between here and our next stop."

"Don't count on it," was the mordant response as Thal called again to discuss arrangements for the pick-up of his people.

"I'm for Selliden. I'll leave them there," Ahxenta told him. "They'll be regarded as shipwreck survivors and will be well-treated."

The dour captain had other ideas. "I've a ship en route to pick them up. If you'll tell me your schedule, the *Moonstone* will rendezvous with you at Selliden to take them on. They'll transfer by shuttle."

Ahxenta could hear Apnis snickering quietly as she agreed.

* * *

In the mess over rations, the first mate heaved a sigh. "Thal didn't want those four on Selliden. He still has trouble trusting the system, Cap?"

"Given what he and his have been through, I'm not surprised. I've sent the fleet what Azular put together, copied to Zillah. She'll send it to the ISA. Thal knows. But why's he sent the *Moonstone*?"

"She's one of the fastest ships in his fleet, if not the fastest, and if she was heading this way from Merkat, it makes sense. She *was* for Mu, so if she was passing Keystone Kell she'd be in the area. And some of her crew were from Thal's original fleet, weren't they?"

"Good points, Tallica. Azular figured *that* when we were aboard her with Grey and his first mate for that meet with Kerrix, Thal, Inks and Levettiza, after we and *Obsidian* had to haul into Starfall for repair."

"You've been aboard the *Moonstone* and know what she's like. More to the point, you'll allow one of *her* shuttles aboard *Arianrhod*: one was sent to collect you and Azular for that meet. And Azular's pet shuttle's Norvallan. Bet it's made his day," Apnis added, nodding over to where the science officer was collecting his rations and talking to Dox.

"I can see the grin from here," Ahxenta returned.

The first mate recalled another issue. "The chat with Kerrix before we left the Web: you said she'd something to say and you wouldn't tell me, though I was partly responsible. As we'll be speaking to her, hadn't you better tell me? Azular knows, I bet."

"He does, and it tickled him," Ahxenta laughed. "I guess Levettiza told him. I don't know why it was done, but Fleetskup's so short of crew he couldn't say no. You've a lot to answer for. *Tallulah's* new chief tactical officer is a Lieutenant Commander Wekki Munnet."

"You're joking!"

"I'm not. How she set up the credentials to get the job I don't know, but she is or was Intelligence. And tactical's right up her space lane."

"But she's a *commander* in Intelligence!" Apnis said, shocked. "And her real name isn't Munnet."

"Exactly. Fleetskup's got a bargain, or maybe the ISA now has a mole in the PSS fleet. Or ISA Intelligence has lost another key op."

"Or the ISA has two moles in the fleet: Levettiza's on the *Moonstone* but hasn't cut all the links to her old unit, given what she can find out."

"Now you know," the captain smiled. "But enough. I want a quick stop at Selliden. It'll take half a day to offload our cargo, and the client wants every part passed fit. As soon as it's off ship, we ready the bays for the Marridani load. Its pods are huge, so grapples. That's a day, *with* our teams on overtime. The *Moonstone* had better be in by then or we drop Spree and his crew with the PA and she can collect them. Once you're back on duty, see what stores we need: we may as well benefit from the rep we have with local suppliers," she said, waving Azular over, the chatty Dox having trotted off to join Box at a side table.

The science officer greeted the two and sat. His cautious glance told them that he expected to be teased, but the captain was more interested in how much he had analysed of the data he had gleaned from the Veil incident, particularly the relevant details from the shuttle records.

"Lieutenant Spree copied all the data from the time he and his crew boarded the shuttle, Captain, but I noted when I was aboard that she'd been primed with the *Kel'Tarn's* data, so that if she made it, that would be available to Starfall. My scanner got it, and it seems the *Kel'Tarn* had been on the bypass that runs from Starfall to K457 when she was called in to search for the lost ship. Spree told us he'd jumped on at a node between Axle Lexo and Dice Gold to make Kell Lyne, so I've assumed a possible route direct from Kell Lyne to K457. I've integrated it into our nav-charts. If it exists, it runs through mostly empty space and would be unlikely to be picked up. I *could* ask Spree if it exists."

As Ahxenta shook her head at him, Apnis gave a snort of laughter. "Or you could ask Captain Kerrix when we meet her at Selliden."

"Very funny, Commander."

"I don't know what Thal said to Spree but I don't expect it was to tell him to tell us everything we wanted to know," Ahxenta said to him. "I doubt he'll answer questions about his ship or Starfall, and Flintlock won't let you lean on him. And you won't likely get a chance to check with Captain Kerrix anyhow; it'll be a short interchange."

"What was Dox bending your ears about?" the first mate wanted to know. "She seemed to have a lot to say."

"She did. And as it relates to an issue that'll have a bearing on other shipboard events, I may as well let you know. The lieutenant has done me the honour of asking me to – I think the official term is *give her away* – at her marriage to Mr Box. To represent her senior family member, in other words. They have other things to arrange, but they have an appointment to talk to you about the ceremony, Captain."

"It's coming home to roost, Cinnabar," Apnis laughed. "You won't be able to dodge that bullet much longer."

"I'd figured that's what it was going to be about," Ahxenta sighed. "I'll be seeing the pair of them just before we dock at Selliden."

"That means you'll have to dig out your dress uniform and make sure it fits, Azular," the first mate continued. "You can use it to impress Captain Kerrix when next you see her."

"Save your breath, Tallica, he won't rise to the bait," counselled the captain. "Finish your rations and we'll go over the lists to see if we can save time at Marridan. We've got the Kanelian arms cargo contract for the ISP yard at Alto Finglas, so Kanelian's our heading after Marridan."

* * *

Arianrhod reached Selliden and settled into her allotted bay. The clients were ready, and goods drop began as soon as Port Authority clearances were in. The *Moonstone* was expected, Ahxenta was told. She also found that the authorities, knowing of *Arianrhod's* human cargo, had deduced that the arrival of the *Moonstone* was related to that. The report that Ahxenta had sent out had come to them via ISA contacts.

The half day specified to complete cargo drop and its related checks was almost gone when the huge trilaterally-shaped *Moonstone* entered orbital space and hove into the bay next to the *Arianrhod*.

"She still causes a stir when she turns up," Apnis said. "Those small transports are buzzing about like bees to get a look close-up."

"Most Starfall ships cause a stir, but there's not another that shape anywhere in the mapped galaxy," Ahxenta replied. "Once she's locked in, we'll say hello. The quicker our guests are off *Arianrhod* the better."

"Cottontail's arranged a big inner bay for her shuttle, as I assume Captain Kerrix will have company. She'll do the honours herself?"

"She will," the captain confirmed. "Flintlock's got the castaways set up with kitbags of essentials to remind them of the nice time they had with us. And she has their med-records for the *Moonstone's* chief medic.

They know they're going to a Starfall ship, but it'll no doubt come as a shock when they see her. As soon as the shuttle's in, they'll be escorted to Cottontail's staff briefing room. I want this done in short order."

"Best have Azular on the welcome team," Apnis said wickedly.

The words were hardly out of her mouth when Lieutenant Bellfish called an incoming link from the captain of the *Moonstone*.

Kerrix was civil in her greetings, keeping her eyes strictly on the two in the centre position. Courtesies over, Ahxenta came to the point.

"We have your castaways ready, Captain, and a berth prepped for your shuttle. You'll meet them in a briefing room near the shuttle bay as soon as you dock. What personnel will fly over?"

"I'll pilot, Captain. My chief medic and my senior science officer will accompany me. That's all."

"Your senior science officer?" Ahxenta echoed charily. She knew he was a Friskianx ex-raider and had once served on the *Kel'Moth*.

Kerrix smiled. "As Lieutenant Commander Nyvallish knows one of the survivors, I thought it wise. And you *have* met him and Dr Mettix. Dr Mettix has their original medical records, and with your permission, he'll run scans before they board my shuttle."

"Agreed. Let me know when you're ready to go."

"I'm ready now. I'll link again when I'm on my way – I'm sure you'll want to run full scans of my shuttle before I come aboard."

"I will. Ahxenta out. Tallica, you have the conn. Tactical, monitor her flight from start to finish and keep eyes on the *Moonstone*. Bellfish, advise Dr Flintlock and her party to head up now. Azular, you're with me. You *will* run full scans of the shuttle and its crew, *and* our departing guests. One of Crizz's team will monitor from main engineering."

"The *Moonstone's* a fellow PSS, Cap," Apnis murmured. "Won't Kerrix think that's a bit strong?"

"I don't care what she thinks, that's what's happening. Goldwash and Hanx will be there: they're escorting Spree and his crew. The doc's given them a last health check. Right, Azular, let's go."

The captain and her science officer were well on their way in the cross-ship transport tube when she faced him squarely. "Right, what is it? I know that expression and you're peeved."

"May I speak frankly, ma'am?"

"I don't know why you're asking, you always do. But go ahead."

"You seem heavy-handed in your dealings with Captain Kerrix," he frowned. "Don't you trust her, despite all our dealings with her?"

Ahxenta sighed. "You damn well know I trust her, or she wouldn't be headed for my ship. And you trust her, and that's good enough for me. But she's Starfall, and Thal's her supreme commander. There are a heap of questions hanging over that fleet and its ways. A lot of ships in it are *not* PSS and some of their crews are suspect."

"That could be said of any ship or any fleet. And if you don't mind me saying, ma'am, your dislike of her seems – personal."

"She bugs me and has done since I met her, as you're also aware. And since *you* met her, you've changed."

"I trust I always carry out my duties to your satisfaction, ma'am?"

"Oh don't pull that crap! If you didn't, I'd tell you to pull your socks up, again as you damn well know." Ahxenta grimaced as she recalled a chat she had once had with her chief medic about Azular and Kerrix. "Flintlock once told me that my dislike was down to her being too like me for comfort. Maybe I should look in the mirror more often."

"She finds you intimidating, ma'am, and copes by being – abrupt."

"Downright rude, you mean. And I know: she told me so. But here we are. Don't worry, I'll treat her with respect. And she rates respect. But you'll still scan everyone that comes off that boat, including her."

The two joined Cottontail in an observation booth overlooking the bay in which the *Moonstone's* shuttle was to dock. The chief stood at a station set to monitor bay activity. The ship was being tracked from *Arianrhod's* bridge and the three outside the bay had a good view.

The *Moonstone's* shuttle made a model landing. It was larger than the one Ahxenta had travelled in belonging to the ship, but it was as sleek, streamlined, and no doubt as luxurious. Ahxenta had posted guards at the bay entry who stood to attention as she and Azular came down. As soon as the space had pressurised, the two stepped in.

Kerrix was first out and down the ramp. She accepted the welcome aboard calmly and presented her officers, waiting while Azular ran the scans his captain had decreed, his only sign of disquiet a resigned look and a fleeting frown as he ran his pet scanner over the visiting captain.

"I take it I'm not an imposter?" she asked him softly.

"No, ma'am," he smiled politely, with a roguish twinkle.

"We've set aside a room for you to examine your people, doctor," Ahxenta said curtly to Mettix. "This way."

They left the bay, the two guards at their heels. Kerrix chuckled as she saw Cottontail at her station above. In the room, the castaways sat at the table, sipping drinks. The four stood as the newcomers entered.

"Captain Xanna Kerrix of the *PSS Moonstone*," Ahxenta introduced. "Captain, if you'll present your officers, Mr Spree will present his."

Kerrix completed her duty swiftly, aware of the high tension around her. Spree had no time to speak, for Nyvallish brushed him aside to face a visibly stunned Lieutenant Olanta. "Soola…"

"You *were* supposed to scan her," Kerrix rebuked her senior science officer softly as Nyvallish and Olanta met in a tight embrace, oblivious to the others. "Doctor?" she asked Mettix, nodding at the pair.

"She's the real thing," the *Moonstone's* CMO confirmed, smiling.

"Lieutenant Spree, perhaps you'd continue the introductions?"

"Aye, ma'am," he responded, clearly nonplussed.

"Dr Mettix will scan you to ensure that you're fit and are who you claim," Kerrix told them. "You'll then head to the *Moonstone* with me. Thank you for caring for our people, Captain," she said to Ahxenta.

"What happens now? You'll take them on as part of your crew?"

"They're not staying with me, I'm for Keystone Kell. They're to be picked up. There's a ship heading in now," Kerrix explained.

The hush that greeted that was not lost on her and she turned. Her face softened as two pairs of stricken eyes looked at her.

"What's your background, Lieutenant?" she asked Olanta.

"I'm a weapons specialist, ma'am."

"I have several, but one more won't hurt," she said. "Perhaps you'd accept a berth aboard the *Moonstone*? I'll clear it with Captain Thal."

The woman could only nod.

"Thank you, ma'am," Nyvallish murmured.

"Care to explain?" Ahxenta enquired as Flintlock joined Mettix to update him on the treatment the four had received aboard *Arianrhod* and to advise both them and him on the next steps to be taken.

Kerrix shrugged. "They'd only been married a month when he was posted to the *Kel'Moth*. Her transfer was in prep when the *Kel'Tarn* went down. He thought he'd lost her. I won't put him through that again."

"You're a romantic, Captain?" Azular asked quietly.

"I'm a realist, Doctor. A cheerful senior science officer is easier to get along with than a grouch, as I'm sure Captain Ahxenta can testify."

Ahxenta looked skyward, shook her head, and left them, to head to where her CMO and Mettix were exchanging data. That complete, the survivors were led to the bay. They boarded with Nyvallish and Mettix whilst Kerrix halted to take leave. After short civilities, she was turning to step onto the ramp when Azular asked for a private word.

His captain's sardonic look and the chief medic's knowing grin left him unfazed, and he waited until they had made the far side of the bay. Whatever he said to Kerrix clearly unsettled her. Her gape and sharp reply resulted in another string of words from Azular that earned him a shake of the head and a reproving finger wagged under his nose.

"You do *not* play fair, Dr Azular!" she accused in a voice so strident that the two at the other side could hear.

He obviously agreed, but in the face of further argument, she finally assented and turned to face him squarely. He took her hand and after a couple of exchanged whispers, he pulled her close.

Bloody hell!" Ahxenta raged from the far wall, to the sound of Dr Flintlock chuckling at her side. "I have a cargo to load!"

"Just as well they can't see what's going on from inside that shuttle, but Cottontail's glued," the doctor observed with an upward flick of her head. "And I bet half the engineering deck is as well."

Azular and Kerrix parted and the science officer watched her board before stepping back from the ramp. He wore a quiet smile as he made his way over to the others, his eyebrows raised, expecting comments.

"Out, now," the captain commanded.

The three made their way to the upstairs obs room, where the chief engineer still held station. She turned to them.

"They're good to go. Tallica's got the details and Gliss has got them on tactical. Got the kiss you were asking for?" she asked Azular sourly.

"Yes, Chief."

"I'd have thought she'd have told you to get lost. I would have."

"I didn't ask *you*, Chief."

The four watched the shuttle safely exit the bay before moving out, Cottontail to engineering and the others to the local transport tube.

"Well?" Flintlock enquired. "What was that about? What were you trying to persuade her to? It wasn't just a smooch in the docking bay."

"That's not your concern, Doctor," he replied, the lustre in his eyes belying his sharp tone.

"Huh!" was the retort as the chief medic stepped out for medbay.

Ahxenta's look spoke volumes. "You keep your private life *private*, mister. My shuttle bay is *not* the place for a public exhibition like that."

"No, ma'am."

"What didn't you play fair about? It annoyed Captain Kerrix."

"It did," he grinned. "I reminded her of her own words: a cheerful senior science officer is easier to get along with than a grouch. So she agreed – eventually."

"To what?" the captain asked suspiciously, her eyes narrowing. "A canoodle in full view of all the engineering personnel looking on?"

His answer caused an explosion that could be clearly heard as the transport tube halted at the bridge. "What!?"

5: CELEBRATION

The bridge crew sat rigidly at their posts, flicking glances at each other and at the two new arrivals. That Ahxenta's face was a study in irritated disbelief did not escape any of them.

"To your station, mister!" she barked at Azular. "What's the status of that shuttle, Commander Apnis?"

The first mate was as amazed as the rest at the atypical outburst but answered calmly that the shuttle was docking aboard the *Moonstone*.

"Our outer bays are ready for loading our cargo for Marridan?"

"Priming now," Apnis told her, tapping the cargo display status on her board. "The first pod will come over by drone in two hours."

"Roger that," Ahxenta said as she sat and hauled her boards across. "I see you've indented for medbay and general supplies."

"Aye, Cap. We got good rates. Here are the lists and invoices."

Kerrix called shortly afterwards. After repeat thanks for the rescue, she told Ahxenta that they were for Idledott, to meet the ship that was to take on three of the survivors. She had left Thal an advisory that she had granted Lieutenant Olanta's request to remain with her ship. She seemed calm, but her eyes were wary as she waited a response. She had scented that something had disturbed the *Arianrhod's* captain.

Ahxenta was cool as she wished her and hers a safe onward passage and hoped to see them again soon. "By the way, Captain," she added, raising a mocking eyebrow, "Congratulations."

Kerrix' eyes widened as she paused for a second before dipping her head in acknowledgement, uttering thanks, and signing off with a sharp final glance around *Arianrhod's* bridge.

"Congratulations on what?" Apnis whispered.

"Mind your own damn business."

After status scans and enquiries, the captain pushed her ops boards aside. "You have the conn, Commander. Dr Azular: my office, now."

"What in blazes has he done this time?" Box murmured to Dox.

"I don't know. But he's still smiling, so it can't be that bad."

"I wouldn't put credit on it. The Cap looks like a thundercloud."

"Shut up and mind your boards," Apnis ordered. "We might be in orbit, but your jobs are to keep us there and plot the next set of jumps that'll take us to Marridan, avoiding all obstacles and possible threats on the way. You copy?"

"Yes, ma'am," was the joint reply.

* * *

By the following planetary day, the large cargo pods for Marridan were locked in, *Arianrhod* was ready to depart and the *Moonstone* was distant. There had been no news of local trouble. Ahxenta's report, backed by one from Thal, had had effects: the ISA, having got it via Zillah, had sent science ships to the sites of the three new worm-pockets. That the Starfall fleet knew of those at Sox and Hervesta and had used them caused fallout, but as far as the PSS fleet was concerned, it was another reason that the TA should rethink its planned contract changes.

The tension between the captain and Azular had amused many, but it had given way to plans for the coming bridal. Ahxenta had stipulated that it take place before Marridan or after Alto Finglas, as those stages would be the quietest in view of their route, its risks, and *Arianrhod's* tendency to attract trouble. That meant in the next four days or thirty down the line. Box and Dox opted for the earlier window. The service and party would take place two days hence, ship time.

"The formalities will be short and sweet," the captain told her first mate over rations in the mess, several hours into their ride to Marridan. "Dox prefers it and Box will do as she says. Gem Ferry's his best man, so he'll keep him straight. And as you're maid of honour or whatever it's called for Dox, you'll have the job of keeping her in line."

"No problem. She's savvier than most aboard, and as we have one smart crew, she's near the top. She says she won't give up her personal quarters, though we don't *have* facilities for legally-hitched crew."

"You're damn right we don't; this is a starship not a cruise liner."

"Here's the proxy father of the bride," Apnis grinned as she spied Azular. "He's taking his duties seriously, but why did she ask him?"

"Tradition: a close authority figure that's older and wiser – though in his case, the wiser bit has taken a few knocks of late."

"What *has* he been up to that's causing you head-scratching, Cap? I know, mind my own business. It's to do with Kerrix isn't it? Whatever it is, *he* seems pleased with himself."

"He won the argument. And stop digging, or I'll take my ears and my rations elsewhere."

"Aye, ma'am. He's coming over, so let's find out how the planning's coming along," Apnis added, indicating the empty chair at their table. "Got your speech ready for the festivities?" she enquired playfully.

"No," he said as he sat. "I've discussed it with Lieutenant Dox, as

I'm not familiar with Stella Viridis Four's marital customs. She says she doesn't want a long eulogy and two sentences will do."

"So what'll it be? I'm not losing a cherished daughter but gaining a son, and as it's Lieutenant Box, she's welcome?"

"Hardly. Is there anything else you'd like to know, Commander?" he asked, aware that there was and it was not about the coming event.

"Got your dress uniform ready? I don't know when we last wore them; we didn't at the party that Captain Kerrix gave after the *Moonstone* became a PSS. You remember?" she said impishly to Azular.

"I remember perfectly. And in that case, perhaps you should inspect your own dress uniform, ma'am. I assume those present at the main event will be required to dress appropriately?"

"They will," Ahxenta told him. "The last time we were in our finery was at the memorial service for Mora Ma'Lappis."

"Yes. We didn't at the memorial for the five lost from the *Firedrake*. That reminds me, Cinnabar: what happens when Flish Ma'Lappis and Felipe Poppet tie the knot? Flick's *Firedrake's* first mate and Flish is one of our best medics, and Axellina doesn't want to lose her."

The captain eyed her first mate wryly: she knew where the question had come from and where she hoped it was going. "I've not discussed it with Ma'Lappis but I'm sure she'll tell me in good time. And since you're here, Azular, do you plan to do more to our cloak? I know you and Crizz finished the initial upgrades before we left for Selliden, the hull sensor work's done and the new data routines are going well. But Crizz told me that the add-on units fixed to our hull plates were tricky to fit, and as we've no spares, we may not be able to get them repaired if they're hit. She figures there might be a way round it."

"The chief *did* have reservations at the time. We've worked on it, and think if we can design our own version, Greffy and Gem Ferry can begin to create it. But we'll need materials we don't have on board."

Azular continued on the same track, thus thwarting further crafty conjectures from Apnis. Ahxenta sat back, enjoying the show.

"That round to him," the captain told her as he left. "But as we've done here, back to the bridge. I have to see Lindell about the balloons and ribbons, and keeping chef on target with the cake. He'd better not overdo it: I'm not made of credit."

"Lindell treats the ship's wallet as his own, Cap; he'll keep track of every button. But you threatened Box and Dox that they'd have to pay for their own party. Best make sure you're not setting a precedent: it might lead to all sorts of trouble," she warned archly.

"Believe me, Tallica, it already has."

"What gives if Flish and Flick set a date and want *Arianrhod* as the venue?" the first mate persisted. "As Pa Ma'Lappis is the father of the bride, he can't officiate if they have it aboard the *Firedrake*."

"They can damn well elope. And you can damn well shut up."

* * *

One and a half shipboard days later, *Arianrhod's* main mess was a sea of floating colour and teeming with a fair portion of her crew. Seating had been reordered and a slow march played. At the far end, an anxious Lieutenant Box stood in front of a draped lectern, his friend Lieutenant Ferry beside him. Captain Ahxenta stood facing the two.

"Too late to change your mind now," Gem Ferry whispered.

"I won't," Box muttered. "But what if Romanna gets cold feet?"

"She's nowhere to run," Gem consoled. "With Doc Azular beside her and Commander Apnis at her back, she wouldn't dare."

A stir behind them warned that the time had come. Box turned to view the advancing vision. His gasp was audible to everyone close, and was echoed by those craning their necks to catch a glimpse of the bride.

"There's a sight you don't see every day," Ferry said softly. "You're a lucky boy, Boxy."

Box was unable to react. Awestruck, his eyes froze as Azular led his bride up and handed her over in the sight of the crew there and those on links. His usual loquacity crushed, Box obeyed orders to speak, read his vows and deploy the ring. He sailed through the ceremony in a daze and at the end had to be reminded by the captain to kiss his new wife.

As the pair set off under a shower of light motes, a double line of friends formed an impromptu honour guard. The captain loosened the neck of her dress jacket, sighed deeply, and turned to her first mate.

"Thank hell that's done. I need a drink."

"You and me both, Cap. What about you, Azular? Do you have to mingle and be sociable before you give your little speech?"

"I do not," he retorted. "Once Lieutenant Ferry has announced the toasts, which he'll do soon, I thank everyone for attending, praise the bride, welcome Mr Box into the Dox family, congratulate the couple on behalf of the captain and crew and raise a toast to them. And that's it. What anyone else has to say is up to them."

"Hell, I hope Box hasn't got his tongue back by that time," rejoined Apnis. "I'd best tell Romanna to rein him in. See you both at the bar."

"Roger that, Tallica. Let's go, Azular. Ah! Gem Ferry's waving at you, so I guess you're wanted. I'll see you when you're done."

As Azular had predicted, his part in the ritual ended with his brief address and a clinking of glasses. Under cover of the ripple of applause, he slid off to join the captain, Flintlock and Cottontail at a side table.

"Nice speech," the chief engineer hailed him. "Short. Gem told me that Dox had said there wouldn't be dancing or any of that stuff."

"Travelling at hyper speed on a bypass where there might be strong currents, unfriendly ships and plenty of nodes where trouble can jump in, I'd hope not," Ahxenta stated. "And the toasting fizz is innocuous, so nobody will be getting drunk at my expense. And on her next duty shift, Dox will be at the helm, newlywed or not. She knows the score."

Apnis came over to repeat the praise on Azular's brevity of speech. "One sip and I'm off to change. I should've kept to dress uniform: it's got to be less tight than this. But Dox asked me to gussy up, as the record's going to her folks on Stella Viridis and Box's at Fyvie Major. You looked the part, *Commander* Azular, every button and ranking pin buffed. Best keep them shiny, in case you need them soon. And now *you* know the ropes, Cinnabar, you'll be ready for the next one."

"Cut it, Commander Apnis, and sit. I've had enough festivities to tide me over for now," the captain growled.

"Come on, Cap! It gives the crew a reason to get together socially. I think you made a very suitable officiator. Didn't she, Azular?"

"I'd quit while you're ahead, Tallica," the chief medic advised her. "Being first mate doesn't stop you from being thrown in the brig."

"True; can you see Murmur Fleetskup as officiator? He'd have more to say than everybody else in total. Or Maris Fleete? Or Race Flintlock – no offence, Doc. Or Captain Kerrix," she added teasingly to Azular.

"Why?" he asked calmly.

"The tongue she has and the formality she hasn't, for a start. And she's not exactly tall and imposing, like the Cap."

"If that's meant to be a compliment, Commander Apnis, stow it," Ahxenta cut in. "And you won't provoke *him*: he's immune."

Azular sat back, his mouth creasing as he smiled into the first mate's face. "Indeed," he agreed. "Lack of formality *is* part of Captain Kerrix' charm. But I'd be grateful, Commander, if you'd keep a civil tongue in your head when you speak of my fiancée."

Apnis dropped her drink.

"*That* was the argument he won," the captain told her, picking up the glass. "You'd better go change. And then I'll see you on the bridge. You too, Azular: you've had enough fun for one day."

As the two rose, Flintlock and Cottontail looked at one another.

"You knew, Cap," the chief engineer stated plainly.

"The spat at the *Moonstone's* shuttle," the CMO guessed. "She didn't have time to argue. Why didn't she just say no? She's quite capable."

"*He's* capable of arguing until the sun turns blue; and I suspect she didn't want to say no. And she prefers a direct approach – she can't be bribed with flowers and bonbons," the captain told them.

"Crew's going to rib him like crazy when they find out, and they will," prophesied Flintlock.

"Serves him damn well right. I've a ship to run. I'll see you later."

Pausing only to congratulate the newlyweds, Ahxenta made for her quarters, squaring her shoulders to relieve the tension as she undid the clasps of her dress jacket, thankful that nothing had spoiled the event.

* * *

The bridge was calm, everyone in post. The captain relieved Earbleat of the conn and sat, glancing over to where Ensign Larai was keeping her eyes on the science station. *Arianrhod* had passed Lesser Kirrin and was on the Swan Two beacon, with Marridan two days away. Comms had been low. Ahxenta looked up as Azular came in, nodding curtly at his dutiful request for permission to take his station.

"You've done it now," she warned him quietly in passing.

Helmsman Lieutenant Oyan Kern looked over at his navigator and raised his eyebrows. Lieutenant Salli Gale pursed her lips.

"Keep your eyes on your ops," she told him sharply but softly. "The currents on approach to the Swan Two beacon are wild because of that variable gravity well. I've set in the best line through."

"On it," he confirmed. "You think Romanna will change her name to Box?" he added conversationally.

"Why should she?" Gale returned.

"Tradition in many places; *you* must have when you married Ezrax."

"Like hell. *He* took my name. So would you if your name had been Ezrax Pinbottom. He got hell in our military college. Why d'you think he chose security as his field and ended up top of his entire year?"

The two broke off as Apnis arrived and sat down. "All okay, Cap?"

"Thus far. Not much on the bypass and nothing close…"

She had hardly spoken when the comms officer called out a distress signal, distant but distinct. It was off the bypass and in normal space.

"Damn! I might have known it was too good to be true!" Ahxenta spat, jumping up. "Can you pin it down, Bellfish?"

"On it, ma'am… It's on a PSS channel!"

"I have a ship on grid, Cap!" Gliss called. "She's trying to jump onto the bypass. Can't confirm status… wait, clearing… she reads as a PSS!"

"Red alert, shields up!" the captain yelled. "Azular, pull up all you've got on that bogus ISP boat that almost got the *Nyx Warrior* and make sure that's not the same. Weapons online; hot up engines, Lacewing."

"No match to the ship that hit the *Warrior*," Azular verified. "Her weapons are powered up but low."

"Got it! It's the *Warrior*! Repeat, the *Nyx Warrior*!" roared Bellfish.

As rushing feet signalled the arrival of more duty officers, some still in dress uniform, Gliss expanded the holo to bring in the latest. "I've got another ship but she's burning up. *She* reads as hostile!"

"Battlestations! Confirm *Warrior's* position, tactical, and send data to navi-helm! Lay in a direct intercept to her position, Gale; get us there pronto, helm! Prepare for speed jump to normal space and remember we're heavy in the beam. Comms, tell her we're on our way," Ahxenta ordered harshly. "Everyone, web in!"

"Another incoming, Cap! It's huge – it reads like the hostile we met at the start of the war by the Orriga Two asteroid field!" Gliss called.

"Confirmed! Positive zukivianite!" Azular broke in as the secondary bridge was ordered on standby. "Greffy, hook long-distance scanners into tactical in case there's another at her back; I'll focus on *this* blip."

"Prep decoy for launch, Azular!" Ahxenta hissed as she scanned the updating data grid. "Pre-programmed sequence and set it to run close to the gravity well off Swan Two: if we can persuade that beast to follow it in, we may have a chance of outflanking her. Earbleat…"

"All weapons stations primed and ready to go, Cap! *Loki VIII* on standby!" the second mate hollered.

Azular called the decoy ready to run on the captain's mark as Greffy reported that the new blip was low on weapons and had no lifesigns.

"Ready for jump!" the helmsman warned.

Seconds later, *Arianrhod* sheared off the bypass on an intercept line. The *Warrior* was cutting a complex course to outwit the new threat, her shield strength failing plate by plate. As *Arianrhod* came about to face the enemy, Azular called that the alien's hull had taken severe damage, but she had begun to rain fire on the fast-moving, dark-hulled PSS.

"So we give her another target! Loose long-range torpedoes! Match *Warrior's* course and speed, helm, but bring us into optimum position for decoy drop at two nine three mark six!" roared Ahxenta. "Ready decoy for drop, on my mark… mark!"

"Decoy away! Sequence running!"

"Gunnery crews, keep up the firepower!" the captain yelled as a shuddering thwack told her that the huge hostile had *Arianrhod* in her sights and its phase cannon fire was breaching her defences. "Tell the *Warrior* to hang back, comms! We've got her."

"Does she bite?" Apnis asked tersely as the huge ship cut off at an angle, her weapons still active.

"Blip's turning to take on the decoy, but we're in her aft sights and she's still got torpedoes!" warned Gliss loudly.

"She's loosing unmanned fighters! Incoming!" Greffy cried out.

"Gunnery crew two, take them out!" Earbleat bawled.

"Damn!" the captain cursed as one fighter cut through the flak to glance off the great starship's flanks and explode like a shell.

"Hostile's caught in the gravity well! She's spinning out of control, but she's still launching torpedoes!" Azular's voice was strident.

"Turn and engage! All long-range firepower to forward batteries, but keep us out of range of that whirlpool, helm!"

The hostile, with no sentient control, had followed the decoy to the edge of the dense gravitational field marking the gravity well, and only then did her onboard systems realise that she was chasing a shadow. By that time her manoeuvring thrusters had failed and, too heavy to turn and pull away, she was caught. Unluckily for *Arianrhod*, so was her decoy, and no power could pull it back.

"Let it go; there's nothing we can do," Ahxenta said. "Stand down battlestations but keep us at alert and keep long-distance eyes online."

"One helluva expensive op, Cap; and now we've lost one of our prime defences," the first mate noted in a low voice.

"A defence that hasn't escaped Nat Holdspan or his senior science officer, I bet. And *he's* sharp, so Azular says. Get us out of here helm, and back to the *Warrior*. She'll need our help to get where she's going."

"This is one wedding day that'll be remembered," Apnis grimaced. "Where are Box and Dox? Sitting in the mess finishing off their cake?"

"No," the captain told her, skimming status updates. "Dox is at the helm on the secondary bridge and Box is with her as navigator."

"We have one helluva crew, Captain Ahxenta."

"Roger that, Commander Apnis."

"Captain Holdspan for you, ma'am," Bellfish advised. "On grid."

Holdspan was grateful: they had been en route to Cygilla Prime and had just made Epsilon when the first hostile jumped onto the bypass at incredible speed, firing blind. It was clear she was uncrewed and thus capable of moves impossible for a typical ship, and though damaged, her approach did not slow: she made direct for them. The PSS, very able to defend herself, was ordered into action, but her captain had the distress sent, knowing he could not outrun an enemy that would stop at nothing. Having recently been refitted, the *Warrior* was fully armed, and despite taking crippling hits, she had got the advantage and taken out their huge adversary. And then his tactical crew spotted the second.

Ahxenta, conning over her ship's status as the damage reports came in, looked at him. "We've lost hull plate, shielding's at sixty percent… but we can shift. Can you make the bypass under your own power, Nat? We *can* set for tow, but we've a heavy cargo and we'll be slow."

Holdspan checked his boards and confirmed that the *Warrior* was spaceworthy and could make the bypass, but tractor stabilisation from *Arianrhod* would help in hyperspace currents. The captains agreed that their best course was Marridan: it was the closest repair and refit centre. It was two days away, but word could be sent ahead and a report drawn up for priority despatch to the PSS fleet, the ISA, and the TA.

The problem of his cargo, luckily intact, was taxing the captain of the *Nyx Warrior*. Ahxenta had sent out links, and by the time the ships had hit the bypass, she had a solution. The *PSS Emerald*, once a luxury liner and now a trader owned by Ahxenta, was on her way back from Bellatrix Station, a holding post of the Interstellar Prison Service, with a half-full hold. She was crossing zone Eta on a bearing for Alpha, for her next drop at Ferris. That route would take her past Marridan.

After talks with Captain Goodsocks, her supercargo Helly Pinkhorn and both sets of clients, it was agreed that the *Emerald* would increase speed to make an earlier transfer at Ferris and then head for Marridan to take on the *Warrior's* cargo for Cygilla Prime.

* * *

Forty four hours later the two ships slid off the bypass for the Marridan system's third planet. Berths were spoken for, a local orbital repair yard was ready and a hospital shuttle was on standby to take on the worst hurt of the *Warrior's* casualties. The joint note of the action had resulted in a request for an urgent briefing by the local ISA office, to which the TA and the Marridani planetary authority would send reps. The topics included the origin of the ships: the presence of two implied more, and as they evoked the ships that had caused such carnage in the war, some must have fled or there were spares; and as both blips were damaged, they had possibly taken out others whose remains still drifted. *That* had prompted the ISA to order active patrols to scour for signs and to send a request to TA-aligned and other shipping lines to scan for debris.

That the ships had no crew was odd; those used in the war had been manned by highly-cyber beings that baulked at nothing to destroy any ship. They had attacked outposts and inhabited worlds with ferocity, pushing some beyond recovery. *Their* technology had been advanced, but from the scans got by the *Nyx Warrior* and the *Arianrhod*, they were less complex than the ships involved in the recent attacks.

Holdspan and Ahxenta had more central tasks on hand and had put off the meet. *Arianrhod* had cargo exchange, repair and resupply. The

Warrior had vital concerns: this was the second severe attack in a short time, she was badly damaged, and her insurers were loath to settle. And her captain was wondering if he was a target on some hit list.

"Welcome to the club," Ahxenta told him dryly at a briefing aboard his ship four hours after arrival. "*Arianrhod's* been on more hit lists than the rest of the fleet combined."

Ahxenta had brought her chief medic and her senior science officer with her, leaving Apnis and Lindell to handle cargo issues and to ensure that all was set for the *Emerald's* arrival. Flintlock made for the *Warrior's* medbay to assist, whilst the others joined Holdspan, Treskitt and Holt.

The two visitors had never been aboard the *Nyx Warrior* before: she was *Vanguard II* class and newer in design than *Arianrhod*, but Ahxenta noted that the decks were as utilitarian and the internal layout virtually identical. She had no idea how Holdspan had gained such a command at his age, but that he was in complete control was obvious from the respect of the officers they passed, most of whom were older than he.

The points of the action were discussed in depth and data and ideas exchanged. Both captains had got sharp calls from ISA HQ for a rapid handover of hard data, and agreed to a joint reply: neither wanted to reveal their ships' full capabilities. The details gone over led to others, and as Ahxenta had suspected, *Arianrhod's* decoy had not escaped the sharp eyes or the sensors of Lieutenant Commander Holt.

A piece of kit that could project a holo around itself and emit signals to simulate the real thing was familiar, and had many applications. That the device could be launched to a set locus, project an image that read as a full-sized ship, project an external image beyond its original *and* be programmed for scanning, resistance and cloaking was certainly novel. Ahxenta told of Cottontail's and Azular's development and upgrading of it over time, but she was not about to hand over the patent.

Talks done and the reply agreed, Ahxenta and Azular left for their ship; Flintlock had agreed to stay on for forty eight hours, as her own medics could cope with *Arianrhod's* casualties.

"What did you pick up of their real opinions of the attack?" the captain asked Azular on the way back.

"I don't believe Captain Holdspan thinks he's on a hit list, ma'am, but he suspects more than chance in the last attacks. He has a point: our fleet *is* harried more than other lines, although we tend to be harder targets. And as he, we and the *Obsidian Sky* are seen as the most difficult to hit, we become the aim of every aggressor that thinks it has an edge."

"Get us and you have the fleet on the run?"

"Maybe. But there's more to it. If we accept the TA's new rules and agree to be called in as active combatants in an emergency, we'd make an effective difference to the state of play."

"Some of us more than others," the captain put in ironically.

"True; and a hostile force would have to factor in Starfall. Thal's PSS ships include the largest, fastest, and most able. And many of them are based on hostile tech and quite capable of taking down similar."

"And the *Moonstone*, a totally new design that's shown she can fight," Ahxenta added. "Good points, and we'll keep them in mind. But we're almost home, so we concentrate on *our* priorities."

* * *

Their priorities took four days. Offloading the delicate cargo needed heavy grapples and careful guiding. *Arianrhod's* outer bays had then to be prepped for their next pick-up. Repair and resupply had to be fitted around it, and as the captain required security at all stages, keeping an eye on how many outsiders had access to the ship or her berth was a chore. The *Emerald* had arrived, but the *Warrior's* damage hindered load handover. It was eventually done, and the *Emerald* waved off.

"I'll be glad to see the back of here," Ahxenta confided to Apnis as they waited final clearance to exit local space. "Our holds are empty, but we can catch up on our schedule. We'll hop back on the bypass as far as Fivepoint and then cross to Kanelian from there."

Ahxenta and Holdspan had sent a short report to ISA HQ after the deferred meeting with ISA, TA and authority reps. *That* had left a sour taste, as Ahxenta had been pushed for facts about Thal by the two TA agents. She refused to comply. The deadline for agreement to the new TA contract was also almost upon the PSS fleet, and both captains had to be part of the process. The consensus, argued over the UV-III, was acceptance on the proviso that the terms be reviewed within a set time period, as that was all that the TA would be likely to accept.

Thal, perforce part of the debate, had his own issues. On advice from Admiral Posettix, he had provisionally agreed to give the TA the access codes to the bypass that ran from a system near Twilight Station to Amity Beacon in Psi, so that it could be added to TA listings. The ISA was also interested, as the bypass ran into its space at three points. The *ISAS Avenger* off his main base had been a strong incentive for Thal to hand the data over. The concessions he had pushed for and got were that the PSS fleet would be given the codes, as his fleet had them in any case, and would not be taxed on the use of any part of the route. He had also stipulated that the codes could not be altered by any but his people and that none of his bases would be approached without the consent of the base commanders. The siting of facilities for use of his bases by outsiders as stop-off posts was left for later.

The last the captain had heard was Thal had left Alto Finglas. Azular guessed he was for Twilight, as in his and Ahxenta's talk with the man, he had admitted that Twilight node was not the endpoint of the route and that it carried on to Gemstone Station. And Azular was sure that Thal had Ambassadors Posettix and Jotakt on line: as Posettix' remit *was* to unite trade relations across the galactic zones, the ISA and TA would have to take her into account. And she and Jotakt *were* there to negotiate the use of bypasses beyond Amity with the TA for trading. As the Norvallans and Telziltic owed Thal for his aid in repelling the hostiles in their areas, and he already had trading relations in zone Psi, he would have a whip hand in many of the dealings.

As far as anyone in the PSS fleet knew, the *NFS Serenity* was still at Alto Finglas. Azular had not heard from Kerrix since the *Moonstone* had left Selliden, but a courtesy link told them that three of the survivors had been relocated to another Starfall ship at Idledott.

The captain sighed as she gave the withdrawal order. The *Warrior* was due to spend five more days at Marridan, but had already set up a trade deal there for transport of a large load to Vreskota Two.

"Steady as she goes, helm," Ahxenta called as, on her final banking turn, *Arianrhod* pulled away from local space. "Best speed to the bypass. Once on, we run with shields up and at amber alert until Fivepoint."

"Unless we meet something on the way," Apnis cautioned.

"Thanks for that."

"Don't mention it, Cap. Where's Azular? He should be here."

"He's checking the gear he and Crizz got for a new decoy and using it as an excuse to contact Kerrix, to persuade her to hand over bits of tech when next we meet. I don't know when: if she's beyond Keystone Kell and heading further out, we won't be likely to meet for months."

"That hasn't affected his inane grin much. On which note…"

"Don't even go there, Commander Apnis. I don't know more, and if I did, I wouldn't tell you," Ahxenta warned.

"And *he's* supposed to be the telepath," she quietly chuckled. "Not much fallout yet, but give it time."

Box turned puzzled eyes to his mate, who was wearing a knowing smile, and cocked his head at her. Dox's smile only widened.

"What is it? What do you know about Dr Azular that I don't?"

"Mind your boards and make sure you set alternate jump lines," she ordered. "It's a short hop to Fivepoint, but given where it is, there's a lot of scope for trouble from half a dozen different directions."

"Aye, ma'am; but you *will* tell me later, won't you?" Box persisted.

Dox grinned. "Maybe," she said.

Apnis traded a wry look with the captain: Box had a mouth the size of a planet. "I give it an hour after the end of his shift and it'll be round the whole ship."

It took a little longer, but by the time *Arianrhod* was almost at the Fivepoint crossover node, half the crew knew that Dr Azular had good reason for his lasting smile. Dox had in fact guessed his secret during their talks over her nuptials, and he had admitted that he had persuaded Captain Kerrix to consider him as a life partner. Dox had said nothing then to Box, knowing that his loquacity was as great as his lack of tact.

* * *

The route from Fivepoint to Kanelian involved a stretch of near empty space, with few systems to provide dens for villains, but the captain knew that that did not exclude trouble. An attack by raider interceptors off the Kanelian beacon many months before had resulted in the near-loss of the *PSS Firedrake* and the deaths of five crew. And although the bypass ran for only a short stretch, the known gravity well close to the dark star Jete had been the downfall of many ships in the past. As it was, *Arianrhod* made the planet safely, and pick-up of the expensive and dangerous cargo for the ISA HQ was smooth.

"Paperwork takes longer than cargo pick-up," complained the first mate. "But we'll get a look at the HQ, which means the old one with a paint job, and a peep at what's in orbit around Alto Finglas."

"That's all we'll get," the captain told her. "They'll have the place shielded and a defence system stretching from planetside to the outer comet belt. But that's our accounts in order, so we're good to go."

Orders given, the ship loosed her struts and made out of local space, heavy with cargo, every sensor on continual scan. As Ahxenta insisted on her most senior crew on the bridge at critical times, every station was manned. Azular was in his usual place, Greffy alongside, and it was the sharp-eyed young officer who spotted an anomaly four hours out.

"It's a small powered source and it's drifting," he reported. "If it's a ship, I can't make out a call-sign; and I can't pull up specifics…"

"I'll link in all we have. I have a feeling about this," Azular hissed.

Even as he spoke, the voice of Bellfish cut across the bridge. "I'm picking up a distress…"

"Bloody hell! Why does it always have to be us?" Apnis demanded.

6: AN UNWANTED GUEST

The expanded holo-grid spun to isolate the distress and nearby power sources. Apart from the mark that was *Arianrhod's* locus in the shifting starfield, one signal was active. The tactical officer judged its source as shuttle-sized, and it was drifting in hyperspace currents.

"Red alert!" the captain called. "She looks solo but we know that trick. Best speed to her position helm, but be ready to jump if need be. Weapons online, prime to lock on. Tactical, all scanners at full. Do *not* answer the distress, comms: I want to know what I'm dealing with first. Any sign of other ships out there?"

"None, ma'am," Gliss replied.

The activity intensified as more officers reported in and Dox altered course to bring *Arianrhod* in a line to the blip. As minutes ticked by and she drew closer, no other active sources were sensed. Ahxenta ordered the alert muted as she skimmed her boards and the ever-shifting holo.

"Any more on that distress, comms?"

"No ma'am, a repeating signal. It's clearer now we're closer... I have a call-sign and it's reading as ISP!"

"I bet it is," the cool voice of the senior science officer cut in.

"What've you got?" Ahxenta asked. "She's too small for a starship so she must be an escape craft, but one from an *ISP* ship?"

"She's an advanced shuttle, ma'am, one aboard. Hull damage has let me past her shields: she's been battered by hyperspace currents."

"Hyperspace currents? How can *any* shuttle, even an advanced one, resist them? Starfall's, maybe. Their shuttles are hellish strong, as we know, having rescued one... but an *ISP* shuttle?"

"We have that shuttle's spec, though few others have," Azular said harshly. "Colonel Myrtleberry's state-of-the-art combat shuttle that we carried from Silverglass to Stinward. *She* could take major stresses and was berthed in our most secure bay with our best cam gear on her. We hadn't been given her full spec, so we scanned and found the colonel's cyber suite. And we've seen that shuttle and *her* recently, in the Web."

The captain stepped over to look at his boards. "She was heading for the *ISPS Repulse*. I want the identity of that boat confirmed! And get your targeting eyes on her, Lieutenant Commander Earbleat!"

Two minutes later and the readings were verified as matching those the *Arianrhod* had on the ISP colonel's personal combat shuttle.

"If that *is* her shuttle, where's the *Repulse?*" Ahxenta asked, settling back into her command chair.

"Not in range," the first mate said. "We've got zip, and our scanners are top-notch, with Azular's Norvallan hand-held tied into his station."

"Dox, cut to dropout speed and get us close enough to get a tractor on her. Bellfish, see if you can raise her. Tell her who we are."

"It'll be tricky getting a tractor on her, Cap; the currents are wild," Apnis noted. "If it *is* her, she'll be pissed when she figures who *we* are."

"If it *is* Myrtleberry, she'll already know," was the sarcastic retort.

"We have a response, ma'am: Colonel Myrtleberry on line."

The frosty face *was* familiar. Ahxenta curtly saluted the woman and advised her to ready for tow. With one sharp look, she obeyed. Despite the buffeting, her craft was stable, but Azular and Greffy had figured that hyperspace currents were not fully to blame for its damage. Scores from a high-energy beam weapon was as close as they could call it.

Exchanges were short as Myrtleberry rigged her shuttle for towing by *Arianrhod's* tractors. Once locked, the PSS and her burden turned in tandem and dropped out of the bypass into normal space. Safe passage confirmed, the colonel was ordered to stand by.

"I want everything we can get on that ship and on *her* before I bring them in," the captain rapped as soon as the comm link cut. "One thing awry and she can stay there until we reach a safe station."

"The closest ISP post is Linza Base, and that's a helluva long way, Cap," Apnis said. "And mostly through Coalition space."

"The space might be Coalition, but the admin's now ISA. Box, plot our onward via Fivepoint, cut a line by Vreskota and the Helix Cluster, and then via Pilt 24 to Merkat. We drop her in the Web or at Linza."

"How much she'll want to make for Alto Finglas?"

"My ship, my rules," was the grim reply. "What've you got, Azular?"

"Odd, ma'am: her hull call-sign reads ISP but there's an overlying signal that registers as ISA – the *ISAS Repulse*. Apart from the damage, she reads almost the same as our last scans of her. As for the colonel, I can't say; but how does the commander of the *Repulse* end up alone in a shuttle a long way from her own ship?"

"*That* situation isn't novel," the captain reminded him tartly. "That was the position Captain Kerrix found herself in that led her to Starfall and then Merkat. But the last we heard of the *Repulse* was in the Web. You were on the *Moonstone*, and Levettiza said that the *Advance* and the *Repulse* were to set out beyond Alpha on an exploratory, after a refit to turn them into ISA boats. But they were to head out via Dryssicon and Jurassa, and that's a hell of a way from here. So how did that shuttle get this far and why's she still got an ISP call-sign?"

"Maybe she *was* in refit but Myrtleberry didn't want her own getting their paws on too much. We can ask when we see her," Apnis said. "Given the comms racket, she has demands, and one of them will be that she wants a ride to a safe place. And she'll be telling us which one."

"Tough: she can tell me how she got out here before we take her anywhere," Ahxenta retorted. "Bellfish, put the colonel through."

Despite the woman's demand for direct pick-up, the captain put her questions. That Ahxenta knew of her task with the *Advance* incensed her, but she confirmed that they had made Jurassa and were en route to Orriga Two's Helleborus outpost when they caught an odd signal off the bypass that implied a large vessel. They dropped out to check, and found the blip a distant mark, its ion trail crossing into chartless territory. As the signal source was a speck on the edge of *their* range, it suggested an unlisted bypass close by. From the data they *did* catch, part of the bypass had to infringe mapped space. They searched, but despite the cutting-edge tech of the *Advance* and the superior resources of the *Repulse*, they found little.

The colonel was in her shuttle, crossing to the *Advance* for a briefing, when the unknown or one similar jumped into normal space from a route other than theirs, again implying a covert bypass across Alpha. She ordered the ISA ships to reply in kind if fired on. They did: as the stranger sent a volley across her bows, the *Repulse* retaliated; the shuttle, caught in the crossfire, was thrown off-course. Myrtleberry had trouble holding her helm, and realised she had hit hyperspace. Her hi-tech ship could cope with the currents but she had no idea of her route. From the fluxes, she guessed she was being hit by random patches of high negative mass-energy density in the Outer Reaches. Guided by that, she pressed on for what she hoped was Fivepoint node, which would put her in reach of an ISP station. She held steady, hoping to reach the node, but the shuttle had lost so much power that she began to drift. She thought she had made Fivepoint, but lacked the control to drop out. She reckoned that she had been aboard for about three days.

The captain was not entirely convinced, but as her stations' updates bore out that the shuttle was in a bad way and the air supply near gone, she gave approval to haul the craft into the bay that had held her the last time she had been aboard *Arianrhod*.

"About damn time!" was the only gratitude expressed.

"You're with me, Azular but set your shuttle's cloak: she's in that bay and you know Myrtleberry. I'll need Flintlock and two guards. You have the conn, Tallica. Arrange a billet and make sure we can track her; *and* restrict her comms to on-board. I don't want her calling anyone. I'll escort her there via medbay as she'll need a full check to make sure she's genuine, and the same as last time she was here. Crizz can go over her shuttle, render it safe and lock it down. Ready us to resume course. Azular, we need to get what data her shuttle has on the unknown and the action she says she was in, whether she agrees or not. We can do it once she's settled, with a security detail posted outside her door."

"I expect we'll have to tell someone we've found her: they might be worried or have search parties out looking," Apnis remarked.

"*Once* we know what we've brought on board."

"Roger that, Cap."

Angry at having had to wait, the colonel vented her ire the second she alighted. The captain gave no apology: the safety of her ship and crew came first. Flintlock and Azular were told to scan her before she moved. Knowing her hosts, she had anticipated it, and submitted. Her eyes flicked to Cottontail, who was probing the shuttle from a console and eyeing the colonel with a dislike that was mutual.

"There's another shuttle here," Myrtleberry snapped as her eyes swept the bay. "Over there, and it's cloaked. Why?"

"What I do with my gear is my affair," Ahxenta informed her curtly, aware that Azular's lips were compressing in anger, but also aware that the colonel had not lost her penchant for needling people to provoke a reaction. "Chief, your team will make sure the colonel's shuttle poses no threat to *Arianrhod*. If you're finished, Dr Flintlock, Dr Azular, we'll escort the colonel to medbay for a thorough health check."

"We should perhaps remove the colonel's arms and scanners," the science officer proposed, raising an eyebrow. "She has two phase guns, two stun bombs and a recorder-jammer inside her shielded jacket."

"*You* haven't lost your touch," she snorted as she dug out the gear, knowing that the captain would have her guards do it if she refused.

"He hasn't," Ahxenta agreed. "This way, Colonel."

"So she *is* who she says she is," the captain said to Azular once the woman had been taken into a ready-prepped iso-bay.

"Aye, ma'am; and she's had no more genetic or physical alteration since she was here last, but Dr Flintlock can confirm. She scanned our bay from her ship, I think; that's how she spotted my shuttle. The chief can check every scrap of hers; I or Greffy can go over the databanks, if they're not locked. And I expect her cyber suite is still in situ."

"I'll bet. But if she's been missing for three days and her ship was hit in zone Alpha, why haven't we heard of it over the usual channels?"

"The ISA wouldn't want to admit it had sent out two premier ships and lost the mission commander. Maybe the ships bested the unknown and are still looking, or didn't make it and had no time to call for help."

"I'll get Bellfish to scour every net now to see if there *was* a report. And once *she's* berthed, I'll contact ISA HQ and give them the good news that we've got her and they can have her back."

"She may know our heading," Azular said as the captain closed the link after talking to Bellfish. "She's ISA and our cargo's for Alto Finglas – she may have still been there when the contract was agreed."

"Good point; we'll see what Flintlock comes up with. And Jute can find new traps for her; the ones she's in could do with an overhaul."

"I take it they won't have *Arianrhod's* logo on them."

"Damn right they won't. One thing I'd like to know is why she took her shuttle out to cross to the *Advance* for a briefing. Why not link in?"

"Given what she is, the Alliance equivalent of an info-sent with the ability to pick up on subtle emotional nuances, I expect a face-to-face will tell her things a comm link won't."

"Spot on," Ahxenta agreed. "Here's Axellina. How is she, Doc?"

"Pretty fit for someone who's spent three days in a boat, even if her augmentations mean she can endure a lot. And her ship's smart: it kept her safe and on course while she took time out to eat, nap and exercise. Her cyber gear's unchanged; Oak's the expert, and he agrees. She wants to speak to you, priority, Cinnabar; she needs to call her ship."

"I'll be there when she does," the captain said grimly. "If the *Repulse* is close enough to catch us up, so much the better. I'm starting to feel that *Arianrhod's* part of some galactic search and rescue squad."

"She needs a shower, a rest and a feed, so I suggest you get her to her quarters and let her do that before you start chin-wagging."

"Huh! I bet she'll have her own ideas."

"So do I; but as she's now *my* patient, I have the final say."

Ahxenta was right: Myrtleberry's immediate priority was the means to call her ship and the ISA, and she made no bones about demanding it. The captain was forthright.

"Aboard my ship, I'm the ultimate authority. Lieutenants Corvus and Ji will escort you to quarters. I'll contact ISA HQ and let Fleet HQ know you're aboard *Arianrhod*. I take it you don't object?"

"Would it make any difference if I did?" was her acerbic rejoinder.

"No – but I *would* record your objection."

"Then I have no objection, Captain."

"So noted. Corvus, Ji, escort the colonel to her quarters and remain on guard. Let me know when you're settled, Colonel, and we can talk."

"Permission to inspect the colonel's shuttle, ma'am?" Azular asked, looking after the party as it disappeared out of medbay.

"No, I want you on the bridge and in on my chat to her. Greffy can start, he's quite capable. You can tell him what he needs to know from your station. And now I've a link to the ISA. And to see how far behind schedule we are with all these shenanigans."

Bellfish found no mentions of the *Advance*, the *Repulse*, or any action in zone Alpha on the usual channels. Cynical, Ahxenta made for her bridge office to contact various associates.

"What's to do, Cap?" Apnis asked on her return. "You've been an hour, the colonel wants a chat, and is pissed she couldn't call off-ship."

"She can wait. As soon as I said we'd got her, I was linked to a fleet admiral in a shiny new ISA uniform. Her story rings true. The *Advance* and *Repulse* were hyperspace for Helleborus when they caught an odd signal in normal space, and dropped out to look. The source shot off but they stayed to search. She *did* take her shuttle out for a briefing on the *Advance*, and as she was crossing, the blip jumped out on them. The ISA ships are state-of-the-art, big and well-armed and beat it off. It jumped back onto the unlisted bypass, they lost it, and then realised they'd lost Myrtleberry: her shuttle had vanished. Their priority was to find it, as it *did* contain the commanding officer of the *Repulse*."

"So why didn't they issue an alert to local systems? They must know there are trading routes out there and it was possible that other ships in the area might spot her."

"I asked. Admiral Trestle's story is that they didn't want hostile ears aware of a missing ship. They assumed she wouldn't be far off-beacon and in normal space, and they'd find her. When they couldn't, the first officer of the *Repulse* called it into HQ and an alert was sent to the ISA fleet. Trestle wasn't keen to tell me why they didn't send a general alert out, but I gathered it was to do with that covert bypass."

"The ISA wants first dibs once it locates it?" Apnis posited.

"That's what I think. The ISA knows there's got to be one. I reckon it's one Starfall uses: at the meet when the new contract was dumped on us and the ISA made public, Kerrix admitted to a hyper-route from a base off Mellifly called Gemstone to Thal's Nexus Station off Theta. She said it was straight but didn't cross the Orriga asteroid field."

"She said bypasses," Apnis recalled. "That struck you at the time."

"She did; and one of them may cut close by the bypass that connects Jurassa to Helleborus and the node for Orriga and beyond."

"Speculation, Cap; You're not going to mention it to the colonel?"

"I'm not; but I'd best hear what she has to say. Trestle will cancel the alert and call the *Repulse*. And he wants to speak to *her*. As she's in command of the *Repulse*, she may be diverted to pick her up. I've told Trestle we're for Vreskota, so she can be collected there. But we're not hanging on, we've contracts. Bellfish, tell the colonel I'm on my way. If Admiral Trestle calls let me know, but not openly: patch it through on my comm link. Tallica, you have the conn. Azular, you're with me; let's go and speak nicely to the colonel."

The dialogue with the ISA officer was as thorny as expected but she seemed pleased that the *Repulse* and *Advance* were safe and that her own knew of her rescue. Calls to her ship and ISA HQ were her priorities, but the captain cut through her demands with her own, for data on the strange ship and the colonel's view of the danger it posed. Trestle's link came as a relief, and Ahxenta halted the talk to take it privately.

"Briefing room five," she told the science officer on exit from the quarters, where Ji and Corvus still stood guard. "We're coming up on Vreskota, so I hope Trestle's put plans in motion and we can lose her."

The plans were that their unwanted guest would be with them until Merkat, unless the captain was willing to hang fire for a day at Vreskota Two. If so, the battlecruiser *ISAS Illustrious* could be diverted.

Ahxenta considered, but only for an instant. "No way," she said. "I have schedules to keep and I plan to keep them."

Azular, busy at an info-station, had found an alternative. She took a quick look, and nodded.

"*Arianrhod* will be up on Pilt 24 in forty hours, Admiral. If your ship can make it there to time, she can take on the colonel and her shuttle."

He checked his charts. "Agreed. I'd like to speak to the colonel."

"Stand by," the captain told him, setting the hold before instructing Bellfish to set a controlled link by which Myrtleberry would not be able to make additional communications.

"The *Repulse* and the *Advance* won't be recalled," Azular remarked.

"Looks like, but get to her shuttle. Cottontail says its fancy sensors *were* smart enough to detect a cloaked ship, but she couldn't work them. Greffy got zip from the databanks as she'd locked them. Her cyber suite's intact and emitting a low signal. You may get more. But sort *your* shuttle. She'll have plans to check hers before she moves out. And I want all you have on the *ISAS Illustrious* – she's a new one on me."

* * *

Forty hours later, *Arianrhod* made the node at Pilt 24, an empty system close to the bypass entry for Beta Zegonia 68. The *Illustrious* had made it in hours earlier. Digging had unearthed that she was an ex-Coalition battlecruiser recently refitted at Alto Finglas. Her captain, Board, was not thrilled to be billeting an ISA colonel and her shuttle, the advantage to *Arianrhod* being that a rapid transfer would be made by tractors.

Ahxenta was happy to see the back of her guest. She had refused to stay in her quarters and Azular had not relished his task of minder. His priority once en route would be to scour the bay for anything left or taken. Myrtleberry had spent two hours bringing her craft to a pilotable spec and had asked to use *Arianrhod's* facilities and crew. Ahxenta had grudgingly agreed: in the bay she was under surveillance. Azular had increased his shuttle's security by adding panels with response plating across her position, and had activated additional cloaking.

"All links secure," Ferry called over as the final tractor of the *ISAS Illustrious* locked onto the shuttle. "Cutting our tractors now."

The tactical holo confirmed locking as the small craft continued on her trajectory to the *Illustrious*. Myrtleberry was aboard: she had refused the offer of a ride in one of *Arianrhod's* shuttles.

"Plot course for Alto Finglas via Linza and Silshoon," ordered the captain. "All speed as soon as she's out of sight, helm."

"Aye, ma'am," Dox acknowledged.

"Do we know where the *Illustrious* is for?" Apnis asked.

"Board wouldn't say. I don't know what he and she jawed over, but he was sour after it. We'll wait for word she's aboard. There's been zip of the action off Helleborus, so the ISA's keeping it quiet. But if the deal out there *is* ISP-led, it won't want an ex-Coalition ship heading that way for a look: reports on trade nets say that the Alliance family's not a happy one, and local issues are interfering."

"Any more on the PSS position over TA contract changes?"

"No, but as the deadline's due, I'll no doubt be in for more chat."

Bellfish cut in with a comm from Captain Board: the shuttle was safe with him and the colonel wanted a word with Ahxenta.

"This'll be the thanks for her rescue and the kindness we extended over her trip with us, I expect," the first mate said with irony.

"I bet. Put her on visual, Lieutenant."

Myrtleberry expressed curt thanks and told the captain that events at Alpha edge and the ISA presence there were not to be revealed in any link. Ahxenta scathingly retorted that her links were personal and none of the colonel's concern. She wished her a safe onward flight, cut the comm and let out the anger that had been building up.

"Cool it, Cinnabar," Apnis advised. "She's out of our hair and we can get back to work. Though it'll be a hoot if the *Illustrious* is headed to Alto Finglas and we see her there."

"Who for? But she's welcome to try her tricks on Board and his crew. If he's savvy, he'll have that shuttle *and* her under constant guard until they ship out. What's the status of the *Illustrious*, Gliss?"

"Powering up and ready to jump back onto the bypass, ma'am."

Minutes later, the ISA ship was a dot on the grid. She had no sooner disappeared when a link came through for the captain. It was the TA.

"Hell! Keep us on course for Alto Finglas, Tallica. And cloak up: we're on a straight road and I want no surprises."

"Will do, Cap. Though you might just be about to get one."

* * *

The captain was three hours at her desk. During that time, Bellfish had had to set up several secure links and patch one through. The chatter on regular nets had been non-stop, implying that the TA summons had been wide-ranging, but no alarms or alerts had been received.

"The quiet before the storm," Box said to his mate as he made fine route adjustments to compensate for bypass currents. "At least we're in ISP space most of the way, with nothing rough until we hit the edges of the Crimson Drapes. Makes it easy for the relief navi-helm crew."

"This is the *Arianrhod*," Romanna Dox reminded him.

Everyone looked up when the captain returned, her face impassive. They waited in quiet anticipation. She sat without speaking and pulled her boards across to assess their current status, although they all knew that updates would have been sent in to her as routine.

"Okay, Cinnabar: what are we up to our necks in?" asked Apnis.

"A new contract with the Trades Alliance," was the cool reply.

"That I'd figured. We've signed?"

"We didn't have much option if we want to keep our flag. But the short notice put so many backs up that the TA's given us an extra thirty days before it comes into effect *and* we have a say in whether a given situation can be classed as an extreme emergency."

"So the TA can't just up and say the balloon's gone up, this is war, drop your business and head into the nearest battle zone?"

"Exactly. The contract holds for a galactic year, when it'll be under full review, but codicils *can* be added. And we have a trade route from Amity Beacon through Starfall, Sunrise and Twilight Exits, with a short link to the ISP sector of Lambda. And the PSS fleet won't be charged fees for any part of it: Admiral Posettix did his work well. He's holding at Alto Finglas, but Ambassador Jotakt is on the way home with a trade deal with the TA on bypass use beyond Amity. Telzilt's still hanging fire about joining in even a loose confederacy with the ISA, though."

"Thal?" the first mate enquired.

"Aboard the *Kel'Moth* at Starfall, with the *ISAS Avenger* off his bows. I called him after the shouting and told him about Helleborus. His fleet *do* use bypasses out that way and he's aware of one that crosses close to the trade route at Alpha edge – there are two crossover points. That there'd been an unknown ship that took on two of ISA's best surprised him, and he *did* seem anxious, so I suspect that it wasn't one of his."

"You realise Myrtleberry will flay you when she finds out?"

"If she finds out: he won't bleat, and seemed grateful I'd told him."

"What else, Cap? You weren't in there all that time just for that?"

Ahxenta smiled. "The *Warrior's* still at Marridan and ready to head out. As she's for Vreskota Two, I gave Nat a heads-up. Vreskota's not too close to Helleborus, but I don't know what other deals he has that may take him that way. And I called Grey, as he was for Delta Iridium last I heard, and some of his clients were antsy over contracts. They've calmed down, as news is spreading that the fleet will comply with the new TA rules, with caveats. *Obsidian's* on her way to the Web. And I spoke to Captain Kerrix. She called me," she said with a look at Azular, who had visibly jolted: it was known that he had had only one personal link from her since they had last seen the *Moonstone.*

"From where? I thought she'd be off the edge of mapped space by now, given the speed of her ship and the way she flies it," Apnis said, as her eyes, and everyone else's, were drawn to the science station.

"Hardly – she's not at Starfall yet."

"But why did she call you?" the first mate persisted.

"Because she had two or three things to say."

"Cinnabar…"

"Just after we'd agreed to sign the TA contract, she had a link from Ambassador Posettix, who'd been following events. They agree in their opinion of Norvalla and its view of things. They talked things over *and* consulted Admiral Posettix; *his* knowledge of Norvallan law is wide and he's been studying the laws of our systems. It had struck them that there might be a way around the clause in the new contract that drafts in the PSS fleet when things get too hot for the ISA fleet."

"Which is?"

"Use us as diplomatic couriers; diplomats and diplomatic ships have immunity from a lot, including having to be ready to jump in and fight when things go belly-up."

"It'll never stand: the TA will block *that* loophole pronto."

"If it spots it. The TA has no right to say what cargo any PSS carries, nor will it have a right to say what any trader from zone Psi holds. But Ambassador Posettix *is* arguing for the right of trading ships from Psi, whatever flag they fly, to use current TA-listed routes without charge, and to use all TA-aligned ports and services without let or hindrance. If that's agreed, the threat by any PSS of telling the TA to go hang and signing on under another flag might be enough to push for concessions rather than lose the levies the TA gets out of us. The TA may find itself having to pull its rules into line with those of the trading organisations it's trying to link to in the new sectors opening up, or it'll lose out."

"That hardly affects us now, so we can leave them to argue it out. But I still don't see why Captain Kerrix called you to let you in on it."

"She had other things to say, but they're none of your business."

* * *

The next three days saw *Arianrhod* pass the Silshoon beacon and make for a crossover node off the Furze system to change course for the final leg of her trip. Her schedule had shifted, as two new contracts had been won, which meant a cross from Alto Finglas to Millet to take on a load for Veximer Prime, and then a trip into Lambda, to Limekiln for engineering parts for a client on Delta Iridium. Ahxenta had heard nothing about other PSS ships bar that the *Nyx Warrior* was now en route to Vreskota Two and would then head for the Web.

The trip was tranquil, despite the misgivings of the more pessimistic of *Arianrhod's* crew that a straight route anywhere usually begot trouble. The captain thus found time for routine matters, including a long chat with her senior science officer. Noses twitching, his fellows dropped hints but learnt nothing, though his smile had not slipped. He and the chief engineer spent much of their time on creating a new decoy with the equipment that they had brought aboard at Marridan.

They were coming up on the Furze beacon, and the misty glow of the Crimson Drapes was within visual range, when *Arianrhod's* long-range tactical arrays picked up a signal off the bypass. The captain, back on the bridge for the course change, ordered shields and cloak up. She was taking no chances. The large and expensive consignment was for the ISA and thus highly classified, but there were sources from which details could be got. That would alert raider operations that it would be worth the risk to waylay her. And that meant taking down the ship, for *Arianrhod's* great outer cargo bays were not easily detachable.

Ahxenta studied the holo grimly. "Amber alert! Get Azular up here, comms. Weapons on line, Earbleat. I don't like the feel of this."

7: HIDING PLACES

The empty Furze system was on the Beta border but inside zone Delta. A small bypass ran from there direct to Alto Finglas. The star-spangled red veils of the Crimson Drapes Nebula provided a glorious backdrop, but the local area of nebulous dust could hide surprises. The PSS *Pearl Shield* had had hull comms gear shot off by raiders near there months before, and other bad lots were known to operate in the area. *Arianrhod* slid off the bypass and held station by the beacon. The regular repeated pulse was active still and seemed to stem from the fourth planet. As tactical and science began a local sweep, the captain ordered probes in rather than commit her ship to a closer study. Azular readied two, and a disquiet nagging, ordered Greffy to begin a scan of nebular space.

"Strange," Greffy mused. "I get a patch of thickening that shouldn't be here, like that anomaly we found off the Ginseng during the war."

Azular checked his data. "You're right! Captain, there's a problem."

Ahxenta stood up for a closer look. "What have you got?"

"On grid: a three-dimensional space resistant to scans. The wall that must be its boundary from our perspective is a nebular thickening that shouldn't exist. But it would've been detected if it had been there long; this is a well-travelled route and a major crossing point into Beta."

"You're saying it's like that glitch at the Ginseng that was actually a holding station for a hostile fleet, but this is a new one?"

"Exactly, ma'am. I don't suggest we send the probes in, unless we want to check out that it *is* similar: it might mean the loss of a probe or it could alert whatever controls it," Azular responded.

"But *it's* not the source of that signal," Greffy pointed out.

"Sensory sweep of the system is negative, Captain," Gliss reported. "All we have is the signal from the fourth planet, but unless we get in closer, we won't be able to pinpoint the locus."

"Then we send a probe to verify the source: I'm not taking my ship anywhere near. Ready an alert beacon to drop as close to that anomaly as you can without it drifting into the nebular mass, Azular. We call this into ISA HQ and it can send a ship. Get what you can and add in our sweep of the area, but *not* the Furze signal. Bellfish, tag the data urgent and link it on a tight beam to ISA HQ. And send it to our fleet, in case any are out this way. Dox, prepare to make for the fourth planet once the beacon's in place, but keep on a clear line for the node. Shields up and red alert. I still have a bad feeling about this."

With the tactical grid continuously updating, and every eye and ear at alert, *Arianrhod* drew closer to the lonely planetary system. An hour had barely passed when a sudden jolt shook the fabric of the vessel.

"Pull back!" Azular's shrill tones rang out. "Now!"

Dox was fast, and without waiting leave, put space between the ship and her target. Azular, spitting orders to Greffy, was upping the range of every sensor as a whirling mass of glowing gas lit the holo-grid.

"What in blazes is that?" Apnis demanded.

"Correlating with current nav-charts," Azular replied grimly. "That, Commander, is an uncharted worm-pocket, but no ordinary one. It has synthetic elements that shouldn't exist in a natural phenomenon."

"You're saying it's *not* natural and it's recent," Ahxenta said tersely. "But how was it created? And more to the point, by whom?"

"Unknown, ma'am; but that's what I get. There *may* be a link to the nebular aberration, as both features must be recent. Very recent, given the traffic that comes out this way en route to Alto Finglas."

"They'd not necessarily jump off, they'd switch to the beacon they want," Apnis argued. "We dropped out to investigate that signal. If the pocket and the nebular glitch *are* new and secret, why draw attention by sending a signal?"

"Good point," Ahxenta agreed. "But there's another aspect to this – if that *is* an active worm-pocket, where does it come out?"

"I take it we won't be heading in to find out?"

"Cut it. Change course to bring us up on Furze Four on a trajectory that keeps us well away from both of those things," the captain ordered her navi-helm crew. "Get all you can on whatever *that* is Azular, and summarise the data for despatch to ISA HQ."

"Aye, Captain. Though there *is* the remotest possibility that the ISA or one of its constituent bodies already knows about it…"

"Explain."

"If it *is* artificial and created to expedite a route from one locus to another, it would make a useful and valuable alternative to a bypass. Though given its location, I can't imagine it's ISP and by implication ISA, as it's too close to home for comfort."

"But how could such a thing be created? I'd imagine it's beyond the capabilities of current science?"

"As far as I know, ma'am," Azular asserted. "I'm not party to all the research in the galaxy. But Lieutenant Spree of the *Kel'Tarn* told us of the worm-pocket near Sox that he expected to take him to Hervesta Tertius, but it didn't, it took him halfway across mapped space. The ISA might be wise to investigate that aspect. As the Starfall fleet knew of the Sox pocket and had used it, *it* may have been tampered with…"

"Can of worms," Apnis put in. "The ISA knows about the worm-pocket near Sox but we didn't pass on the *Kel'Tarn* shuttle's data. But it doesn't solve the mystery of the Furze signal, and we're closing."

"I've a probe ready to drop as soon as we're in range," was the calm response. "It'll home in on the signal."

"Coming into range!" Gliss alerted him from tactical.

"Let it go, Azular," the captain instructed.

"Probe away! It'll take a few minutes to get into range. And our data summary on the rogue worm-pocket is ready to transmit to ISA HQ."

"Send it, copied to the fleet, Bellfish. And copy it to Admiral Zillah. If she's still arguing with the ISA over Freskat's right of first call on its home fleet in the event of major conflict or other disasters, the ISA might drag its feet over sending stuff out."

"Probe data coming in, Captain; transferring to grid," Azular called. "The source is a plateau in Furze Four's mid-northern region. Records indicate that the planet's barely habitable; cold and dry, gravity eighty five percent index norm, atmospheric oxygen eighteen percent and it has little vegetative cover. There have been no in-depth surveys as far as our data shows, and no attempts at resource abstraction."

"Signal still going, ma'am, no change," Gliss notified her. "No scan beams or anything else linked to the source. And our sweeps are clear – no other ships detected in the vicinity."

Ahxenta checked her stations' outputs and pursed her lips. "Drop the cloak, it's using power. But keep our weapons online and maintain amber alert. What in blazes is *that*?"

"It reads as a small habitat dome, ma'am," the senior science officer said, puzzled. "It's the source of the signal. If there *is* someone down there keeping watch, they should have spotted our probe by now."

"Place reads very low in energy, Doc," Greffy put in. "They may not have power for scanning their surroundings."

"If they're sending a signal, they'll want to know who's up here: a response might mean trouble," argued Azular. "I can send the probe in for a tighter scan, ma'am, to check for lifesigns?"

"Do it."

"We have lifesigns! Eight, all inside the dome. But there's an oddity, a modular unit with high power output. Environmental control hub, maybe? But that doesn't track. It seems to be autonomous. And enviro units are usually peripheral…"

"They are, Doc," Greffy agreed, pointing. "*That's* something else. *And* it's reading as alien tech…"

"Alien tech?" the captain repeated sharply.

"Aye ma'am, as is the dome," Azular said. "Sending probe on direct scan. I've seen things like that before. I don't like the implications."

"I'm sending the life readings to medbay," Greffy added, equally harshly. "They're off-beam for standard humanoids."

Ahxenta looked at her first mate. "Seems we have trouble."

"When do we ever have anything else?" she retorted.

"No threat detectable," Azular continued. "Dome has no defensive capacity: the shielding and many external systems have failed."

"More castaways?" hazarded Apnis. "Maybe we *are* turning into the local galactic rescue service."

"Dr Flintlock is on her way up, Captain," Greffy announced. "She wants to take a closer look at what we have."

"What? What in blazes do you think we have?"

The young science officer looked troubled as he glanced at Azular. "The lifeforms, ma'am: I think most of them are children."

"*What?* And what's the unit that's sending out power signals?" she turned to Azular. "You said you'd seen things like that before."

"Yes, ma'am, though not alien. But my scans suggest it might hold cryo-units. Dr Flintlock will have had experience of such facilities, so she should be able to confirm."

"That structure is definitely alien tech or based on it?"

"Yes, ma'am," answered Azular.

"With no defences?"

"None, but there's a large landing pad alongside. And there are silos that may once have contained supplies, but they're near-empty."

"Show me."

As the science officers clarified their results, the chief medic arrived. She had reached the same conclusion as Greffy. She studied the scans that Azular pulled up of the modular block emitting power signals.

"Damn!" she hissed. "They look like a linked series of life-tubes. I don't like it. Why would anyone dump such a set-up on a remote and hostile planet, with a bunch of half-grown guardians to look after it?"

"So that it would remain secret and the creators could return as and when they wanted, for whatever they used it for," Azular posited.

"Used it for?" Ahxenta repeated. "The dome's alien, so it's hostile but defenceless. There's no way of stopping anything that drops in."

"That's one interpretation, ma'am," Azular agreed. "Doctor, what do you make of the enhanced life readings of these entities?"

"The same as you," Flintlock replied darkly. "That place might be alien but those eight read as humanoid."

"It doesn't make sense," the captain argued. "Why would hostiles strand a set of kids on a cold, isolated world but leave them enough to keep them alive? What use... oh hell!"

"Exactly, Captain," Azular said, grimacing. "The hostiles we met in the war used living tissue to repair their own bodies, which is why they scavenged the crews as well as the ships they took down."

"You're not saying that *that* place is a holding area for a ready supply of... that's sickening!" Flintlock snapped.

"The question is, what do we do about it?" the first mate asked.

"We go in," the chief medic said shortly.

Ahxenta mused, scanning her ops. "See if they'll respond to us first. Bellfish, try to establish a link. Give them our name but nothing else."

Minutes passed as the repeated hail was sent on multiple channels, but there was no way to know if it was being picked up.

"If they *are* kids, I'm not surprised they don't want to answer," said Flintlock. "Hell knows how long they've been there and what they've gone through. Or even if they *can* understand us."

"If they *are* kids and it's not a massive set-up," the captain said tartly. "Any evidence of recent ion trails or signs of intrusion in the vicinity?"

"None," Azular confirmed. "The new worm-pocket *and* the nebular anomaly by the Crimson Drapes must both be recent but their creators were maybe unaware of the situation on Furze?"

"Likely, isn't it, given the worm-pocket's practically next door," spat Apnis. "And if *we* could pick up that signal, sure as hell others could."

"That depends on how long it's been running," he pointed out.

"Enough of the speculation," Ahxenta cut in. "Anything, Bellfish?"

"Not yet, ma'am."

"What the..." Azular began. "Gliss, I read a scan beam! It's weak, but it looks like someone down there is trying to see what's up here."

"Got it," the tactical officer verified. "It's standard, rapid sweeps and not powerful enough to read us in any detail."

"Cut our forr'ad shield power by fifty percent," the captain ordered. "But do not power down weapons and maintain alert status. Put me on speaker, Bellfish, and get a visual link if you can."

The captain stated her name and her ship. "We know you're reading us," she said bluntly. "You want a response to your distress, you link now, or we send news of you to the nearest local authority and they'll deal with you – and that will take time."

Whatever debate had been taking place on the surface, it was ended by a sharp voice that cut the ether. "I'm making the link!"

Apnis looked Ahxenta. "Inter-Lan. Looks like they understand us."

The image Bellfish put up caused a few gasps. The dour adolescent face was set in stubborn lines but the eyes were steely as the girl took in what she could see of the bridge and the officer in command. Behind her, a group of youngsters huddled fearfully, eyes popping.

"I'm Captain Cinnabar Ahxenta and this is the *PSS Arianrhod*. Who are you and how did you and your friends get to be where you are?"

"I'm Mara Vetoyn Seer," the girl said grittily. "We were dumped here after we were snatched from our refuge on Kelf Base."

"Have they come to take us home?" a quavering voice asked.

"I've never heard of Kelf Base," the captain said. "Where is it?"

"Sector sixteen of Beta zone," was the brusque reply.

It was clear that the girl was faking bravado to reassure the younger ones as she replied briefly and warily to Ahxenta's questions. They had been taken a long time ago, months she reckoned, by a raiding party that had worn masks. They had been held aboard a ship for some time and then stranded in the dome where they now were. They had been told that people would come back for them, but no-one had, to their relief: their captors had been vicious. They had lived off what had been left, but conditions were so bad outside that they had not gone further than the silos in which they found supplies. Mara had set up the distress using foraged scraps of tech from the enviro-systems that powered the dome; she had tried several times before she had succeeded. What was in the life-tubes they did not know, but they had not touched them.

After a pause, the captain told the group to stay put and she would be down shortly, in a shuttle. She would lift them off and take them to a safe place. Meanwhile, they could talk to Commander Apnis.

"Names and background," she ordered her first mate softly. "Gliss, Greffy, continue long-range and surface scans; Earbleat, keep systems hot. Chief, I'll need you in the shuttle bay. Doctor, Azular, you too."

"I take it you picked up what I did about sector sixteen of Beta?" Ahxenta asked Azular once in the transport tube.

"And other things, ma'am. Kelf may be that hidden base of Captain Thal's in sector sixteen that he once told us was no longer safe, due to infiltration into his set-up by hostile agents such as Lokterix. That was why they set up a new base outside Beta, near Kelfar Keeth, and it was betrayed, invaded and utterly destroyed by hostiles. Thal and his people suffered great personal loss."

"We heard when we first met the *Kel'Moth*, near here in fact. Yes, that struck me. But what did you make of that girl? Smart and tough; and you jumped when she told us her name. Seer? As in Marlin Seer?"

Azular nodded. "Mara *Vetoyn* Seer. I suggest you run comparatives of Ms Seer with Telziltic bio-data and compare her bio-samples at fine scale to those you hold in your med-database," he told Flintlock.

"You what?"

"To those of Captain Kerrix, to be precise."

His face gave Ahxenta a clue and she thought back to an episode in the *Half Moon*, when Kerrix had been arrested by her own. "Vetoyn is one of the string of names she has; but that's circumstantial, surely?"

"Vetoyn is a family name, from her Telziltic side, and limited to her clan. And certainly unknown outside Telzilt Three, which was attacked and overrun by hostiles, and many of its people taken, years ago. And as you know, ma'am, Captain Thal and his people *have* Telziltic links."

"What Telziltic links?" Flintlock wanted to know.

"Not your concern, and highly private," Ahxenta said starkly. "Get to medbay, pick up what you need to make sure those kids are what they seem and ready a team to receive them, as they'll be berthed with you. We'll need our largest shuttle, Crizz. And security back-up."

"I take it you *are* going to let the ISA in on what we're bringing in?" the doctor asked. "Not to mention any folks they have, once we've figured who they are and where they belong – or did belong?"

"One thing at a time, Doc."

"The cryo-tubes, Captain?" Azular questioned.

"Will not be brought aboard," Ahxenta said firmly. "They're hostile tech. And those kids will have nothing on them but the clothes they're wearing. And those will be incinerated once they're up here."

* * *

The shuttle landed softly on the pad outside the decrepit dome. Apnis had kept those inside informed and they were ready, but the wary Mara Seer checked the viewer before opening the airlock. Tests by Flintlock and nurse-tech Jym Kelp on the eight waifs proved that all were human and had not been genetically or cybernetically altered, leading Ahxenta to infer that their original captors had no direct need of them or were acting on orders. They were underfed and ill-clad, but not diseased, dirty or smelly, to the surprise of the rescuers. They were all terrified, Azular told the captain quietly. He probed the inside of the dome, to extract as much data as he could. All the cryo-units were occupied. The bodies read as humanoid and alive, but he could make out little else, as the tubes had clearly been in situ for a very long time.

The captain wanted off the planet as quickly as possible and lost no time in ordering all aboard. Her guards she directed to keep covert eyes on their passengers, but the eight obeyed without question, being too scared to do much else. Apnis, in a private link to Ahxenta, had advised that she was checking on the data got from the children, but it looked as if they had been sent to their late base temporarily, prior to transfer to a permanent home. The first mate had their names, but deemed it wise not to delve into their parentage, feeling that *Arianrhod's* medics and ship's counsellor Lieutenant Parri Millit would be more capable.

There was news: a liaison from ISA HQ had contacted them about their reports of the nebular anomaly and new worm-pocket. The ISA would send a research ship and a warship to investigate. Apnis had not been drawn on *Arianrhod's* actions or ISA cargo, other than to confirm that she was on her way to Alto Finglas.

Once aboard, the children were given into the care of medical staff whilst the captain made for her bridge office, having ordered comms to link to Captain Thal by any means necessary, and Azular to prepare a data shard with all he had on the situation and systems on Furze. The first mate had been ordered to break orbit and set for Alto Finglas with every security measure the ship possessed operational.

The link took half an hour, by which time the guests were settled in medbay and the captain had the data from Azular and Apnis. Thal was in a meeting and not to be disturbed, Ahxenta was informed.

"I don't care if he's in his damned bathtub," the captain snapped at the *Kel'Moth's* duty officer. "I need to speak to him more than urgently, and Commander Seer will have to hear it. Believe me, your head will be in your hands if you don't get him *right* now. This *cannot* wait."

Ahxenta could see the *Kel'Moth's* bridge crew trading glances as she was asked to stand by. Two minutes later, she was told that the captain would take a short link over his earpiece.

"This is Thal," came the cold tone. "What's so urgent, Captain?"

"It concerns a station called Kelf Base."

"What!" the voice was sharp. "Say again."

"Kelf Base. We need to talk privately. Now. Commander Seer needs to be in on it. Be ready to receive a data stream over a secure link."

"Stand by, Captain."

The commander of the Starfall fleet was back in minutes, his equally grim first mate alongside. "Captain. What do you know of Kelf Base?"

"You confirm that it is or was one of your bases?"

Thal nodded. "Yes. In sector sixteen of zone Beta."

Ahxenta rapidly outlined the past hours, the recovery of the eight, the remaining life-tubes and the data that she was ready to send over.

She spoke with little interruption, the two Starfall officers evidently stunned at what they were hearing.

"The eldest one says her name is Mara Vetoyn Seer," she ended. "I see you know it. I have names and limited details on the others. The ISA's planning to send a research ship *and* a warship to investigate the Crimson Drapes anomaly and the new worm-pocket that I reported. I haven't told them of the facility on Furze Four but they'll find out soon enough. I expect you'll want your people in there first."

"I want that data now," Thal told her as he nodded.

"Transmitting. I'm for Alto Finglas with an ISA cargo and I can't delay – the ISA's already asking questions. I'll be there in eight hours, and for no more than a day. *That* would be the safest place in the sector to pass your people over to one of your ships. What's your view?"

Thal chewed his lip. "I don't like it," he said slowly. "I don't trust the ISA and I want no-one there to know of this. And there's no way *I* can make it in time. I'll get back to you shortly. And Captain, again I owe you thanks. But why didn't you call the situation in to the ISA?"

"I trust it as much as you do," she responded forthrightly.

"Mara's my daughter. I want to talk to her," the bitter Seer snapped.

"I'll arrange it," Ahxenta agreed gently. "One of my medics *will* sit in. By the way, my chief medic compared her genetic data to readings we hold on Captain Kerrix, and there's a link on the Telziltic side. Not close, but there *is* association. I'll wait your call. Ahxenta out."

The captain sighed as she cut the comm. She then made a quick call to Flintlock to advise her that Seer wanted a word with Mara and that the doctor should prepare her patient for the link. Back on the bridge there had been no alarms, the ship making good speed to her endpoint.

"You didn't tell Thal we were for Millet after Alto Finglas?" the first mate asked after she had heard the details.

"No. And he knew better than to ask. I don't know what meeting he was in, but I bet he cuts it. We wait for his link and see what he's arranged. He keeps a tight rein on his ops and he won't hang about."

The captain was right, for barely an hour later Thal was back with a request for a private link. The upshot for the *Arianrhod* was given in a senior staff briefing that Ahxenta called soon after.

"We discharge our business from the ship. We don't mention Furze or the kids. Thal's planned their pick-up at Opalite, on Gamma edge. It's a day out from Alto Finglas and it's got mining, orbital holding and resupply facilities that Thal's dealt with. I've got the details of the ship he's sending. You go over them, Azular, to make sure she's the genuine article when we meet her. I'll be having a three-way chat with her captain *and* Thal before and during the rendezvous in any case."

"He's taking no chances, then, but what's he doing about Furze?" Apnis wanted to know. "I guess he'll be sending his own in stat."

"He has two ships already en route. What they'll do when they get there I don't know and he wouldn't tell, but I could see he was seriously shaken. Your priority, Doc, is to ensure our guests are as fit as they can be and aware of what's going to happen to them. And make sure they have plenty of kit: the pick-up ship's a PSS, similar to the *Kel'Beth*, but she's been redirected from a long mission and will be ill-equipped to look after youngsters. How's young Mara, after her talk to Seer?"

"Emotional," Flintlock replied. "She knows he's too far away to be there, and I think she's worked out that not all her friends have folks left, after what happened. But what's the story of their abduction?"

"A sneak attack on Kelf Base. It *was* that one in sector sixteen that they used as their main bolthole before the war, as you guessed, Azular. It *had* been breached by hostile agents once, but they were still using it as a holding area for people and gear being moved out – including to their new base outside Beta, that the hostiles got wind of and took out. The attackers were in and out in less than an hour. A lot of Thal's people on the ground were lost trying to shield the kids. As far as Thal knows, that model of attack wasn't repeated, at least among his, as the perps the defenders *did* get paid a heavy price. They were lackeys sent to do the dirty work. As there were fifteen abductees, he's hoping the cryo-tubes hold those missing, and that they're capable of revival."

"Hell, I hope for his sake he's right," Cottontail cut in. "How will you keep the kids amused until we hand them over, Doc?"

"Mara's got them in hand and Parri Millit's set up a teach and play space in the physio suite. I've got ship's therapy techs cutting hair and suchlike, Lindell's had Perla Jute modifying kit and the crew's pitching in – Gem Ferry handed in a model starship and other gifts keep turning up. But Millit's approving all donations – fake weapons are *not* okay as toys, Whisper Earbleat, and I don't want them in my medbay."

The captain quelled the second mate's reply and gave their schedule for the next hours, after which she dismissed all her officers bar Azular.

"When I spoke to Captain Kerrix four days ago, she was headed to Starfall," she said. "In fact, you had a link from her thirty-six hours ago. Did she mention what we'd talked about?"

"No ma'am, she didn't. And I know better than to ask either her or you. But she's at Starfall and not heading out for her pick-up at Telzilt, as her input's deemed crucial to Captain Thal's dealings with the ISA: the *Avenger's* still around. But the *Serenity* is now on her way to Starfall.

Some issue has spurred the admiral to it, and Ambassador Posettix has no qualms about handling diplomacy from the ship."

"But you don't know what the admiral's issue is?"

"No ma'am; and Captain Kerrix wouldn't tell me."

"I expect not. I spoke to her again, after I talked to Thal. She'd been called in over the link to Mara. You were right: Seer's wife was Telziltic, clan Starwain, *and* Thal's partner's sister. But relations between the ISA and Norvalla are souring, as both want too much and Norvalla's allies are chary of giving strangers sector access. Don't look so worried, we didn't talk about you, much. But now she's got that nifty starship, she's had her scientists and engineers go over her dot by dot. They've figured more of her gear. On top of superior tech, she has a chameleon cloak, top-class weapons *and* a neat escape trick: at high speed, using a local mass-energy density patch, she can in essence create a bypass to jump from one locus to another. It was a safety feature inbuilt for Norvalla's Protector, as the ship *had* been created for him. *And* she's got extended high-spec charts of Psi space, which she's offered to me."

"Why didn't she tell me?" Azular asked, puzzled.

"Because you'd have agreed to take them without asking me. *She* recognises that *Arianrhod* is *my* ship, which some of my officers tend to forget. It'll cost me in new tech for data display and interactive holo-grid updates. And we talked about other things. Did she say anything relevant to ship's business when you spoke to her last?"

"Not exactly, ma'am," was the rather self-conscious reply.

"What's that supposed to mean?"

"We spoke of our official union," he said diffidently.

"You mean *you* did. What are you trying to persuade her to do now that concerns my ship?"

"Sooner rather than later, ma'am."

"And I bet she said no," Ahxenta grinned.

"She advised a delay. She has obligations to the Starfall fleet as well as her own trade concerns, and we have our schedules."

"And?" the captain pushed, scenting a hidden agenda.

"I *would* like you to officiate, ma'am, when the date is set."

Ahxenta looked ominous. "You, mister, are going too far too fast."

Azular smiled faintly. "That's what Xanna said, almost exactly. And she reckoned that you would refuse."

"It's time you washed the stardust out of your eyes. But you might see her sooner than you think. She wants to talk to us both about the worm-pocket data we sent out. She and her senior SO have been going over data from the *Kel'Tarn's* shuttle. *She* was picked off Veil Three by a Starfall ship, and they got what she'd recorded during her final flight. They compared that to what they already hold on the known worm-pocket exit at Sox, and they've worked out that the original readings of the Sox pocket *have* changed. It now has synthetic features that match some of the signals in the data you caught at the Crimson Drapes. She knows we sent an edited version and wants the lot. I won't hand it over on a plate, hence the chat. I'll schedule it in as soon as I can. It'll have to be on a tight beam and I sure as hell won't transmit our data through the ether, so it'll mean a meet. I'll keep you posted. And get that grin off your face: it'll be a scientific meet, not a romantic dinner date."

"Aye, ma'am," Azular agreed, still smiling.

* * *

Arianrhod made Alto Finglas to her revised schedule. Apnis dealt with cargo drop whilst the captain talked to Thal and the command officers of the ship that would collect the children. Azular was there; having studied the ship's spec, she wanted his views on her captain. He sensed that Captain Riven was open, but concerned over the *Kel'Kith's* lack of facilities for minors. His ship had been diverted as she was one of the closest to Opalite and her first mate was a parent of one of the kids. Ahxenta noted that Fay Clearwater bore the facial tattoos of the natives of Sheel Four, and she *was* strikingly similar to one of their charges. Final details for the rendezvous agreed, she cut the link.

"Thal's sending a small attack craft to escort the *Kel'Kith* to Starfall? He's really antsy," she said. "And he'd say zip about Furze Four."

"This is ISA HQ," Azular pointed out. "Our comms security is top-notch and Captain Thal's is maybe better, but with the traffic here, I'd guess that close monitoring is routine on *all* activities."

"And by more than the HQ," Ahxenta replied. "That's a lot of big ships. The ISA wants its insignia on as many as it can, and given the arms we've hauled, it'll be rearming them as well. What are you doing?"

"Checking on ISA ships in port. Data's classified, but I may be able to get visuals on those closest to our position with a routine scan…"

"We've had this argument before, Azular," the captain reminded him. "What have I told you about scanning without permission?"

"I know, ma'am. But we've a short turn time and there may be eyes on our exit line. Ah, I recognise *that* ship: it's the *Illustrious*."

"What? So she *was* headed here. I bet Myrtleberry's jumped ship. Get to the bridge and go over Thal's data. I want to see the doc. It's best that Berrik Clearwater doesn't know his mother's on the way."

"The escort for the *Kel'Kith* will reach Opalite half a day after we get in," Azular remarked. "We *could* wait for her."

"To the bridge, mister."

The captain took her place a good hour later, to find that unloading was proceeding smoothly and rapidly.

"They want us gone," Apnis told her. "When I told the science chief I'd nothing to add to the data we sent on the Crimson Drapes and the worm-pocket, she was riled. And you'll never guess who else called."

"Myrtleberry."

"How in the name did you figure that?"

"The *Illustrious* is here, in a berth close to us," Ahxenta said wryly, with a pointed glance at Azular. "What did she want?"

"Courtesy call, but really to push us for more on the worm-pocket. *And* she asked where we're headed next. She's no wiser. But she was sat at a desk that didn't look as if it belonged on a starship."

"She won't give up on the *Repulse* or her fancy shuttle. You can bet there'll be one similar with her name on it, and she'll be back beyond the edge of Alpha before long – I hope."

They were interrupted by a call from Lindell, advising the captain that he had made enquiries and had found a contract that might be of interest. The supercargo's tone alerted the first mate to something."

"What gives, Cap?"

"Wait and see. Azular, you're with me."

Apnis had to wait some time, for she was off duty before she caught up with the captain. "We depart at oh eight hundred tomorrow," she told her. "Port reps are refusing to release our clearances sooner. We have our fees – though I guess Lindell spilled that."

"Very funny. But we've a pick-up of gem-quality stones at Opalite, for drop at Delta Iridium; *Emerald* will meet us at Delta and take them on to Freskat, with comms gear she's picking up for the Freskat Navy."

"Zillah digging in then?" Apnis asked, spooning up her rations.

"Haven't heard, but Melly Goodsocks may find out something once she gets to Freskat, if not before."

"So why a delay at Opalite?" Apnis asked askance "You put Lindell up to scouting for trade, didn't you? And where does Azular fit in?"

"He suggested it, to let the *Kel'Kith's* escort catch us up, and as an excuse for us to be at Opalite, if us being there is leaked."

"It strikes me that Azular's keen that we stay on good terms with Thal, and I can guess why. But what else, Cap? Whatever you said to him after our briefing about the pick-up of the kids, it left him chirpy. You mentioned a link-up with Kerrix and her senior SO about the worm-pocket data to me the other day, but it's more than that."

"The link's arranged for two hours from now. And then we'll have a meet in person to exchange data and get hold of high-spec charts of Psi – and beyond. Basically, the sectors charted by the Norvallans. And Kerrix has sourced data display tech that she thinks might fit into our holo-grid system to let us use the charts to the best advantage."

"How much will it cost us?" the first mate asked.

"I'm working on it – very little, I hope."

"Good luck with that, Cap. And where's this meet that Azular's no doubt hopeful will give him some free time for a cosy liaison?"

"Delta Iridium," Ahxenta told her with a wicked grin.

"You what? How's she going to get there from Starfall without half the damn charted galaxy spotting that ship of hers?"

"I'll find out tonight. Her last call was to fix details, as she and her senior SO, Nyvallish, were still going over the data they had."

"So where is he now?" Apnis demanded. "Shining his buttons?"

"Wiseacre. He's going over the spec of the *SS Lucent*, the escort for the *Kel'Kith*. She's a small battlecruiser out of Thal's station off Beta."

"You two are going to have a long night," Apnis prophesied.

"Tell me about it. So's Axellina: the kids are hyper over going home. They're used to space travel, though, given the life they've had."

"Poor saps. Want me to sit in on the hook-up to Kerrix?"

"No, you get some sack time. One of us will have to be sharp."

* * *

The outcome of the talk with the *Moonstone's* officers Ahxenta gave to her senior staff on the way to Opalite. More analyses had verified that the Sox worm-pocket had been structurally altered, and the signals emitted were in line with those *Arianrhod* had logged at the Crimson Drapes. Using the final flight data of the *Kel'Tarn's* shuttle, Kerrix had posited that the adaptions had created a bifurcated worm-pocket at Sox, with exits at Hervesta *and* Veil. As the Drapes pocket was new, she suggested that who or what had altered the Sox anomaly may have had a hand in its creation. Her senior SO was not sure, nor did he agree with her that the entity behind it had been trying to create a bypass that had by a physical fluke become a worm-pocket.

"What's your take on it, Azular?" Apnis asked slyly.

"I agree with Commander Nyvallish. The existence of a split worm-pocket has been theorised, it's feasible and could be caused by adaption of an existing one. As the results we got for the Crimson Drapes match those logged for Sox, similar forces *may* have been at work, but the idea that the worm-pocket was created from scratch is speculative. The initiation energy needed would be vast and the expertise complex. It would be difficult to do secretly in such a busy area, though there's the nebular blip: it's been created covertly *and* recently. I *suppose* a minute worm-pocket may have existed undetected, and was used as the origin for the new one, but an attempt to create a bypass that accidentally created a worm-pocket? No. As far as I know, that's never occurred."

"Just because it hasn't doesn't mean it can't," Cottontail put in.

"We're having a meet with the *Moonstone* at Delta Iridium to swop data and take on tech to update our holo," Ahxenta said tetchily. "It'll enhance course projection and include features to display new charts of Psi and beyond that we'll also get. Starfall's larger ships already have it or are being upgraded. We're also being given resources to produce our version of the add-on units for our cloak, Crizz: you had doubts about the ones we have in place, so it'll solve that."

"Is Captain Kerrix handing it over with Captain Thal's say-so?" the first mate queried archly. "Or do we have to cough up? And how's she planning to get to Delta from Starfall?"

"She's getting our data. And it's payback for Furze and for what we didn't pass to the ISA. And she's making for Delta via a covert bypass from Pollens Sentry to Lartzeg Trine."

"You what? How do you know that?" Apnis asked. "I can't imagine she upped and told you. Huh, I might have known: it was you, wasn't it?" she rounded on Azular. "You figured."

"No comment, Commander."

"Cut it," the captain ordered. "And get the gleam out of your eye, Earbleat. The new tech will not include weaponry. Doc, get back to the kids, we'll be at Opalite in eight hours. Everybody else, take a break; I want everybody fresh for the final haul. We… what in hell…!"

The strident tone of the red alert cut the air as the sharp tones of comms officer Lieutenant Rosy Gallus called the captain to the bridge. Ahxenta was out the door at a run, her officers at her heels.

8: KEL'MARR

Arianrhod's bridge was a hive of activity as the captain took her chair to the hail of battlestations and the red glow of the alert. The duty officer, on her feet, had called shields up, weapons online, sensors at maximum and the holo-grid full down. Apnis threw herself into her chair, tensing her webbing and pulling her ops boards over, as other officers assumed posts. Ahxenta could tell by the grid that her ship was not at risk: no blips in local space were marked hostile and her course showed clear.

"Distress, ma'am, PSS channel," Lieutenant Wynna Parlen told her. "It's not a PSS I've heard of. She's under attack off the Beetle system. I've ordered us in to assess and assist but haven't raised our cloak."

"Checking PSS registries, ma'am," Greffy broke in. "I have her, or a ship with that name. The *PSS Kel'Marr*, registered at the Kirtish office in zone Mu. She's only been rigged as a PSS for thirty days standard."

"One of Thal's," Apnis grated.

"Sounds like, but I won't take it as read. Gallus, try to raise her and find out what she's up against. Bellfish, link to Captain Thal if you can: I want to verify if she *is* his, and if so, what she's doing here."

The captain responded quickly to confirm that the *Kel'Marr* was a new PSS of his. She had left Minti for Gemstone, but had been routed to Opalite to await orders. One of Thal's ships near Furze had spotted a battered but active alien off the brown star Altina, close to a node of a little-used bypass out of Lartzeg Trine. It had veered off without engaging. His ship could track it no further, and alarm bells had rung.

Ahxenta cut the link as soon as they had the *Kel'Marr's* spec. Comms had got a signal: the stricken ship was under attack by two hostiles that had jumped her as she had switched course at the Beetle node.

"Got her, Captain!" Gliss exclaimed. "A mid-range ship reading as a PSS! Two others, huge, that match hostile specs. They're closing!"

"Cloak up and make ready to jump off once we get to her position! Gunnery crews stand by. Tell her we're on our way, comms."

"Scanning hostiles!" Azular cut in. "Familiar specs, but ships are *not* identical. Zukivianite in the one nearest, but I can't gauge the weaponry of either. They're manoeuvring, trying to capture her, not destroy her!"

"Dammit! Cook our engines, Chief! Dox, get us up on her location!

Keep the cloak up until we're on them: it may keep them guessing and we've no decoy. *Loki* on standby, Earbleat, we may need her."

The ship's seams creaked as every atom of power was set for speed. The crew were pushed into their seats as the gravity generators strove to maintain balance. The starfield sped by, *Arianrhod's* position on the holo-grid cutting the distance between her and her quarry.

"Dox, ready us to go in at high speed," Ahxenta barked. "Increase energy to forr'ad shields! Prime phase cannons and target that nearest blip the second she's in range. All stations prep for go... now, Dox!"

"Blips closing on the *Kel'Marr*! She's trying to take out their tractors – she knows they want her in one piece!" called Azular.

"They've seen us! Near one's turning to take us on!" Gliss spat.

"Take her down! Launch deflecting drones, target her main arrays! I want her tractors and big guns out! Azular, scan for weak spots!"

As *Arianrhod's* hull rang to phase hits, Dox's skilled hands brought her above the alien, allowing Earbleat's teams to rain fire on the ship's upper hull and main weapons emplacements. For all her size, she was highly manoeuvrable, and spun down steeply to avoid incoming bolts.

"Underside aft, and her port side's lost a lot of shielding!" Azular bawled. "On grid. She reads low on weapons but readings are shifting."

"Then I don't buy it," Ahxenta snarled. "Dox, bring us down across her left flank but keep her targeting eyes guessing. Earbleat, have your crews concentrate on those damaged shields..."

As a wave of torpedoes cut through her flank, the hostile sheared off, an intense bloom of fire erupting out towards *Arianrhod*. Dox had already veered off at a tangent, the ship straining to outfly the wash of energy from her downed adversary. The captain could feel her webbing tighten to breaking point as *Arianrhod* caught the edge of the blast and was hurled off-course. The helmswoman fought with her controls to bring the ship back to an even keel and several heart-stopping minutes later, engines screeching, stability was achieved.

The bridge was chaotic, emergency lights blazing as enviro-systems crashed. Several crew had been hurt and signals on her boards told the captain of problems throughout the ship. As the grid steadied, Ahxenta cursed. The second hostile had the advantage of the *Kel'Marr*, and the smaller ship was now trying to outfly her opponent.

"Prepare to intercept that second blip! Target forr'ad torpedoes on her but keep distance. Ready *Loki* to run: I want this ended now!"

"She's breaking off, Captain!" Gliss roared. "*Kel'Marr's* sent a volley across her starboard and it's destabilised her."

"Hell, Thal's ships know how to fight!" Apnis growled. "We follow that blip or let it go?"

"Let it go. Thal's people will have the spec and knowing him, he'll deal with it. Cut red alert, but keep us on standby. Bring us up on the *Kel'Marr*, Dox. Medic to the bridge!" Ahxenta ordered as she took in her bridge crew, four of whom were on the deck.

"I have Captain Kiff Weaver for you, ma'am," Bellfish broke in.

"On grid."

The PSS had taken heavy damage but could move under her own power, the steely-eyed Weaver told Ahxenta, after thanking her for her aid. He refused more support, citing a mission that could not wait.

"I know; you're for Opalite. I advise you confirm with Captain Thal and we'll escort you. And I'd like the data you got on those hostiles."

"Stand by," he said frostily.

"Rum bunch," Apnis remarked. "I'll go check Azular: his webbing failed and he took a tumble. Greffy's busy."

Most of the bridge crew were at their posts, restoring systems and sending data to the grid. The captain checked her boards. Their status was better than expected, damaged shields had held, and they had no breaches. Plating needed realigned and hull systems restored, but they could source gear at Opalite. The casualty list was stretching, she noted bleakly, but their guests were fine: Flintlock had tied them into life-pods. As the medic arrived, Bellfish called that Thal was on line.

Thal's main fear was the children. Ahxenta reassured him. He had spoken to Weaver and sanctioned the transfer of the *Kel'Marr's* data to *Arianrhod*. Weaver had been briefed and knew of her precious cargo. The Starfall commander had made other plans, as a call for him cut in and after a check of his ops, he ordered a three-way link to bring in the *Kel'Marr*. The *SS Lucent* had been rerouted and was on the way to escort both ships to Opalite, where Thal would arrange emergency repairs at the local yards and cover costs, he told Ahxenta. She had other issues, including her injured crew, and quickly ended the talk.

"He's still a hard customer," the first mate said at her elbow.

"How's Azular?"

"Stubborn; he has a cracked rib, a smacked face and bruising. Kelp's ordered him to medbay, and I bet our people still in post have knocks they're ignoring. I have, for one, but Flintlock has her hands full."

"We've a lot of injured," the captain frowned. "And those kids must be terrified. You hold the bridge, liaise with the *Kel'Marr* and the *Lucent*, and have Lindell check with our Veximer clients: we're behind for our Millet pick-up. I'm heading for medbay, so I'll haul Azular along."

The staff were pushed but coping, Ahxenta found, as she left Azular with a nurse-tech and caught up with her chief medic. No-one needed care off-ship, but there were several critical that would tie up medbay facilities. Flintlock had scant faith in what Opalite could offer, but had drafted a list of essentials. The kids had been freed from the life-pods and left with Parri Millit and Ensign Skimmi Rain of security.

"Rain was on her rounds and got to a web-in site, but cut loose to help when a hatch outside engineering blew and knocked Brook Jentle off his feet: he'd been fixing circuits. She's mobile, and as she has four younger siblings, I made her the child-minder," Flintlock grinned. "I'll leave you to pep talk the patients, I have work to do."

* * *

The advent of three ships caused a flurry in the Port Control office at Opalite, since it was clear that two had seen action. *Arianrhod* had trade and her clearances were granted, but the *Kel'Marr* and the *Lucent* were held off station. As agreed, Thal had linked in an hour out, and he and Riven of the *Kel'Kith* were on line as they made orbit. Thal settled port matters swiftly and sooner than Ahxenta had expected, repair rigs were moving in to deal with *Arianrhod's* distorted hull plates.

"What kind of clout does Thal have with these people that they hop to it so fast?" Apnis asked of the captain.

"Hell knows, but keep an eye on the work crews. I don't want to be here more than a day. Lindell can handle cargo pick-up as it's small, but the company may want a command officer to set the seal. I'll have to oversee the transfer of the kids and Azular's with me. The *Kel'Kith's* shuttle will have two medics, and Fay Clearwater will pilot. Greffy and Gliss will track it every step. *Kel'Marr* and *Lucent* will do the same, and we'll have a live link to the bay. Stress from Port Control you refer to Thal – he'll be on the live link."

The captain stepped into the bay as soon as the shuttle had docked, Azular and three guards at her heels, and in advance of the medbay party. Surveillance gear covered every angle. She greeted the *Kel'Kith's* three as they stepped off the ramp, Azular scanning each one. That done, she called in the group now at the entry.

That the eight youngsters were daunted was clear, but Ahxenta was pleased to see them all looking well. Each toted a backpack. They hove up, steered by Flintlock, Millit and Rain, with a discreet security duo as rearguard. A choked-off cry caused her to turn. It was Clearwater.

The *Kel'Kith* medics quickly moved in, but Berrik had reached his mother, dropping his toy in his haste. The calm Mara Seer picked it up and turned to thank the captain of the *Arianrhod* for her care.

"You're welcome," was the level response. "Look after them," she

100

added, nodding towards the small party. "They still need you."

"Aye, Captain."

The children aboard and leave-taking over, Ahxenta looked around and ordered her people out. She dismissed all bar Flintlock and Azular. The three watched the shuttle's exit from the external view platform.

"Cool customer, young Mara," the chief medic remarked. "I heard what she said to you. She'll make a first-rate officer one day."

"Or a first-rate renegade. Back to medbay for you, Axellina. I'm for the bridge to make sure they get home. Your face still looks like it met the deck, Azular; you'd best have it fixed before we see Captain Kerrix. And I want your take on the *Kel'Kith's* people *and* her shuttle: I noticed you scanning it. As did Clearwater, and I bet Thal did, over his link."

"I know, ma'am. It was so well-shielded that I had trouble, but what I got leads me to suspect that Thal's fitting his craft with zone Psi tech. I'll compare my data with Greffy's. One of the medics was from Vellis, the other I can't say; both had cyber-implants. Commander Clearwater is part-Arrissian despite her facial tattoos. All three were wary, but I sensed no antagonism, just thankfulness."

"I'm off here, Cap; and so are you, Azular," Flintlock broke in.

"I'm for the bridge," he returned as the transport stopped.

"Medbay," Ahxenta ordered crisply. "Now, mister."

The bridge had returned to normal by the time the captain made it. Their cargo was on its way in a small transfer pod, tracked by Lindell's team, and the *Kel'Kith's* shuttle was ready to dock. Work on *Arianrhod's* hull was advancing, as was weapons recharge and resupply, and a pod with medical supplies was on the way.

"*Kel'Marr's* taken a beating; she'll be here four days, her first mate said," Apnis told Ahxenta. "She'll still ride shotgun, so I guess there's not another closer. I've no more on Furze: Thal's close-lipped. What the *Lucent* and *Kel'Kith* will do for now I don't know. We got little from the *Kel'Marr's* data: we've similar specs on file. Greffy thinks the ship targeting us was uncrewed and under the other's control. The smaller one had no zukivianite, was low on arms but big on pull power. Maybe that was why she wanted to cripple and capture the *Kel'Marr*. But there *was* data on the crew. Not a lot, but Greffy's figured them for the highly cyber, human-like clones similar to our ex-enemy Hoxiz, that Thal got. So ruthless, dangerous to cross, and still out there."

"Our pharmaceuticals pick-up at Millet?"

"Sorted. I talked to the senior rep. He was an over-arrogant grouch and Ensign Jute thought an earful of command officer would cut him down to size. I told him we'd answered a distress and if he didn't like it, too bad; we wouldn't ignore a ship in trouble just to suit him. I then linked to the principal company director and told her the same, with the implied threat that she could find another carrier next time. Our load will be in orbit at Millet and the client on Veximer advised."

"Good. As for our Freskat cargo, Azular can check crystal quality once it's aboard. That should keep him out of trouble."

"And if they're not up to scratch?" the first mate asked.

"The vendors get fried and we warn our contacts off their goods."

"This is a new port to us, but they must've heard of *Arianrhod*, Cap. Enough to know that they don't mess with us or you get cranky."

"Cheers. Looks like the shuttle's safe aboard the *Kel'Kith*."

A call from Riven to confirm was followed by one from Thal with thanks for Ahxenta's aid and a promise to let her know the outcome. His people had retrieved the life-tubes and other hardware from Furze, but two ISA ships had reached the area, the destroyer *ISAS Steadfast* and the research ship *ISAS Skimfrost*.

"Haven't heard of either of them," Apnis sniffed. "Recent refits maybe. I expect we'll get the bare bones of what they find, eventually."

"Eventually. But I want us out of here and with all our gear on line, including the decoy. Azular and Cottontail made a start on it with the kit they picked up on Marridan, but it's been on hold due to our other problems. Let's go over the repair schedules and see what's what…"

* * *

Late next day, *Arianrhod*, repaired and resupplied, slid out of her bay. Ahxenta had taken Thal at his word and had brought in all her needs, including the means to complete the decoy. He had not argued and the suppliers had been quick. In Apnis' view, they wanted repeat trade and were going all-out to impress. The captain had heard from Corry Riven of the *Kel'Kith* that the Starfall vessels would refit rapidly and leave in a body, but their forward route he would not reveal.

"They'll make for that covert bypass that cuts through Gamma and Lambda to Twilight Station and make for Starfall from there," guessed Ahxenta. "Less chance of trouble and they can pick up gear and maybe another escort. In fact, they'll be on our tail, as that's the shortest route to Millet. It won't take long, and Veximer's two days beyond. With the upgrades we got at Opalite, we can push the engines a bit."

"Crizz'll thank you," the first mate said. "She's in her lab working on the decoy. I heard her and Azular trading words over it in the mess."

Arianrhod pressed through the dark, every scanner stretched and her crew alert. She met naught en route and made her endpoint during her client's trading hours. The cargo pods, in an orbital holding area, were transferred without a hitch. In hours, the ship was on her way.

Veximer Prime was in central Gamma, and in a briefing, Azular, his mind on Starfall, drew attention to the bypass used by Thal's people that the captain guessed the *Kel'Kith* and her escort would take. It ran close by Veximer and had to flank the trade bypass *Arianrhod* would use to make for Limekiln at that locus. He wanted to deep-scan for it.

"Why?"

"The hostiles must know it as it was one of theirs, and it's clear that they're aware of events at Furze, given the hit on the *Kel'Marr*. And it's possible that Opalite may host hostile agents. If so, three Starfall ships in convoy will be noted and word passed."

"Thal will have it covered," the captain said sharply.

"I know that, ma'am, but another set of scanners would help."

"*You* want to know the precise position of any local node and think you'll stand a good chance of locating it using your Norvallan scanner."

"Aye, ma'am."

"You'll only do it on my say-so and I *will* have a word with Thal in advance. But we don't hang fire at Veximer. We've no pick-up and I want to make Limekiln quickly. And as we need the decoy operative, you and the chief will be busy from here until there. Hop to it, all."

* * *

Veximer Prime was the third planet in the system and the only settled world at a switch node for a major trade route through Gamma. It saw heavy traffic, and *Arianrhod* was known there. She had made in with no glitches and remained only as long as it took to drop her cargo and deal with formalities. Azular and Greffy were on the bridge to operate the science arrays and had drafted Mitt Snow to assist at tactical. Thal had realised that there was more to it than concern for hostile action close to the covert bypass, but did not object. Nor did he pass on data about the precise location of his bypass or nodes close to Veximer.

"Got it!" Greffy crowed as the ship made a curve out of local space. "A patch of negative mass-energy density; it reads like a node off our bypass. It's masked by the gravity pull of the Boxer system. On grid."

"Good call," Azular said. "Boxer was never settled, though nodes tend to exist near inhabited or once-inhabited areas."

"I've got nothing unusual in the area, Doc," Snow put in. "Anything new would've been marked by Veximer's patrol ships."

"True; but now we have one likely node on a bypass used by Starfall, and that's where their ships will enter: it takes a lot less energy than jumping on randomly," he responded.

"We're not hanging here for more," the captain said firmly. "Get what you can in fifteen minutes and then we're for Limekiln via Spinel. It's four days at low loading. You can long-range scan as we go. I want the decoy and our cloak ready to up and run at any peep of trouble."

"*Loki's* in her bay and up to spec, Cap," the second mate piped up.

"Thank you, Lieutenant Commander Earbleat," Ahxenta replied. "I hope we don't need her," she added to Apnis. "We've had no news of local bother and Bellfish has his ears to all the usual nets."

"Any more on the TA contract we're now tied to, or what Admiral Zillah's up to out at Freskat?"

"Nary a thing. We'll find out more at Delta. *Emerald's* still on course to meet us there and Goodsocks may have got news from her Freskat Navy contacts. *Moonstone* should make it in just after we do."

"And after Delta?"

"The Web. Redship Industrial's planetary base is assembling heavy lifting gear for ISA Stinward; it'll be ready to ship in thirty days and we have the tender. And Ottolyx has a batch of micro-engineering kit for Estuary Corp at Yistreen Three. Unless another deal comes up at Delta that we can fit in en route. Lindell's on it; there's a load of cereal seed from Ceres Corp that's bound for their outlier HQ on Bistra that he's put in for. As it's on our course, it'll be easy credit."

"I take it the crystals from Opalite came up to scratch?"

"Azular's impressed with the quality, so we'll keep Gimcrys Mining in mind when we want more. They're a match for Brown Amber's best and the price was keen. Yes, what is it, Azular?"

"No anomalies ma'am, but long-range scans of Boxer Two indicate that despite harsh surface conditions, there *are* structural elements that read artificial, but ancient. No energy signals, so I'd guess defunct."

"Log it, but we're not going in. Set for the bypass, Ms Dox."

"Aye, ma'am. I estimate thirty eight hours to Spinel."

* * *

The hours to and beyond Spinel passed calmly until an alert from the *Obsidian Sky* reported an oddity near Ruby, a zone Gamma system with a node linking Spinel to Millet. A huge ship reading hostile had passed Bluejohn's ship at speed on a route that implied Veximer as its goal. It had not engaged or tried to scan.

"Ruby! Far enough from us, but on a line that might intersect with the Starfall ships," the captain noted starkly. "I hope Thal's picked it up. Get Captain Bluejohn on the link," she ordered comms.

The *Obsidian* had been running uncloaked to Millet from Berry and her captain was surprised not to be targeted. He had caught the ship's spec and at Ahxenta's request, sent it on. One look at Azular told her that it matched the larger ship that had hit the *Kel'Marr*.

"Three Starfall ships are heading that way that may be the target, Grey. I can't tell you more but it's vital they get through. We're too far out to turn back, but the Veximer authorities need to be alerted. It *must* be taken out: it's uncrewed but probably packed with explosive. Have any more of ours called you over it?"

"No, you're the first… wait," he broke off at a call from his comms officer. "Well, well – Captain Thal of the *Kel'Moth*."

"He's at Starfall. Tell him it reads the same as the ships that attacked the *Kel'Marr*. I hope in hell he's got a ship close enough to go in."

"Stay on the link, Cinnabar, and I'll bring him in. Get Captain Thal on line, and keep the *Arianrhod* on," Bluejohn ordered his comms.

Thal *had* called for more, and confirmed that Riven and Weaver of his PSS ships and Jame of the *Lucent* were aware. They had left Opalite for Veximer, via Millet. After a rapid exchange, Thal let Bluejohn know that the *Kel'Kith* was carrying children. The latter mused for a moment.

"Tell your ships to hold at Millet if they get there before me: I'm en route. Once I drop my load, I'll ride alongside until we know the score. I'm switching at Veximer for Stella Triplet, so if your ships are on that track, I'll stay with them. But the authorities at Veximer and its outliers should be warned, if that beast is full of explosive."

"And it's possible that there are more heading in on another tack," Ahxenta cautioned. "These hostiles seem keen to make a point."

"I'd noticed," Thal said tartly. "Thank you, Captain Bluejohn, I'm grateful for your support. Please stand by while I talk to my people."

"Thal's beginning to realise what it means to be with the PSS fleet," Apnis observed once the link was cut. "We help each other out, even if it costs. You think he'll order his ships to keep on the bypass from Veximer to Coral? You'll cut off there for Stella Triplet, Grey?"

"That's right; but what other route would they take?"

"Don't ask," advised Ahxenta. "In fact, don't ask anything about it. I'll give you the details on the flipside, one of these days. But we're for Limekiln and are late as it is. Let me know what happens, if you can."

"Roger that, Cinnabar. I'll see you around. *Obsidian* out."

"Some hostiles know what went down at Furze and they're trying to make Thal's people pay, you think, Cap?" the first mate asked.

"Looks like. And our name's tied to the tale, which'll put backs up."

"Same old story; they never give up. Some lessons they don't learn. But they're still using original-type ships, so they're fixed-up old ones or they've a secret supply; they don't seem to be producing new."

"As far as we know," Ahxenta said darkly. "Give it time. There's a new zone we know nix about, and who knows what's holed up there?"

"Captain Kerrix?" was the arch reply, with a sly glance at Azular.

"Stow it. It's time we were off duty, before the final push. And we've won the Ceres deal to ship the seed from Delta to Bistra."

"A few days at Delta, then, with the Limekiln gear for Rhomb, the gems to the *Emerald* and the meet with the *Moonstone*," Apnis yawned.

* * *

The pick-up at Limekiln and the trip to Delta Iridium was speedy. The *Emerald*, the only other PSS in, was in orbit and taking on her load. A link from Kerrix advised that the *Moonstone* was on the way, but would be half a day late, after a delay at Lartzeg Trine. The call had troubled Ahxenta, as Kerrix had clearly seen action, but she would only say that her ship needed repair. She also said that the *Serenity* had made Starfall.

The gem transfer to the *Emerald* allowed Ahxenta to visit the ship. Captain Melly Goodsocks was upbeat, with local contracts in hand and several under tender. She was to depart shortly for Lambda. Apnis had been left in charge of *Arianrhod*, and cargo drop was done by the time the captain made it back aboard and up to the bridge.

After a swift glance over her ops boards, Ahxenta turned to her first mate. "The Ceres load won't be ready for two days, and we'll need one to load and secure the pods. We'll defer shore leave for the Web, as our deals there will take time. Anything from the *Moonstone*?" she added quietly, aware that her bridge crew were listening in as usual.

"Nary a thing. Why? Trouble?"

"Maybe. We're off duty soon, so I'll fill you in then. I'd best make sure tactical let me know as soon as she gets in. And have a word with Azular. I expect there's no link come in for him lately?"

"Nope. And he's had his scanners at full stretch for hours."

Apnis watched the captain step over to the science station. After a short chat, Azular rose and followed her to the bridge office.

"What gives?" Box whispered to Dox, as most eyes traded glances. "The *Moonstone's* late; wasn't she supposed to get in just after we did?"

"Search me. But don't go asking Doc Azular or you'll find your head in your hands, *after* I've kicked you up the butt," she warned.

Ahxenta and Azular returned in fifteen minutes, but said nothing as they took their places. The watch changed shortly after, and as the crew switched, the captain cocked a brow at Apnis and indicated her office.

"What's the deal, Cap? He didn't look too down in the mouth but he wasn't happy," the first mate said once the door closed.

After a rapid recap of her chat to Kerrix, the captain called up part of the record. "I showed him that. He made no more of it than I did, but her face has met a hard object and her arm's in a sling. She linked from an office, so she didn't want me seeing her bridge. And she was tight-lipped as to what had gone down. She said she'd send an alert to the fleet, but hasn't yet. I checked the relays: nothing for that area, but it's empty. Starfall and the hostiles are the only ones likely to use a bypass from Pollens Sentry to Lartzeg Trine."

"The hostiles? You think the *Moonstone* met trouble from them?"

"No point speculating, but as she's still in one piece, she must have come out on top. We'll find out. But she's…"

A buzz cut her short and the captain quickly tabbed her comm. The *Moonstone* was on her way into Delta Iridium, heading for a repair bay, the duty tactical officer told her. Ahxenta called for a patch-through of the visual, and set her wall grid to full spread.

"Bloody hell, she's been in the wars!" the first mate gasped. "The pride of Starfall and half her hide's in shreds!"

"Hardly," the captain disagreed. "But she's taken a thrashing. I can't see a major breach from this angle and her jammers are still active, as our tactical scanners can't get through. What the… that's our science arrays being pulled in. Damn him! Azular's back on the bridge."

Ahxenta was out of her chair and through the door in an instant. Duty officer Lieutenant Kyvitha Keith quickly vacated the command chair, but the captain made straight past to the science station.

"So what's her status, Dr Azular?" she asked crisply.

"She didn't separate, ma'am, the damage is across the whole ship. She's seen heavy phase and pulse cannon fire and taken torpedo hits, but hull integrity's increasing: she's deploying repair bots even though the bay's restraining struts are not fully engaged. And she's loaded: her main holds are screened, though I can't read the nature of her cargo."

"Life signs?"

"Typical for her size, ma'am."

"And what are you doing on the bridge?" Ahxenta added quietly.

"I was monitoring local space from my lab. I saw her on approach. The bridge science station *is* the best equipped…"

"As you have your Norvallan scanner permanently tied in."

"Yes ma'am. I want to know what happened."

"I'll bet. As do I: there's been no word on any channel, so Captain Kerrix must have a frigging good reason for holding back on sending out an advisory or an alert."

"My opinion also, Captain. I don't like it."

"We'll have to wait until she's fully stable before making a courtesy call," Ahxenta said dryly. "I expect her crew have their hands full."

"Yes, ma'am, I'm sure they do. Her hull arrays are powering up – she's turned her scanners on *us!*"

"She's *what?* Tactical, confirm!"

"Confirmed," Snow called. "*Moonstone's* scanning us *and* every other ship in range, ma'am. Her weapons are online, but not targeting."

"Comms, get me Captain Kerrix!" the captain growled as she made for her chair, exchanging a glance with her puzzled first mate.

The *Moonstone's* captain was in the command chair, her first mate beside her. Both bore signs of injury and Kerrix' arm was still in a sling. Her bridge was bathed in red, techs were carrying out repairs and the gaping bridge crew of *Arianrhod* could see medics in action. Kerrix did not look surprised to see Ahxenta and greeted her equably.

"Care to tell me why you're scanning my ship, Captain Kerrix?"

"I'm making sure you are who you appear to be," was the cool reply.

"And what in hell's that supposed to mean?"

"We've had more than a little trouble with imposters lately. I won't take chances, even with a ship that I know."

"You didn't send out an alert. Why not?"

"One of the imposters was fabricated to look like a PSS."

"What!" Ahxenta hissed. "Which one?"

"The *PSS Pearl Shield,* and she was sending a distress," Kerrix stated.

"The *Pearl!* What happened?"

"The distress was coming from Skart; it's empty, on a line to Lartzeg Trine. We jumped off, scanning. She *was* reading *Valkyrie* class but her call-sign didn't match the *Pearl.* It matched the *Bright Mist,* a ship that's been off the PSS register for a few years: she was lost between Kell Lyne and Tressic Major. It was thought she'd been hit by raiders off the Astrella Nine asteroid field, but no trace was ever found."

"I've heard the name. There was another PSS lost around that area years before her," Ahxenta said harshly, her face twisting. "And there *have* been other ships since. Go on."

"My teams compared our data to the details Captain Holdspan sent on about the *Warrior's* firefight by Idledott: shifting hull comp, power build-up, trace zukivianite hull insertions that *my* senior SO knew were penetrating drones. We rigged to protect ourselves and she knew we'd got her measure: she dropped the façade and came in all guns blazing. She *was* hostile, big, but some of my people have dealt with similar. We held out, but took a heap of damage. We weren't breached but we lost a lot of firepower protecting our hull from those drones. And *they* were taking shots at us. We took her down and jumped for the bypass."

"Didn't you send a distress?" Ahxenta asked.

"After what had just hit us? No, I did not," Kerrix shot back. "I *did* inform Captain Tilius but asked him not to pass it on until we'd made a safe port. But what we hadn't reckoned on was *another* bogus ship. *It* jumped us at Kolm, on the bypass to here. We dealt with it, barely. *It* read as the *ISPS Nomad…* you'll recognise *that* name, Captain."

"Damn straight. She went missing while investigating sightings of a huge unknown ship that we later found out was an alien that had been lurking around the edge of the Starglass. The hostiles got her and used her crew as spare parts for the organic elements of their own anatomy."

"I know the story; *your* people worked it out. Whoever set the fake *Nomad* up to trap us created a call-sign that read genuine, but the ship set up as the *Pearl Shield* used the *Bright Mist's* call-sign: interesting."

"Your reading of it?"

"The hostiles or their agents have got hold of highly-classified ISPS data or they're so damn smart they can produce fake call-signs, like the *ISPS Revenge*; but they're not smart enough to do that for the current PSS fleet. Or they had access to the *Bright Mist,* as why else choose a *Valkyrie* class ship? The *Pearl's* the only one now in the fleet. Is there anything else, Captain? I need to attend to my people."

Ahxenta could see that despite her calm, Kerrix was all-in and Jesse Inks looked as bad. The *Moonstone's* bridge was still suffused in red and many systems were patently out of action.

"Let me know what I can do to help, Captain. The meet we were due to have can wait. Link me at your discretion. Ahxenta out."

Beside her, Apnis gave a deep sigh. "Hell, Cap, how did she get out of two scraps like that? And what's her casualty list like? If the captain and first mate were both hit, what went down on her bridge?"

"Later. Meantime, we deal with our own concerns. Tactical, keep a bead on the *Moonstone* and on local space. Comms, if a message comes in from the *Moonstone,* patch it through to me immediately."

"Mess time," Apnis hinted heavily.

"Mess time. And Azular's with us. Ensign Summers is quite capable of keeping an eye on the science station."

* * *

The mess was busy, as several crewmen had headed in after their stints. The three found a private table, but were aware of the curious glances.

"Word's got round," the first mate noted. "Nothing keeps this crew in the dark for long. And here's the doc: she'll want a lowdown."

"We're not busy in medbay, we could spare some hands," the CMO said, after hearing the gist. "*Moonstone* will be able to source what she needs from Delta. Their medical suppliers are the best there are."

"I won't disturb Captain Kerrix now, I'll send an open link. But we have schedules and I don't want to exceed our stay here. You probed the *Moonstone*, Azular, and you know her spec – what's her real state?"

His brow creased. "Badly damaged; most of her hull emplacements and arrays are wrecked and she's thin on plating, but her repair bots are onto it. Her cargo and launch bays look whole, which implies that her cargo's intact. The worst will have to be fixed here and she can take on arms, but I imagine Captain Kerrix will head to a Starfall base for most of the repairs: they're set up for it and they look after their own. She won't want Delta repair teams to gauge her ship's full capability."

"I bet – Starfall base is probably the only one set up for her ship. But she's a long way from home. Finish your rations, you'll want to keep your strength up. I'll…"

The captain was interrupted by her wrist communit. An alert to the PSS fleet had come in from the *Moonstone*. The four listened to the brief report that told of the attacks. It was enhanced by data on the attacking vessels and the precise sites of the assaults. There was nothing else.

"How long before everybody starts to bleat about them and bug the *Moonstone* for more details?" asked Apnis.

"Captain Kerrix and her crew can handle it," Ahxenta said roughly.

* * *

Several hours later the captain was alerted that a call for her had come in from Commander Jesse Inks. Ahxenta ordered the link sent through directly to her quarters, slightly surprised that Kerrix had not called.

The *Moonstone's* first mate looked better than he had done earlier, she noted, but he was still sporting med patches.

"How can I help you, Mr Inks?" she asked.

He was concise, and Ahxenta listened soberly. She closed the link with a sigh and sat back to think. Shortly after, she made for medbay to chat to her chief medic, after which she made for Azular's lab, where she knew he was still at work.

"Get some sleep. That's an order. You'll meet me and Commander Apnis for breakfast in the mess at oh seven hundred, after which you, I, Dr Flintlock, and a couple of others will head to the *Moonstone*."

"Captain, may I ask…"

"No you may not ask. Sack time, mister."

9: SECRETS

Azular was in the mess when the captain appeared. He sat at a far table which gave privacy, but it was quiet. Ahxenta made her way over with her rations and sat down heavily. They exchanged polite salutations.

"We'll wait for Tallica," the captain said. "I didn't brief her last night as it was so late."

"You've heard from Captain Kerrix, ma'am?" he surmised.

"We'll wait for Tallica," Ahxenta repeated with a quelling glance.

The first mate was punctual and as direct as always. "What's to do, Cap? The meet you've got with Captain Kerrix to trade info and pick up gear is still on? I'd have thought she'd be up to her ears."

"She is: Jesse Inks called last night to say that she wants to pass on the gear, and it makes sense to have the chat while we're there. And he asked if we'd take on the *Moonstone's* cargo: no Starfall PSS is close and the *Moonstone's* not fit. It's small, in company pods, and it's for the Web. I've agreed to that, and to lending him Axellina and two of our medbay staff for the next thirty six hours."

"May I ask why Captain Kerrix didn't call you herself, ma'am, given the nature of the requests?" Azular asked anxiously.

"She was busy trying to contact the families of the crew she lost in their two firefights. They had seven fatalities."

"Oh hell!" Apnis breathed. "That's tough."

"It is. She's lost three engineers, two systems techs, a tactical officer and a medic that had gone below decks to assist. Four were from zone Psi, so getting comms links is tricky. And with the raft of injuries they have, they're stretched. The doc's sorting out kit to take, and there are supplies coming up from Delta. But the *Moonstone's* unique and has gear that no other ship has, and as you said Azular, her captain doesn't want local repair crews getting too close, so patch-up will be a headache. As her nearest Starfall base is Twilight, she'll maybe make for there once she can move, but what facilities it has I don't know. Eat up and make ready to move. You have the data we're handing over, Azular?"

"Yes ma'am. I could stay and assist with technical issues aboard the *Moonstone?*" he hazarded. "I'm familiar with Norvallan tech, I know her spec and I've been aboard…"

"No; you've not been invited, and you're needed here to update our systems with the tech we're getting. If more fake ships are out there, I want all the advantages going to protect my ship and crew. And you'd be a distraction to Captain Kerrix that she doesn't need at this time."

He sighed deeply and nodded. "Aye, ma'am."

Apnis looked upward and swapped a rueful glance with her captain. "Any more news, Cap?" she asked, scooping up a forkful. "I saw from ops that there was more than one link for you last night."

Ahxenta nodded. "Thal was one. He knows about the *Moonstone* but he's holding fire at Starfall, as the *Avenger* is still there. He wouldn't say what his lot did at Furze, but I gather that the ISA hasn't taken a hand. The *Kel'Kith's* convoy has made Twilight. *Obsidian* escorted them on the trade bypass to Freskat: they'd picked up stray transmissions they couldn't pin down, and were suspicious. Grey linked. He was late for Stella Triplet but counts it useful, and Thal *was* grateful. He'd the sense to call Thal before me and get the score, unlike some. Jesse Inks told me that Fleetskup had been yapping in his ears; *Tallulah's* en route to Scuttle Scarp from Peascod and didn't want to meet trouble. And Jesse had an ISA admiral on about the bogus *Nomad*, but choked him off and refused to send more data. Nat Holdspan sent an advisory that he'd caught an erratic signal off Stella Beacon that may have been a distress but there was no trace of a ship or debris, and Nat wasn't going to hang about. There's been no more on the ships at the Drapes either – Thal's heard zip, so the ISA's keeping it quiet."

"Nothing changes, huh," the first mate put in. "Who else is heading over to the *Moonstone*, Cap, bar you, Azular and the medics?"

"That's it. I offered to lend them a couple of engineers, but as they wouldn't be familiar with her systems, Jesse declined."

"And I'd imagine they won't want too many strangers around, given what they've been through."

"No. But if you're done, Azular, grab your gear and head to shuttle bay eight. Crizz and her guys are prepping and loading the *Gadfly*."

* * *

An hour later, the *Gadfly* settled gently in one of the *Moonstone's* inner shuttle bays. The captain had piloted her favourite shuttle and knew that her opposite number would be there to greet her. As soon as the bay had depressurised, with all checks clear and the welcome aboard sounding in their ears, the crew unbuckled and collected their kit.

The *Moonstone's* captain was with her second mate and chief medic but Ahxenta noted two security guards at the back. Kerrix had lost the arm-sling but her hand was strapped and she walked stiffly. Dr Mettix, looking relieved, greeted Flintlock and her team and led them off.

"Lieutenant Commander Nyvallish is in the briefing room, so we'll head there," Kerrix told Ahxenta. "My people have sorted the kit for you. It'll be brought here in a pod. You'll want to scan it before it's put aboard your shuttle. The data's on this shard. You're welcome to check it," she smiled, handing it to Azular. "If you need to know more, ask."

Arianrhod's captain was covertly watching her senior science officer, whom she realised was worried at the changes he could see in his future wife, but was interrupted by Commander Levettiza.

"This way, Captain. We're heading to a briefing room close to our main science facilities. It won't take long."

Ahxenta raised a cynical eyebrow. The Berzic woman clearly meant to distract her and leave Kerrix space for a quiet word with Azular. She agreed however, and let herself be led, subliminally aware of the guards behind them. The passage outside the bay was the first surprise. Gone were the trappings that the captain recalled from her first visit, replaced by storage, but even here the damage the ship had taken could be seen. The few crewmen paid the party little heed, too intent on their tasks, but most of them showed signs of injury.

"How many of your crew escaped without a scratch?" Ahxenta asked her guide levelly.

"I could count them on my fingers. It was bad, but we're here and our opponents aren't. Jesse Inks is arranging the change of carrier with Silversnow Microsystems. You've dealt with them before, Captain?"

"I have. There shouldn't be a problem."

"Thanks again for agreeing to take on our load. As a new carrier in the PSS business, we don't want to upset clients by delay."

"I expect you don't," Ahxenta replied coolly, a quick glance behind showing her that Kerrix and Azular had lagged a little.

"Commander Inks will liaise with your crew over transfer. You'll want every micron checked before the pods are shipped aboard."

"My supercargo has the details. It shouldn't take long, and neither should this meet. You'll have plenty to keep you busy. Have you any idea when you'll be ready to ship out, or where you plan to go?"

"It depends on how fast the teams here work. Our own people are strained. As to where we'll head next – that has to be decided."

The two guards were left outside the room. Shell Nyvallish had set up two linked holo-projectors, both of worm-pockets. The title of one implied that it was based on the Crimson Drapes data *Arianrhod* had sent out. The other Ahxenta guessed was the ambiguity at Sox used by the Starfall fleet. She said as much to Levettiza, who agreed, adding that the data shards and info-pads on the table were for their use.

"Help yourselves to drinks and sit," Kerrix invited. "Many of our ration synths are offline, so I'm afraid that's all I can offer."

They were quickly settled. The *Moonstone's* captain began by asking for the full data set from the new worm-pocket at the Crimson Drapes, to compare it with the *Kel'Tarn's* scans from Sox. Azular handed on a shard, accepting one in return. Nyvallish integrated the new data into his holo and ordered an update and comparative analysis. The readout was transferred to the info-pads around the table.

"A close match," Azular confirmed. "Synthetic adjuncts that should *not* be present in a natural phenomenon."

"Bring up the comparison of the original readings of the Sox worm-pocket with what we now have," Kerrix bid her senior SO. "You'll see what's changed – it's quite clear," she added to Azular and Ahxenta.

After a short exchange of questions and answers, the Berzic science officer turned to Kerrix. "You still think that who or what transformed the Sox worm-pocket into what it now seems to be may be behind the one we found, or even created it from nothing?"

"It's possible. There *are* areas of local high mass-energy that could have been used as a seed. You've seen the data: the synthetic elements are near-identical. You *did* report a nearby glitch, a nebular thickening similar to that one off the Ginseng that *was* a holding area for hostile ships? The Crimson Drapes model must have been hostile-created and recent, and would have needed a vast amount of energy."

"*Arianrhod* seems to be adept at finding odd things," Levettiza wryly noted to Ahxenta. "You reported the Ginseng irregularity to Freskat's ruling council and Admiral Zillah sent it on to the ISP."

"We keep our scanning eyes and ears open," was the acerbic reply.

"Just as well," Kerrix cut in. "We've heard no more on this nebular quirk, but the two ISA ships were still in the vicinity two days ago. And you don't think whoever is to blame for the worm-pocket and perhaps the nebular distortion was maybe trying to create a bypass using some mechanism unknown to us?" she asked Azular.

"I think it unlikely," he said tactfully. "Bypass formation takes a vast amount of energy and needs specialist gear. We detected nothing. And why there, where there's already a known and well-used bypass?"

"That's precisely the point: known. A close *unknown* bypass could be used by hostiles to jump out on any ship that's on or near the known one. And you found nothing nearby? What about a nebular thickening, the likes of which *has* been used in the past to hide a fleet?"

Azular traded a look with Ahxenta and turned back to Kerrix. "You have a point," he conceded. "But I can't see that an attempt to create a bypass, however it was done, would form a worm-pocket instead."

"Short-range bypass genesis to jump from one point to another for rapid transit or for escape is possible. Yes, it has a high energy cost *and* needs complex tech, but it's doable. The bypass is transitory: the energy dissipates to add to the local mass-energy density field. There *were* early attempts to make stable, locus-to-locus jump points in areas of intense high mass-energy using such tech that failed, but some trials created tiny, unstable wormholes. You recall, Captain, that I told you of a huge structure that my ship the *Sunburst* found when we tracked what we thought was a distress to a system on the edges of our explored space?"

"The place the ISP once called K457:003 and the ISA now labels Amity Beacon," Ahxenta stated.

"That's the one: we figured it for an ancient but inoperative bypass node but then we picked up an intense energy signal that our systems interpreted as a small, periodic wormhole. As you know, I went in to check it out and ended up at Starfall Exit."

"Your point?" the captain of the *Arianrhod* asked.

"My point is that whatever tech the hostiles have, assuming they *are* to blame, it may be that they ended up with what early bypass engineers on Norvalla did. But how natural worm-pockets have morphed into tech-enhanced ones I don't know. But it's not our problem. What is, is that if there *are* unknowns tampering with worm-pockets like the Sox to Hervesta in such a way, isn't it possible that they could tamper with others, or with known bypasses?"

"Attempts to spike a bypass would be spotted," Azular interjected. "They're patrolled by the ISA and others, *and* strictly regulated. They have to be, or bodies like the TA wouldn't be able to charge for their use. But you can't prove it, so who do you tell?"

"Vetta?" Kerrix said calmly, looking at her second mate.

"I *could* get some of it into ISA ears. As we *were* contacted about the fake *Nomad* shortly after sending out our alert, the ISA is shaken that somebody's got highly-classified ISPS data including call-signs, or they can create them. What bugs me is that we don't know where the bogus *Nomad* came from. It surprised us, and we weren't flying blind: we had every usable system online. But they were fast. Even if they had been hiding at Kolm, we *should* have picked them up before they hit us."

Kerrix knit her brow, flexing her shoulders to ease the tension. "A pocket within a pocket," she said wearily, clearly tired.

"A hiding place *within* a bypass, Captain?" Nyvallish frowned. "I've never heard of such a thing."

"We'd never heard of synthetic rigging of a worm-pocket until the *Kel'Tarn* fell foul of the results."

"It isn't our priority," Levettiza said succinctly. "If you have all you need, Captain Ahxenta, I suggest we leave it for now. The goods you're picking up will be in the shuttle bay. I'll escort you and Dr Azular."

"*We'll* escort them," Kerrix corrected. "Unless you want to check in with your personnel in medbay, Captain?"

"I'll link later," Ahxenta responded. "Azular?"

"Ready, ma'am," he said reluctantly.

"Take it with you," Kerrix smiled at him. "You've been playing with it since you sat down. It's clearly intriguing you."

He paused a fraction, but swiftly took up the info-pad with a word of thanks. Nyvallish and Levettiza traded wry glances. Ahxenta snorted and gathered her kit, her sharp eyes probing the space and the people. She thanked Nyvallish for his input and turned to Levettiza and Kerrix.

"Commander, perhaps you'd update Dr Azular as to what's waiting in the shuttle bay? Captain, I'd like a few words on the way. I assume your guards will keep a discreet distance?"

"I'll dismiss them; they've plenty to do and you're not about to cause trouble, I'm sure," was the ironic reply. "Mr Nyvallish, you finish up here," she added as the two followed Levettiza and Azular out.

Ahxenta kept a stern silence until they were well clear of the briefing room, before turning to her associate. "Why didn't you form your own short-range bypass to jump out of trouble at the first attack? You have the tech and I assume you had the energy at that point?"

"One, the assault was fast once we'd worked out the ship wasn't the *Pearl Shield* and we *had* rigged our defences; two, such a jump would've alerted the blip to our tech and I didn't want that; and three, and more importantly, there's no way I'd risk my ship or my crew on tech that's novel to us and has never been tested in use in the *Moonstone* – not even during trial flights out of Valla Key."

"Makes sense," Ahxenta agreed.

"And I wouldn't sanction such a manoeuvre except in dire need," she sighed. "My science officers and engineers have been running sims on its use, but that's had to come to a full stop."

"How badly *has* your crew been shaken by the attacks?" *Arianrhod's* captain asked softly. "You're downplaying it, but even the guards have med patches. And for a ship this size, I see very few crew about."

"Badly," she responded shortly. "But it's *my* concern, Captain."

"It'll be somebody else's concern if you don't take time out. You're hanging by a thread and it's noticeable. By Levettiza for one."

Kerrix paused and eyed her. "Why do you give a damn?"

"Don't get cranky with me, Captain Kerrix. *You* know you're all out, but you're trying to hide it. *He's* figured it and he's worried, but he's trying to hide it from you," she went on, pointing ahead to Azular and Levettiza, who were deep in discussion.

As if on cue, the science officer turned round to see how far behind the two were. Ahxenta waved him on. "Making sure we haven't slipped too far back," she said evenly. "He thinks we're talking about him."

Kerrix made no reply to that, but gave her a penetrating look.

"I don't have a hidden agenda," Ahxenta said, half-amused. "What makes you think I do?"

Again Kerrix' eyes searched her face for a clue to a growing sense of disquiet. "You're adept at anticipating my thinking," she said. "*And* Azular's. And he can read me when he's not purposely using his talent, as can Vetta. I get the same feeling with you, and its damn annoying."

Ahxenta's eyebrows shot up. "Really?" she asked acerbically.

"Really," Kerrix repeated. "What *do* you want to talk about? It's not just the health of my crew and how I run my ship."

"Why did Admiral Posettix make for Starfall? I take it his ship *is* still there, and by implication so is Ambassador Posettix?"

"Yes; and his reasons are *his*, and no business of yours or mine."

"Personal then, and not linked to the *ISAS Avenger*. But *you* know," Ahxenta surmised. "And he's keen to help Thal and his people – who now include you. But then you and he go back a long way."

"Why don't you stop digging, Captain? You know I won't tell you. You…" Kerrix paused with a hiss of pain, looking past the tall captain to a spot opposite. She staggered, closing her eyes and shaking her head as if to clear it. "I think I'll sit down for a moment," she said in a ragged voice, sagging against the wall and sliding down.

Ahxenta, concerned, saw her face drain of colour and knelt to help. "Are you all right, Captain? Dammit! Commander!" she roared up the passage as she undid Kerrix' collar. "You're stubborn, is your trouble," she told her in an undertone.

"I think I'll lie down," was the only response as she sank further, to lie prostrate on the deck.

"We'll have to get her to medbay," Ahxenta called as Levettiza came racing up, Azular at her back. "I think it's just a faint, but she's looked wiped out for a while."

"I'll get a medic and a gurney. Mettix knows the score – he advised her to hold off on this meet with you but she overruled him."

"I bet she did," the captain replied as she continued to examine the woman. "Pulse is erratic, but that may be normal for a half-Norvallan."

Azular had knelt and taken Kerrix' bound hand to chafe it gently. "Xanna? Can you hear me?"

"On their way," Levettiza stated. "Mettix is irked, but he'll let Jesse Inks know via the medbay status uplink. I think it's best if we carry on as planned, and you and Azular head out. Once Xanna's attended to, we make for the bay. The crew doesn't need to know more than that she's reported to medbay as advised. They've been through enough."

That advice did not please Azular, Ahxenta noted, but she agreed. She had plenty business of her own aboard *Arianrhod*.

"I'd be grateful if you'd keep me updated on how she is," she said to the Berzic woman as a muted groan let them know that Kerrix was coming round. "If there's anything you need that I can supply, let me know. We're set to leave in less than two days and we can't delay. I'll hold off sending the shuttle over for my people as long as I can."

Levettiza expressed her thanks as the response team from medbay sprinted in. Azular had continued to murmur soothing words but had elicited little response bar her hand tightening in his. He released her to the medics, noting the status controls keenly as she was locked in.

"She's in safe hands," Ahxenta murmured. "Let's leave them to it."

The trip back to the shuttle was sombre, with barely a word spoken. The science officer reflexively checked the pod as the captain notified the *Arianrhod* of their imminent return. A link to her medics on the *Moonstone* told her that they were busy and likely to remain so. Their kit and the cargo stowed, the two made ready to leave. Levettiza carried out the departure checks, set the exit sequence and watched from the obs stage as the *Gadfly* moved out.

Ahxenta sighed in relief and focussed on getting her craft home. In as short a time as possible, the *Gadfly* was settled in her berth. The two debarked with their personal kit, the captain having decreed that the cargo pod be left intact. Azular had been keen to begin an analysis of the holo-grid and cloak tech, but instead, he extracted a data shard of the nav-charts of Psi and its border systems and put it in his pocket.

In token of the new gear, the chief engineer was there with the first mate, eager to begin the cloak upgrades as a first step, as with *Arianrhod* in port, she had the time. She said as much after Apnis had greeted the captain. "And you'll be needed to lend a hand," she informed Azular. "It *is* a joint project after all."

"Yes, Chief, but the holo-grid's a priority. It'll improve data display, and I can incorporate the high-resolution charts of Psi and beyond that I have. If I can source more detailed charts of Alpha through Mu, we'll have the tech ready to use them to advantage. I can begin work on the procedures for holo-grid upgrade from my lab right away, ma'am," he added to the captain. "I have the relevant data."

"On that shard Captain Kerrix gave you when we got in; I know," Ahxenta nodded, as Cottontail began to argue. "Go ahead, but make sure that *is* what you do. You can play with the fancy info-pad she gave you in your own time. Copy the ops data on the cloak to the chief and the holo-grid info to Lieutenant Gliss before you start. I'll be by later, after I've checked cargo status and comms."

"Huh! She gave you new tech, did she?" the chief engineer snorted as Azular affirmed and turned to leave. "And how long do I…"

"Leave it, Crizz," the captain cautioned, shaking her head. "Have your team unload the pod, but shove it in your side-lab for now, it'll keep. I'm for the bridge; I want a word with Jesse Inks."

"What gives, Cap?" Apnis asked as Azular stalked out of the bay. "He's upset over something. His Captain Kerrix not playing ball?"

"Captain Kerrix collapsed and is in medbay. She didn't look good. I'll call Flintlock later, as she'll know more. But don't spread it around. Levettiza's keeping it from their own crew as far as possible."

Apnis' brow creased. "How *are* things over there, Cinnabar?"

"From what I could see, bad; but they're a tight-lipped bunch, like most Starfall people. We have the data and the gear they pledged; they have our data. I'm not holding a briefing over the mission, as there was nothing relevant to our immediate trade bar the upgrades, and they'll go ahead as and when. We'll leave our medics with the *Moonstone* for as long as possible, but our revised schedule is set and I want to be off by thirteen hundred the day after tomorrow, Delta standard."

"That's doable. Silversnow are okay with us as carrier, our team's on standby to bring in the pods and we've borrowed drone grapples from Ceres for transfer, as the *Moonstone's* gear is out of action. Lindell's got the paperwork. We'll have the pods aboard in two-three hours and the Bistra cargo's set to start loading at fourteen hundred tomorrow."

"What about Azular?" the chief engineer wanted to know.

"He's my problem," Ahxenta told her.

* * *

The bridge tactical and science stations were busy next day fitting the add-on data display tech into the holo-grid. Azular and Gliss had spent time the evening before in checking the algorithms and were confident that it would be in place before the ship was ready to leave. The captain was watching the senior science officer: she had stopped by his lab the previous day after having spoken to Commander Inks and to her own chief medic. Captain Kerrix had suffered serious injury, and her refusal to heed her chief medic's advice had increased it, to the extent that Inks and Mettix had relieved her of command. She would be out of action for several days but was making progress.

Azular had gone to his lab the day before to lose himself in work, as Ahxenta had expected. What she had not expected on walking in on him was to find him at his desk, head on arms and near to tears. He had found a coded note on the shard Kerrix had given him. What it said of a private nature he refused to say, but what he had read into a remark she had made alarmed him. Ahxenta pressed, and found that she had legally settled that if anything happened to her, the *Moonstone* would be left to Inks, on condition that the crew was taken care of.

"For a very able telepath, you're oddly naïve," the captain had told him. "She's not expecting to be fired into space down one of her own torpedo tubes or planted in earth just yet. I admire her sense in making provision. And I've a notion that Jesse Inks will make a better captain than she does *and* I bet she knows it. I'm beginning to think she'll make you a good life-mate: she's got some of the savvy *you* seem to lack."

That had snapped Azular out of his misery and the captain's current scrutiny convinced her that he was still cheery. He and Gliss had linked stations to start testing. As the holo-grid dropped, everyone looked up. Their orbital position and the nearby berths showed distinctly, and the starfield beyond sharpened as corrections were made. Box was asked to pull up their onward course and send his projection to the grid. As he did so, the view spun to show the line that *Arianrhod* would take for the bypass and her route to the agricultural world of Bistra.

"Expand to show our line to the Web via Quartic Cross and Berzic, Mr Box," Ahxenta instructed. "You're bringing in real-time data, aren't you?" she asked the two at the tactical and science stations.

"Aye, ma'am," Azular said. "I've linked in recent updates on activity in mapped space from the ISA and others. We'll add in data we find on action elsewhere, and if we set continuous checks on incoming, we can automate the process. That should alert us to potential problems before we're in range of them *and* isolate them on the grid."

The captain nodded. "So we can see what's going on at Furze and the Drapes. The ISA's sent out zip, but other systems *may* have."

"Running it now," Bellfish called. "Nothing from the ISA, ma'am, but news of the Crimson Drapes glitch has leaked: a Berzic carrier on her way home from Alto Finglas spied a huge ship as she passed Altina. She didn't like the look of it so she cut and run for the border, and was caught by a wash of energy that she put down to an unlisted gravity well. The blip followed her but *then* made towards Furze. Berzic news nets picked it up and linked it to the data we sent to the ISA and our fleet on the rogue worm-pocket, however they got hold of that."

"When was that news story sent out?" Ahxenta demanded.

"Within the last two days, if the date signal's accurate. I'll check if there's any supporting evidence to be had, ma'am."

"The ISA will *have* to make a report now, if the local media has got involved, Cap," Apnis remarked. "Thal? One of his spotted a beat-up hostile boat that looked active out that way not so long ago."

"Get what's there into a tight report, Mr Bellfish. I'll send it round the fleet as a note and Thal will get it. He'll act. I've heard no more about what his people did on Furze, but I guess by now they've cleared the place of anything they'd no mind that others should see."

"Nice work on the holo, Azular and Gliss; there's more *and* sharper data," the first mate praised. "But it might get messy. We don't want distracted by non-essential info when things hot up."

"True," Ahxenta agreed. "But from what I can see, there's no action on our onward road. Though what's that blinking red ring at the edge of the holo? Istrel Statice, isn't it? Expand projection, Gliss."

"Expanding. Notice of routine maintenance on a local node. Source is a comm out of an engineering firm, Entech, based on Wisty – it was picked up in a general scan of sector channels."

"What? Why hasn't the TA sent it round?" Apnis asked indignantly. "We pay for that info! We should be told in advance of node overhaul anywhere on any TA bypass route."

Azular set Greffy to raking TA upkeep schedules as he checked his lists. "Entech *is* on Wisty, but it's not a registered TA contractor, it's a dealer in excavation gear; node overhaul is *not* one of its usual jobs."

"And there's no ongoing repair for Istrel Statice on TA schedules," Greffy cut in. "Smacks of trouble to me, Doc."

"Bellfish, copy that comm and ready it to send to TA HQ on Alto Finglas and the ISA, as it's next door," Ahxenta said. "Add in Azular's and Greffy's data and append a request for clarification to the TA on the situation. We won't go via Istrel Statice, we'll take the local bypass to Bistra from here, but some of ours might be in that area."

"Why does it always have to be us, Cap?" Apnis sighed.

"We're so smart is why. And those updates have paid off already."

"But if it *is* trouble, and it smells like it, why put out a warning?"

"Because rigging will be logged by any ship with good scanners on the way in, and a current upkeep order is a way to explain it. Add the name of the party on the job and a ship might be fooled into believing it. Hell knows when the TA will reply, so I'll alert the fleet. Patch a link to the UV-III to my office, Bellfish, and send me the comm when it's ready. And *I've* a link to make. You have the conn, Tallica."

"Aye, ma'am."

The captain was gone longer than Apnis anticipated and had taken several links. She wore a calm expression as she retook her place.

"Who wanted to chat, Cap?"

"Nat Holdspan was one: the *Warrior's* on the way to the Web from Limekiln. He'd planned to head to Istrel to keep mostly in Delta. He's changing course for Quartic to head up through Beta. Given what he and his have been through recently, more conflict he doesn't need."

"Wise man. Who else? Thal?"

"Thal; about the report on the hostile at Altina that may have been on track for Furze. His people destroyed what they didn't lift off. He's had no comeback from the ISA and isn't about to make waves, as one of his ships was sure that that ISA destroyer, the *Steadfast*, had spotted her on the way out. With the ISA's level of tech, it's likely. The *Kel'Kith's* en route to Starfall and should be there soon: Thal's sent one of his big ships to meet her and her escorts. All his people aboard are okay."

"Thanks be. Lindell's talking to Silversnow over a new contract on the table, but he'll have to work around our Redship and Ottolyx deals. It's a cargo of bits for a firm called Sunbeam Services in Cygilla Prime's orbital Resort-Dorm. He's checking out the client, as he's never heard of them. But as Cygilla's on the way to Stinward, it'll be a short stop."

"I know; he sent it in but I only scanned it. I wanted to speak to the doc, to see how things are on the *Moonstone*," she added quietly, though out of the corner of her eye she saw Azular stiffen to attention.

"And?"

"They're coping. Kerrix had her supercargo source the best stock from Delta: the doc's struck by new med-cradles, *and* by the *Moonstone's* primary medbay, though the secondary's apparently as good. Dr Mettix refused to send the worst cases to Delta for care. As they're a mixed bunch, many from Psi, he reckons his own people are better qualified."

"And how *is* Captain Kerrix?" Apnis enquired in a whisper.

"Improving. Issuing orders from her cot, but Inks and Levettiza have got her under control. I tried to speak to Levettiza, but she wasn't available. I'd like to know if she's contacted the ISA on a crack-brained theory that Kerrix came up with at our meeting – if unknowns could fiddle with worm-pockets like the Sox to Hervesta, they might be able to interfere with bypasses in the same way. In view of what *we've* found, it maybe wasn't so far-fetched. Levettiza must have been in on the alert about the Istrel Statice bypass node, and if there *is* somebody with half a brain at ISA HQ, they'll have put one and one together."

"You wish; they're all military types, aren't they? If they do anything, they'll send in a gunship to check it out…"

She was cut short by a call from comms that an ISA alert had come in about Istrel Statice, causing the captain to jump up.

"The ISA? Something's pricked a nerve. Maybe Levettiza *did* find an ear that would listen to her. What's that the holo's picked up now?" she added. "That ring around Istrel Statice is stronger and flashing."

"It's an ISA alert to steer clear of local space around Istrel Statice, no reason given, ma'am," Azular told her. "I added the comms data into the system and it's updated the grid."

"Anybody on that bypass section will be pissed," the first mate said tartly. "They'll have to reverse course or jump off and either swop to another bypass or travel in normal space until they can jump back on – and if they can't use a node, it'll cost in energy."

"Nothing more? Just an alert to stay away?" Ahxenta asked.

"That's all, ma'am," Bellfish shrugged. "Data tags confirm it *is* ISA. It's gone out on the ISA main net to every zone – including Psi."

"Psi is still in the family then, even though Norvalla and the ISA are grumping at each other over who gets what and how much," she noted acidly as she returned to her chair. "I think the *Serenity's* still at Starfall, but Thal would say zip about her. I guess Starfall puts her close enough to Psi to get home without ISA meddling if the treaties fall apart."

"Call for you, Captain: it's the ISA," Bellfish interrupted.

"This'll be a thanks for the heads-up," said Apnis acidly as Ahxenta rose again with an oath, ordering the comm sent to her office.

The first mate told Azular and Gliss to run relevant tests and return the holo-grid to station-keeping as she verified ship's status. Two outer bays would have to be ready for loading their Bistra cargo. It was some time before the captain returned.

"The ISA rep had a lot to say then, Cap?" she greeted her.

"She wanted to know how we figured Istrel Statice; she thinks we've got our hands on alien tech. And she knows what went down with the *Moonstone*, and that we're both here. She pushed me on Captain Kerrix as a source of novel hardware that in *her* expert opinion would be better in the hands of the ISA fleet," was the serene reply.

"I don't like the sound of that," Apnis said suspiciously. "She knew we were here? How? Is this rep someone we know?"

"Myrtleberry. She has spies, as we know to our cost. I think she's at Alto Finglas. I couldn't tell from the link, but Bellfish is tracing it back.

She was in a plush suite, not the *Repulse*, for all she's one of the ISA's best. I guess she'll rejoin the *Repulse*, once she gets a smart new shuttle."

"Or a fancier ride than the *Repulse*," Apnis commented sourly. "Alto Finglas has a shipbuilding dock; if there's a shiny new ship with more guns than the rest of the fleet combined, she'll have first dibs."

"Thanks. I only hope she doesn't go annoying the *Moonstone*, but Levettiza will sort her out. We set for loading at fourteen hundred?"

"Aye, Cap. In which case, a quick bite won't come amiss?"

* * *

Both were back on the bridge for loading. It was a long job that needed precise control, but *Arianrhod's* freight crews were old hands. Azular and Gliss were judging the efficiency of the new systems and gear. The former had pulled in routine warnings of blocks to bypasses and other routes, and local snags affecting trade. He had sent the data to the navi-helm to allow the two there to run sims of alternative routes, but thus far their direct path via a local bypass from Delta that skirted the Triple Pinks star cluster to a node at Ingle, and thus to Bistra, was clear.

"Let's hope it stays that way," the captain remarked, eyeing the holo that filled the forr'ad section of her bridge as Gliss zoomed in to their berth. "Every registered ship in our sights is marked. I'm surprised we have access to PA data to that extent. Does that mean that every other ship in port with similar gear knows exactly where we are?"

"Data is on the arrivals and departures channel, Cap, and any ship in range can scan us; they'll only get our call-sign, but they can mark us," Apnis replied. "Look: arrivals are updating. That's one of ours… it's the *Snow Quartz*. I haven't seen her in over a year, but her home port's Kitty Steel in Zeta. Captain Utterspot won't know the *Moonstone* bar her name and command staff, I guess."

"No, but he'll have heard the rumours and got the report she sent. Once the *Snow Quartz* has docked, send a courtesy, Bellfish. And keep a bead on those cargo pods, Azular. Ceres is an old and trusted client, but I won't assume that those pods or their contents are harmless."

"Aye ma'am."

Loading advanced smoothly under the vigilant eyes of her crew and four hours in, the huge pods were on board, locked down, and guarded by cargo bay monitors. Leaving the final details to her first mate, the captain made for her office to check comms and make links.

She returned over an hour later, frowning. "You'll not believe this," she said to Apnis. "The *Nyx Warrior's* been hit again."

"What! How bad? And where? And who did it?"

"Torch Crux: a beat-up ship jumped *onto* the bypass at the beacon.

It sounded like that blip seen near Altina that seemed to be on a line for Furze; it's possible it switched course and set for down the bypass. It could have made Torch in a couple of days, as those hostiles can go hell for leather with cyber crews, or if they're not crewed. There's been no data on what the crew complement is or isn't."

"But the *Warrior*?"

"Is fine. I spoke to Nat, as he'd left a request for more on what we sent about the Berzic ship near Altina: he knew there was more to it. I gave him the details, plus the sighting by Thal's people, though I didn't mention *his* interest in Furze. The *Warrior's* in shape and Nat had every weapon *and* his cloak on line. So whatever that hostile is, it can detect a cloaked ship. But Nat's read every iota that's come in and was up on it. He was ready and fired first, though his scanners were saying the blip was poorly armed and shielded. He wasn't about to let his crew be caught again. Lucky he did: the hostile took a few hits, threw a barrage at the *Warrior,* and ran. Nat didn't chase her, but he's beginning to think that there has to be more to it than chance. How did the hostile know to jump on there, when the *Warrior* was at that point?"

"Spies in every port. At least he and his are okay. Is he still heading through Beta to the Web?"

"Yes, he's holding for Quartic. I've given him more on the Drapes glitch and the worm-pocket, so he'll be on alert. But as the ISA's still digging there, I don't expect hostiles will be sneaking about. And once he hits Beta, there'll be more patrols, as it's one of the busiest zones in the charted galaxy."

"Who else have you been calling?" Apnis asked in a low voice. "Our people on the *Moonstone*?"

"They'll hang on until tomorrow. The *Gadfly* will collect them at ten hundred. That'll give them time to finish up and settle back here before we ship out. Our clearances will be in place by then or I'll want to know why. Lindell's got the Silversnow deal; we can slot it into our schedule. I talked to Grey after Nat, as I thought he might be making for this neck of space after Stella Triplet. He was: he's for Limekiln and then Alto Finglas. He's had no trouble, but he's not taking chances. We may see him in the Web, as we'll hold there and he's heading in after Alto."

"What's he doing at Alto? Shipbuilding gear for the ISA yard?"

"No, habitat constructs to extend its HQ. Grey figures it's so that the ISA partner bodies can have their own premises and feel wanted," the captain said caustically.

"Too many eggs in one basket. Hit it and you get the lot."

"I'm sure they have it covered. I'd Bee Coxen on as well. *Hexameter's* for there with a heap of hardware for the ISA yards. Classified, but Bee knows it's weaponry. And with the number of half-built warships and the fleet being fitted with new colours and insignia, they're secure. As the Ceres Corp details are settled, Lindell's got Jute hunting more deals, but our schedule's near full. Once we reach the Web the crew can get shore leave in, as we'll need several days for loading and all the rest."

"And I'll make sure we're on the list, Cap."

"Roger that, but leave it for now. I want to go over the manifests we *will* have, so you can lend an eye. We'll do it in the office. Earbleat, you have the conn. Any comms come in, patch them through."

"Aye, ma'am," the second mate acknowledged as she stood.

"What do you really want to talk about, Cap?" Apnis asked as the door shut. "The deals are set and Lindell's okayed Sunbeam Services."

"Sit," she was told. "For one, your remark of spies in every port in relation to the hit on the *Warrior*. It struck me, and I spoke to Levettiza about it. Seems the PSS fleet's being targeted still, but why the hostiles or whoever are picking on the *Warrior*, I don't know."

"Unless there's a spy aboard *her*?"

"No way: Nat Holdspan's a canny commander and he wouldn't let that happen. I've had Rosy Gallus run checks on every comms net she can access for reports of attacks blamed on hostiles. There will be false claims, but she found a few involving PSS ships, including the *Warrior* and the *Moonstone*, but not the *Kel'Marr*. I've a notion that Thal keeps his business quiet, as he has a lot to hide about his bases and ships, and his ongoing face-off with the TA over bypasses. And she caught a note on the buzzing and attempted deep scanning of the *Urania* by two odd fighters a while back, remember, though she wasn't hit."

"Fleetskup told us. But deep scanning?" Apnis said sharply. "Trying to get enough detail to rig up a bogus *Urania*?"

"Good point. But the chat I had with Azular on the way back from the *Warrior* after the run-in at Swan Two: he said that as we, the *Warrior*, and the *Obsidian* are seen as the toughest PSS ships to take out, it makes us prime targets for anybody that thinks they can best us. Thal's PSS ships as well: based on alien tech, huge, can hold their own, and know hostile weak spots. And the *Moonstone's* not afraid of a fight. The rest of the fleet would be less of a contest with us out of the way, and as we've been forced into a TA contract that makes us liable to be drafted in the event of warfare, we'd make formidable allies."

"That doesn't explain why the *Warrior's* so popular in hostile circles. What's she got that makes her a target? More toys than they have?"

"Hardly, Tallica; Nat's worry is that he's taken three bad hits in a short time. The fake ISP boat off Idledott hit him *after* he'd dropped his cargo at Silverglass, so it wasn't that it was after, and there's nothing I've heard that suggests that it was crewed. Then that attack at Swan Two where we came in, and from what we got, they weren't manned; and now this. Though *that* was maybe crewed, if it *was* the blip seen off Altina. Its actions hint at sentience as it didn't hit that Berzic carrier, but did jump onto the bypass to hit the *Warrior*. Which implies that the target was the *Warrior*, or any PSS and Nat was just unlucky."

"It could be they realise that as they'll get nowhere with *Arianrhod*, they'd best try to take out the ships that seem to be next in line. They've hit the *Moonstone* twice after all, but that was in the space of hours."

"Funny; but I'm not betting that we'll be left alone anytime soon, so we'll be fully armed, with all sections running full tilt. Which means your job before you go off is to check what our chiefs need. Lindell's team can source what they can before we leave orbit."

"Roger that, Cap. Except for Earbleat, as she'll want more for *Loki VIII* as a matter of course. And what else?"

"The bogus ships and the minds behind them. Whoever created the cyber-hostiles and their ships must be smart enough to code a ship to track and attack. But there has to be a way of acquiring data to keep it on course. Remember that missile made to look like a small ship that almost got us in the Web? It bypassed the *Tallulah* to hit us, so we were its target, it knew where we were, *and* it got through Web defences."

"But thanks to that nosy drunk in the *Half Moon*, and to Kerrix for recognising what it was, we got the alert in time," Apnis grinned. "But, no offence Cap, it's not explicitly our problem, it's the fleet's, so why are we discussing it here? What else is on your mind?"

"You've known me too long. I'll be piloting the *Gadfly* over to the *Moonstone* tomorrow to pick up our people. I want a private word with Captain Kerrix. And Azular will not be coming with me."

"Whoa, Cinnabar! He'll take that hard. And what do you want to speak to Captain Kerrix about that you don't want him in on?"

"*Not* your concern, Tallica. But she said something odd when we were talking, before she collapsed. She wasn't in a state to push, but I want it explained. She knows I want a chat but she's in medbay, unfit to command, and her CMO won't allow much talk. Nor will Axellina – I called *her* to alert Kerrix that I'd be visiting. But she *has* a lot on her plate that's not easy: arranging committal services for her lost crew for one. But this has to be cleared up before she talks to Azular."

"Now you've raised my curiosity, but *I* know better than to push. You need me to keep Azular out of your hair?"

"Azular's my concern and I'll deal with him. I wanted you aware. Levettiza knows I'll be over to speak to the captain. And we'd best cast an eye over the manifests; it *is* what we were supposed to be doing."

"And then?"

"And then I'll speak to Azular before he goes off duty. I don't want him trying to contact Xanna Kerrix before I do."

* * *

As the first mate had forecast, Azular was upset that the captain would fly to the *Moonstone* solo. That she would bar him from a direct link to his fiancée also caused grief, but he was given leave to send a comm. Ahxenta was firm, but made it clear that his relationship with Kerrix was not the subject of the intended dialogue.

"You'd best send your comm," she advised at the end of their talk. "And don't look like that: I won't tell her anything that'll change her opinion of you. Her opinion of me is another matter."

"She holds you in great respect, ma'am."

"I scare the hell out of her, you mean; she's told me more than once, though I'm not sure I believe her. But I need my rations, so I'm for the mess. I'll maybe see you there. Dismissed."

The captain sat musing for several minutes before making her way out. She had no qualms about what Azular would put into his message, but she knew that he would dig for answers later.

"Azular's not a happy bunny then, Cap?" the first mate enquired as the captain sat, slapping down her tray.

"He'll get over it. How did you get on with the resupply for ship's sections? Are we short of anything we can't get hold of?"

"No. Lindell griped over cost, but that's only because he was over hours and was grumpy. He'll leave the lesser mortals of his team to get the orders in. There *is* one thing: Zaik Oak sent Axellina his supply list for approval and *she* wants two of the new-style med-cradles she's seen on the *Moonstone*. She sent him the spec and the price and told him to add them in. They're not cheap, so I cut it to one, but Lindell's refused to sanction it without your say-so. I've got the details here."

Ahxenta took the proffered reader, scanned it, and gave a whistle. "What's it made of, top-grade meta-jurillium? I'll authorise one. Mark it off and then that's it. We are both off duty until after dark watch."

"Unless there's an alert called at three hundred hours…"

"Stow it, Commander, and eat your dinner."

* * *

The *Gadfly's* berth was busy the following morning as the captain made ready to ship over to the *Moonstone*. She had bid her supercargo retrieve three high grade energy cells to hand over to her fellow vessel, as she knew that such goods were unobtainable from local suppliers on Delta Iridium, and her engineers were at that point fitting them to the *Gadfly's* external carrier skids. Inks had been told of the cargo and would have people ready to unload them when she docked. To Ahxenta's irritation but not surprise, Azular was in the bay. He had put all the data he could find about recent attacks on PSS ships, the hostiles involved, and the fake craft, onto a data shard for Kerrix and Nyvallish, and had searched the PSS register and other sources to dig up what he could of the lost *PSS Bright Mist,* as something was tugging at the back of his mind.

"It *is* important, Captain, and might be worth circulating to the fleet, once you've seen the data for yourself," he said, holding out the shard.

"Were you up half the night?" the captain asked suspiciously as she took it. "Well, give me the gist, but I've little time as I want to get over there. Our clearances are in place so we won't be hanging about once I've got our people back home."

"The *Bright Mist* was lost, allegedly to raiders, off the Astrella Nine asteroid field in Kappa some years ago, but nothing was found of ship or crew. You'll recall from the war that there *was* a hostile base nearby, at Axle Lexo, though we've no clue as to how long it had been there – possibly decades, if not longer. And we now know there *is* an ex-hostile bypass that Thal's people use that runs from K457:003 to Kell Lyne; in fact close to the Sox worm-pocket that's been altered by unknown forces. That worm-pocket that threw the *Kel'Tarn's* shuttle out at Veil."

"You're hinting that hostiles, not raiders, got the *Bright Mist?* And going by the tactics they used in the war, they'd have stripped her down for spare parts and maybe even used her crew to augment their own bodies – or used them as pawns?"

"It's assumption, ma'am, but possible. The *Bright Mist* was lost years ago, but the aliens were active well before they emerged from nowhere to start the war, *and* they'd been abducting people for decades. It's all on this data shard; as the *Moonstone* is part of Starfall, it's pertinent."

"You're still not coming with me, so get the look off your face," Ahxenta told him. "But that's not all, is it? What else is bothering you?"

"I checked the crew records for the *Bright Mist.* She was out of Nyx. Her commander was a Captain Nathaniel Holdspan."

10: MORE SECRETS

The *Gadfly* made berth aboard the *Moonstone* easily. Jesse Inks was there to meet the captain and escort her to medbay. He thanked her for the aid she had given him and his crew, and told her he had a team standing by to unload the energy cells. Dr Flintlock and her people were set to rejoin their ship. His captain was in a private bay, and looking forward to seeing her. Ahxenta very much doubted that, but made sure her own craft was locked up before she left the bay with him.

The *Moonstone's* main medbay was a little way from the outer bay in which the *Gadfly* sat. It was set athwart the mid-section of the ship and smaller than *Arianrhod's*, but Ahxenta was not overly surprised, it being one of two. It was also more vivid than her clinically neutral complex, and the banks of monitors and slick med-cots looked state-of-the-art. What surprised the captain was the apparition that greeted her by name at the entry. Jesse Inks' grave face broke into a smile at her expression.

"Dr Ray, hologram med-assist," he introduced. "He's coded with all our health-related data and is an info-point for the crew. He can't interact physically with us, but he's invaluable: he can save our medics from having to interrogate databases, can demonstrate techniques and can answer patients' questions when no medics are available."

"Can he read them bed-time stories as well?" Ahxenta asked tartly.

"If they ask him to," was the tranquil reply. "Your people are in the staff ready room, Captain. This way."

She followed him to where Dr Jak Wren and nurse-tech Jym Kelp sat, utterly spent and ready to move out. There was no sign of her chief MO. She had gone to say goodbye to Captain Kerrix, Wren explained.

"That's where I'm headed," she told the pair. "I take it the captain is ready to see me?" she asked Inks.

"Yes ma'am. If you'll follow me?"

"You sit tight," she instructed her crewmen. "I'll pick you up on my way out. The *Gadfly* is standing by to get you home."

The bay assigned to Kerrix was small but well-equipped and some wall monitors were displaying ship's ops. The *Moonstone's* captain also had an ops board that linked to her bridge stations. Flintlock sat by the medi-cot, which monitored the patient's every change of condition.

"Good to see you, Captain," Ahxenta began. "I'll join you in the staff ready room shortly, Doctor."

The CMO took that as her dismissal. She bid farewell and left.

"Please sit, Captain. I take it this isn't a social call and you're here on business," Kerrix said without preamble.

Ahxenta looked closely at her. Despite the sharp tone and shrewd eyes, the half-smile gave *Arianrhod's* captain the impression that Kerrix *was* actually pleased to see her.

"I see you're feeling better."

"Much, thank you; although Dr Mettix won't let me out of here. He thinks I'll ignore his orders and get back to work."

"You will, it's your style. I can see by the med-monitors that you're not as fit as you're trying to make out. And you're not playing a game on that console, you're checking status updates."

"I am, as I'm sure you'd be doing in my position. So what's to do?"

"First, I have this for you and your SSO. Azular put it together. I'll send a short version of it to the fleet and relevant authorities, but you'd best go over it and get a copy to Captain Thal."

As she passed over the data shard and summarised its contents, she watched the expressions chasing each other across the half-Norvallan woman's face. Kerrix nodded as she digested the implications.

"Being Azular, I bet he checked the crew register of the *Bright Mist?*"

Ahxenta paused. "I bet you did too. You know what he found."

"I did and I do. I was curious, so I had Commander Levettiza check it out, as she has access to databases that I don't. Nor you, I suspect, although I never discount what the *Arianrhod* can do or find out."

"Thanks," was the dry retort. "And?"

"*Bright Mist* was the only PSS out of Nyx at the time, registered at the Aoria office under a Captain Nathaniel Holdspan. Vetta could only pull a part-list of crew but there were three other Holdspans aboard: a Marienna Janes-Holdspan and a Nathan and a Nortin Holdspan."

"What else? I bet Commander Levettiza didn't stop there."

"She didn't. This won't go further than this room, Captain, or at least no further than those of your officers you think should know."

"It won't. You have my word."

"Marienna and Nathan were Nat's parents, chief tactical officer and first mate; Nathaniel was his grandfather and Nortin was an uncle, an engineer with a bad disciplinary record. They were all lost. But a well-established Nyx shipping firm, the Ember Line, was held by Holdspan until it was sold twelve years ago. Its then director was Ketta Holdspan. As Nat was listed at the same place, we guess she was his grandmother.

But Vetta didn't probe too deeply, in case it was picked up. And she didn't check on his past – that *would* have been noted."

"Wise," Ahxenta commented.

"That's it. But what else brings you in, Captain?" Kerrix asked with a sigh. "I sense you've something else on your mind."

"You sense? Interesting choice of phrase."

"Why don't you get to the point, Captain? I'm not in the mood for a verbal fencing match."

"Nor are you fit. But to get to the point: when last I *was* aboard, you said a few things that caught my interest. For one, you seem to have the idea that I can read your mind – and Azular's."

"That isn't what I meant and you know it," Kerrix broke in. "You're very sharp at picking up what's around you and you've a knack of pre-empting people. Those close to you, you *can* read, I'm sure. That's how you handle Azular, isn't it? A telepath of his skill isn't easy to crack but *you* have his measure. Most would give him a wide berth once they figure his abilities, for fear he'd find out what they have to hide."

"But not you," Ahxenta shot back. "And I bet you've a lot to hide."

"Naturally; everyone does, you included. But Azular knows what he gets with me. If he's annoyed me, he's aware, and it's his problem. It's the same with Vetta, and they're both strong Berzic telepaths."

If that was an attempt to needle her, Ahxenta ignored it. "*You* know when someone's read you, even inadvertently. You knew Azular was a telepath soon after you met him; I bet it was the same for Levettiza, or Vettarista as you knew her then. But you didn't steer clear. And you now figure that I have a similar talent, is that it?"

"You tell me," Kerrix said wearily. "I wasn't trying to provoke you, if that's what you assumed. I was making an observation. It was logical to me, and you were irritating me; and I'm easily irritated, as you know. I *felt* you had a hidden agenda, though I couldn't fathom it. I still can't. I also can't work out why you're bringing this up now. Are you afraid I'll start asking Azular awkward questions about you? You ordered him not to contact me directly: he told me in his comm."

"You tread a fine line. But believe me, none of mine would tell you anything personal about me without my say-so. And they'd tell *me* of any attempt to extract such information. But you: you can sense when there's an attempt to scan you covertly. Now that's a rare talent. Is it natural in Norvallans, or are you an exception?"

"*Now* who's trying to extract personal details?" she shot back. "I'm half-Telziltic, Captain. I found out by painful experience that I *have* a keen empathic sense that's down to my Telziltic origin, and my clan in particular. We're aware of the subtle nuances of others' emotions, and as I discovered much later, we're a tad sensitive to telepaths."

"Painful experience?"

"I grew up in an atmosphere of subterfuge. I didn't understand it, but was aware that behind the smiles was a venom directed at me. And *they* knew that I knew they were playing a part. It made life difficult."

"Are you looking for sympathy for your troubled childhood?"

"Don't be absurd. And you're trying to read me again."

"And you're blocking it… Interesting," Ahxenta said mordantly.

"You *have* telepathic skills, don't you? You're not a strong telepath like Azular or Vetta, but it's there. Berzic?"

"Mind your own damn business, Captain Kerrix," Ahxenta advised her genially. "Making assumptions like that will get you into trouble."

"Trouble and I are old friends, believe me. Answer the questions, Captain Ahxenta. Or leave me to make assumptions."

Ahxenta leant back in her chair, eyeing her opposite number keenly. The eyes that met hers were equally astute. At last, the captain of the *Arianrhod* gave a slow smile as she folded her arms.

"I'm half-Berzic. Where does that leave your assumptions?"

"Half-answered," was the retort. "Azular knows, doesn't he? And your chief medic, she'd have to. And your first mate. Thank you: nice to know that my innate sense isn't wrong."

"But you still find me damn annoying?"

Kerrix laughed softly, sinking back on her pillow. "You know, that's almost an echo of what Azular once said to me? It was in the *Milky Pearl,* just before we ran into the nasty Hoxiz, and the equally malicious Dr Mazy Herta. I'll give you the same answer I gave him: hell, yes."

"It didn't stop you agreeing to get hitched to Azular, did it?"

"He's very persuasive. As I suspect you are. Anything else bothering you, Captain, that you'd like to discuss?"

"Want a list?" Ahxenta asked sarcastically. "What we *have* discussed will not be mentioned to anyone, including Azular, at least for now."

"Certainly not. *Is* there anything else?"

"Where are you planning to go from here, once you *are* able to shift? You won't want to hang around Delta and you'll need a port that can repair your ship effectively."

"Sunrise; Captain Thal's diverted one of ours here as escort. Then Starfall. The *Serenity's* for Psi. Admiral Posettix will convey the remains of my four crew that belong there to their homes: their people asked. We've said our goodbyes. My other three will rest at Starfall. It's as close to a home as they had," she said, her face twisting in emotion.

Ahxenta nodded. "It's not easy, losing crewmen. We've all faced it. And I didn't express my condolences on your losses. That was remiss."

"Captain, there's no need. Your actions towards me and mine have more than shown your concern. I'm grateful, as are my crew. Things around here would have been a lot more difficult without the help of the *Arianrhod*. And her crew, particularly your medics."

"Welcome. And now I'd better get back. We're due to ship out in a couple of hours. Take care. Will I tell Azular to expect a link?"

"Please ask him to call me when he has time. I'm sure he's busy and I've been told I have at least another thirty hours in here."

"Roger that, Captain."

Ahxenta made her way out to where her officers waited. That they were curious as to what had held her up was clear, but she said no more than necessary. Inks had been told of her return and came in to attend them to their shuttle. Ahxenta was not sorry that he said little. She felt the need to be alone with her thoughts, which were troubling enough.

The trip to *Arianrhod* was quiet, the medics realising that the captain was pensive. Once back aboard, she dismissed them to rest and left the *Gadfly* with her engineers. Flintlock held back: she knew that Ahxenta was brooding on something and wanted to know what it was.

"Go to hell," was the answer to the CMO's gentle probing. "I have to see Azular. He's on the bridge, and that's where I'm for. You are off duty: that's an order. I'll speak to you once we're on the road to Bistra."

"You'd better," was the parting shot as the doctor stalked off.

The bridge was humming. The stores indented for were aboard, including one advanced med-cradle, Apnis told the captain. "Suppliers are quick when they scent profit, but expect comeback from Lindell: he reckons he could source another one at two thirds the price."

"Clearances?" Ahxenta asked.

"In place. We can leave for Bistra as soon as we're prepped."

"Hold for now, while I talk to Azular. And then he'll make a link."

"And you're still not going to say what the chat to Captain Kerrix was about, are you?" the first mate surmised in a low whisper.

"No," was the short reply as the captain stood and walked off.

"Captain Kerrix is expecting a call," she said softly to Azular. "She's in medbay and will be there for a while. Go do it now, as I want you on the bridge when we leave orbit. You have one half hour. Scoot."

"Yes ma'am. Thank you, ma'am."

The captain stretched, gazing round. Everyone sat rigid, not daring to look up as Azular trotted off. She grinned and returned to her chair.

"What else is new since I was off ship?" she asked her first mate.

"Crizz's started on cloak upgrade. She *has* asked Azular for help and he's input some. She figures it's not a long job, and will be almost done by the time we ship out. Where's he gone, or need I ask?"

"To talk to Kerrix; she's in medbay, so she's a captive audience. The *Serenity's* due to leave Starfall for home, but I still don't know why she stayed so long. She's taking the *Moonstone's* Norvallan dead home."

"And things aboard the *Moonstone*?"

"Could be better, but they'll cope. Kerrix was grateful for our help. I see Lindell's sent up a tender he thinks we could bid for. Any good?"

"Silversnow has a batch of micro-tech for Polstarn's orbital comms relay facility. It's not huge and the profit margin's light, but Polstarn *is* on the way to Stinward and its industrial assembly arm *may* have a deal for us by the time we make it in: Lindell's called a friend in its supply unit. We'll have the hold space for the Polstarn tech, even with the heavy Stinward gear, as our other two cargoes are small."

The captain mulled the idea over as she took in her supercargo's figures. "Okay. We know Polstarn and it won't lose us time. We'll need a quick turnover in the Web, but we'll have a few days. We'll go for it."

* * *

The *Arianrhod* was well on her way to Bistra, with no alarms to disturb her. Three days in, the CMO invited the captain to her office to brief her on matters she had picked up during her stay on the *Moonstone*, and to satisfy her own curiosity as to what Ahxenta had been so keen to chat to Kerrix about. She had deduced that it was personal and it had bothered her. The captain thought it wise to partly enlighten her.

"She figured I was Berzic, or at least had a link there," Ahxenta told her bluntly. "And *she* has a secret, but I'm not telling Azular for now, so keep it close. She's an empath; not strong, but it's a trait inherited from her Telziltic side. It may be relevant if we have her in our medbay again. But there *was* a thing relating to Nat Holdspan. I'm not bringing anyone but you, Tallica and Azular in on it, as it may not come up, but it might clarify a couple of things."

"Poor Nat," the doctor sighed, once she had heard. "It explains his drive to be the best in the fleet, with the fastest ship, the sharpest tech, and everything in place to protect his crew. And how he can afford to outfit her, if he inherited a shipping line. The *Warrior's* the only ship in the fleet apart from us and the *Obsidian* to have a cloak, isn't she?"

"Apart from Thal's PSS-rigged ships," the captain replied, straight-faced. "And the *Moonstone* has a chameleon cloak."

"That lot are a case apart," the chief medic parried. "But I haven't heard much about the TA's attempts to hijack Thal's bypasses. Does it still want the codes to list as its own, to charge for their use, the strap line being that the credit's for upkeep and patrolling? *And* it wants nearby systems to set up facility ops along the way for the comfort and convenience of the rest of us, for which we'll have to pay top whack."

"Cynic," Ahxenta said. "Thal *did* hand over the codes to his bypass from Twilight via Starfall to Amity for TA listing, on Admiral Posettix' advice, but he pushed for concessions. The TA had to agree that the PSS fleet would get the codes, and as we did, we won't be taxed on the use of any part of it. And Thal's insisted that only his people can alter codes and nobody can approach any of his bases without the say-so of his base commanders. And believe me, he won't let hostiles loose on it if he can help it. As for facility stops, that's on hold. But there's been nix more: I'd have said at a staff briefing. I *will* contact Thal, and bring it up. I've heard no more on the *Kel'Kith*, though I'm not surprised. Until she's safe at Starfall, he won't mention her in any comm."

"On another note, how's Azular? He's been avoiding me in case I ask about Kerrix, and I bet he's ducking others, as he doesn't want to field the chat, however sympathetic it looks on the surface."

"Burying himself in work. He's sent out and had at least one link since we've been out. The *Moonstone* was still at Delta last I heard, but she's for Sunrise, then Starfall. And we're headed on an opposite track. It's unsettling him, and he won't talk about it."

"*I'll* make him. If he thinks separation anxiety magically disappears once you're hitched, he's in for a shock. But others can manage it, and he will. I've had no sign that Flish wants a move to the *Firedrake* after she and Flick Poppet tie the knot, and he can't transfer here as he's first mate and essential to his own ship. Elsey Gunn's partner is a pilot on the *Comet* and they only meet five or six times a year, but do okay. And there's my brother; but as Race never shuts up from dawn 'til dusk and often not even then, I'm not surprised Mercy sticks to her post as the *Quarkstorm's* CMO. I sometimes wish I'd never introduced them."

"I get the picture and I'll leave it to you. I have to get back to the bridge for the final push before we make port. Keep me updated."

"Aye, Cap. And don't forget you've got your med-check in a couple of days. I'll send you a reminder."

"Hell, it's not long since the last one: why are they so frequent?"

"Ask the captain; she's the one that sets the rules," Flintlock shot back wickedly as Ahxenta stood.

"One day I'll dock your pay for impudence," was the sharp retort as she swung out of the door and smiling, set off for the bridge.

There was nothing to report bar course tweaks for random shifts in hyperspace currents, and an advisory from the *Tallulah*, who had spied a bulky ship cutting across her path at distance. It did not engage, but readings got in passing bore a resemblance to those of known hostiles, and a trace of zukivianite had registered.

"Fleetskup sent that round?" Ahxenta asked in surprise. "Are his command skills improving or was it a fluke?"

"It came from Juke Spickle," Apnis told her. "*Tallulah* was coming up on the Sevolb beacon. Sevolb's near the Crimson Drapes and being Coalition, it's always been dubious, so Spickle must have set his sensors to full. But whatever it was, it was on course for the nebula, maybe to skirt across the top at Obit, and it was in a hurry."

"*Tallulah's* at Sevolb? She's for the Web if she's come from Scuttle Scarp. Dandy. She may still be there when we get in. Spickle's earning his pay if he's sharp enough to keep a lookout along that stretch. Or maybe it was Munnet that spotted it. Did he send on the readings?"

"He did. Azular's checked them, and added the data to the grid. It's not enough to match the ship to a specific hostile design but there are parallels. Which rings an alarm: is it aiming for that likely holding area near Furze and doesn't know that the ISA has got eyes on it?"

"If it's unmanned, that's possible. I suppose Spickle sent the gen to the usual camps as a memo as well?" the captain asked.

"*Tallulah* must have got the recent data that was sent round, so she will have. It's standard for general alerts. I could check up?"

"Do it. Word it as a thanks for the data and ask if there's any more," Ahxenta advised. "For all that Fleetskup's not the savviest commander in the fleet, his ship is top notch and he likes to keep her in trim, so his tactical and science arrays will be up to scratch. Use the office."

"Will do. It'll give me a chance to stretch my legs," Apnis said.

She was back shortly. "It was sent to the ISA, the TA *and* the Sevolb authority, as Obit's one of its posts. Fleetskup was pleased I'd linked; he made as if it had been his idea to send word out. He asked after you; I told him you were busy. Tallulah Tommy wasn't in his usual spot aft of the command chair. Maybe Spickle is keeping him in order as well?"

"That'll be the day," Ahxenta snorted.

"Anyhow, I got all their science and tactical data. Fleetskup ordered it sent over, so comms should have it by now. I had to let out we were near Bistra, but I hinted we'd be on his tail soon, and asked if he'd had any trouble by Pixel Point, so he's assumed we'll head in by that route. He said he'd see us in the Web, as he'd be there for a stretch."

"In that case we make for Quartic Cross and straight on. It puts us close to Furze, that worm-pocket and that ship that *Tallulah* reported, if that *was* its heading, but what the hell. It's a straight run, and as we'll only have the *Moonstone's* Silversnow cargo, we'll be light in the beam."

"It'll take about eight days after Bistra," Apnis warned. "A lot can happen in that time. That might be the start," she groaned as Bellfish called out an incoming for the captain from Captain Thal.

"My office," Ahxenta instructed. "Good news for once, I hope."

The news was that the *Kel'Kith* and her cargo had made Starfall. The parents of two more of the children had been traced. The other four would be found new families, but all would stay at Starfall for now. Thal also said that the *ISAS Avenger* had left in the direction of Amity, which was another reason that the *NFS Serenity* would move out soon. There had been no more on the TA's taking advantage of his bypasses, but he was keeping a tight rein. He told Ahxenta nothing of his own trading matters, but he thanked her for her aid to the *Moonstone* and hoped their paths would cross one of these days.

"Saved me calling him. He was in his office aboard the *Kel'Moth*," the captain told Apnis. "I expect he'll stay at Starfall until the *Serenity* leaves. He's heard zip about what the ISA's doing, but says he keeps his ears open, which I bet means he still has a network of spies. The *Kel'Beth* will escort the *Moonstone* from Delta. Anything new here?"

As she spoke, a note came in from Lindell: a food load for Merkat Three was almost ready at the Bistran firm to which they were hauling the seed, and he had been asked if *Arianrhod* would take it on. It could be in pods at their target holding station inside three hours of arrival. The fee was generous, as there would be an early delivery bonus.

"We'll take it," Ahxenta stated, once she had read the details. "It's only an extra half day. But we'll be slow to the Web: that's a big load."

"In which case we'd best keep our eyes and ears open en route, as we'll be close to hot spots near the Crimson Drapes," Apnis said.

"I agree. I'll call Zillah, as we've not spoken lately and she may have news about the ISA and its doings out her way: there's nothing on the usual nets. The holo will warn us of things to keep tabs on. I see it's clear by Bistra. What's the power usage on the upgraded holo, Azular?"

"Barely eight percent above previous, Captain," he replied. "For the gain in data depth and clarity, it's a worthwhile addition."

"Good. Once we're on our way out of Bistra, we set it to maximum all the way to the Web. We might be headed into more well-travelled territory but that tends to make it more of a target for troublemakers. How long until we make the local node at Bistra, helm?"

"Twenty two minutes, Captain," Dox replied. "I estimate one hour and ten minutes to Bistra from there at expected post jump speed."

"Then I'll wait until were in orbit before I contact Zillah."

"Best check local Freskat time, Cinnabar – she won't thank you for disturbing her out of hours," the first mate advised jocularly.

"Thanks for that, Commander. I suggest you liaise with Lindell and make sure our teams and bays are ready for a quick turnaround."

* * *

The turnaround *was* rapid. The thought of a bonus and free time in the Web spurred on *Arianrhod's* teams. Cargoes were switched seamlessly, and the ship was soon on her way to Quartic Cross. Ahxenta had talked to Zillah, and in exchange for more data on recent clashes involving the PSS fleet, was given food for thought. Freskat was now saddled with the upkeep of an ISA office near its fleet HQ and the company of two ISA warships in its naval dock. As the main centre in the ISP sector of Lambda, and the only large power in an empty area of space, the planet was seen as vital. Zillah's take on that was that as Freskat had managed itself for decades with no trouble, why add layers of regulation to burden taxpayers and annoy local authorities?

That a station under Thal's aegis was off her doorstep did not upset Zillah, nor did the proximity of the once-covert but now listed bypass: it could get her ships to zone Mu in double-quick time. One thing that did bother the admiral was the incessant stream of hints from ISA HQ that her fleet should keep its beady eyes on Starfall's local activities, as it was suspected that other covert routes might exist in the area.

"Zillah's not sure what the ISA's up to at the Crimson Drapes, but she was called into the new ISA office for talks about the holding area the hostiles set up off the Ginseng during the war," Ahxenta told her senior staff. "She had the raw data on the energy fluxes at the anomaly, and more analysis has shown that it's close to what the ISA's got for the Drapes. The inference is that it means trouble. From what Zillah's been told, the Drapes isn't hiding a huge force, but that's not verified. You know she seeded the perimeter of the Ginseng with fusion mines to slow the fleet that jumped out of there for the assault on Skyrtek, but that didn't stop it. What's bothering you, Azular?"

"Thal needs to know that ISA eyes are on his fleet's actions near Twilight, and it suspects that other covert routes exist in the area."

"Because they do," Ahxenta said. "But I agree. Zillah's not keen to put her own in the position of watchman, but she has little say over what ISA ships do – except that she'll have to order hers in if they hit trouble. I *will* alert Thal. But the ISA's certain there's a hostile holding area at the Drapes. Zillah got a copy of the report on the worm-pocket I gave her from the ISA, and she's been asked about it and us. The ISA figured we'd held back but may have told her more. That implies it *has* explored and has got data that's worrying it. It sent out a research ship, and its experts know the pocket has artificial elements, as we reported it. The *Skimfrost* and her escort are still there, but I doubt they'll hail us in passing. I didn't mention Furze to Zillah and she didn't bring it up, so it may have escaped ISA notice, but I wouldn't bet on it."

"You'll also alert Captain Thal to that, ma'am?" Azular asked.

"I will. But back to work, all. We'll soon hit Quartic and we need no glitches in the switch for the Web. Not you. Azular, I want a word."

"You heard from Captain Kerrix again," she said as the door closed. "I don't want to know the personal details, but I do want to know how she and her ship are; you've been avoiding that issue, amongst others. The *Kel'Beth* should have made Delta by now."

"She's back in the command chair," he said with a brief smile. "Not fully healed, but she's stubborn. And yes, ma'am, the *Kel'Beth* has made orbit. She brought supplies *and* had a Starfall defence craft at her back. The Delta authorities are annoyed, but there's a reason: pieces of intact shielding with sensory inclusions were stripped off the *Moonstone's* hull, and the captain's furious. She's demanded their return, halted ops until the theft's investigated and warned the repair base that she'll take legal action and send out an open report unless it settles the matter. As Delta has a name to preserve, the Port Authority's involved. It's asked her to keep it quiet until it's sorted, but she *will* notify the PSS fleet, so we'll get an advisory. Internal repairs are ongoing, but the ship's fit to move out, and Xanna wants to make Sunrise Base as fast as possible."

"Somebody's filched some of the *Moonstone's* tech? No wonder she's pissed, as that's a hull like no other. Is somebody trying to make a fast credit on novel tech, or is it something more sinister?"

"That *is* the question. I'd be grateful if you don't mention it, ma'am. Xanna *did* say I could tell you, but she doesn't want it spread around."

"You mean she knew you would or I'd work out something was up," grinned Ahxenta. "She won't post it on open channels, as it would alert others that she has hull tech worth lifting. But the bluff will work on the repair firm if the PA's breathing down its neck. It's an issue: we have add-on hull tech that's novel and could bring in credit if any sharp bods spotted it, could remove it, and knew where to sell it on."

"We have sensors that tell us if our gear is being tampered with."

"If they're on line. But another thing: Sunrise is a long way from Merkat and we're for the Web," she said, eyeing him closely. "You may not see Captain Kerrix for a while. What do you plan to do about it?"

"Have you been speaking to Dr Flintlock, ma'am?" he asked warily.

"She's been speaking to me. And you've not answered the question.

"We'll have to live with it for the present," he grimaced. "And live with long-distance comms."

"I'll sanction unlimited comms," the captain said softly. "As I have for Dr Ma'Lappis. I'd meant to have a chat with Captain Kerrix, but I will sooner rather than later, after what you've told me. But let's get to the bridge before we come up on Quartic."

All bridge stations were at alert, as the route shifts for the switch to the main trade bypass for the Web were complex, Quartic Cross being the hub of four galactic zones. In the event, the switch was painless. As their route would take them past Furze and within reach of the new worm-pocket and the Crimson Drapes, the grid was at full stretch. As the hours passed, Ahxenta ordered her senior crew off watch in relays, to ensure they were fresh for that sweep of bypass.

* * *

The captain's eyes raked the holo-grid as they made the Furze beacon. She had deployed the cloak despite its energy use, to make her ship as undetectable as possible. She heard Apnis suck in a breath as the holo shifted with the ship's forward route and the marker for the rogue worm-pocket came into view. It had an ISA alert tag. There were other indicators that they would have to get a handle on, Ahxenta knew, as she eyed a warning ring off the edge of the bypass beyond the Furze system, at the edge of the redly-glowing nebula off starboard.

"An alert's in place for that as well," she said to Apnis. "Keep away. Have we any more details on what the ISA reckons it is, Azular?"

"No, ma'am, it's marked *unknown hazard*. There's no note of an ISA presence in the area, but long-range scanners have picked up two ships holding out of range of the anomaly; neither is logged hostile."

"I bet they've spotted us, cloak or not," the first mate said acidly. "Think they'll say hello?"

"I don't know, but we don't give them any reason to suspect we've detected them," the captain said shortly. "Continue on course, helm, but be ready to jump off the bypass if we need to."

"Aye ma'am," Dox replied. "Get jump lines plotted," she told her mate. "With the Drapes on one side, a worm-pocket on the other and a hole in space that I bet hides nasty surprises, we don't want slip-ups."

"You got it," Box replied genially.

The words were hardly out of his mouth when Azular called, "One ship's on the move and on a line that'll bring her across our bows! The larger one. Her outline implies a destroyer, so I suspect it's the *ISAS Steadfast*. The only data on the register is that she's in active service."

"She knows we're here! What kind of scanning gear does she have that she can get a bead on us from the other side of Furze?" Ahxenta snarled. "Drop the cloak, Dox, it's not helping."

"Won't that let them know we've marked them?" Apnis asked.

"Do them damn well good. Tactical, get a bead on that boat. Shields up! Warm up our weapons, Ms Earbleat but do *not* target – yet."

"Aye ma'am! *Loki*…"

"Will stay where she is. You will not deploy her. As soon as we have that ship in our short-range sights and have verified her call-sign, hail her, Mr Bellfish. Have you got anything more, Azular?"

"Very little. She's closing, increasing to jump-in speed… she'll jump in aft of us. I have her call-sign: she *is* reading as the *Steadfast*. Locking in my Norvallan scanner… she has a range of weaponry, an inactive cloak and sufficient scanning arrays to know who we are, *and* what our capabilities are, although our jammers should block her scans."

"Hailing now, Captain!" Bellfish advised. "Got her! I have Captain Mitz Reddish of the *ISAS Steadfast* for you."

"Put him on speaker and on visual. Keep us on track, Dox, we don't want to look like we're running away. And keep his ship in range of our aft torpedo arrays' targeting eyes, Ms Earbleat."

"Very shiny," Apnis drawled quietly as the image of the ISA captain appeared and details of his spanking clean bridge could be seen.

After greetings, Ahxenta abruptly queried the reason for the arrival of an ISA destroyer on her tail that was matching course and speed.

Reddish was equally blunt. He had been waiting for her. He knew she had left Bistra for the Web, and it was a sound guess that she would run via Furze. He wanted words and had decided on a direct approach.

"Direct meaning you have your guns up my stern," Ahxenta cut in. "I don't know you, Captain, so perhaps you'd fill me in on you, your agenda and why you in particular want words with me."

"I have my orders."

"From whom?"

"My superiors."

"That covers a few. Colonel Myrtleberry wouldn't be one of them, would she, if not the main one?"

His eyes blazed and he said nothing, but Ahxenta could see his first officer looking at him sideways, a perturbed look on her face.

"Not saying?" she continued. "If you don't hear what you want, what's your next move? Gentle persuasion or another direct approach that involves your forr'ad torpedoes up my butt?"

"That is not how the ISA operates, Captain."

"Really? I've had a taste of how the ISA operates and I beg to differ, Captain. But let's hear these words you want to have."

Reddish wanted to know how she had spotted the fake maintenance order at Istrel Statice that hid node-rigging. That she had caught the spurious comm from a local engineering works rung oddly in his ears.

"And in Colonel Myrtleberry's ears," Ahxenta interjected. "I've told *her* all I plan to on the subject; and *you* can keep your scanning eyes off my hull. Is that why you've hauled in alongside? The colonel had her own notions and you're here to check them out in your state-of-the-art warship? She thinks I've sourced equipment that she would like for the ISA fleet and you're here to press the issue."

"You're very friendly with the Starfall fleet and many of their ships are now on the PSS register. The *Kel'Moth* and the *Moonstone* for two," Reddish returned tartly. "They have high-end tech, and we know some of it is alien. And your ship seems to have an edge that many don't."

"My ship's *always* had an edge. You want to know what tech Starfall ships have, I suggest you ask it; not that you'll get far. If there's nothing else, Captain, I'll be on my way. I have commissions to fulfil."

"There was a ship that smacked of Starfall design leaving Furze in a hurry a while back. I had other priorities but I *did* check Furze. There was a recently-wrecked structure down there. Do you know anything about it?" Reddish asked, his eyes narrowing.

"I don't keep tabs on Starfall's activity, so how would I know if one of its ships was there? But what's this about Furze?"

"You reported the nebular irregularity *and* the worm-pocket in the area, Captain, so you *were* there. Surely you spotted something?"

"I was switching at the Furze crossover for Alto Finglas, as I'm sure you know damn well, as I was hauling a large and costly cargo for ISA HQ that would make my ship a target for raider ops. My gear is always online as I always expect trouble, and given I've been waylaid by you, I'm clearly justified. We spotted the nebular anomaly in a long-distance sweep. As we'd met similar, off the Ginseng in Lambda during the war, we went in to look. Once we realised what it was, we set a beacon and took a wide line out – and struck the uncharted worm-pocket. It almost pulled us in. I alerted ISA HQ, as you know, as it's the reason you and your research ship are here. If you've been here ever since, *you're* more likely than most to know the score. Why you need me to corroborate your findings puzzles me, unless you have a hidden agenda. Do you?"

"I'd like to know more about the two attacks on the *PSS Moonstone*," he said coolly. "We have what she sent out, but that's not much. You were in Delta Iridium at the same time and you *did* render aid."

"You know I was at Delta when the *Moonstone* came in: Myrtleberry called me to push for the data you think I have. As I've told you, I have nothing more to add to what I told her, but I'm curious as to why you or she thinks I have; and why she figures that sending you on my tail will change that. And why you're still trying to scan my hull."

"And I can't. You have exceptional tech and jamming gear."

"You haven't answered my questions. Do you plan to?"

"My senior officers and my orders are no concern of yours."

"My business and my ship are none of yours. And unless you plan to restrain me by force, this talk is over. I *will* send a formal complaint to the ISA, copied to the Trades Alliance and others as I see fit, about this – dialogue. Do you have anything else to say, Captain?"

"Not at this time, Captain. Have a good day."

"And you. Ahxenta out."

"Not that it can get much worse," Apnis said, once the link was cut.

"Keep targeting eyes on her, Earbleat. Gliss and Azular, maintain scanning. She's heading off, but I bet she's still trying to probe us."

"She is ma'am, but our jammers are foiling her," Azular stated. "I'm scanning her path and local space. She's jumped off, but she's left us a surprise: a probe, possibly set to track and scan us! It's got a chameleon cloak – *our* cloak add-on arrays have identified it."

"Take it out!" Ahxenta said shortly. "Get Reddish back on line."

"Captain... perhaps we'd do better to capture it?" the senior science officer interrupted. "We could analyse it..."

"And update it and send it back to him better than it was before," the first mate added facetiously.

"Stow it, Tallica. Engineering, prepare a tractor to haul it in as soon as Dr Azular confirms it's safe. And keep a mark on it, Earbleat. One wrong move and it's stardust."

"I have Captain Reddish for you ma'am," Bellfish called.

"On screen... you forgot something, Captain," Ahxenta said coldly. "A tracking probe. Care to tell me why you set it to trail us out of this sector, or shall I take it up with your senior officers at ISA HQ when I call them about your intercepting and scanning us?"

"What are you talking about, Captain?"

"Dr Azular, send what you got on the *Steadfast's* probe to Captain Reddish. It seems he's forgotten he left it behind. I'm picking up your probe, Captain, and you won't get it back until you tell me exactly why you released it and what you were hoping to get from it. Your call."

Ahxenta folded her arms and waited as Azular, scans complete, sent them to her boards and to Bellfish for transfer to the *Steadfast*. In spite of its cloak the probe held no harmful elements and, deeming it safe, Azular bid engineering set the tractor to capture it and bring it in.

The infuriated Reddish icily told the captain that he held her and her ship an irritant, and he was not bound to explain his actions.

"In that case, I'll retain your probe until I find out exactly what it is and what it's coded to do. And I will. And I *will* contact your superiors to raise a formal complaint about your actions. Ahxenta out."

"We're getting the hell out of here, once that probe's aboard. Lock it in an outer bay and kill any signal it's sending," she ordered. "I'd like to know what his game is, and who the other players are."

"We're an itch that he and his chums can't scratch and they don't like it," was Apnis' summation.

"I'll bet, Myrtleberry being the chief. He didn't deny it, so I'm damn sure she's the instigator. Once we're out of this sector and away from that ship and her antics, I'll need tight-beam transmissions set up, Mr Bellfish. And you'll be with me on a few, Azular," she told him. "I want words with Colonel Ellin Myrtleberry, if she's still at Alto Finglas."

"Maybe she's got a super-shiny new ship and will soon be on the way to remote parts, and wants a last shot at getting something out of us or out of Thal and his lot," the first mate suggested.

"That might not be so far from the truth. My first link will be Thal – he has to know that the *Steadfast* did spy his ship leaving Furze and that the ISA now knows about the base that was once there."

"And then the *Moonstone*," Apnis grinned, glancing at Azular. "Since Reddish wanted to know what we had to do with her. And then you'll take Myrtleberry and the ISA to pieces. You're going to be busy, Cap."

"And so will you, Commander. You'll have the conn."

* * *

The plan differed in that the captain's first contact was Myrtleberry, as the woman linked after speaking to Reddish about his abortive attempt to track *Arianrhod*. Ahxenta was incensed, for as she had suspected, the ISA colonel had been at back of the idea. Myrtleberry was unrepentant: she had ordered the *Steadfast* to obtain data that she suspected the PSS captain had and was holding onto, data that Myrtleberry believed was vital for her next mission into unknown space. That Reddish had used the methods he did were not her concern. And she still wanted what she supposed to be supplementary data.

Apnis had been near the bone with her off-the-cuff remark about the colonel's ride for her next mission. The ISA had judged it crucial to send a third ship to join the *Repulse* and *Advance* in searches beyond zone Alpha, in view of the trouble that the two had met when barely into their task. The colonel was to command the third, the latest off the production line, and equipped with all the ISA could throw at her. Myrtleberry would be the ranking officer of the small flotilla.

A polite query by Azular had not elicited the name of the new ship, but digging whilst the colonel and the captain were trading icy words over Ahxenta's refusal to hand over extra data, and her intent to lodge a protest with the ISA Defence Department, copied to its Council, told him. The *ISAS Peerless*, a custom-built explorer-destroyer and class ship of a new unit, had been launched five days before. Her first trip, to join her sister ships at the edge, would be her shakedown cruise.

That he had readily found the data through ISA press office lists made the colonel hiss in fury, and his conjectures as to the presence of a new high-spec shuttle with an inbuilt cyber suite as her personal ride enraged her, but she had not denied it. She cut the link wrathfully.

The captain made good on her threat, and her protest, copied to the PSS fleet and the TA, was sent in short order. Ahxenta expected rapid results, but her talk to Thal was next. That Reddish had detected a ship that he figured for Starfall on the way out of Furze meant that high-spec ISA vessels now had the tools to penetrate the jammers and cloaks of Starfall ships. Their internal cloaking was probably effective, but it could not be taken as read, and Ahxenta had no idea what the ISA ship had caught of the load the ship carried. That the *Steadfast's* search had led to the discovery of the remains of the base that Thal's team had left was an added concern, as there would be fallout: the ISA would not let that kind of mystery lie untouched if it could help it.

Thal was perturbed over the news and of the ISA's interest in his fleet. And he was anxious that a radical explorer-warship with an info-sent in command would be heading for a sector where he had a base, and active bypasses. The new ISA presence close to Twilight was also taxing him. He had little to say on the *Moonstone* other than that the issue of the stolen shielding was only partially resolved, but the ship and her escorts were on their way out of Deltan space and on track for Sunrise. As for the contents of the life-tubes that had been recovered from Furze, he was not open, but did say that they did not hold those missing from his base. They did however, hold humans that his people would try to reanimate, should they be alive, once they could do so safely, as their significance was likely to have far reaching effects.

The captain and her senior science officer traded glances as the link to Thal was cut. Ahxenta could not crack the meaning behind his cryptic remarks, but felt that an issue was biting him. Azular was no wiser, but sensed that what Thal suspected was acutely troubling. He hoped for clarity from the call to Kerrix. He had not heard from her since the *Kel'Beth* and her escort the *SS Schiltron* had made Delta. As the *Moonstone* had left there, she was obviously fit to travel, but the part-resolution of the theft of the missing hull units sounded ominous.

Kerrix had been off duty but found a private space to talk. She had an inkling of what part of it might be, as she had read Ahxenta's latest protest to the ISA. That one of Thal's ships had been sighted at Furze made her uneasy, but she would say no more, and had no data on the life-tubes that were disturbing him. She was open on *her* problems: the missing bits of intact shielding were set with high-tech micro-sensors linked to her ship's science arrays. They were new, recently fitted, and under test, and could sense and counteract threats by emitting blocking signals. One goal was to stop attachment and penetration of insidious weapons such as the coded limpet drones that had recently been used on the *Nyx Warrior*. As those had been more complex than any earlier known examples, Kerrix had set the Norvallan and Telziltic engineers of her crew, and the *Moonstone's* science labs, to produce the sensors.

That Kerrix had instantly frozen the repairs to her ship and ordered every op off her hull had irked repair company reps. Her alerts to their managers, the Port Authority, the PSS, and her own fleet irritated them even more; and her demand for the direct return of the missing tech was met with blank faces. The PA had intervened to advise that the repair yard get enquiries underway at once, and Kerrix had directed her second mate to investigate and to set up the initial steps in legal redress, but she had held off notifying the TA and the local press until she got some answers.

The tactics had had partial success, as had routine security measures on the *Moonstone*, as the timing of the theft had been resolved. The ops tasked with repairs near the affected plating had been quizzed and their lockers searched; part of the stolen tech had been found and three ops detained. They admitted that the theft had been to order, but refused to name their paymasters. They had held back part of the loot in hopes of netting profit *and* had sold pieces on. They had no idea of what they had, but in Levettiza's view, people linked to the company had to be involved. She had asked a friend, an ex-colleague, for help.

That had been the situation when the Starfall ships left Delta, with the *Moonstone* only just able. They were on a local route to Lartzeg Trine and Pollens Sentry. Kerrix was sure her stolen tech was in criminal if not enemy hands, but the felons would be ignorant of its use, and even if not, with no ancillary gear or codes, the pieces would be tough to fit. She had set some her own to recoding the micro-sensor units still on her hull, but could do little else. Her recent clashes had left her acutely under-crewed, as with so many injured, she had other priorities.

The nature of the micro-sensor units had made Azular's ears prick: Ahxenta could feel him restive as she told Kerrix of the radical gear the *Steadfast* must have used to detect *Arianrhod*. The probe they had got was now in Azular's lab. He had studied it and judged it safe, but that was all. That the *Peerless* was to head beyond Alpha caused Kerrix a little interest, but her main concerns were her crew, her ship, and safe passage. All Thal's ships along her course had been contacted and had reported no problems. Local nets, and the hostile listening posts en route that Starfall had converted to its own use, also read clear.

Ahxenta frowned at news of Starfall's listening posts but kept quiet. Most civil and military bodies, *and* criminal factions, had them; and most outfits monitored rivals' ops and were in turn spied on.

"Anything else, Captain, apart from the micro-sensor tech that's now part of my shielding? I can see that Dr Azular's interested."

"I'll bet, though I doubt you'll be sending me a detailed spec. But it sounds like handy kit if we're faced with more of the high-end limpet drones that caused Captain Holdspan such grief not so long ago."

"True. My concern is that if the no-goods that created those drones *have* got sticky paws on them and worked out what they can do, they'll figure a way to get round them," Kerrix said.

"Unlikely," Azular disagreed. "I expect the thieves were ordered to abstract strips of intact hull. It's known you have novel tech and any piece would be fair game. If Colonel Myrtleberry *is* keen to know about it you can be sure others are, both inside and outside the law."

"You're not suggesting that her or her lackeys are involved?"

"No, but if they were, Ms Levettiza would find out. But the attempt by an ISA ship at tracking *Arianrhod* by probe shows the lengths that lawful parties will go to, to get what they want."

"Good point, though I query the lawful," Kerrix smiled. "But I will *not* pass plans on over a link. Don't look so down, Azular, I'll get them to you. I'll talk to Captain Thal. If our kit can be easily replicated and integrated into standard shield plating, the whole fleet could benefit."

"You could sell it on the open market. The Starfall fleet are traders, after all," Ahxenta remarked sardonically.

"The market wouldn't last; some wiseacre would figure out how to side-step it," was the equally terse reply. "Anything else, Captain?"

"Yes. But it's a private matter, so I'll ask you to leave now, Azular. Unless you've anything related to our current situation to add?"

After a few technical queries, he was obliged to say goodbye, with the promise of a personal comm later. Ahxenta waited until the coast was clear before turning back to the screen.

"I want to continue the discussion we had at our last face-to-face."

"I thought you might. Please go ahead."

* * *

Ahxenta made the bridge an hour later, by which time *Arianrhod* was well on the way to Berzic, and on target for the Web.

"You've had words with a few of our fleet ships?" Apnis asked.

"Yes; I thought I'd update them personally. Azular's back in his lab, I take it, working on that ISA probe?"

"Yup; and you'll be thrilled to know the *Peerless* shipped out. Bellfish got it from the new ISA Central Office channel: it's upholding the ISA tradition of boasting about itself. The shakedown cruise of a squeaky-new boat is big news, though heading and crew data are classified."

"I'm sure," the captain agreed ironically. "But if everything's going on well here, I'll do the rounds and stretch my legs."

"And talk to Azular? He said you were still talking to Captain Kerrix when he left you. He came back here to see what Greffy was up to."

"Typical. I'll see you later, Commander."

"Aye, ma'am."

"What did the Cap say to Captain Kerrix that she couldn't with Doc Azular there?" Lieutenant Box whispered to his mate at the helm.

"It's none of my business or yours, big ears! Mind your boards. Just because it's quiet out there doesn't mean it'll stay that way for long."

"Aye, ma'am," Box said woefully. "But we can talk about it later?"

The captain tracked Azular to his lab. The ISA probe was on a side bench with most of its innards removed. The shell was high-grade meta jurillium from Beta Zegonia 68c, he told her. Many parts were standard but the probe *did* contain top-quality sensing and tracking gear that was more common on the hulls of long-distance explorer ships and military hunter-destroyers. And on ships like the *ISAS Advance*, with a remit of first contact and links to the ISA Intelligence Division, he added.

"Alien tech?" the captain asked.

"No, ma'am. But Psi tech: Norvallan navigation sensory arrays, like my shuttle, and a simple part-cloak that's smart enough to stop most scans, though not ours. Do you plan to return it to the ISA, Captain?"

"Yes, when we've got what we can out of it. We'll circulate its spec to the PSS fleet. But I sense you're not overly impressed by it?"

"We have better aboard, ma'am."

"I bet. But sit: I want a word before you call Captain Kerrix again."

His face told her that he had been expecting a chat, but had no clue as to theme. He sat calmly until she spoke of the exchange the two had had in the passage, when Kerrix had fallen. Their talk in medbay and what had arisen from that caught him by surprise.

"You hadn't figured her for an empath, then?" Ahxenta asked.

"No, ma'am. I guessed she had some *telepathic* ability, as she could often read me. When I first met her, after she'd jumped into that fight to help me, she knew I'd given her a false name. It didn't register then, other than it told me she was sharp, but she often knew when I had an agenda in our meetings, *and* used it to outflank me at times," he smiled.

"I'm sure she has telepathic talent," Ahxenta said. "She figured her friend Vetta, though not for an intelligence agent, I think. She had *your* measure: if she hadn't been out of it at the time, you'd not have figured *her* for a starship captain. And she can block me, most of the time. So now you know. The doc's aware, but no one else, and it stays that way. Revealed secrets lead to trouble, as we both know only too well."

"Aye, ma'am. Was there anything else?"

"She was off duty when we spoke, so now might be a good time to call her. Get Bellfish to set it up: once the *Moonstone* reaches jump point for the Pollens Sentry bypass, you may have trouble picking up a relay."

"Yes ma'am; thank you, ma'am."

She left him to his link and set off to finish her rounds. As she trod the deck, she mused on the months that stretched behind. Life in the lanes had not been easy for *Arianrhod*: she was a maverick among the fleet, a situation down to her idiosyncratic captain and contrary crew. Ahxenta had always given rascals and rebels a second chance, and she had been repaid in loyalty and reliability. But since the war that had shaken the mapped galaxy to its core, times were harder. The hostile legacy was there still, and likely to remain, and her people were targets. Shrugging, she stepped into the transport tube for medbay.

* * *

Skoon and Linza Base were behind them and *Arianrhod* was two hours from the Web. Little had arisen to disturb the even tenor of their ride, the captain reflected as she pulled her ops boards over to check status. She flexed her shoulders and skimmed through the order of business.

"We deliver the *Moonstone's* cargo for Silversnow as soon as, but we prep for taking on our own," she said to her first mate. "Our bays are on standby for the Redship gear, but that won't be for a day or so: they won't release it until the admin's in order. But it's en route to holding."

"I'll chase up Lindell before we head to the harbour office," Apnis replied. "Silversnow's stuff is in company pods, so it'll be easy to pass to company or trade grapple drones – once we've got the fees."

"Roger that. We have the spec of their pods of bits for Sunbeam at Cygilla, and Polstarn's comms gear; they're small hard alloy shell, but we'll use outer bays, and the same for the Ottolyx load for Yistreen. I want our inner bays free in case we pick up delicate or high-security cargoes. Jute's been checking ISA needs: its Alto Finglas and Stinward shipyards are short on jurillium-protected crystal wafer arrays for their fancy comm units, despite the ISA array assembly unit at Alto Finglas. With few suppliers or skilled array-setters, we'll be in with a chance, *if* we can get hold of high quality crystals *and* gem-grade jurillium."

"Jurillium-set arrays? What are they expecting will happen to them, grand theft or cosmic meltdown?" demanded Apnis.

"This is the ISA, and now zone Psi is part of the family, its defence department reps have got lots more tax credits to play with and grander plans. Their idea of galactic defence is bigger ships than the enemy and plenty smart gear to fit them up with," replied the captain cynically.

"About to jump off the bypass now, Captain," Dox warned. "We'll have Merkat in our sights in ten."

"Roger that, helm. Sound the tie-in alert, comms," she ordered, tightening her webbing for the expected jolt.

"Smooth," Apnis noted as the ship slowed to jump-off speed and made the shift to normal space. "Our new grid tech's paying its way; those visuals are super clear. We'll be able to tell who's in dock before we get there, and get a heads-up on who to try to avoid."

"Hah! We'll be lucky. *Tallulah* will still be here," Ahxenta groaned. "*Obsidian* should be in too. The *Warrior* was heading in a while ago, but she may be out again: Nat's no slouch. I haven't heard of many of our own over the nets and there haven't been any big scuffles in this neck of space for a while. Steady as she goes, Dox: everyone that's due will get shore leave as soon as Commander Apnis organises the rotas."

"Already done, and you and I are on that list, Cinnabar."

"I should hope so. Right, let's go over supply and get the lists done. But not another med-cradle for the doc, even if Lindell can source one. And get that gleam out of your eye, Whisper Earbleat; upgrades for *Loki* you will not request. The bits you've got haven't lost their shine."

The usual expectant buzz ran around the bridge as the vast outer meshes of the Web began to glow on their horizon.

Apnis gave a deep sigh. "Back again," she said in satisfaction

"It looks the same," Ahxenta mused. "The last few weeks have been a haul and we all need time ashore. Send out our call-sign; bring her in easy, helm, don't overcook the auxiliaries. On speaker, comms. *PSS Arianrhod* to Merkat Three Port Control: request permission to dock."

"You're on our screens, *Arianrhod*: welcome back to Merkat Three Free Port. Stand by docking instructions," came the response.

"Docking instructions coming in, ma'am," Dox confirmed. "Stand by clearance… we have clearance, and our bay. Powering down," she continued as she brought the great ship into the specified path.

Her call rang out in fifteen minutes that docking struts had locked and station-keeping was achieved, allowing the bridge crew leisure to examine the holo-grid to see what other traffic was in.

"Why do we always end up next to the *Tallulah*?" Apnis complained. "She seems in fine trim. *Firedrake's* the next berth over. Who planned that? It's maybe time to shine your dress uniform buttons again, Cap."

"Stow it," she was advised. "We've a visit to the harbour office, a cargo to shift and trade talks. Lindell's registered our arrival with our usual clients here, as it's well within standard business hours."

"And standard drinking hours," the first mate hinted. "Lindell's speedy. He wants to get deals done and his shore leave in. You'll need Azular for talks. *He* won't want leave, and Greffy won't either, as Merry Jetty's on the *Moonstone* as ship's counsellor – *those* two are still an item."

"What *is* it about that damn ship?" Ahxenta grumbled as Lieutenant Box was heard to remark pithily that he'd be hauling Greffy down for a break whether he wanted one or not, as he was sure it was needed.

"You want to get him oiled enough to let slip what he and Merry are up to and to find out what he knows about Dr Azular's and Captain Kerrix' business," Dox accused crossly. "You won't be doing it while I'm around. Shut down your main console and pull in the latest online nav-charts. We pay enough for accessing them, so we'll be doing it."

"Yes, ma'am! Have you heard from Merry lately? You've kept in touch ever since Captain Kerrix was spirited away from the *Half Moon* by that admiral and Commander Thal, as he was then. Greffy told me."

"It's time *he* learned to keep his mouth shut as well," Dox retorted.

"I'll tell you later," she added in a conspiratorial whisper.

Ahxenta and Apnis exchanged wry glances. Very little escaped the crew of the *Arianrhod*, it seemed.

"Who else is in?" the first mate asked, eyeing the arrivals update on her board. "No *Warrior*, *Zephyr's* due, but there's *Obsidian*, *Nova Stella* — and the *Kel'Torc*. That's a new one. Starfall, a carrier I guess; I can't see Thal slapping PSS plates on his battlecruisers. He'll want them to keep an eye on the TA, not to hand over fees to it for the honour of flying its flag and making use of its services, including his own bypasses."

"Very funny. But the business of the rest of the day starts here, and I need to talk to Lindell before anything else."

* * *

The *Half Moon* was busy as usual when Ahxenta and Apnis walked in after business. They had left their supercargo in marketing with an old friend, in pre-arranged talks. Azular had set off alone, but planned to join them in time for a quick dinner before their return to the ship.

"Nice to see you back, Captain, Commander," Ally greeted the pair, dredging up two mugs. "We heard of trouble out by. Captain Fleetskup was in and told us about hits on the *Nyx Warrior* and *Moonstone*. *Tallulah* had no problems this bout. He put it down to his command of her and her super spec, but Mr Spickle said they'd just been lucky. Mr Buntle was there. *He's* back to normal," Ally grinned.

"Too bad," Apnis said satirically. "They're not in here now as far as I can see, so they must have other important things to do."

"Don't speak too soon," Ahxenta warned. "Now they know we're in, they won't miss a chance to dig up what's been going on first hand."

"They're not the only ones," groaned Apnis. "I spy Captain Fleete and her first mate, but they're bending two pairs of ears in the corner."

"They're new reps from the TA office," Ally put in. "The office had to expand due to extra work, so I hear, and they drafted in new blood. They'll soon learn who to talk to and who to avoid."

"Extra work? That would be Starfall and the routes the TA aims to take over, as well as the fresh trade it hopes to pick up in Psi," Ahxenta grunted. "And all the new rules and levies it's trying to slap on us."

"You've all signed up to it now, ma'am, so I hear," Ally stated.

"You hear a lot. Have you bugged them or do they talk too much?"

"They like to talk," he admitted. "Especially to PSS officers."

"I wish them joy of Pa Ma'Lappis: he's not slow to give anyone the rough edge of his tongue," Apnis chortled, gesturing to where a few of the *Firedrake's* crewmen, including her captain, were seated.

"You want to eat here, Captain?" Ally continued. "The dinner rush is starting, so you might be better putting your orders in soon."

"Dr Azular's joining us, so we'll wait. Put our orders in as business dinners on my tab. But we'd best find a table, Tallica. A small one: we don't want to encourage company. We'll order at the pad."

"Roger that, Cap. That one?" she suggested. "Good all-round view, plenty far from Maris Fleete, and we'll see Azular when he heaves to. What was he up to that he shot off like a rocket after our meets?"

"We'll no doubt find out," was the ironic response.

"That's Ahxenta and Apnis back, Malty my lad," remarked Jurry to his mate from the depths of their usual wall booth, from where their shrewd eyes had been taking in the action. "In for dinner, by the look of it. *Arianrhod* hasn't been in that long, so they're fast-footed."

"They always are. But there's a few Privates in, so maybe there's a meeting or something?" Malty conjectured.

"Don't be soft, there's always a few Privates in. It's the stop-off for most of 'em when they're not out in the space lanes. Why do you think there's a local TA office? Profit, my lad. Talking of which, these mugs are dry: who can you see that might fill them for us?" Jurry asked.

Malty scanned the *Half Moon's* large, dim interior, his head turning slowly, like an old hunter scenting game. "Hmm, not many. In fact, not one. It'll have to be Ally and he'll charge us."

"Hold a bit, Malty: that's *Tallulah's* new senior science officer, out of Milkit Major and green, by all accounts," Jurry observed.

"And on her own! Why Fleetskup picks them straight out of the academy beats me. How do they know about life aboard a starship?"

"They've all been through compulsory military service, same as us," his friend told him. "I could still handle a shuttle if I tried. She's a cheap option as far as credit goes, she'll have good credentials and she won't know the *Tallulah* or her captain well enough to know that she should steer well clear. Once she's figured it, she'll be off, just like Yellowfork. *He* did a bunk to the *Emerald* with a handful of Fleetskup's crew when Ahxenta set her up as a going concern. Fleetskup's still sore over it."

"Hand over your mug and I'll go and introduce myself."

Malty was back in minutes, two small mugs of ale in his hands and a deep flush on his face. "For an attractive young lady, she has a tongue that'd flay a squad of scrapyard scavengers. She was waiting for a friend anyway – and he's the *Tallulah's* new chief medic, Dr Steen."

"So I see. Better luck next time," Jurry soothed. "There's Dr Azular, heading for the captain's table. He doesn't look over-happy, but that'll be because that Captain Kerrix isn't about. *They're* still an item."

"Maybe it's the two at his back: Fleetskup and his best pal Tommy

Buntle. I see they've lost Juke Spickle, or maybe he lost them," Malty grinned. "They've spotted Ahxenta and Apnis. Though *they're* hard to miss: the whole place spotted them the second they walked in."

Azular had been quick to spy his colleagues and as rapid in excusing himself to the duo at his tail. He strode over and was invited to sit.

"How long have those two been bending your ears?" the captain asked as she began tabbing her order into the menu pad.

"I met them in the transport tube on the way up from green nine, ma'am, so not long. They'd come from their shuttle."

"And what were you doing on green nine?" Apnis probed. "There's not much there but shuttle bays, company offices, dorms and bars. And that big market that seems to be open all hours."

Azular cleared his throat, flushing slightly. "It was a private matter, Commander, and with respect, none of your concern."

"But aren't you still on duty, Dr Azular?"

"Can it, Tallica, and order your dinners, both," the captain directed. "Here they come and I bet they choose that empty table next to this."

Ahxenta was right and the two sat down. Captain Fleetskup leaned over at once to greet the officers. He would be in the Web a few more days, he explained, as the cargo he was due to load had been delayed. Spickle was aboard expediting matters, and his supercargo was in a late marketing meeting, setting up a new long-term contract.

Ahxenta gave him free rein to talk until their meals arrived and then excused herself as she had urgent matters to discuss. She set privacy, with a promise to chat later. As she unpacked her cutlery, she took in her science officer's face. The irritated look that Apnis' question had caused had gone and he seemed quietly content, but there was an edge of wariness, as if he expected more chaff. He was justified, for the three had no sooner begun to eat than the first mate returned to the chase.

"We'll find out what you were up to in the end, so you may as well tell us, Azular. What *were* you doing that you raced off the second our meet was done? It didn't take long, so it can't have been difficult."

He eyed her crossly. "I said it was a private matter, Commander, and there is no reason for you to concern yourself in it."

The ensuing silence lasted several minutes, until a noise at the entry heralded the arrival of a group of *Arianrhod's* crewmen. They collected drinks, found a table, and sat. The captain nodded over.

"They got here, then," the first mate laughed. "Box was first in with his leave request as usual, and he must've been able to persuade Greffy. I couldn't deny them, they were due the time. But what's Box nudging him about and looking at you for, Azular? Dox is trying to shut him up. She'll have that mug over his head if he's not careful."

The science officer exhaled sharply and exchanged a glance with his captain, who was watching the scene with an amused gaze.

"You'd best tell her, Azular. She won't give up, and if Box *is* in the know, it'll be all over the ship before we leave. *Is* Box in the know?"

"Lieutenants Box, Dox *and* Greffy were in the green nine market at the same time as I was, and I've no doubt they have *some* clue as to my business, though I was in a secure booth," he sighed.

"So what *was* your business there?" Apnis asked slyly.

"If you must know, Commander, I was buying a gift for Captain Kerrix, and a couple of other items."

"Is that all? So why the cloak and dagger? What did you buy?"

"A piece of jewellery. Why is it anyone's concern but mine? It *was* to be a surprise, but that's probably shot," he snapped, peeved.

"I can't imagine she's the sort that wears a lot of trinkets," the first mate remarked. "They don't go with the uniform for a start."

It was Ahxenta's sly tapping of the back of one of her own fingers that gave Apnis the clue. "Aha! An engagement ring! It was to be a surprise? Then a ring's not a custom of her people?"

"Not the Norvallans. For people of her rank, betrothal includes a legal exchange of assets, a visible exchange of costly symbols and a big festivity, none of which she approves. The Telziltic consider a promise as sufficient and binding, and Xanna favours that approach."

"Wise woman. What were the other items you mentioned?"

"Leave it, Tallica," the captain advised. "You've had enough fun at his expense. Eat up, we have things to do aboard. We're not on shore leave and I want to check what Lindell's arranged by way of trade. Our next trip may be a long one, so we'd best plan for a big resupply."

"I hate to point this out, Cinnabar, but Murmur Fleetskup and his pet minder are still there. You promised a heart-to-heart."

"I didn't say when, so he can wait," was the caustic response. "I'll let Lindell know we're heading to green twelve. He can meet us there."

Ahxenta called her supercargo and then had a quick word with the eager Fleetskup before settling her tab and heading out, her officers in tow, for their shuttle. Lindell was there, having fruitfully finalised talks with his friend, he told the captain. Apnis, nose twitching, was given no clue and once aboard, Ahxenta took the helm for the trip home.

Back on ship the first mate was ordered to the bridge, as the captain was going with Lindell to his office to check the latest deals. "I'll need to call you in, Azular, if Jute's made progress on the jobs left with her."

"Aye, ma'am; I'll be in my lab," he replied, turning for the exit.

"Off to hide the goods in case we rag him," Apnis observed to the other two, to Lindell's puzzlement. "I'll see *you* later, Cap."

"I'll call a senior briefing once things are settled, but I'll bring you in beforehand," Ahxenta told her. "Hold off on the Ottolyx cargo for now: we may need hold space in the outer bays for another big load."

"Aye, ma'am; I'll see which of our supplies are ready to ship in. It'll be tricky if all our suppliers want to send our stuff up at the same time."

"I'm sure you'll cope," the captain told her. "Let's go, Lindell."

* * *

The first mate had to wait for the story until the ship had settled into the dark watch and she and the captain were taking their usual nightcap in the mess. They had been reviewing the day's business and mapping out next day's when Ahxenta began. A Redship friend of Lindell had told him some time ago that his company had begun a new product line: high-grade agricultural gear. Its first orders were now ready, and as *Arianrhod* and her like were amongst the largest carriers, they were an obvious choice. Lindell had heard of a contract that might suit them and had brought it to the captain. She had given the go-ahead.

"It's for Wester 287," Ahxenta told her first mate.

"Wester? The far end of zone Mu and off most beaten tracks."

"Exactly. The Westies are a recent colony and still import food, but Wester's fertile, with a lot of land it can put under crop. The authorities want to switch to high output, and export the excess. It's isolated, but there are markets in the local group and they can get their produce to distant centres via the Mu double bypass. It's worth importing the gear from here: it's top-notch and the price is competitive, as Redship wants to establish its rep as a producer of agro gear. And the fees are decent."

"All very well, Cap, but that'll take us to system edge and... close to Starfall! Is that why you wanted Azular in? Bet it put a smile on his face. Was that part of his reason for that trip to the green nine market?"

"No, it damn well wasn't! He was called in for another reason. You know that Perla Jute found out that the ISA wants ready supplies of jurillium-protected crystal arrays for their new boats' comms?"

"And your buddy on Freskat can produce them if we can find the bits. We can pick up premium crystals at Brown Amber, not that we'll be anywhere near there, but gem-grade jurillium? That's asking a lot."

"That's where Azular came in. There's a source of quality gems not far off route. We're for Yistreen via Keystone to Wester, so we cross Kappa and take a minor cut into Eta for Xerophyte IV. I've not dealt with its mining outfits, but Lindell can sound out his pals for contacts. Xerophyte gem quality *is* a byword, but Azular can test the goods."

"Doesn't help us with the jurillium," Apnis pointed out.

"Azular again: there's a fairly small but quality meta-jurillium source on Kirtish that the Starfall fleet use for their shipbuilding needs. And it *does* supply gem-grade meta-jurillium, ready-processed."

"We're not heading to Kirtish!" Apnis interjected in surprise.

"No. But Thal's people trade in Kirtish; Azular will ask Kerrix to persuade him to bring a shipment into Starfall for us."

"Starfall!"

"Keep your voice down, Tallica. Yes, Starfall. We may not have to make in there, but we'll see."

"Xerophyte and Kirtish were Azular's idea, weren't they? Once he knew that the ISA needed the stuff, he started to dig. And thought he'd organise his personal life, just in case, and splashed out on the ring… and another couple of items. What items? You know, don't you?"

"I can guess. But it's his business, not mine."

"They wouldn't be the rings to go with the engagement ring, would they?" Apnis asked askance. "The Norvallans and Telziltic may not go in for rings but the Berzic do. Is he planning a wedding?"

"You'll have to ask him. But no word of this, Tallica. It *is* his private life and he's had to put up with a lot of ribbing for the past while."

"He enjoys it, Cap, whatever he puts about otherwise. He's been a very happy bunny since his precious Kerrix came into his life."

"Captain Kerrix, and don't you forget it."

"I'll try not to. Talking of which, I see from your log that you've a meet with Dr Ma'Lappis tomorrow. As the *Firedrake's* in and she's not put in for leave, what's going on? Are we going to lose a medic?"

"I am not second-guessing my crew, Commander Apnis. And as it's been a long day, I'm going for a run and then I'm hitting the sack. And I suggest you get some sleep. We've plenty to do in the morning."

* * *

Plenty to do was understatement and both command officers saw the prospects of shore leave receding. The captain elected to stay on board for the duration, feeling that her senior officers were entitled to leave, and once the set briefing was over, she ordered most of them off.

"Axellina headed down with Flish Ma'Lappis and they were toting big kitbags," the first mate remarked later. "What's in the wind?"

"There's a conference on the latest gear and surgical methods in the main medbay that they're attending. CMOs from other fleet ships will be there. *Obsidian's* Enaid Gunn for one – Grey told me when we last spoke. And Ashet from the *Firedrake* and Steen from the *Tallulah*. As for the kit, there's likely to be a dinner, so they'll need a change."

"And the band played believe it if you like," retorted Apnis. "We'd best get on with the necessary here, since half our crew's down there."

"We have gaps between the Silversnow, Ottolyx and Redship loads, so we can work around it, unless Lindell pulls in any more deals."

"He's supposed to be on shore leave. And where *is* Azular? Having yet another chat with Captain Kerrix?"

"He's checking up on Xerophytic mining firms and products. After our last trip there, I don't trust many from that neck of the woods."

"You could get him to talk to chief tactical officer Wekki Munnet of the *Tallulah*. Wasn't she once a native of those parts?"

"Don't push it. And anyway, he's already suggested it. I've left it up to him, but I've had Fleetskup asking when we'll be in the *Half Moon*. He spends more time ashore than he does on board, that man."

* * *

The daily round aboard the great ship when in port continued until the third day, when a lull allowed the two senior officers a trip to the *Half Moon* for a quick lunch and an earful of idle chatter from the *Tallulah's* captain. They could stay only a short time, Ahxenta told him, as they had a task that required both of them aboard. The puzzled Apnis said nothing, but the captain's wily smile suggested something on the cards.

"What *is* the deal, Cap?" Apnis asked back at the *Gadfly*. "Why leave me with Fleetskup when you slid off and came back with that packet?"

"Wait and see. But don't worry, we're not right back on duty. We've enough seniors to look after the bridge for a few hours."

"A few hours? Now you've got me worried."

The first mate had to wait until the two were settled in the captain's office for a quiet chat. "Don't get too comfortable in that seat, Tallica," Ahxenta told her. "You have an hour to get ready."

"For what?"

"To sort yourself out and get your dress uniform on: we're headed to the *Firedrake* for a little party, and the *Gadfly's* standing by."

"What!"

The little party, as Apnis had guessed, was to mark the marriage of Dr Felicity Ma'Lappis to Commander Felipe Poppet. The service was quiet, for close friends and associates, as the *Firedrake* had recently lost five crew, one of whom was Flish's brother. Dr Flintlock was the only other one there from *Arianrhod*, and would fly back with the captain.

Ahxenta's reason for the packet was a surprise for her young medic, and only Apnis, Flintlock and Captain Ma'Lappis had been told. At the end of formalities, Ahxenta was called on. The essence of her talk was the presentation to Dr Ma'Lappis of a set of stat bars, with the news that she had been promoted to Lieutenant Commander and given a secondment to the *Firedrake* for one duty tour as a bonus. She would re-join *Arianrhod* at the next suitable opportunity. Meantime, she would serve as a medic aboard her father's ship.

"You know how to drop a bombshell, Cinnabar," Apnis laughed when the *Arianrhod* trio were aboard their shuttle. "And now that Flish is promoted, there won't be an opening on the *Firedrake* for her."

"No comment. But she deserves it. She's been with me for years, she's a top-notch medic and Axellina backed it. There isn't the same opportunity in the PSS fleet for promotion as in a military fleet, unless you head out to a new berth – or there's a war on."

"Now that many of the Starfall fleet are on the PSS register, that might change. Thal seems to have plenty of ships low on personnel."

"Stow it, Tallica. But I'll be glad to get back aboard. It's been a tiring day. Let's hope tomorrow will be easier."

"Who you kidding? The Redship ops are on standby to start shifting the first part of those two loads up, and they're huge."

The *Gadfly* made a swift return and was left to the hangar crew to check and lock down, for on the way up the captain had been advised that a link had come in for her from Captain Kerrix, who wanted an urgent word. Kerrix would be available whatever the hour.

"I'd best see what it is she thinks is so urgent. I'll take it in my office. You two head to the mess and I'll join you there for a nightcap."

"Roger that, Cap. But first I'm ditching the jacket," Apnis told her.

* * *

An hour later and with no sign of the captain, Apnis turned worried eyes on Flintlock. "Cap's not answering her wrist comm or office link. The duty officer reckons she's still *in* her office, but the link to Starfall's been cut for half an hour. Something's up. I'm going to check."

"I'll come with you. Best use the outer passage door, we don't want to alert the bridge crew. She's maybe fallen asleep: it's been a long day."

"I don't believe that and neither do you. Let's go."

The two trod the quiet decks of the huge ship and made their way to level one and the entry to the captain's bridge office. The occupied sign was lit but a discreet buzz produced no reply. Apnis hit the access panel and quickly stepped inside, to see the great Cinnabar Ahxenta, her head in her hands, staring down at a flickering info-pad.

12: BOOM

The captain's dress jacket was draped over a chair and her shirt blouse was disordered, as if she had torn it open at the neck. The view grid that linked into the comm relay for incoming and outgoing calls was empty. She had received data and sent it to a shard that slotted into the projector port of her desk viewer, Apnis surmised, as the data port was active. The viewer was dark, so she must have closed the record. What was on the captain's personal info-pad the first mate could not see, as Ahxenta had quickly flicked it off. Flintlock and Apnis traded anxious glances as they walked over, the doctor digging out a medi-scanner that was always part of her kit. The harsh injunction to go to hell affected neither. The first mate put an arm round the captain's shoulder. She had never seen her so affected before.

"What is it, Cinnabar, what's happened?"

"Leave me be; I'm fine."

"I'll be the judge of that," Flintlock said firmly but gently.

A rapid scan later and the doctor nodded, satisfied. "The news from Captain Kerrix, then. What's wrong, Cinnabar? Something at Starfall?"

The answer was a shake of the head as the captain gave a shuddering sigh and straightened. "Sit down," she said gruffly, turning her chair to them. "Some of it will get out, and you two know part of it anyway. You remember the cryo-tubes from Furze that Thal's people lifted?"

"He was hoping that they were the kids missing of the fifteen that had been stolen," the doctor said. "But they weren't."

"No. He didn't say much after I spoke to him about the *Steadfast* and told him that one of his ships had been spied at Furze, but he *did* say he aimed to revive the humans in the tubes if he could do it safely, as there were serious implications. He asked Kerrix to update me. They found more. He was advised not to revive them. Medics drafted in from the *Serenity* had worked out that a few *were* alive but in such a bad way that revival was liable to kill them. They weren't quite whole. They were of various origins, and had had things done to them. Organs, bio-materials from other humans, had been grafted or implanted, some of their own removed; and they had cyber implants, probably to ensure compliance with what had been planned for them."

Apnis made a face. "That's gruesome! But what else, Cap?"

"They tried to get IDs on the victims using extracted tissue samples to check bio-markers. Thal didn't have access to relevant data, but he asked Levettiza. As ex-Intelligence, she has contacts *and* database links that most don't. She dug around, and asked an ex-colleague for help. She had to tell him part of the story, but Intelligence *is* a closed shop. She persuaded him to dig into past fleet records. He'd to go way back for details, and use a lot sources, as the medics had worked out that the victims had been in the tubes a long time, years in fact."

"And they got some IDs?" Flintlock asked as the captain paused.

"Only a few and much of it came from military academy archives. Everybody going through compulsory military training, which is most of us, have bio-records. The data's meant to have a finite shelf life and the record's patchy: some places set more store than others on privacy. And many records are untraceable, as after training, most people head into civilian life and stay there. But there were a couple that linked to planetary fleets, and one or two that needed more digging into other databases to turn up answers. One led to the *PSS Bright Mist...*"

"Oh hell, not one of Nat's?" breathed Apnis.

Ahxenta shook her head. "No, an officer listed as a senior engineer. No Holdspan was linked to any sample, intact or part, but Nat will be told what *has* been found – he has a right to know."

"But?" Apnis asked, sensing more. "Something's got you rattled, Cinnabar, and… I don't want to pry, but – personal?"

"One record came up that matched the captain of a PSS lost years before the *Bright Mist*, in the same area, near Peart. Nothing of the ship or anything related to her was ever found. The incident was blamed on raiders. She was an early *Vanguard* class trader called the *Wing Skipper*."

"I don't recall the name," Apnis stated, eyeing the captain closely. "But then I'd not heard of the *Bright Mist* either until Captain Kerrix told us of her, in relation to the bogus *Pearl Shield*."

Ahxenta turned the info-pad she had been nursing towards the first mate, flicking the holo on. It was of a huge trading ship, similar to the current *Vanguard* ships in shape. Apnis took the pad and extended the holo, scrolling past the ship's spec and insignia to reach the standard record of her command staff. She halted, stunned.

"Oh hell, Cinnabar! Oh, Cinnabar, I am *so* sorry…"

Flintlock leaned over to see and read the entry. "Current Command Staff: Captain Reder Ahxenta, Commander Kelva Ocean. Reder was your father, I take it," she said softly. "And Commander Ocean?"

The captain nodded. "Yes, he was. Kelva Ocean wasn't a relation, though I called her Aunt Kelly. She'd been booted out of ISP service on a spurious charge she didn't bother to fight. My Pa took her on, as she was a known quantity and a damn good officer."

"A known quantity?" the first mate repeated.

"A friend of his wife's. *She* served aboard the *Wing Skipper*. She was his senior science officer and very adept, as far as I remember."

"Your mother," Apnis deduced.

"Yup. So now I know." She smiled crookedly. "I need a drink."

"Kerrix told you. So now *she* knows."

"She knows. She was very… understanding," Ahxenta sighed. "She had a few other things to tell me. I was pretty cool with her."

Flintlock had taken the info-pad and was flipping through the short list. "Senior science officer, Dr Merretissa, lieutenant commander," she said delicately. "A Berzic name. You said that *one* bio-record came up that matched the captain of the *Wing Skipper* – any other matches?"

"No, that was the only one. One's enough," she added grimly. "And it was linked to a tissue sample, not a body."

"We'll get you that drink," the doctor told her. "But we'll head to medbay. I have a private supply, for medicinal purposes. There may be one or two night birds hanging around the mess."

"Helluva way to end what was meant to be a happy day, Cinnabar," Apnis remarked with a sigh. "What can we do to help?"

"Keep your mouths shut," was the testy reply.

"Azular…"

"Will not be told, at least not yet. Kerrix and Levettiza will keep it quiet or I'll have their ears. But part of the story *will* be filtered through to the ISA. It seems a stash of life-tubes was found a couple of months ago on Skota, on the Epsilon-Zeta border, by an ISA patrol ship sent in after the report we and Nat Holdspan despatched after the *Warrior's* run-in with hostiles near Swan Two. The ISA ordered a lid on it."

"When we jumped in," the first mate recalled. "Any idea what was in the life-pods the ISA ship found?"

"No and I don't want to know. I know too much already," Ahxenta told her. "I'll take that drink, doctor. But no word of this to anyone. The past is the past and there's naught to be done about it."

"Except deal with the aftermath," the first mate said as she retrieved Ahxenta's jacket and handed it over. "You want to talk, Cinnabar, you know we'll listen. Let's go."

The captain had no intention of talking but medbay was quiet, the chief MO's office peaceful, and after a tot or two of medicinal spirit, it was a relief to shed the load of years of lack of knowledge. After the

Wing Skipper had officially been declared lost, Ahxenta and her brother Rede found that they had been left well provided for. The plain, solid family house on Freskat remained their home until military service and an engineering career took Rede to Stella Marina and then to Limekiln, with his partner Jo and their son.

The captain, then in school, spent most of her free time in searching for answers and in hard training in a local cadet corps drill centre. Her main aim at that time had been to find a way of paying the raiders back for what they had done to her family. Her brother's and Jo's deaths at the hands of raiders had reinforced her resolve. It had also left her with a young nephew to rear. Her enforced military service was hard to bear, as the authorities refused to cancel or let her postpone her warrant to allow her time with the only family she had left.

"Hard times," she admitted. "But I got through it."

"Was that why you didn't go military as a long-term career option, Cinnabar?" asked Apnis. "The fleet's got no heart. But you must have gone through the ranks to get your captain's commission at least, or did you join the merchant service?"

"I stuck with the fleet," she disclosed. "With the system squabbles in Delta zone and increasing raider activity close to home, the fleet sent out a lot of ships and needed crews. There's more scope for command on the smaller corvettes and patrol ships, and I was driven."

"You still are," Flintlock observed. "Just like Nat Holdspan. But you didn't have enough to set you up with the *Arianrhod*, surely?"

"Not quite. But I got there. And now I'm here," she smiled at them. "Thanks for the ears. And the drinks, Doc."

"And nobody else knows?" the first mate asked tactfully. "Azular must know some of it: he has the longest service record of anyone else aboard *Arianrhod*, apart from you."

"He came with me from my first ship; she was a Freskat trader, the *Molly Star*, big and well-armed, but not on the PSS register – I couldn't afford the fees then, nor the levies the TA charged. Azular had been a fleet science officer; he was as disillusioned as I was. I met him when I was given command of a patrol runabout, the *ISPS Rue Twelve*. There was little hope of a step up in rank for most of the crew, or of a move to a bigger ship for me, unless I resigned my commission. So I did. I'd got hold of the *Molly*, as she was up for refit and resale. I didn't need a science officer, but Azular signed on as tactical officer and assistant supercargo. I rigged him a step up in rank. I'd gauged his skills by then. I knew he wasn't happy on the *Rue* and that he'd find it tough getting out of the service or promoted: his personnel record had a disciplinary attached. And I'd a few trusted contacts I could call on for more crew."

"And Azular could suss them out as good or bad bets," the doctor put in. "I'm not surprised about the disciplinary; he goes his own way now and then. In fact, most of the time. You didn't tell him what had happened to your folks or how you got to be where you were?"

"None of his business. It was my burden and I wasn't about to put it on anyone else… or at least, there was one friend from fleet academy that knew much of it, but he's kept it close for years."

"Grey Bluejohn," Apnis said. "I'd guess he's gone through similar."

"And that's why you're my first mate: sharp, smart, and not slow to use your tongue when you have to," Ahxenta smiled, with a return to her usual irony. "And now I'm heading to the sack. Tomorrow we start bringing in the Redship loads, and we'll have to be on our toes."

* * *

The next day ran as expected and the ship was still buzzing hours later, at the close of business hours. The Wester freight had been loaded and locked; another day would see the second Redship cargo moved into place. The captain and first mate were obliged to use the break to head down to the *Half Moon* for an evening sortie, on the instructions of the chief medic. Flintlock had also tried to persuade Azular down, but he had business of his own aboard and refused.

"Thought you were going to duck out, Cap," Apnis greeted her in the small docking bay that held their shuttle.

"I linked Kerrix to see how things were her end, and to find out if more had been found. And to apologise for my shortness yesterday."

"I'm sure she didn't take it personally. *Was* there more?" she asked in barely a whisper, although the bay was empty bar themselves.

"Nothing more about the contents of the life-tubes. I got the feeling that Thal's been let down by it all. He'd hoped there'd be good news for his people and… well, it was what it was. His people are going over the tubes and attached tech: there's something else causing worry, but I don't know what. Kerrix had to deal with the transfer of her late crew to the *Serenity*, so she wasn't happy. And the internment of the others. Not a good time at Starfall."

"At least she's safe there. Azular will be pleased. I guess that's why he wouldn't be coerced by the doc into coming with us."

"I guess; but let's head down. Flintlock's probably keeping tabs on us from medbay."

The *Half Moon*, when the two made it, was lively. Ally was not to be seen, but one of his ex-staff was leaning on the bar: chief tactical officer of the *PSS Tallulah*, Lieutenant Commander Wekki Munnet.

"It's a change for you to be this side, Commander," Ahxenta said to her. "Your captain's busy, I take it?"

"My captain, Commander Spickle and supercargo Skillet are in the *Subspace Diner* talking business with a rep," was her dry reply.

"What, no Mr Buntle?"

"Mr Buntle's in the brig."

"You *are* joking!" Tallica Apnis cut in.

"I'm not: Mr Spickle found out he'd tried to cream a percentage off one of the deals we have on the table, brought it to the captain's notice and locked Buntle up before he could argue or the captain intervene. Buntle will talk his way out of it, but it'll put the scuppers on his antics for a while and the disciplinary *will* go on his record."

"Spickle's turning into an efficient first mate," Ahxenta observed. "Captain Bluejohn rated him as a skilled tactical officer and reckoned he'd make a good commander one day. Seems he was right."

"He's finding his feet," Munnet agreed. "The crew's taken to him and discipline's a lesser problem than it was. Can I buy you a drink, Captain, Commander? If I can find anybody to serve us."

The two accepted and Munnet collared a passing waiter.

"Ally's in back sorting stores," Jez said, inserting himself behind the bar to pour their drinks. "They were late. And one of our new staff's not here. She's late and he's annoyed, but it can't be helped."

Ally appeared moments later, to vent his ire on a panting girl who had run in. "What time d'you call this? You were due ten minutes ago!"

"It wasn't my fault! Half the local transport tubes are down. There's been an explosion outside a shuttle bay on green twelve and it's taken out a tube control unit; place looks like an overturned ants' nest. Isn't it up on the internal channel monitor yet?" she asked.

"I haven't had time to look," was Ally's tetchy retort as the officers looked at one another and then at a holo-grid behind the bar that was usually set to the latest Web-side news.

"Get on!" he snapped at the girl, turning to activate the blank grid.

"I'll check in with tactical," Apnis said, flicking up her communit. "They can link to our shuttle from the bridge and get a signal on her."

"You can read her from your bridge?" Munnet asked. "Your tech must be top-notch. I'm impressed."

Ahxenta's only reply was a raised eyebrow as her first mate snapped off her comm to say that their shuttle read normal. The grid was giving the latest, and the two from *Arianrhod* were relieved to see that the blast was well away from where their craft was docked.

"Maybe we're off the usual round of hits lists, Cap," Apnis drawled.

"The local hooligans have found somebody else to pick on."

"They're saying it's a system fault and there are no casualties," noted Munnet. "Too quick a diagnosis. That's the third in as many days that's caused explosive disruption and they've all been in inner two."

"I hadn't heard," the captain remarked.

"Sections thirty eight through forty two of the lighting grid on green ten went down yesterday due to a massive short. It blew out the system but the backup kicked in. One of our shuttles was berthed in a nearby bay but wasn't affected. A volatile discharge in an industrial unit near the blue five tube terminal was blamed on a botched repair job, but the bang was heard over two levels. No casualties in any, just disruption."

"And you reckon it's a put up job?" Apnis asked her.

"I don't reckon anything, it's not my job. But if I worked for Merkat security, I'd be suspicious," Munnet replied.

"Not our problem," the captain said, lifting her drink. "Any other crime outbreaks we've missed, Ally?" she asked the barman.

"One or two, ma'am. Mainly petty theft and punch ups in the wilder sections. But the *Port in a Storm* had a fancy mirror behind the main bar shot to flak by a gun-toting drunk from Seedly, one of the ropier patch-up yards. Just after you made port. But this *will* interest you Captain, now I think of it. He'd got given his notice for using a false ID to get the job, and for sabotaging a couple of the tatty runabouts they fix up. My partner got it from a mate that knows a hand in the yard. He'd only been there a few months; he'd gone for a job in the main repair sheds, but failed the interview for Guild membership. The fake ID was caught when he applied again later. The Guild told his boss and he was sacked. His mates took him out for a send-off. Seems he was popular as he paid for rounds, but some say it was because you'd cop a broken nose or worse if you crossed him, as he'd a nasty temper and hard fists. And *that* was because he was more metal than bone. Turned out he'd got cyber implants, and real high-class jobs at that."

"How did you find that out, Ally?" Apnis wanted to know.

"Two off-duty security bods that drink here," he whispered. "They were narked as two of their mates came off badly in the scrap with him when they arrested him after the shooting. One of them compared him to a real hard-nose they had in high security ages ago, the one sent off in a prisoner transport that vanished and was never seen again. The one arrested with that senior medic from medbay, who escaped…"

"What!" Ahxenta exclaimed. "Are you sure?"

"That's what they said, Captain. Their two guys that were punched about suffered severe injury. The bastard's still in the cells, as he's been charged with resisting arrest *and* serious assault. But they said he was like that other guy, though they said not as smart or dangerous. *That* guy was the one that shot Dr Azular, wasn't he?"

Apnis let out a long breath. "Bloody hell, Cap! We knew that Hoxiz, or Berg Brack as he was called when he was got for your and Azular's attempted murders, wasn't one of a kind, he had clones, but still…"

"I'd rather you didn't spread this around, Ally," Ahxenta said. "Let's have a seat, it's been a tiring day. You'll join us, Commander Munnet?"

"Of course."

"Three on my tab, Ally, over there," Ahxenta pointed.

The trio made their way to a wall table and sat down. They were the focus of several pairs of eyes as the haze of the privacy shield grew and they began to talk, halting only to allow Ally to set down the mugs.

"Never fails, Malty," Jurry muttered to his drinking chum minutes later. "Ahxenta heaves to, Fleetskup and his train trot up behind. He'll be as welcome as a headache, though I see Tallulah Tommy's not there. What d'you think Ahxenta and Apnis are yapping to that Ms Munnet about? *She's* a dark horse: used to be one of Ally's hired helps and then joins the *Tallulah* as a lieutenant commander and chief tactical officer, now that Juke Spickle's first mate. Like that Kerrix: *she* turns out to be an alien ship's captain with a title; and now she's in command of a PSS, and a rum one at that. Ally knows how to pick them."

"Aye, that Munnet's another story. It pays to drink in the *Half Moon*, Jurry, lad. If we could get to the bottom of *her* tale, we could dine out on it for weeks. We may, if we can corner one of the *Tallulah's* newer hands. But not that Dr whatever it is, the senior science officer," Malty reflected. "Kirri Scumble, isn't it, she of the flip mouth. And she's only a lieutenant. If that Dr Steen is keen on her, he'll have his hands full."

"His ears, you mean," Jurry corrected.

The *Tallulah's* captain spotted Ahxenta and Apnis with his tactical chief, and waved over, miming an offer of drinks. The three refused with smiles and head shaking, although the language behind the privacy shield's haze was fruity. In minutes, Fleetskup, Spickle and Skillet had stepped up to their table. The captain slipped into a chair.

"Do sit, Murmur, you and your crewmen," Ahxenta invited with irony. "How are things aboard *Tallulah*?"

Things were going well, he claimed. He and his team had been in a late meeting that had resulted in a new contract. That and other trade would take them away from the Web, once the details were arranged.

"No Mr Buntle?" Apnis asked disarmingly. "He's usually in on trade meetings, isn't he?"

"He's back aboard," was the quick reply. "He's indisposed."

"Nothing serious, I hope? As your exec, I know you rely on him."

"He'll be fine, Commander," Fleetskup replied a shade too quickly, before turning the talk to their last trip out and the formal protest that Ahxenta had sent out on the attempt by the *ISAS Steadfast* to track her ship, as well as the *Tallulah's* input to fleet safety in terms of the alert issued on the sighting of the alleged hostile off Sevolb.

* * *

Arianrhod's shuttle was as Ahxenta and Apnis had left her and the berth and its vicinity were clear. The captain had made sure by scanning every micron of their route from the *Half Moon*. There was no sign of trouble on green twelve and the local transport tube network was operational. Security and maintenance people could be seen poking into regulator units and peering down hatches, but that was all.

The two had left Munnet with Fleetskup, their talk half-done. They had food for thought. Ahxenta had brought up the reliability of mining firms on Xerophyte, and the quality of their goods. She had been given names, and a promise of more. The presence of a possible hostile agent in a Web repair shed was disturbing, and Munnet agreed to pass word on. Ahxenta had no mind to contact security over the issue, as she did not want her actions to be noted or reported to the wrong people.

"Munnet's still working for Intelligence in some role, she must be," Apnis declared. "She wanted details on the *Moonstone* that you wouldn't give, but you'd think she could get them from Levettiza. D'you think it was wise to tell her we'd found out that Myrtleberry had a fancy new ride and was set to join the *Repulse* and the *Advance* on their travels into unmapped space beyond Alpha, Cap?"

"I'm sure she knew. She certainly knew we still had the probe the *Steadfast* set on our tail. And as for Levettiza, *she* has Intelligence links, but for whatever reasons, *her* loyalty is to her ship and her captain."

"And talking of Myrtleberry and her ISA chums out by Alpha: Thal has at least two bypasses out there and a station, Nexus, isn't it? I guess he's warned it, but will he send in warships to reinforce the peace? If he has any spare, that is. And what's keeping him and the *Kel'Moth* at Starfall? She's a trading ship and a huge one at that, bigger than we are, so why isn't she out trading?" Apnis asked. "It can't all be down to protecting what he sees as his borders off Zeta and Mu in case the ISA sends in another warship to keep an eye on him."

"He's up to something that needs his ship at Starfall," surmised the captain. "It *is* the base that's closest to Psi and I bet the ISA and TA are trying to up the ante in establishing local presences. We'll find out soon enough. But let's get home. I'll have to find Azular and pass on the details of the Xerophyte companies."

"Xerophyte for gems is go, then? What about the jurillium? Have we heard any more about a source on Kirtish?"

"No; Azular hasn't got back to me and as Kerrix is up to her ears with other things at Starfall, I imagine he hasn't raised the subject."

"I expect so. Want me to take her up, Cap? You've had a long day and it'll be longer still once we're back aboard, if you're planning a chat to Azular about Munnet's data."

"There's no need to mollycoddle me, Tallica. I *am* coping."

"Cinnabar, you don't get over a shock like that in a day, however you try to pretend otherwise. And if I can see what the score is, you can bet you last credit that Azular will. You'll have to let him in on it. I know Kerrix won't say a word, but..."

"Huh! You're not slow at butting in, are you? And yes, I've been thinking about it, and he has more nous than I do when it comes to data searching and analysis; and other issues might come up."

"Other issues?"

Ahxenta turned to face her. "I'm not giving you all the details, but I had to put a link in to Grey late last night, after our stop in medbay. I asked him to get back to me when he could, on a personal matter. I wasn't about to wake him up at that hour, as I know the *Obsidian Sky's* in the middle of loading, as we are, and he's had his hands full aboard."

"And he called back right away?" Apnis guessed.

"He did. You were spot on when you guessed he'd had to deal with a similar loss. His father was the owner and captain of a *Vanguard* class trader called the *Obsidian*, out of Arrissia, that flew under the TA flag. She was lost, allegedly to raiders, near the Enigma Nebula, on a trip to Canna. She'd got out a distress, but no remains of ship or crew were ever recovered. It was just before Grey was assigned to the Point Freen military academy in Delta, at the same time as me. They wouldn't give him time out on compassionate grounds either."

"Point Freen? Both far away from home then," Apnis observed.

"Yup. After basic training we were assigned to different fleet ships, but we kept in touch. Grey has family on Arrissia still, but not close."

"You called him on a personal issue? What else did Levettiza pick up on her trawl through records? A link to the *Obsidian*? You did say that Kerrix had other things to tell you."

"You're smart. Yes, and again a bio-sample, not a body. It matched the record of a Ferry Izland, first mate of the missing *PSS Obsidian*. As she was lost near the Enigma and the other two ships by Astrella Nine, it looks like the early hostiles *did* have bypass links that could get them across the mapped galaxy – which is why they were so successful when first they jumped out on their rampage."

Apnis looked uneasy. "So nobody was safe from them, even though we didn't know it at the time. I'll take her up, Cinnabar. I need practice and we've both had more information than we're comfortable with."

The shuttle made the short trip swiftly, to be met with the news that the *Nyx Warrior* had docked. Ahxenta had called Azular to tell him she wanted a chat. He stepped down from the raised obs platform as soon as the bay had repressurised, and met the pair at the entry.

"You didn't have to come all the way over, Azular. I'm capable of finding your office."

"I was checking up on the *Xanna*, Captain, so I thought I might as well wait," he said. "And I had some news that Captain Kerrix thought you'd want to hear sooner rather than later. It's about the ops systems of the life-tubes from Furze Four, and their contents."

"My office," the captain decreed. "Your day stops here, Tallica. I'll maybe see you in the mess later. If not, enjoy the rest of your night. I've a feeling I might not enjoy mine."

"See you later, Cap," the first mate acknowledged.

"The life-tubes' systems?" Ahxenta asked when once in the cross-ship transport tube. "A technical issue with them?"

"Yes, ma'am. Captain Kerrix sent me part of the data, at Captain Thal's request."

"He had his people going over their specifics, as he had concerns. They've found something that's got them rattled?"

The details Azular kept until they made the office. The inert humans in the tubes not only had cyber implants to force compliance, they had *live* trackers. Thal's engineers and the *Serenity's* medics had blocked the signals and excised the units for study. The life-tubes were trackable, but that tech was already disabled. However, other elements in place were more sinister: fixed micro-drones akin to limpet drones that could detach and then reattach to other types of tech to cause disruption, and could remain viable indefinitely. Luckily, one of Thal's people working on the tubes was a Norvallan nano-engineer who had seen such pieces before and recognised them and their implications.

"Did you know that an ISA ship found a stash of similar life-tubes on Skota a couple of months ago, and the ISA hushed it up for reasons best known to itself?" Ahxenta asked curiously.

"Captain Kerrix told me: Ms Levettiza got it from an Intelligence contact. The ISA could get no clues as to the contents of the tubes. It may do now: Levettiza felt that Intelligence should be told, because if the Skota tubes have trackers…"

"The ISA could be in trouble," Ahxenta finished. "That's a problem for Thal; if there's an inquiry into where the data came from, it's bound to come out. But if the trackers in the bodies were active and tabs have been kept on them, or they're on an auto-surveillance system… there might be a record of where they ended up."

"It's a risk, but the tubes *are* old and had been untouched for a very long time. And the hostiles have had setbacks, including losing the war to the Alliance. But Thal's rescue ships were hindered at every step, and that suspected hostile ship by Altina may have been heading for Furze. It *was* spotted more than once. But it, and others, may have been making for what looks like a holding area by the Crimson Drapes…"

"Things are getting complex, and it's not our problem," the captain said sharply. "What might be is that we found them and alerted Thal, and there are some out there that must know it and may take action. We stay alert. Another thing: Tallica and I met Wekki Munnet in the *Half Moon*. Tommy Buntle's in *Tallulah's* brig, but that's an aside. And Ally had a piece of news that may concern us."

Ahxenta told of the inner two troubles and of the Hoxiz-like being. It was news for Thal, although his worries were elsewhere, but Munnet would pass the details to the ISA. The captain then gave him the names of reliable Xerophytic mining firms and advised him to expect a link.

"Be canny in what you tell her," she warned. "She pressed me for specifics on the *Moonstone*, which she didn't get. I told her that we knew the *Peerless*, with Myrtleberry in command, was to head out after the *Repulse* and the *Advance*, but she gave no sign that *she* knew – though she must. But did you get any clues as to when the *Kel'Moth* will leave Starfall? Thal seems to have dug in, and for someone who claims to be a trader and runs a PSS, he's not doing much business at present."

As Apnis had suspected, Azular knew intuitively that the change of tack was deliberate, and the issue of the life-tubes was still troubling the captain. That Kerrix had insisted that she be told the details sooner rather than later had also exercised him, and he deduced that there was a cogent reason behind it. Being Azular, he had his own ideas and was not averse to expressing them and digging for more.

The captain clicked her tongue in irritation, but in a few words, with a curtness close to rudeness, she told him most of the tale. She was not surprised that he had guessed much of it long since. Having known her so long, and with a shared heritage, she realised it was inevitable.

"And Xanna knows," he sighed, having expressed his sympathy. "I thought there was something behind her urging that you *had* to be told, but this I hadn't foreseen. Maybe it's better that some mysteries remain unsolved. But as for Captain Thal and his lengthy stay at Starfall: he *is* base commander, but he has other motives than the current ISA crisis and the *Kel'Kith's* cargo. The *Kel'Moth's* being refitted using Norvallan and Telziltic tech. Her hull's having shielding like the *Moonstone's*, with inbuilt array-linked micro-sensors to stop attachment and entry of alien drones. Chameleon cloaking, or the ability to create a transitory bypass is beyond Thal's people, but it may come… A halt at Starfall for the gem-grade jurillium that Xanna's sourcing from Kirtish *is* an option, after our halts at Xerophyte and Wester, Captain?" he added.

"You don't give up. On top of seeing Captain Kerrix, you want a close-up of the *Moonstone's* tech, and figure your chances will be better in a ship under refit. I doubt that, at Starfall. She promised to give you the details in any case and she was going to sound Thal out on a version of it for the fleet. Tallica was right: Thal *was* up to something that he and his ship were delaying at Starfall. It seems he's setting up a network of PSS vessels that'll be tougher and smarter than the rest of the fleet, and other trading fleets besides. I give him credit for that. But it's been a long and tiring day, so I'm off to the mess for a nightcap. Are you coming? In fact, let me rephrase. You *are* coming."

* * *

Early next day saw the cargo for ISA Stinward moved into a spot that allowed *Arianrhod's* massive grapples to get a grip and convey the load into her outer bays. Her teams, used to the work, soon had it running. It was as well, Ahxenta told her first mate: she had had a link from Nat Holdspan, who wanted a private word next time she was Web-side, or on the *Warrior* if it suited, but he stipulated that Dr Azular be present.

"Why has he asked for Azular?" Apnis wanted to know.

"Search me, but much as I'd like another look round the *Warrior*, a trip will raise curiosity. It'll have to be the *Half Moon* or marketing."

"*Half Moon*," Apnis advised. "Everybody will have a good look, but it won't result in nudging and speculation – much."

"They'll certainly be taking a good look at Nat," the captain grinned. "You what?"

"Wait and see. But after this show's on the road, which means late lunchtime. Nat can make it then, and I need to see Parket in security."

"I take it you've told Sergeant Parket you want a word with her?"

"I have, but not the gist. She's expecting me late afternoon, and as I need Azular there, he'll be with us anyhow."

"In that case, I'll link Kit Biernop. If he's free, I'll call a meet to talk about the bogus repair guy that tried for a Guild ticket. As Kit's Guild security liaison, he can find out; *and* if any of the same that are more than they say on their personnel records applied, and *did* get in."

"Good call, Tallica. If he can't make it today, arrange another date. Meanwhile, the cargo…"

The hours specified by the captain stretched and well after midday she, Apnis and Azular made the *Half Moon*. Holdspan had not arrived, but he had meetings, Ahxenta knew. She had made tactful enquiries as to his knowledge of the fate of the *Bright Mist* at hostile hands when he had linked; his face told her that he not only knew, but knew that *she* was aware of his ties to the ship. Kerrix had called him about the Furze victims and told him the truth of how she had uncovered his past. She also told him that other partial IDs had been got from the tubes, and he was acute enough to realise that Ahxenta had interest in the matter.

A rising hum as the holo-veils of the *Half Moon* parted to allow entry of three officers from the *Nyx Warrior* alerted those from the *Arianrhod*, and Ahxenta waved over from their table at the far wall.

"*That's* a new look for Nat," Apnis remarked, raising her brows as she ditched her lunch plate. "Not many fleet captains go for a beard. It suits him. Sol Treskitt will have been in marketing with him, but why has he brought his senior SO, Holt, isn't it, to this meet?"

"We're about to find out," the captain replied as the three at the bar scooped up their drinks and made their way across.

After greetings, Holdspan asked for privacy and came to the point. He had stopped off at Iridis, a dependency of Delta Iridium between Needle Beacon and Bistra, for resupply and to allow his crew time out. A well-known layover in an otherwise sparsely-settled sector, Iridis had a large flea market. His senior SO had visited it, and on a hunt through the stalls, had picked up an odd piece of allegedly ancient alien junk.

Holt explained that the vendor, a buyer and seller of curios, claimed it had come from beyond mapped space, and he had bought it in from a freelance archaeologist friend who made a living by trawling deserted worlds for artefacts. As the seller refused to name his contact and had no certification for the piece, the friend was probably a scavenger, but Holt, after inspecting and probing it, had been curious enough to buy it. He had worked out that it *had* been in space and was possibly part of a ship, but it did not read as any hostile tech known to him, and the attached inclusions intrigued him. Back aboard, he had carried out in-depth testing and reported his finds to his captain who, recalling the message sent from the *Moonstone*, had contacted Captain Kerrix.

"Captain Kerrix told me that *Arianrhod* was on her way to the Web, and asked me to get all the analyses that Bix got, *and* a part of the piece, if we could cut it off, to you in person on the QT, as you knew more of the details," Holdspan told Ahxenta. "She asked that Dr Azular be included, as he has extensive files that include hull specs of Norvallan and other alien ships, *and* he's familiar with Norvallan tech."

Holdspan paused to look at the Berzic officer curiously, but carried on. "Captain Kerrix said that you could verify if the slice had come off the *Moonstone's* hull, Dr Azular, as you have scans of her, though the insertions *are* new additions. She also said that you could tell me more about the inclusions, Captain, and why the theft of intact pieces of hull should give rise to such a fuss."

Ahxenta gave Azular a dry look before responding. That the stolen shielding flakes included inbuilt jamming micro-sensors linked to the *Moonstone's* science arrays was no surprise to Holdspan. That they had been created by her crew as a means of foiling the binding of complex limpet drones and such missiles to hull plate did. He was also surprised that she sought to develop the tech to enable its addition to standard hull shielding and to make it available to the PSS fleet.

"I have a small slice of the piece and the data shard with me but we don't hand them over here," Holdspan said firmly. "Too many eyes."

"I agree," Ahxenta nodded, looking around at the avidly-watching faces. "We can find a private booth in marketing, if you've time, Nat? Dr Azular and I have a meeting later on, as does Commander Apnis."

"Fine by me," the young captain agreed. "My supercargo's finalising a deal there, and I'd planned to catch up with her anyhow."

"I'll have to shoot now, Cap," Apnis said as she scanned her wrist unit. "That's my contact. Buzz me when you're done with your other stuff and I'll meet you and Azular either there or at the shuttle."

"Roger that. We'll see you later."

Apnis made her farewells and left the others to collect their gear.

"That was a set-up if ever there was one," Jurry remarked to his mate as their eyes followed the five officers out of the *Half Moon* from the safety of their dark corner booth. "What did they want two senior science officers there for, if not for cloak-and-dagger?"

"The *Half Moon's* not a place for a secret tryst," contradicted Malty. "Too many nosy types that'll put one and one together and get three."

"Exactly. That's why it's so handy. Who'd think people like Ahxenta and Holdspan would talk shop in a place like this, privacy or not? So, we keep our noses to the ground and see what else we can dig up. Like why Nat Holdspan's grown a beard. What's he hiding?"

"A scar?" his friend hazarded. "Or maybe he thinks it makes him more attractive. Though with the looks he has and the ship he has, that shouldn't be a problem. I was as good-looking, once," Malty mourned.

"Didn't get you anywhere though, did it? You've lost the looks and never had a ship to call your own. You never had anything to call your own, not even a career. If you'd kept your nose clean you could've stayed with the ISP fleet, poor as the pay was. Then you wouldn't have had to join a freebooter like Oaky Logan aboard the *Riptide Dexter* on the promise of wild times and plenty of credit."

"Too late now. I never got beyond ensign in the service and I'd to leave anyway, but I was ranked lieutenant aboard the *Riptide*."

"Were you hell, you just had the pips. You were lucky to be off on a spree when the marines caught up to her for lifting the cargo drones off three Crimson Ensign Line carriers in the space of a week. Oaky's still in Skene Starn Penitentiary and the *Riptide's* hull is rusting away in a Sevolb wrecker's yard. If you hadn't managed to hook that job aboard the *Brill Lugger* as a loading op, you'd have been scuppered."

"Old days, old ways," Malty sighed. "But isn't that Tallulah Tommy Buntle out on his own? Though he'll not stand us a jar; he's too fond of credit to splash it where it won't bring him in a bonus. But where's his captain? Juke Spickle got a leash on him at last?"

"Hand over your mug, lad, and I'll see what I can find out," ordered Jurry. "I'll play out the chat line and press a couple of his buttons. You never know what might pay dividends."

Jurry was back in his seat in ten minutes, clutching two small mugs. "It's our lucky day," he beamed. "Buntle's so lost and lonely he's been spilling his troubles to Ally. His captain and first mate are in marketing with their supercargo and he's been given a spell of leave to think on his sins. At least, I figured that, though he's playing it down. Told Ally he's been under par and was told to take it easy, but he looks fine to me. It's probably only his conscience that's under par. I waited 'til Ally slid off and then dropped hints about the cosy chinwag that Ahxenta and Holdspan had, with their science officers and first mates chipping in. He was all ears. Passing data shards by the look of it, I told him."

"But they didn't, they were just talking," Malty disputed.

"I had to feed him a tale or two to make him pony up the ale. I told him about Holdspan's face fuzz and hinted at a reason. And I pointed out Lieutenant Whittle of the *Zephyr* as another lonely soul: Jez said she had a row with her boyfriend over his eyes looking the wrong way, and told him to get lost. He took her at her word and did. But as Trigger Whittle's a handful, he was maybe thankful to see the back of her."

"Buntle won't get far: his rep follows him wherever he goes," Malty snorted. "And as Whittle's one of the top weapons officers in the fleet on duty and off, you duck if you see her coming. Wonder *what* Captain Ahxenta and young Nat Hotshot are up to? They shot off pretty fast once Commander Apnis had hightailed it."

The officers were in a booth in marketing. Azular was analysing the piece that Holdspan had handed him. It was Norvallan meta-jurillium, quality, with an internal structure that was standard for top warships. It bore a residue of outer defence cloak, a superfine net infused with minute flecks of a radiant element that gave the *Moonstone* her lustrous glow. She was the only ship of any fleet he knew that had such a shield.

"So *that* is definitely off the *Moonstone's* hull," Ahxenta said. "And it found its way from Delta to Iridis. Captain Kerrix will be pissed."

"The *Moonstone's* a one-off; this can't be mistaken, Captain," Azular said. "It's off her hull. And these two micro-sensors must be the add-ons that Captain Kerrix' people created for added protection against alien weaponry. She'd no option but to haul into Delta for repair, given her heavy damage, and even in such a reliable centre, larceny will exist; in fact, it's probably endemic. But it *was* to order, the culprits admitted it, and they couldn't or wouldn't name their clients, who had to know the *Moonstone* was there, either because she was known to be heading for Delta or she'd been tracked that far; or they knew that the two attempts to take her out had failed. The latter *would* suggest that they *are* hostiles, or guided by them, but it's not a given."

"What are you implying, Dr Azular?" Holdspan asked. "People out there want the tech she has and would go as far as stealing it?"

"It's possible. Now she's a PSS, many know about her and want the super tech she seems to have," he replied, turning the piece around in his hand. "A ship that can do as *she* does? Protection so far in advance of the norm that the beating she took didn't bring her down? A hull that can split into two autonomous units and act as very efficient ships in their own right? A chameleon..."

"A what?" Holt interjected. "A hull that splits in two?"

"Now you've done it," Ahxenta warned. "Captain Kerrix will thank you for that."

"Captain, the hostiles have seen the *Moonstone* in action, off Wester 287. She responded to the *Obsidian's* distress, as we did. We took them out, but word will have got back — we know *that* from what they know of *our* technology. And yes, Commander Holt: she's twin-hulled and we've seen her operate as two units. My point is that she's a target for any who want novel tech. And they may not necessarily be alien."

"*You've* seen her work as two units? But how did the piece Bix found end up in a flea market on Iridis?" Sol Treskitt asked.

"The thieves didn't know what they had, but it *had* to be valuable, as the theft was to order; so they stole it," Azular said bluntly. "One of the ops maybe had a contact on Iridis and *this* looks strange enough to be an alien artefact. As no standard scanner could read what it was, the label would stand. Though you scanned it and found it sufficiently intriguing to pay for it," he added to Holt.

"My scanner's the best that credit can buy – at least I thought it was. I'd like a look at that one you have."

"You won't get it," Ahxenta told him. "Captain Kerrix gave it to him and he doesn't let it out of his sight."

"The thieves didn't know what they had," Holdspan broke in. "But do others out there now know what that is? And if they do, it won't be long before they'll find a way past it."

"No doubt," Ahxenta sighed. "But for now, Nat, no word of this to anyone. And as we have a meet on green one, we have to go."

She thanked him for the data shard and hull piece, promised to keep him updated, and released privacy. Azular folded up his gear, stowed the piece and shard in an inner pocket and clipped his scanner within easy reach on his belt, grinning at his opposite number impishly.

The five had just quit the booth when a call signalled the advent of the *Warrior's* supercargo, Lieutenant Ettis Book. That was the last thing they heard before a dull boom shook the fabric of the walls around them, and they and everyone close were blown off their feet. As shards of building fabric shot off in every direction, a siren began to scream.

13: MATCHLESS

Ahxenta raised her head a fraction. It felt heavy, it hurt, and there was a taste of dust in her mouth. That and the dull ache down her left side told her she was alive. A soft groan to her right sounded human. The siren was muted now, and cries echoed in the distance. She forced her eyes open against the stinging dust. Visibility was poor, and sporadic flashes, heat, and the burnt smell of blown power boards assailed her senses. A nearby body in a dust-covered dark uniform was moving and cursing quietly. She recognised it as Nat Holdspan, and inched over to check on his status, aware that her left leg was refusing to cooperate.

He half-turned when she called his name and tried to heave himself semi-upright, but was having trouble. She got to him, coughing in the clouds of powdery residue that caught her throat and made her stinging eyes water. An inadvertent cry left her lips as a scrap of metal caught at her damaged leg, and she swore.

"Captain? Are you okay?" His voice was concerned.

"I'll live," she told him. "You?"

"I'm fine," he lied as he looked into her face and then turned slowly to scan what he could through the rising, dirty fog. "My people – where are they? I need to find them."

She indicated a dark mass shaking itself in the gloom. "Over there."

They could hear sounds of movement, of feet, of shouting. Intense spikes of light flashed through the murk, the torches of the mobilised emergency teams cutting into the dust and scattering its particles. Fine jets of suppressant liquid were hissing as they drowned the fires that had shot up from systems and units that had blown or had been caught by the energy that had unleashed chaos. The two crawled towards their target, which had now sat up and was gingerly testing its coordination.

"Sol!" Holdspan called in relief and the head of his first mate slewed in his direction. "Where are Holt and Book?"

Ahxenta had her own concerns and missed Treskitt's reply: Azular had been behind her and must be close, but she could not see him. She felt her way around, cursing again as flakes of debris caught her, cutting her hands. The moving shades of light and dark were coloured now, red emergency lighting adding to the stippled effect. Tall shapes moved like restless ghosts among the shadows: the search teams, working their way through the wreckage. Her voice catching, she called his name. A shrill note at the edge of hearing made her turn and repeat the call as she crawled towards what she thought was the source, as other noises, voices in the dark, made a jumbled mass of echoes. A large panel block had fallen across what once had been a bench seat. Part of it rested on the floor and there was a form crouched alongside, tugging at a shape under the collapsed screen. Through the pulsing red-orange glow of safety lights along the bulkheads, she could make out a uniform.

"Azular?" she cried again as she pulled herself along, her useless leg dragging. "Azular?"

A grating voice answered and a pair of eyes glinted in the dark. "It's Lieutenant Commander Holt, ma'am. Dr Azular's trapped under this board. I don't want to haul it out in case it shifts or more comes down. If I raise it, do you think you could pull him out from under it?"

The captain tried to lift herself up and failed. "Dammit! I've hurt my leg and it won't support me properly," she told him in a rough, low tone. "Let me slip under that board, and I'll make it up on one knee. I can use my back as a prop and lift it."

With some manoeuvring, Ahxenta was able to wedge herself partly under the panel; bracing herself, every muscle aching, she arched her back and pushed up on her hands and her uninjured knee. The board gave and she felt it rising step by step. Holt had grasped Azular by the shoulders and was hauling on him. An age seemed to pass before the young officer finally pulled him free.

"I'll take the weight now, ma'am!" he gasped.

Ahxenta sensed the burden slacken and rolled out of the way as fast as she could. Her first thought on sitting up was her science officer. She slid over to where he lay immobile, repeating his name and feeling for a pulse, her mind drawn back to the last time he had been in this position, when the alien agent Hoxiz had shot him in the back. That had been in the Web too, and they had almost lost him then. The slow beat of blood in his veins reassured her and she sighed in relief.

"The rescue teams are closing," Holt assured her, and she turned to see that he had not escaped unscathed: blood was running down his face from numerous cuts and his uniform was torn in places.

"Your captain and Commander Treskitt were looking for you," she said in reply. "They're both around and are more or less in one piece. I don't know about Lieutenant Book."

Holt tabbed his communit. His captain replied at once and Ahxenta could hear the relief in Holdspan's voice. He and Treskitt would head their way, he said. Lieutenant Book was slightly hurt, as she had been further from the blast source, and was helping rescue teams search for victims. The Web medbay was preparing for an influx of emergencies.

The comm had awoken the captain to other issues and she reached for her unit to send a quick query. Apnis and Kit Biernop were already on hand, her first mate told her. They had been in the nearby *Sunlight Subspace Diner* when the blast hit. Ahxenta brought her up to speed.

"Get the ship to lock onto my comm and you'll find us. Azular will need to be taken to medbay and I've busted my leg. I see lights heading in, so we've been located. The teams are shifting rubble as they go, and they'll have to be alert to the possibility of another big bang."

"Hang in there, Cinnabar; we'll be with you as soon as we can."

The captain had little time to wait, for a thankful Nathan Holdspan and his first mate were with them in minutes, a paramedic at their heels. She had tried to establish Azular's status, but in the dim light of a small torch that Holt had dug out, she could see little. There was emergency med gear on the way, she was told, but as this explosion was the largest in the recent spate, it would take time.

Apnis arrived next. She had left Biernop with the team looking for the cause of the blast. *Arianrhod's* duty officer knew the score and their medbay was on standby. Ahxenta and Azular were their only crewmen caught in the turmoil, but those on shore leave had been told, *and* warned to mind their backs, she told them.

"I've done the same," Holdspan put in. "We'll head to the *Warrior* once we see you safely to medbay," he said to Ahxenta.

"And I'll be taking the shuttle up, Cap," Treskitt told him firmly. "You've taken a few knocks, and so has Bix. Dr Caslyn's been told and she'll be waiting for you when we get there."

"Have it your way," Holdspan grimaced. "How's Dr Azular?" he asked of the paramedic, who had set to immediately to assist him.

The para, having set Azular's head in a brace and attached a portable breather unit, was methodically prepping the officer for removal to a med-trolley. The extent of his injuries could not be gauged at present, but he was stable and breathing, was all the para would say. Ahxenta, by this time exhausted almost to immobility, had hauled herself to an upright post and was sitting against it, supported by her first mate.

"You three get home," Apnis said gently to Holdspan, whom she could see was in a bad way. "I'll cope here and let you know the score. Go on, Sol," she nodded at Treskitt. "Here comes the relief party," she added as a medic and an assist pulling a trolley rolled up.

Ahxenta's world now ran in hazy slow motion. Azular was assessed, strapped in, and borne off. Apnis' voice in her ear reassured her as she was helped to lie down on a gurney, tied in, lifted. Her first mate had collected her phase rifle and other gear, and trod alongside as the group made their way past curious onlookers to the main medbay on green three, emergency overrides in place all the way. The party was met at the emergency entrance by their own Dr Zaiklyn Oak; he had been on shore leave and had been sent in by second mate Whisper Earbleat.

"Half inner two knows ours were caught in it," Oak told Apnis after the captain had been taken to admissions, and the two sat in the waiting room. "I was in the *Half Moon*; so were crewmen from the *Warrior* and the *Obsidian*. Captain Fleetskup, his first mate and their super were in marketing, but they're safe. I don't have anything on other PSS crews, though I saw two faces I didn't recognise on the way in. The badges said the *PSS Kel'Torc*, so Starfall, but I don't know what gives."

They were fated to find out, as a pair of strangers walked in. Captain Turret and her first mate had been on the way to meet their supercargo when the blast went off. The latter had been caught in it, but was pulled alive out of debris near a bank of power boards halfway down the main area. Her ID had been found and her ship notified.

"Last time I was here, I was with the Cap and Dr Flintlock, waiting for news of Azular," Apnis said. "Now it's the Cap and Azular. Back last time, Nat Holdspan was with us: he'd brought Kerrix in…"

Apnis gave the two from the *Kel'Torc* a summary of those events as time stretched. Oak had left to seek information, and came back to say that a medical officer was on his way to bring them all up to date.

* * *

Earbleat sent the *Gadfly* for the captain and the first mate, as Ahxenta had insisted on returning to her ship despite her injuries. She left Oak to monitor Azular. He was conscious but had multiple injuries, and the attending surgeon had advised that he remain in medbay for three days.

"He'll make a full recovery," Oak assured the captain as he checked her mobile chair for the trip to the shuttle bay. "I've sent his last status report to Dr Flintlock and she concurs. She'll be ready when you get in, ma'am. Here are Nurse Kelp and your guards."

Earbleat had sent an armed escort, and a pilot waited in the shuttle. Apnis heaved a kitbag of the captain's and Azular's discarded uniforms and other kit onto her shoulder and took a last look round. The captain of the *Kel'Torc* was at a wall comm. Apnis waved and the party set off. Their ride had been berthed as close to medbay as possible, but news had spread and groups of gossipmongers held up every corner.

"Vultures are thick," the first mate sniffed. "You can bet a few will have recognised *you*, Cap. And that looks like a reporter," she snapped.

She undid her small phase pistol and took deliberate aim at a roving cam that a sharp-suited man had let go and which was drifting closer. The device shot back and its owner, hissing, snatched it out of the air.

"Let's get the hell away from here," Ahxenta said wearily, her eyes missing little. "We'll take the transport tube across."

"Roger that, Cap. And if anybody tries to hop in beside us, you and Ensign Hanx persuade them otherwise, Lieutenant Ji."

"Aye ma'am," Ji responded, lifting her rifle.

The party made the *Gadfly* unmolested and boarded quickly, the first mate ensuring that the captain was strapped in and that every atom of the area read clear. The *Arianrhod*, she knew, would monitor the flight from the bridge. All set, she gave the departure order.

The *Gadfly's* berth was a welcome sight, and as soon as the bay had pressurised, Ahxenta was wheeled out. Flintlock, med-scanner in hand and an anxious look on her face, raced in at the entry.

"Don't start," she warned before the captain could speak. "You're for medbay, and there you stay until I say otherwise. You're with me, Jym," she said to the nurse. "You'll be wanted on the bridge, Tallica."

"I'll say. I'll have to give the gear Azular got from Holt to Greffy, and I've links, to security for one: Parket will have figured our missing the meet was down to the bang, Cap. And I said I'd let Nat know about you and Azular. And links will have come in: the news will be all over local *and* stellar nets. You take care: I'll stop by when I can."

"Don't forget our loading schedule. The second Redship cargo…"

"Can damn well wait," Flintlock finished irately. "There are other priorities, and as of now you're mine, Captain. Let's move. You'd best be off to your post, Commander Apnis."

"Aye, ma'am. Don't worry Cinnabar, our teams know their jobs. I'll round up ours on leave and we'll be set to go once we get Azular back."

Apnis was aware of every eye on her as she walked onto the bridge. Whisper Earbleat rose from the command chair, a question on her lips.

"Cap's in medbay, doing fine," the first mate said in a tone caught by everyone. "We'll have Azular home soon. What's our status?"

Earbleat speedily brought her up to date; Apnis then made for the office to send out links. It took forty minutes, as the latest outrage had spawned a cluster of incoming messages.

"You'd think I was an info point," she groused to the second mate. "But I need to speak to the Cap about an issue that's cropped up, so keep our loading on track. I'll be back as soon as I can."

The first mate overrode the chief medic's injunction of no work-related matters and snapped the iso-bay panel shut on her complaints.

She hauled over a chair, sat, and cast her eyes on what Ahxenta was doing. "No work, the doc said. You're checking ops updates."

"You got me. I'm fine, apart from the leg, the ribs, and all over cuts and bruises. My mind works so I'm using it, and I see Earbleat's got us on target. What is it? You're not here with flowers and sympathy."

"Kit Biernop knew about the gunplay in the *Port in a Storm*; he was brought in when the fake ID came up on the perp's Guild application. He's smart: he checked the records of other ops that joined about the same time as the guy arrived in the Web, a few months back. He ran scans and picked out oddities, like three casual tickets for short-term Guild membership issued close together. It's not unusual, the Guild's always got openings, but all three said they'd previously worked for the same outfit: a shady orbital repair yard at Mellifly. And they all hailed from the same place – Brittle, in zone Mu. Remind you of anyone?"

"It does," the captain said shortly. "But go on."

"Kit checked the Mellifly link. The repair yard exists, but he got zip on it apart from location. You want to speak to a human, you have to go there; and they only deal with local traffic. You slot names and IDs into an auto system. *That* verified the three casuals and the dates they claimed to work there. Kit then ran a Guild check to see if others from the Mellifly place had applied at the same time – and found the name of the guy who'd tried to get in later, with the fake ID. The Guild had him listed as having worked at the Mellifly yard, but he was rejected, as the personnel rep interviewing him didn't like what she saw. But the ID tag and the employ record he'd used to get the Seedly job *and* for the second Guild application didn't mention the Mellifly place, it was some other yard at Salt Three, though he'd used the same name."

"Which is why the ID registered fake, as they'd have contacted Salt Three," the captain nodded. "But why did he go for a Guild ticket again using the same name when he'd failed the first time?"

"Who knows, but wherever he got the new ID, it got him the Seedly job, so maybe he thought he'd chance it to get into the Guild. Kit tried to find out what a search of the guy's billet turned up, but got nothing. He's passed the details of the original ID the perp used to try to join the Guild to security, but not what he'd dug up on the three still on the roll, in case it gets into the wrong ears and brings him trouble. He's still on it, but it means that there are at least three shady characters working in the belts that could potentially be hostile agents."

"The perp can't be that clever if he used the same name. Hoxiz was very dangerous and very smart."

"That struck me; didn't Ally say that the security bods that told him of the *Port* attack say he was similar to Hoxiz, but not as dangerous or clever? I asked Kit to pull up the guy's face from his records."

"And?" Ahxenta asked.

"I *thought* I could see a similarity to Hoxiz types we've met, but with no direct comparison to the original, how do you tell? When I called Parket to explain your absence, I asked her to see what she could find out on the QT. She'll have the guy's bio-checks. He's still in a cell, and with the charges against him, he won't get bail. I didn't bring Kit into it, as his link to me might come out and the fewer that know about that the better, for his sake. All we can do is wait to see what happens. Parket told me that the marketing blast was the worst to date. There's one fatality, a rep from one of the Web-based shipping companies."

"And they've all been in inner two," Ahxenta sighed. "The quicker we're out of the Web the better. Any more on Nat and his crew?"

"He's the worst hit of his own and is in medbay. Treskitt's holding the bridge; he took minor hurt. Holt and their supercargo are okay. I sent a courtesy call to the *Kel'Torc*: her super's still in the Web's medbay but the captain wants her back aboard as soon as she can be moved. Grey Bluejohn linked to ask after you and Azular: some of his got the news from ours. I gave him the latest. Fleetskup buzzed in too. I think Juke Spickle put him up to it, but he *was* civil. *Tallulah's* heading out soon, but where I don't know. Another thing, Cinnabar: a private link from Captain Kerrix to Azular came in. *We* can't access it, but I don't think it's wise to pass it to him in Merkat medbay. Word of the blast won't have hit Starfall yet, but it *will* get through, and if there's no reply from him… I plan to call back and let her know. What do you think?"

"Yes," the captain nodded. "But don't say too much."

"Roger that, Cap. You take care and I'll see you later."

* * *

Later turned into much later, with loading time extending and the first mate being interrupted by calls as word of the explosion spread. She found that Kerrix *had* heard, via a note to Starfall from the *Kel'Torc* and a link from Sol Treskitt. Apnis also had Parket on line: security medics could tell that their prisoner was cyber-enhanced, but not to the extent of the original Hoxiz, though he could cause serious damage. He had meta-jurillium implants and had recently undergone genetic alteration. His origin had proved to be zone Mu, possibly Minch Fettin. A search of his quarters had turned up the first ID he had used, pieces stolen from the Seedly yard and its clients, and a stash of explosives, although *that* had not been linked to the four incidents in inner two.

"Security's treating them all as criminal," Apnis told Ahxenta when she made time to visit. "Parket's got site teams filtering what they can, but as the damage for the first three's been patched, it's difficult. The marketing hit's been classed as sabotage with intent to cause damage and loss of life. If it *is* down to the guy in the cells, it's a murder charge, as well as multiple assaults with intent to cause serious bodily harm."

"Doesn't help us, though it's curious that the last hit caught ours and Nat Holdspan's people. Azular did once say that *Arianrhod, Warrior* and *Obsidian* were seen as the toughest PSS fleet ships, so major targets – and the bang goes off when we and Nat's guys are in? And *Obsidian's* in port, though Grey wasn't there. But what's Flintlock at out there?" the captain asked. "She's been lecturing her staff on something."

"It's that med-cradle she got at Delta. She wants to take it down to Merkat medbay to transfer Azular. I think it's more to give it a run and her staff training in its ops, as Oak says he doesn't need it, though he will have to transfer by med trolley. He wants to come home, whatever the doc in Merkat says. Axellina can sort it out. He knows about Kerrix' message and that she knows about him: I told Oak to tell him, after I'd spoken to her. She was worried about him, I thought. And about you; she sends her regards and hopes you'll be back on both feet soon."

"I bet she didn't say it like that," Ahxenta retorted. "What's going on in her neck of the galaxy anyway? Has Thal moved out yet?"

"He'll soon be on his way to Kirtish, where he'll pick up a load of processed gem-grade jurillium, some of which will be diverted our way at trade cost. Kerrix didn't enlarge on how much, but she's no fool and realises its uses. I can see Thal's fleet using jurillium-protected arrays in its comms systems. And as Gemstone Station is only a jump on and off his bypass that passes Brown Amber, I'm sure he can get a deal on a bucketful of the needful as and when he wants it."

"Cynic," the captain responded. "The *Serenity*?"

"Is to head out soon, so I reckon the *Kel'Moth* might act as escort, to Kirtish, if not Amity. There's no more on the *Moonstone's* stolen hull pieces, apart from what Holt found on Iridis. But Treskitt was quick off the mark: he passed on word of the explosion, and that we and his team had been caught in, it in the brief he sent Kerrix to tell her that the goods Holt had picked up had been verified as she'd asked and a piece handed to us. But I'm leaving you to rest, or the doc'll have my head. We won't ship out without Azular, so we have time to make sure all our loads are secure and our route is as safe as possible."

* * *

Two days Merkat standard later, *Arianrhod* let go her docking struts and set out of the Web, her sights on Cygilla, on the near edge of Zeta. The trip meant crossing zones Alpha and Epsilon, but the route was clear, Box told Dox in an aside as she set for the bypass. The captain was in her chair, leg brace in place, under threat that any lapse in the strict orders placed on her by the CMO would lead to a return to medbay. Greffy was at the science station. Azular was still in care. He had borne the trip in the med-cradle well, and Flintlock was pleased by its ease of use, but irked over her patient's lack of fitness and scathing of his care Web-side. *He* was cheerful, using his time working out how the micro-sensor relays on the *Moonstone's* hull section could be adapted to link to *Arianrhod's* arrays, and how they ran in situ. As the gear was innovative and held rare elements, he was finding it tricky. The doctor had vetoed a trip to his shuttle to carry out tests.

"This route will put us on a line to Skota, as it's almost bang on the Epsilon-Zeta border and straight up the bypass from Cygilla. It's where the ISA found the stash of life-tubes, so our holo had best be at full all the way," Ahxenta murmured to her first mate. "It's as well we brought our weapons up to max while we were in the Web. As the ISA ordered a clampdown on the life-tube find and everything about it, I wonder if it has a presence at Cygilla? It *is* the main centre of those sectors, and the info sure as hell won't be on any updates we get from ISA HQ."

"True; but it's the fastest way and we're late. We'll be in line for a quick getaway if we meet trouble, as the client's orbital. But if the ISA *has* a presence there, it'll be nice to us. We still have that ISA probe the *Steadfast* set on us. We can wave it at any pests."

"Thanks for that. Steady as she goes, Ms Dox. We may be in a hurry but I don't want to overcook our engines."

"Roger that, ma'am. Forty two minutes to bypass."

Although the ISP, Coalition, Non-Treaty, and United Independent parties of the charted galaxy were now units within the ISA, the bodies still held sway in their own sectors and had their own rules. The course to Cygilla involved crossing Alpha from a small ISP-majority area into a large swathe of Coalition-held space before making the mainly ISP-held Epsilon. Having met trouble on the route in the past, Ahxenta ordered cloaking on reaching the ISP-Coalition cross-point of Wheen.

The hours after Wheen became days, Lesser Kirrin was passed, and *Arianrhod's* holo-grid was working well. As the captain had expected, no alerts or reports had come in from any ISA source.

"And just what do you think you're doing back on duty?" Ahxenta demanded of Azular as the Epsilon border was reached and Dox made ready to negotiate the beacon and bypass crossing at Cygnet.

He had appeared and asked leave to take his post half an hour after the start of the new watch. He was keen to see the holo-grid in action in the last stage of their trip, was his excuse, but the captain was having none of it. "Flintlock's last update said you'd been let go from medbay but you'd need two more days off, and that was barely an hour ago. Back to your off-duty pursuits, mister. What *were* you doing anyhow?"

"Deep-scanning and imaging a section of the *Xanna's* hull to make a tri-dee holo, ma'am. I can use that to create a composite that mimics the shard of *Moonstone's* hull that we were given. A larger piece than the current one will help in figuring micro-sensor layout and linkage to our science arrays. The details will have to wait until we have a full spec of actual sensors, but if I can work out the best layout for *Arianrhod*, and we can source the relevant materials for the sensors…"

"I might have known! Off duty means off duty, not hiding out in a shuttle and playing with bits of kit. I'd have Flintlock fit you with an implanted locating pin, but you'd find a way around it, I bet."

"Captain, I feel perfectly well…"

"You don't look it, and I have your med report right here. My office *now*. Commander Apnis, you have the conn: keep us on track."

"Oops! He's in trouble," Box muttered over the navi-helm console.

"When's he ever in anything else these days," Dox responded. "But keep your eyes on your boards. We're coming up on the Cygnet beacon and node and anything tricky at the last second, I need to know. And then it's a tight pass of Swan One for Cygilla, and nasty things have a habit of hiding in the shadow of planetary or stellar bodies."

"Tactical will have a bead on it and we'll be able to see every last moonlet on that grid," the navigator shot back. "But I'll set in a couple of jump lines just in case we hit a bump."

The captain returned in minutes minus Azular, and retook her chair gingerly, settling her injured leg at a comfortable angle.

"He's thinking better of it, then?" Apnis asked.

"I wouldn't go that far, but he's for medbay. The doc will hold him until I find time to shout at him. He can play with his shuttle scans and design a composite. He *has* a point: if those sensors can foil new-style limpet drones and are easy and cheap to fit, they'd be a handy add-on."

"At that rate, our hull will look as glitzy as the *Moonstone's*," Apnis protested. "She looks like a slice of frosted cake. And with them linked to our arrays, will we have the tech to decipher what they pick up?"

"That's what Azular's paid for," Ahxenta replied dryly. "But as the *Kel'Moth's* now fitted with a shield-net of them, it can't be difficult."

"We *are* heading to Starfall, eventually," chuckled Apnis. "If Azular sweet talks Captain Kerrix into sweet talking Captain Thal into handing us the needful *and* allowing us free use of his fitting bays…"

"Cut it," the captain ordered. "Here comes the crossing. Eyes open, tactical, all long-range scanning gear at full stretch. You too, Greffy. We want to spot anything before it spots us."

In the event, the node was passed and the route to Swan One set. Local space was clear, and in twenty hours, the outer beacon of Cygilla Prime was in range. The captain had ordered her most skilled crew on duty for final approach, and had let Azular take his post, realising that he would otherwise monitor it from medbay. *Arianrhod's* loading teams were ready for a quick cargo drop as soon as clearances were in order.

The cargo for Sunbeam Services was in company pods. Lindell had contacted the clients on the way in to ensure that they were ready to collect and had secured the first part of the fee, the balance to be paid once the pods were in the grip of trade grapples at the orbital Resort-Dorm facility. The planet was the main stop for several routes through three zones, and was generally a hive of activity.

"Plenty of traffic in orbit," Apnis noted as she took in the holo-grid that had now located the docking points for large- and medium-sized ships. "What's the boat with the fancy trim? Colours look ISA to me, but she's got a lot of shielding even in dock, and she's huge."

"She's reading as the *ISAS Matchless*, Commander," Azular notified her in a ringing tone. "The sister ship of the *ISAS Peerless*."

"You *are* joking," the captain growled.

"No ma'am, I have her call-sign. And I don't think she's a phony. There can't be many bespoke explorer-destroyers with ISA insignia on their hulls. I don't have details on her command staff, it's classified."

"I wonder if *her* captain's an info-sent with a showy shuttle that'll ride hyperspace currents?" Apnis asked acidly. "It's not Myrtleberry at least. She must be well on her way to outer Alpha by now – I hope."

A small chuckle from Azular interrupted her.

"What is it?" Ahxenta demanded.

"I've pulled up the new ISA press office events list, ma'am; another launch is due, the *ISAS Dauntless*, the third in a new class of explorer ships built for long-range survey and first contact missions."

"Maybe they'll call the next one the *ISAS Worthless*," Box sniggered.

"Hush it, and keep your eyes on that mooring grid," Dox ordered. "I need to angle my approach to let our teams have easy access to those frigging grapples, and they're still on the move… That's us locked in place for cargo handover, ma'am," she called out with a relieved sigh. "We can go ahead at your discretion."

"Roger that, helm. Keep your eyes on that ship and everything else in local space that might attempt to scan us, Mr Gliss. You too, Azular. If her gear is anything like the *Steadfast's*, it'll be good."

"And if her captain's anything like the *Steadfast's*, he or she will be sneaky," Apnis added. "D'you think we should give them a call and ask them if they want the *Steadfast'*s probe back? They're ISA after all."

"Zip it. But let's ready to loose cargo. Lindell, make sure we've got our residual fees before we let go our final grapples," she charged the supercargo, who was on a link on her ops board.

"Aye, captain. It's all in order thus far."

"Good. Loading team four, release cargo pods at your discretion."

Cargo release was smooth, and after civilities and sign-off, *Arianrhod* needed only final clearance to drop her docking traces and move off. The go-ahead had just been given when Bellfish gave a cry.

"*ISAS Matchless* on line, ma'am. Captain Kresta Goldcriss for you."

"On visual," Ahxenta said, raising inquiring brows at her first mate.

"We want our toy back now?" Apnis hazarded as Azular called over that the ISA vessel had begun a scan that was getting through.

"Hold comms! Increase jamming to block those scans!" the captain snapped. "She'll be several notches up on the *Steadfast*, so her gear will be the ISA's best. Azular, return the favour and scan the *Matchless*!"

"Scanning," he called as the power to their jammer net was upped. "She has a lot of scanning arrays, most trained on us. They're shielded, *and* she has active hull jammers. I can get a partial through. Her scanner shields read as Norvallan response plate tech, so they could get partial scans of us, despite *our* jammers and response plate! Her weaponry's formidable and she's locked targeting eyes on us, but she's not arming. But I'm sure her cloak contains chameleon elements similar to those we've seen before – on hostile hulls."

"Put Captain Goldcriss on viewer, comms."

"On screen, ma'am."

"Captain, why did you initiate a scan of my ship?" Ahxenta queried. "Why are you still scanning, and why are your targeting eyes locked?"

"You're carrying an ISA load to an ISA base. This is an ISA vessel and I have every right," the woman said acidly.

"You damn well don't," Ahxenta shot back hotly. "You've no right to know who my clients are, what my loads are, or what my route is. And that doesn't answer my question. I repeat, why did you initiate a scan of my ship and why have you locked your targeting eyes?"

"I want to know how you can pick up salient facts and figures that escape everyone else and how your ship has the knack of avoiding or dealing with the kind of trouble that's clogging space these days. Your ship has a range of weaponry and smart devices that most don't – apart from some Starfall ships – and I want to know how you got them."

"*You* want to know?" Ahxenta spat back. "You mean the ISA wants to know. And this is yet another attempt to extract that information by subterfuge and duress. Did you track me or did you know I'd be here and plan to intercept me, like Reddish of the *Steadfast*? In a very fancy ship that you believe is so capable of taking on mine that it might make me more inclined to comply with your demands. Well?"

"My mission and my being here are none of your concern, Captain, and I want answers," rasped Goldcriss.

"And my mission and my presence here are none of yours, and you won't get them," Ahxenta returned with a frosty glare. "I owe neither you personally nor the ISA any account of my business or my resources and I advise you direct your scanning eyes and your big guns elsewhere. Your advanced ship might be more than a match for mine, but don't be misled into believing that I won't use what I have to prevent your unjustified snooping or any further intimidation."

"You already have; your jammers are highly effective and you have insertions on your hull surface that are very efficiently masking the tech beneath. And your scans of *my* ship have been quite thorough."

"They have," was the calm return. "And your ship has similar. Your scanner shields have response plating you don't find this side of zone Psi and you've got a chameleon cloak based on hostile tech that your experts no doubt acquired from the hostile ships that the ISA has taken down and taken to pieces at one of its secret bases."

"That is preposterous!" Goldcriss hissed.

"Really? I recall Colonel Myrtleberry, with a hostile interceptor tied up in the *ISPS Repulse's* tractors, inform me that she was headed to an ISP base, where the ship would be taken apart bolt by bolt. It was after two aliens attacked the carrier *Marjenna* by Triple Pinks; we'd answered her distress. The colonel insisted that we and the *Marjenna* hand over the tactical and science data we had on the attacking ships. The *Repulse* had been tracking them, and jumped in to grab the one live hostile left before we reduced it to flak, or it did the same to us."

"I have no idea what you're talking about. And I demand you cease scanning my ship."

"Really? But as you're still trying to scan my ship *and* your eyes are locked, my scanners and my eyes stay on you. I intend to send *another* formal complaint to the ISA about this, copied to the TA, my fleet and the Cygillan authorities: I'm sure they frown on such irregularity going on in their space. I object to my doings and my ship being under illicit scrutiny by the ISA because certain parties want their hands on what they assume I have. I consider it an invasion of my privacy and that of my clients. Your attempt at coercion by locking targeting eyes verges on criminal. You'll remove them now or I *will* despatch an alert to the Port Authority that I consider you hostile and will arm in response."

"You wouldn't dare!" Goldcriss snapped.

"Lieutenant Bellfish, ready alert; despatch it immediately to the PA. Lieutenant Commander Earbleat, weapons online, target the *Matchless*. Shields up! Red alert!"

Acknowledgements rang around *Arianrhod's* bridge, the siren began to wail and a voice on the bridge of the *Matchless* confirmed targeting.

"PA wants to know what's going on, Captain," Bellfish said loudly. "It's preparing to initiate the outer defence grid!"

"Stand down targeting eyes!" Goldcriss yelled angrily as her comms reported the same message and planetary defences began gearing up.

"*Matchless* has ceased targeting," Gliss called from tactical.

"But she's still scanning," Azular observed.

"Stand down targeting, but keep our weapons online. And keep our shields up," the captain ordered. "Cut red alert to amber and maintain scans until the *Matchless* ceases."

As the wash of red light bathing *Arianrhod's* bridge cut out, Ahxenta looked at her opposite number grimly. "Your move, Captain."

"Your actions were out of order, Captain, and I intend to make a full report to my HQ."

"Please do. *I* certainly intend to make a full report to your HQ. It'll be attached to the formal complaint I'm sending, and it'll be copied to all relevant bodies. Anything else?"

"You are in possession of ISA property – a probe that you captured from the *ISAS Steadfast*. I demand its return."

"A probe the *Steadfast* set to tail me covertly and that I picked up to prevent it. I'll return it to the ISA at Stinward. And you're still scanning my ship. I demand that you cease."

Goldcriss gave the relevant order and Ahxenta repeated the same to Azular, who immediately cut his scan.

"You haven't heard the last of this, Captain," Goldcriss told her.

"And neither, I suspect, have you. Ahxenta out."

"Whew!" Apnis breathed. "That was some party, Cap."

"It's not over yet. Tell the PA that I'll send a report shortly, Bellfish. The alert's still on, but the defence grid's powering down. As soon as we're en route, I'll be scorching ears at Alto Finglas. This had better be the last, or there'll be hell to pay. It's time the TA stepped in to protest this harassment of shipping. What in the name is it all about?"

"ISA's science and engineering experts went to the Norvallans for fancy new tech and think they've been short-changed, as we've still got better than them, is what it's all about, Cap. She's still looking us over, but she's not moved. We'd best keep our eyes on her as *we* move out."

"And we're going now… Lieutenant Dox, alert Port Control that we're preparing for departure. I take it we still have our clearance?"

"Aye ma'am, it hasn't been withdrawn," Dox replied.

"They wouldn't dare. They're probably glad to see the back of us," the first mate remarked.

"Let's hit the trail. Gliss and Azular, keep all we have on that damn ship; Earbleat, don't drop our defences until we're out of local space. Once we're out of direct range I'll get on to Cygilla PA and see if I can speak to someone with sense. And then I have links to make."

"And the first one is to the ISA to tell it its name is mud yet again *and* it's in for another formal protest over the *Matchless*," said Apnis. "Box was right, but *Worthless* isn't quite the right name for the next one off the production line. Maybe it should be called the *Witless*."

* * *

The captain spent so long in her office that the first mate was tempted to step in to see what was going on. *Arianrhod* was by then well on her way to Eta, with a long trek across empty reaches to come. The distant shipyard and industrial facility of Polstarn, for whose orbital comms relay post the cargo was destined, was just over the border in Iota.

"Got all your reports and links done, then, Cap?" Apnis enquired at her eventual reappearance.

"I did. One of the problems was that people kept linking back. Hell, I'm not an info-point of the entire charted galaxy! And an Admiral Best I finally spoke to at Alto Finglas might be Myrtleberry's twin: he claims that the *Matchless* has a right to scan ISA cargoes. That our other loads weren't ISA and her scans breached clients' privacy cut no ice, until I told him I'd instruct my legal rep to instruct my clients to publicly sue the ISA for its breach of confidentiality. And I told him I'd return the *Steadfast's* probe at the ISA office at Stinward."

"Did you ask if he wanted it upgraded to a better standard?"

"Funny, and no. I'd had enough by that time. But Best knows that a formal complaint with his name attached is on its way to the council, copied elsewhere. He didn't like it, but tough. I did it as soon as I'd cut the link; some were caught right away, which led to the influx of calls. The head TA rep at Alto Finglas was one: he wants the incident played down to avoid a fuss. I spiked that notion for him. It's too late anyhow, as Cygilla Port Authority plans to lodge a complaint about the *Matchless*. I told him, and he was pissed. And two of ours are close: the *Comet* and the *Firedrake*. Sarie Jikelleli's at Selliden en route to Marridan, but Pa Ma'Lappis is at Bella Six. He'd planned to stop at Cygilla for resupply, as he's got a big load and smaller ones for ISA Stinward, but he'll head to Spelter, though he'll get less. But Stinward Central Logistics holds a huge range, as it supplies every ISA post across most of mapped space, so he's hoping to pick up the rest of his necessaries there."

"At a price. But you've left a couple of burning ears and a few pretty annoyed PSS captains out there, then," Apnis declared. "I did wonder what was taking you so long. I was going to send in a rescue party."

"Thanks for the thought. I seem to spend more frigging time in my office drafting and sending reports and yelling at people long distance than I do in my command chair," the captain complained.

"You should maybe hire an exec, Cap. It works for Fleetskup. You could always see if Tommy Buntle has a brother that needs a job?"

"That is not funny, Commander," Ahxenta reproved.

"My apologies, Captain, that *was* in very poor taste. You'd be better looking for an exec at the discard door of a convict reform centre."

"Cut it and tell me how things are out there. I take it there's been no trouble as far as our forward route goes?"

"Not yet, but give it time. We have a lot of empty space to cross."

* * *

The hours became days as the dark star deserts of Eta were navigated, to the hum of distant bypass traffic. Most systems were Coalition, but a courtesy link to the independent New Zegonia gave no cause for alarm. The quiet gave the crew free time, and the captain ordered it spent in fine-tuning systems. As it was that or drills, most labs, work rooms and task areas were busy. Azular spent much of his time in his lab tweaking a model hull section he had built that mimicked that of the *Moonstone*. He was in the throes of aligning a surrogate micro-sensor lattice that he hoped to link to the science arrays on *Arianrhod's* hull.

About this time, several messages came in. One for the captain told her that as the *Firedrake* would stop to supply at Stinward and would be there when *Arianrhod* docked, Dr Ma'Lappis would like to rejoin her ship. A skim of her schedule showed that the ships *would* meet, and Ahxenta agreed. She told Flintlock and Apnis over a bite in the mess.

"I heard from my brother," was the CMO's input. "He's in the Web to pick up Redship gear for Salt Three. As he has stops at Silverglass and Barfit, we may see him at Xerophyte, as they're all in Drosophila.

194

But somebody at Redship let out we were for Stinward and Wester, so he reckoned the bypass will take us close to Salt, even without halts. I pled ignorance and told him we don't tend to use main routes, but don't be surprised if the *Karillion* turns up off starboard at some point."

"You love him, really," Apnis snickered.

"I do, but mostly at a distance," was the acid retort. "Though it's a pain if the Redship reps can't keep their mouths shut and word of our doings are out there. Has Azular heard from Captain Kerrix? I had him in for a check-up the other day and he was humming like an out-of-tune harp. He wouldn't say why but he had a twinkle in his eye."

"Yes he has," the captain groaned. "He's got a mock-up hull section and he's trying to work out how the sensor units connect to each other and relate to the science arrays on the hull of a typical Norvallan ship."

"But our arrays are nothing like the *Moonstone's* and she's not like any ship in any fleet," Apnis objected. "She's hardly typical."

"Tell me about it. He reckons if he can get his head around that, he can work out the most effective alignment of sensors or sensor units for *Arianrhod*. Then all we need are the bits to build the sensors. Hence the chat to Kerrix and a promise from her that he'll be given a couple of units next time we're within spitting distance of the *Moonstone*."

"Which means when we get to Wester or even Starfall," sighed the first mate. "And I bet that's not all he and Kerrix had to talk about."

"Mind you own business, Commander Apnis."

"I hear a lot of 'mind you own business' when Azular's the topic."

"Tough. He forgets these sensors will cost and will need fitting, and nifty tech on *Arianrhod's* hull means hassle when it comes to repair and refit. The reason the *Moonstone* lost plate to sticky fingers was because she's draped in fancy tech that somebody thought was worth stealing."

"And no more word on that either, I bet," Apnis said.

"Nope. The perps have been charged and fined but not locked up. They've lost their jobs and have been sent for rehabilitation."

"Huh! That'll help… what the…!"

Ahxenta rose cursing, slapping her mess tray into the recycle hatch. The soft wail and the flashing lights denoted amber alert, but she was out of the door as fast as her injured leg allowed, her communit at her lips demanding answers. Apnis was two steps behind.

14: SANCTUARY

Arianrhod's trail was clear in the holo-grid and the captain and first mate could hear the hum of rising engine power as they reached the bridge. Other senior officers were already in post, tracking all that their arrays could pull in. Comms had picked up what registered as a distress, duty officer Mitt Snow stated as he released command, but it was unfamiliar, distant, and tactical and comms could not pinpoint the source, though it was coming from the general direction of Polstarn.

"It can't be Polstarn," Apnis panted, sliding into her seat. "The yard and repair base will have ships that can turn and fight if there's trouble, even if they aren't fully fitted. And Polstarn's in the middle of mostly nowhere, so where can trouble hide out?"

"Polstarn's nigh on the Fourpoint intersect of Theta, Eta, Iota *and* Kappa, so there'll be plenty unknown hidey holes," the captain rapped as she gingerly sat down. "I don't like this. The data's updating at a rate of knots and the holo's showing a hint of the source, but I can't make out if it's off or on the bypass. And why hasn't somebody at Polstarn noticed? What have you got, Azular?"

"Locking findings into grid now, ma'am. Damn!" he snapped as a spinning accretion of radiant gas took shape in the holo almost at the spot that marked the automated Fourpoint station. "Our current nav-charts are in the system and *that's* definitely not logged."

"Damn!" Ahxenta echoed. "It's another one of those fizzing newly-created worm-pockets, isn't it? Start pulling in what you can, Azular; you too, Gliss. Red alert and shields up! Weapons online and ready to go, Earbleat. Decoy on standby. Ready engines for fast action, Chief. Slow us, helm – we don't want pulled in if that beast's got more power than that last one," she called, tightening her webbing.

"Plot me jump lines to get us out of trouble, whatever way we have to jump!" the helmswoman ordered her partner as she complied.

"On it."

"Distress still going!" comms called. "Triangulating; data to grid…"

"It's close to the worm-pocket," Azular confirmed. "But I still can't match it to any record we hold in our databases. Greffy?"

"No sir," the young science officer replied. "But it now reads as off the bypass. We'll have to jump off if we head in."

"Slow to jump-off speed as we come up on Fourpoint," the captain ordered. "Earbleat, prime weapons for action, all stations."

"All weapons stations ready to go on your mark, Cap! *Loki* standing by!" the second mate roared in reply.

"Plot the best jump-off spot without coming into range of what's sending that distress, or near the mouth of the worm-pocket," Ahxenta directed as the signal stabilised in the holo-grid. "I need more data. I'm not risking sending a response until I know what in blazes it is."

"Worm-pocket's definitely not natural, Captain," Azular stated. "I now get synthetic signals, but they don't read the same as those of the Crimson Drapes pocket. Odd: I estimate that *this* singularity's smaller! Synthetic elements do *not* read like hostile inclusions we've met before. I advise we stay well clear, as the gravity field will be strong. Sending projected minimum safe distance area data to grid."

"Get the doc's data, Box, and make sure we keep well away from it!" Dox said sharply.

"You got it… locked in now."

"I get that signal as very close to that pocket!" Gliss cut in.

"It's a ruse, Cap?" the first mate hazarded.

"Or someone or something that's caught is trying to get out."

"Or get in and isn't sure how," Apnis said. "Or maybe it's the ones that created it, caught in their own trap. If these things pop up because who or what's creating them is trying to make a bypass, it's possible."

"Hell!" the captain breathed. "You have a point. Have we anything more on the source of that distress?"

"Off the pocket is all we can get, ma'am," the senior tactical officer replied. "If it's a ship she may have shielding and cloaking in place."

"Why would you cloak if you're sending a distress?" retorted Apnis. "Doesn't make sense."

"You don't want people to know who or what you are until you're sure of them," Ahxenta replied grimly.

"Coming up on Fourpoint, ma'am; ready to jump," Dox alerted her.

"Roger that. Keep us well away from interaction with the pocket as we come off. Tighten up all, and ready for leaving bypass. Hit it, helm!"

"Jump-off!" Dox sang out, and the huge ship cut off the bypass on a curving path that took her out of zone Eta and into Iota.

Her people had done their work well, the captain noted as *Arianrhod* met normal space with only an abrupt bump and the noise of straining seams whining below the red alert. Every sensor eye was set as the grid confirmed her current position. She was the only ship in the vicinity bar whatever was still sending the regularly pulsing distress.

"Haul back!" Azular's strident voice cut through the din. "Power discharge from worm-pocket increasing!"

"Get us distance helm!" Ahxenta rasped. "Weapons batteries ready to fire at anything in your sights. Three hundred sixty degree sensor sweeps in every direction! What are we picking up of that distress?"

Dox had anticipated her and the *Arianrhod* was already arcing away from the power source.

"Got a discrete entity now, Captain!" Larai's voice cracked as she called it. "Small, no more than transport-sized. She's heading our way, trying to outrun that wash of power from the pocket! She's veering off, trying to avoid us! Looks like she's just spotted us!"

"Huh! I wouldn't bank on that!" the first mate snorted.

"Want me to send a shot across her bows, Cap?" Earbleat roared.

"Negative, Lieutenant Commander! What in hell *is* she?"

"Getting readings now," Azular advised her. "I get a positive signal for trace zukivianite! She's of an old-style…"

"Worm-pocket's destabilising!" Greffy interrupted in a loud voice. "I read massive power fluctuations – it's going to collapse!"

"Helm, get us out of here! Set a course for Polstarn, top safe speed!" Ahxenta thundered.

As *Arianrhod* banked and turned at a steep angle to outrun what was expected to be a volatile energy burst, the odd craft shot away, but with her power almost gone she was slowing, and it was clear to those on the bridge that she was too close to the whirling mass of light that was now sparking colours and spewing gouts of fire.

"What the …" Words failed the captain as there was an outburst of searing light and then a sudden dark, as if a switch had been turned off. A hazily expanding flak field grew in the holo as *Arianrhod's* sensors attempted to make sense of their readings.

"It must have imploded," Azular reckoned aloud. "The force of the energy burst blew back through the pocket, in the direction of where it comes out, I imagine. But where's that ship gone?"

"Got her!" Greffy cried. "She's all but dead and the distress has cut. I still read trace zukivianite and a hull comp like the alien ships we met early in the war. But she's smaller than a ship, more the size and shape of an escape transport… like the ones from that huge battleship that nearly got the *Obsidian Sky* by the Orriga, the one we took out! And she *has* hull defences, but no power readings from any of them."

"Lifesigns?" Ahxenta asked. "Someone's piloting that thing."

"Internal shielding, Captain, but it's failing, as is everything aboard,"

Azular told her. "She's seen serious action, but the scoring on her hull's not all due to the fluxes through that worm-pocket, if that *was* her entry into this sector. Getting through her hull… one life sign, no specifics."

"Stand down red alert but keep us on heightened status and do *not* drop shields," Ahxenta ordered as she undid her restraints. "Slow, get us close enough to get a better view, helm, but keep targeting eyes on her, Earbleat. One wrong move and you send that warning shot."

Arianrhod had no sooner moved towards the hostile craft and taken up position astern of her when Gliss let out a cry.

"Another ship's coming in! Distant yet, but from the trajectory, I estimate she's from Polstarn!"

"On it," Azular responded. "She's not trying to hide. Call-sign says she's the destroyer *ISAS Iris Quartz*. Checking registry: she *is* in active service but I've no more, as it's classified. She's shiny as a new pin, so recently refitted. Her design matches a standard ISP destroyer."

"Keep a bead on that transport, Azular. I want…"

"Ma'am! Hostile is hailing us!" the voice of Bellfish rang out.

"What? Get me a visual! Earbleat, keep targeting; Azular, send out a probe to analyse her hull and what's inside. I'm sure as hell not going closer until I get answers. And keep that ISA ship in your sights, Gliss. She's still heading this way and I'd like to know what *her* game plan is."

The face that came into view over the holo-grid was thin, haggard, and pale, but unmistakeably humanoid. "You're the *Arianrhod*?"

"We are; I'm Captain Cinnabar Ahxenta. Who are you and what do you want with me? And how do you know who I am?"

"My name is Dexel Thal. And everyone's heard of the *Arianrhod*."

"You still haven't said what you want with me," the captain stated, her eyes narrowing in suspicion, laced with surprise.

His answer was a single word. "Sanctuary."

"You what? I'll need a helluva lot more than that, mister," Ahxenta told him sharply. "Who you are, where you come from, what you're doing in a hostile ship and what your business is for a start."

"My name *is* Dexel Thal; I'm Friskianx. I was in command of a ship taken down by three hostile ships, I guess over a year ago. Most of my crew were killed in the fight. They towed the wreck of my ship to Axle Lexo; we couldn't stop them boarding. Those of us left put up a fight, but they cut us to pieces. Four of us survived, badly injured. They kept us on their base, did things to us, to make us useful to them, I think. They questioned us for days. We told them nothing. I don't know what became of my ship, but their base was under threat and we were moved to a ship. We were in space a long time, then dumped in a holding area, no idea where, and left, for months…" His voice trailed off, the data he was picking up clearly disturbing him as his eyes skimmed his ops.

"And now you're here. There's a lot I still want to know," Ahxenta rasped as she scanned the readings Azular had sent to her board. His ship was hostile and closely akin to one of a fleet of transports that had fled a huge battleship that *Arianrhod* had finally downed after a cat and mouse chase on the edge of the Orriga Two asteroid field.

"I *will* tell you, Captain, but I request sanctuary."

"From what?"

"That ship coming in. It's ISA and I can imagine what'll happen to me if I'm taken whilst aboard a hostile ship, or any unauthorised ship come to that, anywhere near here."

"You're not making sense," the captain snapped.

"That worm-pocket I escaped from is an experiment, a trial set up and engineered by the ISA."

"You what?" Ahxenta was incredulous.

"It's mechanically engineered and I'm sure it's an ISA trial."

The captain's eyes flicked to the track of the *Iris Quartz* on the main holo. The ISA ship was closing and would be up on them soon. "Drop all your shields, internal and external," she ordered, with a quick look and nod at Azular. "I want readings of you as well as your ship."

Azular nodded in return and made ready to confirm from his probe if the man *was* Friskianx. As he did so, he recalled another meeting that he, the captain and the first mate had had in the Web not long before a blast that had been set to take out *Arianrhod's* shuttle, in fact not long before he met Xanna Kerrix for the first time. On impulse, he pulled up a data set that he thought might have a bearing on the matter.

The captain had the data on her board in moments. The man was part-Friskianx and his readings closely matched those of Captain Vexin Thal, who had also been modified by hostiles. The probe data showed that the almost-defunct ship had no weaponry left that could harm them and bore no traces of limpet drones or other harmful tech.

"Cut every power source you have," Ahxenta told him. "We'll bring you in. But you'll be taken straight to my brig until I know more about you, your story and how you came to be here. And if it turns out to be a heap of hogwash, you'll be handed over to the authorities. And in this neck of the galaxy, that means the ISA. Do you copy?"

"I do, Captain. I'm cutting everything now, including life support."

"Azular?"

"Confirmed: she's completely dead, Captain. I'm getting no power emanations bar comms. My probe's still scanning."

"Stand by for tractors," the captain warned. "Cut comms. Dox, get us close enough for our tractors to get a grip. Azular, keep your probe on her. Crizz, activate tractors once we're in range. And ready inner aft bay three: it's big enough to take her, our inner tractors and grapples can draw her in, and there's firepower there. Tactical, secure cams on her as she comes in *and* once she's docked. Ahxenta to security: I need a fully-suited and armed detail in inner aft shuttle bay three now. You'll deal with one cyber-enhanced male coming aboard. He's to be escorted to the brig immediately he disembarks and a full guard placed."

"The doc'll have words to say about that," Apnis remarked.

"She'll be on hand to meet *and* scan him, but he's for the brig. You'll be there, Azular. He'll have nothing on him but the clothes he's stood up in, and not even those if I find aught amiss. Hold the bridge, Tallica. I suspect the captain of the *Iris Quartz* will want a word. She'll soon be in range and you can bet she wasn't sent out to meet us. It's probably to do with that ex worm-pocket. And maybe *that* ship."

"What about that ship once she's aboard?" the first mate asked.

"Crizz's engineers will go over her, make her safe and tie her down. And until *we* get the whole story, the *Iris Quartz* gets nothing."

"Roger that, Cap. Did the ISA really think we'd miss that worm-pocket? Or we'd figure it for another like the one at the Drapes?"

"It seems to be a piece of work that wasn't meant to be here, or at least nobody was meant to detect it, but it's got out of hand. I'm going down to meet Dexel Thal. Tell Flintlock to meet us outside the bay."

"Aye, ma'am, and be careful on that leg. Another Thal? Maybe he and Captain Thal are clones and there are more of them out there."

"Cut it. You're with me, Azular. And we break out arms once we get there."

Inner aft shuttle bay three was large and brightly lit. A closed upper obs room allowed an inward craft to be seen and scanned as it docked. The captain and her teams were ready, and as the ship entered, locks moved to secure her and bay monitors to scrutinise her. Cottontail had left Gem Ferry on the bridge to control the tractors and was in the obs room to make sure there were no risks. Ahxenta and Azular stood by.

"Security goes in first," the captain said to Cottontail. "Axellina's on her way: she'll be here in a tick. She knows the score."

"That's her secure now, Cap. And boy is she in a mess! She couldn't hurt us if she tried, she hasn't a torpedo or pulse cannon to her name. I think she once had slicer beam ports, but it's hard to tell. No shields operative and her hull scanning arrays read dead."

"Just make sure she can't wake up," Ahxenta said curtly. "That's us pressurised," she added, tabbing her comm. "Goldwash, head in now. Approach with care. Any trouble and you shoot first. Do you copy?"

"I copy, Captain. Goldwash out."

The three in the obs room watched as four suited and armed guards slid in and spread out. They halted within a few steps of the ship and waited. Moments later, the panel slid over, a ramp dropped and a tall, dark-clad man appeared, his arms raised and his hands empty. He was bareheaded, and stumbled as he stepped slowly down to the deck.

"We go now," the captain said starkly, limping to the door. "Crizz, stay here and monitor that boat. One peep and you hit the alarm."

"Aye, Cap."

The other two made their way to the bay floor, Azular's Norvallan scanner in use as he advanced. They heard the bay door open behind them to admit the chief medic, who was soon on their heels.

"I'm checking him over before you take him anywhere," Flintlock murmured to the captain. "He looks in a bad way."

"He's probably cyber-enhanced and genetically altered. Don't get too close. And he's for the brig, no matter how bad he is."

The man let fall his arms, waiting, unsure of his reception. Ahxenta introduced herself and her officers and moved aside to let Flintlock in.

"He's undernourished, dehydrated, and has unhealed wounds from beatings," the doctor noted. "He's had at least two infectious diseases, but isn't carrying harmful microbes. He's exhausted, and needs primary aid before he'll be fit for medical and surgical treatment."

"Which he'll get in the brig," Ahxenta said firmly, although she saw he was in no state to be quizzed. "My guards will escort you. Azular?"

"Our guest *is* Friskianx, but only partly: readings are indefinite, so I can't pin down his exact origin. He has cyber implants, but trace meta-jurillium absorption products suggest that they were inserted months ago. And trace serocepcin in his system; *that* implies genetic alteration, though I can't gauge nature or extent. I read no zukivianite, but he *has* what I take to be an inactive tracker."

The man looked at him in surprise. "What kind of scanner have you got that tells you that?"

"Is it accurate?" Ahxenta demanded sharply.

"Yes. I told you Captain, my people and I were taken and they did things to us. We were unconscious for much of it and couldn't object. We realised we'd had implants and guessed we'd been tampered with genetically as we were… different. That's all I can tell you."

The captain sensed truth, and could see metallic glints at his temples that she associated with hostile fitments to ensure victim compliance.

"Take him to the brig, Lieutenant," she ordered Goldwash. "And you, Doc. Get him cleaned and fed, and fix his immediate hurts. More treatment and questions can wait. I've an ISA ship to deal with."

"Thank you, Captain Ahxenta," the man said with a deep sigh.

"Don't thank me yet," she warned. "Your story had better stack."

She waited until the group cleared the bay before she and Azular made for the obs room, where Cottontail was still scanning the craft.

"All clear, Crizz?"

"All clear, Cap. She's not going to blow up on us. I'll have my team go over her with a fine-toothed comb and get the results to you as soon as I have them. You staying here to help, Azular?"

"No he isn't," the captain answered. "He's for the bridge. The *Iris Quartz* will be off my bows by now and I want to know what she's up to. Let's go, Azular."

Ahxenta used the trip up to question her science officer on the man. Both had noticed his likeness to Vexin Thal, and the closer readings Azular had made confirmed a common origin, if nothing else.

"As his alterations were relatively recent, I deduce that he wasn't an original victim of the hostiles," Azular said. "Thal by his own account was taken over twelve years ago, standard galactic. If *this* Thal is related, he didn't meet a similar fate."

"We'll find out, and see what Crizz comes up with on that ship. But he reckons that that worm-pocket was an ISA set-up? Where did they get the gen to base it on? The Drapes? Is *that* why the *Skimfrost* spent so long there, *and* why she had a destroyer like the *Steadfast* as escort?"

"Possibly, ma'am. The ships were there for a while and didn't seem to spend time checking Furze, as Captain Thal was anxious they might. And Commander Thal, if that *is* his name, says he escaped that worm-pocket. He also claims to have commanded a ship that was taken out by hostiles over a year ago close to Axle Lexo, which would place it near the Astrella Nine asteroid field in zone Kappa."

"That hadn't escaped me, and it smacks of a hell of a coincidence. The *Kel'Tarn* was downed when she was sent in to look for a ship of the Starfall fleet that had been lost in that area," Ahxenta said tartly.

"Aye, ma'am. It did cross my mind as to why Thal would send in another to search for her. If he figured she'd been got by hostiles, why send in another that might suffer the same fate when your fleet's under threat and you're short-handed?"

"There's a person aboard that means a lot to you, and you've already faced losses that would mentally and emotionally crush most people."

"Thal *is* driven to take down hostiles in a way that most would find vindictive; and we know his crusade against them *is* personal," Azular said, his face creasing in pity. "He'll go out of his way to take them out, whatever the cost. And if this Dexel Thal *is* who he claims, he would know of the *Arianrhod* and that Thal has had dealings with us, although not of the *Kel'Tarn* and the events after that."

"Exactly. Though how come he knows of the ISA? It's a recent set-up. But we're here. Let's see what the status is. Apnis hasn't alerted me to anything as yet, so the *Iris Quartz* won't have opened a dialogue."

The ISA ship had not called, but had come in off starboard and was holding a parallel line. The first mate had ordered their course set for Polstarn, she told the captain. Ahxenta had barely taken her chair when comms called a link from Captain Morgen Gulley of the *Iris Quartz.*

"Will this be the third formal complaint to the ISA or has it learnt its lesson?" Apnis asked quietly as the captain ordered a visual.

"I'll see. I'm Captain Cinnabar Ahxenta. How may I help, Captain?"

The man was abrupt. He knew of the advent of a small hostile ship in the area and had logged the *Arianrhod* hauling it on board. He wanted to know why Ahxenta had taken that step, and more to the point, what she had done with the pilot.

The captain was equally terse. The ship was in a bad way, could not harm hers, and the pilot had requested aid. She would not refuse a ship in distress. The assumption that it was hostile was beside the point.

"It's obviously hostile!" Gulley flared. "With the superior gear *your* ship has, I'm sure you're very well aware of what it is."

"Our rep precedes us," Apnis murmured.

"Be that as it may, Captain. What is it to you? What interest do you have in a severely damaged vessel that can in no way harm yours?"

"I want that ship and its pilot."

"Why?"

"That's my business."

"What do you plan to do with that ship and her pilot?"

"That's not your concern," Gulley told her coldly.

"Until you tell me exactly why you want that ship and her pilot, and what you aim to do with them, I will not accommodate you. If you'll excuse me, I have a cargo to deliver and I plan to do just that."

"Not so fast. That's a hostile ship in ISA space and close to a major ISA facility at Stinward. I have a right…"

"So has that pilot and I don't plan to hand anybody over to anyone who clearly does not have good intentions. I have a cargo to deliver," she reiterated. "Do you plan to hinder me?"

Gulley bit his lip. "No I do not. But I *will* escort you to Polstarn."

"You know I'm headed to Polstarn: interesting. But as you wish. I advise that you steer well clear of that extinct worm-pocket: the energy currents in its immediate vicinity are erratic. Ahxenta out."

The first mate began to laugh softly. "He didn't like that, Cap. Now he's sure that we're sure that there was a worm-pocket and now there isn't. And he'll be wondering who we plan to tell and when."

"The fleet will get an advisory as soon as I have time."

"And the Polstarn authorities: Polstarn's in ISA space and on a line to Stinward, but it's not military, so Gulley will have no jurisdiction. If a new worm-pocket's been set off close to their business premises, I'd imagine they'd be pissed."

"Good point. And I'll have to contact Thal. He'll thank me," she sighed. "Ready us for the bypass and all speed to Polstarn, helm."

* * *

Arianrhod reached Polstarn with the *Iris Quartz* at her back. The *Quartz* settled into an adjacent bay, but made no contact as the PSS completed admin and began offload. Lindell had been busy on the way in and had the specifics of the deal alluded to by his friend in supply. It dealt with a batch of sonic cleaning units for Hervesta Tertius, twelve hours from their next but one stop of Yistreen. They could make it with no cost to schedule if despatch times at Polstarn and Stinward were minimal.

"Go for it," the captain agreed when the supercargo sent in the data. "I've had nothing from the ISA about our run-in with the *Iris Quartz*, and she's still sitting there, but I'll have to deal with the ISA office in Stinward, as I'll be handing over the *Steadfast's* probe."

"But not that wreck of a ship or her pilot," murmured Apnis.

"Not that; and I have to talk to Captain Thal. Axellina won't let me quiz Dexel Thal: he's in a bad way. She's planning surgery with Oak as assist to dig out as much of his cyber hardware as possible, as it's a danger to him and maybe to us."

"What does he think of that?"

"He's grateful; it causes him pain. The doc says it's because it was inserted quickly and inexpertly, a hack and splat job with no aftercare, so it led to infection. He's caused security no trouble, and his ship's a tin can taking up space in my bay. Azular's been extracting what he can from its databases and ops systems. Captain Thal can have it."

"Talking of ISA Stinward, Cap: the disappearing worm-pocket that this Thal figures for an ISA experiment?" Apnis said softly.

"Hearsay. I won't mention it; and nobody else had better breathe a word," she added balefully, aware that the inveterate eavesdroppers of her bridge crew had got the gist. "Everything's on track, so you have the conn, Tallica. I'm going to have a quick word with our guest in the brig and then I'm going to try to raise Thal."

The quick word related to answers that the captain wanted before she spoke to the commander of Starfall. Flintlock sat in to ensure that her patient was not unduly stressed, and was satisfied. An hour later, Ahxenta was in her office, a link to the *Kel'Moth* set up.

"You've been a time, Cap," the first mate noted dryly on her return. "Drop's done and Lindell's on pick-up. Reactions to your advisory, I guess; I had Polstarn PA on about it and about the *Iris Quartz*. I told the rep to talk to Gulley. I take it Thal could confirm our guest's claims and clarify the points that were bugging you."

"He did. He'd lost contact with a ship called the *Kel'Mor* around the Astrella Nine and sent the *Kel'Tarn* in after it. She'd been carrying vital top grade gear from Hervesta Tertius and was making for Sox and their bypass through Kappa and Mu to Starfall."

"Hervesta? So Thal's lot were trading *there* at that point?"

"Looks like. They must have had the credit. I've shown him Dexel Thal's ID and the bio-spec that the doc got and he's verified them. I've also had checks made of Friskianx trade and military fleet records: now that the Coalition's in the ISA, they *can* be got."

"How in blazes did you manage that?" Apnis wanted to know.

"I got an associate to do it," was the grinning reply.

"Levettiza. Thanks be for the UV-III. And?"

"Dexel Thal was career military, lieutenant commander on a Friskie Coalition fleet ship. He resigned his commission and vanished after Skyrtek. That's when he joined Starfall. With Vexin Thal in charge, he got command of the *Kel'Mor*. Thal needed all the able officers he could get and he knew he could trust his kid brother."

"His brother? They *are* related then?"

"Yup. Dexel Thal says he and his mates were left in a holding place until they and two life-tubes were hustled into that transport by a few cybers and a human-type. It was flown aboard a battleship that cut and run. The human-type used Inter-Lan in stroppy links between himself and a base, which let the prisoners work out that they'd been on Skota and were now on a bypass and headed to a base at Sella…"

"Bloody hell!" Apnis exploded.

"Exactly. As far as he could tell, the hostiles had just lost two auto ships and the dispute was about crews, as unmanned ships were so easy to outfox. Supplies for repairing what they had were wanted urgently, hence the life-tubes. Thal then realised that he and his people would be part of the equation once the ship made Sella."

"That's… just a sec, unmanned ships? The *Warrior* at Swan Two?"

"He didn't know, but it fits: Skota's not far off. But once they knew what they were in for, they decided to fight it out, whatever it cost. I'll never get the full story, but Thal says they played compliant, waited 'til the transport was being unloaded and then made a break. Their cyber implants gave them strength but two of them went down before they could grab enough hardware to make it count."

The captain was interrupted by an update from her supercargo that their contract was on and the Hervesta cargo ready. She gave the go-ahead and scanned the other notes on her ops board. Ordering the first mate to handle loading, she left for medbay to talk to her CMO. She was back within an hour, to find the task almost complete.

"We can be off in two-three hours, Cap," Apnis told her. "Still zip from the *Iris Quartz* and she's been sat doing nothing but trying to scan what she can. Not us, though she *has* had her eyes on the client's pods. No alerts or calls. I'm surprised Captain Thal's not linked, or ISA HQ. You going to make a formal complaint about Gulley's antics?"

"That depends on his next tricks. Stinward's ISA, so I bet he'll make tracks the second we do, and his won't be the only ISA ship there. And we won't be the only PSS. The *Firedrake's* waiting for us, and given the advisory I sent, we'll have the *PSS Kel'Lath* from Nexus."

"What? That'll put the wind up the ISA if she's no trade at Stinward. And I can't imagine the ISA would use a Starfall ship."

"The ISA wouldn't but the New Zegonia independents would and they're the suppliers. It's meta-jurillium plating for the Stinward yards and Captain Dun's putting a spurt on to get in at back of us."

"What else?" Apnis asked, scenting a hidden agenda.

"We leave with the *Kel'Lath*. The ISA can make of that what it will."

"*Kel'Lath* won't be taking on our lodger?"

"No, she'll head back to Nexus, but the ISA won't know that. The doc's setting up for surgery, as Captain Thal's okayed it."

"What *of* our guest? How did he find out about the ISA's attempt to make a worm-pocket, or what in blazes it was up to? Or even about the ISA, as he'd been out of circulation for so long?"

"There were aliens in and out of Skota near the end and they were nervous, so he'd heard of the ISA and its expansion into Psi. But later: first we finish here. It'll take us over a day to Stinward, as we're heavy in the beam with its cargo. And I won't discount trouble on the road," the captain said heavily.

* * *

Later meant in the mess, with duty hours done, the cargo stowed, and the ship en route. Ahxenta had decreed alert status all the way: the *Iris Quartz* had slipped out to shadow them, and a call to her from Gulley had advised that he would attend her to Stinward. She did not object, but advised him that her eyes would be on his ship from here on in.

"Come on, Cinnabar, what's the rest of Thal's story?" the first mate urged. "How did he get away from the hostiles and end up out here? It's a long way from Sella, *if* that's where he jumped ship."

"The ship hadn't made Sella. He'd no clear idea of a way out – they meant to go down fighting, taking as many out as they could, which may be why he *did* make it. His story is that they were in a hangar with fighters and shuttles, but few aliens. They got the ones they could, but then realised that the space doors were rigged and the bay set to blow. He made back to that transport, his mate to a fighter. They shot their way out. He made it but she was taken out. The transport was hit but could survive the bypass, and having flown Starfall ships, he could handle it. He worked out he was close to Sella, so he jumped off the bypass and cut an angle back on, to aim for a hub called Flit, where he knew a local crossover bypass to Portal, on the Eta-Theta border."

"Never heard of Flit *or* Portal," Apnis said. "How come he did?"

"Eta's mostly Coalition and he'd been part of their fleet: Flit's a base for fleet survival training, so he knew he could hide out and cross to Portal once it felt safe. Portal *is* in a line to Fivepoint, so he reckoned he'd make for Nexus from there, if he could lift extra gear off Portal – it's an auto post and he knew the systems. But he didn't reckon he'd run into a rebranded ISA research ship with an interceptor escort just off the bypass at Portal. I checked the call-signs he said he got and the names stack: *ISAS Sparillia* and *ISAS Adamant*. And he logged a large mass-energy density locus in an area known for random fluxes, but this was stable, rotating and infested by a raft of tech. The *Adamant* spied him and started firing as soon as she was in range, so he knew he'd get no quarter. He made back to the bypass and she followed him. He says the *Sparillia* came about as well, so they wanted him down."

"And?" the first mate prompted.

"He jumped off again and used every atom of energy he had to dive down the mouth of the rotating energy mass – it looked to him like a worm-pocket. He knew the transport was unlikely to survive and he'd no clue to what he'd find. He says he's no idea how long he rode the currents, but he shot out where we found him. He set off the distress as he'd nothing left. He was amazed to be alive and even more freaked when we showed. But as he was an ISA target and we weren't ISA, we were a reasonable bet. And then he spotted the *Iris Quartz*."

"Hell, the ISA must have got its alert out quick *and* had the *Iris* close to hand to get it en route. I wonder if Gulley's been told why they want that transport and Thal. But has Azular confirmed the readings he says he got of the worm-pocket and the actions he'd been in?"

"Some. The data we picked up of the glitch at *this* end matches what Thal got of the other. As it blew, whatever the ISA experts have been up to, they haven't sussed the technique. But I recall Kerrix saying at the TA show where the ISA was unleashed that the ISP, the Norvallans and a Mu ship were up to mischief at K457. She didn't know how the ISP first found K457, but guessed it knew short bypasses or similar that it kept under wraps. She was maybe onto something."

"Be that as it may, Cap – the ISA will *have* to be told about Sella, if there's an active hostile base there. And *we* can't spill," said Apnis.

"I know. Levettiza can. I'll get on to her later, though she may know already through Captain Thal. But enough; we'll need to be fresh for the next leg. If that isn't trouble," Ahxenta groaned as an urgent cheep of her communit told her that something was up. "What is it, doc?"

"Get down to the brig, and bring Azular with you: there's a problem with Thal. I'm prepping him for immediate transfer to medbay."

15: AN OLD ACQUAINTANCE

Apnis had raced to the bridge and was grimly waiting news. She faced an inflexible Captain Gulley; he had been called to his bridge when the *Iris Quartz* picked up an unknown signal rated hostile by his science team that had been traced to *Arianrhod*. The PSS had quickly killed the bleep, but Gulley wanted answers that Apnis was not about to supply. She had called shields up, weapons on standby and the ship to alert in reply to the scans that Gulley had ordered, and *Arianrhod's* tactical and science stations were keeping a close watch on their opposite number.

Gulley had inferred that the signal was related to the alien transport or its pilot. Apnis had deduced the same, but was not minded to allow the *Quartz* to probe *Arianrhod* to find out. She had sent Cottontail to the bay to verify that the craft was dead, which she had. The first mate's refusal to cut jammers on Gulley's demand infuriated him. He ordered his ship closer to the PSS, a risky move that had the seething first mate insisting he haul back. At his refusal and an energy rise that read as his weapons charging, she called red alert and defence systems on line.

Gulley's eyes bulged as the alert wailed, red light flooded *Arianrhod's* bridge and calls rang out as duty officers assumed station. "I have not targeted your ship!" he bellowed.

"You're dangerously close to my hull *and* you've powered weapons, Captain. I regard those as hostile acts and am preparing to defend my ship. Comms, despatch a distress, all channels! Lieutenant Commander Earbleat, target the *Iris Quartz*! Ready to return fire on my mark!"

Apnis had already cut the link to the *Quartz* when Ahxenta sprinted in to claim the command chair. "What's he done?"

"Committed an error I bet he's regretting. Tried to snuggle up close and thought I'd not notice him sneakily arming his big guns from his ops board. Any response to our hail, Gallus?"

"No ma'am, but Captain Gulley wants a word."

"His ship's not a patch on the *Matchless*, but she'll have a few tricks," the captain said tersely. "And she *is* damn close. Helm, get us clear of her. Put her in sight of our aft batteries: that should give him a fright."

"She's not matching our line, she's slipped back. This'll be the third formal to the ISA, then?" the first mate surmised.

"Too true. Keep a bead on her, Earbleat; his weapons are hot, but he'll not be rash enough to use them. Cut the noise, but maintain alert."

The ships held for Stinward, now under ten hours away. After a rapid exchange with Gulley, Ahxenta ordered the distress cut: the *PSS Kel'Lath* had caught it, responded and was on intercept, a tactic that had the ISA captain livid. He had powered down his weapons, and the *Iris Quartz* was holding distance but matching pace with *Arianrhod*.

"Drop to amber, but keep our defences ready," the captain decreed. "Rotate the duty crews, Tallica, and get sack time: we need to be sharp for Stinward. I have to talk to Olith Dun *and* send a protest to the ISA; I won't hang fire on it and I'll copy the fleet in. That's the doc, spitting quarks over Thal," she groaned as a message lit her board. "I'll have to defuse it, though I see she's got him to medbay. I'll update you later."

Ahxenta despatched her first two tasks quickly. The formal protest to ISA HQ she copied to its Stinward office, as she anticipated fallout, and to the TA, along with a request for TA action on ISA intimidation. The *Kel'Lath* was now an hour behind and catching, and the *Firedrake* was aware of the situation. Medbay was quiet when she reached it. The chief MO was viewing the monitors outside Thal's iso-bay, there was a nurse-tech in attendance on the man, and two guards at the door.

"How is he?" Ahxenta asked.

"Better than he was but worse than he should be," was the icy reply. "I'll get Wren to take over here and then we'll talk in my office."

"I'll get Azular in. He'll still be in the brig, I expect."

"It's you I want to speak to, not him."

"That's enough," the captain warned as Flintlock marched off.

The CMO reached her office to find two hot drinks on the table. "Sit," Ahxenta said. "Say your piece and then I'll haul Azular in."

As she had guessed, her chief medic needed to let off steam about events in the brig. Flintlock had been summoned over a sudden decline in the man, who appeared to be in intense pain. The doctor had picked up on the reason at once: Thal's inactive internal tracker had kicked in. She had put him out and called for a med-cradle to take him to medbay. Azular, on reaching the brig, had grasped the problem and blocked the tracker by upping the cell's secure field and setting off a counter-signal, but the means were fixed; he and the CMO had been locked in dispute when the captain came in. Her command to cut the device out of Thal in situ, as she would not risk her ship and crew if the signal was caught, was met with disbelief. Ahxenta was inflexible: *Arianrhod* had the *Iris Quartz* on her tail and was heading for an ISA station. She backed her order with security. Flintlock had complied, but was positive that the stopgap surgery had damaged Thal. She held the captain responsible.

"I'm calling Azular in, but before he arrives, let's get one thing clear: *I'm* in command here, and you will not dispute when I give you a direct order. And now I'll tell you what went down after that tracker signal."

Flintlock's fury had abated by the time Azular arrived. He had taken the tracker apart and stored the bits separately. It was meant to be read at distance, and though he believed it unlikely that the signal that got out would have been caught by hostile ears, he did not discount it.

"Somebody in the ISA will figure, and long tongues will spread the rumour that we were involved," Ahxenta said sourly. "It'll reach hostile ears one way or another. The moles in most of the big outfits that think they run the damn galaxy will see to it. You'll check Thal for anything else that might emit a signal and you'll remove anything that shows as soon as safely possible, Doctor. Damn! What now?"

"You're getting grouchy: time you were off," Flintlock advised as the comms officer informed the captain that the *Kel'Lath* was up with them and that Captain Dun was on line.

* * *

Arianrhod's Stinward berth was strategically placed to allow several ISA vessels to keep her in their lines of sight. Ahxenta had no doubt they were keeping tabs on her. She had declined a civil call to head directly to the ISA office for talks. The gear she was set to deliver was a priority, and on a tight schedule, she had no room for irksome chat. The facts that *Arianrhod's* targeting eyes were online and all but her operating cargo bays were shielded were other sore points with the authorities.

The captain was amused to note a shuttle leaving the *Iris Quartz* for the orbital ISA office, although Gulley had not called. The *Kel'Lath* had been directed to an outlying bay to drop her cargo, but her captain had linked for news, as had Ma'Lappis of the *Firedrake*. It had been agreed that Dr Ma'Lappis would be picked up by the shuttle that Ahxenta was to take to the ISA office to deliver the *Steadfast's* probe and explain her actions; she had already had a spat with Admiral Best, who had linked supra-light to argue over Fourpoint. A TA HQ rep had also called her about her request for an official response to ISA intimidation.

"You're popular, Cap," Apnis greeted her after a lengthy absence in the bridge office. "Half our cargo's offloaded already. I think the crews have been told to get a move on. Maybe they want us gone asap."

"They want me in the ISA office. I get the feeling that the top brass is desperate to know what Thal knows and what he's told us. Best was pushing for answers, so he knows the score as far as Portal's concerned *and* he mentioned Sella, which means word of that's got through. And the TA doesn't want to annoy its chums in the ISA: I've been told the TA Council won't pursue my claim of harassment."

"Huh! The TA doesn't want to lose its fancy Alto Finglas office and the rewards it gets from its links to the ISA. You sent that to the fleet?"

"I did, and a note on Sella, lest any of them are near. Captain Kerrix told me Levettiza got word to the ISA. She's busy on repair, there's no more on her stolen hull tech and our jurillium's heading to Starfall. Lindell has the costs and says it's a bargain. *Quartz's* shuttle home yet?"

"No sign. What did Nat Holdspan and Grey Bluejohn have to say?"

"*Warrior's* just left Cressel for Polstarn, so Nat was asking about the vanishing worm-pocket, and if we wanted back-up here. I said no, but warned him why he should watch *his* back. *Obsidian's* for Limekiln and is past Quartic. Grey had no trouble at Furze, but recorded activity off beacon. But I'd better get down to see what the ISA reps want their ears tickled with. Azular's with me. He should have the probe ready."

"You're taking an armed escort and you'll all have locating pins."

"Azular will have that info-pad Captain Kerrix gave him. It'll tell us what the reps had for lunch," was the dry retort.

"Armed escort and locating pins," the first mate repeated. "Azular's toys or not, we both know the ISA and its tricks. And mind that leg."

The captain was wise enough to take heed and she, with her science officer and two guards, set off in the *Gadfly*. They were met by an aide and led to a meeting room. Ahxenta left her security outside as she and Azular turned in. That Captain Gulley was there was no surprise, but one face that met them caused both to halt. The senior rep had hardly opened his mouth when *Arianrhod's* incensed captain rounded on him.

"What's *he* doing here?"

"Excuse me?"

"You heard me: what's *he* doing here?" Ahxenta repeated.

"Lieutenant Horn is here to check that our probe, ISA property that you refused to return to the *ISAS Steadfast*, is in original condition and has not been tampered with," the man announced.

"Dr Azular, scan him!"

The captain upheld a grim silence until the process was complete. Gulley and the reps watched in perplexity whilst Horn stood immobile.

"Mr Horn's talents are active, Captain, and his cybernetics still allow him to throw a formidable punch," Azular concluded.

"You try anything, mister, and there'll be a fourth formal complaint heading to ISA HQ. You copy?"

"I don't know what you mean, Captain," Horn said icily.

"You damn well do. Here's the *Steadfast's* probe, the one set covertly on my ship's tail by the ISA, for purposes that Captain Reddish refused to explain," she told the senior rep. "Perhaps *you'd* edify me as to why this probe, with high-spec sensory and tracking gear, a partial cloak and navigational arrays based on those used in zone Psi ships, was set to tail my ship from Furze? You'll find it *is* intact: my science officers have better things to do than play with your cast-offs."

Horn sullenly examined the probe as senior ISA rep Bell denied any familiarity with the incident and Azular checked that his info-pad was logging every iota of the meeting and relaying it to the *Arianrhod*.

"You know Lieutenant Horn?" the second rep, Ringlet, asked.

"The last time we met Mr Horn, he caused Dr Azular severe injury in an unprovoked attack. I was told he'd been relieved of duty and was to be charged. The ISP, as it then was, never did follow it up. And now I find him here. Why? What's your remit?" she asked Horn.

"To analyse this probe… Captain," he added at the glint in her eye.

"A pilot of advanced military craft? Interesting," Ahxenta remarked acidly. "Have you completed your analysis?"

"Yes ma'am. It's intact, and hasn't been interfered with."

"Good. Get out."

"Captain, I protest," Bell interjected. "Lieutenant Horn will sit in."

"Why?" Ahxenta enquired equably.

"As an observer and technical expert."

"On what?"

Bell had only a string of pretexts and it was soon clear to the visitors that Horn was there to dissect every word with regard to Fourpoint. It was also clear that the ISA badly wanted its hands on the alien ship and pilot that *Arianrhod* had rescued, and more information on them.

"Admiral Best of fleet command has been briefed, I've sent reports, and I will not give a badly-injured shipwreck survivor into hands that won't explain their intentions," Ahxenta told him. "The ISA would do better to help the Polstarn people clear the mess at that extinct worm-pocket. And I refuse to discuss anything with Mr Horn at my elbow."

"This is uncalled-for, Captain! Lieutenant Horn is an ISA officer and an expert in stealth technology…" Bell stuttered.

"He's also an info-sent with a short fuse," Ahxenta cut in.

"He's what?" Gulley snapped.

"Are you saying you didn't know? Mr Horn, you will tell me exactly why you're here and who sent you, or this meeting is at an end."

Horn was clearly furious, but asserted that he was there to analyse the probe and to assist the ISA office to clarify events at Fourpoint.

"Your list of jobs is expanding. And you still haven't told me who sent you. Or when. Rather a coincidence that you turn up when I do."

"I have no more to say to you, Captain," he said stiffly.

"In which case, any further dialogue will be a complete waste of my time. I have duties aboard my ship. Good day."

With that, Ahxenta gathered her gear and turned, Azular behind her, ignoring Bell's furious mutters but aware that Gulley was readying to move. As she limped to the door, she heard the ominous shirring of a weapon being released from its sheath.

"What in hell are you doing, man?" Gulley barked as he grabbed Horn's arm and twisted it savagely.

Azular had instinctively pushed his captain aside. She fell heavily as a phase shot hit a wall and *Arianrhod's* guards raced in. Bell and Ringlet had ducked, Bell calling for aid. Horn was disarmed and restrained in seconds, his strength no match for the stun that Ji dealt him. Ahxenta's quiet cursing alarmed the already concerned Azular.

"Get a medic in here *now!*" he hissed at the cowering Bell.

"I don't need a medic," the captain growled.

"I beg to differ, ma'am. Captain Gulley, your assistance please."

The two helped Ahxenta sit up as two ISA guards pounded in. Horn was handed over with a rapid exchange of words, and hustled out as a medic arrived. He dropped to his knees by the captain whilst Azular replied to Apnis, who had been anxiously calling for details.

Gulley called his ship and then faced the ISA reps. He was unaware of Horn's info-sent status and incensed that he had not been told, but astute enough to refuse to reveal his remit when Azular civilly asked. The Berzic then turned to the captain let her know that Apnis had sent a shuttle down, with Dr Flintlock and a pilot for the *Gadfly* aboard.

Ahxenta's level gaze met his and then dropped to his upper left arm. "That bastard didn't miss, did he?" she grated. "How bad?"

"It's not serious, ma'am. The bolt grazed me before it hit the wall."

"Doctor, please attend to Dr Azular. Lieutenant Ji, tell Mr Bell that I want to speak to him. Now."

Bell had been expecting the summons but was taken aback by the one word thrown at him. "Explain."

* * *

A relieved Apnis stood at the end of the *Gadfly's* ramp as the captain was wheeled down, Flintlock and Azular behind her. "You have a habit of finding trouble," she greeted them. "Elka Reef's bringing our other shuttle in via the *Firedrake*. We got all of what was said and done – you didn't shut down your info-pad," she said to Azular. "Those ISA reps won't have a leg to stand on when I bawl them out later."

"Save your breath," the captain sighed wearily. "Bell's a prating yes-man that does as he's told, as you no doubt picked up from our chat. His sidekick's no better and the ISA will close ranks around Horn."

"How can they? And how in hell was he let loose to practice his art after his actions last time? What's he doing here anyhow? He's a pilot, or was when he flew Myrtleberry's shuttle up from Silverglass, way back. And dished *you* a broken jaw, Azular."

"Later," Flintlock cut in. "The Cap and Azular are for medbay."

"Horn's an expert in stealth technology," the Berzic mused. "He's maybe also an expert in worm-pocket technology."

"Button it," the doctor said brusquely, setting the captain's chair in motion. "You either walk, mister, or I get the guards to carry you."

"I'll see you both later," the first mate grinned. "We've cargo drop to finish. And I bet Captain Gulley will want to talk – his shuttle headed out same time as the *Gadfly*."

Word had travelled, and in addition to Gulley she had the local ISA office and its HQ on, as well as Captains Dun and Ma'Lappis. She dealt curtly with the ISA, in no mood for its warping of facts. She relayed the gist to Ahxenta when, work done, the ship was prepping to leave.

"Best was on; I told him there was a fourth protest heading in, with assault charges attached. And I sent the TA a note, as it'll be pulled in. We have Flish back, but you know that. Pa was on good form: he's demanded a full account of the action from Bell and a promise that it'll be dealt with, not that he'll get it. *Firedrake's* for Keystone Kell, but she'll escort us to the bypass. Captain Dun will head out when we do and the *Kel'Lath* will be with us as far as Yistreen, in case of trouble."

"Gulley?" asked the captain.

"Is shook. Whatever his orders were, that the ISA set a flawed info-sent to spy on us, who tried to down you, has given him a jolt. He still wanted info on Thal and his ship, but got zip. He asked after you and Azular, *and* how you knew Horn. I told him you were both in medbay, and to ask his own about Horn, as I expect he'll be called in over it. I got the base medic's report – Bell was put out, but I told him our legal rep needed it as evidence, and if he refused to hand it over, the court would want to know why. Our guys got the security facts: Horn's gun was set to cause damage. But I'm for the bridge, as we're off soon. Doc says you're here for the next twelve hours, so be good."

* * *

Arianrhod, having waved off the *Firedrake*, was with the *Kel'Lath* on the way to Yistreen through virtually empty space. Apnis had agreed with Dun and Ma'Lappis that they cut a wide line by Fourpoint after leaving

Stinward, but scan for what they could in passing. They got little: the area was tight, with alert beacons in place. Ahxenta had resumed her chair soon after but found she had a stack of comms, reactions to news of the attack on her at the ISA base.

"I seem to be popular, or a lot of people out there are worried about me," she told her first mate after another stint in her office.

"Does that include the ISA?"

"Does it hell. Its upper ranks only want to make sure I'm not going to publicly sue it. Our legal rep says its legal unit is playing the line that the ISA has the absolute right to guard its own from any possible threat by any means, though Horn's been charged with two counts of serious assault and removed to a med facility, allegedly."

"You won't win against the ISA," Apnis cautioned.

"I know, but I can annoy it big time by what it thinks I might do."

"You realise we won't win any more ISA contracts? At this rate we'll be banned at every ISA post in the mapped galaxy."

"We won't. The ISA's still desperate for protected wafer arrays for comms for its new ships, and who do you think will soon be one of the few suppliers with materials *and* expertise?"

"That'll be fun," the first mate prophesied.

"It will. What now?" Ahxenta asked, as comms called a link for her.

"It's from the ISA, ma'am, and tagged important," Bellfish replied.

"My office. I'll be back," she growled, rising.

The captain returned thirty minutes later. "Important my boot. It was about the glitch at the Crimson Drapes and that dicey new worm-pocket. The ISA's sent in its best research scientists to find out what they are, how they work, their dangers, and how to put a stop to them."

"That would be the sterling work done by the ISAS ships *Skimfrost, Steadfast, Sparillia* and *Adamant*, no doubt," the first mate cut in.

"Yup. The logic is that there might be more of them. The ISA wants the edge on how to find and deal with them, for everyone's safety, of course. The ISA press office will notify every allied system, but those directly involved, such as all the main fleets, are getting first dibs."

"In case we scream, or come across ISA ships where they shouldn't be, doing what they shouldn't be," Apnis snorted.

"More or less. But the link from Starfall that came in was to tell me our cargo's arrived and it'll be kept for us."

"So Captain Thal's back then?" the first mate questioned.

"Captain Kerrix didn't say, but *did* say we're welcome to stop when we're out that way. *Moonstone's* up to scratch; she's testing new kit that's been fitted, *and* the tech she came with that her crew has to get a handle on. Starfall *is* the repair and build centre for the fleet. Kerrix didn't give much away, but other ships are due in. Thal's upping his fleet round it: as the TA's got the access codes from Twilight to Amity, he'll have to patrol the route. ISA and other fleets will use it, as they'll want into the new sectors, but they won't be wanted at any Starfall base *and* Thal will need to spike any plans by the ISA fleet to send in patrol boats."

"Anything else from that neck of the galaxy?" Apnis asked slyly.

"The link didn't say: it was short. We can make straight from Starfall to Twilight, and maybe cut off there for Freskat, if we can get Thal or whoever's in charge to hand over the codes for the bypass that links Twilight to Gemstone. Unless trade comes in to take us elsewhere."

"Cinnabar! You plan to use the bypass to Twilight? That'll be a new one for us and mostly in unmapped space. And then ask Thal if we can use the node that cuts up to Freskat and then on to near Mellifly?"

"Exactly. We may as well get used to the new routes. It won't cost, it'll advantage us time-wise, and for now there won't be many ships on them. The bypass to Gemstone crosses into mapped space near Brown Amber, so if we get the codes we can make for the Web from there, unless we have other business. Lindell's on the hunt."

"You're relying on Thal to hand over the goods, Cap? We might be giving him his brother back, but will that make him trade?"

"*I'm* not second-guessing him. But we've our loads to shift. We'll be up on Yistreen in thirty six hours at our current rate and Hervesta's only a hop beyond. Ah! Here's the note from the doc: she's finished surgery on Commander Thal. I'll head down and see how it went."

"That was some stint: she and Oak and their team will be done in."

The first mate was right and the captain found the exhausted CMO in her office with her face in a mug of coffee. The rest of her team she had sent off. Dr Ma'Lappis was monitoring the patient.

"He stood it well," she answered to Ahxenta's query. "He'll be out for a while and on life-support for twenty hours. I've kept the bits for Azular. We had to leave the hardware merged to his skeletal structure, but it won't cause him trouble – Oak's seen to that, and added repair patches where there was bone injury. The micro-parts fused to his skull were the worst to deal with as we'd to cut links, but he's now clear of anything that could be used as a control."

"Learning curve for you?" the captain asked.

"And then some. And since *you're* here, we'll get your med-check and physio done. Leg still holding up?"

"Thus far. But I need to get back to the bridge."

"You damn well don't; Tallica's more than able. I'll let her know you'll be here for a bit. Lettis needs the practice, so he can do it."

The captain submitted with good grace, aware that Flintlock would else nag, and the scans and therapy were carried out by her junior medic. She was back in her command chair in less than an hour.

* * *

The peace lasted over the rest of the trip to Yistreen, and by the time *Arianrhod* had made orbit and bid the *Kel'Lath* farewell, their efficient supercargo had found a contract that fitted into their existing schedule. Ahxenta laughed as she called up the details on her ops board.

"You deal with cargo drop, Tallica. I need see Lindell. I don't know how he orchestrated this, but it's a good one."

"What is it?" the first mate asked curiously.

"A pick up at Hervesta: a cargo listed as scientific instrumentation, but no other details. Very delicate, so it'll be in a highly-protected pod."

"Which means we won't know what's in it and we might not be able to scan. You sure that's wise Cinnabar? Who's it for?"

"The commander of Starfall base," the captain grinned.

"What!? A cargo for Starfall? One of their own can't pick it up?"

"We're heading there, and as Captain Kerrix for one knows, I guess she might have had a hand in it. And we *are* headed to Starfall. It makes sense. And profit," she added wickedly. "Keep us on track."

"Roger that. Bet Azular had something to do with it," she muttered. "Making sure we *are* going to Starfall, come hell or high water."

The clients were planet-based but had sent a cargo carrier to collect and Lindell's team dealt with the accounts. Apnis handled the whole, for three hours had gone without the captain's return. Links had come in for her that Bellfish had patched through, but just as the first mate was giving way to anxiety, she was called into the bridge office.

"Sit," the captain invited. "I've been dodging high-rankers from the ISA that want to chew my ears over the protests *and* other things I've sent – and the TA. Remember the Skota life-tubes? Levettiza got word to ISA Intelligence to test them outside and in for trackers and micro-drones; a few were found and disabled, but Intelligence bods have been sifting evidence, and our name and Starfall's has come up as knowing more than most, *and* Furze has come into it. I'll to have to call a briefing and let our people in on some of it, once we're on the road."

"Has the ISA linked any tissue samples to known missing persons, do you know?" Apnis asked delicately.

"Probably, but Levettiza wasn't told – whatever her links to her old job, there must be limits to what she can find out. The alien presence on Skota's gone and the ISA's digging. There's nothing on the Crimson

Drapes pocket or nebular glitch, but I got a comm from Nat Holdspan: he was waylaid by the *ISAS Adamant* on his way out of Polstarn, and warned off getting too close to a string of warning beacons…"

"*Adamant?*" Apnis echoed. "Wasn't she at Portal?"

"That struck me *and* Nat, but she'd have run via the bypass and got in at his back. He was quizzed about us and told them off. He's for Flecket, then Keystone, so we may see him at Xerophyte. But that's our clearance in, so back to the bridge for us. Next stop Hervesta."

The captain called the staff briefing two hours later, as she had other issues to clear before *Arianrhod* made her next port. The first was a talk to Thal, and she made for medbay soon after. Flintlock, insisting that her patient remain in care, had settled him in an iso-bay. The captain's response to that had been to post a watch and she nodded to the guard as she stepped in. The man looked markedly better than he had when first they met, she noted. He tried to stand and she waved him down.

The captain repeated the kernel of the talk, and others that she had had later with Azular, to her first mate in private. Thal had recalled as much as he could of the places he had been held, the tech he had seen and the hostiles he had met. He had come across human-like forms, and when Ahxenta showed him an image of Hoxiz, he knew the type. There were various versions, always in supervisory roles. Of the life-tubes he had seen, he could tell her little — they had never been worked on in his presence and seemed old.

Thal held to his story; Azular thus compared the data the man had got of the ships he had met, and both ends of the worm-pocket, with data *Arianrhod* held, and verified that the ISA ships *were* the *Sparillia* and the *Adamant*. The synthetic worm-pocket elements were non-alien, and Azular read them as attempts to replicate what had been found at the Crimson Drapes. Some inserts logged intrigued him, until he searched his lists of Norvallan tech, and linked Kerrix for more facts. She agreed that overall, the structures were similar to her people's trials to short-cut bypass building by using gravity wells and similar as step-off points. She had also asked to speak to the captain.

"She wanted to pass the tech details to Admiral Posettix, to see if he knows more on Norvallan-ISA shenanigans at K457, and if there's a link. I okayed it, and she got back to me not long ago. The upshot is that the ISA has to be nice to Norvalla and its colonies, and agree deals that'll benefit them and their Psi allies if it wants closer scientific liaison and useful tech, to stop its tests blowing up in its face. There *has* been liaison, but the Psi bodies won't hand out something for nothing."

"Happy days, Cap. What about the bits Axellina took out of Thal?"

"Azular says they're too broken to make anything of; he's made sure they're inactive, and encased them in resin to make sure they stay that way. But we're for Hervesta in a few hours to offload, and haul in that pod of Starfall gear, and we'll both be on the bridge. So break time."

* * *

After a swift cargo drop, the protected pod for Starfall was shipped in. The captain had her people go over every micron before allowing it on board, and once cleared, it was tied down under continuous scan in an inner hold. Leave to depart being given, Ahxenta gave the ready order.

"We're still heavy with the Wester gear and this'll be a long pull across a lot of empty space to Xerophyte," she remarked.

"Some of which might be less empty than it looks," Box muttered.

The captain agreed and once underway, *Arianrhod* ran at alert, her cloak up and her hull arrays at full stretch. Science and tactical used the time to test the holo-grid, pulling in data from their arrays and outside sources. They were two days out when Azular, checking ISA press and info nets, found an item noting four new areas posted dangerous and off-limits. The first ran from Furze to beyond the new worm-pocket, taking in the assumed hostile holding area; the second was at Fourpoint and the third off Portal. The attached bulletin stated that the ISA was upping scrutiny of the anomalies in the areas, as they posed potential shipping hazards. The fourth area was around Skota.

"Looks like the ISA is still pulling out what it can from Skota since it found the life-tubes, and it's begun on Furze," the first mate said to the captain as they read the data. "*And* it's at Portal: part of ISA or not, I bet the Coalition's pissed that one of its auto-posts has been ring-fenced. Has the bulletin been widely circulated, Azular?"

"No ma'am," he replied. "As far as I can tell, it hasn't been sent to any zone or system authorities or shipping lines."

"Keeping it quiet," Ahxenta said cynically. "Azular, log the link and have comms send it to the fleet, copied to the TA."

"The TA should already know, as its Assembly HQ is next door to ISA HQ at Alto Finglas," Apnis pointed out.

"So why didn't it send the news out to all the fleets under its flag?"

"Maybe it did and we fell off the list."

"Can it. Azular, add a query to the TA asking it to clarify its policy on projected hazards to shipping in those areas," Ahxenta directed.

No-one was surprised by a lack of response hours later, although a few enquiries from the PSS fleet had come in. The captain left the first mate in command of the bridge, as a link from her chief medic asking for a chat called her to medbay. The topic was Thal, now fit enough to be discharged to a private billet. Flintlock wanted to do that.

"He'll need regular physio, so he'll be back here every day, and he'll need more stimulus than looking at four walls for hours or jabbing at info-stations that won't let him access much. He's not asked to talk to his own at Starfall, which I thought he might."

"And Captain Thal hasn't called to ask either, probably as he figures we'd listen in," Ahxenta remarked. "Nor would he want to run the risk of a link being intercepted, even with our and his secure systems. Dexel Thal can have his old billet in the brig back."

"Cinnabar! That's not an option. He's a fellow fleet officer…"

"He is not – he might be Starfall but his ship wasn't a PSS."

"You're splitting hairs, Cap," the doctor argued. "He's been in here long enough, you've checked his credentials and you've talked to him. What *do* you make of him?"

"Deep, like his brother. Okay, I'll sanction a change of quarters, but I'll post a guard, he won't go anywhere unescorted and his info-use will be monitored. He can use the officer's mess. You'd best sort him gear other than medical scrubs. Azular can keep an eye on him. That might take *his* mind off other things," she grunted.

"Like what, apart from the obvious?" Flintlock asked.

"That hull section mock-up with micro-sensors to detect and block limpet tech: he says he's grasped how the sensor units link to Norvallan hull arrays and to each other. He's been in Crizz's lab in his off-duty making a fine-mesh overlay of simulated sensor units that he wants to test in situ on a couple of *Arianrhod's* hull science arrays."

"You told him in his dreams, I bet?"

"Damn straight I did. He won't be sending out bots to stick patches of flashy matter to my hull! He can run sims and chat to Thal instead. Let Thal know he'll be moving. I'll get Lindell to arrange a billet and then I'm for the bridge. I'll see you in the mess later."

"Aye, Cap. Who'll be telling Azular he's Thal's minder?"

"I will."

The captain informed her senior science officer of his task on return to the bridge. He agreed calmly. Dubious as to why, she asked outright. That he hoped to dig up more on Starfall did not surprise her, though she figured that Thal was likely to find out more on them than Azular would on him and his. Something else bit and she regarded him keenly.

"What else? You want to know how Vexin Thal ticks and think you might get some clues from his close kin? You'll be lucky."

"Data exchange, ma'am," he said. "He'll find out about Starfall's PSS ships when he speaks to Captain Thal, so keeping it from him now is pointless; telling him might make him open up."

"You tread a fine line and I bet there's more to it, but you're right. Keep a tight rein."

"Yes, ma'am."

"What's he up to now?" Apnis asked when the captain resumed her chair. "He's got a grin on his face and that usually means trouble."

"Later. What's our status?"

"No change, apart from we're nearer Xerophyte and *Warrior's* on a line for Keystone and may pass us by the Eta-Kappa border. And the *Karillion* was on; she's navigating the edges of the Silverglass Nebula en route to Barfit, so crossing Zeta. I told Captain Flintlock we'd a halt at Xerophyte, though we might be off before he gets into Salt. Nothing from the TA about our query. What did Axellina want? Thal?"

The captain nodded and outlined the next steps. "Once he's settled I'll try a call to Captain Thal, as we're not close to systems with listening posts. Wherever the *Kel'Moth* is: she'd been escorting the *Serenity* last I spoke to Thal but that was a lot of days ago. I suspect he'll want to get home to be on hand in case the ISA or TA try anything at Starfall, or on the Amity to Twilight bypass: it's a long stretch to keep an eye on."

"And as we'll be paying a visit, I expect he'd want to be around for that. We and the *Obsidian* are the only non-Starfall PSSs that have seen the place – as far as we know," Apnis said.

* * *

The next days passed quietly as the ship sped on. Thal's move to crew quarters was smooth, a secure watch ensuring the man was never alone when on the decks. A private link to Captain Thal had been sanctioned, but not data transfer. Azular's task gave *him* more puzzles: Dexel Thal was as taciturn as his brother, and seemed to share the same traits of reserve and a nature fiercely protective of his own people.

"He *was* surprised that part of his fleet's now PSS," Azular told the captain. "He also figured I'd been set to watch him, and he told Captain Thal when they spoke, as the captain told him that he'd met me in the Web, and on the *Moonstone*."

"And that you were upright and honest, and could be trusted, up to a point," the captain added sardonically.

"It didn't come up, ma'am. But as *this* Thal was a second officer and weapons expert in a war cruiser of the Coalition fleet, he was fitted for a command in Starfall. But I sense he thinks we still don't trust him."

"I do, up to a point," Ahxenta said. "*I* spoke to Captain Thal after he'd talked to him. He was okay with what we'd done thus far. He'll be at Starfall, so we keep Thal until then. Which means he'll need to be occupied: I doubt that physio spells, the inside of his quarters and your company will amuse him for long. Any suggestions?"

"There's his transport," Azular said, after a pause to think. "There's not much to it, but if it's to be ditched at Starfall, he could bring it up to a state to fly. Without weapons," he added at a dangerous glint in the captain's eye. "Interaction with crew other than myself, his guards and medical staff *would* help him."

"What? To make him feel wanted, or to give you time off to get back to playing with that hull model of yours?"

"Hardly, ma'am. But I and our engineers can help with the ship if you give the go-ahead. And the bay *is* secure and monitored."

"I'll discuss it with Crizz and the doc – and Jay Goldwash, as he *will* need security at his back. Then we'll see."

The captain had her senior officers in for a chat over Azular's ideas. The result was that Thal would be given access to his transport for four hours a day, after the *Arianrhod* had left Xerophyte. As the plan was to make Wester 287 by main routes, the ship would skirt the longest edge of zone Kappa. It meant a lot of time in near-empty space, and any large carrier would make a good target if her route were known.

Thal was surprised but keen when Ahxenta let him know what she had decided. Although his injuries were not yet fully healed, he had felt frustrated in being limited to a small space for hours on end. She left him to think, as the ship was almost at the node for entry to Eta.

The transition at Lynx Lace was barely made when a call came in for the captain from Holdspan of the *Nyx Warrior*. She was ten hours behind them, on a line for Keystone Kell and her next stop. Ahxenta was gone for twenty minutes and was grave on her return.

"We hang fire at Xerophyte 'til the *Warrior* gets in," she told Apnis. "She was hit by a scuffed-up wreck with little protective gear but plenty weaponry – one she'd met before, at Torch Crux."

"You what? Again!" exclaimed the first mate.

"Yup. It jumped onto the bypass at Jagg and let loose. Nat's got the spec locked into his tactical and science arrays, so his gunners threw all they had at it. But he had his cloak up, as he had at Torch, so it was up to scratch despite its looks. He's wondering if he's been getting false readings, and it's got a chameleon hull that can emit signals to make it look like a wreck; or there's more than one. He wanted it down, but he wasn't about to pursue it, in case it was a trick to make him follow…"

"And run into more trouble. Why the *Warrior*? And at Jagg? That's close to here. No wonder Nat thinks he's on a specific hit list."

"That's as maybe, but we wait for him: he's not far behind us. We'll be up on Xerophyte IV in a few hours, but we run cloaked and at red until we're in port. I won't risk that blip's scanners seeking us."

"Nat sending an advisory out?" Apnis asked.

"Not yet – we'll have a word once we're in port. But we stay sharp."

Arianrhod made the hot, dusty world safely. Ahxenta had opted to fly the *Gadfly* down for the small load. The firm they were dealing with was new to them, but as Munnet had okayed it and Lindell and Azular checked it, she had no qualms, although she had two guards as well as Azular and Perla Jute with her. Drum Mining, on the fringe of Xeroph Township One, was easy to reach.

The shuttle was left in a company bay. The captain was surprised to see a well-equipped main market unit, and stepped in, to be met by two senior reps, clearly on watch. Greetings over, and offers of refreshment and a tour refused, they were taken to the despatch area to check cargo quality. Ahxenta could see Azular eyeing the place and guessed that his info-pad was in use. Their pod was open for review in the huge zone, a part of its contents set aside for closer scrutiny.

The science officer was used to gem testing, and if his kit surprised the reps, they were too polite to say. He confirmed that the stock on show was of the quality claimed, and that the rest of the load that he could detect through the pod case read similar. Once aboard *Arianrhod*, he would make a detailed analysis, he told them.

"It'll be done before we leave orbit," Ahxenta explained as the team was ushered out to complete formalities in the marketing area. "We'll store the goods and you can have your pod back."

In fifteen minutes the captain was advised that her cargo was ready for transport to her shuttle, and quickly settled business. Azular was at ease with the outcome and young Ensign Jute unruffled by the security measures related to credit transfer and warranty.

"I'm surprised they didn't wave us off at the door," Ahxenta stated on the way to the bay. "They seemed a tad eager to please. Did we get a bargain?" she asked her science officer.

"The quality of the crystals I scanned was high, as good as the best Brown Amber can produce, ma'am. But I think we unnerved them, as they're not used to dealing directly with carriers; and they were curious, possibly as to why we would want such merchandise."

"Good. And they were honest enough to point out the pod's live tracker. But as long as they don't bleat about it to other clients – there *are* a couple of non-company shuttles here, and marketing was busy. And there are a few traders in orbit, but Xerophyte's a big place."

"One or two in marketing *were* eyeing us up," Azular told her. "But here's our pod," he added as a guarded goods car rolled up alongside.

"Check it again before we load," he was instructed.

The pod passed muster and the escort gave a hand to load, taking a good look at the *Gadfly* as they did so. The captain saw them safely off before she gave the command to board. She took the helm for the trip home, pleased to hear that there had been no alerts in her absence.

Azular's first task on arrival was to escort the pod to his lab, empty it and examine every crystal. He had the indent from Lindell and knew exactly what should be there. It was all in order, though he noted wryly that the best crystals had been left out for his initial inspection.

"I put the packing back in the pod, Captain," he told Ahxenta when she stopped in. "I'm sorting the crystals by quality. They can be locked into these small cases and secured in an inner hold until needed."

"Good. Lindell's dealing with pod return. It'll go down in *Arianrhod Six. Warrior's* on approach, so I'll hear from Nat soon. I don't plan to head planetside again: Xerophyte IV is not one of my favourite places."

"I imagine not, ma'am," he replied. "Given what happened…"

"I'm for the bridge," was her only comment as she turned, but her face told Azular that she was recalling a very painful brush with three thugs in the main township's dusty streets almost two years before, one of whom they met later as the nasty Len Lokterix.

The bridge was quiet. The holo-grid was down, updating as it took in the systems beyond Xerophyte and Salt Three. As the holo stretched past Eta and into Kappa, and systems condensed into a thick mass and then cleared to show details, the captain's brow wrinkled.

"What gives?" she asked of her first mate.

"Greffy, Larai and Bellfish have been fiddling with data: a story on a minor channel about a clash at Karret struck a chord with Greffy. He'd been looking at data from the *Warrior's* scrap at Torch Crux and reports on the sightings of a beat-up ship near Altina, and Bellfish had been trawling through recent comms for grid updates. Seems a pair of Friskianx League loaders were hit by a single, huge but dented hostile off Karret. That a damaged ship would target two fully-operational ships is odd, but the loaders took bad hits before they saw it off, so the damage on the blip wasn't as bad as it read, or it wasn't damage."

"That smacks of a rare coincidence," Ahxenta sniffed.

"That's what Greffy thought and why the three of them are going over all the data they can haul in. They reckon the ship at Karret could be matched to the one that hit the *Warrior* at Torch Crux, though they haven't got enough data to be sure; and I don't think the Friskie League would hand any over even if we asked nicely. But the report went out as an alert to local fleets – it's a fluke that Bellfish picked it up."

"Karret's a way from here, but it's possible that any ship there could have hightailed it as far as Jagg…"

"That's the puzzle, Cap: the Karret hit was barely half a day ago – the alert went out on hyper-channels in case the blip had other targets in mind. But *no* ship could get as far as Jagg in such a short time."

"Unless there's a worm-pocket from there to here," Ahxenta said.

"No way, Cap. *That* would be a coincidence too far."

"So what have our three come up with?" the captain asked. "There are more blips out there with hulls reading like dented biscuit tins?"

"That's as close as they can get," Apnis told her.

"I'll need to speak to Nat Holdspan. Get Azular up here once he's done with the crystal cargo. He can add his nous to theirs."

"Roger that, Cap. But remember a while back we had an incursion of a hostile convoy off Kelfennig into our sectors at zone Zeta? The *Kel'Beth* spotted it and asked us to pass it to the ISP, as it was then. The five ships read beat-up by local probes *and* by Starfall ships and they were tracked as on course for Zeta Dixt."

"*You* suspected they had chameleon cloaks that hid their real nature, like that rogue, the *Seafoam*, that almost got us; and you were right, they *were* big bangs ready to go off, as the ISP found when it sent in a pawn to find out. Get Greffy to compare what he has with the specs of the *Seafoam* and similar, to see if there's a match on hull comp. I'll call Nat. Patch through any data that comes up."

Ahxenta was an hour, as other links had come in. One was the tardy reply to her query about TA policy on potential shipping hazards in the areas listed by the ISA. She also had comms to send, and *Arianrhod Six* had dropped the cargo pod at Drum Mining and returned to base by the time she had done.

"Nat's sent the data on that rogue at Jagg. I told him what our guys had dug up and that we'd compare it with his data and pass him the lot," she told Apnis. "The TA's sent a strap line that we should refer to ISA bulletins for details on areas that the ISA's listed out of bounds, so it's washing its hands. And I spoke to Zillah. She still has a camp of ISA reps next door in an office her people have to pay for, and a brace of ISA warships in her backyard. The reps were whining that she won't give them the time of day, but she will now: she'll quiz them on the four off-limits areas, as no-one told *her*. And she'll have questions on the high-spec ships with high-spec comms that the ISA's building for its own ends. *She* wants Freskat's home fleet top-spec, if any old boat can travel the mostly uncharted super-bypass from Amity to Twilight."

"To just off Lambda and close to her neck of the galaxy; and Nat's, as Nyx is even closer to zone edge. But how did that come up, Cap?"

"I told her. If she can get specifics on the jurillium-protected crystal arrays urgently needed for the new comms linkage systems, we can get them custom-made for whatever clients want them…"

"And charge top credit for them."

"That also," Ahxenta grinned. "But if Zillah's dockyard wants first dibs, it can have them – I owe her that. Yes, Azular, what is it?"

"The *Warrior* caught a clear spec of her assailant's hull, ma'am: trace zukivianite, and tiny inclusions similar to those I recorded on pieces of plating off the *Seafoam*, after it attacked us off Merlin last year. I thought then that they might be sources for chameleon ability and fake signals, and work I've done since on a model of the *Moonstone's* hull and other bits imply structural parallels. The *Seafoam* wasn't crewed, but given the current hostile's attack mode and the fact that it *does* pull out when it's outwitted implies it's crewed, as were the five outwardly damaged ships tracked into our space and taken down by the ISP last year. What we have look similar but larger, *and* there may be more than one."

"Another thing, Cap," Apnis cut in. "Those five ships were crewed by a few cyber-hostiles but they were led by a remote control ship with a human-type in charge – and remember what he looked like?"

"A Hoxiz clone," Ahxenta said grimly. "So a ship may be out there controlling these beasts?"

"I disagree, ma'am," Azular said. "The course and tactical data the *Warrior* got implies an intelligence that isn't the pre-set responses that we've seen in purely cyber-controlled ships. And as the *Warrior's* arrays are superb, I don't think she'd miss a control ship."

"Get what you have into a tight report for the fleet and relevant authorities. I'll get back to Nat. Ready us for moving out, Tallica. We'll be with the *Warrior* as far as Keystone Kell and then we'll see."

Ahxenta called on Azular to explain what he had found and worked out. Holdspan had his SSO, Holt, in on the chat. The data to the fleet and other parties they agreed to send out jointly: if hostiles posing as wrecks were out there intent on mayhem, the more legitimate bodies that knew about them the better. The main issue remaining unresolved was why the *Nyx Warrior* had been targeted so many times.

16: STARFALL

The *Arianrhod* and the *Nyx Warrior* left Xerophyte in tandem. The ships were two of the best-kitted in the fleet and both had cloaks, which they engaged once on the bypass, as the data in their joint report had hinted at the *Warrior's* location. If *that* reached hostile ears, it might provoke a reaction. Ahxenta had told Holdspan more of Dexel Thal, as he knew what had happened after Polstarn, but she had not revealed his identity or the level of his surgery at alien hands. Azular, musing on things, had come up with an idea that might benefit their current position.

"It strikes me that the ship that hit the *Warrior* might be an advanced type of *Seafoam*," he told the captain when she walked over to see what he was doing. "Larger, mainly with cyber-crews, but with human-types in control. It would be useful to know what the crew mix might be."

Ahxenta scented an agenda. "How would you find that out?"

"Ask Commander Thal: he's had contact with both types, he's come out alive, he's been aboard hostile ships, *and* escaped one. And being Starfall, he's familiar with hostile tech."

"You have a point," she sighed. "You've spent time with him since I told him I'd let him work on his ship: what's his take on us now?"

"He's more open and at ease. His health's better, which helps. And if we ask for *his* help, it puts him in a position of trust. When do we let him loose on his ship, ma'am? He *has* asked about it."

"I bet. And it's *his* ship now, is it? He's welcome: the sooner it's off mine, the better. What does he know of our mission?"

"Very little. He knows we'd a stop at Xerophyte but not why, and that we're en route to a location near Starfall – he got that from Captain Thal. But he doesn't know about the *Nyx Warrior*."

"Tell him; it might make him more likely to open up. He can start on the ship tomorrow but he'll still have a guard. I'll clear it with Crizz. We've a long ride, and thus far nothing to take us out of our way."

"I'll let him know, ma'am. Thank you."

"What for? Are you about to pick his brains on something else?"

"That depends on what he knows, ma'am."

"Just don't give too much away," Ahxenta warned as she made her way back to her command chair.

"What's he up to now?" the first mate asked.

The captain gave the gist. "I'll be glad to see my rations," she added, scanning her boards. "Lindell's sent news of a cargo, Bluekey to Rettik; profit's good, but it takes us out of our way, to the edge of Coalition space. We'll pass. I want rid of what we have. If the bypass is clear we can make Wester from Keystone in twelve days at top safe speed."

"That'll use power, Cap. We'll need a resupply stop soon after we make Wester at that rate. You thinking of Starfall for resupply?"

"We may as well. Thal should be there and he'll owe us."

"Can I be there when you tell him that?"

"Cut it, Commander. Here's the duty crew, so chow time. Or maybe not. What is it now?" she asked as comms called a link for her.

"See you in the mess," she said to her first mate. "I may be a while."

* * *

The captain was twenty minutes, which she reckoned good going, she told Apnis and her CMO when she made the mess. Her caller had been Captain Flintlock. He had made Salt trouble-free across Eta, but given the hitches at Jagg, he wanted more data: his next port was the watery Pleck in Iota, and he would come close to Jagg en route.

"Thanks for the notice," the doctor said. "I left my unavailable code on, but I won't pick up any transfer link. I'll respond later."

"You think he'll call you?" the first mate asked.

"He will; he always does. He'll already have dropped links to Mercy and the boys. But what's Azular chatting to Thal about? That's the first smile I've seen on that man's face."

Ahxenta advised her of the plans for him and she was content. Talk then turned to news of their route, from Keystone via Stook and Green to Wester 287. The *Warrior* was for Fyvie Major and Vellis Prime, so she would cross Zeta, the captain said, pushing her plate aside.

"Unless that's trouble," she groaned as her communit flashed a note that Captain Holdspan would like a quick word. "I'll be back," she said.

Her return was rapid and it was only to tell her officers that she was for Lindell's office, and that her first mate should keep Thal company, as Azular was wanted. The two were out of the door at a trot, leaving those who had been witness to wonder what was going on. The senior officers found out at an unscheduled briefing called shortly after.

"Nat Holdspan's a savvy man," she told her team. "His super was offered what seemed a good deal that would only take them a little off-route. Nat had a close look: after recent upsets he was leaving nothing to chance. It was a load from Bluekey to Fyvie Minor."

"What!" exploded Apnis. "Weren't we offered a deal to ship a cargo from Bluekey to Rettik?"

"Exactly. I had Lindell check: he couldn't tell who all had been sent it, but that's common. But it *was* sent direct to us, so targeted. The load was typical: heavy-duty pods of industrial parts. Nat's super contacted the Bluekey rep for more but he was cagey and told her that she'd get full details if she agreed the contract. Nat was suspicious: as he's for Fyvie Major, just over the border from Fyvie Minor, it smelt fishy, so he linked me, to warn me that something was off and to be on my guard. We compared what we *did* get – log numbers and such…"

"And they were the same," the first mate posited.

"Yes, so shady; and people know where we and the *Warrior* are, *and* where we're for. Nat alerted the fleet and told the Bluekey authorities about Nest Holdings. We'd never heard of them, but they're listed as parts suppliers locally. Azular ran checks, got zip, and analysed the link Lindell got: it *was* from Bluekey and the tags read true for Nest."

"Where's Azular now?" Whisper Earbleat wanted to know.

"Busy," was the short retort. "But from here to Keystone Kell, we run at alert and the *Warrior* will do the same. I've heard no more from the ISA on the Crimson Drapes or other likely hostile hidey-holes, nor of new worm-pockets or off-limits areas, despite its promises, but I've had word from Captain Thal: one of his ships, probably from Nexus, spied a huge blip near a node called Zenith, beyond the Outer Reaches, off Theta's border on that side. It didn't engage and his ship figured it was on a specific track. Given *where* it was, Thal called it in to ISA HQ, as Myrtleberry's fancy flotilla is scouting in the area."

"Won't that make the ISA start pestering him on what his ship was up to there?" Apnis asked.

"He can cope. I've not replied. But that's all unless anyone has any questions. We'll be up on Keystone soon enough and I need everyone on the ball all the way if we're on some hit list."

* * *

Despite likely dangers in passage, the two ships met no obstacle over the days to their goal. Nothing had come in on Nest Holdings, and as *Arianrhod* had no trade at Keystone, she left the *Warrior* and set for the main bypass through Kappa. She remained at alert, as Bluekey, though not on her direct track, was close enough to it to cause concern.

Azular spent much of his time with Thal and had queried him on advanced hostile ships with mutable hulls capable of deceiving regular sensors. Thal knew of such craft, and knew that most of the crew were cyber-like, but those in control posts tended to be humanoid. Azular also asked about hostile weapons: Thal *was* an expert and might be able to help in judging the nature of the binding and piercing rogue drones that had now been involved in several attacks. Azular hoped to use any input to refine his micro-sensor net, but kept *that* aspect quiet.

Thal on his part was curious about recent events involving hostiles, as he had been out of contact with his people for so long. Ahxenta had refused him more links to them, as she judged the interception risk too high. That *Arianrhod* had been to Starfall surprised him, though he, like most of the mapped galaxy, had heard of her. His contact with some of her crew told him why she had the reputation: their help in restoring his ship was skilled and rapid. But he knew that they were learning as much about it and him as he was about them. He was also aware that he was under scrutiny, and his minders never slipped. The captain took nothing on trust, and in talks with her, she gave little away. He thus did not know that Azular and Cottontail had spoken highly of his skills.

Arianrhod had passed Stook and was closing on Green, just off the bypass in Kappa and with a view of the Greenstar Nebula in adjacent Zeta. Ahxenta, in the mess before her next shift, had halted by Thal's table to ask after his health. She had hardly spoken when a voice cut the air calling her to the bridge. The red alert had already begun to wail.

"Dammit! Azular, you're with me. Hanx, see Commander Thal to his quarters. Tie yourself in," she warned Thal. "Let's go."

She and the science officer sped off, other feet pounding after them. "Thought it was too good to last," she panted as they squeezed into a transport tube with three others. She banged the tube link to demand details, aware that *Arianrhod's* engines had been cranked up a notch. It was a distress on an ISA channel, was the response.

"I'll believe it when I see it," she said sharply.

"What's the score?" Ahxenta called the second she made the bridge.

"We picked up a distress off the bypass on the Kappa side, ma'am," the duty officer reported as more arrived to man their bridge stations and Tallica Apnis raced in. "Any more, comms?" he demanded.

"She claims to be the *ISAS Crusader*, sir," the officer replied. "She says they're under attack by two vessels, configuration hostile."

"Got her!" the newly-arrived Gliss called. "Battlecruiser, call-sign *ISAS Crusader*, two huge blips, can't pin down their types. On grid!"

"Don't respond to the distress!" Ahxenta snapped, tying herself in. "Battlestations! Keep the cloak up, Dox; ready us for jump off bypass! Earbleat, hot them up. Chief, make sure our shielding's tight. Azular, get everything you can on what's out there; it may be the *Crusader* and it may not, but we have her spec, we've met her before. And if she's a damn battlecruiser, she should be a match for most blips."

"Scanning! Greffy, tie in auxiliaries… two hostiles, big, and reading like the ship that hit the *Warrior*… with a *lot* of explosive firepower."

"Confirm that – they've loosed a barrage at her!" Gliss yelled.

"I still won't take it as read, but drop the cloak and ready us to jump to as near to her as we can, Dox. Shields at max! Keep all three in your targeting eyes and ready phase cannons, Earbleat! Prep the decoy, but I won't deploy unless I have to. All positions at ready… hit it, Dox!"

Arianrhod swept off the bypass at speed, weaving an intricate course towards the trio. Even at distance, space was alive with explosive light. They had been detected and were being scanned by the hostiles, Azular warned. Their readings matched the ship that the *Warrior* had met, but with full arsenals. The ship under fire still read as the *Crusader*. Greffy, scanning long-distance for other threats, caught nothing.

Ahxenta's keen eyes scoured the holo. "Prime forr'ad phase cannon and fire as soon as we've got the range!" she hollered as one of the two turned for them. "Send two long-distance torpedoes in her face!"

"She's attempting lock-on!" Gliss yelled.

"Launching deflecting drones!" Earbleat bawled in reply. "Station one, target her forr'ad arrays, they're fully active! Station two, get those port emplacements out, they're still firing! Gliss, get me a bead on her fighter bays, I don't want them on line!"

"Tallica, man auxiliary weapons," the captain ordered as Dox pulled up into a tight spiral to evade incoming fire and *Arianrhod* shook to a glancing hit off her flank. "That beast's huge, she's not letting up and our fire's not slowing her. Azular, find her weak spots and send them to grid. *Loki* on standby, Earbleat. Status of *Crusader*, Bellfish?"

"Comms may be down Cap, I can't raise her," was the reply as more bursts caught *Arianrhod* and she juddered, sending her crew slewing.

"She's taken heavy fire… trying to run, but she's slowing," Azular rasped. "She's not got much left – her opponent's got her tied up in its tractors and it's hauling her in…"

"Damn! Earbleat, send *Loki* after the ship on the *Crusader* and make it count! Comms, send a distress, all channels! Ready the decoy, Azular. Secondary bridge, stand by! Weapons, throw all you have at that thing!"

Arianrhod's seams creaked as she zigzagged, flinging the crew every which way as they tried to keep hands on controls and eyes on screens. Suddenly, a small swarm of bright objects shot from the alien ship's hull in a direct line towards them.

"What in hell's that?" Ahxenta demanded.

"She's set off limpet drones, Captain!" yelled Greffy.

"Tallica, get those drones! I don't want one getting through! Any response to hails, comms?"

"No, ma'am. Still sending."

"Dox, get us above her but keep starboard phase cannons in range!" the captain ordered as the chief engineer roared that port shielding had taken a pasting, hull integrity was down twenty percent and an aft cargo bay mesh had buckled.

"*Loki* closing on second blip!" the second mate screeched above the din. "Got her! That's one engine out, but she's got more!"

Arianrhod spiralled down to outfly the equally fast hostile, but it was mirroring every move, its relentless firepower searing the pink ship's hide and shearing off flakes of hull plate. Amid the chaos, Azular cried out that he had located a destabilised area of starboard shielding and was sending the coordinates to the weapons stations.

"Use fine-beamed disruptor fire!" he bellowed to Earbleat. "Just do it!" he screamed at her query. "Now, damn you!"

"Station two, hit it, fine-beamed disruptors! I've got my hands full!"

"What in the… there's a massive energy surge just off the bypass!" cried Greffy. "Can't get an ID on *what* it is, but it's big!"

Ahxenta's eyes hit the holo-grid. A hazy halo of spinning light that read as an anomaly and query hazard was brightening as its dark centre contracted to a dense, dazzling bluish-white core. It dimmed as a streak of shadow shot out. The captain saw no more as bridge lighting flashed and cut, its energy cell emplacement blown, and the holo died.

"Secondary bridge, stand by for transfer of control!" she yelled into a dark that suddenly became red-lit as emergency units kicked in.

"Still have helm!" Dox shrieked. "Pulling away from hostile!"

"Grid stabilising!" called Gliss. "Restoring!"

"Hostile has veered off to face whatever *that* is heading in," Greffy's voice cut through the confusion as the holo-grid's glow grew. "But her underbelly's on fire! We got her!"

Earbleat's yell of triumph drowned the rest as the ship that had the *Crusader* in its tractors blew amidships. The second mate had sent her cherished guided missile, set to self-destruct, down the main engine of the alien, and it had blown a critical emplacement.

"Hold her steady, helm!" Ahxenta roared. "Cut firepower, Earbleat, that beast thinks it's downed us and it's making for the thing that burst out of that worm-pocket, or whatever it is."

"Capturing data!" Azular's voice rang out. "It's not a worm-pocket, ma'am; it's a rotating mass of negative high energy density, but without the strong gravity well I'd associate with a wormhole or worm-pocket. But *something* was ejected… got it! It's a ship! What in the…!"

As Gliss expanded the holo view of near space, they could see the ship that had targeted them. It was aflame and spiralling out of control, a huge chunk of its flank spearing off at a tangent. The main body of the thing suddenly blew apart, sending shards of wreckage outwards.

"Get us out of this flak!" Ahxenta barked.

Dox was swift to comply and *Arianrhod* banked upwards and as far from the expanding bloom of lethal fragments as speed could take her. As the ship's course stabilised, and the stand down battlestations order was given, Apnis made her way back to her own chair and sat.

"The updates to the grid were worth every credit, Cap, and the time spent on it," she groaned. "That's some view, with nary a limpet in it. Where's the ship that jumped out of that hole? It *was* a ship?"

"It's a ship all right," the captain said acerbically, her eyes raking the grid. "What she's doing out here *and* how she did it is anybody's guess, though I bet Azular has an idea: he's cranked up the visual. But where's the *Crusader*? Comms, ascertain status of *Crusader*," she called over.

"She's still just about in one piece," Apnis noted as Gliss pulled the stricken ISA ship out and into focus. "She was damn lucky they wanted her whole or she'd be in bite-sized chunks. The way those blips blew, they must have been packed to the gunnels with explosives."

"We've a lot of damaged plate," Ahxenta frowned, flicking through arriving damage reports. "Our cargoes are intact but three outer holds have taken hits and our hull's got more holes than a pepper pot. No major breaches, but we've emplacements wrecked in engineering and medbay's calling in wounded at a rate of knots."

The captain was interrupted by Bellfish, who had at last raised the *ISAS Crusader*. "Captain Flute for you ma'am."

"He's still in command?" the first mate asked, surprised.

The ISA ship's red-lit bridge was in disarray, with consoles sparking fire and techs and medics busy. Slices of superstructure were down and blocking salient stations. Captain Jolion Flute tendered his thanks, but his pressing concern was the intentions of the ship that had jumped in from what his science officer read as a sporadic wormhole.

"She's not here to blow us to pieces, Captain," Ahxenta said mildly. "She's a PSS and she *did* take out that hostile that was on us."

She had no sooner spoken than Bellfish cut in. "Captain! I have Captain Kerrix for you."

"Stand by, Captain Flute; if you draw up a list of your immediate needs, I'll see what I can do. Hold the link to the *Crusader*, Mr Bellfish, and put Captain Kerrix through."

"On grid, ma'am."

"Captain Kerrix. Good to see you."

"Likewise, Captain Ahxenta. We're making to your position. Let me know what you need and how we can help. I've hailed the *Crusader*, but she's not up for contact. Have you been able to raise her?"

"I have her on hold; she's a tad wary of you – she's not sure what you are or how you got here. How *did* you get here?"

"Technology; we made our own bypass and jumped," was the wry reply. "We *were* on the way to escort you anyway. Captain Thal thought it wise, in light of information that came his way, but more of that later. We picked up the *Crusader's* distress, and yours, and I figured we'd best shift. We used a patch of mass-energy density at an orange star tagged S32X as a locus and aimed to come out near Green. We made it, more or less," she smiled crookedly. "I won't be doing it again in a hurry. What help do you need? We'll have to leave here at speed."

"I'll bring in Captain Flute of the *Crusader*; we've met him before, so he knows us. Stand by."

Flute was still wary after introductions, but sent his list of needs to both PSS vessels. After a quick exchange with her supercargo, Kerrix agreed to ready a pod of supplies for the *Crusader*. The *Moonstone* was closing and would be in range to send it to the ISA ship in ten minutes. *Arianrhod* could cope until she made Wester, Ahxenta decided. She was sound and could move under her own power. The *Crusader* was able to manoeuvre but would need stabilisation in hyperspace. Flute proposed the ISA base of Kellybar as the destination as that was where he had come from, but it was vetoed by Kerrix. *She* insisted on a direct run via the main trade bypass to Wester. Deviations to smaller routes would take time and would involve crossing empty spaces, which could be dangerous, given data recently picked up by the Starfall fleet.

Kerrix was terse when asked for the logic: one of her fleet had spied a convoy on line to Minch Fettin in Mu, and estimated that it had come from Psi via the Amity to Starfall bypass, and jumped off at Canna. Its four vessels read derelict, but the *SS Fire Opal* had not taken the bait and made off without making a closer appraisal. Thal had no idea of its endpoint, but later data picked up implied that the convoy was now heading for Wester 287, which would put it in a line to cross into Zeta.

"Or hit Wester," Ahxenta remarked.

"I don't think so, nor does Captain Thal. Wester has no home fleet but *has* planetary defences, and can call for aid: from us, from Wild, or Kellybar One, though it's further on. We've got little to go on as to the specs of the ships, so we can't say if they're parallel to the ones that hit you. But we need to leave now: if either of those two got a comm out, we don't want to be here if backup arrives."

"Why hasn't this Starfall fleet sent the data to the ISA? And where's it getting the added input?" Captain Flute asked suspiciously.

"Not your concern, Captain," Kerrix said. "The ISA *and* other fleets will get the data once it's verified. Prepare to receive your supply pod. We're coming into position and will send it over by fine-beam tractor. Please send me the coordinates of the bay for reception."

Flute complied and the delicate shifts needed for the transfer were quickly made. The captains were in the midst of coordinating the move towards the bypass and helm tie-in to respond to the currents when a call came in for Kerrix from Thal. She left the bridge to Inks to take it privately. She was back in her command chair in minutes.

"The convoy's put a spurt on and has made Zeta," she told Flute and Ahxenta. "It's confirmed hostile. Captain Thal is preparing an alert to be sent to all relevant bodies. If all's go for jump, we go now. And I recommend you both keep every scanner you have online."

Commands were given and the ships set for the nearby node and a tricky leap. After several bumps and course tunings, the trio, stabilised by tractors, settled to an even tempo as fast as was safe. The captains had their own concerns, and it was an hour later that Ahxenta decided that a call to the captain of the *Moonstone* was warranted.

The reason Thal had sent an escort was her first query. The sighting of a hostile convoy was only part of it, Ahxenta was sure. She was right: Starfall base had lately been subject to visits by two ISA ships, one the newly-launched *ISAS Dauntless* and the other a research ship, the *ISAS Ingenious*, despite Thal having closed his border to ISA ships. The stop offs were superficially courtesy, as the two had been on the bypass for Psi, but where they had jumped on was a mystery, as Thal's people had not detected them. They had questions about PSS ships in general and *Arianrhod* in particular, some of the latter in relation to the rescued pilot and the ship Ahxenta had refused to hand over. Given their slant, Thal was sure the captain of the *Dauntless* knew part of *Arianrhod's* route, but he would not talk about *his* mission or that of the *Ingenious*.

"So the ISA's still interested, and Captain Thal suspects that we may be waylaid by one of its ships," Ahxenta mused. "I haven't heard much from it, despite the protests I've thrown at it. But how come Starfall can get hold of all this data on the moves of hostile convoys on track through our zones? You've got Flute foxed."

"You know we have listening posts in various zones. They're set to scout for atypical signs. But as the four spotted are now in Zeta, they're unlikely to bother us en route to Wester. That *is* where you're for,

Captain? I suggest we leave the *Crusader* there and she can yell for help from her own. If she hasn't already: the ISA *has* ships in this zone. Is there anything else I can help you with? You took a lot of damage, though I doubt the ISA will compensate you for it."

"I won't hold my breath," Ahxenta said sardonically. "We'll make it to Wester and take on supplies there. But Azular's keen to hear about the tech that enabled you to make the jump to Green."

"You'll be welcome to resupply and refit at Starfall, but Azular can wait. We've the aftermath of that experience to deal with."

"Aftermath?"

"I've a lot of injured crew, as well as damage and serious drains on many of my systems. It was a rough ride."

"And I haven't thanked you for riding in," *Arianrhod's* captain said ruefully. "Thank you – on behalf of my people and the *Crusader's*."

Kerrix shook her head. "There's no need for that between us. You'd do the same for me and mine. But if there's naught else, I'll sign off."

Ahxenta put one or two further questions and then cut the link. Her brow creased. That the cost of the jump would be high in energy terms she had realised, but that the *Moonstone* and her crew might be put at considerable risk she had not.

"What's our status?" she asked Apnis on return to the bridge

"Holding steady, clear ahead. We're fixing what we can, medbay's coping and I've started on lists of repairs and supplies. Lists are getting longer. Got the answers to your questions?"

Ahxenta glanced towards the science station. Azular had turned and was listening intently. She briefly shook her head at him before relating a part of what she had learnt. Her tone alerted Apnis to a problem, but the first mate did not press. The captain checked her updating boards and then stalked over to speak to her senior science officer.

"A couple of things you said during the firefight's got me curious," she told him. "You isolated an unstable area of starboard shield on that hostile and you insisted that Earbleat use fine-beamed disruptors on it. How did you find the spot and why fine-beamed fire?"

"A tip Commander Thal gave me when we discussed hostile weak points: some ships have a starboard tech site that generates chameleon cloaking. I showed him the spec of the ship that attacked the *Warrior* off Torch Crux, and he figured it for one like that. When the cloak's active, the site's vulnerable to finely-focussed fire. I remembered."

"And it worked, as the beast was already afire when she turned to take on the *Moonstone*, fortunately."

"Talking of which, Captain…"

"You will *not* contact Captain Kerrix about non-essentials for now," he was told severely. "She has her hands full."

"There's something wrong, isn't there, ma'am?"

"I'll speak to you in the mess later. I'm going to speak to our guest."

The captain found that Thal had been following events as far as he was able from the limited means open to him. She updated him; as his medbay check had been cancelled, he guessed that *Arianrhod* had taken heavy casualties, and offered to assist in repairs. The captain agreed to consider it. As Azular and Cottontail rated him and security had made no adverse report, he could be useful. She then visited medbay for a status report before heading to the bridge for watch handover.

Apnis and Azular joined Ahxenta in the mess, both keen to know more of what Kerrix had said. The *Crusader* was not the only ISA ship around, she told them. A Starfall ship had logged a battlecruiser, *Merrin Free*, on the main bypass from Barfit to Keystone days before.

"Just a sec, Cap: if *that* ship was on that line and the *Crusader* was at Green and heading the other way via Kellybar, wouldn't that have put us in an ISA sandwich?" Apnis asked.

"That struck Captain Kerrix, once she knew the score here, though she didn't mention it to Flute. *He* wouldn't give away his mission, but it might've been to meet up with the *Merrin Free*."

"There would be no point asking," Azular said. "But what's wrong on the *Moonstone*, Captain? I haven't been able to take detailed readings because of her shielding."

Ahxenta was not surprised he had tried, but she passed on what she had heard from Kerrix about the cost to her ship and crew of the jump to assist. "We'll be up on Wester in two days, or sooner if we can coax more out of our engines and the *Crusader* holds up. I sent a note of the action to the fleet, the TA and the ISA. I've had no more from Flute, but I bet *he's* sent a report to his HQ. If the *Merrin Free* is high spec she'll be fast, but I doubt she'd make Wester before us."

"But something out of Kellybar One might," warned Azular.

"I'm aware of that, as is Captain Kerrix. Our bridge stations will be on alert, as Kellybar *may* send an escort for the *Crusader*. We'll get vital repairs done at Wester, but the rest can wait until Starfall, after we've passed on their gear and picked up our treated gem-grade jurillium."

"And resources to produce and fit micro-sensor tech arrays to our hull – Captain Kerrix *did* promise," Azular added.

"He doesn't give up, does he?" chuckled Apnis.

"He's not the only one: Earbleat's already left me a memo on what would be useful improvements for *Loki* the ninth."

"She'll want a new top-spec cargo pod as a shell, that circular gun port enhanced with what she can filch at Starfall, a cloak, and a net of sensors that'll spot a fly up an alien's armpit," the first mate told her.

"She's got the pod already but that's all she's getting on my watch," Ahxenta retorted. "She snaffled a prime pod that Lindell had parked in shuttle bay alpha five in the hopes she'd miss it. But another thing: Thal's offered to help with repairs. Your take on that, Azular?"

He was in favour; he could imagine the man's tedium, cooped up in a small billet, his every step shadowed when out of it. And his freely-given information *had* been useful in coping with their late opponents.

"Sort it with Cottontail and Goldwash," he was told. "But do *not* let up on security; though if the doc has a spare minute, she can insert a tracker and he can be monitored that way. But he *will* be accompanied to the mess and to and from engineering."

* * *

Despite unceasing scans, nothing had been seen on the bypass as the ships came into range of Wester. They were heading for prearranged repair bays when *Arianrhod's* tactical station caught the call-signs of two other large ships in port: the *PSS Obsidian Sky* and the *ISAS Trueheart*.

"*Obsidian* was for Limekiln, the last I heard," Ahxenta mused. "Grey may have had business closer to home if he's out this far. But what's an ISA battlecruiser doing here? Shopping for grain?"

"Come to take the *Crusader* home," Apnis suggested.

"I'll bet; Flute said little the twice I spoke to him and zip about what he planned to do here," the captain said. "Keep our eyes and ears on the *Trueheart*. Steady as she goes, Dox. Once we're secure, we'll set for cargo release: our clients are on standby and our teams are ready."

"I see repair bots on the *Moonstone* already," the first mate noted. "They'll be her own. Captain Kerrix won't have more than the bare minimum done here, given what happened at Delta. And now she has an audience! The *Trueheart's* changing her berth!"

"Scan that ship!" Ahxenta called. "She won't take up a repair berth, but there are several free near here, or she may just maintain orbit."

"Westies won't like it if she gets in the way. They've small carriers shifting loads and local shuttles on the move," said Apnis.

As soon as Dox called station-keeping, the captain told Lindell to send the requisite files and her teams to begin moving cargo, a delicate process due to the damage sustained. Bluejohn had called, but Ahxenta deferred a reply, though she took an urgent link from Kerrix: *she* had been called by Captain Chance Drevell of the *Trueheart*, who wanted a full account of the recent firefight and the parts played by the *Moonstone* and the *Arianrhod*. She had cut him short and referred him to the report sent out or to the *Crusader*, at which point the ISA ship had severed the link, began to move, and started scanning. Her protests had elicited no response, but her jammers were blocking the scans. Drevell might try to contact the *Arianrhod*, but Kerrix had sent a link of her own that she hoped would assist the situation.

"What's she done?" the first mate asked as the comm faded. "She'd a smile on her face, so she figures it might rock the boat?"

"I reckon so, and I don't think it's a formal protest to the ISA. You carry on here, Tallica; I'm going to have a word with Grey."

The captain was gone an hour; a call *had* come in from Drevell. Her only reply was that if he tried to scan *her* ship as he had the *Moonstone*, she would send a protest to the ISA, copied to every galactic body in reach. Drevell was arrogant enough to argue, but Ahxenta cut him off to contact Flute and give *him* an earful, before linking Bluejohn.

"Grey got my report; *Obsidian* was at Wemm and was for Arrissia, but he figured I'd be for here and made in to see if we needed help. He can spare us a few energy cells. He'll hold for a couple of days. It'll take us and the *Moonstone* that long to get done what we need. But we don't need the *Trueheart* or any other ISA boat on our tails."

"Like the *Merrin Free*."

"That's my concern, but I don't think they'd hinder us – they've too much to lose, after our aid to the *Crusader*."

"And the number of times we've bested them," Apnis observed.

"And that also. But how's unloading?"

"Two more hours, despite our dented bays. We *could* get mesh repair done but they're short on materials, so I suggest we stick to plate patch. Grey's energy cells will help a lot. Weapons spares we *can* get. Crizz is moving ahead on internal repairs and says Thal's pulling his weight."

"Good. If we can't get the needful at Starfall, we can stop by Aoria Six on the road to Freskat to get our weapons emplacements and arrays up to scratch. Meanwhile, back to work…"

The next hours were full but fruitful. *Arianrhod's* tired work crews were given respite but the captain refused to slacken security whilst Wester repair ops were on her ship's hull. The promised gear had been sent over by the *Obsidian*, and she kept her position: the *Merrin Free* had come in and was holding, but had not contacted the PSS vessels.

Late the next rotational day, another visitor made Wester 287 space, one that had the planetary authorities in a lather and nearly every ship in the place stunned. *Arianrhod's* cool captain sat riveted as a Norvallan war cruiser, permission to dock given, slid into a bay near her ship.

"Captain Kerrix," Apnis muttered. "How'd she pull *this* string?"

"Friends in *very* high places," Ahxenta said. "But she must've been on her way in; she'd not have made it this fast from Norvallan space, which is where she was headed last time I heard of her."

"One helluva quick turnaround," the first mate observed. "Why?"

The *NFS Serenity* was an unusual sight. Any diplomatic ship was rare in Wester space and one from zone Psi was unheard of. Her consular status was evident from her relevant insignia and her call-sign. Twenty minutes later, Captain Kerrix was on the comm.

"Escort to Starfall," she replied to Ahxenta's query. "She *was* on her way there, en route to Alto Finglas. As she has the ambassador aboard, I don't expect to be tailed by an ISA ship out of here."

Ahxenta frowned. "What's her agenda? A consular ship doesn't go out of her way to escort a pair of traders out of port for the hell of it."

"To make waves, Captain. You'll recall that access codes had been swiped from the wreck of the *Twin Star* with Norvallan complicity, and with ISA and Mu contacts, the plan was to use them to pilot the Amity to Starfall bypass. And the Mu bypass add-on from Kollaskin to Amity: the ISA used *that* as leverage to pull the Independents into the Alliance and remove part of the need to use our bypass to reach the zones this side of Mu. Extension creation *is* gearing up with Norvallan input, but one of our ships spotted activity off the Selky system between Kirtish and Canna five days ago; it looked like a node being built to link *our* bypass to another, maybe the Kollaskin to Wild slice of the Mu bypass. There were three ships: a Norvallan survey, a Mu-listed carrier, and an ISA science ship. Starfall wasn't alerted, nor was Ambassador Posettix. *She* sent queries to her government and the ISA, with no response. The Norvallan was off Selky as the *Serenity* came by so she hailed her; her captain wouldn't say what his mission was, but it seems the Norvallans and the ISA have a project that's being kept from the diplomat whose job is linking trade relations in ISA zones to those in Psi, and brokering trade use of Psi bypasses. Whatever's up, somebody stands to profit, but who and why? We don't know if the TA is aware, but why are ISA ships like the *Crusader* and the *Merrin Free* touring trade routes? On the same stretch? And the *Trueheart* hauls in and tries to scan *my* ship?"

"I take it somebody on the *Serenity* will ask them?"

"The admiral will. He's for Starfall as soon as we're ready to go. I'm not for more repair here, and I see your repair bots are off your hull."

Ahxenta grimaced, but said only that *Arianrhod* would be ready to go as soon as word was given. The relevant details were exchanged and it was agreed that the two would take their lead from the *Serenity*.

"Posturing," the first mate commented as soon as comms were cut. "The ISA and the Norvallans setting up shop off what Thal looks on as his byway? I know zip about Selky bar the name, but where's the profit? Surely a track from Canna into zone Kappa would be a better option? What've you got there, Azular?"

The Berzic had set up the section in the grid and marked lines. "The Selky and Kilda systems; Kilda's at Kappa edge, close to the Kollaskin-Wild section of bypass. Neither system is settled but both have nearby pockets of high negative mass-energy density, so useful for building a node, and both are mineral-rich. A recent survey found meta-jurillium deposits on Kilda. The Norvallans and the ISA were part of underhand bypass dealings at K457:003 in Psi, so it seems there are still links there. Norvallan tech for ISA concessions, perhaps?"

"Political chicanery's not our remit," the captain said firmly. "That's what Ambassador Posettix and her like are paid for. With her ship here, no ISA boat would dare follow us, but *is* all this just to get us and our guest before we make Starfall? The ISA may want its paws on that alien transport *and* Thal, but it's got others. Thal's seen things ISA would rather he hadn't, but why are we now flavour of the month in it all?"

"Because they reckon we know about it, Cap," Apnis grinned. "And our fleet, because we'll have told them. And a few Starfall ships fly the PSS flag. The ISA's senior bods are pissed and are afraid more of their secrets will come out. If a bit of the ISA's keeping things from the rest, fur will fly. But here are our marching orders from the *Serenity*, so we'd best get on. *Obsidian* coming with us, or is Grey heading home?"

"He's for Arrissia, but he'll wait a couple of hours to keep eyes on those three ISA ships, in case they're brash enough to trail us. Ready us to follow the *Moonstone*, Ms Dox."

The trio of ships moved off from Wester 287 on a parallel course, their endpoint Starfall base. They had all been there before and all were armed with the best tech available, but none of them assumed a quiet ride. Wester PA's farewell was muted but there was no courtesy call from the ISA ships. None of their captains had given Admiral Posettix acceptable answers, but he expected his queries to be sent to ISA HQ.

* * *

Arianrhod's most skilled team were on the bridge for the ride to Starfall, via a direct hyperspace track that came out close to Thal's huge orbital HQ. The lifeless planet to which the station was bound still read the same, but the place had transformed since last Ahxenta had seen it.

"Captain Thal's been spit-shining his base," Box observed as Dox brought the ship into her allotted berth. "These struts are new, there are more bays and there must be ten spanking-new small carriers. And look at all those other ships on grid!"

"Keep your eyes on your boards," he was directed irately. "I'm still locking us in, the *Moonstone's* just off starboard, and those are movable repair rigs. More bays there might be, but space is tight… *Arianrhod* at station-keeping, ma'am," she called a moment later.

"Roger that, helm. Now for the fun," the captain added. "I've talked to Dexel Thal and he's ready to ship out, but we still have the logistics of repair and resupply, as well as Starfall's cargo, the goods we have to pick up and that beat-up transport of Thal's. This'll be a long haul, and I expect Captain Thal will want a meeting in short order."

Things began quickly, and as soon as their repair wants were listed, the rig was moved into position. Ahxenta insisted that *Arianrhod* had a link to it to track the work, and that her scanners were active. Starfall's highly-protected pod of science gear was moved first; Thal's transport was then shifted into the arms of waiting grapples. A team had the pod of gem-grade jurillium ready and it was stowed in a secure inner hold before repair drones and bots began work on *Arianrhod's* damaged hull.

A meeting with Starfall's commander had been set for later, to allow respite for the participants and to give time for responses to the various despatched queries and messages to come in.

"Wonder what the Selky fallout will be," Apnis said as she rose to hand over to the next watch. "If the ambassador and the admiral have raised hackles *and* an ISA ship was there, it'll have to say something."

"Or do something," Ahxenta retorted as she released command. "Four hours and then to Thal's main office. I expect he left Seer with the *Kel'Moth*, but he's expecting his brother. Crizz will prep our shuttle and Azular's coming. He's got stuff to give Kerrix."

"What sort of stuff and do we have to give them personal space?"

"Funny, and no: he's got holos of his hull section model with micro-sensor units and the mesh overlay, and data on how he thinks they link together on Norvallan hull arrays, and how they'll work on *Arianrhod's*. He can hand that on and they can work out the odds later. His personal business he can sort out in his own time, not in mine."

"Where is he anyhow? I haven't seen him for a while."

"Checking over the gem-grade jurillium we got," the captain told her. "And its pod: as it's Starfall, I bet it'll have a surprise or two."

"He'd best watch out," the first mate warned. "If it's that good and big enough, Earbleat will hijack it for *Loki* number nine."

"Like hell. She's started in on the pod in bay alpha five; bits are all over one of Crizz's side labs, including a new type of circular gun port that she'd been rigging for the last *Loki*. Let's go, it's chow time."

* * *

The bay in the huge complex of Captain Thal's main HQ was sparse. *Arianrhod's* shuttle had been directed to a single berth. The captain left her pilot aboard; she had brought no guards but she, Apnis and Azular were armed. Dexel Thal toted a kitbag with his newly-acquired effects.

Two of Thal's officers were there as escort. Ahxenta was surprised not to see him, but realised why at his office: Kerrix, Inks and Levettiza were there. Whatever the plan for the reunion, it broke as soon as the brothers saw one another. Vexin Thal gave a choked cry and embraced his younger sibling. He recovered quickly and led him into a side-room, leaving the others to find coffee and seats.

Greetings and updates were traded until the hard-faced commander reappeared alone. He thanked Ahxenta for her actions and care, and told her that Admiral and Ambassador Posettix would not be there, as they were busy aboard the *Serenity* with links to ISA HQ and Norvallan consular and fleet HQs. *His* concerns were the events at Polstarn, his brother's rescue, the ISA's interest in worm-pocket creation and action at Selky. He had news, sent in by a monitoring post on the border of the ISP and Non-Treaty Alliance sectors in Zeta: the hostile convoy had passed Pearl, on the edge of the Greenstar Nebula. An alert was on the way to ISA, TA, and local authorities, copied to the PSS fleet. His inference was that there might be a hostile holding area in or near nebular space, similar to the anomaly at the Crimson Drapes.

Ahxenta had finished her account of her contact with various ISA ships and events at Cygilla and Polstarn, and had begun on the conflict at Green when they were interrupted by an urgent comm for Thal. He took it by earpiece and his face alerted them to a significant incident.

"Tell them to hold station. Alert Admiral Posettix *now*, although I expect the *Serenity's* logged them. Keep tabs on them; one slip and you act. I'll have a word with Captain Kerrix and get back to you."

"Two ships have come in off the Canna side of the bypass," Thal told them. "A Telziltic war cruiser with a diplomatic crest. Ambassador Jotakt's aboard. Captain Heltakt's in command," he added to Kerrix.

"The other?" she queried.

"Is the Norvallan survey ship that was last seen off the Selky system: the *NFS Sunburst*. You *certainly* know her."

The holo ship spun atop the table, her flat shape and fin-like extrusions evoking a sea creature. The hull was hazy, and as Azular caught its fine detail on his info-pad, he could see a cross-linked net overlain with tiny fur-like projections. He drew out to show the inlaid emplacements and arrays over her flanks, screened by the misty glow of shielding.

"So *that's* the *NFS Sunburst*," Ahxenta said dryly. "She's not very big for a survey ship. Quite a jump to command of the *Moonstone*," she said to Kerrix, who had been looking askance at the science officer.

"Not exactly," was the equally tart return. "My previous command was an explorer with two hundred crew and a very wide remit."

"What happened?"

"Broke the rules, faced a disciplinary board, and was demoted. How did you pull that up so fast?" Kerrix demanded of Azular, as Ahxenta traded a wry glance with her first mate.

"I linked to my station on *Arianrhod's* bridge and used her hull arrays to bring in the data: she *is* scanning local space."

"I'll have to stop giving you toys: you're too good at adapting them for your own devious purposes. But you won't get through her hide, even with a Norvallan info-pad and your ship's top-notch gear."

"Including Norvallan scanning ability," he smiled. "But you're right, I can't: she's got good jammers."

"I advise you to stop. Captain Sallix is probably whining to Captain Thal about it now – it won't have missed *his* tactical ops, believe me."

Thal had left to talk to the captains of both ships. He knew and trusted Captain Heltakt; he had not met Sallix, but Kerrix had warned him that the man had a temper and an inflated ego, and was unlikely to give him straight answers. Neither would he be open with her there: they had never been friends. Her advice had been to outface him and threaten him with Ambassador Posettix and Admiral Posettix, as both outranked him, and to give him no leeway whatsoever.

"What was your link to Captain Sallix?" Ahxenta asked curiously.

"He was my first officer on the *Sunburst*. He thought the command should have been his. Now it is, but I doubt his attitude's improved."

"He was the one that abandoned the search for you to head home for some fly-by carnival for the new head of state?"

"He's the one. In his book, he was following fleet orders. Which he was, in a way. But here's Captain Thal. It must have been a short chat."

"The *Zetkalt's* for Alto Finglas. Ambassador Jotakt has the authority of several Psi worlds to negotiate on alliance with, but not membership of, the ISA. And he'll meet with the TA. He and Ambassador Posettix are in session now, as she got nowhere with the Norvallan authorities. As Sallix won't say why he's here, he's not welcome. I told him so and referred him to Admiral Posettix. He can hang fire until I know what he's at. And I want to know what he and the ISA, with Mu collusion, are up to near Selky," Thal said darkly.

"As for that," Ahxenta began. "Azular's come up with an idea that might explain where the bypass – if it *is* one – will lead. Azular?"

The Berzic set up his holo of a likely line from Selky to Kilda, with facts of the recent find of a rich meta-jurillium source on the latter, the sites of local high negative mass-energy density pockets and his notion that an exchange of Norvallan tech for ISA benefits in the area might be the key. Levettiza leaned in for a closer view.

"Kilda's outside ISP and Mu borders, in Non-Treaty space, but not claimed," she said. "The NTA's part of the ISA, so it won't raise dust. The Norvallans get a fast route into Kappa via Mu without having to come via Starfall *and* dibs on the ore source."

"They could use Canna," interrupted Apnis. "The Brittle to Minch Fettin bypass cuts through there."

"That wouldn't get them leverage for an ore supply *and* it's close to here and to Minch Fettin," the commander pointed out.

"And it'll be slower and riskier to navigate to Kappa, if you keep to Mu space," Jesse Inks observed. "The hostiles that slipped off at Canna and are now en route to the Greenstar must have spied the activity on the way through, and I bet it's been sent into hostile ears."

"Good point," agreed Kerrix "I'll pass it to the admiral, but he may have figured and is beating the ISA with it. I doubt he's found out what it's up to at Selky or why its ships are prowling around harassing PSS ships. I'd like to know why the Norvallan authorities are part of it and why it's being kept from their ambassador. Her job *is* trade relations."

"Didn't you reckon some time ago that the ISA *and* the TA would try to get their toes in the door here and near Psi by setting up locally, Cap?" Apnis asked Ahxenta. "This Selky deal may be the start of it for the ISA, but where does the TA fit in? *It* won't be far behind if profits are on the cards. And they will be if Kilda's so rich in ore."

She was interrupted by a sharp chirp indicating another link to Thal.

He quickly inserted his earpiece, but the message was short.

"Commander Seer," he said. "The four blips that passed Pearl have been traced no further, but four hostile signals were caught by the *Snow Quartz* as she skirted the Greenstar, en route from Kitty Steel to Silf. She'd got the alert I sent, so Captain Utterspot scanned on the way by. He's sent the results: four signals that cut, with a small spurt of energy, next to what read as a patch of thickened nebular matter. He didn't go in for a close look, but he's sent round a note and warned the ISA."

"It *must* be a holding area," Ahxenta said. "I've heard zip of what the ISA made of the area at the Drapes, but it'll be under surveillance."

"Wonder if it's been mined," Apnis remarked. "It's what Zillah did at the Ginseng, and that spoked alien plans a bit."

"Not our problem, but we need to be aware. Once we leave, we're for Lambda," she informed Thal. "We'll use the route to Twilight Exit, and then take the cutoff to the ISP sector, and make for Aoria. But I'd like to know where the *Sunburst* plans to head," she added to Kerrix.

"You *and* me. I can try a link, but I suspect that any comm from me to anyone aboard will be monitored. Admiral Posettix may be able to help. I'll keep you updated if I hear anything. I don't want the *Sunburst* or any other ship on my tail when I head out."

"When will that be?" Azular asked her anxiously.

"When I've done what I've to do here," she smiled. "Refining the recoding of my hull micro-sensors for one: I've had no more on my stolen hull pieces since the slice found on Iridis. And the *Kel'Moth's* will need recoding. My people are on it, but we've had to shelve creation of a version for standard hull plate. You'll get a couple of trial units, once I've seen the bits you've made. Our ships will be here a few days, so we'll have time. But if that's all, Captain, I've a lot to catch up on aboard my ship, including crew-related issues," she said to Thal.

The talks over, the officers and their escorts set off to the shuttles. Ahxenta and Levettiza chatted on the way, leaving Apnis to Jesse Inks. Azular and Kerrix took up the rear; he was asking about the *Moonstone's* injured crew. She still had two badly hurt, but they were mending.

Once aboard *Arianrhod*, the three made the bridge. All was in order, with repairs and resupply on target. Starfall had charged for materials, Lindell stated, but the rates were fair and set against cargo exchanges. Repair crew time had not been charged, and on that basis, Earbleat had drawn up a list of items she deemed crucial for *Loki Nine*, now nearing completion. Starfall's supply section apparently had the gear.

Ahxenta groaned, but given the alerts about the Greenstar, which *Arianrhod* had got, Earbleat told her, and the recent arrivals at Starfall, she agreed, on the rider that *Loki* would be ready for action in days.

"You'll regret it," Apnis warned, laughing.

"Thanks. But I'll call Zillah; she'll have the ISA data, since she has a pack of reps living next door. She *may* know more than we do."

The Freskat fleet admiral did. Two ISA ships on the hunt for hostile signs were heading to the Greenstar; and activity had been spotted near the Crimson Drapes holding area. Zillah had heard zero of Selky and had not been invited to ISA meetings, but she *had* seen an increase in ISA ships in Lambda: the *Dauntless* and *Ingenious* had come and gone from Freskat, and two more were in orbit. Zillah had dug up details of the protected arrays wanted for ISA ships, and the ISA was in quest of sources. Greskitty, her fleet's supplier, also wanted array wafers to fulfil military orders. As Ahxenta signed off the call, another link came in, which Apnis had sent through. She was not surprised that the captain was some time in answering.

"What did the rude Admiral Best want?" she asked when Ahxenta returned. "He looked like he'd swallowed a frog."

"A lot," was the wary return. "He knows we're here. I bet he found out from the ISA ships at Wester: they'd have guessed. Or the science ship with the *Sunburst* at Selky. And he's worked out that as we didn't drop Thal or his boat en route, this is where they are. I gave him zip, but I told Captain Thal that Best is pushing. But *I* pushed Best on my complaints. He won't play, but he's pissed about that. And that his HQ is about to have political visitors: he's heard that the *Serenity* and *Zetkalt* are here with tetchy ambassadors aboard. He asked what I knew about them and their affairs. I told him to ask them, and that I'd pass on the news that he'd enquired. He didn't like that. I dropped a line to Kerrix and asked her to send it on. Where's Azular?"

"Upgrading our nav-charts to integrate bypass routes beyond Amity Beacon at this side *and* zones Beta and Alpha at the other – in fact the ones Starfall use *and* ones the Norvallans use. And he's putting in the speculative route from Selky to Kilda. He says it's easier from his lab and he can keep tabs on his station from there."

"I'll bet he did. And where did he get the data, or need I ask?"

"He was being cagey, but a link for him came from Captain Kerrix while you were chewing Best's ears off, *with* a huge data stream."

"Hold the conn: I'm going for a walk," the captain growled.

"Oops!" Box whispered to his mate. "He's done it again."

"Hush up and mind your boards; if Dr Azular's updating our nav-charts, the outcome's going to be landing in *your* lap soon."

As Ahxenta had expected, her Berzic officer had got the new nav-data from Kerrix, but where *she* had got it baffled her. That Thal would hand on his fleet data to *Arianrhod* surprised her, but he *had* authorised the transfer, on the proviso that it would not be passed on. New route data from Psi and beyond had come from the admiral, as the *Serenity's* nav-charts had been revised on her last stop at Norvalla.

"The bypasses through and outside mapped space *are* the ones you figured," the captain said, scanning the holo. "We have the codes. But *that's* the route to Nexus: in uncharted space, way off Alpha."

"Aye, ma'am. If Myrtleberry's ships *are* there, they may spot one leg of it, but Thal and his base commander will be aware. Here's the Kell Lyne to Amity route that Thal's people use. It crosses Flemm, and the Sox worm-pocket's marked as risky, so the data's recent."

"Anything else I should know? I expect Captain Kerrix is still busy."

"She is, but she plans to speak to Captain Sallix: he called her ship while we were with Captain Thal. We didn't discuss personal matters."

"I bet. I see the *Zetkalt's* near the *Serenity*, but where's the *Sunburst?* Is she still in high orbit above the ball of rock Starfall's anchored to?"

"Yes ma'am; Captain Thal hasn't approved a berth. That's maybe what Sallix wants to talk to Captain Kerrix about."

"She'll give him short shrift. You're on the bridge for your next duty shift and this time you'll stay there."

"Understood, Captain."

By the time Ahxenta made her station, it was close to handover. She glanced over her boards. "On track," she said to Apnis. "We'll chat in my office once we've signed off. And I want Azular there."

Fifteen minutes later, the three were seated in the bridge office.

"Admiral Best," the captain began. "He brought up the Skota life-tubes and the tracking and other gear found – and suspicions that there was a link to Furze through Starfall *and* us. The ISA's evidently combed through what was left on Furze and found enough to warrant interest. He wanted to know what I knew about Furze; he said he knew there *had* been life-tubes there, and hence remains."

"Cinnabar…" Apnis began, putting a hand on her arm.

The captain shook her head. "And he's figured whatever *was* there was taken to Starfall."

"Thal's ships were chased all the way home from Furze," recalled Apnis. "Somebody knew about it and if it *was* ISA, that means a leak. Best might be one of the plants the ISA's looking for – he's nasty piece of work and too like Myrtleberry for comfort."

"Unlikely," Azular put in. "It was hostile ships that…"

"That's *not* the point," Ahxenta cut in. "What is, is what he let slip.

True or not, Kerrix has to know. The last I heard, Levettiza didn't find out what was in the Skota tubes. She may know now, but I doubt it."

"Cap?" Apnis queried.

"Similar to what Thal's and the *Serenity's* teams found for Furze, but some Skota remains were Norvallan The hostiles *were* active in Psi."

"What! The ISA teams could distinguish Norvallan remains?"

"The *Advance* was at Norvalla, after that clash at Telzilt where the *Twin Star* was badly hit. She assisted, and Levettiza was aboard then. The ISA knows about the *Moonstone*, and that she has Norvallan crew. But I'm going to link Kerrix now, before Best gets there."

"If he hasn't already," Apnis said grimly.

Best had not called the *Moonstone*. Ahxenta told of her talk with him and what he had said. Kerrix looked troubled and called Levettiza in. *She* had heard no more on Skota after her comm to ISA Intelligence, other than that the trackers and drones found had been disabled. Her links to her old unit were being eroded, she admitted, possibly because she was now serving aboard a PSS of the Starfall fleet.

"I'll have to tell Admiral Posettix," Kerrix stated. "*Serenity's* due to leave for Alto Finglas. Captain Thal's sending an escort with her and the *Zetkalt*. The admiral will make waves: he'll be subtle, but he'll dig. Vetta, contact anyone you think can help and see what you can find. I'll bring Thal in. The ISA won't be able to bawl security and hide its doings on worm-pockets and secret ways for much longer; and if it tries to use its influence to undermine Starfall, it'll run aground."

Ahxenta was surprised at her intensity but rather than pursue it, she asked if Kerrix had spoken to Sallix. She had: he still refused to explain the *Sunburst's* presence in Mu space, but as his ship was part of an ISA-allied fleet, he had asked that she intercede with Thal to accord him the usual civilities. She had told him to stick it, referring him to Posettix and Thal. But in going over her record of the chat, she sighted a known face on his bridge: a systems engineer skilled in bypass initiation.

Kerrix ended the talk by telling Ahxenta that she would take the news to the admiral and Thal, and link back any results.

"She seemed thrown," Apnis observed to Azular. "And you didn't bring up the bits and pieces she's promised for the hull arrays."

"It wasn't appropriate, Commander."

"But the news shook her for some reason," the captain broke in. "Any idea why, Azular?"

"No ma'am, and I don't intend to ask. We've another four days here so more may come to light. I'd like leave to visit the *Moonstone*, if I can. I can take the model micro-sensor mesh that I developed. I sent Xanna an updated holo and she has spare trial units and resources we should be able to use to produce our own and fit them to our hull arrays."

"Run it by me first," Ahxenta ordered.

* * *

Azular set his shuttle down gently in the bay aboard the *Moonstone*. The stash of goods he had brought was tied in behind him. As soon as his boards read stable, he unclipped his harness and eased out of the tight seat. As he had expected, Kerrix was there to meet him, but to his mild irritation so was Nyvallish, the *Moonstone's* senior science officer.

"Dr Azular," she greeted him formally. "Your units are stacked over there. We've others we can use to explain their workings in our labs. I take it your model's in the shuttle?"

"Yes, ma'am. I can fetch it out now if you wish."

She agreed and he stepped back up the ramp. Nyvallish was eyeing the *Xanna*. Despite her insignia and the rad-repelling glaze that cloaked her in the pink of most of *Arianrhod's* shuttles, she was an odd craft.

Azular reappeared toting a kitbag and the soft case that housed the model. "I brought my info-pad and hand-held scanner lest you have any updates I can add," he explained.

That was greeted by raised brows and the instruction that he attend the two to the lab where the work on the micro-sensor units was being done. The transport tube across the main hull to the science unit was fast and the walk to the lab broken only by the nods of passing crew. The *Moonstone* was still under-crewed, Kerrix said, but she hoped to be at full strength when she left Starfall. Azular could see little of the harm caused by the jump through the self-made bypass, but he sensed an air of anxiety in the techs active in the large lab into which they turned.

"Let's get down to work," the captain grinned.

Two hours later, the three stopped for a break. Nyvallish and Azular made for a rest area while Kerrix called the bridge, as she had had two links whilst they had been busy. On her return, she sent Nyvallish off to medbay and sat by Azular. She and her techs were impressed by his model, she said, and his input had been valuable. She now wanted his opinion on her lab and the work he had seen.

"There's a pod of pieces for *Arianrhod* that will help you with micro-sensor production," she told him when he had done. "Captain Thal's cleared it. We *could* do it here, but your captain wouldn't sanction it, as we'd need details of her hull science arrays that she won't give. You won't get full hull coverage, but that you don't need. I suggest you use your own codes. Thal's had it done for the *Kel'Moth's* units and those for fitting in our ships will have unique coding. What's the look for?"

"I'd hoped for a little private time with you, but this place is public. And you didn't actually set a time limit on my visit…"

"I'm still on duty, and so are you," she smiled at him. "You're back to my lab while I see what my crew's been up to. You'll join me for dinner in the mess. Take your gear and speak to Negynn Olirix: he'll get you updates. Meanwhile, finish your drink and I'll have mine."

He could tell she was edgy but knew he was not the cause. He dared mention Skota and was treated to a frosty stare and a warning to back off. Admiral Posettix had been advised and would take it further, and the ambassadors had been told. The admiral had had harsh words with Sallix *and* Norvallan fleet command: the story was that the *Sunburst* had been sent to aid the ISA on covert technical issues. That the diplomatic corps and other authorities had been excluded from the process was creating discord in Psi, and reports from there to the ISA Council were about to upset non-ISP ISA members, as it looked as if ISP interests were taking the lion's share in most ongoing profitable enterprises.

"I'm for medbay to see my people," she ended. "I'll send Nyvallish back and you can talk to him about the units. I'll pick you up later."

Later was much later and Azular had begun to wonder if she would reappear. He had learnt from the lab team that their tasks were almost done, and those from the *Serenity* were due to leave. Nyvallish had been visiting his wife in medbay: she had been hurt in the action at Green. He also found that the ISA ships sent to the Greenstar had made it days before, but no report of their findings had come in. Thal was back on the *Kel'Moth*, the *Sunburst* had been given a berth where an eye could be kept on her and the *ISAS Elucida* had arrived. *Her* captain had told Thal that she and the *Sunburst* were heading for the Greenstar.

"Dr Azular," Kerrix said on entry. "You'd best pack up now. I've arranged guest quarters for you, as you'll want to contact your ship. This way. I take it you've updated your info-pad and scanner?"

"Yes ma'am," he confirmed, his eyes lighting as he collected his kit and made ready to follow her.

"Guest quarters?" he murmured as they strode along the deck.

"We *have* spare berths for visitors. On the command staff level. I've assigned you the one next door to mine. And get the grin off your face – trust me, it's not luxury."

"And then dinner?"

She smiled impishly. "Yes. With four of my senior officers. How much time do you reckon you still need to familiarise yourself with the systems, fixing and use of the sensor units and their gear?"

"At least a day, ship-time."

"You can have until twelve hundred tomorrow," he was told.

"Xanna?"

"Azular?"

"I'd like a quick word in private before I contact my ship, if you don't mind. In my quarters – or yours."

"Don't push it," she warned as they reached the transport tube.

The quarters she brought him to were small but well-furnished. The means to link to *Arianrhod* had been set up, she told him as he dropped his gear on the sofa. He gave her little time to point out the rest before catching her in his arms with an inarticulate endearment.

"I've missed you too, Azular, Azular," she whispered in return.

A minute ticked by before she extricated herself. "Any more of this and the crew who saw me come in will start talking. Make your link. I'll be back in half an hour and we'll head to the mess. What now?"

"Before you go," he smiled, his eyes crinkling up wickedly. "I have something for you."

* * *

The senior mess of the *Moonstone's* main hull was large but smaller than *Arianrhod's*, Azular noted as he and Kerrix made for a wall table. The four there stood as they came up. He recognised them: Levettiza, Inks, Mettix, and chief engineer Morrow, a grizzled Marridani he had met in the Web when first the *Moonstone* had been rigged as a PSS.

"We usually collect our own rations," Kerrix clarified as they settled into their seats. "But for guests, we offer table service."

"Is that to impress them?" Azular asked quizzically.

"If my ship hasn't impressed them, they're not worth impressing," she shot back. "Your menu, Dr Azular. I left it to Cookie and his team, but if there's anything you don't like, feel free to let me know."

"If your chef is anything like *Arianrhod's*, I wouldn't dare," he smiled gently at her before scanning the list.

Jesse Inks, looking keenly at his captain and a clearly happy Azular, traded a glance with Levettiza, who grinned and gave a quick nod.

"If I may ask, ma'am, are congratulations in order?" he asked.

"Can't keep a savvy crew down," Vetta told her. "Berzic tradition, I see: the tricolour ring. How long has *this* been on the horizon?"

"Since Selliden – when we picked up the *Kel'Tarn* survivors."

"And you've kept it quiet since then? Well done."

"On *this* ship yes; I suspect that most of the crew of the *Arianrhod* know by now, don't they?" she asked Azular wryly.

"Yes ma'am, I expect they do. But they *are* discreet, in general."

"In general," she repeated. "And yes, I guess congratulations *are* in order, Jesse," she smiled, looking down at the token on her hand.

"Captain Ahxenta knew at Selliden; she congratulated you then," he said shrewdly. "Should I order a bottle to mark the occasion?"

"No way, the crew is eyeing us up as it is. And there's wine with the meal. Another perk for visitors," she said to Azular. "I inherited a stock with the ship and Cookie locked it up before I could ditch it."

The chat ran on until the food was served, and then turned to ship issues. The price of creating a bypass was high in energy costs, and the jump speed had caused intense stressing of the *Moonstone's* systems and fabric, Azular found. Morrow's teams were still repairing damage, and he was exploring ways to limit any future impacts. Kerrix asked about the *Arianrhod's* decoy: Thal had told her of it, and she figured a similar device would benefit her ship. Azular explained briefly, and spoke of his use of the response plate specs she had given him soon after they first met. A buzz on her wrist comm interrupted.

Kerrix inserted her earpiece to take the link. It was from her bridge. Her irritated look told her colleagues that the message was unwelcome.

"Urgent my boot. Tell him to stand by. I'll call from here. Excuse me," she said as she rose. "This won't take long. Please carry on."

They watched as she made for a wall comm booth, her second mate noting that someone was in for an earful. She was back in ten minutes.

"*That* was Captain Sallix. The *Sunburst* and the *Elucida* are off in two hours. He was peeved I knew they were for the Greenstar. He wouldn't say why, but they'll be checking it out. The call was a last-ditch attempt to find out more on Starfall, its commander and the ship and pilot that *Arianrhod* brought in, and to rile me. But you're right," she told Azular. "ISP and Mu factions in ISA and Norvallans in the bypass-building trade *are* making a link between Selky and Kilda. Sallix called from his bridge. Bad move: systems engineer and bypass expert Kinnitix at his back had a holo-sim running, possibly deliberately. I taxed Sallix on his and the *Elucida's* mission to join Selky to Kilda and the deals Norvallan groups would get on Kilda's meta-jurillium. He was rash enough to ask how I knew, but naturally I didn't tell him it was mere speculation."

"You think the bypass engineer was deliberately running the sim, Cap?" Levettiza asked. "Why?"

"I told you I recognised him in my last chat to Sallix. He's not part of the *Sunburst's* crew. He got to be a senior officer by sheer hard work, not rank; he's ethical, dislikes Sallix intensely, lectured at fleet academy and served on constructor and science ships, including mine. I think he's been brought in for this project, as he should be retired by now."

"What *did* you tell Captain Sallix?" Azular wanted to know.

"Not what he wanted to hear. He used the line that as a Norvallan, my duty to my world overrode any personal agenda. I'd to remind him that I wasn't a citizen, nor had I any rights on Norvalla or its colonies: *he'd* seen to that when he spoke for the prosecution at my court martial. And as he'd demanded info on Captains Thal and Ahxenta, I'd send a copy of our talk to them. And to Ambassador Jotakt, as I'm a Telziltic citizen. I wished him a good trip and cut the link."

"There must be close links between the Norvallans and some ISA bods if Sallix knows about Dexel Thal's ship," Levettiza pointed out.

"That struck me, but I wasn't about to pursue it. Norvallan input *was* maybe sought after the imploding worm-pocket at Fourpoint, but I'd be surprised if the ISA gave away any details. Once we're done, I'll speak to those involved here. I've had the records sent to them, copied to Admiral Posettix, in case Sallix is unwise enough to make contact."

"He wouldn't, surely?" Inks queried.

"He *was* arrogant enough to link me from his bridge. I've ordered tactical and science ops to watch him and the *Elucida*, though I expect Captain Thal will track them as far as he's able," Kerrix replied.

The chat carried on while the six quickly finished their meals. They had almost done when another alert for the captain came in. As she listened, her face showed shock and surprise.

"What…! Dammit! I'm on my way. Send a comm that we'll render immediate aid, though I expect Captain Thal and Captain Ahxenta will have got there first. Kerrix out. Jesse, Vetta, you're with me; Doc, get to medbay; Chief, you're for main engineering until we know more. Azular, make for your quarters and stay there: you'll have a clear line to your ship. The *Kel'Kith* and the *Kel'Torc* are towing the *Nyx Warrior* in," she told them. "She's badly hit, but that's all I have."

Azular found his way to his berth and arrived just as an amber alert was declared. He made for the comm to link to *Arianrhod*. She was also at amber, as lights were flashing in the background.

"You'll stay there for now," the captain ordered. "We know it was a hostile attack near Wester 287 on the Zeta side. The *Warrior* was en route to Wester via Vellis Minor and Silf. She passed by the Greenstar, but as she'd got the alert from the *Snow Quartz*, she gave it a wide berth. She *did* scan, but logged no sign of the ships the ISA was to have sent in. Thal's contacting the *Elucida* to see if he can find out more, but the two that hit the *Warrior* were on a track that implies they'd come from nebular space between Silf and Pearl, on a direct line for Zeta or Mu. *That* puts them in a line for Starfall. Thal's listening posts in the area had been recording zip for the past few days, so he'd sent in the *Kel'Kith* and *Kel'Torc* to check. The *Warrior* was barely holding her own by the time they found her; she'd sent a distress but it'd been jammed. They downed the blips and are heading in, but it looks like Thal's posts have been inactivated or subverted. The data implies that the hostiles were crewed. What is it?" Ahxenta asked as the comms officer called out.

"Captain Thal's sending two defence craft into Zeta to see what they can find," Bellfish announced.

"The *Lucent* and the *Schiltron*," Gliss added from tactical. "We have them on grid. *Kel'Kith*, *Kel'Torc* and *Nyx Warrior* are now in range."

"I'm cutting now," Ahxenta told her science officer. "You'll be kept updated by Captain Kerrix, I'm sure."

Azular could follow what was going on via the *Moonstone's* channels, and busied himself linking his info and scanning kit into the unit in his billet until the entry buzzed. It was science officer Olirix, asking that he accompany him to the lab to assist in tracking events and taking any necessary action. Azular agreed, suspecting that the order had come from the captain. He soon knew why. Dusker of the *Elucida* had told Thal that two ships in the now-verified Greenstar Nebula holding area had burst out on a line across the ISP sector of Zeta, towards Epsilon, bypassing the ISA ships in the area. It was inferred that they were en route to Arrissia or Heligon; the ISA ships were in pursuit. In Thal's opinion, it was a ruse to draw Alliance ships away. He suspected that his base was the target, and was upping his defences in response.

* * *

The next hours were busy. The *Nyx Warrior* and her escorts had made it, and Starfall's ops and the PSS ships were assisting as they could. The *Warrior's* plating and arrays had taken massive damage, and three outer cargo bays were out. Holdspan had ordered one blown to jettison its payload of heavy gear for Wester in the face of an enemy ship to slow it and give the *Warrior* more speed, but by the time the *Kel'Kith* and the *Kel'Torc* had got to her, she was down to her last defences and had taken multiple casualties. Thal had mobilised his HQ medbay to take in the worst, and requested aid from the visiting ships for his under-equipped centre. The *Arianrhod*, *Zetkalt*, *Serenity* and *Moonstone* had sent medics and supplies and the *Moonstone* had lent the *Warrior* three high-spec med-cradles for patient transfer. Dusker excused the *Elucida* from assisting as she was due to depart, but told Thal that he and the *Sunburst* would hold until the situation at the Greenstar was clearer.

Ahxenta had ordered her staff off in relays for rest once she was up to date on conditions aboard the *Nyx Warrior*. Holdspan and his first mate, both hurt but adamant that they would stay on duty, were facing the loss of two crewmen; nine others were gravely injured. Thal, having assessed the damage, had the *Warrior* tied into his best-equipped repair bay and deployed his most able crew, but he did not spare her young captain from the problems facing Starfall when an urgent call came in from the *Lucent*: she and the *Schiltron* had reached their closest listening post in Zeta. It was inert and had a crude alien jammer attached. Thal, taking it as a sign of imminent danger to his HQ, had alerted his bases, recalled his ships on non-urgent missions and had the jammer blasted. That post restored, the ships had set off to inspect others. Thal warned the ISA that an alien force at the Greenstar was likely to be priming for assault, and urged that activity at the Crimson Drapes be watched.

Ahxenta, sent off-duty by her CMO, used the break to call Azular. He was in his quarters, having been ordered to gather his gear and head to his shuttle. He informed the captain of the *Sunburst's* agenda and told her that two micro-sensor units and a pod of bits to produce more were set to load. His hull section model he would leave. He was calm, but she sensed frustration at the undoing of his plans. Their chat was interrupted by a buzz at his door. It was Kerrix, who had come to escort him to the shuttle bay. He linked off, and Ahxenta, grinning to herself, alerted the bridge that he would be over shortly.

* * *

The captain was on the bridge when the next alert came in. The *Lucent* and *Schiltron* had tested and restored two more jammed listening posts, and, now in range of the Greenstar, had logged rising energy signals from the holding area. Their science officers had concluded that more hidden ships were on the move. The two were ordered to drop probes and head home. And faint hostile signals on an incoming vector had been sensed on the Amity to Starfall bypass by the Mu carrier off Selky. She had sent an alert and retreated towards Kappa. Thal had launched a probe and rallied Starfall for defence. His ships were already moving to set positions across the base. The *Moonstone* was one and Azular was keenly tracking her progress from his station.

"What do you make of it?" Ahxenta asked at his back.

"The *Moonstone's* been moved closer to the diplomatic ships to flank the *Sunburst* and the *Elucida*, despite her ongoing repairs. Captain Thal has positioned the heavy cruisers *Fire Opal* and *Amber Flash* off an inner ring of his main HQ. Much of *that* is heavily fortified, so he must have valued things to protect down there."

"Such as?"

"The cargo delivered by the *Kel'Kith*," he answered raising his eyes to hers. "She's still based here, as is the *SS Lucent*, and if I recall aright, the *Lucent* was out of Thal's Gemstone Station originally."

"He's not breathed a word about the kids. Or the life-tubes from Furze, and *they* must be stashed here. If the kids are there… no wonder he's sending his best in to protect them. No word of this to anyone. And the *Warrior*? I've not spoken to Nat Holdspan, bar to offer aid."

"She won't be able to help in any action we might face, despite the speed of her repairs," Azular said grimly. "Captain Thal's going all out on them, from which I reckon he's expecting trouble, and soon. Has he said anything, ma'am?"

"No. But I'm off to make calls. Anything changes, you let me know. Gliss, get our grid full down and plot anything and everything."

The captain was back in her chair in forty minutes. There was little to report, the first mate told her, bar the repositioning of ships within the meshes of Starfall and the advent of several more.

"I was checking in with some of ours," Ahxenta said. "*Obsidian's* at Arrissia still; there's no sign of alien incursion into local space, so the blips from the Greenstar weren't heading there. As I've had zip on the ISA ships trailing them, maybe they've lost them. Grey was taking on weapons, so I advised he take on extra and reroute here, if Thal's okay with it. *Obsidian* could hop on at Sunrise and come straight through. Grey's agreed."

"I bet Thal will say yes. Who else did you get on line?"

"Not many in this locale; the only one close is the *Snow Quartz*, and she's heading home to Kitty Steel. She got the general alert Thal sent out on the UV-III. And I spoke to Zillah. I got her out of her bed, but I figured it was worth it. She'd seen the alert from Thal to the ISA and heard of the Greenstar action, but not any outcome. She's sent two of her fleet to scout the Ginseng, in case. There's been no reports of other possible holding areas, but two blips *were* seen near the Stoorie Nebula between Jete and Mica, by a Kanelian carrier. Theta's thinly settled and ill-patrolled, so the ISA's antsy. Zillah thinks if there's another positive sighting in the area, the *Peerless, Repulse* and *Advance* will be recalled."

"Myrtleberry and company? That'll help," Apnis said scathingly. "The ISA would be better drafting in its ships that are keeping eyes on the likes of us, or sneakily building worm-pockets and bypasses. How long until the *Lucent* and the *Schiltron* get in?"

"I reckon twenty five hours," the captain replied. "But trouble may come from the Selky side: if Canna's avoided, then Starfall's the target, and if the incoming blips are uncrewed, they'll be fast and deadly. Our people need to be ready. *Arianrhod's* repairs are done and she's fit, but I want our decoy and *Loki* prepped as well. This is a tight space to fight from, but we'll deploy them if we have to."

"So much for the TA's threat that the PSS fleet could be drafted in to fight if there's major conflict," Apnis sighed. "We're in it anyway."

"Yup. I'll call a briefing on all that's relevant and warn the crew that this is the calm before the storm. We'll need reinforcing patches on hull shielding and intensified energy fields for our open cargo bays."

* * *

The calm lasted less than expected, for a supra-light link to Thal came in ten hours later from a contact on Canna that three large alien ships had come into range. Canna's outer defences had powered up in reply. That was followed by an alert from the Starfall probes at the Greenstar that a huge energy outwash had been detected. The masked signal had split in two: one arm was on track past Silf for Mercy Four, the second was headed deeper into the ISP-majority sector of zone Zeta. Thal had alerted Sunrise, Arrissia Five and Heligon Station as the main habited loci, and the ISA. He followed that up less than an hour later with the warning that the signal heading his way from Mercy had dropped its masking and had coalesced into five recognisably hostile outlines.

"He's included the *Elucida* and the *Sunburst* in his alert; so the *Elucida* will update the ISA on what's going on," Ahxenta noted tartly.

"Including what's pulled out for Starfall's defence," Apnis snorted. "That won't have missed Thal. And there's been no word on what his probe headed to Canna has found."

"Yet," Ahxenta cautioned. "If those blips pass Canna, we're in real trouble. I'd best alert the doc that we'll need boosts to keep us awake."

Those at Starfall had little time to ponder, for the hostile trio skirted Canna and the probe logged them as coming in. From its output, Thal could tell that they were heavily armed and manned. He thus ordered Sunrise Base to ready for assault and to send out scouts to track those blips on a line deeper into Zeta, lest Sunrise was their objective.

Ahxenta had sent her senior bridge crew off for short breaks, as she wanted them in place if Starfall *was* the target of the incoming convoys. She included herself, and had barely had two hours when an urgent link came in from Zillah. The ships surveying the Ginseng had detected a glitch matching the nebular thickening that had hidden a hostile fleet during the all-out conflict that had resulted in a battle off Freskat. The admiral had alerted the ISA. And another report had come in of two huge strangers prowling the spaces near the Stoorie in Theta. As it was ISA in origin, Zillah suspected that the trio of advanced explorers led by the *Peerless* was already heading back into habited parts.

The captain cut the link quickly and called Thal: if hostiles *were* ready to jump out at the Ginseng, his Twilight base might be on their hit list, and Nexus was in the vicinity of the Stoorie. She recalled that a Starfall ship in uncharted space near Theta had spied a huge hostile near the Zenith node on the bypass off Nexus, at about the time *Arianrhod* had been dealt the bogus job offer by Nest Holdings, and wondered about a link. Gemstone Station had no nebula nearby, but there were ample hiding places in the vast accretion of asteroids in the general area and the unsavoury dens of Mellifly and Brown Amber were close.

The harsh leader of Starfall was grim. All his bases and ships were at alert, he told Ahxenta, and every listening post he could call on was operational. If the situation *was* the prelude to an attempted recovery by the hostiles of their ex-bases, his people were ready, but he doubted that aliens still active and out for revenge against him would have the ships or resources for such a coup. Their plan was probably chaos, as in such a climate, especially under the guidance of superior, human-like types, their kind could prosper.

Thal was still online when a note from Zillah was patched in: the *Merrin Free* and the *Trueheart* had been rerouted to pursue three ships crossing Zeta. ISA listening posts had tracked the group past Foxbat, an empty system in the centre of the ISP-majority area; its current line would take it to Parkin, a newly-established, manned ISA station.

"I'm not taking it as read," Thal declared. "But I *will* warn Sunrise. If the ISA station's the target and those ships are as big as the ones we have coming in, those two ISA battlecruisers will need help."

Ahxenta felt it essential to update her senior staff in a quick briefing and called one two hours later. She had heard from Captain Bluejohn: the *Obsidian Sky* was heading in with as many arms as her holds could carry and supplies for Thal's main medbay. The ship was running full tilt and expected to be with them in eight hours. Ahxenta had barely called dismissal when the distinctive wail of the red alert hit her ears.

"Here it comes!" she said harshly. "Everyone to station!"

18: STORM

Arianrhod's bridge was washed in a red, pulsing light as the captain and first mate took their seats and drew their ops boards across. Sounds of scurrying feet flowed round them as officers raced to their posts, and the holo-grid flashed as data flooded in from all points. Greffy, at the science station, was analysing hull science array input and exploring the probe data of the three blips on a line from Canna. Azular slid in beside him and began a review of the ships and resources available at Starfall.

Reports flashed across Ahxenta's board telling her that all her ship's sections were set for go, but she could see no explicit threat in the fluid holo. An alert from Captain Thal, directing the field from the *Kel'Moth*, notified all ships and base posts of an ops channel that would send out data as it came in. They were ordered to link into it and to update it as they could. Directives would be sent to specific ships to aid Starfall's defence. All commanders were asked to confirm readiness to comply.

"Send an affirmative, comms," Ahxenta ordered. "And keep your ears open for anything from the non-Starfall ships here."

"You think the diplomatic ships or the *Elucida* or *Sunburst* will refuse to take orders from Thal and hold fire, Cap?" Apnis asked.

"*Serenity* and *Zetkalt* will comply: they've shown their commitment to aid Thal. But I have my doubts about the other two. I expect…"

"Hail from Captain Thal, Captain!" Bellfish cut in.

"On grid."

Thal wanted the *Arianrhod* to take point at the northern polar sector of the planet around which Starfall orbited, and hold position on the line at which he expected the five hostiles heading his way from Mercy to emerge. Ahxenta would have free rein to take any action she judged appropriate and would have two of his heavy cruisers, the *SS Firestorm*, and the *SS Glenblaze*, as backup. Thal had placed reinforcements at strategic positions. Ahxenta agreed, with the proviso that she was given a full schematic of Starfall: she did not want to risk damage to sensitive locations. The data was with her in minutes.

Apnis checked the inward stream. "*Captain* Dexel Thal's at the helm of the *Firestorm*, so he's with us. How long before the storm hits?"

"Not long," Ahxenta replied curtly as a note lit her ops screen. "The five making for us are fast, uncrewed and with no jammers. No control ship either, so they'll be coded to take out everything in their path."

"Meaning they could cut through us like paper and head in to raise hell at our backs. What's our plan? Get them before they get us?"

"Exactly. But we don't go hunting, we wait, for them and anything else that might sneak in this side: the route from Sunrise crosses a lot of empty space *and* a slice of Zeta, where anything could jump on."

"Such as the blips coming in from Mercy. *Obsidian's* on that bypass."

"I don't think the five making in will divert, but Grey will have every scanner he's got online and he'll be ready. What's that, comms?"

"Alert from Admiral Zillah, ma'am! The blips tracked past Foxbat are holding course and have been engaged by two ISA ships! The ISA's sent out a request for aid from allies!"

"Patch it through to Captain Thal. There's no allied system near but he's put Sunrise on alert and it may have ships in the area."

"Patching through."

"Tactical readouts updating, Cap," Apnis warned. "The five blips are coming in – they're forming a fighting wedge! The speed of those things! How long until they're in range, Gliss?"

"At that speed, fifteen minutes tops!" the tactical officer sang out.

"Battlestations! Shields to max! Earbleat, hot up weapons, targeting eyes online! Chief, I need manoeuvring thrusters. Prep decoy and *Loki* to run," Ahxenta ordered. "Thal's reserves are coming about to protect our flanks," she noted, fingering the schematics on her board to bring up *Arianrhod's* position. "Comms, get me *Firestorm* and *Glenblaze*... Captain Thal, you're on my starboard, Captain Green, you'll take port, but mark me and keep your distance. We go in directly they're in range. *Arianrhod* has a fireship and a decoy that I *will* deploy if needed, so be aware, but I will not launch fighters. Azular, what have you got?"

Azular had drawn in all he could of the inbound five and had spied an oddity. "They read like the ships the *Warrior* faced at Swan Two, so no crew, but the leader's hull comp's unstable... chameleon! It's hiding tech! Breaching drones, like those that hit the *Warrior* at Idledott, so lethal. And I think it's manned, despite its approach speed."

"The damned ISA captured that beast from Idledott and sent nary a line on what it found! Get that data into a tight stream and send it out over the ops channel now! Did you get that, Thal, Green?"

They did. "So our priority's the lead ship," she snapped. "It must be in control, so crewed or not, we take it down."

"Hostiles slowing! They're marking us, Captain! Homing in on our position!" Gliss called. "Leader's holding course, outriders diverging!"

"Trying to outflank us!" snarled Ahxenta as she took in the pattern on her board. "*Firestorm*, *Glenblaze*, match the lines of the two closer flankers and engage at your discretion; *Arianrhod* will mark the leader," she ordered as Bellfish called that their reserves were forming into a defensive wing to protect the orbital installation at their backs. "Helm, come about to three seven nine mark two! Hold course but be ready to veer sixty degrees to port on my mark! Tallica, take auxiliaries and target any drones let loose: I don't want one getting through. Ready *Loki*, Earbleat! We're going in fast! Hold her, Dox, hold her…"

"She's launching a torpedo spread straight at us!" Earbleat warned. "Station two, target and take them out! All forr'ad batteries, fire!"

"Power surge from lead ship!" Azular's voice rang out. "She's about to unleash something! A bay's opening… it's a huge projectile ship!"

"Damn! Earbleat, get a bead on it and launch *Loki* as soon as it's in your sights! Helm, sixty degrees to port: get us into optimal position for launching *Loki*! Hold phase cannon until we're closer. Get those torpedoes down the tubes!"

"Hostile cutting off to flank us!" Gliss called. "Missile ship holding course to intercept – it's moving as we do."

"*Loki* away!" bawled Earbleat. "On target… give me covering fire, Bottle, high intensity, that beast's marked her, it's aiming to strike!"

The small craft twisted up and shot down to come within range of her quarry as Earbleat brought her circular gun-port array into play, its deadly beams merging into a tight burst of fatal fire. As a gout of flame burst from the projectile, she ordered one of her team to send a high energy torpedo down its throat and pulled her precious craft out of range of its mothership. The missile ship exploded in an intense gush of fire so bright on the grid that the bridge crew was dazzled, but as Earbleat reeled *Loki* back into her hold, *Arianrhod* shook to a massive torpedo impact that sent a shock wave through her hull.

The crew were thrown about in their seats as Dox fought the helm to steady the ship and get her out of the line of fire of the huge hostile, without impeding their backup. The captain ordered the missile ship's spec sent out on the ops net, and scanned the grid, hanging on tightly as Dox set *Arianrhod* into an upward spiral to confuse enemy targeting. The hostile spun up to match, letting loose a rain of pulse cannon fire.

"Face her out!" Ahxenta snarled. "Launch reflector flak at her main arrays, set forr'ad torpedoes to run! Dox, get us in range of her comms; tactical, assist targeting! We cut her links to her convoy. Damn! She's launched drones! Tallica, get them! Gunners, make your shots count!"

Arianrhod's hull shook to multiple phase cannon strikes despite the intricate path Dox was carving to outfly the enemy and the shield fields that her engineers were boosting in failing areas, but even as *Arianrhod's* firepower bit and slices of flak sheared off the hostile's keel, Azular's keen eyes spotted a weakness in the ship's flight path.

"She's guarding her aft port side! It's maybe her ops centre. Sending data to grid. Suggest targeting of highlighted area!"

"On it!" Earbleat exclaimed before the captain reacted. "Crew two, mark that guide point and hit it with high energy torpedoes! Floss, take station three and assist Commander Apnis, enemy drones are getting through! Dammit! Keith, get fine-beamed fire on upper hull section three one five, we have a breaching drone attaching!"

"No we bloody don't!" Crizz Cottontail yelled. "Ejecting hull plate section! Gem, intensify that damn field!"

"Hostile veering off!" Gliss called. "She's losing control!"

"We end it!" Ahxenta thundered. "Dox, bring us round to give our forr'ad batteries a target. Loose high energy torpedoes! And take out all those damn drones. Where are the *Firestorm* and the *Glenblaze*?"

"Holding their own, ma'am," Azular said loudly as *Arianrhod* slewed and everyone clung on. "Once the leader's influence is lost, they should have an advantage. Our reserves have slowed the other two, but they're still active, despite crippling damage."

"That's her down!" Earbleat's shrill voice cut across the bridge.

"All stations, report!" the captain ordered. "Dox, get us out of this flak field and come about to assist our reserves! What is it, comms?"

"Alert from ops, ma'am! The three blips from Canna have raced in all guns blazing and another two are coming in off the bypass from Sunrise! They're forward of the *Obsidian*! She logged them and she's on their tails but they'll get in ahead of her!"

"They'll have jumped in at Wemm! But the four in our sights are our priority," Ahxenta rasped, scanning the schematic. "Tactical, locate the two blips on our reserves. We can't let them get close to that orbital platform, it's Thal's engineering and science hub and it's a main storage area. Helm, prepare to move in on the nearest blip at speed. Hit it!"

Used to fast manoeuvring, and with a fine instinct for finding the perfect spot, Dox took *Arianrhod* steeply down upon her first mark as Earbleat charged her teams to target with phase cannon. As multiple flak hits stung and *Arianrhod's* shields strove to cope, Gliss yelled that the second blip had come about, a small Starfall carrier at her back.

"Get her in our aft sights and launch deflecting drones!" Ahxenta roared as *Arianrhod* pitched to intensifying shocks against her hull.

Dox held her steady to let their firepower bite; the shocks waned as enemy fire declined, and Azular, scanning the ships closely, called that the arsenals of both were running dry, but the two were still advancing and probably aiming to ram.

"Punch a hole through that ship!" the captain yelled. "High energy torpedoes. Aft torpedoes, get that second beast!"

As the two exploded simultaneously, the sky lit with an intense wash of light. The impetus of the shockwave sent *Arianrhod* into a spin that had Dox wrestling the helm. As she brought the ship back on line, the captain checked the status of the *Firestorm* and the *Glenblaze*. Both had destroyed their targets and were intact. The *Glenblaze* had caught the small carrier in her tractors as she reeled out of control, to prevent her crashing into the orbital facility. Others of Starfall's tactically-placed small ships raced in to sweep up the debris that littered the battlefield.

"What's happened to the other incoming?" the captain asked as she eyed the complexity of data that shifted within the holo-grid.

"The *Kel'Torc* has taken on the three from the Canna side, with the *Serenity* and *Zetkalt* as backup," Azular told her. "*Kel'Moth* is making for the two coming in from the Sunrise side, given her heading."

"Then we give her a hand: we still have firepower enough. Get me the *Glenblaze* and the *Firestorm*. Captain Thal, you're with me to aid the *Kel'Moth*; Captain Green, remain here and assist clean-up. Any more trouble and assist at your discretion."

The two ships made swiftly to where the *Kel'Moth* was moving into position to cover the parts of the base close to where attack was likely, in a direct line to the node that was the end of the Sunrise to Starfall section of bypass. Vexin Thal set his ship to take point, and ordered *Arianrhod* and *Glenblaze* to cover his flanks. The three assumed position just as the warning of an imminent strike sounded. The alien ships had jumped off the bypass at top speed and had not slackened pace.

Azular recognised the forms. "Interceptors, raider design, large and well-armed with phase cannon, torpedoes and slicer beams! We've met their like before, as has the *Kel'Moth*, when she came to our assist at the Kolly Beacon asteroid field! I can't get clear readings as their hulls are solidly-shielded, but the Kolly ones were uncrewed."

Comms called in the same, as Thal, knowing the type, sent an alert and ordered his ships in at full pelt to take them out. As the defenders formed into a tight wing, one alien swept up and over them and the other cut under at such incredible speed that *Arianrhod's* skilled gunners could not get lock-on. As a stream of phase-missiles tore towards them Earbleat let out a yell of frustration.

"They're too damn fast, Cap! Suggest scatter mines to slow them!"

"Do it!" the captain bellowed.

"Station two, load port torpedo tubes with scatter mine clusters and set for wide spread! Helm, get us on a line to launch them! Damn these blasted phase bolts!" Earbleat cursed as *Arianrhod* rocked under enemy fire. "Set to go on my mark! Mark!"

The spreading field of mines cut into the rain of fire heading their way from one oncoming alien and caught it in an explosive spray partly caused by its own artillery. A searing flare signalled its end as *Arianrhod* banked and veered out of the expanding flak field.

"Where's the other?" the captain demanded.

"*Kel'Moth* and *Glenblaze* have it on the run," Gliss responded.

"Helm, get us out of the firing line," Ahxenta rapped. "This place is awash with debris. What the hell is it now, Bellfish?"

"Ops alert, ma'am! More blips on a line from Wester! *Moonstone* and *Kel'Kith* are heading to intercept!"

"That's the far side, nearer the Canna intersect," frowned Ahxenta, her hand flicking across her board. "There are other ships closer. And we're low on arms and our hull's taken a beating."

"Captain Vexin Thal on link ma'am!" Bellfish broke in.

Thal was short and swift in his thanks and, aware of the damage to both ships, ordered them to stand down and make for the base's mid-section repair bays. The *Obsidian* was closing and other help was due. His smaller craft would clear debris and dump it on the planet around which his station was constructed, to be dealt with later.

Ahxenta acceded and stood down battlestations, but told her tired crew that the ship would hold at red alert. As *Arianrhod* changed course to her allotted berth, the captain turned to damage assessment. From the mounting list of reports, she realised that refit would be a long job.

"Hell knows where we'll source the gear," she said to Apnis, now back at her side. "The ships here will have taken a helluva battering."

"Except the *Elucida* and the *Sunburst*," Apnis scowled. "They're still in their cots watching as space burns around them. What's new on the nets? About the hostiles on track for Parkin for one, and the two than lit out from the Greenstar with two ISA boats on their tails?"

"And the likely holding areas at the Ginseng, and off the Stoorie," the captain sighed. "We've had no more from Zillah; that might mean she's got her hands full. But our concerns are here."

Arianrhod made berth and was soon in a mesh of holding struts, but the repair rigs were down, their teams busy on more seriously-damaged ships. The *Nyx Warrior* was one, and Ahxenta could see from the holo-grid that the PSS was still badly injured. *Arianrhod's* science and tactical teams had tied the ops channel into the grid: the cut and thrust of the action around the base was visible, the defending ships marked clearly.

"Getting the upper hand, do you think, Cap?" Apnis asked.

"*Kel'Torc*, *Serenity* and *Zetkalt* seem to be holding up, but I can't see the *Moonstone* and *Kel'Kith*. A bit of the Wester edge is out – jamming, maybe. *Firestorm's* still guarding the north polar sector: expecting more trouble, though *Obsidian* should be in soon. And the *Lucent* and *Schiltron* are closing; they're marked as expected."

She was interrupted by a cry from Azular, who had also figured that jamming was causing signal loss from an area off the massive Starfall Base. One of the ships in the zone must have taken out the blocking vessel or gear, as that part of the grid came alive again to show several blips entangled in a scrap. Four were marked hostile and three friendly, but no IDs were clear. One hostile cut suddenly out of the pack and through the defensive line, on a bearing towards the inner base area.

"Hell! That'll put it damn close to us! Battlestations! All shields up! Secondary bridge online! One of ours is on the blip's tail! Which one, Azular? I can't make out the shape."

"It's the *Moon*," he replied dourly. "The *Moonstone's* split and her two hulls are operating as self-reliant ships."

"Risky move if she's not fully functional," Apnis said over the alert siren. "Kerrix will have her work cut out to stop *that* beast."

"Too right. Cut us loose from our struts, helm!" the captain roared. "We can't do much, but we'll add our firepower to hers. Comms, send a request to the *Elucida* and the *Sunburst* for aid; they're hanging off our bows doing damn all."

"Captain Thal already has, ma'am, over the ops net," Bellfish told her. "I'll add ours as urgent."

"Incoming hostile has taken a deal of damage, but it's *not* slowing!" Azular called. "It still has firepower, but I read it as low."

"*Nyx Warrior's* powering her aft tubes!" Gliss cut in. "She can't do a lot from there but pitch a couple of torpedoes this way! *Glenblaze* has cut loose from her berth! She's heading in!"

"Struts retracted; we have manoeuvring power!" Dox confirmed.

"Come about to face that beast! Our forr'ad arrays can still sting. Keep our power up, Crizz, but do *not* divert from shields."

The *Moon* had caught up to the advancing hostile, which had begun to spew fire at the meshwork that made up the section of repair berths, catching two empty bays and sending spears of metal spinning off. The joint firepower of the three defenders was enough to cause the huge craft to bank and turn to protect her port. The reason was soon clear, for as shards of her hull sheared off and fire erupted amidships, a small projectile shot out of a side bay. It wove a convoluted course but it was clear that the habited sections of the inner ring was its target.

"It's a damn missile ship!" Earbleat bawled. "Get it in your sights, all stations! Target at will!"

"It's too small and fast, Chief!" Ensign Floss hissed. "I can't get lock-on. Readings are unstable and she keeps changing course!"

The cry was echoed by the other weapons officers as they strove to target the swiftly-twisting dot in their sights. As Gliss warned that the *Fire Opal* and the *Amber Flash* were on the move, another voice cut in that the *ISAS Elucida* and the *NFS Sunburst* were powering up.

"The *Moon's* come about to tail her!" Azular spat out. "She's smaller, but she'll have the same problem we do!"

The part-ship had come within a fraction of *Arianrhod* in passing, but she tilted and cut speed, to turn port-side to her fellow PSS, causing Ahxenta to demand what in hell her captain was playing at. The game was clear when the *Moon* banked again and stood off. She had released her own projectile: a fighter that shot off on the track of the missile ship at a speed that had most of those watching amazed. The captain of the *Arianrhod* had other concerns.

"What are the *Elucida* and the *Sunburst* up to?" she demanded.

"Snooping," her first mate sniffed. "*Elucida's* come in to see what we're at and what we have that she doesn't. Is she arming, Azular?"

"She's powered weapons, but as she's well-shielded, it's difficult to tell," he replied. "She *is* scanning us."

"Block scans! And keep an eye on her, and the *Sunburst*, tactical," Ahxenta growled. "Where's that fighter? I can't see her in the grid."

The Berzic had tracked the small craft and had her pinpointed. She had caught up to the missile ship barely in time to prevent it from unleashing its power against a large housing segment of the inner ring. A well-aimed and relentless stream of energy took its toll and the alien burst apart, the outwash of energy catching the fighter and forcing her outwards in a dizzying whirl towards the section of repair bays.

"Dox, get us at an angle to catch her in our main tractor if she can't regain control," Ahxenta ordered. "The *Moon's* on the wrong side and we don't want her colliding with us."

"She's pulling out of the spin," Azular reported. "Her auto controls must have taken over: the pilot would've blacked out at that speed. I can't get clear scans of her hull. Her shielding's formidable and I don't recognise the design. The *Moon's* coming around to retrieve her. The *Sunburst's* moving this way!" he added indignantly. "What's she at?"

"It's getting busy around here," Apnis noted trenchantly. "Those two Starfall cruisers are holding off; damage limitation, I guess. This whole area's littered with flak."

"Intensify our shielding, Crizz," the chief engineer was instructed. "And hold that tractor at the ready. She's braking but she's still fast."

The small craft had continued to slow but her progress was erratic, as if her engines were cutting out. Ahxenta cursed and ordered comms to open a channel to the pilot. A link was achieved almost at once.

"Fighter *Red Moon One*," Bellfish announced.

"*Arianrhod* to *Red Moon*: we have you in our sights and are prepared to deploy a tractor to bring you in," the captain stated.

"Copy that, *Arianrhod*. My engines are almost dead. I'll cut them and use my thrusters to get into a position to let you get a grip," the pilot replied in crackling tones. "At your discretion, *Arianrhod*."

"Hold us steady, Dox: she's coming around," Ahxenta directed.

"So's the *Sunburst*," Apnis remarked. "What the hell…! That damn Norvallan's deployed a long-range tractor! She's caught the fighter!"

"Get the *Sunburst* on line!" the enraged captain ordered.

A voice sparking with static broke over the speaker before Bellfish could comply. "Fighter *Red Moon One* to *NFS Sunburst*: I suggest you release me from your tractor, *Sunburst*."

"*This* is Captain Sallix," a sharp voice said. "Why should I do that?"

"One, because you have no right to hold me, and two, because my finger is on the firing button of a pulse cannon that's set to take out your main tractor array if you don't. Your move, Captain."

"You don't frighten me with your threats! You will cease targeting my vessel immediately, or I'll have your captain up on charges."

"Wrong answer, Captain," was the mordant reply.

A fine-tuned spear of energy lanced from the small fighter and burst in a scattering of stars on the *Sunburst's* hull. Seconds later, the freed craft shot off at an angle that took her up and across the forr'ad section of *Arianrhod*, her hull seared by a swiftly-fired bolt from the *Sunburst*.

"Missed!" the pilot hissed down the line. "Enjoy the rest of your stay here, Captain, which I expect will be short. And the rest of your career, which I expect will also be short."

"Crizz, get a fix on that fighter and haul her in!" Ahxenta roared. "And get that damn fool Sallix on the link! What the hell's he doing, releasing a bolt in a confined space at a friendly ship *and* in our face?"

The *Sunburst's* captain was popular, for the *Glenblaze* and the *Moon* were both demanding answers, but Sallix was refusing to respond. His targeting eyes were homing in on the fighter despite her proximity to

Arianrhod, and the captain of the PSS was incensed.

"Target *Sunburst's* scanning arrays! She so much as twitches, send a shot across her bows! Have we got that boat yet, Crizz?"

"Got her! I'm bringing her into inner alpha four, Cap. That grazing shot's split her hull and she's breaking up. Lacewing, containment field up! Safety team on standby. Pressure-up the second the airlock's tight. Cottontail to medbay: emergency team to shuttle bay inner alpha four! Emission *and* explosive hazards, so suit up. Get those tractors on line, Jentle, I can't risk grapples! Easy... almost there. Good going, Jentle. Transfer to magnetic pad and pull her into the field. She's secure! Bay pressurising... that's it. Safety team, head in now, damp down volatiles and crack open that hull! Gem, you sit tight here: I'm heading down."

"Captain, permission to accompany..." Azular began.

"You stay right there, mister!" Ahxenta rapped.

The chief engineer had no sooner raced off than Bellfish called that Commander Levettiza of the *Moon* was online. The Berzic second mate looked worried as she asked after the fate of their fighter and its pilot. Ahxenta knew why: she had recognised the distorted voice.

"We have them aboard and my people are there. They're trying to cut the pilot free, but we can't get clear readings of that fighter. Is there anything we should know about it? We're not familiar with the design."

"It's Norvallan, it has a dense, highly-shielded hull and it's bonded to the pilot; *and* it has intrusion detectors designed to prevent entry. I'll send you the spec we have, but it's partial. I guess its ops have shut off, but we lost contact after the *Sunburst* fired that shot."

"So did we," Ahxenta said grimly. "It's bonded to the pilot? That's why your captain was flying it then – nobody else could."

"Precisely. But later: I've been ordered back to aid the *Kel'Kith* and the *Stone*, so I have to go. Please keep me informed."

"Will do. Good luck. We'll take care of her," Ahxenta promised.

"Got the spec, sending it to you, doc," Bellfish told Azular. "*Elucida* has also been asked to head out to aid the *Kel'Kith*," he added.

"Not that she's moving," Apnis said derisively. "Grid's updating – what's that on track from the Wester side? Ours or theirs?" she said in a tone so sharp that several heads turned to scan the holo as it flickered and shifted. "Ours! It's the *Kel'Marr*! And the *Obsidian's* just made it in. And there's another at the Canna side! What in blazes is *that*?"

Azular was quick to scan and check it against every database he had. "It's Telziltic, Commander. She's the *Jekzilt*, Captain Heltakt's previous command. And the *Elucida's* now making headway. I have the fighter's spec, Captain," he added anxiously. "I could assist the Chief..."

"Go," she said harshly. "Get us back into our repair bay without smacking into any of that junk out there if you can, Dox."

"Roger that, ma'am. Plot me the quickest way through," she bid her mate. "It's like swimming in a trash-infested pool round here."

"Where any of the scraps might go bang," Box commented as he adroitly complied. "I'll give the *Sunburst* a wide berth. She's still sitting sulking out there but there's no saying if she'll lob a shot at us."

"She tries and Commander Earbleat will have her hide," Dox darkly replied. "Cowardly bag of bolts…"

"Why did Sallix grab the fighter?" Apnis asked the captain in a low voice. "It was the *Moonstone's* and he wanted a stick to beat Kerrix with? Or did he think it was tech he didn't have and thought he should? It sounded to me like he hadn't figured it was her."

"Hell knows, Tallica; but *where* did she get it that it hasn't a full spec, and why did she jump out to take on that travelling bomb?"

"It *had* a target," the first mate pointed out. "The two heavy cruisers Thal posted were quick to shift, so he really wants to protect what's down there. *She* must know. They got her yet?"

The captain was swiftly flicking through status notes on her board. "They're through the hull… Axellina's with the med team. Zip yet bar there's lifesigns. But Kerrix is a survivor, she'll make it."

"Or Azular will tear Sallix' head off with his bare hands and shove it out an airlock. Our injured are mending, thanks be, but our repair bay's still got no work teams. The damage to Starfall will take months to fix, clearing up's only half of it. But how are Thal's other stations?"

"We'll find out when the dust settles. As backup's got here, I guess they either haven't been hit or are holding their own. The grid's shifting again… another blip riding in at back of the *Obsidian*. It's the *Kel'Seth*!" Ahxenta exclaimed. "We've never met her but the *Warrior* did, a long while ago now, near Wemm, if I recall aright."

"Yup… *Elucida's* got to the bust-up at the Wester end, but *Kel'Marr's* raining fire, so *those* three will be space dust. You think *Elucida's* trying to figure how the *Moonstone* can split in two and come out fighting?"

"Maybe; but Jesse Inks will burn Dusker's ears, and as Levettiza's ex-Intelligence, she'll intervene if he meddles. *Kel'Moth's* back near HQ and the *Lucent* and *Schiltron* are in, so the action must be all but over. Those few small ships zipping in and out must be clean-up details."

The action *was* all but over, for the order to stand down came within ten minutes. Ahxenta called off the red alert but held her ship at yellow. As Thal called in data from his bases and news nets came alive, a clearer picture arose of events across most galactic zones. Starfall was the only base of Thal's that had been hit, but sorties from the Crimson Drapes, Ginseng, Stoorie and Greenstar nebulae had occurred. Freskat's home fleet, backed by two ISA ships and two from Twilight, had dealt with the aliens in Lambda, and the recalled explorer group under Colonel Myrtleberry had halted those from the Stoorie. The Crimson Drapes, close to Alto Finglas and other habited parts, had caused major alarm. Despite the rapid deployment of ISA and other ships, heavy losses had been taken before the attackers were routed, as their numbers had been boosted by ships from other alien hideouts.

Assaults by the ships hidden at the Greenstar and nearby were also serious, but not as bad as they might have been, thanks to Thal's early alert and the help of his ships. Two on the way from Sunrise to Starfall had caught a distress from an Arrissian trader headed home. A hostile trio had burst out of the Flint Wolf system and were making for her. The Starfall ships had come about to assist, and the ensuing firefight took them into Arrissian space. Sunrise Base was left near defenceless as its commander had sent a ship to Parkin, but the attackers there had been downed, as the *PSS Snow Quartz*, delayed on her trip home, had jumped in. Lesser assaults in other sectors had been put down to aliens, and local authorities were picking up the pieces. A note via the UV-III verified that no PSS ships had been lost.

"Thank hell," Apnis sighed. "But so many parallel strikes must have taken action and time to organise. Why wasn't it spotted?"

"Too much petty squabbling amongst the ISA and its pals trying to set up their own versions of mapped space, worm-pockets included," was the captain's view. "Too tied up to notice. But we should be clear for a bit. Crizz's lot are clearing inner four and we have patch-up going on all over. If you get the duty crews off to grab some sack time, I'll head down to medbay and see what the deal is there."

"Roger that, Cap."

Arianrhod's medbay was busy, as the ship's own injured were many, and Ahxenta stopped to have a word with those she passed on her way to find her chief medic. Flintlock, as she had expected, was directing the care of the pilot of the *Moonstone's* fighter.

"How bad is she?" the captain asked, nodding through the iso-bay portal at the recumbent form under a bank of medical monitors.

"She'll do," the CMO said shortly. "What was she doing flying that crate anyhow? And why? Azular wouldn't say."

"Long story, and I only have a fraction of it. Where's *he* gone?"

"I kicked him out as he was underfoot. He's back in the shuttle bay. The boat had cracked like an egg. *She* was in a protective inner capsule, so she was damn lucky. As her gear had an inbuilt air supply, she was spared toxic rad levels. Crizz said the hull had breached as the forces on it had been severe before the hit, and the fuel core had split."

"I know, I got her report. Sallix will have to explain *his* actions to a higher authority. And you've not answered my question. How bad is she? Jesse Inks won't take flannel and neither will Levettiza."

"Severely concussed, bruised, two stress fractures. I'll send a report to her CMO, but I'm keeping her under and I won't relocate her just yet. How's the *Moonstone*? Azular said she'd separated, to leave one half to help the *Kel'Kith*, but another of Thal's had shown. As we've been stood down, I guess the fight's all but wrapped up."

The captain reeled off all she knew of the situation. "*Obsidian's* here with arms and medical gear. I've not spoken to Grey, but he'll unload as fast as he can. Thal's dumping the drifting wreckage on the planet, but he'll want to sift it out, to see if anything non-hostile has survived."

"Like in life-tubes, you mean," the doctor put in.

"Unlikely. But he can salvage useable materials – this base *is* set up for it. But you must be due off-shift, as is half your staff, so move it."

"You can talk," was the irate reply. "I've no time, with Wren and Ipvy still on the *Warrior*. When do we leave? Our scuffles won't have improved our shape and I've seen nary a repair bot in action."

"Hell knows. That sounds like more news," Ahxenta continued as her wrist comm gave an insistent buzz.

It was Apnis. Thal had called in favours: safety gear, deck and cabin goods, rations and tech stores were on the way from Arrissia, Wemm and Canna, carried by his ships. As for the outcome of the battle, Sallix had been relieved of command by Admiral Posettix and confined to quarters. Supported by the ambassador, the admiral had reported the *Sunburst's* actions, and lengthy inaction, to his fleet, and insisted on her recall. The *Elucida* had been told to go: her late entry to the final assault had not altered the result, she had tried to record the reversion of the *Moonstone* into a single entity, and when Dusker realised his scans were being blocked, he had had the gall to demand her spec. Thal had copied his dismissal and the reason for it to ISA HQ, and deputed the *Schiltron* and the *Lucent* to escort the *Elucida* to the edge of Mu space.

"This isn't the end of it, despite the heavy losses those bastards took," the captain sighed in reply. "And we've heard zip from Psi. But as it's quieter here, our people can take time out. You too, Tallica. I'm off to see how Crizz and her teams are coping. And then we'll see."

* * *

Twelve hours later the captain was on the bridge studying a list of the urgent repairs needed to *Arianrhod's* hull fabric. Three loads of repair gear were on their way from Kimi, on the edge of mapped space. The *Warrior* and the worst-hit of Thal's ships would have the largest part, but she had been promised as much as could be spared.

"What's the payback?" her first mate enquired. "Thal doesn't hand out stuff without good reason, despite our help here."

"He knows we wanted the gem-grade jurillium he got for us for the protected crystal arrays the ISA is so keen on, *and* he knows we can get the arrays made. He wants that kind of tech for his fleet. I've agreed to divert some his way, but he knows Zillah's top of the list. And he can get us more supplies of gem-grade jurillium."

"Win-win. And yet another link to bring us back to Starfall. I know who that'll please. Where is he anyway? In medbay?"

"He'd better be in his lab: Grey's lending us a cluster of repair bots, but they'll need recoded with our call-sign. He'll be over with them and to get the story on what went down, as he doesn't believe half of what he's heard. But as *Obsidian's* in fighting trim, Grey can head out and get anything we need from local systems, so get our chiefs to send in their lists. He's for the *Nyx Warrior* after us, to see how he can help Nat."

"And the other PSS ships here?" Apnis asked archly.

"Thal can look after his own. I *had* a link from him: he's not calling a meet over what we've been through, but he said thanks for our help, and passed on news. The Arrissian authorities were grateful for his aid but he's had no word from the ISA. It's probably pissed that he sent the *Elucida* packing with a flea in Dusker's ear, courtesy of Jesse Inks. The *Sunburst's* off, with one of the *Serenity's* senior officers in command; and the admiral's going ahead with his mission in these parts."

"The ISA owes Starfall for the alert on the Greenstar and for diving in to tackle the hostiles in its territory," the first mate grated. "Not that their upper bods will see that: they'll reckon Starfall was the target and everybody else was just unlucky. And as for the display by the *Sunburst*: on the basis of Admiral Posettix' report, Sallix will face a court martial. And as the *Elucida's* last-ditch crack to salvage her rep backfired, she'll be full of red faces once the story gets out. Did Thal give away what's holed up in that inner ring that Kerrix risked her neck for?"

"*Captain* Kerrix," Ahxenta corrected, aware of her listening bridge crew. "He asked after her, so I dug. The kids *are* there. He's nowhere safer to transfer them. As for other things there, he wouldn't say. But the TA sent a memo to all ships that fly its flag: a reminder that we can be called up in extreme emergency. The conflict we've gone through wasn't classified as such, but the clause is still in our contracts."

"But we have a say in whether an emergency *is* extreme, don't we?"

"Supposedly, but I'd not rely on our views being accepted. There's the note that Grey's on his way in. I'll go meet him. Comms, have Dr Azular report to inner aft shuttle bay three."

By the time she reached the bay, the *Obsidian's* shuttle had docked. Azular was in the obs area with Cottontail; her team was ready to take in the bots. Bluejohn was alone, and waved as he stepped off the ramp.

"We'll head up to my office, Grey," Ahxenta greeted him. "I take it you trust my people to deal with your cargo?"

He laughed. "As ever. I noted *Arianrhod* looked a tad worse for wear as I came in. You had a rough ride."

"We did. And thanks to your bots, we'll be out of here quicker than we thought. Thal's got his hands full, and we've meets on Freskat that might lead to a contract. My supercargo's on the hunt for more trade."

Bluejohn stayed aboard for an hour and a half, long enough to find out what had happened, cover personal matters, and pick up a list of *Arianrhod's* needs. Ahxenta saw him off and then stepped into medbay. She had heard from Flintlock that Kerrix wanted a word.

The *Moonstone's* captain was visibly better, Ahxenta saw, but looked drawn and tired still. She was grateful for her rescue and care but the captain sensed other issues, and asked bluntly what they were.

Kerrix smiled. "My fighter: you're curious. And Azular's hinted that if I left her here, he and your engineers could try to fix her up…"

"Like hell!"

Her laugh was genuine. "I figured you'd say that. And with only a part-spec, even *he* would have trouble. He's told you her story?"

"No, he hasn't. I want to hear it from you."

"We found her and other bits of tech silting up a lower storage bay that I've only recently had time to check. She was set up to bond to a human and would only fire up with a DNA-based link that fit a subset of Norvallans; I'm one, but no-one else aboard. And I had trouble. Her defence level was a problem, but from what we *could* read, she was superior to our other fighters, in fact to any we know of. You can run sim flights in her. The missile ship: we knew it would take a small ship to get close enough to take it out. No other fighter had the power."

"So you left the bridge to your second mate in a war situation and jumped in, in a ship you'd never flown before?" Ahxenta said starkly.

"I did. You don't approve?"

"That's not the issue. Why? There's more to it than taking out an explosive device that was set to blow out a piece of superstructure."

"That thing would have caused massive damage and led to knock-on effects on other parts of Starfall. And you've spoken to Captain Thal," Kerrix said acutely. "You know."

"I know about the kids. What else is down there?"

"It's Thal's business, not mine, Captain."

Ahxenta realised that she would get no more on that and eyed her guest keenly. "What else?" she asked.

"I need to get back to my ship. I've a lot of injured, every section's taken damage and we're still under repair. I'll take my fighter, as my crew may be able to salvage something…"

"Your CMO won't sanction your removal yet and neither will mine. They reckon another thirty six hours."

"My CMO I can overrule; yours I can't."

"And you don't want to overstay your welcome," the captain said shrewdly. "You think you're a burden."

"You *can* read me like a book," Kerrix grinned dourly. "Am I?"

"You are not. I once said you'd be welcome aboard *Arianrhod* and I stand by that. I think you haven't grasped what it means to be part of the PSS fleet, you and the other misfits of Starfall. We look after our own, even if they *are* pains in the arse."

"And that's how you rate me?"

"Yes, Captain Kerrix, I do. But you'll always be welcome aboard my ship. And as *I* have a number of injured, ship's sections that need refit and *we're* still under repair, I have to go. And you're staying here. I *can* overrule my CMO, but in your case I don't intend to."

"Your ship, your rules," Kerrix smiled softly.

"Damn straight. Take it easy. I'll see you later."

The senior science officer was on the other side of the iso-bay when the captain stepped out. He looked anxious.

"And how long have you been there? You're meant to be recoding those bots and getting them out on our hull."

"A few minutes," he admitted. "The bots are recoded and Chief Cottontail's dealing with their deployment. Dr Flintlock said you were talking to Captain Kerrix, ma'am, but that you wouldn't be long."

"So do you want to talk to me or her?"

"To you first, ma'am, and then Captain Kerrix."

"The doc's office," Ahxenta sighed. "And you're not hanging onto the bits of her smacked up fighter, before you ask. That bay's only just been made safe and the pieces are crated for transfer."

"I understand, ma'am."

The first matter discussed caused the captain such irritation that the CMO heard the blast of invective from her desk in the main medbay.

The second related to Kerrix' interest in *Arianrhod's* decoy. It included Norvallan tech, and as Kerrix thought that such a tool would be of use, Azular had posited handing over its basic spec to her and Thal.

"Crizz'll have something to say on that," the captain noted.

"The chief knows what we owe to Captain Kerrix, and to Starfall in some measure," he replied stubbornly. "And if *her* science officers can upgrade it, we would stand to profit by their work – and their tech."

"You have a point. Run it by Crizz and let me know. We won't be here much longer: another few days if Captain Bluejohn gets back with supplies and Starfall's repair teams move it. What's the look for?" she asked as his face fell. "You planning another dinner, alone this time?"

"We've had very little time together, despite my trip to the *Moonstone* and Xanna's stay here, ma'am; some privacy would be appreciated."

"The iso-bay is as private as it gets, Azular. Sort the details with the doc and take time out. But that's it. Your personal life will not impinge on your main duties aboard my ship. As for what you suggested: you've not talked it over with Captain Kerrix?"

"No ma'am. I thought it best to raise it with you first."

"You know *my* answer and I suspect hers will be similar. I have to go. I *will* see you later."

The captain was out of the door before her science officer was on his feet. He looked after her and shrugged stoically. Beyond the entry, Flintlock, still at her desk, looked up.

"What was the shouting about?" she asked.

"You heard?"

"Only the shouting. What's he been up to now?"

"Hatching loopy plans. Don't give Kerrix any portable gear: she'll hit him with it. But let them have time together if she's fit. He'll talk to you about it. I'm for the bridge, but I'll see you in the mess later."

"I'll look forward to it," Flintlock wryly replied.

The bridge was busy but orderly when the captain arrived, with the stations tracking the repair bots. All was on course, Apnis told Ahxenta as she sat down heavily. No direct comms had come in. An ISA memo had listed the known clashes and their outcomes, all of which had been logged as positive for the Alliance. The reasons for the wave of attacks, and the level of damage to Starfall, had been recorded as unknown.

"Despite the ISA presence here at the time," Ahxenta said acidly.

"That's about it. Thal hasn't sent a correction, but then he wouldn't. Azular heading up?"

"No. Greffy can handle the science station for now."

The first mate looked quizzically at the captain, who shook her head imperceptibly. "He's due the time," she said.

"But what's he using it for?" the first mate murmured in reply.

"Later."

* * *

Three hours down the line, the captain, first mate and CMO met in the mess. The ship was on dark watch, repairs ongoing under the vigilant eyes of her cargo teams. Ahxenta had had a link from Thal apprising her that as the ships from Kimi had made it in, he had assigned some of his ships' crews to repair teams and had allotted a squad to the rigs at *Arianrhod's* berth. With no wish that the *Obsidian's* repair bots be under scrutiny, she had withdrawn them. And Holdspan had called in to tell her that as his injured crew were on the mend, he could dispense with the services of Dr Jak Wren and nurse-tech Velli Ipvy. Repairs to the *Nyx Warrior* were also advancing apace.

"So good news," Apnis said. "You reckon we'll be clear in three to four days, Cap?"

"I do, all being equal. Grey should be back soon with what he could get for us and the *Warrior*, though Nat will have to hold longer. Thal's boosting all his bases' outer defences, but from what he's found out, the known hostile forces have been smashed – though so have a few Allied taskforces. Zillah's okay, so we're for Freskat. Azular figures we can fix the two micro-sensor array linkage units he got from Kerrix to one of our main science arrays. He's recoded them and Crizz's techs can fit them once Starfall's people are off our hull: they have the specs and have been going over them, so they know how they attach. And they have part of the tech to produce more."

"Talking of Azular, Cap," Flintlock cut in. "What was the uproar in my office? He saw Captain Kerrix after his one-to-one with you, and came out later with a smirk on his face, so something chirked him up."

The captain looked at her CMO. "What? I can't imagine she agreed with him, so what's he got up his sleeve?"

"You can ask him; he's come in – he's picking up his rations," Apnis tilted her head and waved. "What would Kerrix not agree to?"

"That I push through the details at full tilt and perform a marriage service in medbay, before she heads back to the *Moonstone*."

"What!" the first mate whistled. "That's nuts."

"She wouldn't agree to *that*," Flintlock said. "But here he is, and still sunny, so she didn't tell him to get lost. I'll ask him."

Azular *was* smiling quietly, and clearly aware that he was being talked about. Kerrix *had* firmly vetoed his rash plan, he admitted. She did not like lavish ritual, and had told him of the Telziltic custom of hand-tie, a simple exchange of verbal consents before two adult witnesses, and its entry in a valid register such as a ship's log. Azular was in favour, and *had* wanted to proceed before she left *Arianrhod*.

"Where's the point and why the rush?" Apnis wanted to know.

"That's personal, Commander. But it *is* an accepted form of union on Telzilt, in place of or as a prelude to a traditional ceremony."

"And she's agreed that you two get tied here, before she heads back to her ship?" the first mate continued sceptically.

"She didn't agree," he conceded. "But she didn't say no."

"And you figure you've enough time to persuade her," the CMO snorted. "You'll be lucky."

"Eat up," Ahxenta advised. "And then you and I are going to chat."

Azular looked askance, but obeyed. Apnis continued to tease, but was ignored as the mess began to empty, and the meal was spun out in small talk. The captain finally pushed her crockery into the hatch.

"Finish up and scoot, Tallica, Axellina," she told them. "You stay," she ordered Azular. "I'll fetch us a couple of coffees."

The captain returned with two steaming mugs and sat. She paused for a moment before sighing deeply. "Want to tell me what in blazes is going on with you and Kerrix?"

19: FRESKAT

The captain had been on duty for half an hour next day when a private link came in for her from Levettiza. Her brows raised in surprise, she made for her office. Back in ten minutes, she told Apnis she was going to medbay, and to patch through a link due for Captain Kerrix from the *Moonstone* immediately, on a secure line. Dr Flintlock was aware.

"Azular, you're with me," she added sombrely.

He complied promptly, acutely aware of his crewmates' glances as he and the captain stepped into the transport tube.

"Levettiza got a link from an Intelligence contact in an ISA lab, at HQ probably, though she wouldn't say," Ahxenta told him. "It's about the gear and remains on Skota; they've got them where they can analyse them. The contact needs info on issues that have cropped up. Levettiza wants leave to pass on specifics, once the *Moonstone's* medics have fully checked the data she got. But she's hinted that some of it has personal significance for Captain Kerrix."

"Personal? What have they found, ma'am?"

"I don't have all the facts. Levettiza was cagey, but you know some remains are Norvallan? Others aren't, but they think they're zone Psi, maybe Telziltic. Levettiza had dealings with Telzilt and Norvalla when she was with the *Advance*, so the contact's figured she'd have bio gen. It's known that the *Zetkalt*, with the ambassador, is here, but the ISA's chary of contacting him, given the bypass fiasco. There's another issue, what I don't know, but it involves the Norvallans. Levettiza spoke to the admiral, he checked the data and advised she contact Kerrix, with the caveat that there may be upset. He's going to bring Ambassador Jotakt in, and their ships will make headway for Alto Finglas to kick up a fuss shortly. Flintlock has the basics and wants me there. And I figure you'd best be there as well. It sounded serious."

The call had come in by the time the two made medbay. The CMO was waiting it out in her office, and they joined her. They spun out half an hour in chat, until word came that the link to the *Moonstone* had been cut. Flintlock told the others to stay, and rose to check on her patient.

She was back shortly to say that Kerrix had ordered Levettiza to send a shuttle for her and the ruins of her fighter. She meant to return to her ship, and despite Flintlock's protests, she was preparing to leave.

"I can't talk sense into her; maybe you can, Cinnabar. I'll call Mettix and get his views. I've got her last readings here. Go for a walk, Azular, this is private."

The captain rose with an oath and set off to the iso-bay, her senior science officer on her heels. A look in the bay window confirmed that her guest was up and about, though still in medical scrubs.

"Make yourself scarce," she ordered Azular as she flicked the entry toggle and strode in. "Captain Kerrix: I'd like a word."

"Dr Flintlock told me to expect you," she said calmly, but Ahxenta could tell that the woman was strung as tightly as fine wire.

"Sit down before you fall down. My CMO says you're not yet fit to transfer, so what's the hurry? The *Moonstone's* not going anywhere, your crew are capable and your chief medic won't sanction a return to duty."

"It's not your concern, Captain," she said, dropping onto her cot.

"It's what was found at Skota, isn't it?" Ahxenta said bluntly. "It's rattled your people and spooked you. It's about past alien activity, and as Admiral Posettix and the Telzilt ambassador are caught up in it, it's big. Want me to call Azular in and you can tell him?"

"No!" she said sharply, glancing up.

"Why not?"

"I don't need his concern – or yours."

"You think I wouldn't understand," Ahxenta said tartly.

Kerrix paused and looked away, her face creasing. She cursed softly, shaking her head. "Wrong. You more than most *would* understand."

Ahxenta frowned as she pulled up a chair and sat, a chilling unease growing. "I'll find out sooner or later, so you may as well tell me. Your problem is you're so used to having no-one to lean on that you have trouble asking for help when you need it – and trusting people."

"Just like you, you mean."

Ahxenta smiled dourly at that. "You have a point," she conceded. "I learnt the hard way. Which doesn't answer my question: what's been found in the Skota life-tubes that's so disturbing?"

The captain could see the warring emotions flitting across her face. "It's not only life-tubes," she said at last. "Other things were dumped – derelict hostile shuttles, gear scavenged long ago. You know some Norvallan remains were found?"

"I know," Ahxenta said gently. "And some unknown. Telziltic?"

"Yes. After the ISA got the alert on trackers and micro-drones in bodies and tubes, it sent in a team to analyse and shift the stuff to Alto Finglas. As Vetta was the alert source, an Intelligence agent called her to clarify bio-signs and bits related to the stuff found. They know she's on the *Moonstone* and we're Starfall, so it's a safe bet she'd be able to."

"But that's not all, is it?" the captain asked quietly.

"No. Of the metal alloys got, a fair bit were off Norvallan ships. No call-signs, but part-insignias fit a ship called the *NFS Valla Sun*, one of three sent to answer a distress from Telzilt, when it was attacked by a huge alien force bent on take-over. All three ships were lost."

"*Valla Sun?*" Ahxenta repeated, thinking back to a conversation she once had with Azular about Thal's *and* Kerrix' links to Telzilt and their reluctance to talk of it. "Your mother was aboard one of the three lost ships. You think the hostiles captured the ship, not destroyed it?"

"My mother's ship *was* the *Valla Sun*," Kerrix said bitterly. "What I didn't find out for years was that no trace of her was ever found. The other two, but not her. Reports at the time said she'd played a key part in the fight and had been disabled. So she must've been taken, but to where and why? Some bits the ISA's found match the *Valla Sun's* hull: the right vintage, her class of ship… what am I meant to think? Mettix has analysed a part-profile of Telziltic DNA Vetta got; it matches mine. It's not conclusive, but the admiral will try to get more at Alto Finglas."

"Hell," Ahxenta hissed, eyeing her. "I can say nothing that'll make it better, but I'm *so* sorry. I'll let my bridge know to expect your shuttle; your fighter's ready to go. I'm sending Azular in. Sit tight, I'll be back."

The captain rose, pressed Kerrix' shoulder in sympathy, and turned to go. She found her science officer perched at the nearby task station in the passage and inclined her head.

"Go in and sit with her but don't ask questions. Don't," she warned him. "Just be there for her. I'll be back shortly, I've things to see to."

Her next stop was the CMO's office. Flintlock had talked to Mettix, who, to her surprise, backed Kerrix' transfer, though he refused to say why. Ahxenta only nodded and started on her links. That done, her next demand of her chief medic caused the latter to spit fire.

Moments later the two looked through the iso-bay window. Azular sat, his arm about Kerrix. Her head was on his shoulder, her face steely. The captain buzzed and walked in without waiting an invitation. She sat down, and looking at her intently, held out a glass.

"Drink," she said.

The ghost of a smile flitted across the woman's face as she returned the look. "So I see," she said, reaching out to take the glass. "Jetfuel?"

Smiling faintly, Ahxenta gave Azular a glass and turned to take one from Flintlock. "Medicinal spirit," she said. "It'll do you good."

"It will. Thank you, Captain."

"Any time."

"I *have* told him," Kerrix said, glancing up at Azular. "But it goes no further for now, except to those you think should know."

"Understood. Your shuttle will be here shortly. Dr Mettix is aboard to oversee things. Drink up and I'll leave you with the doctor. I'll escort you to the bay when you're ready, Captain."

"Thank you, ma'am."

* * *

The captain returned to the bridge without Azular after the *Moonstone's* shuttle left. She claimed her command chair, reading the quizzical look her first mate gave her. She shook her head and Apnis got the message.

"Everything's on target, Cap. Repair crews have been busy all night and *Arianrhod's* beginning to look like herself. Wren and Ipvy are home. Grey called: he's on target and will get in late tomorrow. Our gear will be in pods, so a straight transfer. I told him you'd link later."

"Roger that. I'll wait for word that the shuttle's made the *Moonstone*. I see the *Serenity* and *Zetkalt* are for off, with the *Jekzilt* as escort."

Word came swiftly, and Ahxenta crossed to her office to make and take links. It took two hours. Apnis was curious as to the inward calls, but deferred enquiry until she and the captain could take a break.

"Crew's curious to know what's up," she said as Ahxenta set privacy at the table. "Where's Azular? He was due on the bridge."

"He's in his lab sorting the micro-sensor units to attach to our hull arrays so that Crizz's guys can do a quick job. With luck, they'll help us spot and block anything thrown at us by way of limpet drones. And he's drafting a simple spec of *Arianrhod's* decoy for Kerrix and Thal."

"You didn't want him on the bridge," Apnis said astutely. "What's the deal with Kerrix? I take it things didn't go as planned?"

"Captain Kerrix," the captain corrected. "And no…"

The first mate listened in concern and shock. "Hell, that's tough," she breathed. "How many more are affected the way that you and… sorry, Cinnabar, I didn't mean to bring it up again…"

"I know. But his other plans were scuppered, so he's pretty upset."

"She wouldn't have agreed anyhow. But why's he in such a hurry to put a ring on his finger? He's managed without all these years."

"Because he didn't think he would; no-one stayed, once they knew he was a telepath. He knows Kerrix is for keeps, no ulterior motive. And what I hadn't realised: he's lonely. Oh, he has friends, but no kin as such. This goes no further, Tallica… his own cut him off after he joined the *Molly Star*. They'd never been close, and after his disciplinary there was a rift. Leaving the fleet for a trader was the last straw. As for her: being a hybrid, she knew she was seen as a ticket to rank and credit among her peers, but little else. Another solo soul."

"So *Arianrhod* brought them together, like Greffy and Merry. We're a dating agency for lonely scientists, then, and tied to the *Moonstone* and Starfall. But what was the call from Admiral Posettix? Bellfish had the sense to link it in without saying, so the bridge crew don't know."

"It showed on your board," the captain said. "We had a word about Azular and that's all *you* need to know. Thal's called a meet for senior PSS officers about what we've gone through, and what's next. There'll be his own, us, the *Warrior* and the *Obsidian*, and it'll be two hours after *Obsidian* docks, so late tomorrow. Zillah knows we're for Freskat, we'll be there several days, and that she'll get the jurillium-protected crystal arrays in short order – the long-distance locked link was to my contact there. He's got details of the Xerophyte crystals and the spec of what's needed: he's set up the gear for array-setting. Azular will liaise with him to ensure the product's quality and it *will* have secure tags."

"You told Azular your contact's your nephew?" Apnis asked.

"No; he probably suspects a link, being Azular, but he and Jon have never met. The TA link was a contract note to its tied ships: given the impact of the recent conflict, the clause that says we can be called up is to be altered to define what is or isn't an extreme emergency. Which means we're in it when the TA says we are," Ahxenta ended.

"Oh joy. Anything else, Cap?"

"Admiral Best wanted to bark. He wants the charges against Horn dropped, as they'll lead to a court martial. He meant that Horn's info-sent status would come up. I refused. He couldn't push, as he knew I was logging the link. He griped about Dexel Thal, so the failed wormhole fiasco is still hot. And he knows the ambassadors are heading his way to kick ass, so he's nervous. I'd to remind him that as we're just out of a major conflict, *his* matters were trivial – he didn't like that, but it gave him the chance to ask how we and Starfall had done."

"Bet you told him to ask his own; *Elucida* was told to push off and I expect fleet HQ's had a word with Dusker by now," Apnis grinned.

"Spot on. I spoke to a couple of ours over the UV-III, and it seems that the action is about done for now. Nobody's sanguine that it'll stay that way for long, but we'd better get back on duty – we've a lot still to do, including prepping Grey's repair bots for return."

* * *

It was late when the captain and first mate landed in Thal's main HQ. Two guards were at the bay to escort them to the assigned room, where they found Thal, Seer, and the captains and first mates of the *Kel'Torc* and the *Kel'Marr.* Those from the *Kel'Seth,* the *Kel'Kith* and the *Moonstone* were due. Small talk was made to news that the *Nyx Warrior's* shuttle had docked, with one from the *Obsidian Sky* close behind.

"The *Warrior's* repairs are advancing rapidly but she still needs a lot of work," Thal stated. "I trust the *Arianrhod's* are on track?"

"They are, thanks," Ahxenta replied. "Your teams are efficient. I'm shipping out for Freskat in two days but I'll keep in touch about your comms arrays. We've trade concerns, but I can work round them."

"Good," he said, and turned to greet the two from the *Nyx Warrior.*

Ahxenta and Apnis traded looks. A scarred Holdspan was moving stiffly and Treskitt was limping. They had no time to chat, as Bluejohn, Stone, Kerrix and Inks all trooped in. The *Moonstone's* captain was edgy, Ahxenta thought, despite her smile. She had no time to ask, as noises at the door heralded the last four, and everyone was invited to sit.

Thal wasted few words. The last spate of attacks bore out that the hostiles were inclined for war and capable of it, which meant they had bases, ships and spies. In view of their targets, they were out to destroy what they held to be the main threats to them, but an urge was driving them to remove those they deeply resented: Thal and his people. The catalyst for the alien resurgence after their last defeat was possibly the rising unification of charted space. Discrete alliances that had joined forces to defeat them were now welded by treaty into the ISA; *that* had brought other bodies into a union that could halt them for good. As to why the *Nyx Warrior* was a popular target, he would not speculate.

"You pointed out when last I was here that the aliens are avid for total control," Ahxenta told him. "To stay on top, they need the means: cutting-edge tech, the biggest ships, the advantage over anyone that is or has more. That's why Captain Kerrix was tracked and attacked when she first made the Web. Bearing grudges is inbuilt in the hostile psyche, which is why *we've* had such a heap of flak. We've spoked their wheels too many times, and as they've not been able to stop us thus far, we've proved they're not invincible. As have the *Obsidian,* the *Warrior* and the *Moonstone.* We can put up a fight and win. So we become targets."

"The attacks on the *Nyx Warrior* seem to have a particular element – she's been very pointedly targeted," Thal argued.

"So was *Arianrhod,* and my crew," Ahxenta said bleakly. "*And* you. The attack on Starfall was aimed at you: your other bases weren't hit. Didn't you once say that after the war, a lot of hostiles, their allies and hangers-on took off to other bolt-holes, *and* they still had bases capable of building ships? Worlds they'd subverted or overrun over the years. You told us you were wearing them down. Where are these places?"

"I don't have a map to every hostile hiding place," Thal snapped in return. "And I don't have the resources or time to go hunting. I protect my own and I will assist as necessary for the common good."

"Or when the TA orders you to," Apnis added in an undertone.

"I *would* like your views on the latest troubles," he continued. "And any conjectures as to the aliens' next moves, how we can forestall them and keep our own safe. I can't imagine the ISA and its allies will act to up patrols and sniff out hostile threats."

Ahxenta listened intently. The Starfall officers agreed that *their* ships were more likely to be hit than other Privates, as many were crewed by freed hostile victims that had fought off alien control; and Starfall had taken over several hostile bases. None expected that they had seen the last of the conflict. New hostile types now to the fore were less liable to throw in their all, were clever and vindictive, would bide their time, *and* had to have hidden bases that had not yet been called on.

"If the ISA could be stirred to use the gear it has for creating worm-pockets to destroy holding areas at the Drapes and wherever else it's assumed the blips have ships, it would be useful," Kerrix remarked. "If it has the credit for that, it can up the ante. But it *would* be handy to be able to positively identify holding places and other hidey-holes from a distance. Pre-emptive strikes."

"That's not helpful, and not our remit," Thal reproved. "But I'd like a heads-up on their hideouts and what they're up to. My data's limited."

"Do you have other listening posts they may have got to?" Ahxenta asked suddenly. "Your ones in Zeta were spiked."

"We're checking, but it takes time. But that's not a PSS concern, it's strictly Starfall. The Norvallans and their allies must have recent data on potential hostile hideouts," he added.

"They probably do but they haven't told me," Kerrix replied. "I've limited data, but I'll dig. Ter Kinnitix would be a good bet, and Captain Heltakt. Though you'd be quicker asking a hostile. Didn't the ISP get its paws on a crewed ship a while back and took it for scrutiny, Captain Ahxenta? I recall Vetta told me that you were part of the action."

"At Triple Pinks, yes. And more than one. It got the control ship of a group on a line to Zeta Dixt that had a Hoxiz-clone in charge. Ms Levettiza told me *that*, so you must know. She was with the ISP then, and I heard no more. But *you* got the original Hoxiz, Captain Thal. Care to tell us what you got out of him? And that agent Flatt that you got?"

Thal was narked but told her that Hoxiz had thwarted a grilling by selectively wiping his own memory, a cyber trick. Flatt had been easier to crack but knew little, as he had also part-wiped his own memory.

"So the ISA's probably got zip," Turret of the *Kel'Torc* snorted.

"It'll have something, Kiv," the captain of the *Kel'Marr* cut in. "But as it must still have moles, the gen won't have been circulated."

"I bet," Ahxenta said sharply. "But I have a list of sites, sent me by Ms Levettiza when she was aboard the *Advance*," she said to Kerrix. "It included Zeta Dixt, Peden Post, Axle Lexo and others. Some had once been Alliance listening posts. I take it Captain Thal has those?"

"He does," she said curtly. "The new nav-data I gave you with the data display tech for your upgraded holo-grid has them marked query dangerous. It includes known sites in Psi and beyond the charted zones that may still be active," she continued more civilly. "But the nav-data is not to be passed on – that was agreed when it was handed over."

"What new nav-data?" Nat Holdspan interrupted. "If it has *that* sort of info, it's useful to the fleet and we need it."

"Azular agreed to the proviso, and I stand by it," Ahxenta replied. "Sorry, Nat: you'll have to take it up with Captain Thal."

Bluejohn had a few words to add, as had captains Weaver, Mint and Riven, but Thal cut them short ruthlessly. "Accurate information is the surest way to stay on top of the issues that affect us as far as the hostiles are concerned, but exchange of it poses its own problems."

"As does misinformation," Kerrix added mildly.

"Infiltration's a major problem; and I don't discount that the UV-III can be cracked," Thal continued starkly.

"Damn!" Ahxenta hissed. "You're not alone. When *our* every move was being tracked, Azular reckoned the same, as new tech kept turning up in our zones. And now Psi is in the mix. All we can do is keep our comms secure and minimise long-distance data transfer. We'll have to pass data on as and when possible – which means personally."

"I agree; and to that end, Captain Holdspan, Captain Bluejohn, I *will* give you that nav-data: it includes bypass routes outside recognised charted space, and routes across Psi that my fleet uses. But you will *not* reference the data or pass it on to anyone whatsoever. Is that clear?"

It was, and more than the two captains expected, but they gave their thanks and agreed. Ahxenta studied Thal and Seer closely, and inferred that the matter had been discussed earlier and the action decided. The leader of Starfall clearly realised he would need more PSS allies, and the three non-Starfall captains there were the best to be had.

The meeting was wound up with exchanges on the plans of the nine ships. The *Kel'Moth* would stay at Starfall; the others were set to leave. The *Obsidian* was for Arrissia but would be days behind *Arianrhod*; once his ship was fit, Nat Holdspan intended to head home to Nyx.

On the way back to their respective shuttles, Ahxenta caught up to Kerrix for a quiet word. The gist she shared with her first mate on their trip back to *Arianrhod*. The *Moonstone* had residual repair work, and then trade at Letik, a colony world of Telzilt, and if it went to plan, it meant a rapid turnaround. Kerrix expected that her next trip would lead her back into the inner zones, probably to zone Lambda.

"Lambda? Catching up with Azular? But she still looks rough. She was mighty snippy over possible hostile holes still out there."

"It wasn't personal," Ahxenta said wryly as she brought the shuttle in. "She's hurting. As is Nat Holdspan. That beard's hiding more than skin. But our trip to Freskat is to collect the crystal arrays I've promised Thal, *if* the timing can be agreed. We'll have to hold fire until the work's done, but as our people need a break and most of them like Freskat, they can catch time out there."

"I take it that includes us?" Apnis asked.

"I damn well hope so. We'll see. But I'd best get to the bridge, late as it is: I bet I'll have Grey and Nat on the link over the nav-data."

"And I bet you'll have Azular at your door over Kerrix."

"Stow it, Commander. And get to your sack."

"No way, Cap: I want to see what the crew's been up to."

The ship was quiet, but as expected, the captains of the *Nyx Warrior* and *Obsidian Sky* called over the talks and the data. She cut them off civilly and she and Apnis set out for their customary night-cap.

"Told you so," the first mate chuckled quietly as soon as they made the mess. "Wonder how long he's been sat there?"

"I'll have to change my habits: he knows them too well," the captain rejoined as she waved over at her senior science officer.

* * *

The next two days brought *Arianrhod* back to fighting trim, one science array fitted with the micro-sensor units that Ahxenta hoped would foil limpet drone threats. Her repairs were as full as Starfall could achieve, her stores likewise. Thal had not charged for repair or resupply, as he regarded the aid given in the fight for Starfall as payment enough.

"I've never been so keen to see a place in our aft scanners," the first mate sighed as the order was given to break from Starfall space and on to the bypass. "This has been one hell of a spree."

"The road from here to Twilight is clear as far as I know. Steady as she goes, Dox," the captain directed. "It'll be a long haul. We can use the time to get clued-up on what's been going on out there, and with our usual clients. Lindell's had very little sniff of trade thus far."

"It'll pick up; it always does. Grey will be at our back in a few days and the *Warrior* will be on the move before long. As will the *Moonstone*," Apnis added, with a quirky look at Azular.

"*We'll* definitely need shore leave after this," Box said to his partner. "*We* haven't had much personal time with all this on the go."

"Tell the whole frigging bridge, why don't you?" Dox retorted.

"And Doc Azular didn't get much time with Captain Kerrix either, though this *is* her home port and she was aboard awhile," he persisted.

"Button it and mind your ops. You'd best get your head round the new nav-routes; there may not be trouble on this bypass now, but there are plenty places where it can jump on."

"Yes, ma'am. What say I take you to the Halcyon for our leave?"

"What say you plot our onward route from Twilight Exit to Aoria, Mr Box," the captain said mildly. "And keep your private life – and everyone else's – off the bridge."

"Aye, ma'am," the navigator gulped contritely.

"Halcyon, aye," Dox murmured, setting her controls.

Apnis caught the captain's eye and grinned. It seemed that very little dampened the spirits of *Arianrhod's* crew.

The even tenor of the next days lasted and little Starfall news bar that the *Moonstone* had left for Letik came in. Elsewhere it was different: most authorities had claimed victory in the assaults in their sectors, but there had been extensive damage to ships and stations. Parkin had got off lightly, but the Coalition's main shipyard by Settle was badly hit. The Veximer, Vrackin, Vellis and Delta Iridium fleets had seen heavy action, with lesser clashes at Marridan, Vreskota and Berzic, but most settled planets were intact. The patch-up would take months, and as the ISA had had to deflect so much flak for its lack of immediate relief, it was said to be recalling its ships on explorer and other missions for patrol duties. The *Peerless* had been seen off Fivepoint by one of Thal's ships, implying that the *Repulse* and *Advance* were close by.

The data on likely alien dens spoken of by Kerrix as part of the new nav-data was clear in the holo, and the captain was sanguine that their path was free of threats. The ship ran at alert even so, and she ordered regular comms scans: Freskat had seen action and the Ginseng was a hot spot. *Arianrhod* made Twilight in fifteen days, to be met by base commander Ver, captain of the *Kel'Beth*. Twilight had not been hit, and its ships sent to aid Freskat had returned safe. *Arianrhod's* ensuing cut-off via the ISP sector to Aoria was efficient, and with no stop for extras thanks to Starfall, she made swift work of the two-day ride to Freskat.

"Sunshine!" Box beamed to his sidekick as she brought the great ship to station-keeping in a tight berth over the main settlement.

"Work for us, Tallica, and then a meet with Zillah," Ahxenta sighed. "But get the leave rotas started: every last one of us needs furlough."

"Roger that, Cap."

"It's past noon below, so I'll call my contact and see how he's fixed to store the stuff: the crystal load's small but the gem-grade jurillium case isn't. I won't head in until a few of ours are down: you never know who's keeping tally. There's an ISA boat in orbit, so our eyes had best stay on her. The *ISAHS Red Mercy*, a hospital ship," the captain noted. "Wonder what she's doing in this backyard?"

"Zillah will probably know," Apnis reckoned. "When's the meet?"

"Early tomorrow, for a roundup of news and a talk about array-sets for her fleet. She's heard that Alto Finglas still needs suppliers, which means that once her fleet gets a stock, the ISA will want to know the source, which means us," Ahxenta said as she rose.

"Hah! Maybe it'll improve Admiral Best's manners, if he thinks he has to be nice to us."

"Doubt it. You have the conn."

The captain would head down with the cargo early evening, she told Apnis on return. Azular was needed, as his contact with the young man had exposed tech issues; and as Jon had recruited a trainee fresh from college, Ahxenta wanted Azular's views on him. The *Obsidian* had left Arrissia for Vellis Prime, the *Warrior* for home, and the *Serenity*, *Zetkalt* and *Jekzilt* were crossing Delta to Alto Finglas. The *Moonstone* had made Letik but was soon to leave. The UV-III had little, but PSS trade was up because of the damage taken by so many.

"Lindell's aware," Ahxenta said. "We can get arms on Aoria, though their repair yards prefer to fit their home produce on site."

"Bet Nat Holdspan's worked that out, and if he's for Nyx, he'll be handy for pick-up. Unless we fit in a quick about-turn from here?"

"We don't; I'm not leaving our people here and taking the ship out. If I hear of anything trade-wise, I'll pass it to Nat. He'll need the credit, as I expect Thal had to charge him for the *Warrior's* repairs."

"I guess... Doesn't Form-tech on Limekiln deal in habitation units? They'll be in demand for damage-patch for sure, and we know them."

"Good call; he may be onto it, but let him know. I've to see Azular."

* * *

Ahxenta, Apnis and Azular met Zillah at her HQ for a rapid review of news. The three had heard most of it bar details of the Ginseng clash, but a supply of first-rate comms array units for her fleet concerned the admiral more. The captain had found in talking to her nephew that the first batch could be ready in ten days: the new recruit was skilled and

Azular was sure he was reliable. That timescale suited Zillah, and once accord was reached, Ahxenta alluded to Alto Finglas. The ISA had sent out feelers, the admiral said, but until her fleet's needs were met, she was loath to pass on information. The captain was clear: the ISA could be told that she could source the goods, but that was all. Array set-up and the supplies for such was no-one's business but hers.

Ahxenta then brought up the *ISAHS Red Mercy*. She had come in four days ago, a shuttle had visited the local ISA office and returned to the ship hours later, but no other sorties had been made as far as Zillah knew. A call had elicited only that the *Red Mercy* was on an ISA mission, but she had been the third ISA ship in Freskat space in a short time: the *Strongbow* and the *Trueheart* had left the week before, after stops of less than a day to resupply and check in with the local office. They had come from the Star Desert and had set out again on the same track.

"What is it, Azular?" the captain enquired, aware by his face after a scan of his info-pad that his quick brain had sparked.

"I wonder if the ISA's found something in the Star Desert, ma'am. You'll recall hostile action near here months ago? Freskat was under attack by ships apparently from an unknown base near Peden Post *and* from a hide-out in the Star Desert, but we heard no more about it. We were for Silverglass Station, and were hit soon after by two aliens from a base in Ochre Valley. *Trueheart's* a battlecruiser, the *Strongbow* a science ship. Have they found something that needs a hospital ship? In light of recent hostility, there must have been ISA and other ships crossing the ISP-majority sectors of Lambda, and there has to be several still-active alien bases we don't know of."

"Assumption; the *Red Mercy* may not be linked to them," Ahxenta said slowly. "But you have a point. It won't affect us, but it's something that you need to be aware of, Admiral. If there *is* a problem in the Star Desert, it could affect your people."

"A hospital ship's not usual here," Zillah mused. "I'll enquire, but I can't promise to keep you informed. Freskat *is* an ISP-allied world."

"Understood. If there's nothing more for now, I'll take my leave."

There was little, and the trio made for their ride, where the captain called the ship; the *Red Mercy* had not changed orbit nor tried to scan or contact *Arianrhod*. As soon as the shuttle was home, they set off for the bridge, where Ahxenta planned to make a few private calls.

"What's to do, Cap?" the first mate asked on the captain's return from her office after a lengthy absence.

"A lot," was the grim reply. "For one, more stolen pieces of the *Moonstone's* hull have turned up."

"What! Where?"

"Starfall, on one of the blips downed on the planet below. Thal sent in probes and then hunter craft on sorties; the bits were crammed with other goods in a wrecked hold. They don't know if it accounts for most of the missing plate, but it's a reasonable haul."

"You spoke to Thal?" Apnis queried.

"No, to Captain Kerrix. She's had words with that systems engineer chum of hers about zone Psi's alien hides. He *was* deliberately running a holo-sim of a Selky to Kilda bypass when she was talking to Sallix, so that's a go, but as the *Sunburst's* back at Norvalla, he's off-ship. He's only aware of the logged hostile bases and the usual rumours of others, but he's now a link and we'll get anything he finds out."

"What else have Thal's scavengers pulled up?"

"Piecemeal hulls that are amalgams of others; mostly vintage, and Thal's people don't have the data or expertise to pin them to known ships or types. Minimal crew remains, she said; but that's it."

"That's enough," Apnis said in distaste.

"Thal's got more to do than turning over wreckage, so it'll be a slow job," Ahxenta continued. "I told her about the *Red Mercy* and asked her to tell Thal. Levettiza and Admiral Posettix will ask awkward questions. I don't know what she was at on Letik; she'd only say trade. Not much on PSS nets but the *Warrior's* on her way home to bury her dead: they were both from Nyx, Nat told me, when I called him."

"Who was the ISA-tagged link?" the first mate enquired. "Best?"

"No; it didn't come from Alto Finglas. It was from a ship."

"The *Peerless*. Myrtleberry?"

"The same. I don't know where she is; back in settled parts, I guess, and she's party to all that's been going on at her HQ, including Best's gripes. She called over her ex-pilot Horn, to request a tad more politely that I drop the assault charges against him. He'll stay an info-sent, but he'll be sent for therapy and then be office-based."

"You believed her?" the first mate asked.

"No, and I refused again."

Apnis shook her head. "She can string it out."

"I know; we clashed over it, but she agreed to clarify points if I gave way a bit. Not on the Selky-Kilda bypass, but she's admitted to a *mishap* at Fourpoint in tests by ISA brains to kick-start a worm-pocket. That led to Dexel Thal. She's realised she'll get zip out of me, but the ISA knows we brought him to Starfall and some bright spark's linked him to the news of a hostile base on Sella. The *Red Mercy* lit a fuse when I rode her on two of ISA's best scouting the Star Desert. She and hers are sure there are still several well-hid alien bases that are keeping low, or ex-bases that hide surprises, hence sorties by escorted science ships. But she was peeved, so I guess the *Mercy's* part of it in this locale."

"Alien hunters," Box remarked to his partner. "Maybe they've dug out that criminal senior surgeon that used to be in the Web's medbay from the prison they put her in, to lend a hand. Wasn't she into aliens?"

"Don't be a fool! And finish your updates before we hand over to the next watch, or you'll sit there until you do," threatened Dox. "We won't go near the Star Desert, but you'd better get all you can on it. Trouble from there hit this neck of the galaxy a while ago, remember?"

"I suppose. But there's nothing in it except a chunk of the Ginseng and a lot of dull planets orbiting boring stars," he grumbled.

"That's not what your charts are saying," Dox pointed out. "Bell 2 for a start: it's marked off-limits."

"That wasn't there before!"

"What wasn't there before, Mr Box?" Ahxenta, an amused listener to the exchange, demanded sharply.

"Yellow star Bell 2, ma'am: it's in ISP space in Lambda, close to the Delta border. Sending to grid: a keep-clear warning, but no reason. It's been there less than twelve hours, if my comparisons are accurate."

"No known habitable planets," Azular chimed in. "But that didn't bother the hostiles before. If the *Trueheart* and the *Strongbow* left Freskat over a week ago, they could have made it there by this time – assuming they know a route through."

"Big assumption," Apnis stated. "But what sparked their interest?"

"We'll not find out," the captain replied. "I'll pass it to the fleet and Zillah, as she may not be aware. We'll be here for another eight to nine days after Zillah's order's ready to go: my contact says he can produce another batch with the supplies he has in six more days; those are for Thal. The *Moonstone* should be in by then, but I don't know her plans. The arrays may not be taken home straight off, as Captain Kerrix told me there's an issue pending that may change her schedule. But *we* have a draft contract with Form-tech to ship habitation units from Limekiln to Berzic that suits us time-wise. That was a good call, Tallica: Lindell's contact says Form-tech's flooded with orders for ground *and* orbital units from as far as Epsilon, and is working flat-out to fulfil them."

"It should be safer to Limekiln if we take the Starfall bypass: it cuts into the main trade route linking Lambda and Gamma zones. And then Berzic via Quartic Cross," the first mate mused. "That'll take us near Furze. And then the Web, if nothing else comes up. Did anything else come in, Cap? You were gone a while."

"Not much," was the evasive answer. "I sent an alert to the fleet on the Star Desert, but I've had naught back bar notes of receipt. Grey's left Arrissia for Stella Marina and will cut by here, but won't stop. He's impressed by the new nav-data from Thal and curious about the data display tech we had from Kerrix, but he won't get that."

"What did you give way on when you spoke to Myrtleberry?" Apnis queried in a low voice.

"I've agreed that the assault charges against Horn will go to an ISA fleet medical hearing, but I'm not dropping the case. It'll no doubt be filed with my other protests and hang fire in some comms list."

"And when do you head for your leave?" the first mate persisted.

"When I've dealt with all the business silting up my comm."

* * *

The captain's leave was long in coming, as ship's affairs took up much time. The *PSS Emerald* had called in with energy cells from the NTA-run Tress, by which time Lindell had won a contract to carry mining gear to Limekiln's main satellite, Orea. And the *ISAHS Red Mercy* had just left Freskat when Ahxenta had the ISA supply unit chief in her ear, requesting a sample shielded comms array wafer, with a view to placing and order if it came up to scratch. The Freskat ISA office had got wind of Zillah's supplies and had passed the news to its HQ.

"He wasn't polite," the captain grumbled to her first mate after the chat. "And if he thinks I'll stop off at Alto Finglas to hand over a free gift, he can think again; he'll damn well pay. But *Emerald's* for Minti, so she'll be close enough to pass it on. I'll get one ready; Azular can set in trip codes and adjust the jurillium signature to confuse source analyses. It won't be long 'til the ISA's bods start making their own, but we may as well get first dibs. *Moonstone's* on her way in; she's speedy, that ship. Kerrix wants a word directly she docks, business *and* private, but she won't give details over an open link. The rumour that the UV-III's not as secure as it was has filtered down, and a lot of PSS captains are antsy. Thal's units are almost done, so I've got Lindell on to hunting quality crystals and gem-grade jurillium. The Kirtish supply's small and it's out of the way, and we need to go through Thal to get it."

"But before the *Moonstone* gets here, you're for furlough. I'll be with you as far as the main settlement to make sure you take the time out. Azular's put a request in, but left it fluid, and so's Greffy."

"That damn ship's got a lot to answer for. But things are going well and we both need a change. Still, my first stop will be to get an array — Azular can come with me, as he wants to test new gear he's tied into his shuttle. He can bring it back up and get on with the work."

The plan ran as agreed and both senior officers were able to factor in personal time before the news came in that the *Moonstone* had made Freskat space and was on her way. It was no surprise to Ahxenta that Azular offered to pilot the shuttle for a trip to the Starfall ship, whence she had been invited by its captain, but she did query Kerrix about the plan. Captain Kerrix had expected it, but told Ahxenta that their initial talk would be private.

"You'll be with me for the main event," Ahxenta advised her first mate. "Inks will be there, but who else I don't know. The trade talks are about Letik, but that's all she'd say. The *Moonstone's* trip to Psi was clear both ways, so the last run-in's stalled hostile activity. Not ISA and Norvallan activity, though – the Selky-Kilda bypass build has started."

"Huh! That was quick!" Apnis snorted. "There must be a lot to gain. Ambassadors Posettix and Jotakt will have shouting to do when they see the ISA Council. They'll be in deep at Alto Finglas."

"Politics is not our remit, but we'll no doubt be updated if it affects us. But make ready to shift: we're leaving in two hours with the crystal arrays for Thal. Azular's packing them aboard his shuttle now."

Two hours later, Azular made the run to the *Moonstone*, which had been assigned a berth near *Arianrhod's*. Kerrix was there to meet them, take custody of the goods for Starfall and lead them to a briefing room where Inks and Levettiza were waiting, along with a new crew member. The trek to their endpoint took time, and Ahxenta and Azular spotted changes since their last visit. Apnis had not been aboard the *Moonstone* before, and was struck by some of her fixings.

The briefing room was comfortable and Kerrix presented her new officer to her visitors before offering refreshments. "Commander Ter Kinnitix, systems engineer and bypass creation expert, including short-range bypass systems for ship use. You know the *Moonstone can* create such. Ter was influential in the prototype developed for the *Moonstone* when she was designed for the Protector of Valla Key, but he was cut out of the loop well before the build was complete."

"May I ask why?" Azular queried as he saluted the man.

"My social credentials were inferior when the *Valla-Brilliant*, as she was then, was first authorised," was his ironic answer.

"If you'll collect your drink, Captain, I'd like a talk before we begin on business. In here," Kerrix said to Ahxenta, indicating a side-door.

The captain of the *Arianrhod* could sense disquiet, and followed her with no more than a nod and a raised brow.

The two returned in fifteen minutes, Ahxenta carrying a flat box that she stowed by her chair. The others were listening to Kinnitix, who had a holo set up that Azular was eyeing intensely. The attached symbols meant nothing to Ahxenta, but Apnis muttered that it was part of the system the *Moonstone* used to create her own bypass.

"Stop for now, Ter," Kerrix directed. "Captain Ahxenta has the gist of our trade plan and we'll discuss it. The samples can be analysed here, or taken away as she sees fit," she added, with a quiet smile at Azular.

The talk dealt firstly with the *Moonstone's* next moves. The arrays for Thal were to be taken on by the *Kel'Torc*, as she was for Limekiln to pick up habitation units for Starfall. On the back of that, the *Moonstone* had been contracted to ship more units, now being built, to Vreskota Two, after which she would make for the Web, if another deal under discussion at Starfall could be agreed.

Kerrix, with a quick look at Ahxenta, then moved on to the venture on the table. Her mission to Telzilt's Letik colony had been to pick up gem-grade jurillium and quality crystals that had been assessed and bought by an agent of Thal's at very good rates. The *Moonstone* had left them at Starfall on her way in, but samples had been extracted to check if they were usable by Ahxenta's contact as supplies for his trade. The logic was simple: Thal was keen to be involved in array-production, to thwart the ISA's scheme of becoming the main supplier in the mapped zones. The ISA was planning mass-production on site at Kilda, as the planet's ore seams were proving rich in meta-jurillium, it was in NTA space near to the ISP area that housed the ISA's Kellybar One station, and it was on the Kappa border with ISP-UI linked zone Mu. Once the Selky-Kilda bypass was complete, the goods could be transported anywhere, including Psi, with the ISA calling the shots.

Kerrix would not give her sources, but told them that the Norvallan circles involved were backing off because of awkward questions about keeping zone Psi Ambassadors and other parties in the dark over the Selky-Kilda bypass. Queries raised of similar tactics in respect of other joint issues had resulted in acute governmental embarrassment.

Ahxenta's doubts related to the part her contact's small business would be expected to play, but Kerrix was adamant that he could name his terms as far as the immediate future was concerned. Letik was close to Telzilt and Amity Beacon in Psi, and there was consultation ongoing at colony level of setting up production there, where ore *and* crystals were available. Her main task at Freskat was to ascertain if the quality of the raw materials were such that the end product would be viable as a trading commodity, hence the samples for analysis.

"In other words, my contact's take on gem and jurillium quality and suitability for purpose, and supplies for his use if fit," Ahxenta said.

"Precisely. The ships being built to replace those lost will need the ability to take disruptive hits. *That* makes shielded array sets for comms and other ops crucial. And meta-jurillium's the best protective stuff for a host of purposes. Letik's a growing colony, it has the materials, but at present it doesn't have the skills. That's changing, as Telzilt lost so much during years of hostile occupation that many of my people want to relocate to Letik and our other colonies. If the arrays can be made to order here, in small amounts at first, it would be a start. But it's your call. I know nothing of your trading here and it'll be in your hands to deal with as you see fit. I'll be here for as long as it takes, as my people need time out and I'm waiting for my next cargo from Limekiln."

"Food for thought," Tallica Apnis put in as her captain mused over a data holo of inventories and timescales that Levettiza had called up. "*Emerald* could be called in as local transport."

Azular had been listening intently, but his interest was drawn to two cartons he had spotted on a side table, surmising that they held the ore and crystal samples. Kerrix directed her first mate to open them for his inspection while she waited the response of *Arianrhod's* captain.

"I'll take the data and the samples with me," Ahxenta decided. "I've a lot to discuss and check, and I'll have questions. I'll get back to you. And as we've got two days before my next cargo will be in place, maybe you'd be my guest on *Arianrhod* for our next meet?"

"I'd be honoured, Captain," Kerrix agreed.

Ahxenta could see Apnis smirking as Azular's eyes lit up, and ended the talk: she had work to do. The three were led to their shuttle, and as soon as she had launched, the first mate turned to the pilot.

"I expect you'll want shore leave, starting now?"

"Hardly, Commander: I have to analyse these samples and Captain Kerrix is busy aboard her ship, as she's only recently docked."

"Cut it, you two," the captain broke in. "We've work to do and the first is a call to my contact. And then a meet with Lindell and his team over this and the Orea load, and *then* a senior staff briefing. You'll be going nowhere bar your lab for a time," she warned Azular.

As they were gathering their gear from the *Xanna*, Apnis spied the package that the captain had stowed amongst her personal kit.

"What's in the box Captain Kerrix gave you, Cinnabar?"

She realised the question was a mistake when she saw the pain in Ahxenta's face as she stiffened visibly. "Sorry, not my business."

"That's all right, Tallica," she sighed, stopping dead. "It *is* personal. And as you both know part of the story… you know Thal sent in teams to hunt the wreckage of the crashed ships? They found shards of hull that were fusions of others, some old… one big section with multiple repairs had an intact call-sign still. It was the *Wing Skipper*. Kerrix heard of it, had the slice extracted and brought it out here to give to me…"

"Thal knew," Azular said softly. "Was there anything else, ma'am?"

"Not as far as I've been told, but they've only scratched surface. No word of this to anyone," Ahxenta added roughly. "Get your gear."

The two obeyed and the craft was left, as Azular preferred that no-one handled her when he was not present. The captain sent Apnis to take the conn; her primary task was a long talk with her nephew.

* * *

The details of Starfall's proposal took most of the two days the captain had specified as their remaining time on Freskat to sort out, on top of loading their cargo. As Azular had found the goods to be prime quality and Jon had agreed, she allocated another thirty six hours to set up the contracts and collection and delivery systems. She was grateful for the bustle, as it occupied her mind and numbed heavy thoughts. She was in the mess eating alone after another session with her supercargo when she was accosted by her chief medic, who sat down uninvited.

"What's bothering you, Cinnabar?" Flintlock demanded. "You've been avoiding me, and that means trouble."

"Ship's business," was the short reply.

"Like hell; the *Moonstone's* in port and Azular hasn't been pressing for leave? Tallica's looking after you like a cat after her kitten? It started when you three got back from the *Moonstone*, so what gives?"

"This damn crew's far too nosy and you're one of the worst."

"That's what makes us the good crew we are, Cinnabar, and you know it. So, what is it?"

Ahxenta sighed, realising that she had little option but to explain. She had hardly done when the chirp of her wrist comm interrupted. It was Apnis, to tell her that Captain Kerrix had linked to request a chat at the captain's convenience. Apnis had not asked the topic with the bridge crew listening in, but had sensed urgency in her tone.

The captain chose to link back immediately and made for her office. Kerrix was in *her* bridge office and came to the point. She had had news from Admiral Posettix; he had found out that the ISA had sent a band of warships to Zeta to take out anything found on Sella, and move in. And Posettix had been contacted from the *Peerless* by Myrtleberry and grilled on the events at Starfall and on the whereabouts of the hostile transport and its pilot that the *Arianrhod* escorted in. The admiral had referred her to Captain Thal and had called Thal to warn him.

"Thal knows Myrtleberry's an info-sent," Ahxenta said abruptly.

"But does the admiral?"

"Thal can handle her, but I'll warn the admiral, though he's canny enough to treat her warily. And he outranks her. As for the *Red Mercy*: Vetta and Admiral Posettix both probed. The admiral was blocked at every turn, but Vetta's found that she's for Bell 2, in the Star Desert. The ISA's spotted what it thinks is a deserted alien base with a storage facility that its scientists figure holds life-tubes. The *Mercy's* for there: if they're active, they'll be brought up. Her contact didn't know if there were experts aboard that would attempt to revive any occupants, but it's possible. And your name was part of the gen that she picked up as having queried the *Red Mercy* and Bell 2, Captain."

"Myrtleberry!" Ahxenta spat. "The *Mercy* didn't scan us or attempt contact before she left, but there was activity around her. I won't alert Admiral Zillah to this, as she knows about Bell 2. Any news on the remains from Skota?" she asked softly.

"The admiral's people haven't been given leave to examine them," was Kerrix' pained reply.

"Anything else of note, Captain?"

"Nothing that affects your ship, or the fleet, Captain."

"But you'd like a word with Azular?" Ahxenta guessed.

"Is it *so* obvious? I would, ma'am," she admitted. "My people have started on a decoy and his input would be useful. And he *did* want a closer look at my fighter, or what's left of it. My engineers haven't had time, but as Ter Kinnitix is now involved in that and in several science ops as well as our bypass capacity, things are moving ahead."

"Two good excuses to get him back aboard the *Moonstone*," Ahxenta deduced. "I take it there's a motive."

"I'll keep you updated on anything relevant," she smiled.

"He can have one day, Freskat standard."

"Thank you, Captain."

"You're welcome, Captain," Ahxenta replied, and severed the link. "I bet I'm going to regret this," she muttered to herself.

20: TYING KNOTS

The issue of logistics was testing the captain as she stepped out of her office. Her first mate looked up to gauge her expression: she had heard that Azular was to head over to the *Moonstone* to liaise with her science officers on the decoy and other issues, once he had cleared things with the chief engineer.

"What's the score, Cap? The *Moonstone's* started on a decoy already? I thought her people had more important things to do. And I bet that's not all Captain Kerrix had to say."

"No; I'm holding a briefing on it shortly. Myrtleberry's been stirring it, and we're part of the equation. But we leave on our revised schedule, as our goods will be ready to collect by the time we hit Limekiln. And I've agreed that only us, the *Emerald* or named Starfall ships will carry out cargo drop or pick-up of goods here. I've set up a secure depository for local storage and exchange, Thal's guaranteed security at his end, and only his TA-affiliated ships will bring Letik supplies in here."

"Watertight as can be, then," Apnis said. "But what else is Azular up to, if he's flying off to the *Moonstone*?"

"We'll find out when he gets back," was the sour reply.

The captain was fated to find out before his return, for she had a call from him five hours later, asking for a private word. She was about to go off duty, but diverted to her office. Apnis opted to remain on the bridge, but to her surprise, she was called in ten minutes later.

"Sit," Ahxenta said shortly. "It's a four-way link. The *Serenity's* on line with Admiral Posettix and Ambassador Posettix, and the *Zetkalt* with Ambassador Jotakt and Captain Heltakt."

"You what?"

"We'll get the story later. I've set to log the comm."

The first mate took in Azular, Kerrix and Inks in what looked like an office aboard the *Moonstone*, and gaped as she settled into her chair. "They're wearing dress uniforms!"

"Welcome, Commander," Kerrix smiled at her. "Everyone's here, Admiral, so perhaps you'd begin?" she added to Posettix.

He nodded, and with no ado stated that those watching were invited to witness a hand-tie ritual, to be carried out in line with Telziltic law.

It entailed an exchange of verbal consents, with or without reasons for the same, and the recording of the event in official records.

"Which means four ships' logs," he explicated. "Captain, Dr Azular, please proceed with your consents, and statements, should you wish."

Kerrix smiled softly and looked up at Azular. "I consent to be hand-tied to you, Azular of Berzic, from this moment on, because I love you. I could search the galaxy from Alpha to Psi and never find your match. You're unique. Even if you *are* damned annoying at times."

Azular laughed as he raised her hand to his lips, kissing it gently. "And I consent to be hand-tied to you, Elistya Xanna Sethina Vetoyn Bet Kerrix, Daughter of Clan Starwain of Telzilt, from this moment on. I love you, Xanna. I believe I have done, since first I met you."

With a gentle smile at him, Kerrix tied a ribbon around their clasped hands, and both looked round at their observers. Admiral Posettix was first to attest to witnessing the rite. As the others also affirmed, Azular slipped a ring onto his new wife's finger and she did the same for him. Formalities over, the pair embraced.

The first mate of the *Arianrhod* hissed softly. "Our people will be pissed," she murmured. "They were looking forward to a party."

"Can it," her captain advised.

Kerrix gave her and Azular's thanks to the witnesses, accepted the good wishes of those on the *Serenity* and the *Zetkalt* and politely cut the links. She then turned an amused gaze on the *Arianrhod* officers.

"That was short and sweet," Ahxenta remarked sardonically. "You realise you *are* due back aboard in twelve hours, Dr Azular?"

"Yes, ma'am," he replied, his smile not wavering.

"Congratulations to you both," the captain continued. "I'll hear the details later, but for now, I expect you all have things to do."

"We do, Captain. Jesse and I are for the bridge, and you, Dr Azular, have fine-tuning to do on our decoy before mess time. *And* you wanted a look at my wreck of a fighter," she grinned impishly at him.

One eyebrow shot up and Apnis laughed at his startled expression.

"You want the Cap to spread the good news, Azular, or will you do it later, when you fork out for drinks for the entire crew?" she teased.

"I'll consider it and let you know, Commander," he replied.

"My people will have it figured by the end of this watch," Kerrix said dryly. "I'll let you both get back to duty," she continued. "I'll speak to you before you leave, Captain."

"Count on it," was the reply. "Ahxenta out."

"Duty?" Apnis echoed. "Like hell: I need a stiff drink. Azular *has* been noticeably nuttier since he met Kerrix, but this beats all."

"*Captain* Kerrix," the captain corrected. "Let's go. I wonder what prompted it," she mused as the two set off. "She was itching for a word with Azular after she'd spoken to Admiral Posettix; and she was upset that the admiral wasn't allowed to examine the Skota tubes."

"I imagine she was. So Myrtleberry's still local enough to annoy? I'd have thought *she'd* be itching to get back to her mission to the back of beyond, in her fancy new ship at the head of her little flotilla."

"She's maybe hanging on to see what's in the sample the *Emerald's* taking to the ISA supply unit. She'll want to know how it's constructed, and where and how we came by the materials. And as she knows we're here, she'll work out that Freskat's involved in the chain."

"She was quick to muscle in when we told Zillah about that hand-held probe to detect trace zukivianite linked to cyber-organic bodies that our people came up with after Skyrtek. She was on the link before we could turn, yelling that the ISP, as it was then, should've been told at the start. Then she high-tailed it from Alto Finglas to snap up our stock and take over production. She even brought her own lab gear."

"We made her pay," Ahxenta recalled. "If the ISA wants a stack of arrays, *it* can pay for them at going rates. It won't be long until it has a regular source of ore for making its own, but until then, we can profit. And we don't tell Myrtleberry *or* anyone about it. But I can't imagine she'll chase us down just to find out how we did it."

"I see Axellina's made it in before us," the first mate noted as they entered the mess. "Do we spread the news or keep it quiet?"

"We play it by ear, but least said, maybe. Though if you're having a shot of the strong stuff, she'll want to know why."

"I'll leave it until after my rations," Apnis grinned.

The two joined the CMO and talked of general matters until a short time later, when Cottontail stalked in, her face a mask of perplexity. Spying her senior colleagues, she made a rapid sortie to round up her rations, stepped over, and sat down heavily.

"So what's Azular been at now?" she asked the captain directly. "He calls me up from the *Moonstone* with a question about fine-tuning their decoy, he's grinning all over *and* he's in dress uniform. What's up?"

"Where was he, in a lab?" the first mate cut in.

"No, an office. He's just off the link. I asked about the get-up but he'd only say he'd been busy and had to finish the tuning in a hurry, as he'd other urgent work on. What's so funny, Tallica Apnis?"

The first mate continued to laugh. "I'll go get us drinks, Cap, we'll need them. Maybe you'd better fill Axellina and Crizz in."

"I'll wait 'til you get back," Ahxenta said acerbically.

The captain was succinct when the drinks had been set down. "Pick them up. To Dr Azular and Captain Kerrix: they've just got hitched."

"They've *what?!*" the chief engineer exploded, in a voice so loud that half those in the mess turned their heads.

"They've got hand-tied, the Telziltic equivalent of a low-key knot-tying," she explained, and then gave an account of the proceedings.

"Short honeymoon, then," Cottontail said scathingly. "No wonder he'd a face like a sunrise. He'll be impossible to live with now *and* we'll have to put up with that endless humming. But why the rush? I'd have thought *she'd* have put the scuppers on it."

"I'll find out when he gets back. Don't spread it around yet."

"Half the crew in here are wondering what's up, Cap: they'll figure," Apnis warned. "If he tells Greffy, *he'll* tell Box, and the whole ship will know by tomorrow."

"Not my look out. Damn!" she exclaimed as her wrist comm trilled. "It had better not be Myrtleberry. I haven't finished my rations."

It was not, she found when she listened by earpiece. Her response was curt. "Copy the admiral's note to the *Moonstone*, in case she didn't get it. And send the lot out on the UV-III to the fleet, priority."

It was an ISA alert to all posts and ships in zones Lambda and Delta of hostile action off Peden Post: a carrier out of Milkit Major had been hit as she switched from the main bypass to the local track for Hespera Two. An ISA ship had answered the distress and taken out the alien. There was an addendum for Ahxenta from Zillah. The carrier was the *PSS Tallulah* and she was being towed to Hespera by the ISA ship.

"Hell!" Apnis exclaimed. "We won't know how bad she's been hit. Does Jesse Inks or any of ours on the *Emerald* have friends aboard?"

"No idea," the captain said. "But it means hostiles are still out there ready and able to fight. We're too far out to help, but one of the fleet may be nearer. She's taken a hiding if she needs towed. Fleetskup's not the savviest captain, but he keeps her in good trim."

"Gem Ferry's from Hespera," Cottontail put in. "He may have kin that can find out more. I'll check."

"There's zip we can do, so finish your dinners," the captain ordered. "The ISA will send in scouts to search for the hidden base. With *this* trouble and the upshot of the last, it'll be stretched, which might stall its worm-pocket and bypass-building shenanigans."

"Bet it won't," Apnis said. "It'll still be sending explorers out into unmapped space at tax-payers expense – which means us."

"As long as there's not another hostile den on the way to Limekiln," Flintlock added. "I'm done, so I'm for my rounds. I'll catch you later."

"Likewise," Ahxenta sighed. "I'd best see what else has happened since we've been in here. Tallica, you're off duty."

"I'll come for the walk, Cinnabar. I've never been fond of Murmur Fleetskup, but I'd miss him if anything happened to him."

* * *

The *Xanna* settled into her bay two hours before *Arianrhod* was due to leave. Azular, toting his kitbag and a small case, stepped off the ramp. The captain was on her way towards him.

"You're for my office and a chat," she greeted him. "I should offer my congratulations, but that'll keep. What's in the box?"

"Ma'am," he said formally. "It's a couple of bits of tech for the chief to look at: add-ons for the decoy that might enhance its ops."

"That you and the *Moonstone's* engineers came up with," she said. "Let's go. You can speak to Crizz later. She knows, by the way, as does half the crew: you shouldn't have let it out to Greffy."

On their way up, Ahxenta made discreet enquiries about links that Jesse Inks had to his previous ship. The *Tallulah* had been hit by a huge, old-type hostile warship augmented by heavy shielding and an array of weaponry. The brain aboard was intent on destruction and heedless of self-damage. The *ISAS Matchless* had come to her rescue.

"He *has* friends aboard," Azular said. "The chief engineer and one of the medics; they took minor hurt. But *Tallulah's* serious casualties include her first mate, chief tactical officer and other seniors, and the ship's very badly damaged. The ISA's main concern is the upgrades to the hostile. If there *are* similar out there, where are they and where are they finding the added tech *and* having the ships fitted? It suggests a well-equipped base that has thus far gone unnoticed."

"I sent a link, but got no response," the captain told him. "I expect Captain Kerrix did the same. Gem Ferry has kin on Hespera, but they know nix, apart from there's upped local traffic. Melly Goodsocks is anxious, as she and some of hers have mates aboard. But what you've been up to and why Captain Kerrix agreed is making noses twitch here: I can't imagine it was entirely down to your persuasive ways."

Azular smiled but refused to say more until the two had reached the bridge office, at which point the captain bid him be seated, unlocked a cabinet, and pulled out two glasses and a small bottle. She poured a generous tot into each and grinned wickedly.

"So?" she asked, raising her glass. "How did you persuade her?"

"I didn't," he said tranquilly. "Admiral Posettix did."

"You what?"

"He called *her*," he explained. "He'd had a link from a legal friend on Valla Key about efforts to nullify the contract between Xanna and the Protector after her court martial, where she lost her citizenship and assets, but got the *Moonstone*. It seems that her hereditary property did *not* legally revert to her Norvallan kin, and wrangles are ongoing for it, as an Equity Justice ruled that her Telziltic kin had rights. It's proposed that Xanna be legally allied by proxy to a mid-ranked Norvallan; *that* may allow the Protector to annul the contract and claim the assets, but it will challenge Xanna's rights to the *Moonstone*. The admiral was livid, he warned her, she asked *his* advice, and he advocated that she be hand-tied as soon as possible and leave the other parties to fight it out."

The captain shook her head incredulously. "A tangled web, and it sounds inane. She's not Norvallan now, so it'll never succeed."

"So the admiral thinks; but she's still part of a Norvallan family in name, and the best legal minds *were* called in to devise the contract. It's not likely that her Telziltic clan will want to be drawn in. But there are other concerns: the admiral's been told that Dr Kinnitix resigning to join the *Moonstone* is enraging certain parties, as they think his skills will make the *Moonstone* more cutting-edge, and Starfall will benefit."

"So they're put out," Ahxenta snorted. "Tough. Weren't they the ones that said he wasn't high-ranking enough to join their party?"

Azular laughed. "Exactly. But plugging one legal loophole will foil the Protector's plans somewhat. And Xanna had no objection."

"I'll bet. And that's why the ambassadors of Norvalla and Telzilt were called in as witnesses – the stamp of high authority." The captain stood and raised her glass again. "Congratulations, and the best to you both, Azular. You've got yourself a good mate, even though I find her as damned annoying at times as she finds you."

He chuckled. "Thank you, ma'am. I *am* very happy."

"I can tell. And believe me, everybody else will too. Go sort your gear and then head to the bridge. We're due out shortly."

Ahxenta shook her head at her departing officer and stepped onto her bridge. The hum of systems gearing up for departure hit her ears as she slid into the command chair and pulled her boards across.

"So how is he, apart from grinning ear to ear?" the first mate asked.

"Chipper and contented," was the reply. "He'll be here shortly. He's brought back some tech add-ons for our decoy to up its performance."

Azular had no sooner made the bridge, to knowing grins from his crewmates, when the comms officer called a link from Captain Kerrix. The captain opted to take it in her office: with all the ears around her alive with anticipation, she felt it wise. She was gone for half an hour.

"Anything new?" Apnis asked on her return.

"Not much. The *Moonstone* will be three days after us, as the *Kel'Torc* won't be in until then, but her load from Limekiln's not ready yet."

"And after that?"

"Nothing's confirmed, but given her look, something's in the wind. She *may* see us in the Web. Once we're en route, I'll call a briefing."

The first mate had to be content with that and it was hours until the seniors were called in for an update. The news related to the *Red Mercy* at Bell 2; she had been sent in because the partly-buried alien structure found there *had* held active life-tubes. They had been brought aboard the *Mercy*, and Levettiza's contact was sure attempts would be made to revive the bodies. Given the voids of the Star Desert, the ISA Council was uneasy that other covert bases might exist. One of its directors had called Thal to ask if he knew of any. He did not, but due to the sceptical tone of the ISA man, he warned his captains, lest they were contacted.

"The ISA top-brass didn't believe Thal, then," Apnis deduced. "But what's it to do with us?"

"We've been associated with queries over the *Red Mercy* and Bell 2, we've links to Starfall, and the admiral and the ambassadors are ruffling feathers at Alto Finglas," Ahxenta stated. "Those ISA ships are almost at Sella, and they've been joined by two more that were on patrol, so it looks like big trouble. No word's out over the usual channels, as the ISA doesn't want to alert any hostiles on Sella to an imminent attack."

"They'll know," Cottontail said sourly. "They always do. And what about Cygilla and Marridan? They're the nearest big centres and might find themselves in a firing line if there's a showdown."

"Zip we can do," Ahxenta told her. "We continue on track and keep our eyes and ears at full stretch. Dismissed. Not you, Azular."

The perpetual smile on the senior science officer's face faded, but the additional news was only that the Norvallan and Telziltic ships at Alto Finglas had now been given leave to inspect the Skota life-tube data and to have their own experts examine the physical evidence.

* * *

Comms channels were quiet over the days to Limekiln, but unloading the mining gear for Orea was quick once in orbit. *Arianrhod* was obliged to change bays to take on the habitation units from Form-tech orbital storage and the loading took most of two days. They were nearly done when news came in of the ISA attack on Sella. It had been decreed a success, but had cost an ISA heavy cruiser and the disablement of three others. There *had* been a flight of small ships fleeing Sella, but it was assumed that warning had been received and many others had already left. Of the escaping ships, one was still loose and was being pursued.

307

"No data on its heading," the captain reported in her subsequent briefing. "Nor of the pursuit; but the blip's a small transport. We're far enough away, but there may be a couple of ours in the area, as it's close to busy sectors. Nothing of what was found *on* Sella; and I've little on the *Tallulah*. She was towed out of Hespera four days ago, for Delta Iridium's repair and med facilities, as they're the best in Lambda."

"Anything on what the *Red Mercy* found?" the first mate asked.

"Yes; but this goes no further, as it's unverified and is from various sources. The medics revived what was in two of the intact tubes. They *were* partially-altered hostile victims, but they'd once been raiders that operated in Beta *and* in The Belts by Jurassa. They've been questioned, and they've told of bases outside Alpha, including Nexus, and another that might be home to the ship that attacked the *Advance* and the *Repulse* way back, and led to Myrtleberry being our guest for a while."

"I take it Thal knows?" the chief engineer put in.

"He does. But the ISA Council's beset by in-fighting, and it's meant that reports are not sent or sent late, so there's likely more. But that's it for now, we're for Berzic. Back to posts. Azular, stay."

The Berzic officer frowned, suspecting the reason. The captain was sympathetic: experts from the *Serenity* had analysed the remains in the life-tubes from Skota to which they had been given access. The part-profile Telziltic DNA that Dr Mettix found to be close to his captain's had come from a tube holding a semi-cyber being; a new tissue sample had tested identical to that of Dr Jerettila Vetoyn Sethina Bet Kerrix, a senior science officer aboard the lost *NFS Valla Sun*.

"Captain Kerrix told you *that*, ma'am? Why didn't she contact me?"

"She didn't tell me, Admiral Posettix did. He's had to pass the news to the Norvallan fleet, so that any kin of the crew lost aboard the *Valla Sun* can be informed. At least all the life-tubes were defunct, so there's no question of revival. But it's still a shock to those involved. There's more work, and more Telziltic remains have been found, so Heltakt will have a similar job to do for his fleet. But I have to say the admiral seems driven, as if he's still trying to find something."

"The unknown number of bases and hostiles out there are the main headache for the Alliance and the ships that cross free space," Azular rasped. "How many more life-tube stashes are there? Raiders we've always had and dealt with, but these aliens are more dangerous. Captain Thal has said there are hostile hideouts on occupied or annexed worlds that can build ships, but he doesn't know where they are."

"So we keep a step ahead. You and Crizz will handle hull defence systems, arrays, and the decoy. Gliss can manage the holo and Whisper has *Loki* in hand. We're for the bridge and the haul to Berzic. You can contact Captain Kerrix later: she'll have a lot to think on right now."

The science officer trailed the captain to the bridge. All the stations were at full alert, Apnis had brought the main holo-grid full down, and their forward path was clear. The off-limits alert around Furze was still active, and the nearby worm-pocket marked, she noted.

"No word that ISA ships are still at Furze, but the ISA won't have given up on it, as a lot traffic goes by that way: tabs would be kept."

"*And* the glitches at Fourpoint and Portal," Ahxenta said. "And Skota," she added gravely.

Azular, listening, pulled the Zeta-Eta border region by Skota into a discrete frame: Sella was shown as off-limits. Ahxenta sighed and gave the order to move out. Slowly, the great ship powered up, and docking traces sliding away, she turned to face the spaces beyond Limekiln.

"Steady as she goes, helm. Time to bypass entry?"

"Hour and ten, ma'am," Dox replied. "Check we've no alerts for Torch Crux," she bid the navigator. "It's smack on bypass edge. Or Quartic Cross – that's been a pain in the past."

"You got it," Box replied amiably. "It should be a smooth switch, and as long as nobody jumps *onto* the bypass anywhere near Furze this time around, we'll be up on Berzic to time, or even sooner."

"You get jump lines plotted just in case," his mate said darkly. "That worm-pocket and the Crimson Drapes are still kicking, and who knows what's still in that nebular hidey hole we found way back? The ISA said it had got them all, but how would we know? We've a long ride ahead."

* * *

The long ride also involved drills, essential upgrades to ship's systems and addition of alerts to the bridge holo as they were received. Nothing was detected off the Furze beacon and the area near the worm-pocket read clear, but Azular's probing with arrays he had boosted with extra micro-sensors got from the *Moonstone* implied that shielded ships were out there. Lindell's team, scouting for contracts, had found two that would mean meetings in the Web. The *Emerald* had dropped her cargo at Minti and the trial comms array wafer at Alto Finglas. She was now Web-side to pick up a cargo for Silshoon.

"We may pass her on the road," the captain remarked as she settled in her chair after a lengthy session in her office, where she had called in Azular to assist. "*Moonstone's* got her cargo and is set for Vreskota. She's faster than us, but won't catch us. The *Kel'Torc's* almost at Starfall with Thal's gear, *Obsidian's* for Silverglass, *Warrior* left Nyx before we left Freskat and *Tallulah's* safe at Delta Iridium, but that's all I've had on ours, apart from a link from the *Hexameter.*"

The tone alerted Apnis to something else. "About what?"

"You'll find out at a briefing I'm calling once the watch changes."

The details the *Hexameter* sent to the PSS fleet were sparse. She had been en route from Spelter to Cygilla Prime and near Cygilla when she caught signals hinting at action off the bypass. Coxen ordered her ship in, as she had had no word of conflict in Cygillan space. The jump took the ship within range of an ISA explorer-destroyer with a small, beat-up transport in her tractors. As the ISA ship began hauling the craft in, it opened fire. From what Coxen's science officers got, the interaction of weaponry with the tractors' energy caused an implosion that cracked the transport's hull open. The ISA vessel hauled the remains in, but the *Hexameter's* team had been able to identify the craft as hostile, and link it to the one that had escaped Sella. Coxen *had* hailed the ISA ship to verify her suspicions, and was sternly rebuffed by her commander.

"Ellin Myrtleberry of the *ISAS Peerless*," Ahxenta said gruffly. "Bee figures from the ion trails her guys picked up that the blip jumped off at a local node from Mull to Cygilla, with the *Peerless* on her tail. I asked for the data; Azular confirms the transport as a match to Dexel Thal's."

"You've passed that on to Captain Thal?" Apnis asked.

"I did. So the ISA has Sella sewn up. How much damage was done and what can be saved of what's left I don't know. I assume the *Peerless* is for Alto Finglas, but we shouldn't meet her. We'll be up on Berzic in eight hours, so grab some sack time and be ready for duty in seven."

The senior officers were on the bridge as orbit was made. That the habitation units were needed was clear: many orbital facilities had taken damage, including the offices of the company that had ordered them.

"Lock us down, Dox. Stand by for credit transfer, Lindell. Confirm when received," the captain ordered.

File and credit exchanges were made, and the cargo teams given the go-ahead to begin. The work would take a day, but Ahxenta had no qualms. She left Apnis in control to check with her supercargo, who was touchy over increased levies said to be down to recent hostilities.

"They don't miss a trick," Box said huffily to Dox. "Bet the cost of ale's up in the *Half Moon*, and Ally will claim it's due to tax increases. Dr Azular not calling in on his people here? It *is* his home port."

"Don't be nosy," Dox retorted. "He never has before when we've been here, so why should he now? He may not *have* people here."

Apnis could tell that the senior science officer was aware of the chat and patently ignoring it. He had had to put up with a deal of ribbing over his marriage, but she knew he relished it. The news had not gone beyond the ship, but once *Arianrhod* made Merkat, that would certainly change. She flexed her shoulders to ease the tension and settled into her chair, her eyes on her boards to ensure all was on track, but cargo drop advanced smoothly, and bar routine updates from Berzic Port Authority, nothing disturbed the process.

* * *

The next days were peaceful, the only interruption to passage along the bypass a courtesy link from the *Emerald*, now on her way to Silshoon. *Arianrhod* had passed Linza and was nearing the node for Merkat when another call came in, and the captain learnt that the *Moonstone* was less than a day behind. The gist of the link Ahxenta thought best to discuss with her first mate and senior science officer in private, and once off duty, she called the two into her office.

"The *Moonstone* will stop off in the Web before her trip to Vreskota, hence the turn of speed," Ahxenta told them. "Captain Kerrix wants a private word with Nat Holdspan, on an issue she won't talk about or pass on over any channel, so she'll haul in to catch him. The *Warrior's* due shortly, in fact she may make it ahead of us. Whatever it is, it sounds serious, but she wanted to know if I'd heard from Myrtleberry, or any of her ISA cronies from Alto Finglas, so I suspect that's part of the deal. She'll speak to me when she gets in – again, she'll say zip over a link. That's it. I don't know if you'll get a chance to catch up, Azular, as she won't be in long."

Once the ship made port, the Berzic officer was bid down with the captain to the harbour office and then to a marketing meeting arranged by Lindell. Ahxenta had noted the *Nyx Warrior* in when *Arianrhod* hove to, but she must have only arrived, as Holdspan and his first mate were also in the harbour office. After cordial exchanges, the four set off for their shuttles, both heading to inner two belt and marketing.

"We'll maybe catch up with you in the *Half Moon*," Ahxenta said to Holdspan as they reached the bays. "Our talks should be short."

"Maybe," he parried. "I have an urgent meeting with Captain Kerrix and the *Moonstone's* due in shortly."

"I know. She wants to talk to me too. Any idea what it's about?"

The young captain paused, his brow wrinkling. "No I don't, but she was very emphatic about not responding to any ISA links, particularly from Colonel Myrtleberry, on any account."

"What? She asked if *I'd* heard from Myrtleberry, which I haven't, but that was it. I wonder what she and the ISA have been up to now?"

"We'll no doubt find out. Excuse me, Captain."

Ahxenta glanced after him. "He's anxious. *Did* Myrtleberry try to contact him, I wonder? Let's find Lindell. The *Moonstone* won't be here until near the end of standard Merkat business hours."

The captain was at lunch with Azular and her supercargo in the *Half Moon in a Puddle* when noises nearby signalled new arrivals. Holdspan saw her and waved, and after talking to Ally, he and Stone walked over to the distant table, followed by two pairs of curious eyes.

"Well, Jurry, lad, I see young Holdspan still has the face fuzz," Malty sniffed. "He looks to have aged a bit. It's been tough out by, from what I've heard: fights all over the place and a heap of damage."

"Lucky it didn't come near us," his mate replied. "They've been out a while; haven't seen Ahxenta in months, but her ship's shiny as a new pin, from what I saw on the holo as she hove in. There's more here: *Urania* and *Pole Star* are in, but none of their crews are here. *Arianrhod's* won't be long to ship over, though: they're always up for shore leave."

"It's started: here's the advance guard," Malty observed. "But looks like there's another big boat coming in, going by the buzz at the grid and pointing fingers. I'll get us a couple of pots and see what's up."

"Good idea," Jurry agreed. "I'll stay here and keep my eyes peeled."

Malty was back in five minutes. "Would you believe it!" he rasped softly as he slid into the bench. "That's the *Moonstone*, but what a story! Dr Azular has gone and got hitched to her captain!"

"Who told you that?" his disbelieving friend demanded.

"I heard Lieutenant Box, he of the big mouth, telling Ally. His mate bid him hush, but he didn't. Seems it happened on the quiet on layover at Freskat. Box thinks now she's here, there'll be a party, but Dox told him to dream on. Couldn't get more, Ally shooed me off," Malty said in disgust. "But if I'm not mistook, doesn't Azular have a shiny trinket on one finger that wasn't there before?"

Jurry eyed the far table narrowly. "You're right, mate. Now there's a tale we might make profit of, if we can get more details."

The rising chatter at the bar had also disturbed the table of officers, as a trill of Ahxenta's communit told of a link. It was her first mate, to tell her of the *Moonstone's* arrival. Ally, rolling up with orders, repeated the news. The captain of the *Warrior* immediately excused himself, to make a private link. He was back with word that Captain Kerrix would make her way over once all necessary ship's business was complete.

Kerrix, her first mate at her heels, walked in an hour later, to be met by a surge of chatter and sly glances from the tables of *Arianrhod's* crew spread around. Ally quickly poured two mugs, told Kerrix they were gratis, and offered quiet congratulations. The two accepted the drinks and set off for the back table, where room was made for them.

"You must have travelled at max speed to get here so fast," Ahxenta saluted the captain. "You were near a day behind us at Linza."

"I didn't want to miss you or Nat, and I've deadlines I don't intend to miss," she answered.

"Are you going to let us in on any of it?"

Kerrix shook her head. "Not in here. This place has more eyes and ears than the Web's secure-cam system. But finish your meals: I'm not going to haul you away in the middle of lunch."

"When do you have to get back to your ship, ma'am?" asked Azular.

She smiled up at him. "When I've done what I have to do here."

Despite the light tones, Ahxenta could tell she was edgy and made short work of the last of her meal. Holdspan had already cleared his mug into the recyc hatch. The trivial chat was strained and soon gave way to the issue at hand, Kerrix debating on the nearest private space.

"Ally's office," the *Arianrhod's* captain said abruptly.

"He'll be charging me rent if I commandeer it for a chat again, and the regulars will speculate at a rate of knots," she said wryly.

"You walk out of here alone with Nat and they'll speculate anyway."

Conceding the point, she made for the bar to talk to Ally, returning to say that they were welcome. The two captains had been right in their opinion of the curiosity of the *Half Moon's* clientele: avid eyes watched the two officers as they made their way round the back of the bar.

"What do you reckon to that, Malty?" Jurry asked from the shelter of their dark booth.

The two conjectured in murmurs, and were further puzzled half an hour later when Ahxenta rose and set off on the same track. That tryst lasted another forty minutes and the three looked serious as they at last reappeared. By that time, most of the eyes and ears in the *Half Moon* had left or been drawn elsewhere, and it had settled down into its usual post-lunch torpor. The three returned to their table without a sideways glance, but almost at once, the group stood to leave. In minutes the table was empty. The quiet buzz of the *Half Moon* rose to crescendo.

"Well, they haven't been arranging a party," Jurry told his mate.

"More like a wake," Malty observed. "Where are they for now?"

The seven were destined for their respective shuttles, all berthed on level four. Little was said, but by tacit consent, Azular and Kerrix were given space to slow down and talk. The *Moonstone* was to leave the Web shortly, but would return once her cargo for Vreskota was delivered. The *Arianrhod* would still be there, for a number of meetings had yet to be held and, in view of the long time they had been away, her captain had decreed a spell of shore leave for every member of her crew.

The trip back to *Arianrhod* was silent bar the exchanges needed for flight in the tight spaces of the Web and docking aboard. Ahxenta had called a senior staff briefing for two hours hence, but wanted a closed session with Apnis and Azular beforehand. She brought the shuttle in on a tight arc, and prepared for the tractors that would draw her inward to her allotted bay. Wasting no time, the captain left the final lockdown to her engineers and set off to the arranged room, Azular at her back. The first mate was waiting, coffee at the ready.

"I'll rinse off first," Ahxenta said roughly, slinging her gear on the table and removing her jacket before slipping into the hygiene closet.

"What gives?" Apnis demanded. "Cap looks a tad distracted."

Azular shrugged. "I don't know, Commander."

The two sat, but the captain was gone only moments. "Hell," she breathed as she settled, looked at the pair and abstracted a data shard from a leg pocket. "Details of that wrecked alien transport from Sella that the *Peerless* chased, caught and hauled in to Alto Finglas, and what was found in it," she said shortly.

The first mate's eyes bulged. "How in blazes did you get hold of that, Cinnabar? Captain Kerrix?"

Ahxenta nodded. "Via Admiral Posettix and a contact of Thal's that *he* won't talk about, not even to his own. Xanna Kerrix suspects a plant in ISA HQ. The *Peerless'* remit was to capture the boat and get its pilot alive, but it failed. The pilot was killed as the hull of the ship split, but the ISA experts got most of it, *and* him, intact and dissected the lot at Alto Finglas. And what I've got to say now goes *absolutely* no further, either of you. It's why Kerrix didn't want Myrtleberry to get to Nat."

Ahxenta sighed and looked away. "The pilot was a part-alien, part-humanoid like no other they've ever found. The highly advanced cyber parts were so meshed to the soft tissues that they were indivisible, but the fleshy parts contained human and alien DNA. Most of the human part's been explicitly linked to one person. They trawled through hell knows how many files to get a name, and they did: Nortin Holdspan."

"Shit!" Apnis exploded quietly. "Poor Nat!"

"It gets worse," the captain said harshly. "The ISA's digging rung alarm bells in a few quarters, including the registry sections of the Nyx and Freskat home fleets; and their local PSS registry records had been ransacked, so hackles were raised, and that's how some of it leaked out. Jesse Inks is from Nyx, Levettiza has a contact there, so the *Moonstone* was drawn in; and Captain Kerrix brought the admiral in. *He* dug and with his people on Alto Finglas and up to their necks in it, *and* in the relevant sections of its facility, they got more info."

"Hold a sec, Cinnabar," Apnis interrupted. "You said the Nyx and *Freskat* home fleet registries?"

"I did. The body had other merged tissue that was identified. Freski. Captain Reder Ahxenta," she said bitterly. "And traces of Berzic tissue, but no specifics. A few other fragments."

"Oh hell, Cinnabar! That was something you didn't need to hear," the first mate whispered, putting a hand on her captain's arm. "I am so, so sorry. But why did Captain Kerrix call you in while Nat was still there? Surely that sort of thing should have been private?"

"Nat asked her. He was completely in shock. I wondered why she'd a bottle and three full glasses on the table." Ahxenta's voice was tight and hard as she pushed the data shard into the reader slot of her info pad. "She made me sit and take a shot before she began."

The holo melted into what looked like pieces of hull, burnt and so flecked with damage that little could be seen, but Azular's keen eyes could pick out the molecular signatures of a fusion of materials and he activated the console to bring up more.

"Well?" the captain questioned.

"Meta-jurillium, ages old, from more than one source I think," he said softly. "Not all of alien extraction. Without comparisons, I can't attribute any of it. And other fragments, including zukivianite."

Ahxenta nodded. "Bits of hull from the *Bright Mist*, but not the *Wing Skipper*," she said. "And other items in the ship, relics of the *Bright Mist*, including ranking pins: lieutenant."

"That's not all, is it, ma'am?" the Berzic officer asked gently, brow creasing as he looked intently at her. "There's more."

"Damn you," she sighed. "Poor Nat for sure. I think he wanted it off his chest. Nortin Holdspan was his uncle, a nasty piece of work, and aboard the *Bright Mist* on sufferance; his last chance to make good. He'd a poor record and held grudges, not least against his older brother – Nat's father. But he was sly *and* smart, as far as Nat remembers."

"Cinnabar, should you be telling us?" Apnis asked anxiously. "Nat must have meant it to be in confidence, and..."

"Believe me, there's a reason. It's possible that this Holdspan wasn't a forced dupe of the hostiles. Among the data found in the wreck were lists of trade routes, carriers, recent contracts; mostly TA. The *Warrior* was on it, *at the top*, us, the *Obsidian*, others. Levettiza did some checking and she reckons the data was got from the UV-III."

"What!" the first mate hissed.

"Exactly. The inferences being that this part-alien was working for the hostiles, and he and his have cracked the UV-III. That would give them enough to track a particular PSS, and as the crusade *was* directed against Nat, it's likely that this pilot was in authority and held a personal grudge. It's a lot of assumption, but if the UV-III *has* been cracked, the ISA knows, and can figure the way it was done – and replicate it."

"That's bad," Azular whistled. "And leaves the problems of alerting the fleet without bringing this into the open, *and* solving the issue."

"*You* suspected the UV-III might have been cracked a while ago, when that Dyne-Bek woman gave our gen to the hostiles for her own gain. And Thal's of the same opinion. What's to be done?"

Azular mused. "First, let the fleet know but without the details. If there's a breach, other ears will hear, and flak from that might give us a clue as to who's listening. And then devise a new code-decode system in a way novel to most of the fleet, so possibly based on zone Psi tech. Commander Kinnitix might be a good bet. I worked with him on the updates to our and the *Moonstone's* decoy; he's astute and quick at seeing unusual solutions to problems."

"Why's the onus on us?" Apnis wanted to know.

"Us and Starfall," Azular corrected. "The system has to be PSS and not registry-linked, and like it or not, Starfall has more PSS vessels than any other concern, as most other Privates are independents."

"Our seniors need to know about the UV-III," Ahxenta declared. "With minimal details. Holdspan and Kerrix are doing the same – and Thal. I'll link to the two here on a private channel and put your ideas to them. Kerrix will have a way to reach Thal. Unless that's trouble," she added as a link from Bellfish alerted her to a comm. "Damn!"

"Cap?" queried the first mate.

"The chief of the ISA supply unit," was the reply. "I'll take it here. You two get back to post and I'll see you at the briefing."

* * *

All the seniors were at the briefing. Ahxenta updated them and asked for comments. Cottontail condemned the actions of the *Peerless* and the ISA and was scathing of a possible breach of PSS comms.

"Plant a story and see how far it gets, Cap," she advised. "One that'll have Myrtleberry in a spin. She'll get back to you fast enough."

"Not helpful Crizz, and I've better things to do," she was told. "For a start, sorting out comms arrays for ISA HQ's shipyard; that means you'll be busy, Lindell. The supply chief wanted a lot more than he got, such as data on our sources, but he's ordered plenty to give him a head start and he wants more. That makes me suspect there are ships ready to launch soon, and his own haven't got the materials to up production. Where the ISA's credit comes from I don't know, unless it has outside deals, but as long as we get fees on delivery, it's not our problem. I've had no word on the beast that hit the *Tallulah* and zip on the hidden base that was thought to have launched it. I'll contact Zillah and see if she knows more once we're done. I'll need to see how *Emerald's* trade is, as she'll be the carrier for the goods from Freskat; and you'll have to give our contact the heads-up on how to set in trip codes and tweak the metal signature, Azular: we don't want the ISA getting above itself. More markets for the arrays would be welcome, Lindell."

"Shouldn't be difficult: I'll send out feelers," he replied.

"I've not heard back from Captains Holdspan or Kerrix on ways to sidestep UV-III hacking, but they need time. *Moonstone's* ready to leave, but Vreskota's a straight run and she won't be gone long. And there's a deal with Starfall been in the wind since Freskat, but what it is I don't know," Ahxenta told her people. "We seem to figure in it, but as we've plenty to keep us busy and a leave rota that stretches the length of the ship, we'll be here when she gets back."

"That'll please *you*," Earbleat remarked flippantly to Azular.

"Naturally," he grinned at her, impervious to sarcasm.

"Cut it," Ahxenta told them, as a buzz from comms interrupted.

"Request my boot," she groused when the duty comms officer told her it was Colonel Myrtleberry requesting a private word. "Dismissed; I'd best see what she wants. And then I'll call Zillah."

The captain was back on the bridge an hour later, in a sour mood. "She's still harking on about Dexel Thal's transport," she said to Apnis. "They've got scans of it, and she reckons it's a match for the one off Sella that her ship captured – which of course it is."

"She's admitted the ISA's taken that boat apart?" Apnis murmured.

"As *Hexameter* was in the area, she assumes the PSS fleet's now in the know, but she was holding back. Though I bet she knows *we* know more than we're saying. She didn't get on to personal details," Ahxenta added quietly. "But she *did* ask if I'd talked to Nat Holdspan recently. She's still trying to reach him, so she knows he's here. I'm not assuming a comms breach, as ISA's eyes and ears are all over, but I warned Nat. I got hold of Zillah: she says there are Coalition ISA ships scouting for more bases in the Star Desert. The *Red Mercy's* hauled into Freskat, so she's left Bell 2. And the Selky-Kilda bypass is on track, supported by two Norvallan ships. Admiral Posettix is irked and Thal's got probes in the area, as his ships are often on the Starfall-Amity bypass."

"Apart from that, the galaxy's quiet," Apnis snorted. "When do *we* get our shore leave?"

"After our marketing meets and after I've read a contract missive the TA's sent, and passed it to our legal rep. It's about upping levies to fund a series of new bypass routes, so look out for repercussions."

"New routes? Capping the ISA in the Mu double bypass and Selky-Kilda stakes, or building alternatives to Starfall's? And trying to make us and the other fleets that fly under its flag pay for them?"

"Looks like," the captain agreed. "There's been little over the UV-III or other nets about the state of trade, though Monto Strong sent a memo that two local carriers were hit in Marridani space. Both got off lightly, but it seems the bad guys are still around and up for a scrap."

"*Pole Star's* home base *is* Marridan, so he'd know. *Moonstone's* off, by the by, and as the *Firedrake's* on her way in, I've told Ma'Lappis to take her leave as and when. Azular's in his lab tweaking decoy ops, he says, but I bet he's got other stuff ongoing. Otherwise, we're on target."

* * *

The next days were busy as the captain and her team agreed contracts and set schedules. Despite the rounds of talks that absorbed her, and the physical exertion inherent in organising the ship for cargo, Ahxenta had a feeling of something in the offing.

"Time out," she decreed, when, another set of manifests dealt with, she handed over to the next watch. "I don't know about you, Tallica, but I'm for the *Half Moon*. We've rooms booked in green four, and I've nobody to see 'til tomorrow. Azular wants to head down: the *Marjenna's* in and her supercargo's an old friend of his. You?"

"I'll come with you, if only to hear our people pull Azular's leg — *Moonstone's* due in soon. I'm meeting Kit Biernop for dinner, but that's it. Axellina's down. I saw a couple of cargo pods heading to the *Warrior*, so I guess she'll be off before long. Let's hope she won't meet trouble."

The *Half Moon* was humming when the three made it. Several more traders were in, Ally remarked as he poured their ales; many of their own crew were in and other PSS vessels were represented.

"Family reunions," Apnis noted. "That lot are from the *Cresset*. Her captain's Kym Bottle's aunt and Axellina's nephew's a science officer. *Green Comet's* in, so I guess Elsey Gunn will want time out, as her mate's one of her pilots. And isn't that Captain Jedinlok of the *Marjenna?*"

"It is," Azular nodded, his eyes lighting as he waved. "The man on his left is my friend Zelujmar. I'll say hello: I haven't seen him in ages."

"And here's Box with a handful of mugs. Best get a table before they're all gone and Box opens his mouth," the first mate said.

"Roger that," agreed the captain. "We'll sit over there. You eating here, Azular, or do you have other plans?"

"I'll eat here, ma'am, but first I'll have quick word with my friend."

"Off to flash the ring," Apnis grinned as she and Ahxenta claimed a table. "I'm not meeting Kit until nineteen thirty, so I'll stop for a bit."

Azular was gone twenty minutes, as he was waylaid by others. He came back with word that the *Marjenna* and the *Cresset* were off in three days, but the *Comet*, *Firedrake* and *Urania* would stay longer, by which time the captain had chosen her food and discussed a crew matter with Apnis that had the latter shaking her head in mock annoyance.

Azular quickly ordered his meal, with a quizzical glance at the two. The captain would tell him, Apnis told him as she set off to change for dinner. Just as she reached the bar, raised voices and pointing fingers made her pause. An event in the Web's outer docking bays had caught the locals' attention, as Ally's bar holo-grid had been set to its widest extent, and the host was working the controls.

"The *Moonstone*," he said. "I thought she wasn't due yet. But what's up? There's a small ship flanking her. Looks like a Starfall one."

"It's the *Schiltron*," Apnis replied. "She's a defence craft, but she was at Starfall last I heard. And *Moonstone* isn't due for hours. What's got her in so fast, and why under escort? Is there any damage?"

"Not that I can see," Ally replied. "But two huge ships are holding off the outer meshes; waiting permission to come in, I expect."

The first mate looked over at the captain, who was taking a call on her communit and had risen. Azular, frowning at what he was hearing, was glancing at the bar. Apnis beckoned them across.

"*Moonstone's* back early with the *Schiltron* at her back," Apnis said as the two hove up. "Any idea what gives, Cap?"

Ahxenta shook her head. "The two out there are shielded, so we can't raise a call-sign. We'll see once they're in, but *Moonstone's* jamming everything in sight, she's got shields up and she's targeting."

"Shields up in port, targeting? What's been going on?"

"Sounds like Earbleat's found out… yes, what have you got?" the captain asked her second mate, aboard ship and watching every move.

"They're moving, so they've been granted permission to come in," Azular observed as he craned his neck for a better view over the others at the bar, who were equally as interested. "What in the name…!"

"We can see them on grid here," Ahxenta informed Earbleat grimly. "If she'd *them* on her tail, no wonder she flew in at light speed."

The crowd at the *Half Moon's* bar gawped as two huge ships spun into adjacent berths near the *Moonstone*. Ally, his voice hoarse with ordering them back to allow the PSS officers in, gave up and poured more ale.

"We've seen *them* here before," *Arianrhod's* first mate said icily. "A top-range explorer and a battleship: the *ISAS Advance* and the *ISAS Repulse*. They were recalled along with the *Peerless* when things got out of hand around the Stoorie Nebula."

"Earbleat says they're scanning the *Moonstone*, hence her shields and jammers," Ahxenta replied. "She's sent protests to the Port Authority, Merkat's Central Advisory Council, the TA and the ISA, and alerted every ship in port. And returned the favour by scanning them, though she'll get nowhere. I've told Earbleat to add our voice to hers, notify every ship in the fleet and send a formal complaint to the ISA."

"You'll be popular," her first mate told her.

"Looks like a stand-off, as she's still targeting," the captain went on, tapping her earpiece. "The PA will have to intervene. Ah, the *Warrior's* sent a protest and complained to the TA. Bet she won't be the last."

She was correct: every PSS followed suit, as did ships of other lines in the Web. The result, as Earbleat reported with glee, was that the ISA vessels cut their scans. Azular had meanwhile been using his info-pad and talking to Greffy, and Apnis had left for her dinner date.

"No point in us hanging on here holding up the bar," Ahxenta told her science officer. "Let's get back to our table and get our dinner. I'm sure you'll find out what went on later. What were you digging up?"

He had been searching for the latest on the two ISA ships, but had found little. They had been cited as assisting in actions in zones Theta and Alpha during the recent conflict, but that was all. Neither he nor Greffy could find any allusion to Sella, but as the *Peerless* had been part of that, it was possible that they had taken a hand. He could find no other mention of them, nor of any ISA action in Vreskot space.

"But?" the captain asked, scenting something.

"But as Captain Thal's Nexus Station *is* in uncharted space between Alpha and Theta, that may be a reason for their being in the area."

"That won't have escaped Captain Kerrix. And here's our food. I'm famished. Tell me what your Berzic friend had to say about your latest doings – and everybody else that caught you on the way by."

Azular was happy to do so, leading Ahxenta to infer that he enjoyed it. By the time their meal was done and passing friends spoken to, the *Moonstone* had begun to offload cargo, the *Schiltron* had left, and comms had linked over a request from Captain Kerrix to Captain Ahxenta for a talk when she had time, about a contract matter.

"Tomorrow," she decided. "If there's cargo moving, she'll have her hands full. And as I see Cobalt Mikbeam and his first mate are in, I'd best go and have a few words. You coming?"

"No thank you, ma'am. I have a few things to arrange."

"Don't get into trouble," she adjured as she set off to speak to the senior officers of the *PSS Urania*.

* * *

Ahxenta and Apnis sat in the *Half Moon* at breakfast. They had agreed to meet Azular, but he had not arrived. As far as they knew, he had not seen Kerrix nor any of the *Moonstone's* crew. Inks had been sent to the harbour office the previous night for the usual sign-in but had returned directly to his ship. Kit Biernop could not shed light on events, as the Dockers' Guild had not been called in, nor had Guild security. Both ISA ships were in port still, and preserving a moody silence.

"The meet with Captain Kerrix is at twelve hundred in marketing," the captain apprised her first mate. "She's booked a private room. And here he comes at last. Sit down," she greeted Azular. "Been busy?"

"Yes, ma'am. I've been talking to Captain Kerrix. She's been having words with Captain Birk Crossox of the *Repulse*. He was irritated at her actions of yesterday, and by her refusing to take his calls then."

"Order your breakfast and let's hear the details."

"The *Repulse* and *Advance* caught the *Moonstone* at Vreskota," Azular said, poking the menu-vid. "Xanna had heard of them from Captain Dun, as the *Kel'Lath* had met them at Velish on *her* way to Nexus. The captain of the *Advance* had called Captain Dun on the excuse of local hostile action, but started to dig on Nexus and Starfall ships in the area. The *Moonstone* was one, which alerted Captain Dun, as she knew of the *Elucida's* action at Starfall. She refused to answer, warned Captain Thal, and sent the *Schiltron* from Nexus all speed to Vreskota."

"How'd the ISA know the *Moonstone* was at Vreskota?" Apnis asked.

"She'd come from Freskat via Limekiln, and there were ISA ships there," Azular posited. "That she halted here would be known, but the UV-III was maybe part of it. The ISA ships made Vreskota and began a scan, with *Norvallan* gear. The *Moonstone* blocked them and objected.

Tranger of the *Advance* contacted Ms Levettiza to try to get data from *her* on the basis of her ISA past. She got an earful and the news that a protest was on its way to ISA HQ. The *Moonstone* released her cargo and she and the *Schiltron* set for here, with the ISA ships at their backs. Crossox claims that as he's part of an Alliance taskforce to protect the charted zones, he has every right to scan anything in his path."

"Or anything he can get a bead on that he thinks might have one over on him. Who gives him his orders, I wonder," Ahxenta mused.

"One more thing, ma'am," Azular added. "Captain Kerrix had a call from Captain Mint of the *Kel'Seth*, who's at Skoon. An ISA ship going all out in this direction passed him en route: the *Peerless*."

"I hope she told Nat," Ahxenta growled.

"She did. The *Nyx Warrior* will be gone before she arrives, and not by that bypass. On another matter, Captain: the issue that you and the commander were discussing in here yesterday?"

Ahxenta looked round, but it was early, quiet, and privacy was set. "Promotions. We've a few due, primarily Earbleat and Gliss. The doc's suggested Velli Ipvy for second lieutenant and Jak Wren for first. Crizz wants Gem Ferry stepped up; there are others. Your proposals?"

"Greffy. He merits his first lieutenant's pips," Azular said promptly. "Whisper Earbleat a full commander?"

"That was Tallica's reaction. She deserves it, despite her attachment to weaponry and annoying habits. Greffy it is. I'll arrange the pips and the party, but it will be aboard. And now to business. I don't suppose Captain Kerrix spoke about this meet with me at twelve hundred?"

"No, ma'am. Did you want me there?"

"No, it's private; but I want you and Tallica hard by. You can check in with the ship when you're there: that big cargo for Selliden is set to load first and then the one for Cygilla Prime. Lindell's polishing a deal of parts for Keystone with Ottolyx, but it's small. I'm holding off on other potentials until I hear what this Starfall business is about."

"Starfall?" questioned the first mate.

"It has to be. Once I'm done here, I've a few things to see to before twelve. I'll meet you two in marketing at eleven fifty hours."

* * *

The two were prompt; the captain found them in the main reception area of the marketing facility with the lately-arrived Kerrix. Greetings were swift, and the *Moonstone's* captain led her opposite number to a small briefing room off the main hall to which she had the key.

The captains had been gone over an hour, by which time Apnis and Azular had been sought out by their supercargo. He was perplexed: he had had a call from the captain to hold fire on the Ottolyx contract for Keystone, to resume another with the firm to ship small parts to Delta Iridium, and to ascertain the current trade status of the *PSS Emerald*.

"I've spoken to the Ottolyx reps and they're okay with it. The Delta cargo's a priority, but they're busy, so I've had to leave the details until fifteen hundred. *And* they want the captain there. *Emerald's* got a pick-up at Berzic for the main medbay here, so she'll be in soon. But Captain Goodsocks has put in a bid for a contract that would take her to Stella Marina in Gamma. That would put her on a line for Freskat, where she could pick up the goods for ISA HQ, if they're ready."

"You can let the Cap know; there she is, with Captain Kerrix. That must have been some meet," the first mate said.

The captain refused to discuss the matter publicly and accepted the key to the room she had just left from Kerrix, who had to leave. Azular, disappointed, trailed the others to the place.

After Lindell's update, Ahxenta called the *Emerald* via the *Arianrhod*, to tell Melly Goodsocks to delay on the Stella Marina tender, until she spoke to her face to face. She then turned to her mystified officers.

"If we can secure the cargo for Keystone Kell, and Ottolyx agrees, *Emerald* will ship it," she told them. "It's a profitable deal, *Emerald* has the hold space, and if we take on the Delta Iridium shipment, it'll take us in the right direction for our next couple of cargoes."

"Which are?" Apnis asked enquiringly.

"A load of medical gear from several sources on Delta, and as many habitation units from Limekiln as we've hold space for," was the silky reply. "Form-tech are already building the units."

"Habitation units, ma'am? For Starfall?" hazarded Azular, trying to read what the situation was from the captain's quirky smile.

"No – for Letik."

"Letik! In zone Psi?"

"The same. I agreed, after a heap of arguing. Thal was brought in – he's at Twilight and on the way to Limekiln. We'll be a convoy of three ships from there, and we'll pick up two more at Starfall."

"A convoy of three to Starfall, ma'am?" Azular queried askance.

"*If* we get our contracts in place. We drop our Cygilla cargo, then the Selliden gear. We then head for Delta, by which time most of the pieces should be in place for the pick up at Limekiln."

"But Cap, the comms arrays for ISA HQ?" Apnis interrupted. "The *Emerald* was to be the carrier."

Ahxenta smiled maliciously. "The first batch of shielded arrays for Alto Finglas are nearly ready. I've agreed with my contact *and* Thal that the *Kel'Torc* will take them on and ship them to ISA HQ."

"Whoa, Cap!" Apnis whistled. "The ISA supply chief will be livid; so will the whole place, when a Starfall ship shows up with its goods!"

"The goods *will* have my endorsement, so not my problem. But the logistics *are*, and the Ottolyx meet is now. Lindell, Azular, you're with me. Tallica, you're back aboard. Start sorting our teams and holds. I realise you're all missing shore leave, but we arrange it later. We'll need a quick start once we *are* fully loaded."

"A convoy of three to Starfall, you said, ma'am," Azular repeated.

"Yes," she grinned at his look. "Us, the *Moonstone* and the *Kel'Moth*. We'll discuss it fully once the pieces are in place."

"We're for Psi, then," the first mate breathed. "New territory, and a heck of a long way from the Web *and* civilisation for all our people. There'll be a few anxious moments."

"More than a few," the captain agreed. "But the route's not new to the Starfall ships, so we'll be in good company."

"Yet another tie to Starfall," was the sarcastic reply, with an oblique glance at the senior science officer. "Cheered *you* up, I see."

"I'm always open to the new, ma'am. I'll have to make sure our nav-charts are current and that every hull science array is running at max."

"I'll bet," was the ironic reply. "You want me to pass on the news to the seniors, Cap, or will you do that when you get back?"

"I'll brief them as soon as I can. Let's go, you two. I'll see you on the flipside as soon as we're done, Tallica."

"Roger that, Cinnabar. What in the name's going on out here?" she added, as an uproar in main marketing caught their ears.

Azular spotted his Berzic friend and hailed him in passing. The man pointed to one of the info-screens floating above. "*That's* just come in, and there are two more behind her, apparently."

"Damn!" Ahxenta hissed. "She's made it. Just as well Nat's shipped out. Two more like that, Lieutenant?" she asked the officer.

"I'm not sure ma'am, but a services rep told me they're ISA and big. They'll be using marketing for meetings, their crews are for shore leave and most vacant billets have suddenly been listed as taken. We've been asked to vacate our quarters early, as the *Marjenna's* due out tomorrow. And a few of the big inner two shuttle bays are now marked off-limits. My captain's arguing it with the facilities office."

"He'll get nowhere, but thanks for that, Lieutenant. We must head to our meet," she said to her team. "Find out what's up, Tallica, and link me. If that's not a call to say Myrtleberry's hanging off the comm."

Ahxenta tabbed up her communit as Zelujmar took his leave. It was

Earbleat to say that the *Peerless* had made it in and that two more berths were being prepped. The *Advance* and *Repulse* had made no moves, nor launched shuttles, but the *Moonstone* had raised her shields.

"That'll go down well; the *Peerless* is next to her two pals, which may be why," Apnis noted. "I'll head off before the other two get in."

"Tallica's on her way," the captain told Earbleat. "Keep our eyes on those ISA boats *and* the other two, and block scans. I'm in a meeting if Myrtleberry calls, and not to be disturbed on any account."

"Roger that, Cap," the second mate roared cheerfully. "And I'll get my teams onto running weapons diagnostics to pass the time."

Ahxenta groaned as she closed her link. "Keep me updated, Tallica. We'll finish as soon as we can. Warn Melly about the high jinks. Any meets we have will be aboard *Arianrhod*. I'm not coming down here if the place is swarming with ISA grunts and their officers. And yes, you can take time off after the talks, Azular."

"If my berth hasn't been commandeered," he said glumly, eyeing the scurrying around him. "I made it provisional."

"You can use mine: I'll be heading back aboard. Let's go."

In the event, Azular had no need of a berth, for Kerrix was too busy to spare the time. Before he had time to repine, she invited him aboard the *Moonstone* to work with Kinnitix on an upgrade for the UV-III, until a new system could be devised. The ships would be in port for days, and Kinnitix had ideas *and* the tech to begin testing. Ahxenta agreed, and left him and his kit to hitch a ride with his partner.

The captain set for the bridge as soon as her shuttle landed, whilst Lindell made for his office to work on contract revision. Ottolyx had agreed to the Keystone cargo transfer to the *Emerald*, now in dock, and *Arianrhod's* loading teams were pulling in her first load. Ahxenta had barely sat down when tactical called that the ISA ships *Matchless* and *Mirk Arrow* had made it in and were heading to berths close by them.

"*Matchless* is a long way from Lambda," Apnis said sourly. "And I've never heard of the other one – a destroyer, but a big one."

Greffy had been scouring databases. "She's a deep-range destroyer, ma'am. That's all I have."

Seconds later, comms called that Colonel Myrtleberry was on line and asking for the captain.

"I suppose I'd better see what she wants, but this'd better be short. Patch it through to my office, Mr Bellfish."

The talk was less short than hoped, for the captain was not back for an hour. "She wanted to know where the *Warrior* had gone, where we were for next, what the *Moonstone* was up to and how the contract for the comms arrays was coming along.”

“She keeps her fingers in a lot of pies,” Apnis commented. “Why does she keep trying when she knows you won’t tell her?”

“She thinks she’ll win by riling me. One of her stings was that the ISA’s dropped the charges against Horn, his defence being diminished capacity. But she won’t tell me the hearing outcome, it’s classified.”

“Huh! Did you make her day by letting her know that the *Kel’Torc* will be delivering the comms arrays to her HQ?”

“No; I’ll let it be a surprise. But she and her fleet may miss it. They look to be set for a mission beyond mapped space, given the number of ISA crewmen hijacking Web facilities. *Moonstone* hasn’t dropped her shields, and I bet her jammers are at full stretch.”

“They are,” the first mate said, eying her closely. “One of her stings, Cap? She had others?” she asked in a low voice.

“A couple, but nobody else’s business.”

Apnis let it rest. “How long’s Azular staying on the *Moonstone*?” she temporised. “He’d planned a cosy time in the Web, but that didn’t happen. So had we, for that matter. *Our* billets are retained.”

“Our people still to head down can use them, if most of the dorms are earmarked for ISA crews. Though I don’t expect the average grunt will expect to lodge in the inner belts, they’re too expensive. But all the bars will be hotbeds of the usual punch-ups from here on in.”

“*Half Moon’s* used to it, and our people can take care of themselves. Got news of the *Tallulah* while you were jawing with Myrtleberry. Most of her crew are mending and her repairs are half done. I’ll call Murmur to see how he is once I’m off duty. I may be able to dig up more than has been put out – and warn him about potential UV-III safety issues.”

“Good idea; that’ll chirk him up,” Ahxenta smiled. “I’ve a link or two to make as well.”

* * *

The captain and first mate met as usual in the mess for their late meal. Apnis had got a direct link to Fleetskup; he was at Delta Iridium still, and hopeful that his ship would be back to capacity in twelve days. He had been badly shaken, and only thankful that he had not lost any crew.

“I warned him about the UV-III, but only obliquely; but you know Murmur, subtlety’s lost on him. Spickle’s back on form *and* he’s been efficient, as he’s put together a spec of the hostile that hit them. I asked Murmur to send it to me, and he did. I’ll get Greffy to copy it to Azular. But he told me that the *Matchless* demanded all their data, from the time they detected the blip. She didn’t get it: his stations were so badly fried they couldn’t call it up. But his people *have* dug up stuff; not verified, but the ship that got them may've come from Blox. A boat from Milkit Major spied a heap of ISA activity near there and was warned to keep off. Blox is close to Milkit, the ship called it in; Fleetskup's from Milkit, and his Ma's there. How did your links go?" she probed delicately.

Ahxenta looked at her. "Nat and Kerrix, about Myrtleberry and her attempts to grill me; *and* her insinuations."

"About the pilot of the Sella ship," the first mate guessed. "I figured she'd been riding you on it. That woman has a nasty streak. She worked out you knew and had got the info via Admiral Posettix?"

"She did, but that's all she got. I called Grey but didn't say much, given what we suspect; I'll tell him later. Why the *Serenity's* been so long at ISA HQ I don't know. *Zetkalt's* still there, so it's maybe diplomacy. And I'm still sure Posettix has an agenda, but Kerrix won't say."

"*Captain* Kerrix," Apnis corrected mischievously. "How's Grey?"

"*Obsidian's* for Silshoon, then here. I didn't mention contracts as I used the UV-III: he knows about it. If Azular and Kinnitix *can* create a fix, we'll pass it by hand to the ships here. It'll have to be circulated to the fleet that way, so it'll take time. But the ops of it are beyond me."

"And me," the first mate confessed. "Any news from Thal?"

"No, but as he's cautious, it's no surprise. Starfall *can* link to its own ships covertly, so if something was up Kerrix would've said."

"Maybe Azular and Kinnitix could use the Starfall system as a base for a new UV?" Apnis suggested.

"No way. Thal wouldn't sanction it, and as it's based on hostile tech, it's not a good idea. Hostiles are out there, and as Thal's often a target, it may have intrinsic snags. What now?" she asked as her wrist unit trilled and a holo-note flowed out. "Azular; he's working late. I'll check what he's been at and let him in on what you found out about Blox."

Azular and Kinnitix did not have a UV-III fix, but had an idea. It needed specific parts and tools, and a tech used to delicate work. Parts were available on the *Moonstone*, but Azular wanted gear from his lab and consent to use Gem Ferry, who was known for fine work. As he thought it unwise that a shuttle from *Arianrhod* be seen to cross to the *Moonstone*, he suggested a meet in the Web next day. Ferry could return to the *Moonstone* with him. Greffy could sort out the kit.

"Gem will jump at the chance to have a look at the *Moonstone* from the inside," Apnis said. "And he's had his shore leave, so he won't miss out. But what's Captain Kerrix got to say about all this?"

"I'll find out. I may as well link from here. You want to sit in?"

"You bet."

* * *

The *Gadfly* had been left in a secure bay near marketing. It was ultra-busy, the captain saw, as she and Apnis walked in with an excited Gem Ferry. Azular, Kinnitix and the *Moonstone's* supercargo were in a booth. The super, there for trade talks, excused himself and left.

"*Moonstone* taking on cargo or is it a blind?" Apnis asked.

"I've no idea, Commander," Azular said smoothly. "I take it *that's* the kit I requested from Greffy, Lieutenant?"

"Aye sir. I've brought my gear as well, based on what's expected."

"Good. We've bits to pick up before we head up, ma'am," he told Ahxenta. "You're with me, Gem. Commander Kinnitix has to go, but will meet us at our shuttle in two hours; then we head to the ship."

"That was short," Apnis said as the three shot off. "He's desperate to get back aboard. *Half Moon* for us, to see what's washed up there?"

"Similar to what's washed up in here, *I* bet: half this lot have ISA uniforms on their backs. They're not here to trade."

"Spying on the people who are," the first mate came back.

The *Half Moon* was busy despite the early hour, with many ISA crew breakfasting. Most seemed to be upper rank. The muted conversation rose as the two officers walked up to the bar, from which vantage point their eyes swept the place. Several pairs of eyes looked back.

"Can't help themselves, Cap. Anyone in PSS uniform is fair game. Pa Ma'Lappis and his mate are over there: they probably got the same," Apnis laughed shortly as she returned stare for stare.

"Good morning, Captain, Commander," Ally's dulcet tones cut in as he hove to behind the bar. "Here for breakfast?"

"We've eaten," Ahxenta told him, turning back. "We'd early meets. What's with the ISA brass? You giving discounts for bulk-buy?"

He smirked. "No ma'am. But there *have* been a lot of ISA people in, from those ships up there. Most of them are hanging off *Arianrhod's* bows, I see," he added. "Looking for trouble?"

"They look hard enough and they'll find it," she replied. "We'll have ales. Any of these parties been asking questions?"

"Aye ma'am. The captain at the table by the holo-vid, the one with red hair that's sat with two others; *she* asked if you used my place, when you last were in here, and how long you'd been in port," he said darkly as he set two full mugs on the bar. "I told her I didn't keep tabs on my customers and to ask your people if she wanted details."

"Kresta Goldcriss of the *Matchless*," Apnis drawled. "She has a fancy boat with high-class scanners that she's not afraid to use."

"I take it *Arianrhod's* had a run-in with her, Captain?" Ally asked.

"Just let's say we've met before and leave it at that. Put these on a tab, Ally. We'll sit over there. They can all look if they want."

Two topers in a dim recess in the far reaches of the *Half Moon* were doing just that. "I see they're both armed to the gunnels," Malty noted.

"So I see," Jurry agreed. "Setting privacy won't stop the nosy types, but I doubt anybody'll scan: every ISA officer knows the *Arianrhod* and her skipper. And what she's liable to do to them if they cross her."

Malty belched. "Nobody here we can dun for a mug, they're all high rank. Can't have much to do if they're sat filling their faces. Might be worth heading to outer nine: the grunts billeted there will be silting up the *Frozen Sunbeam*. This place'll get lively later, once the big guns have drifted off to what they usually do. What's *that* coming in?"

The stir heralded a face familiar to Ahxenta. "Hell, what's *she* doing here? I wouldn't have thought the *Half Moon* was her style."

"She heard we were in and wants a chinwag?" Apnis guessed. "And who's the captain along of her? *Her* first mate?"

"Extra pair of ears," the captain replied as she set a jammer in view, glowering at the ISA colonel, who was shrewdly looking about.

Myrtleberry noticed the two, and gave a curt nod. Ahxenta returned it coolly. The colonel turned to speak to her associate, and call Ally. He filled two beakers and the pair took them up, but their eyes were drawn by a buzz as two others, in black PSS uniforms, came in. Ally looked relieved, smiled a greeting, and slid down the bar to speak to them.

"Captain, Commander, what can I get you?"

They ordered ales, and ignoring the stares of the ISA duo, looked around. The captain spied Ahxenta and set off with an aside to Ally.

"May we join you, Captain?"

"Please do, Captain," Ahxenta replied swiftly, resetting the privacy shield she had released when she realised who they were.

"Myrtleberry's vexed," Apnis noted. "Bet she still comes over."

"Ally's bringing drinks," Kerrix said. "Azular told us you'd be here. I'd like a few words, but this is *not* the place, with all those ears pricked. And one scanner on a direct line," she scowled, checking a wrist device.

"Who?" Ahxenta demanded sharply.

"The one I'm going to stop," was the sharp retort as Kerrix stood up and set off deliberately for a table in their line of sight, the warning from her first mate going unheeded.

"Whew! What's to do there, Jurry?" Malty rasped as he took in the sight. "Captain Kerrix looks mighty put out. And given her style when she worked in *this* place, my credit's on her to win the argument."

The argument was short, ending in weapons fire and a furious tirade by the captain of the *ISAS Matchless* that Kerrix ignored as she marched back to her table, her face set like stone.

"You fried her scanner," *Arianrhod's* captain greeted her. "You're lucky she or one of her subs didn't drop you."

"One was about to, but spied my backup," Kerrix smiled. "Captain Ma'Lappis heard every word and set his phase rifle; *and* his first mate recorded the incident. I doubt an ISA captain would sanction a scrap in here anyway. I'll copy you in on my data – the spec of the scanner, its targeting, and the person using it."

"Neat, but there goes *her* boss to find out what went on," warned Apnis, inclining her head towards the fuming colonel. "She's trouble."

"Tough," Kerrix replied, as Ally stepped up with the drinks and the news that the livid Myrtleberry had threatened words with her, once she had learnt the cause of the ruckus.

The four at the table were ready. Ahxenta reminded her opposite number of the info-sent status of the colonel, and advised caution.

"I want a word with you!" Myrtleberry snapped, eyeing her badge. "It's Kerrix of the *Moonstone*, isn't it? What was that farce about?"

"That captain was spying on us with a scanner-recorder of recent Norvallan fleet issue. She refused to desist. I ended her illegal intrusion into our business. She objected to my actions, and one of her officers tried to shoot me. He was foiled by the actions of fellow PSS officers. Their evidence *and* mine will be in my protest to your fleet HQ, copied to others as I see fit. Your move."

"You haven't heard the last of this!" the colonel barked.

"I sincerely hope not," Kerrix shot back.

"Where's the device you used to detect what you imply was used to scan you? And what is it?"

"My property," was the equable reply. "The output of which *will* be used when I bring charges."

"You're bluffing. I suggest you get back to your own business and do not interfere with my people."

"I am not bluffing, Colonel, and I *will* interfere when I and mine are put at risk or spied on by anyone, *your* fleet included."

"You've not heard the last of this," the colonel reiterated.

"Good," Kerrix said astringently to her back view.

"You've made an enemy there, Cap," Inks told her.

"To be honest, Jesse, I'd rather have her as an enemy than a friend. Gives you candy one day, stabs you in the back the next."

"You realise if you *do* put in a formal complaint, you'll end up in an endless round of argument," Ahxenta said to her.

"Not if I send it by Admiral Posettix and ask him to handle the legal issues," she grinned. "There are two Starfall ships due in here, one of which is for Alto Finglas. I'll use her as courier, in the event she does try to scupper me, or the ISA *has* cracked the UV-III."

"A Starfall ship for Alto Finglas?" queried Apnis.

"Perhaps we'd best finish up here and make tracks for somewhere private," Kerrix suggested. "And here's Captain Ma'Lappis."

Ma'Lappis had come for details, and to pass on his first mate's data. He sat until the others had done, all aware that they were the mark of every eye. In the murky booth at the back, Malty turned to his mate.

"I reckon we'll be able to hang in and profit from that action. Word will fly round quicker than a flea with a rocket up its arse."

"You got it," Jurry agreed. "There they go. More talking, I guess."

Talking was deferred until the four cleared the *Half Moon*. Marketing was chosen, as the gear the PSS officers carried was adequate to assure privacy. Once secure, Kerrix handed over a shard of the data her wrist scanner had caught, and then came to the point: the Starfall ship for Alto Finglas was the *PSS Kel'Lath*. She was due in from her home port of Nexus to pick up pods of goods for transfer to the *Serenity*. The view of some people at ISA HQ was that the Norvallan ship had outstayed her welcome, and supply being a sticky issue with the ISA, *Serenity* had decided to bring in her own. The second Starfall ship due in had been sent by Captain Thal to escort the *Moonstone* and the *Arianrhod* to Delta Iridium; there, each would take on a cargo of medical supplies and then head out to meet the *Kel'Moth* at Limekiln. The escort was not a PSS but a newly outfitted heavy cruiser: the *SS Firestorm*.

Ahxenta caught her breath. "Captain *Dexel* Thal's in command?"

"He is. He asked for the job," she smiled wryly. "The five ISA ships are taxing Captain Vexin Thal: neither he nor Vetta can find out what their mission is. Their top guess is that they're for an exploratory cruise and they'll head out past Alpha, but our Nexus Station's in the area, so we have our suspicions. And as we'll be setting out for Cygilla along of you – I've a cargo for Spelter – their eyes will be on us."

"So we provide something to focus on?" Apnis put in cuttingly.

"More or less," she replied, but her eyes were on her fellow captain.

"You've a cargo for Spelter. That must have passed my supercargo by. May I ask what it is?"

"I didn't pick it up here, Captain, I got it at Vreskota. Part-exchange for the cargo I dropped there. Small pods of rare cereal grains for trials on Spelter. I'll leave you and the *Firestorm* at Cygilla and rejoin you there for the trip to Selliden, as I've heavy medical gear for them. We'll settle our onward route to Delta later, as things will change."

Ahxenta did not disagree, and the four debated the next steps for both ships, up to the time they planned to leave the Web. As they were wrapping up, the captain of the *Arianrhod* brought up an issue that had raised her curiosity. How did Kerrix read Goldcriss' scanner-recorder's output so accurately if it was of *recent* Norvallan fleet issue?

"Simple," said Kerrix. "Admiral Posettix gave me this wrist-scan at Starfall. As you're aware, most data-based fleet kit can self-update by linking to relevant already-updated units within range, including handhelds. My unit linked to hers the second I walked into the *Half Moon*, and did just that. I doubt she was even aware."

"I thought there were measures in place to foil covert updating."

"There are, but this is senior command level kit, it's bonded to me, and will operate if attached. And I keep it set to rove for new data."

Ahxenta shook her head ruefully and the group set off to the level four shuttle bays, where they parted company amicably.

"The *Firestorm*," said Apnis, once she and Ahxenta had reached their ride. "Dexel Thal thinks he owes us?"

"Could be. But he's Starfall, he'll have top range anti-scan gear and the best of weaponry. Myrtleberry and her chums won't get anything he doesn't want them to get."

"What's the betting she'll find out when we're due out and make sure she and her happy band are at our backs?" Apnis grumped.

"Her crews are on shore leave," the captain reminded her first mate as they stepped aboard the *Gadfly*. "And as agreed, we'll be set to move as soon as our cargoes are loaded and the *Firestorm* gets in."

"The *Moonstone's* supercargo in marketing *was* a blind!"

"It was, as Lindell will be when he goes down later. Our billets will be held until we ship out and I've booked a meeting room for two days after we leave. As Grey will have meets here when *Obsidian* gets in, I'll transfer it to him. He's due late tomorrow."

"You're getting to be sneakier than Tallulah Tommy, Cap."

"Wash your mouth out with soap, Commander."

* * *

Over the next three days, the *Obsidian Sky* made port and Ahxenta met her captain for a private talk and to hand over a short term fix for the UV-III. She had met Goodsocks and the captains of the other PSS ships still in the Web for the same purpose. The latter included Captain Olith Dun of the *Kel'Lath*, which had arrived two days before.

Azular and Kinnitix had had partial success, and had created a data shard that worked as a plug-in code-decode device. It would randomly scramble outward links in such a way that they would be decoded when received by a vessel with UV-III send-receive tech and the plug-in. The device used complex crystal-based tech that Kinnitix had scavenged from his captain's wrecked fighter. They had produced several shards and were hopeful that more could be got from Letik, as that planet was upping its assembly of advanced crystal tech as well as supplying gem-grade jurillium and quality crystals for other markets. However, both officers believed that a totally new system was the best option for the PSS fleet, but were little forward with a concept. *Arianrhod's* captain called a halt to the work: she needed her science officer in post.

The *SS Firestorm* was also in. The flutter her arrival had caused in Port Control was soothed by her captain's calm compliance with rules. She had declared no cargo manifest, but paid her fees at the harbour office as required. No ship tried to deep probe, but surface scans were activated and sustained by the *Peerless* and the *Matchless*.

Ahxenta had done her tasks and she and Apnis were set to catch up to Azular and Kerrix in marketing. The latter had Levettiza with her, and after final tactics had been agreed, the five made their way out, aware that several ISA personnel had eyes on them. They made for the *Half Moon*, where they intended to fill listening ears with fiction.

Ally was quick to fetch Ahxenta's order. "Business over for the day, I take it, ma'am?" he asked.

"It is," she agreed. "You're busier than usual this early."

"We have been, ever since the military came in. They've not caused much upset. The lower ranks stick to outer belt bars early on, but roll in later, to visit the green twelve nightclubs. Eating here, ma'am?"

"We may as well," Ahxenta said. "You all right with that, Captain?"

Kerrix smiled. "I am. I know the high quality of the food in here."

Ally preened, pointing out the quietest spot. "I'll get your orders as soon as I can," he promised. "Most of this lot haven't ordered yet."

"I'll set privacy," Ahxenta said as they sat, looking sharply round at the nearby tables "Too many eyes and ears tuned in."

Most of the faces attached to the eyes and ears pursed their lips and make comments to one another, some meant to be overheard.

Apnis grinned. "They're taking it personally, Captain."

"Good. Set up that list of Redship tenders, Commander, and we'll see what we can bid for," the captain replied, activating privacy.

Their meals ordered, the five talked over likely contracts and sipped ale, Azular's primed jammer-scanner clearly visible. No-one interfered, but many stared. Soon after their food arrived, Ahxenta took a holo-note that told her that *Arianrhod's* loading was complete. She smiled in content. She knew the *Moonstone* was already prepped.

The meal was laced with chat as the *Half Moon* filled, until the noisy arrival of a bunch of non-comms sparked activity. Ahxenta and Kerrix made to the bar to settle tabs, their looks and loose phase rifles quelling any approach, though they were eyed by an officer whose insignia placed him as the captain of the *ISAS Mirk Arrow*. His colleague, also a captain, stared coldly at Levettiza, who smiled tranquilly in passing.

Once clear of the bar, Kerrix drew a deep breath. "Tranger of the *Advance*," she said. "Looking daggers at *you*, Vetta."

"She's not forgiven me for leaving her ship after the battle at Telzilt, for the *Moonstone*. She's a good officer, but a stickler for rules and loyal to the service. I don't know Tatter of the *Mirk Arrow*, but he was giving you and Captain Ahxenta the once-over."

"I noticed. Let's hope he picked up on the vague promises we made to Ally to see him in a day or so."

"Others will have," Azular put in as they turned down a side way, to come face to face with a group of well-oiled troopers.

The leader of the pack bowed facetiously as he and his cronies made way for the five, but he made the mistake of grabbing Kerrix' arm and insisting that she dance with him, to the hoots of his chums. Before a furious Azular could intervene, the man hit the deck, clasping his groin. Ahxenta's left hook floored two others who had jumped in as the battle began. It was soon over: Apnis and Azular had drawn hand-guns as Vetta replied to her attacker with a well-aimed kick. The gunfire alerted those nearby, and a stentorian voice rang out over the racket.

"*What* is going on here?"

Ahxenta looked up, wiping a streak of blood from her face. "Yours, I believe, Colonel," she said caustically, pointing to the heap of bodies on the floor. "The evidence of their assault on us will have been caught by that security cam. I *will* be in touch over the matter, believe me."

The captain turned on her heel and set off, followed by the others, Myrtleberry's voice echoing along the passageway.

"We're still the flavour of the month, then," Apnis noted.

"As ever," Ahxenta replied. "Those lower-deck grunts will be in for epic ear-bashings and disciplinaries. Want to call Kit Biernop, if he's about, for a quick chat? He's not security but he's close, and he'll be able to get the output of that cam before Myrtleberry's lackeys."

Apnis nodded and sent the call. "He'll meet us in marketing," she said. "He'll be there in ten."

Kerrix and Levettiza left as Biernop arrived. The talk was short and the issue quickly settled. A call and a trip to security yielded the relevant footage, and after a swift farewell, the three set off for their ride.

"This nonsense will tighten our schedule if Myrtleberry's up for a jawing to persuade you to drop it, Cap," Apnis warned once aboard their shuttle. "I expect she's still ranting at that bunch of hooligans."

"She'll have the evidence as soon as I'm aboard; what she does with it is up to her. But we follow our plan."

* * *

Hours later, the metallic Web of light and power of Merkat Three Free Port was dimming as the mighty structure prepared for planetary night. *Arianrhod* sat fast in her dock, the tiny lights of search and repair drones winking on her hull. The ship was darklit, but soft illumination behind her engaged fine-mesh cargo bay safety shields cast flickering shadows. The captain sat hand on fist in her chair, having earlier fended off the insistent Colonel Myrtleberry. Every bridge station was manned and each officer in turn called out operational readiness.

"Bring in our drones," Ahxenta ordered. "Links to *Moonstone* and *Firestorm* active, comms?"

"Links active, ma'am," Bellfish confirmed.

"Course plotted and laid in for Cygilla, helm?"

"Affirmative, ma'am. Ready to go on your mark," replied Dox.

A scan of her boards confirming that the drones were retrieved and secure, the captain gave the ready engines order. Seconds later, comms called that the *Moonstone* had applied for and been given clearance to depart. Ahxenta pushed the relevant toggle and requested the same, but was asked to hold. As tactical verified that the *Moonstone* had cleared her berth, *Arianrhod's* authorisation was issued.

"Power us up, Crizz. Ready to take us out us, helm."

Slowly, to a rising thrum, the ship awoke, the glow of her pink hull intensifying as each exterior locus made ready to engage. The lancing red lights of her berth picked out her shape, and one by one melted to green as *Arianrhod* broke free of her struts and slid out into free space.

"Turn us about and make to follow the *Moonstone*, helm."

"Affirmative, ma'am," Dox responded as she brought the huge ship in a tight arc into optimum position and set course.

"I see the *Firestorm's* powering up," the first mate noted. "How long until Myrtleberry realises she's been outfoxed?"

"Not long," Ahxenta grinned. "Get me the *Moonstone*, comms."

All was set, Kerrix stated. They would hold as agreed at the outmost beacon for their escort to catch up. At that point, Azular called that the *Peerless* had sent scan beams after them. The warning was echoed by Nyvallish of the *Moonstone*.

"They'll get nothing," said Kerrix. "Captain Thal's aware that he'll be a target, so he'll be shielded. I have him on screen," she added.

"Roger that," Ahxenta agreed, her eyes glued to her tactical grid.

The *Firestorm* reached their position in twenty minutes, and the three ships formed into a tight wedge, *Arianrhod* in the lead.

"Lock onto the local bypass beacon and set for Cygilla, helm. Match course and speed with the *Moonstone*."

"Locked on, ma'am. Links to *Moonstone* and *Firestorm* secure. Time to bypass approximately fifty minutes."

"So when does the fun begin, Cap?" Apnis asked archly.

"Once somebody tells Myrtleberry."

It did not take long for word to reach the colonel, for a call came in for the captain shortly after the three vessels had made the bypass.

"She wanted a face-to-face over the bust-up *and* a guarantee that I'd not press charges. She was put out that I wouldn't play ball, tell her our heading or why we're in company," Ahxenta told her first mate. "I rode her over the *Peerless* and her scans, but you know Myrtleberry."

"I do. *Will* you push over the scrap with her minions, Cinnabar?"

"I've left it to our legal rep, but Web security may file charges. The TA and our fleet know, and I don't give a damn, but if it riles the ISA, all to the good. We've plenty to keep us busy from here to Cygilla."

* * *

The activity over the ten days to their first stop included a promotion ceremony. The party meant a break, but comms home were forbidden, as the captain did not want a hint of their position to get out. The three ships made Cygilla Prime on time, where the *Moonstone* left to continue to Spelter and her cargo drop.

"The Redship cargo's big," Apnis remarked to Ahxenta. "It'll take us two days local time to despatch it. Inspections and admin will mean another one. We hold for the *Moonstone*?"

"We do. Spelter's just down the bypass, so she'll be quick. There's been zip from ISA fleet HQ on the protest over Goldcriss and her spying in the *Half Moon*, or the gun her sub pulled. I checked the detail Pa Ma'Lappis got: the gun was set for heavy stun. Myrtleberry's not responded to the security evidence of our run-in with those grunts, but she wants to know where she or her rep can contact me in person."

"She still wants to know where we're headed."

"Yup. If she and her squadron are set for outer Alpha, she shouldn't come close, but hell knows where other ISA boats are on patrol, with our name and the *Moonstone's* on their list of ships to look out for."

"Just as well we got our holo-grid upgraded," grinned Apnis. "ISA news will be added in as we get it."

The two were interrupted by a call from the *Firestorm*. The captain took it in her office and was gone only minutes. On return, the bridge holo was ordered to full stretch and Bellfish told to stand by for a link from the *Firestorm*, the data to be added to the holo immediately.

"You're psychic," Apnis was told. "Thal's sending a bite caught by a Starfall ship skimming the edges of the Star Desert near Milkit: huge energy washes and an expanding flak field at the Lambda-Delta border. She closed in to check and it was Blox: five ISA battlecruisers and two hostiles fighting it out and half the planet ablaze. She left them to it and called it in to Twilight. Once we've got it, I'll see if Zillah's available and can shed any light, but I'd guess that an ISA patrol found a hidden base and the ISA ordered the troops in before the aliens could react."

Ahxenta was close: a Freskat fleet ship had spied activity off Blox and sent in a probe, which had read surface and orbital craft. The ship reported it, the admiral notified the local ISA office and the chief there ordered every warship in the area in, without waiting HQ go-ahead.

"The result she's not heard, but the action got rid of two of the battlecruisers hanging off Freskat. She expects the ISA press office will put it out as a victory for the good guys and pat itself on the back. I won't send it out on the UV-III lest the wrong ears pick it up and it's traced back to Zillah. She's one contact we don't want to lose."

"No: we trade on Freskat regularly. But no comm is totally secure, so wrong ears may have caught your link to her," Apnis said.

"It's always a risk, but space is a big place. Delivery going ok?"

It was, the first mate assured her, and the two settled down to keep their eyes on the work ongoing and catch up with other issues.

It took a full three days for the task to be completed to the standard Ahxenta required. She had Lindell search for new contracts and make enquiries; she had no intention of raising curiosity in those who spied on the PSS fleet. She was glad she did: as the final invoices were signed off, her tactical officer alerted her that a ship was on approach to Cygillan space. It was the destroyer *ISAS Iris Quartz*.

Ahxenta checked her boards and ordered the meshes of her openwork aft cargo bays down. That would protect the cargo left there, close the bays to prying eyes and ready the ship for departure. She also had her stations keep their eyes on the inward-bound ISA vessel. Space around Cygilla Prime was usually busy and a new arrival would raise no dust at Port Control, but this one worried her.

"I bet this isn't a social call," her first mate grunted.

"You and me both. Last time we met *her* was after Thal's transport shot out of that failing worm-pocket, and she followed us to Polstarn and Stinward then. Get me the *Firestorm*, comms."

"He'll have spotted her, *and* he'll remember her," Apnis was sure.

Thal *had* recognised the *Iris Quartz* and had set to jam. The captains agreed not to initiate contact, but both wanted to know her intentions. Ahxenta tried to find out, and shortly after had a partial result.

"She's not for resupply or talks in the ISA office," she said to Apnis. "But Cygilla's on a direct line to Silverglass, so she maybe has business there. And we're close to Skota and Sella: the ISA won't have finished with what's there."

"But she might have another motive – us."

"Possibly. Lindell's contact will keep her eyes and ears open, but we may find out more at CP Met Systems' orbital office. The client knows us, there are tenders available, its contracts office has hinted at more and we've a meet in two hours. Lindell will be there, as he knows the reps. We can't accept this time, but we can keep them sweet. And then we visit the *Spectrum Bar*: it's in the orbital business sector, it's clean and people involved in local trade use it."

"Does this *we* include me?" Apnis asked slyly.

"Yes, and Azular. We'll wear locating pins as a precaution. Earbleat will have the conn, but I don't expect the *Iris Quartz* will try anything."

"With Whisper in charge, she'd be rash just to look us over," Apnis chuckled. "But a trade trip is an excuse for our being here. I bet Gulley will get a jolt when the *Moonstone* comes in. Are you letting Thal in on what Lindell picked up from his friend?"

"I'll do that before we leave. In fact, I'll do it now, as we have time.

We'll take the *Gadfly*. Gulley will no doubt track us, but he knows better than to try any tricks. He was fairly reasonable once he found out about Horn and what the ISA had pulled at Stinward, so he's got integrity, but he's firmly ISA. I'd like to know who gave him his orders."

"You're not likely to find out, Cap. There's been no move from that ship since she got in, but it's early yet."

The *Gadfly* was prepped when the four made her bay. Ahxenta had decided against a security escort, but she had their locating pins tracked from the bridge. The client's orbital office was easy to reach and had a docking station. Two reps awaited them, one of whom was Lindell's contact. After two hours of talk, they had a fifteen minute walk along the corridors of the business sector to the *Spectrum Bar*, but they found the place quiet and placed their orders at their table.

"The CP reps don't know any more of why the *Iris Quartz* is here, then, as far as you're aware?" the captain asked Azular.

"No ma'am, they were baffled, as was the senior manager we spoke to. She wasn't expected, but being on a line to Silverglass and in a busy sector, there must be a regular stream of fleet traffic in and out."

"Possibly," Ahxenta agreed. "None of her crew are in here, so not a furlough stop. Earbleat will tell us if she sends out a shuttle."

Their waiter had no idea of why the ISA ship had hauled in, though her presence was leading to talk. A chat with customers at nearby tables produced nothing, and as the captain preferred to be aboard if the *Iris Quartz* attempted any move, she soon called a halt, and the four made ready to leave. They had barely stood up when Ahxenta took an alert from Earbleat: a shuttle had exited the ISA ship and was heading their way, possibly for the local ISA office. It was at the other side of their current location but it used the common docking facilities.

"They've got to know we're here," the first mate said. "Though I don't suppose we're the object of their business."

"I want to make the *Gadfly* before they get in, so move it," Ahxenta said. "But where's the *Iris Quartz* come from and where she's headed? Cygilla's handy for a lot of places, such as that Flit to Portal bypass on the Eta-Theta border that Thal told us of, that led to that tech-ridden whirlpool of a synthetic worm-pocket he dived into. And the *Iris* was part of the equation then, once he'd shot out the other end."

"You reckon it might be more on that stuff? The sneaky Admiral Best of fleet HQ pushed you on that, didn't he, Cap? And isn't Portal, as well as Skota, Furze and Fourpoint, still marked on the ISA alert list as off-limits because they pose substantial risk to shipping?"

"They and Sella were highlighted on the grid when we hauled into

Cygillan space, which suggests that the ISA still has a presence at each of them. But we'd not be party to that kind of info, and they'd want the likes of us keeping well away."

"In other words, things are still going on there and snoops are not welcome," said Apnis. "But we're traders! Why would we want to poke our noses into what the ISA and it's chums are doing?"

"Unless they affect us personally, Commander," Azular told her.

She continued to argue, but they could only guess at the purpose of an ISA destroyer off a planet where the major concerns were tourism and trade, despite a small ISA office, there because of the bypass route to the major ISA holding station of Silverglass.

"Enough," the captain warned. "Here we are."

"And there *they* are," Azular added mildly, nodding towards three individuals that had just stepped through a bay door.

Ahxenta recognised Captain Morgen Gulley, nodded as he spotted them, and turned to open her bay. She halted when he called her name.

"Parley?" Apnis whispered in her ear.

Ahxenta's greeting was short. "Can I help you, Captain?"

His formal reply and trite remarks on trade in the area hid an agenda that was clear to her. He noted casually that the *Arianrhod* still had the *Firestorm* as escort, but the *Moonstone* was no longer with the group that had set off from the Web, and asked after her whereabouts.

Ahxenta was incensed but kept calm. "May I ask how you knew I'd come from the Web, and with whom?" she asked, a dangerous glint in her eyes. "*And* why you want to know where the *Moonstone* is?"

"I receive reports," was the ambiguous reply.

"So do I, but not on the private dealings of ships or people that do not or should not concern me. Please answer my questions."

"You were in the company of two Starfall ships, one a heavy cruiser. Starfall's increasing its role in the PSS fleet if it's sending escorts out."

"Several Starfall ships fly the Trades Alliance flag. If you want more details on it and them, I suggest you call Starfall HQ and don't waylay me. And you still have not answered my questions," she reminded him. "Please do so."

Gulley was no fool but nor was he inclined to give her answers. He bluntly stated that he would not give his sources nor outline his orders but his enquiries related to the ISA and he was within his rights as an ISA officer to make them. Ahxenta doubted *that*, she told him shortly, but whatever *his* rights were, their infringing on *hers* was a breach of her privacy and that of her fellow vessels. She bid him a curt farewell with the warning that any further violation of her liberties would be answered by a complaint to his superiors and a protest to the TA. The buzz of her wrist communit sped her steps, and she and her crewmen turned into their bay, watched by the three ISA officers.

The captain said nothing until they were locked in the *Gadfly*, when she called *Arianrhod* to talk to Earbleat. A note from the *Firestorm* with Starfall news had come in, she was told. The arrival of the *Kel'Torc* at Alto Finglas to drop the crystal arrays had caused a stir, and it was likely that the ISA supply office would raise the issue with her.

"Best get home," Apnis grinned. "When the news gets to Gulley, more sparks will fly, especially as the *Kel'Lath* won't be far behind the *Kel'Torc*. The ISA must have been notified by its Web office that we'd left with the *Moonstone* and the *Firestorm*, and I bet the ISA office here let out that we'd pulled in a few days ago but the *Moonstone* had left. The *Iris Quartz* was likely still in the area, so she was sent in to ask rude questions, as Gulley knows us. The ISA wants to know what we're up to, as our links to Thal, and his links to Psi concerns, and his bypasses, are irritating its upper echelons. *They* still have two ambassadors in their hair that they must want rid of, but on the best of terms, as well as an admiral that's digging into ISA secrets."

"And they can't tell them to leave. The ISA Council signed treaties: ripping them up isn't part of the equation. And from all I've heard of Norvallan nature, they're for long term diplomatic chit chat. What did you get from Gulley, Azular?" the captain asked as she set her engines.

"He was uncomfortable with what he was asking, ma'am. He'd been given his orders, I'd guess, but didn't relish carrying them out."

"I felt he was ill at ease, but his agenda was to find out what we and our friends are at. The sooner we're off the better; once the *Moonstone* gets in, he'll have more upper brass on his back. Though I don't think he'd be ordered to trail us — that would be a step too far."

Lindell was puzzled by another aspect. "Curious coincidence that we were set to leave just as he and his arrived. Who told him we'd done our meet and had stopped off at the bar?"

"The local ISA office," the captain said. "The complex is rife with security cams; it has to be, as it's so busy and there's a lot of trade and thus credit about. He didn't scan us, but you can bet we had eyes on us. It's happened before. And *Arianrhod* is the only PSS in at present."

In the short time it took for the shuttle to reach the ship, Earbleat was again on the comm. She had heard from the *Moonstone*. She was on her way from Spelter and would be with them in six hours.

"That'll make it close of business hours in this sector," the first mate noted. "I take it we'll head out as soon as she gets in?"

"That would be my choice, but I'll call Captain Kerrix. I expect she knows we have the *Iris Quartz* in our sights."

Once the *Gadfly* was docked, the captain made to her office to call. An hour later, *Arianrhod* was readied for departure. It had been decided that the *Moonstone* would halt at the beacon. She would be seen, as the ISA and others had local surveillance posts, but it would prevent undue interest; and as the shuttle from the *Iris Quartz* had not returned to her ship, it was unlikely that the *Quartz* would attempt pursuit.

The request for exit clearance by the *Arianrhod* and the *Firestorm* was a surprise; a flurry of activity ensued before it was granted, but when it was, they made good speed once clear of Cygillan space. The *Moonstone* reached the beacon barely half an hour behind them, and their course set, the three made the bypass jump for Epsilon, where most systems were aligned with the former ISP and could thus be regarded friendly. The crossing to Selliden was well-travelled and alarms were unlikely, but all three ships ran cloaked and silent. Their advent at Selliden *would* be reported: the resident ISA office would see to that.

There was little news of the Web or Alto Finglas over the four day trip. *Arianrhod* had her cargo of engineering parts ready for fast release. The captain estimated two days turnaround, which would provide time for a talk about the route to Delta Iridium with Kerrix and Dexel Thal, given no ISA interference.

Kerrix was first to hear of the events at Alto Finglas, and passed the details to Ahxenta and Thal in a short three-way link. The Starfall ships had caused an outcry, in spite of their PSS tags. Turret, refusing to wait until the supply chief had checked with Ahxenta that the *Kel'Torc's* load was bona fide, had called his bluff on delaying its delivery. His bosses had overruled him and the goods had been sent down, but the fee had not been paid on receipt, on the excuse that the arrays had to be quality tested. Turret's protest was copied to the TA office, which had to act: her second position had been immediate and public legal action. The ensuing entry of the *Kel'Lath* into local space had raised hackles when the *Serenity* told the port office she was there to deliver a cargo to her. As a diplomatic ship, the ISA had no right to question or scan what the *Serenity* intended to bring aboard, but Admiral Posettix agreed to probing of the pods and contents, explaining that they were essentials that the ISA supply depot had refused to provide.

"It caused acute red faces," Kerrix said. "And the admiral got my protest over the deeds of Tranger and her trigger-happy sub in the *Half Moon*. Captain Dun handed him the evidence personally, and he'll act. The ambassadors are still trading talk with the ISA. One catch is the security of links home, which both distrust. But as Norvalla wants a preliminary treaty of alliance with the ISA ratified and Telzilt doesn't, it's tricky. Trade and other contracts have been agreed, but the doings at Amity, Kilda and elsewhere have clouded the issue. The admiral and Captain Heltakt see eye to eye: they want a rapid exit from ISA space, but they're tied by protocol."

The next stage of their journey to Delta was talked over and agreed, whilst *Arianrhod* was unloading under the eyes of her first mate. A holo-note sent into her office towards the end of the chat caused the captain to smile: the *Nyx Warrior* had come in and hailed them. Kerrix had got the same news from Inks, and she and Ahxenta decided that a talk to her captain to pass on a plug-in code-decode device and explain its use would be a wise use of time. Ahxenta undertook to contact him.

The captain of the *Nyx Warrior* realised that his peers had matters they did not intend to share in ship-to-ship links, and agreed to early talks with them and their aides in the aptly named *Skipper's Rest*, a well-known hostelry on the outskirts of Selliden's main city that had plenty of landing bays. As he had been asked to bring along his senior science officer, he left his first mate to oversee his own cargo drop.

"You're looking well, Nat," Ahxenta greeted him, pleased to see that none of his injuries were apparent and that his step was easy and light as he and his science officer walked over from the bar.

Azular and Kinnitix were with their captains, and after a round of small talk, the six found a quiet table. The *Warrior* had come in from Vrackin with gear for Selliden, Holdspan told them; he would resupply before making for his next pick up in the Web. He had had no trouble en route, nor had impolite comms on his business come from the ISA. Ahxenta warned him that she had been quizzed on his movements, her own and that of the *Moonstone*, by Myrtleberry, and gave a rundown of events in the Web and at Cygilla. The ISA was clearly keeping tabs on various ships, particularly theirs.

Ahxenta then came to the point, and as they sipped drinks, Azular and Kinnitix described the concept of the code-decode device, handed over two, and explained that they *would* produce more, but their current resources were limited. As the *Warrior* was for the Web and many of the PSS fleet used it as a base, it being the largest trade centre from Alpha through Mu, Captain Holdspan was likely to meet another PSS that would benefit from the spare, and could use his discretion.

Ahxenta and Kerrix thought it wise that he remain ignorant of their next moves, but he was sure it involved Starfall, given the *Firestorm*. He had a cargo to pick up from Redship, he said, and would then head to

Epsilon for more, his final stop, via Wester 287, being his home port of Nyx. With a mutual exchange of civilities, the group parted.

Ahxenta found on return that Captain Bluejohn had called to speak to her. He told Apnis that the five ISA ships had left the Web in a body thirty six hours before on a heading that would take them to the bypass node on a line for Quartic Cross. That implied an onward route to Alto Finglas, but the captain of the newly-arrived *Equinox*, whom Bluejohn had met in marketing, told him that the five had passed *his* ship on the direct bypass to Jurassa station, in the opposite direction.

"I passed *that* to Jesse Inks and Dexel Thal," the first mate told her. "That course will put them damnably close to Nexus, so Starfall should know. Grey didn't elaborate on what he wants to speak to you about," she added, her brow creasing. "He said it wasn't exactly vital, but you should hear it sooner rather than later."

It *was* important, and to more than her, Ahxenta realised, when they spoke. Two of Bluejohn's senior officers had been waylaid separately by Captain Vint Skarfin, first officer of the *Peerless*, and quizzed on the *Arianrhod* and her route. The colonel allegedly needed an urgent talk with her captain and had to know where she could be reached. Skarfin had no success, but Bluejohn was then called by Myrtleberry, whose remarks included personal details about Ahxenta, and finds on Sella by the ISA said to be relevant to her. *That* led Bluejohn to suspect that the UV-III had been breached, and the link Ahxenta had made to him from the Web about the Sella incident, and the attempts by Myrtleberry to extract information from her, had been intercepted.

"Damn!" she cursed. "I called Nat Holdspan over the UV-III about the same thing, as it was relevant to him. At least *this* link's safe; and as the *Warrior's* here and I've given Nat the code-decode fix, his ship will be secure from here on. I'll pass your news to him; and we'll have to get it out that the UV-III should not be used to pass on private data or information. We're running low on the batch of shards that Azular and Kinnitix made, and won't be able to get more materials until we make Starfall. Did Myrtleberry push you on what the ISA found at Furze?" Ahxenta added delicately. "She must know *we* know, which implies that we have the means to find out what the ISA and its chums are up to."

"She did, in an indirect way," Bluejohn confirmed. "That's maybe why she's really pushing you and Nat, and possibly Captain Kerrix and the Starfall ships: as you know more than most, especially about her doings and the ISA's, she reckons you've got a way of finding out."

"We have, but it's none of her damned business. It's called watching your back, as *she* should know more than most," Ahxenta replied. "But she will want to put a stop to it, as we want to pull the plug on her and the ISA's infiltration of the UV-III. Azular and Kinnitix are right; they see a totally new comms system for the fleet as the only way to halt the info leak. Their fix will hold for a bit, but some bright spark *will* crack it. And like it or not, the ISA has a lot of bright sparks in its pocket."

She was interrupted by an urgent hail from Apnis: Captain Kerrix had had a link from her home base that the *ISAS Iris Quartz* had left Cygilla and was racing through the bypass on a direct line for Selliden. The news had come in via a Starfall carrier. The *SS Cymerilla* had been scanned in passing by the *Iris Quartz*. She had blocked the scan beams, but her captain's protest at the incursion had been ignored.

"Looks like she's on a mission and Selliden's her target," Apnis said angrily. "Captain Kerrix has told Nat Holdspan. I've had our teams up speed on cargo drop and told Lindell to expedite the admin. We'll be ready to shift in six hours, which will be plenty time to get out of this sector before she shows. The ISA office here probably called it in. It looks like every frigging post in the Alliance is on the watch for us. What in hell have we done to deserve the favour?"

"I can guess," was the bitter reply. "Stay on line Grey," she told him when she restored the link. "Tallica, get comms to patch me through to the *Warrior*, *Moonstone* and *Firestorm*."

Once on, Ahxenta told the captains that the UV-III was positively open to ISA and hostile intrusion and no comm was secure. She asked their advice on circulating the news to the fleet: the main problem was that the ISA would find out almost right away that its secret was out, and that the captain of the *Arianrhod* had been the source.

Bluestone was firm: news had to be passed on personally and in no other way. The ships with the temporary fix could be told and asked to tell others when they could. The trail would eventually lead back to the *Arianrhod*, but it could be kept quiet in the interim. All agreed.

"Never stops for us, does it, Cinnabar?" the first mate sighed when the captain had returned to her chair. "We'll be out of here as soon as we can. I take it the *Warrior* will make her stop short and sweet?"

"She will. Nat's as narked as us. What else did the whizzes at Alto Finglas pick up from that damned alien transport? They must've had a high time dissecting it. As Admiral Posettix' people were given partial access, they may know more, but I bet it wasn't much and beady eyes were kept on their every move. I won't check it now: we've a ship to move. We know our next stages, and they're complex. The *Moonstone* will send over the route switches and our navi-helm team will integrate them. We'll change them if the need arises. But we're for Delta Iridium, top speed. As our holds are near empty, we should make good time. The *Moonstone's* not hauling a lot of cargo, as far as I know."

"Roger that, Cap. But what in the name could Gulley do if the *Iris Quartz* did catch us? Throw eggs and tell us to stop and spill the beans or he'll tell the colonel we won't play ball?"

"Hell knows. But I've no time for the ISA, Myrtleberry or any of its or her hangers on, or their antics. Enough is enough."

"You could try another formal protest?" Apnis suggested.

"Can it, Commander, and pay attention to your boards."

* * *

The route to Delta Iridium was not as intricate as the captain expected, nor much longer than the one *Arianrhod* would have taken. The convoy set off by a short local bypass deeper into Epsilon, to the deserted Melt system, and then joined the ex-hostile bypass used by Starfall that led to the extinct Lartzeg Trine. Switches at Kolm and Iris Three led them into Deltan space from a rarely-used track. As the zone, apart from a small Coalition area, had been firmly ISP and was now as firmly ISA, the captains had no doubts that their presence would soon be widely known, but meanwhile they could arrange trade matters.

The port of Delta Iridium Colony was less formal than Merkat Web and visits by senior officers of arriving ships to the harbour office were not obligatory, as long as manifests and IDs were in order and docking fees paid promptly. To Ahxenta's surprise, the *Tallulah* was in port still, and looked to be up to spec, as her berth had no repair rigs. She put in a courtesy call to Captain Fleetskup, who was back in his chair. Spickle was now whole and alongside. They would be leaving for Milkit Major in a few hours, Fleetskup told her.

As Lindell had begun to arrange cargo drop and pick up before they reached orbit, the pieces were in place for rapid transfer of the Ottolyx micro-engineering parts to the clients as soon as *Arianrhod* made berth. The company from which they were to take on the large shipment of medical supplies was on standby, with the goods hanging off an orbital transfer point awaiting *Arianrhod's* cargo pods. The *Moonstone* and the *Firestorm* had made ready to pick up their payloads, Ahxenta noted.

"Starfall *is* efficient," Apnis said. "But there's a big ISA presence here, bang in the middle of ISP-run ISA space: the Point Freen military academy's churning out recruits, there are listening posts and location beacons. But it's too good a chance to miss: *Tallulah's* here, Murmur thinks there's a UV-III breach, we know there is *and* we have a fix."

"I know," Ahxenta muttered. "I'll risk heading over. I don't know his senior SO, but Juke Spickle's pulling his weight. I'll need Azular, but Fleetskup will be more likely to bite if you're there. Earbleat can cope here. I'll call privately, *and* link to Captain Kerrix. She'll have spotted the *Tallulah*, so she'll have figured."

Fleetskup was keen to have visitors, especially Apnis. Ahxenta had told him she wanted to talk PSS issues and check in with him socially, and had agreed to head over after cargo delivery. She was disturbed by a flurry at the tactical and science stations.

"What's that?" she called as Gliss pulled down the bridge holo-grid, to show the data updating at a rate of knots.

"More places posted off-limits by the ISA, ma'am," Azular replied. "As well as Furze, the Drapes, Portal, Skota and Fourpoint, we have Sella, Bell 2, Green off the Greenstar, Klam off the Stoorie, and Blox. Others marked *approach with caution* include Sox."

"Sox!" Ahxenta exclaimed. "Vexin Thal will need to know, as that's the end point of one of his bypasses – *and* that compromised worm-pocket. If the ISA's got a presence there…"

"Preparing copies for the *Moonstone* and the *Firestorm*, though they may have it. I'll do one for the *Tallulah*. Mr Bellfish found it in a trawl through ISA open channels, but it hasn't been sent to shipping or local authorities. ISA fleet command may be drafting a detailed version."

"I wouldn't count on it," Ahxenta growled. "Send your copies when ready, but we'll take the *Tallulah's*. Here are the approval docs and the drones to catch Rhomb Systems' cargo. Lindell's verified them."

The captain gave the orders to release the cargo to the drones, and watched as the transfers were made and the drones locked down. Once delivery was approved, she authorised the release of two of *Arianrhod's* secure-tagged pods to the transfer point specified by their next clients, Preens Medical. After checks and file exchange, the pods were loaded, secured, and set to make their way back under their own power. Once in reach of *Arianrhod's* tractors, they were pulled in and safely restowed.

"We'll head to the *Tallulah* now," Ahxenta said. "Earbleat, prep our outer bays for the Limekiln load. We've dealt with Form-tech and Lindell has the details of habitation unit size. As the *Moonstone's* picking up her supplies from Preens now, she'll be set to move, and I see the *Firestorm's* taking on cargo even though she's not a transport. Ready the ship for departure. Nobody from the ISA office has sent as much as a hello, so they may not want to talk; but they'll have noted every iota of our doings and they'll have been told about us. If a link comes in from the ISA, be civil, tell them zip and tell them I'm too busy to chat."

"Aye ma'am," the second mate replied with alacrity as Ahxenta rose and signalled to her first mate and her senior science officer.

"We lose the *Firestorm* at Limekiln, I expect," Apnis said on the way off the bridge.

"Yes, as far as I know. I'll need a chat with Captain Kerrix anyway, as we need to agree the route to Limekiln. It'll be a long haul to Starfall after that. Thirty days standard depending on the track, and assuming no trouble. And we'll be heavy loaded and vulnerable."

"Habitation modules are hardly high class articles, Cap, but raiders will steal anything," Apnis agreed. "Not that anyone should know what we *are* carrying, but word gets out."

"Crizz has *Arianrhod Six* prepped, so we take her. The noses in our business can make of it what they will."

That ISA noses were sniffing was apparent, for a call came in almost as soon as the shuttle reached the *Tallulah*. Earbleat wasted little breath, cut the ISA rep off mid-sentence, gave him the captain's message, signed off, and sent an update to Ahxenta. By that time, the three were comfortably seated in a briefing room aboard their sister vessel.

The chat to the voluble Fleetskup took two hours, but the time was well spent, in Ahxenta's opinion. They met the senior science officer, acid-tongued Dr Kirri Scumble, who seemed to be shrewd and smart, and quickly grasped the intricacies of the code-decode device. Juke Spickle was also well-informed, and having been chief tactical officer, was able to make use of the ISA data on the new sites posted off-limits. He also took in what the problems of the data and the undermining of the UV-III would mean for the PSS fleet rather better than his captain, and had many pertinent questions.

"Fleetskup's got himself a damn good first mate," Apnis observed to the captain once they were in their shuttle and readying for return to the ship. "I wouldn't have thought it before, but he's quick on the uptake *and* knows it would be better not to talk to ISA reps, however nice they are. What's your view of him, Azular?"

"I agree, Commander. I think he has the measure of his captain, but there's respect – and gratitude for giving him the position."

"Grey Bluejohn figured he'd make a good first mate, once he'd got used to making himself heard," Ahxenta put in. "But has that science officer got the savvy to keep on top of the UV-III breach? She'll need to liaise with their comms senior and keep her eyes and ears open."

"She's clever and also has the measure of Captain Fleetskup, ma'am. But over-confident, I think."

"Just like someone *I* know," Ahxenta told him ironically. "And you managed to slip in *your* news very adroitly, I noted."

"It made Murmur sit up," Apnis laughed as the shuttle slid into free space. "I was glad to see him upbeat, but he seems to have aged. The shock and his injuries have told on him. He'll be glad to get to Milkit."

"And I'll be glad to get home to *Arianrhod*," the captain replied.

Back on the bridge, the news that there had been another link from the local ISA office met the captain. "A jumped-up jack-in-office called Lieutenant Commander Chert Burnet," Earbleat said. "Didn't want to speak to *me*, wanted you, Cap. I told him *again* you were far too busy, but he reckoned you must be on the *Tallulah*, so they've been keeping track. He wasn't happy when I told him to mind his own business."

Ahxenta grinned: her second mate was not subtle. She reviewed the ship's departure status and checked in with her fellow vessels before deciding that she had better find out what was so important.

The alleged reason for the link was the complaint and security cam copy that the captain had sent Myrtleberry of the assault in the Web. Those responsible had been disciplined, Burnet told her. He wanted to know to whom she had passed the material and what her next steps were. The talk was stratagem: Burnet was trying to find out what she and the other ships were up to, and why she had crossed to the *Tallulah* rather than calling. The form of the questioning and the tone gave the captain another clue as to Burnet's nature.

"He's an info-sent," she said to Apnis on return. "Not Myrtleberry class: he just about kept his cool when I tried to provoke him over the added off-limits spots the ISA's posted. The mention of Sella, Bell 2, Klam and Blox made him fizz. I pushed him on the *approach with caution* notice for Sox and asked why it had been added; I was told to back off. But he cleverly slipped in guesses about what we and Starfall are up to. He'd heard about the *Kel'Torc* at his HQ and wanted to know why I'd recruited – his expression – a Starfall ship to deliver a cargo I'd agreed to deliver. Which I hadn't. I'd promised a cargo, the ISA got it. I didn't say I'd hand it over personally with ribbons and bows."

"But why is the ISA so interested in us, Cap? We can't undermine its ops or affect its business in any way."

"But we have friends who can. An admiral and two ambassadors from Psi, others. And we can supply goods it can't source, but they're necessary for its fancy new ships' comms. And as you said, we worry it, and the fact that Myrtleberry can't get one over on us pisses it."

"Sounds reasonable when you put it that way. But that's us set to move. We wait word from the *Moonstone*?" the first mate asked.

"Yes; she must be ready for shipping out, or close to it."

As if in response, comms called a link for the captain from Captain Kerrix. She had heard from Admiral Posettix about the protest to the

ISA fleet HQ on the attempt by Goldcriss to bug their conversation, and the wanton use of a primed weapon by her officer. Charges against the two would be pursued *if* captains Kerrix and Ahxenta attended the hearings in person. Posettix had agreed on their behalf, but only on condition that the ISA officers would be there to answer the charges. The admiral had been told that as the *Matchless* was on a mission that meant she could not return to Alto Finglas any time soon, it would not happen. The result was stalemate, but it suggested that the convoy of ISA ships *was* on the way to the Outer Reaches.

The other part of the admiral's message was that the *Kel'Lath* had left as soon as she had passed on the pods of cargo; the *Serenity*, *Zetkalt* and *Jekzilt* were to ship out soon, heading for Starfall and then home. Ambassador Posettix had a draft alliance treaty in her pocket as far as it concerned Norvalla and its colonies, but she was set for long debate with her people before it was settled. Telzilt did not intend to sign up to an alliance until much more had been thrashed out, but its accord with the TA on the use of its listed bypasses past Amity still stood – although the PSS fleet could use the bypasses without let or hindrance, whatever the TA tried to push on the ships that flew its flag.

Burnet had called the *Moonstone*, Kerrix told them, using the excuse of the bugging attempt in the *Half Moon*. She had Levettiza sit in, for a very good reason: she knew him, having met him on a posting years before. The Berzic had been struck by a marked personality shift in the man she had once known, and on a close view after several questions, had reached the same conclusion as Ahxenta: the man was now an info-sent.

"Commander Levettiza didn't push," Kerrix said. "But it looks like the ISA *is* using info-sents in key locations to gather info – Delta's an important centre. But how many ISA offices have them planted? And do their colleagues know what they've got?"

"Can of worms, and we can do zip about it," Ahxenta responded. "We'll just have to be aware. And we can't warn our fleet, as only a few have the UV-III fix yet. But you're ready to ship out?"

"We are. The *Kel'Moth's* on the way to Limekiln and should be there when we get in. We've a straight run on local bypasses and there's no sign of trouble, but I don't discount there being ISA patrols out there."

"Me neither," Ahxenta said darkly. "Let's get the show on the road and give Burnet something else to sniff over."

As orders were given and the three ships made ready to leave Delta, Apnis leaned over. "Interesting: Levettiza figured Burnet's personality had changed to what she remembered of him? Does that imply that the alteration to info-sent status causes a personality flip?"

"That's what I figure, Tallica: Horn's adjustment was especially bad and caused his natural short fuse to worsen *and* his judgement to cloud. Myrtleberry needles people to get what she wants – is *that* a trait that has been intensified in her? And what other unwanted changes did she have? Looks like the ISA hasn't got its procedures right."

"Or it's what happens when info-sents are created. Maybe our old chum Bick Micklemouse was a nice guy once."

The captain snorted. "That runt was never a nice guy. But it could be a reason why the likes of Myrtleberry keep pushing when they know they'll get nothing. They think they will, eventually. But we're off. Ready to link to the *Moonstone's* helm at your discretion, Ms Dox."

* * *

The trip to Limekiln was regular and the three ships made berth in five days. The *Firestorm* stayed only hours, as she had other business. Form-tech's vast orbital handling facilities were loaded with the sections that made up the habitation units, and the admin was in order. The *Kel'Moth* had already begun cargo pick-up. The loading of the two newly-arrived carriers would take four days, during which time the captains were to hold talks. Ahxenta had authorised shore leave for as many of her crew as possible, as she knew that it was likely to be a long time before they would have another opportunity.

"At least Limekiln's NTA-run, even if it's now part of ISA," Apnis observed to Ahxenta, as she stretched to relieve muscles after a long spell at rest. "Lambda's a long way from the centre of things, so the tentacles of the ISA won't do much damage here."

"The Limeys have always been an independent bunch; and though Freskat sits in an ISP-run sector, it's never bowed to ISP authority and won't to the ISA, despite the office next door to Zillah."

"I wonder if there's an info-sent in *her* backyard?" the first mate mused. "Though I doubt Zillah would be swayed if there was."

"I've no way to warn her, but she's a hard nut to crack and a canny officer," Ahxenta replied. "Snow has the conn for the next watch, but we're on track. I've the meet with Kerrix and Thal tomorrow at eight hundred local time, so for now I'm off duty."

"You taking Azular over to the *Kel'Moth*?" Apnis asked slyly.

"Like hell; he wants a date with his other half, he can make his own arrangements. I'm taking you, so be prepared."

"Aye, aye, Cap. Axellina wants a chat about med supplies, so we can talk it over in the mess. She needs another of those med-cradles from Delta, but we didn't get the chance to pick one up."

"We'll take on air and ship's goods here, but she won't get gear like that. Our main resupply is Starfall, but as that place can source high-tech goods, she may be lucky. It'll be a long haul, thirty days, even with free use of Starfall's bypasses and Thal's ships keeping the way clear."

"I'll set drills to keep the crew up to scratch, but it may be wise for them to get their heads round what we may or may not find in Psi. It'll be a new experience for us all. Azular will have a heap of data on it, and he can dredge up more from Captain Kerrix."

"I'm sure he has and can, and that's a good call. *I'll* need to be up to speed on the trade routes for one thing."

"So will you," Lieutenant Dox whispered to her partner.

"I am," he said testily. "I've run nav sims ever since Doc Azular put in self-updating nav-charts; I knew we'd be out there one day. And the grid will have all we need to look out for: it goes well into Psi."

"Okay, keep your hair on! *I'll* have to get the facts into my brain on the positions of bypass nodes and other jump points, and I'll need to know about worm-pockets, gravity wells and other nav hazards; and we'd best be aware of boundary disputes, unfriendly local authorities, raider hidey holes, off-limits areas, and other stuff to steer clear of."

"Like that ship the *Sunburst*; if there are other boats out there with captains like that Sallix, we'll *really* be in trouble," Box warned.

Apnis looked at Ahxenta, raised an eyebrow and grinned. "Can't keep a good crew down, Cap."

"Looks like. That's us set, and here's our relief. You have the conn, Mr Snow," she told the lieutenant. "Keep us on target."

∗ ∗ ∗

In just under thirty days, the vast station that circled the dead planet welcomed them. Thal offered his repair facilities to bring the *Arianrhod* up to peak, as the *Kel'Moth* and the *Moonstone* would be making use of them. Ahxenta agreed, and once docked, took time to check around. She was surprised at the level of activity, with ships coming and going, including small craft down to the surface – scavenging what was left from the attack on the base, she inferred. She speculated on how Thal could keep track of such a large number of ships and those at his other bases, although she knew he had local commanders. The ever-curious Azular had spotted that the inner belts that housed the more important Starfall services had expanded.

Arianrhod's resupply began at once. Off-ship, the means to make more code-decode devices were limited, but Azular and Kinnitix were allotted a Starfall lab and staff to produce as many as possible. Thal wanted them for his newly PSS-registered ships, which would use the

UV-III. He had authorised PSS status for several of his larger carriers, but he had *not* affiliated them to the Trades Alliance, Azular told the captain at a senior staff briefing after his return from his first sortie to the lab. Although the TA was the only duly-authorised body in zones Alpha to Mu that issued bypass-use clearances, port entry permits and port-use insurance for registered private starships and other mercantile fleets, and it operated in most ports, it did not have universal control. In free ports such as the Web, anyone could trade; many small ports were free and Starfall had its own system of bypasses that could link to local hyperspace routes that did not need TA clearance.

Thal's carriers had been registered as PSS in an approved centre in Kirtish, in Mu. His plan was that he would fly them under the flag of a Telzilt-based trades association that supplied free use of the bypasses in its jurisdiction, port entry and use assurance, and guaranteed rights to new fields in what was now zone Psi, and in sectors beyond it.

"Clever," Apnis approved. "The port authorities in our zones need to keep a handle on the numbers of privates that operate in free space, which is why the PSS registration scheme was set up in the first place, to let the PAs know they have bona fide ships coming in – and have comeback if things go belly up. I expect Psi and the sectors on the far side of it have a similar sort of insurance."

"They do, and Captain Thal may have to register his ships there as well," Azular told her. "The difference in Psi and its allied sectors is that as hyperspace bypasses are deemed to benefit all the allied sentient systems, all share the expense of their building and upkeep. The outlay can be recouped from the levies that many worlds attach to use of their port facilities by non-local traffic, but some larger planetary authorities provide free port facilities and chains of local bypasses, as they know the trade will boost their own economies. The equivalent of the TA in Psi is what translates as the Free-Market Trades Exchange, and flying under its flag will entitle new Starfall PSS ships to free entry to a large number of allied ports, as well as benefits that would be gained in our zones from TA alignment. But Dr Kinnitix told me that the Exchange isn't closely tied to the political body that unites many of the sovereign powers in Psi: the Union of Federated Systems, the equivalent of the ISA. The ISA wants to pull the UFS into its confederation, as it will bring a lot of the zone Psi systems into line."

"Too much politicking for me," Apnis declared. "What affects us is access to trade routes and ports without being hauled into rows over territorial rights or forced into being cannon fodder when the political wing thinks the hostiles are getting out of hand and its ships are faced with too much. Which reminds me, Cap: have we heard more on the changes to the TA contract that would mean our loads levies would be upped to pay for the new bypass routes the TA wants to introduce?"

"Our legal rep figured it was sound; the TA got approval to add codicils when it felt like it back at the start of the caper, though I didn't damn well vote for that. The standard year that the contract's meant to hold for still has a few months left to run, but what in blazes a full review of it will achieve after that I don't know. But our priorities are resupply and upgrading. What's the medical position, Axellina?"

The chief medic had been able to source two high-spec med-cradles and was happy with the additions to her other stores. The overhaul of the hull weapons arrays pleased Earbleat, but the lack of permission to bring in add-ons for *Loki* was tasking her. Other ship's departments were on track with their renewals. The other main issue that concerned Ahxenta and the other PSS captains was the UV-III position.

Azular assured her that they could collect a batch of code-decode plug-ins from Letik. The blueprint had been sent via a Starfall channel and the devices were already in manufacture. He and Kinnitix would have final adjustments to the pieces to make, but that was all. As for a new comms system, the two were convinced that a totally new design, with integral complex variable coding, might be the best way forward. Such a board could be plugged into the existing comms system of each partner vessel, and each ship would be able to set its own encryption ciphers. The two were working on it as and when they could.

The captain nodded. "Good. As for us, all being well, we ship out in three days. Our escorts will be the *SS Amber Flash* and the *SS Lucent*. They'll both carry small cargoes, but they'll be well armed and their job is protection – though Captain Thal isn't expecting trouble, he won't take the chance. I'm meeting their captains before we leave."

She was interrupted by an update from tactical: three large ships had entered Starfall space and had been given permission to dock. They were the *NFS Serenity*, the *TSS Zetkalt* and the *TSS Jekzilt*.

23: NEW HORIZONS

Arianrhod sat quiescent in her bay. She had been due out the day before, but Captain Thal had authorised a delay, as the embassy ships and the *Jekzilt* had requested escort as far as their routes led together. It would take them to Amity Beacon and then Telzilt, where the Telziltic ships would halt. The *Serenity* was for Norvalla, the Starfall convoy for Letik. The Psi ships had resupplied, and shuttle trips from the *Serenity* and the *Moonstone* to Thal's HQ had been observed. No word of a meeting had come in and Ahxenta assumed it was Starfall or personal issues. Azular was equally in the dark. He had had little contact with Captain Kerrix since the three Psi ships had got in.

The two at the navi-helm were running sims of starfields they would cross and routes they might take once the convoy reached Amity. The only update to the holo was notice of a new worm-pocket beyond Mu, at Greel, a system between Canna and Brittle, but it would not affect them. Their main puzzle was how it had been found, but as the data source had been unidentified, no-one could guess.

"Probably from one of Captain Thal's probes, the ones he sent into the bypass to monitor it, as his ships use it; and there's the racket along it due to the bypass the ISA's building with Norvallan and other help," Box conjectured. "Or maybe a Starfall ship: they're the only ones likely to be outside Mu."

"Don't count on it," Dox said sternly. "With all the ISA and other uproar on the Starfall-Amity link, and the high-speed build of the new Selky to Kilda track, with outside ships in on the action, a lot of sneaky sorties could've been made. Look at the number of nodes on the main route: loads of places to jump on and off with low energy use, and no known places to make for, as it's not marked, apart from numbering and coordinate data. And Greel's bang on Mu edge. But what's up?" she asked, pointing to the holo that was showing local activity. "Looks like a transport's coming up from the surface of that planet. That's the third one today. What *is* down there to find?"

"I don't think I want to know," Box replied. "Bits of wreckage and dead bodies, or parts of them, I expect."

"Grim," the first mate said softly. "There's been a lot of shuttles up and down, and the labs are busy. Maybe they're onto something."

"We've got our orders, so not our worry," the captain returned as she scanned her boards, to a frisson of excitement that ran around the bridge. "Cut the chat, people: here we go. Ready engines, Chief. Helm, have you got course and line data and our positioning coordinates?"

"Aye, ma'am, locked in."

"Comms?"

"We're linked into the relevant Starfall channel, ma'am, and to every update link that comes in," Bellfish responded.

"Good. The *Kel'Moth* will take point, we and the *Moonstone* will fall in behind and the two diplomatic ships will come in at back of us. The *Amber Flash*, *Lucent* and *Jekzilt* will protect our flanks and rear. We take route and speed data from the *Kel'Moth*. We have one stop to take on air before we leave Mu. Grid full down, Lieutenant Commander Gliss. We keep it down the whole way. All stations, confirm ready status."

As her officers complied and the impersonal voice of Starfall base control issued the go ahead, Ahxenta gave the command to release the struts tying *Arianrhod* to her berth. She powered up slowly to the rising pulse of her engines, her pink flanks beginning to glow as the exterior arrays of scanners, comms, navigational and weapons gear made ready to engage. In minutes, she slid out into free space. Her initial heading was a rendezvous point where the eight ships that made up the convoy would form into the most efficient travelling wing.

"Here we go," Apnis breathed as Dox set the ship on the trajectory, and *Arianrhod* began to pick up speed. "The great adventure. With this entourage, it should be interesting."

"That's one word for it," Ahxenta said dryly, feeling her restraining webbing tighten. "Steady as we go, helm. All long-range scanners set to full from here on in. I want every eye and ear we have at alert."

"You don't discount trouble, then, Cap?" the first mate asked.

"I never discount trouble. And given the company we're keeping, we're more than liable to find it."

The phalanx of eight settled into the agreed formation, their helms linked to maintain their positions within the group. This was the largest convoy that *Arianrhod* had travelled with, but the highly experienced helmswoman, trained in a military fleet, was undaunted, and the initial ride to the node of Starfall Exit was smooth. With hardly a bump, the bypass that would take them on a trip through the uncharted reaches of space that led into zone Mu at Canna was achieved.

"Once we get to Kirtish, it'll be almost the furthest from home that I've ever been," Box muttered to his mate.

"Almost?"

"I was at Kollaskin Ambit once, as an ensign on a training ship. We were only there because we'd been on manoeuvres to Kellybar station and the captain wanted to give us rookies the taste of a tough ride. We made for the Kollaskin system, as the asteroid belt's really close-packed and needs smart navigating. Ambit's the third planet and it's a colourful place: it's got a pink ocean. All *I* got was trouble for plotting a course that took us too far into Kollaskin space; the authorities were miffed because we were ISP and they hadn't given us permission. Got an ear-bashing and a negative point on my record," he added dolefully.

"Bet it wasn't the first," Dox remarked.

"No," he admitted. "It wasn't the last either."

Ahxenta grinned at Apnis. At least half of her crew had fleet records blemished in one way or another. "We should be quiet as far as the Mu boundary," she said. "But from the holo, there's activity before Selky. And we'll cause a stir when we show up on the marker beacons that I bet the ISA and its chums have planted in the area."

"Thal will have a bead on it. The problem with any bypass is that no-one can claim it entirely as theirs unless they actually built the whole thing, or were major funders, as the TA claims on its main trade routes, to make us pay for their use. We know *this* one was used by the hostiles we met in the war, but they for sure didn't build it, it goes back a lot further. Thal might have upgraded it so his fleet can use it, but he can't claim absolute right, and it doesn't stop anybody else, including the bad guys, from riding on it as well."

"Given the ISA and their allies have the codes, he can't stop *them*," the captain agreed. "But he sees all this construction off it as incursion, and he has a point. The Selky to Kilda operation could've been kept as a separate entity, but it would have cost more."

"Looks like the bypass is on the way to being usable," Apnis said, pointing to the shifting holo. "Thal's probe data, I bet. Those blips are ships, and a couple of them are huge. I don't recognise the design."

The listening Azular had pulled up two outlines from his databanks to set in the holo. "Two are Norvallan constructors: a new design class to move huge loads of building gear. There's another constructor I'd guess is Mu, as it's less high-tech And three more: a small Norvallan science ship and two ISA heavy cruisers or equivalents."

"Any ID on the ISA boats?" the captain demanded.

"Trawling the banks, ma'am; as I don't have their specs, I can't get names, but we may be able to tell as we get closer. The science vessel I *do* know: she's the NFS *Sunburst*, or one like her."

"That'll bug Captain Kerrix," Apnis snorted. "In fact, the holo's updating and it's got her pinned as the *Sunburst*! I thought she'd been sent home with her tail between her legs. Maybe she's back with a new captain: many of her crew *have* been here before."

"We're not changing course or speed," noted Ahxenta. "Thal will want us ready by the time we make their position. His probes *must* be smart. We'll make the Mu border in two hours, and then we'll see."

The *Arianrhod* saw little over the time it took to reach and pass into Mu. A link from Thal confirmed that there had been no trouble in the local area, according to a contact of his on Canna, although the run of bypass beyond had been busy with ships that were using a cut-through hyper route on the zone Kappa side near Wild to make Minch Fettin, and thus to access the Starfall to Amity route.

The peace continued over the days to Selky, but once near, comms came alive with requests for IDs from a centre on Selky and from two ships close to the planet.

"It's a base, ma'am; a habitation dome with land tunnels radiating to landing pads and outbuildings," Azular confirmed. "There are small transports around it and ships in orbit."

"They're really serious about this place," Apnis breathed.

"Looks like, Tallica, with so many ships. Hold on confirmation, comms," the captain ordered. "They can read our call-sign; they know who we are. Constructors are still in range, but further towards Kilda," she said, her eyes scanning the holo. "Those are storage depots and processing sheds, maybe for the ore they hope to get from Kilda. *That's* the *ISAS Elucida*, researching whatever's going on here, I suppose."

"Huh! So you can bet the news that three Privates, three cruisers and two diplomatic ships are en route to Psi will be sent out, with our names attached, and the ISA will be on it. And they'll know *we're* heavy loaded," the first mate sniffed.

"We're carriers, it's what we do. But I suspect they know already, as Thal's probes won't be the only ones out there. And *I* bet the ISA's set up a listening post. Here's a big boat heading in, probably to make sure of us. She's tagged as ISA, but she must be heavily shielded as the call-sign's not been picked up yet. Ah! It's the *Crusader*."

"Long time no see," Apnis said derisively. "So why do they need a battlecruiser on a building site?"

"To make sure nobody steals the building blocks?" Box suggested.

"Keep your eyes on your boards, Lieutenant," the captain reproved mildly. "It's the ISA's style."

"Captain Thal has sent a response to the Selky base and the ships in the area, ma'am," Bellfish advised her.

"Let's hear it."

Thal's steely tones replied that the convoy was passing through, and he would like an update on risks in the area. That resulted in a demand from the *Crusader's* captain to be told his business, the cargo he carried, its destination and his schedule. In icy fury, the captain of the *Kel'Moth* reminded Flute that his group was on a Starfall bypass, and entry to it by ISA and other ships had only been made possible using access codes that had been, with Norvallan complicity, illicitly taken from a wrecked Norvallan ship in an attempt to forcibly annex the bypass from Starfall Exit to Amity Beacon. And as Thal was protecting the two zone Psi consular ships at his back, he warned Flute that neither the *Crusader* or the other ships should attempt adverse action, or delay them. Thal was followed by Ambassador Posettix, who advised Flute that as she and Ambassador Jotakt of Telzilt were on diplomatic missions, it would be unwise to interfere.

The *Sunburst* had made no attempt to scan or link, though Ahxenta wondered if she would try to call the *Moonstone*. No notice had come from the Starfall ship of such contact, but a chuckle from her senior science officer told her that something had happened.

"What is it, Azular?"

"I'm scanning the *Moonstone*, ma'am, there's no jamming…"

"Captain Kerrix will have your head for that," she interrupted.

"I suspect she knows, ma'am. The *Moonstone's* Norvallan and there's a datastream being sent to her from the *Serenity. She* has been linked to the *Sunburst* for a time. As we know, some database-related tech aboard Norvallan fleet ships can link to updated units on other ships to update their own. As an ambassadorial ship and entitled, the *Serenity* has done just that, and is sending the revised records to the *Moonstone*."

"And does that mean we can have those records at some point?"

"I hope so, Captain. Admiral Posettix will have no objection, as he knows of our Norvallan technology. I'll certainly enquire."

"But not until we're out of this sector and on the road to Kirtish," Ahxenta bid him. "Whoever's in command of the *Starburst* is probably hacked off as it is, but he or she can't gainsay an admiral of their own fleet. I wonder who *is* in command over there. I bet it won't be Sallix."

"I could enquire of the *Moonstone*?"

"Don't even think about it. Any more directed at us, comms?"

"No, ma'am."

"They wouldn't dare," the first mate said. "They're chary of Starfall, and they know what we're capable of and what we'd be liable to do if they hindered us. With a zone Psi admiral and two ambassadors along, Flute's probably quaking in his boots in case he drops himself in it."

"Especially as one ambassador has a tentative treaty agreement with the ISA in her hands, though Flute may not know that. The ISA won't want slip ups," Ahxenta replied. "What now, Mr Bellfish?"

"A general alert from Captain Thal, ma'am, to all ships in the sector, with the request to pass it on as they see fit: a note of the traffic at the Selky node and an advisory to take care. Sending to your board."

"Point to Thal," Apnis chortled. "They can't argue or recall it; now it's not the secret they hoped it was. Wonder how work's going at the Kilda end? They'd need the node up and running as a priority."

"There'll already be a node, Commander," Azular put in. "Kilda's in Mu and close to the line of the second arm of Mu's double bypass to Kappa, so it's a logical place for one – there's a local patch of high negative mass-energy density to assist building."

"In that case, why didn't they exploit Kilda meta-jurillium sources, and ship them to Wild in ISP space using the Mu bypass?"

"Selky's also mineral-rich, and the Norvallans are key players in the scheme; they wouldn't want to cross into Kappa to get their hands in at Kilda. And the Norvallans *did* connive with the ISA to gain access to Starfall's bypass. Though now there's an extension of the Mu bypass to Amity, via the three way split at Kollaskin Ambit."

"The quicker we're out of this hotbed of political chicanery and off this building site the better," the first mate grouched. "I'm beginning to think zone Psi and Telzilt may be civilisation without the knobs on."

"We'll find out when we get there," the captain cheered her. "Seems Flute and his group are afraid to say more, or to detain us. Thal's given the continue on route order, no detour or slow down as we pass. Keep on track, helm, but keep all our options open. If we need to jump off, I want to be ready."

* * *

There was no need to jump anywhere over the four days to the major node at Kirtish. In that time, the new technical and strategic data taken on by the *Serenity* had been passed on via the *Moonstone*, and Azular had set it into ship's systems, including response plate and hull array add-ons. They had also heard that the *Sunburst* had been totally refitted and sent out with a new captain and additional crew. She had two bypass engineers, three science officers, added medical, tactical, weapons and other staff, and a linguistics expert. Kerrix had known her captain from academy days, and though never close, she knew Captain Mettoryn was shrewd and capable, and would run a tight ship. An astrobotanist, she was a native of a Norvallan colony, Valla Port, and not a highly-ranked, fast-tracked typical fleet captain.

As the convoy made its approach to the Kirtish node, Thal ordered the ships to slow to jump-off speed and set for an independent fly-past of an oxygen-rich world in a nearby system to take on air, as had been agreed earlier. This was their one detour, and once over the Mu border, the next stop would be Telzilt. As the group reformed after the pass and made the jump back onto the bypass, *Arianrhod's* bridge crew let out a collective sigh of relief and elation: this was it. They were now in a sector new to all of them.

"Looks the same as inside," Box observed brightly. "What do you think is waiting for us at Amity Beacon?"

"A lithium rich red-orange star for a start," Dox retorted. "It has a string of dead planets, with a heap of tarted-up tech around the fourth that's supposed to be an ancient bypass node, but it's been reactivated to allow jump off or crossovers to other bypasses, and we have the codes. Didn't you read the stuff related to it attached to the new charts you're supposed to have committed to memory?"

"I can't remember every bypass track or node in the whole frigging mapped galaxy or outside it!" Box said hotly. "That's what the charts are for. And as I've never been here before, they're all I have to go on until I get the hang of the ins and outs. But I know that: I meant who'll be there apart from us? There were plenty of ships at Selky."

"That wasn't part of the info-stream," his mate said tranquilly. "But as it's *Arianrhod*, I bet there'll be a surprise or two."

"No deal," Apnis grinned at the captain. "Didn't Captain Kerrix say way back that a Norvallan heavy cruiser, an ISP survey and a Mu heavy constructor were mooching around and up to no good?"

"That was ages ago; she and Thal suspected that the idea was to link Kollaskin to Amity, so that Thal would have no leverage on their use of the Starfall bypass. I've heard zip more, and as the grid hasn't got a link from Kollaskin to Amity charted as far as I can see, they're either not telling anyone, or they've given up on it. And as Thal's people have been in and out since then, they would have spotted something."

"Near the node yes; but if they started from the Kollaskin end?"

"Someone would have seen it. But isn't that a gravity well close to Amity? It's not exactly next door to the K457 system, but it looks close by on the holo. I don't recall seeing it before. *Was* it in the previous update of this sector that I saw, I wonder? Azular..."

"On it, ma'am... there *is* a gravity well listed now. Homing in... I don't think it's as close to the K457 system that it would cause trouble on jump off or on, though we'll have to take it into account. But you're right: it wasn't on the last but one update. I'll try to find out the source of the data. I'll send a query to the duty science officer on the *Moonstone*, as that's where our updates are sent from."

Nyvallish was back in minutes. *That* data had been got by a Telziltic fleet ship and was part of the latest update. As few ships tended to use the region other than as a bypass crossing, and the re-energised Amity was a recent node as far as the ISA and the Union of Federated Systems were concerned, it was possible that it had been overlooked in UFS nav-charts in the past, but he doubted it. He had been told to pass the puzzle to their cohort ships and ask if anyone had more.

"Seems you've opened a can of worms, there, Cinnabar."

"It'll give the science officers and navigators something to do until we make the next jump," Ahxenta replied. "I want every senior duty officer off for a two hour break, though. We need to be fresh for the crossover, as it's new to us."

"Tell that to Azular: he'll be playing with all the data he can get his paws on. But *I* need a drink and a stretch, for sure. And so do you."

"I'm going to check in with medbay: I'd hope we wouldn't need the doc and her team, but they'd best be on their toes."

"You know your crew, Cinnabar; we always are. Maybe it *is* because you drive us all along with a whip?" Apnis said impishly.

"Zip it, Commander, and take a break."

As soon as a duty crew was in place, the captain set off to medbay. It was as well-prepared as always, and with no patients under care. She repeated her time out orders to her chief medic, although her first mate had already circulated the directive to every department.

"I got the message," Flintlock said. "You expecting trouble, Cap?"

"*Arianrhod* has a knack of attracting trouble, so I won't discount it, even with the other ships around us. I'll see you later."

"I'll take that as a promise," the doctor called after her.

* * *

The final push was smooth as the convoy made Amity and the jump off the bypass. With Dox at the helm, the crew of *Arianrhod* felt hardly a bump as the ship crossed into normal space, her companion vessels with her and still in close formation. The views caught by their external scanners and set by tactical as a separate holo expanded as data poured in, and the bridge crew stared in fascination.

"Wow! It takes your breath away!" gasped Box. "I'm speechless!"

"Nothing takes *your* breath away," Dox disagreed. "And the only time you're speechless is when you're eating or sleeping, and often not then. But it *is* some sight. That planet's close to the node and I've never seen a setup like it: there's a heck of a lot of superstructure and a lot of interference coming off it. It's as well we're following Captain Thal's lead," she added as she kept on course in the wake of the *Kel'Moth*.

"The size and colour of that star!" the navigator breathed. "It looks so big from here. But this place doesn't look friendly, it looks spooky. So why did they call it Amity Beacon?"

"Renamed by the ISA when it was tempting the Norvallans?" Dox suggested. "Or trying to lay claim to it, more like. At least we've made it thus far and are safe off. You got the jump-on spot marked for the Telzilt bypass? It's a bit of a ride from here."

They were cut short by simultaneous calls from Bellfish and Azular. The *Jekzilt* had detected an energy surge at their backs and sent an alert and the request that rear scanners be set to roam aft. Azular spat orders to Greffy to extend their aft science arrays to detect specifics.

"Got them!" the junior science officer verified.

"Damn it!" the senior science officer swore as he sifted through the data at high speed and the holo shifted. "We've got synthetic elements we've met before! We'll outrun that surge, but it's close!"

"What in hell is it?" the captain demanded, as the hazard showed as a spinning vortex of light and power, with pulses of energy thrusting outwards and inwards like the beating of an immense, bright heart.

"It's a small worm-pocket with high gravitational energy and light rhythmic outflux that may signal instability. It's riddled with synthetics that *don't* occur in a natural pocket or gravity well."

"Like Fourpoint, you mean," Ahxenta said grimly.

"More like the readings that Captain Dexel Thal got from the stable mass-energy density vortex off Portal, ma'am. That was infused by tech that didn't contain visibly hostile inclusions but *did* contain Norvallan additions. My monitors show pulsing energy surges from this example, but they're not like the readings we got of the huge destabilising power fluxes that resulted in the implosion of that artificially-created pocket at Fourpoint. But as these pulses are highly variable, the gravity field will fluctuate strongly, so the further we get from it the better."

He had hardly spoken when urgent links came in from the *Kel'Moth* and the *Moonstone*; their science officers had taken similar readings and had reached those conclusions. Vexin Thal had already sent an alert to his base to warn his fleet ships. The *Jekzilt* had done the same, as had the *Serenity*, and Admiral Posettix was already making waves.

The next alert was again from the *Jekzilt*: she had logged three ships behind them, flying in at speed from the path of the anomaly. She was trying to identify them, but two were neither Telziltic nor Norvallan. The Starfall ships and the *Arianrhod* could assist there, Azular called out loudly, for they could read their call-signs.

"The *ISAS Sparillia* and the *ISAS Adamant*, Captain: those logged by Commander Thal at Portal. The *Adamant* accosted the *Nyx Warrior* later near Polstarn, and warned Captain Holdspan to keep away from the warning beacons that the ISA had set up in the area."

"So what are they doing out here? Or is that a stupid question," she muttered. "The same as they were doing at Portal and Fourpoint, but this time they've got help, if there's another boat with them."

The answer came in seconds: the *Serenity* called the third as the *NFS Skelfinnix*, the class ship of a new heavy cruiser cum science vessel type with exploratory and analytical capacity, a crew of over two hundred and the best that Norvallan science and engineering could supply. As far as Admiral Posettix knew, this was her first assignment after her shakedown cruise. She had been in the final fitting stages when he had seen her last, and he knew her captain. He sent over the spec.

Thal had no intention of deviating from his mission to swap details with the advancing trio, but he did want to know what they were doing in the area. He opened a link to the ISA ships, leaving contact with the *Skelfinnix* to the admiral. Captain Delver Swilf of the *Adamant* was cold and brief; his task was not Thal's concern, but he would drop warning beacons, as the unstable gravity well at back of him that he had been exploring had erupted suddenly and was so close to the Amity Beacon node that there was risk to shipping. He could not shut down the node at once without hazard, but it might have to be done. Thal was livid, but reminded him just as coldly that the node signalled the end of a Starfall bypass, passage through which by ISA and other ships entering from Psi was by permission, and any attempts to interfere with the bypass or any parts of it would be considered criminal.

Swilf's rejection of that was instant and accompanied by threats of reprisal, but Thal had taken the step of having his convoy ships on line during the dialogue and bluntly accused the ISA of another attempt, with Norvallan complicity and tech, to create an artificial worm-pocket such as those at Fourpoint and Portal. The readings his fellow vessels had caught had decisively confirmed it – and of course, one of those *had* been present at the disastrous end of the Fourpoint experiment.

Swilf was aware that the *Arianrhod* was with the convoy; and he was familiar with the part she had played in the escape of a hostile from the *Iris Quartz*. He accused the *Arianrhod* of hindering the *Iris Quartz*, and as Starfall had had a part in the outcome, Thal had to know what had come of the escapee and his ship. The impassive Starfall captain failed to rise to the bait, his only response a raised eyebrow. Swilf continued to deny the rumours rife after Fourpoint, or that the local gravity well between Amity and Kollaskin was a better-informed repetition.

"A local gravity well that had *not* been recorded in that area on any navigational or other chart until a ship of the Telzilt fleet spotted it only fifty five standard days ago," Thal said coolly.

As Swilf began at once to doubt the fact, the captain of the *Kel'Moth* carried on. "The *TSS Zetkalt* and the *TSS Jekzilt* are on line. I *can* bring in their captains to confirm the data as accurate. If you have doubts of *their* veracity, you can request to speak to Ambassador Jotakt of Telzilt: I'm sure he'd assist you. Or as you have Norvallan allies there, perhaps you'd prefer to talk to Admiral Posettix of the *Serenity*, or Ambassador Posettix of Norvalla."

Swilf refused, and demanded an account of why the convoy of eight ships was in that part of space. Thal again referred him to the admiral and ambassadors, and in return asked why the three ships were tailing him. Swilf claimed to be putting distance between his ship and the gravity well, and that his forward course was classified. He ended by telling Thal that he had not heard the last of the issue, and was set to cut the link when Admiral Posettix came on line, identified himself to the ISA officer, and suggested that he hold. Swilf complied.

Posettix had spoken to Captain Treskillik of the *Skelfinnix* to insist on answers, and had been told that the gravity well had been a patch of high negative mass-energy density, intentionally intensified to form the seed of a trial worm-pocket. The reason for the experiment was cross-collaboration and the exchange of ideas, and to instruct their ISA allies in methods, demonstrate Norvallan technology and understand ISA trial methods. Treskillik would not speculate on results, nor the political or other strategies behind the test, but his ship and the *Sparillia* had been working in concert, using Norvallan and ISA sourced tech. The *Adamant* was an escort. Captain Treskillik's orders had come from Norvallan fleet command and he had not questioned them.

Swilf made little reply, and it was obvious to those watching that he wanted done, but he upheld his refusal to clarify his orders and their source, or his next steps. The admiral let him go, promising enquiry of ISA and Norvallan fleet commands and their political arms.

"What do they get from these devious schemes?" Apnis asked as, the three intruders set on another course and links to them cut, the order came in to prepare for jump onto the bypass for Telzilt.

"Possibly a route from Kollaskin to Norvalla without using Amity,"

Azular surmised. "It's been alleged that the ISP exploratory fleet had ways into and through what's now zone Psi – one of theirs *must* have used such a way to cross Mu's limits to find K457:003 initially. Captain Kerrix ended up off Starfall when she was exploring what she took to be an unknown, ancient, defunct bypass node; it activated, and sucked her shuttle into a high energy vortex. I used her shuttle's nav-data and raw data from early ISP star charts of areas it *had* explored beyond Mu, that we got from Admiral Zillah, to cross-compare star alignments. An ISP ship had logged K457's type and position in the starfield; it *was* close to a patch of high negative mass-energy density that extended on a direct line to Kirtish…"

"And once you'd figured its location, you realised that Kirtish was a node on a line to Starfall Exit. And then you and she worked out a route to Norvalla. I remember," the captain said. "What you're saying is that the ISA may have secret bypasses that few can access, and it and its Norvallan chums are using them to get about, *and* using parts of them to create worm-pockets for extension into official, taxable, hyper routes. Interesting: Captain Kerrix said similar months ago, at the party that created zone Psi. She wondered how the ISP had charted K457 if it was in unknown space, as even explorers wouldn't reckon on making a full run from Mu in normal space. She assumed the ISP had to know some hyper routes, as she knew that *her* people used little-known short bypasses and durable wormholes."

"Curious that a mass-energy density spot mutated into a gravity well and not a worm-pocket. It can't have been a known cut-through, but the phenomenon *is* in a suitable spot: if they *are* looking for shortcuts in bypass building, it was worth a try," said Azular.

"Could be, though they've got it wrong if it *was* that energy outwash that had them scooting out of the way. It was maybe a fluke that they ended up on our tails. But enough. Are we set to jump, Dox?"

"Ready for jump, ma'am."

"Engines at ready… at your discretion, helm."

The jump onto the bypass made, the three days to Telzilt left time for the comms that the clash with the *Sparillia*, *Adamant* and *Skelfinnix* had created to produce flak. One impact was that Ambassador Jotakt had had notice that his government had suspended unrestricted use of its bypasses by ISA and Norvallan fleet ships, but agreements with trade fleets still stood. Its Council had also deferred activity on moves to join the ISA. And Telzilt and other UFS partner bodies had issued a joint enquiry to the Norvallan authorities asking for clarity on the issues brought up by the action at Amity.

The results for the *Arianrhod* were as her captain had predicted: one or two enquiries from her own fleet, and a note from Zillah, to whom Ahxenta had copied a joint statement prepared by the three PSS ships; the admiral had sent *that* to the ISA office next door to her HQ.

"Do we expect ISA repercussions?" Apnis asked when she heard.

"Maybe," Ahxenta said. "But they can't do much to us out here."

ISA repercussions were swift but caused the captain no pain. By the time the eight ships had jumped off the node for Telzilt and were on the way, the supply office at ISA HQ had rescinded its follow-up order of more shielded comms arrays for its shipyard.

"So what do we do with the batch that's next to ship?" Apnis asked.

"We see if Zillah needs more for her navy, we send as many on to Thal as he wants, and Lindell will find other markets. Many of our fleet wouldn't say no, though retrofitting might be tricky."

"I bet Starfall could set up in that trade," the first mate smiled. "It's one of the best yards we know, if not the best."

"You can talk to Captain Thal at our next meet," Ahxenta told her. "Meanwhile, we're for Telzilt. I'm looking forward to seeing the place. We've heard a lot about it and we'll be there for three days local time, as we and the *Kel'Moth* will pick up a few small loads for Letik. That's only a short hop away on a local bypass, so it won't take above half a day. The *Moonstone* is to take on live cargo – technical and other experts heading out to help the colonists in building and expanding mining and manufacturing activities. And specialist supplies for a new tech school that's been set up."

"There for three days? Do we have meets planned, or trips down to the planet?" enquired Apnis. "If so, we'll need translators."

"Thal hasn't scheduled briefings and will only call one if anything comes up. We'll get updates on Amity and other stuff as they come in, but as we'll have plenty to do once we reach Letik, the crew can take time out aboard, so no drills. But no shore leave. Telzilt is still picking up after years of hostile incursion, and it *is* an unknown planet to us – it's not set up for interstellar tourism and I don't want anyone falling foul of local customs and causing trouble."

"Best make sure Azular knows," the first mate chuckled. "Captain Kerrix calls this home. She may have plans for a family reunion, if she has any, and as *he's* officially now family, he'd have to be involved."

"It's not been discussed," Ahxenta said dryly. "I'll let you know if it is. The *Serenity's* holding here as the ambassador has official talks, but Norvalla's two days away in hyperspace and there's a direct link."

"That's us now in local space," Apnis observed, indicating the holo.

The order from Thal to disengage helm links and break formation on approach to the third planet came in. Dox complied, bringing the ship in on the coordinates sent out by the Port Authority. Several ships, most of which looked local, were in orbit at the approach side, but the planet had no structure that could be orbital docks, although there was construction in progress.

Arianrhod's bridge crew stared curiously at the surface forms of the planet visible from their approach angle, as tactical brought up the fine detail on a section of the grid. It seemed a typical terrestrial world, with bands of polar ice and temperate zones, but from a lower orbit, derelict areas within habitable parts were visible. The second continent, above which the ship had assumed final position, had several scarred sectors inside city boundaries.

"The last battles to take back their planet left it badly hurt, by what I can see," Apnis remarked as she drew up an area on her board. "But they're back in business and gearing their colonies up for action? They must be a hardy breed. Our first job will be preparing our inner holds for the extra cargoes. Do we have the specs of the pods?"

"We will have shortly," the captain told her. "A contact of Thal's is organising it; they'll be sent up on local transports and we'll haul them in by tractor. They're endorsed by Thal, but I want them thoroughly scanned before they come anywhere near my hull."

"Which means Azular will have to be at his station with his gear at the ready." The first mate tilted her head to the senior science officer, whom she was sure was listening to every word.

"Here's the payload schedule coming in now," Ahxenta responded. "We're first to load, and there aren't many pods for us. Thal has things to do planetside, and he wants all his pieces in place quickly."

"I'll bet. *Zetkalt's* sent out a shuttle; the ambassador and his staff, I expect," Apnis said. "Her crew will be glad to be home: they've had a long haul. But I don't see an orbital shipyard. Are they building new, or do they source ships elsewhere? They must have a home fleet."

"Ask the expert," the captain advised.

Apnis did just that, and Azular was able to tell her that the Telziltic bought ships in from their allies and refitted them at orbital yards at one of their colonies that had not fallen under hostile influence.

* * *

The captain had not been surprised by Azular's appeal on the day after arrival to take his time out off ship. He and Captain Kerrix had a task in the main city of the largest state of the second continent, and he *had* to attend, he told her. Ahxenta had not asked why, knowing she would hear eventually. Cargoes loaded, there was respite before the PSS ships and their escorts would head to Letik. Azular also asked to go with his partner to the *Moonstone*: he had fix issues to talk over with Kinnitix in relation to the batch of code-decode devices ready at Letik.

"We know that those we're to collect are an advance on our own: the crystal quality of the shards is better, internal crys-linkages are finer, and the binding matrices are gem-grade jurillium, which means greater stability and strength," he explained.

"So they'll be practically indestructible," Ahxenta cut in.

"Exactly; or hurt only by extreme force. We want to tweak them to increase the number of random coding options. If we can figure a way to do that now, it'll mean a quicker turnover of usable devices."

"But you both think that a novel, virtually unbreachable system, is the only way to stop our data finding its way into the wrong ears."

"Aye ma'am. The main problem is that comms ops are similar the galaxy over: Psi ones are much like ours. Only the scrambling methods keep the links secure, and there are ways around that, as we know from the UV-III breaches. I'm looking into the Starfall system: it uses micro-crystalline lattices within flexible cases filled with conducting fluids…"

"I'm sure it does," the captain interrupted. "Spare me the specifics. You're the scientist: *I* don't understand the finer points."

"Aye, sorry ma'am," Azular smiled. "But semi-organic conducting fluids might make the difference."

"Any new system will be a headache to integrate into our ships. Keep on top of it; but it will not interfere with your work on *this* ship."

"Of course not, Captain. I may pick up a few tips in New Tekrynith, the Tekrynith State capital, where I'll meet Captain Kerrix. There are places there worth visiting."

The gleam in his eyes told her that he was looking forward to it, and that he would welcome questioning. "Places worth visiting? You're not going sightseeing. That's not the purpose of this urgent visit. Come on, you're desperate to spill the beans. What are you two up to?"

The pair were to meet the chief and seniors of Xanna Kerrix' clan, Starwain, in order that Azular be received as a son of the clan, his right, as he was tied to one of its daughters. The event would be entered in clan records, giving an added level of legitimacy to block interference from Kerrix' Norvallan kin over her property: she had had requests for links from their advisers, which she had ignored.

"Hell, I didn't know what I expected, but that wasn't it!" Ahxenta exclaimed. She was, however, intrigued by another aspect of the news. "Wasn't Captain Thal's partner Telziltic and Clan Starwain? Did he and she go through the hand-tie procedure, do you know?"

His face creased. "Yes, as did Commander Seer: his late partner was Telziltic, and of that clan. They're both sons. Mara Seer is, by blood, a daughter. She's obviously not aboard the *Kel'Moth*, but Captain Thal and Commander Seer will be with us, to have her inducted."

"It'll give her something to belong to," the captain said. "That was one of the main griefs facing all Thal's people – losing all they had, and never being able to get anything back. It'll be a big ceremony?"

"No ma'am, only two hours. The Telziltic don't go in for long ritual. With a history of invasion and occupation, much was lost. Ambassador Jotakt will be guest of honour, as witness to our hand-tying. He'll speak for us and Mara, and for Captain Thal's son, who was killed with his mother when their base off Gamma was destroyed."

"Congratulations – I guess. And *you'll* have somewhere to belong that's not Berzic."

"I hadn't considered that, but I will. With your leave, I'll stay on the *Moonstone* overnight. I'll take the *Xanna*, to bring in any bits and pieces."

The captain gave her consent, as the stop had been quiet. The plan for Letik was now set as cargo off-load, talks to suppliers of the comms array bits, crystals and meta-jurillium that would form their next loads, and future trade deals. Letik was small but long-established, Ahxenta realised as she studied the limited details Azular had dug out for her, but it was set up in a modest way for the stopover of ships and crews. *Arianrhod* could top up her air there for free and take on supplies.

* * *

The day leading up to departure from Telzilt space consisted of coming and going between ships and planet, though *Arianrhod's* crew did little. The captain noted that the *Kel'Moth* had had several visitors, including shuttles from the *Serenity* and the *Moonstone*. Azular knew that there had been comms traffic between the three ships, but his partner would tell him only that it was personal, though Azular had observed that Captain Thal and Admiral Posettix spent much time talking. The shuttles to the *Moonstone* were easier to explain: they had brought up the human cargo for transfer to Letik, and their goods.

Azular and Kinnitix had resolved the fix issues of the code-decode device, and were optimistic. He told the captain that Captain Kerrix' fighter was now in good trim, as she had been able to find many parts locally, and with flight engineers and Kinnitix working on it, had got it up to a fair spec. He had brought back a highly modified blueprint of the craft and one or two pieces for Commander Earbleat. Ahxenta had a suspicion that it was a ruse to keep the weapons chief off his back over the other tech he had got, but let it rest: Azular and Kinnitix had also made inroads into a pilot design of comms system, and with Thal's permission, he had brought back an assortment of small parts used in the Starfall system to tinker with.

The admiral and the ambassadors had pushed over Amity, but were no further on. Queries had gone to Norvallan and ISA fleet commands and governments, backed by data and a copy of the talk with Swilf. All refuted underhand activity, Telzilt Council's move of denying free use of its bypasses to their fleets a strong incentive. A clarification request on the issues raised by Amity by other members of the UFS had been met with a promise of an official inquiry by the Norvallans.

"Political flannel," Ahxenta growled. "The bigger an organisation is, the more attractive it is to self-servers that want a cut of any pie and will use any relevant means to get it. In other words, profiteers. We've an hour left in port and that's us, so let's get to it."

The hour sped by, and the PSS ships, with the *Amber Flash* and the *Lucent*, made a swift run for the local node and the short trip to Letik. The bypass was the same as most others and routine for a ship such as *Arianrhod*, well able to handle massive hyperspace currents. The captain had therefore no qualms in leaving the conn to Apnis when an urgent comm, to be taken at once, came in from the TA central office.

She was gone for two hours: that link had been followed by several more, to the *Kel'Moth* and the *Moonstone*, to Admiral Zillah, and then to several of her own PSS fleet contacts, but only those on board ships that had been given the code-decode fix. Her face was black as thunder on return, as she sat heavily in her command chair and roughly pulled her status boards across.

"What in the name's going on, Cap?" the first mate enquired in a low, anxious voice.

"The TA has temporarily revoked our right to its flag; as of now, the *Arianrhod*, the *Kel'Moth* and the *Moonstone* have no trades association backing, and around half the trading ports in zones Alpha through Mu are closed to us."

24: TRADING PLACES

The remainder of the flight to Letik was sombre. It was obvious to her bridge crew that the captain was livid at the injustice, but resolute. She had circulated the news ship-wide, backed by a calm assertion that their livelihood was not at risk and they had many trade routes open to them. The three excluded ships had the support of their PSS colleagues, who intended to raise protests with the TA.

Apnis was the only one who dared ask questions of their iron-willed captain, the first being why the step had been taken. The TA was not obliged to give a reason for any decision, Ahxenta had been told, but evidence given by the ISA had been key, and until enquiry was made and issues settled, the ban against the three ships would remain.

"I figure the main reason is that we've narked the ISA and its friends so often that it's dragged the TA into the mix in the hope that we can be bullied into toeing its line," the captain snapped. "As the ISA has a major beef against Starfall, penalising its leader is one way to stress its own importance; or it may be the way it sees things."

Ahxenta had taken steps to secure her trade standing, the first being to ask Admiral Zillah to raise the possibility with its planetary authority of making Freskat a free port. *Arianrhod* had been registered as a PSS at its registry centre and was thus entitled to use it as a trade stop, but the same would not apply to the *Kel'Moth* or the *Moonstone*.

"Freskat's out of the way in Lambda, it has little to do with the TA and has no TA office, so the authority may bite. Lamella and Limekiln are trade partners and free ports. Delta Iridium's the biggest free port in Delta and that's a bonus, as we trade there a lot. Some concerns *will* be chary of using us and we won't be able to take on loads for TA-controlled ports. The puffed-up prig that took delight in giving me the news sent me the official annulment, which basically says damn all. I've sent our legal rep a copy and got him to start action on the reasons for the ban and the means to reverse it, but it'll take time. Thal's done the same for his ship and the *Moonstone*. The temporary bit was part of the title, so I expect the TA will use it to beat us up from time to time."

"How long before the TA withdraws the flags of all Captain Thal's ships?" Box asked his partner, once the news had sunk in. "They're all part of the Starfall trade fleet, aren't they?"

"I give them two days. That should be long enough for their teensy brains to work out that he can pass the Alpha to Mu trade to them; as he has free passage in zone Psi, he'll be fine," was the sagacious answer.

"Good point," Apnis agreed with a smile. "Maybe we should ask Thal if we can join the Starfall fleet, Cap?"

"Very funny, Commander. But we *have* options. There's more than one way to send a shuttle into orbit than set it off on a launch pad. But as we're closing on Letik, we ready for action. The habitation units will be offloaded first. Most, apart from the new hospital modules, will stay in orbit until the ground bases are ready; rigs are on standby. It'll take two days, as it needs careful handling. The medical supplies can sit until we empty the outer bays. We shuttle them down: the Letik authorities are still adjusting to having a larger population and logistics is a crucial issue for them."

"Roger that, Cap," Apnis replied, eyeing Ahxenta keenly, aware that there was something else on her mind.

The plan ran to schedule and the five ships made orbit three hours later, to be welcomed by a relieved ruling council. News of the troubles with Norvalla had raced in before them, as had two heavy cruisers out of Valla Key: *they* had passed the local node on a line for Telzilt without as much as a hail, and the council members were concerned.

Delivery of the huge living modules *was* drawn out, but unlike most centres, the form filling was the least of it. At the end of the release of the second batch, the captain called a halt. Her crew was exhausted and she was feeling the strain of fourteen hours on duty with only two short breaks. Once the next duty shift was in place, she and Apnis made for the mess, stretching taut muscles and yawning all the way.

"Right, Cinnabar," the first mate began as the two settled at a table with their steaming rations. "More than one way to send a shuttle into orbit? And do you think the TA would be stupid enough to revoke the rights to its flag for every registered PSS in the Starfall fleet?"

"Your second point first: I think Box and Dox are right and so does Thal. He's got plans in motion to carry on trade in the original zones, and he's got allies on Telzilt. The ISA badly wants to pull the Telziltic into the Alliance, as they're prime influencers in Psi, and this isn't going to improve its already shaky relations with them. Thal's had trade links with Psi before ever he put any of his ships on the PSS register, so this ban will give him little trouble. It means his PSS ships will have to trade further out is all, but that's no hardship, as Starfall and his other bases are the only places they can call home. As for us: we have the *Emerald*, until some ISA or TA bright spark remembers she's under *Arianrhod's* flag. And I have friends in the fleet. Grey Bluejohn and Nat Holdspan have already been on saying they'll do what they can to help us."

"Ah, so if there are batches of high-spec comms arrays and the like to shift, we can ask them to pick up or drop off, if they can."

"That's already taken care of: if the *Emerald* does fall foul of the TA, she can still trade at Freskat, as that's where I registered her as a PSS. People *will* want those goods, they're not huge as cargoes go, and the Web's the biggest free port there is, so we can trade there."

"But not with the ISA."

"Exactly. It's set up array production at its HQ yard but it still needs supplies and skills. And by what's going on here, Letik will be a primary supplier of gem-grade meta-jurillium and quality crystals."

"And it's a Telzilt colony. Smart thinking," Apnis said, spooning up a mouthful. "When do you head down for the meets Thal set up with the parties that produce the crystals and the jurillium we're to pick up? And there's the place that's started on the new spec comms array parts. Azular will have to be there, as he has the gear for crystal testing, and he can check the quality of the arrays."

"I'll head down at ten hundred local time tomorrow, and you'll be with me: if this turns out to be a regular contract, you'll need to know the clients. Now we know the ins and outs of cargo drop, Earbleat can cope. The med supplies and small pods we took on at Telzilt we ship later. Azular's with us, Nyvallish will act for the *Moonstone* and Thal will use his judgment. But I need some sack time, I'm bushed."

"You and me both, Cap."

The captain put her cares aside for six hours, but found a request for a link from Captain Goodsocks awaiting her when she awoke. With an inkling of what it might mean, she had her duty comms officer link to the *Emerald* and patch it through to her quarters. Half an hour later, she was on the bridge.

"Missed you at breakfast, Cap," Apnis smiled. "Melly Goodsocks?"

"You saw the log. *Emerald* got the same news as us. I sent a note to the *Kel'Moth*, but I bet Thal's had the same from his TA-aligned ships. No word on why, but we'll soon have the excuse. Things are moving and the Letik reps are efficient: Lindell's sent a note that half the fees are in our coffers, the rest on completion of delivery. And as trade here will give us a foothold in Psi, there may be other deals we can pick up on the back of it without relying on our links to Starfall."

The captain had a call from Thal twenty minutes later: his other TA-linked ships had been barred, pending inquiry. He had told the TA to stick its flag, and would register all his PSS ships with the Free-Market Trades Exchange. That would give them free bypass access in Psi and beyond, insurance and other protection, and guaranteed rights to new trading fields. The body had offices on several Psi worlds, though not on Letik, but he was in negotiation with the nearest, on Telzilt.

"Norvalla has a big FMTE office, and if it commits to the ISA treaty Ambassador Posettix has on line, the FMTE will *have* to be accepted in our zones," Ahxenta said. "One of her key remits was trade."

"This web of intrigue is getting more tangled and stickier with every passing day," the first mate replied. "We're set for our trip down?"

"We are. We'll take the *Gadfly*. Thal's guaranteed safety, so we won't take an escort. He and the *Moonstone's* people will meet us in the shuttle park at the head office of the first place; we use local transport for the others. It's you, me, Azular and Lindell: he'll deal with contract issues if the goods are up to scratch. Kinnitix will be there, to evaluate the code-decode shards that the local company have come up with."

"Sounds good. Will we be down there long?"

"I'm sure we'll find a decent diner. It's usually one of the first things set up on any new colony, and Letik's been established for a long time. As it's expanding, the need for food and drink in a friendly setting will expand as well. They probably have a thriving lunch and liquor trade."

The captain was right: on arrival at the first of their meetings at the Letik Crystal Mining Corp, an offer of refreshment was made by their hosts, and accepted. *Arianrhod's* crew had already been struck by the glittering façade of its office; it included many of the types of crystal elements produced by the company, the leading director assured them, and more were available for trade inspection on the way in.

Azular, Kinnitix and Nyvallish took advantage and quickly had their scanners busy. Azular's raised eyebrow and positive nod told Ahxenta that the goods were quality, but taking nothing as read, she insisted on the future cargo being examined in detail. The senior rep had expected it, leading her to believe that he had been briefed. After the short stop for drinks, the group set off to the product despatch depot.

Their next visit meant a trip to the edge of the settlement by local transport. Letik Aggregates was located close to a large jurillium mine, and its main building was less grand and more industrialised than their previous stop, but the processed meta-jurillium sheets were top-class gem-grade and the reps friendly and eager for trade.

Thal proposed lunch and a talk at a diner he knew of near their third and final destination, where they would be assured privacy. By the time they reached it, Ahxenta had had enough of a chat with Azular to know that he judged the goods he had examined to be very high quality and fit for use; as Nyvallish and Kinnitix were of the same opinion, their advice was to accept the goods at the set, non-negotiable, price.

Thal wanted to discuss the logistics of cargo transfer off planet. The loads were not huge, but it made sense to split them between the three ships for safety. Such being the case, the ships would have hold space for more freight; its source was another matter.

The comms company creating the code-decode shards to spec was a short walk away. The group was expected, and while Azular, Kinnitix and Nyvallish were taken to the labs to study the methods and results of shard assembly, the others talked terms with the directors.

The three experts were enthusiastic and full of ideas on their return. The data shards were precision-built and durable, but Metriklon labs had other projects, and had been testing different materials as integral elements of comms systems. Azular and Kinnitix had asked questions, studied test results, and traded ideas. Their hosts had been refining a system similar to the Starfall set-up to render the units more tamper-proof and to carry greater comms loads. They had implanted nano-crystalline lattices into flexible cases bound with meta-jurillium, Azular explained, and were testing them with various conducting fluids. He and Kinnitix had advocated a semi-organic matrix as a way forward, and the researchers were eager to try, as they had materials to hand.

"New toys," Apnis muttered to the captain as she listened, but she could tell that both Ahxenta and Thal were interested.

The talks were extended to discuss the potential of the comms units as tradeable goods, and ended with the deal for the data shards agreed and the batch handed over in two cases. An arrangement was made for Azular and Kinnitix to return to Metriklon shortly to see the progress of the comms unit adaptions they had proposed. Nyvallish had other priorities, Captain Kerrix told them, and would not be there.

Ahxenta had no chance to find out more, as Azular had claimed a seat next to his partner for the ride back to the shuttles. Thal had been in contact with the *Kel'Moth*, and had heard of two deals for shipping industrial goods to Telzilt. More contracts were available for larger loads, which might benefit the PSS vessels. Another message he had taken privately, and Ahxenta soon found out why: a call from Earbleat shortly after told her that the *Amber Flash* and the *Lucent* had left orbit.

The captain waited until the group had been deposited at the shuttle park and their transport had gone before asking Thal for the reason. He was sharp: the *ISAS Adamant* and the *NFS Skelfinnix* had entered Telzilt space and Commander Seer had thought it wise to act, in view of the Telzilt Council's restrictions over the use of its bypasses by ISA and Norvallan fleet ships. Those two, and the heavy cruisers recently arrived from Valla Key, were all now in breach of the directive.

* * *

The next day was as busy as the one before, but by its close, most of *Arianrhod's* payload was out, the goods from Letik Crystal Mining Corp aboard and processed meta-jurillium sheets from Letik Aggregates on the way. Azular and Kinnitix were with Metriklon, helping advance the comms work, and repair rigs had been placed by the *Moonstone* and the *Kel'Moth*. There was rising tension at Telzilt as the Norvallan ships and the *Adamant* had refused to apply for retrospective permission to use Telziltic bypasses. The Norvallan government had been asked to take a hand or risk sanctions by several Federated systems. The *Serenity* and *Zetkalt* were still there, but the *Jekzilt* had left on a mission.

The reason for the repair rigs was visible some hours later. The skull and crossbones that was the age-old Trades Alliance symbol had been erased from the two Starfall ships. Azular, back aboard and in a private chat with Ahxenta, could say why: both were now allied to the Free-Market Trades Exchange. It did not insist on the display of its insignia: a registered call-sign marker and a secure holo identified its members.

Azular had also brought up a prototype comms unit. The Metriklon team had worked all night to produce a small number. For the device to be quickly usable, the researchers had designed it as an external unit, for attaching to typical comms consoles. For fitting into new ships or comms utilities, a tailored version could be made. A current hitch with the bolt-on model was that a dedicated hull array was needed, but that could be an advantage if standard hull comms arrays had been disabled.

The captain could see where it was going. "You've got the array as well, haven't you, and you want it fitted to *Arianrhod's* hull?"

"Aye, ma'am; it's not a big job. Our engineers could probably do it as an external. I'd have to check with the chief, but as we *are* in port and liable to remain here for another three or four days…"

"Another three or four days? How do you figure that?"

"The *Kel'Moth* and the *Moonstone* haven't finished offloading, and Dr Kinnitix told me that there were more cargoes for Telzilt. Two deals have been agreed for the *Kel'Moth*, and extra contracts are on offer to shift bulky batches of raw jurillium sheets for processing; as we're the largest carriers here, it's a trade opportunity. I'm sure Lindell will be notified as soon as the specs are known and the details finalised."

"Huh! Well, in the event he isn't, you can drop into his office after we're done and tell him. With no TA flag over our heads, trade might be thin once we're back on our own patch. As for a new comms array on my hull, I want to know more about this unit you plan to attach to my main comms station before you go any further. Anything else?"

"I'd like to work with Dr Kinnitix on the data shard adjustments. It makes sense to fine-tune all our shards at one time; once it's done, we can work on the problems that might crop up in integrating the new comms unit into our present system, if that *is* the agreed way forward," he added hurriedly at the glint in her eye. "Ter – Dr Kinnitix – has passed the details to Lieutenant Commander Zel, Captain Thal's senior science officer. One thing I suggest, and Dr Kinnitix agrees, is that we fit two: one in our main bridge, the other in our secondary bridge. The *Moonstone* would have two in any case, one for each hull. How we'd persuade the remainder of the PSS fleet to take on the new system, I don't know, but as it's certain that the ISA and others have cracked the UV-III, it may not be too difficult."

"Most Privates are mavericks, as we have no fleet body as fall back," Ahxenta said. "Any means of keeping our business from the ISA and TA is a plus. Every ship registering as a PSS knows the score and most captains are savvy. But there's no point in extolling the virtues of a new piece of kit unless it's been shown to work *and* cause no harm to the current system or the ship. And until I'm absolutely sure of that, you'll be fixing nothing to my comms consoles or my hull. Clear?"

"Yes ma'am."

"Good. Now get to the super's office. I expect you'd like to work with Kinnitix aboard the *Moonstone*?" the captain added sardonically.

"Yes, ma'am," he replied eagerly.

"Agree it with Captain Kerrix. Greffy can cover here. Now he's first lieutenant he'll be keen for more responsibility, and he's able."

Azular was out of the door in a flash, grinning. The captain sat back with a sigh to check the status updates. She had a lot of thinking to do, much of it requiring soul searching. She tabbed her comms console.

"Mr Bellfish? I want a long-distance link, on the modified UV-III, to Captain Bluejohn of the *Obsidian Sky*."

Her next task was to plan a briefing to inform her seniors of the latest and call for ideas and opinions. If the deals were as stated and agreed, the crew would be busy over a longer stop. She decided on the next day, to allow time for Azular and Lindell to carry out their tasks. By the time it was set, her call to the *Obsidian Sky* had gone through.

* * *

The captain and first mate met as usual for a late meal, to discuss ship's business. Ahxenta had called for status reports from her section heads in advance of the briefing, and was reading them as Apnis arrived.

"Everything moving along okay, Cinnabar? You were locked up in your office for a while, and a heap of comms were coming and going. And you've set an early briefing."

"Everything's up to speed. We've no acute issues in medbay, we've all the supplies we need to keep us going until Telzilt, and the contract to pick up two batches of jurillium sheets from Perk Metals is sealed, so we start loading late tomorrow. The outer holds are ready and Chief Hardbake's teams are on standby. Thal's dealt with Perk, he's vouched for them, and they have the gear to get the loads into orbit. I've had a note from Azular that he and Kinnitix have done with the code-decode shard changes and he'll bring our set back with him. Those two and Zel are still scratching their heads over the prototype comms piece they figure can be the basis of a system to replace the UV-III, but Azular says its looks promising, and the add-on hull array part that's needed can be set up on its own in advance of insertion of the module as a useable piece of kit. I've told Cottontail to have her people check the hull piece and its links in depth and its suitability for use, and I want input from Bellfish on the comms unit."

"It's lucky most of our crew are experts in their fields," remarked Apnis. "Azular's staying over, then? He'll have to be up and across first thing to make the briefing. But even supposing this thing works and is cost effective, it won't be in place before we leave here, surely?"

"The team in the Metriklon labs are working overtime on the pieces; they see them as a big step forward, and thus very saleable, *if* they work as advertised and can be shown to be simple to retrofit. Because of the organic parts, their range of variable parameters is, in effect, unlimited. As far as I understand, it means that each system produced for a client is specific to them and won't overlap any other. As the client sets the security level and the final coding, even the producers won't be able to override their own systems once they're in place."

"Sounds to me like you're buying into this gear, Cap. But our Azular can be persuasive when he's excited about something, especially tech."

"You don't need to tell me that, I know him too well. That's why I've asked around. Kerrix and Thal trust the instincts of their experts, and have brought in *their* senior comms officers to check the bits. The consensus is that if the things can be shown to work well, we go for it. One advantage is that the company will give us the prototype working gear free, provided we check it out as a useable system and send them regular reports of its efficacy. They want it done inside three months."

"That's doable? And Thal and Kerrix have agreed?" Apnis asked.

"Yes and yes; I've run the ideas and the science by Grey Bluejohn, and he's up for it. He reckons things are getting stickier with the TA. He'd heard about our problems from Melly Goodsocks, and other PSS captains he's met are getting antsy *and* narked. The TA keeps squeezing its contract to get more for less. I've run another couple of ideas by him too, but asked him to keep them close for now."

"And what might they be, Cinnabar?" the first mate queried quietly. "I figured something was up after you'd cut the link to the *Obsidian*."

"I won't keep it from you, Tallica, but we're not discussing it here. We'll head to my office after this. It's all up in the air anyhow: I need a meet with Thal and Kerrix to clear the details, but they've got things on at Telzilt. We *could* make for home once we've delivered, but if this comes off, I'll have to be on the surface for talks. Our first stop after Telzilt is Starfall, as we'll have gear to drop there."

"Any more on what the deal is at Telzilt? I've heard zip about the *Adamant*, that fancy Norvallan science boat and those heavy cruisers."

"Stalemate; but it's politics and I'm not sticking my nose in unless it gets personal. Though I've an inkle of what the TA's beef is against us. Levettiza's been in touch with old Intelligence mates, and it seems that certain ISA parties are leaning on the TA to reduce our clout in the PSS fleet and elsewhere. We're seen as a disruptive influence, as we spotted the uproar and got the better of their people at Fourpoint, *and* worked out what their ships and their zone Psi allies were up to on the sly. And told the mapped galaxy about it, which caused red faces and fuss. And now we're riding with Starfall ships, trading in Psi, and have acted as escort to two ambassadors that the ISA had been wooing, as it wants them, or rather their governments, on board."

"Hell's teeth, Cap, we're only one ship! Although she is *Arianrhod*. But Starfall's already a thorn in the ISA's side, hence its attempts to annex Thal's covert bypasses that criss-cross known space. The ISA doesn't want ships in and out of its playground that can't be tracked."

"Too true. But finish up, and we'll head to my office. I'll welcome your input, and I *will* bring it up at tomorrow's briefing."

* * *

The briefing session was lengthy, and the officers returning to post had serious faces. The captain left Apnis to manage final preparations and contract issues for their loads and shuttled alone to the *Kel'Moth* to meet Thal and Kerrix for talks and links to Telzilt and elsewhere. She was gone five hours and sorely in need of a break on her return, but she insisted on an update meeting with her senior crew.

It took the time set aside to finish loading and other trade, but that allowed prototype comms units to be fitted to the stations of the three PSS vessels, and attachment of the new hull array element. During that time news came in that the *Adamant* and *Skelfinnix* had left Telzilt on a line to Amity. Retrospective consent to use Telziltic bypasses had been granted, and relations were said to be mending between the Union of Federated Systems and Norvalla, but the *Serenity* still held at Telzilt. She was to be escorted home by her fleet's two heavy cruisers.

"It's been quite a haul," the first mate said to the captain as they set to leave Letik. "Our people need shore leave, but that won't be an option at Telzilt. Nor at Starfall, but as we'll now have a stop at Freskat after that, we could maybe factor some in?"

"We will; I'll have a bit to organise there, and I want a meet with Zillah, but that's in the future," Ahxenta told her.

Apnis grinned. "We'll cause a stir when we make Freskat, especially as there's an ISA office next to Fleet HQ. It's as well the *Adamant's* left – she'd have a thing or two to report home. Though it's possible we might meet her at Amity Beacon. We'll have to navigate that carefully, if that man-made pocket-thing's still spewing energy every so often."

"We will, but Starfall ships have been through recently and we have their nav-data, thanks to Captain Thal. Swilf's threat of closing it has crashed, as the ISA knows that any attempt will blast fresh negotiations with Psi authorities out of the water. That's the signal. Helm, ready us to follow the *Moonstone* out, at your discretion. Steady as she goes."

"Aye ma'am. Setting orbital release. That's us loose," Dox stated, as she brought the massive ship up in a wide curve. "Keep us on a tight line," she ordered her sidekick. "Next stop Telzilt."

"Next stop Telzilt," Box echoed. "It won't take long – we'll be there before we know it."

"Ever an optimist," the first mate chuckled. "But it's only ten hours away and our route's clear. We'll catch up to the *Amber Flash* and the *Lucent* once we get in. I take it they'll be heading out with us, Cap?"

"They will. Thal wants escorts through Amity, as he suspects that the *Adamant* and her friends will still be about. You'll take the conn for now, I've things to arrange ahead of time. Azular and Bellfish will run tests on the new comms add-ons once we're on the bypass. A series of trial comms have been set up with the *Kel'Moth* and *Moonstone*, using all the units. Greffy and Gallus can run the secondary bridge system."

"Roger that," Apnis replied, settling into her chair to sift through her tasks as the ship picked up speed to follow her sister vessels out.

With one change of watch, the three made good time and were soon locked into low orbits round Telzilt, to simplify cargo handover. The captain remained on the bridge to oversee discharge of the first load, and as that ran smoothly, she left the rest with Apnis and set off to the surface with Lindell to meet Thal, Kerrix and other parties. The issues to be discussed, argued and possibly agreed would take most of the residual hours in the Telzilt business day and carry on into the next.

Ahxenta and Lindell returned to the ship the next afternoon. Lindell had two trade deals in hand. The captain found she had more in hers, as a private memo awaited her. She let it rest to attend to priorities. As the drop of the Letik loads had gone to plan, she ordered *Arianrhod's* two massive outer holds stripped out for work to be done. Her inner holds held the treated gem-grade jurillium and crystals taken on at Letik. Much of it would be left at Starfall for safe keeping, as Thal had borne part of the cost, but the rest was for Freskat. The inner hold space still free was to be readied for a batch of nano-parts for Starfall.

One of the effects of the long dialogues and hard thinking the crew could see twelve hours later, when two small repair rigs that had been set into place and anchored at the exits of *Arianrhod's* open outer cargo bays became hives of activity. A suited-up ship's loading crew was in post and ready to assist the Telzilt team carrying out the work.

"End of an era, Cinnabar," Tallica Apnis breathed three hours later, as secure cams in the bays, tied into the bridge holo, showed the repair rigs slowly retracting, to reveal the results of all the hard work.

The emblazoned Trades Alliance crest was gone, the slip track that led into the body of each great bay now smoothly polished. The captain took her eyes from the spectacle and sighed.

"Put me on ship-wide audio, comms... Captain to crew. *Arianrhod* is no longer part of the Trades Alliance. We are now members of the Free-Market Trades Exchange, registered at Telzilt. We will fly under its flag and use its registered call-sign. An FMTE identity holo will be transferred to all crew wrist comms. A list of our rights and benefits as a member of the FMTE is available on the intra-ship info net. The *PSS Emerald* has also been registered under the same terms. Captain out."

"So how long before the nuisance calls start?" the first mate asked.

"We might make it as far as zone Lambda, but I doubt it," was the dry response. "Melly's having the work done on the *Emerald* at her next stop, Keystone Kell, so she'll be in for flak before we will. She's picking up small arms for Starfall, so I've ordered her to hold off on call-sign integration until she gets there, and wait for us. We'll both head out to Freskat, as I may need her before I'm done. Grey knows what's gone on and has leave to pass it on to whom he sees fit, but only in person. Now our outer bays are shipshape, our teams will ready them to receive

Captain Thal's new shuttles. Loading's set for ten hundred tomorrow. They'll taxi in on auxiliaries and our people will shut them down and remove their energy cells for the ride to Starfall. Azular will check them as they come in. They're just off a production line on Rom Litra, and as that's a trusted ally of Telzilt, they should be bona fide."

"These shuttles: are they up to Starfall's standards of highly shielded and tough as old boots, *and* made of that hull material that most of Thal's ships are?" Apnis asked slyly.

"Yes they are; and no Commander Earbleat, you won't be making sorties into the bays to give them the once over," she told the second mate, whose ears had pricked. "Once we're at Starfall and they move out, the last one will be put into one of our inner shuttle bays. Crizz's team will have the job of making her ours. You have the blueprint of Captain Kerrix' fighter and some of the bits she was so kind as to hand over; you can play with them and make sure *Loki's* up to trim. We haven't had to use her in a while, and she'd better be ready if we do."

"I hope that's not prophetic, Cap. But it's been one hell of a day. We've a lot to digest. And I for one am ready for mess time."

"You and me both; I've heard things that I'd rather not have. But we can talk tomorrow's loading schedules over our rations."

"Thanks for that, Cap."

"Welcome; let's move it."

There were a number of things to discuss, including certain comings and goings between the *Moonstone* and the surface that were taking up much time. It was apparent that it had upset Azular's plans, but he was no wiser as to the reasons. The captain and first mate made early to their billets however, as the next day would be busy and would be a prelude to departure back to more familiar territory.

* * *

Loading the new shuttles for Starfall was simple, as they were efficient, sleek and fast. That and the pick-up of the nano-parts were finished by late afternoon, and the crew had leisure to reflect. Azular used his time to try to reach Captain Kerrix, who had been planetside but was now back aboard ship. It was hours before she returned the link, and in the interim the *Serenity* had left Telzilt with the two Norvallan cruisers at her tail. Kerrix had news that Azular thought best his captain was told at once and in private. He tracked her down in main engineering.

"You'd best use my office if it's so confidential," Chief Cottontail told him. "I've no shortage of work to do out here."

Ahxenta indicated the door and the two made in. "To do with the trips up and down," she said, pouring coffees. "Let's hear it. I saw the

Serenity and her shadows decamp, so they're for Norvalla?"

"Yes, ma'am; the ambassador needs to discuss treaty details with her government, and with recent events, there's a lot to argue over."

"The admiral will be glad to get home as well, I suppose."

"The admiral's not gone with the *Serenity*, Captain; he's resigned his commission in the Norvallan fleet and is aboard the *Moonstone*."

"He's what?!"

"That was the gist of Captain Kerrix' link, and what's taken so long, and so many sorties up and down."

"I bet that went down well with his fleet. But surely he *has* a home?"

"The fleet *and* the authorities are livid because he's party to a lot of fleet data, he's one of its most highly ranked officers and he's an expert in fleet law, so he's often called in on legal issues. As for his home, I don't know; but I'm sure it's a personal matter that prompted the step. He'll stop off at Starfall but his station will be on the *Moonstone*, as an advisor, Captain Kerrix told me."

"I bet: she won't have him in authority over her. A Norvallan fleet admiral in the Starfall fleet, aboard a PSS? No wonder the powers that be are hacked off. And once it hits ISA ears, there'll be major fallout," she chuckled. "I'd like to be a fly on the wall when the big guns *do* find out. I take it this is to be kept quiet for now?"

"Aye ma'am; the *Moonstone's* crew know, but only the senior officers of the *Kel'Moth*, *Amber Flash* and *Lucent* are to be told."

"I'll let ours in before departure. That's set for eleven hundred. The *Amber Flash* and *Lucent* took on cargoes; for Starfall, I expect. But why would an admiral leave everything behind, including home and career, for Starfall? There must be a lot more to it."

"I agree, ma'am; and Captain Kerrix wouldn't say. But the admiral is of age and has the right to retire, I understand, which means that his fleet has very little hold over him."

"People like him rarely retire," the captain noted with a short laugh. "They keep going until they're tied to a desk or fall off the perch. I've certainly no plans to hang up my uniform."

"I'm glad to hear it, ma'am."

The first mate was similarly surprised when she heard the news, as were the ship's seniors when they were told at the wrap-up session before withdrawal. Earbleat's main concern was how one would deal with the admiral face-to-face, rank being rank.

"I've met Admiral Posettix, and he'll tell you if you step out of line, believe me," the captain assured her. "We've three days on the bypass from Telzilt to Amity to get used to the idea. It won't affect us. What's waiting for us at Amity on the other hand, might. Starfall's watching, and Captain Thal's Kirtish contacts update him. The *Adamant, Sparillia* and *Skelfinnix* are lurking about trying to fix what they did wrong at the gravity well cum worm-pocket, but normal space is chaotic as it's still subject to random energy and gravity fluxes. Work was at a standstill the last Thal heard. I want all departments at full alert all the way, and that means that *Loki* and our decoy must be ready to run. And *we* need to be aware that the *Moonstone* now has a decoy; if she launches it, we'll have to mark it as friendly and not shoot it down. Have you got that, Commander Earbleat?"

"Aye, Cap. Gliss can lock in its spec and it'll show on the grid. And the *Moonstone* and the *Kel'Moth* – and the others – will have to be alerted. We don't want to lose the decoy or my *Loki* to friendly fire."

"Good point; Azular, you'll deal with that once we're on the bypass, as I'm sure you'll be in contact with the *Moonstone* at some point."

"Affirmative, ma'am," he smiled.

"What does a PSS admiral's insignia and ranking pips look like, Cap?" the first mate queried on the way to the bridge after the briefing. "Can't say I've seen any before."

"Search me; but I'm sure we'll recognise them."

The bridge was prepared, and the captain saw that the holo-grid had been updated to show an unknown navigational hazard close to Amity. Box had devised and run sims and plotted jump lines to avoid potential threats, and Dox had increased power to the ship's main stabilisers.

As before, the five ships locked helms to run as a convoy, the two smaller covering their flanks. It had been agreed that the new comms units, attached and tested as far as ship's ops were concerned, would be used during the trip to Starfall, to assess in-flight use. The exchange of chat between the ships prior to leaving orbit allowed Ahxenta a clear view of the *Moonstone's* bridge, and as her eyes raked the ops section at the back of the dual command position, she noted that the admiral had been assigned a station next to Ter Kinnitix. He was in a PSS uniform but his ranking pips were not visible. From the quiet chuckle of Apnis alongside, it was obvious that she had also spotted him.

The removal from Telzilt was routine and the ships soon made the node. Once in hyperspace, the journey settled into an even tenor. The crew of *Arianrhod* were used to long periods of tedium, but the captain had decreed no drills: she wanted the new gear tested, and she wanted to give her crew time to get used to being part of a new trade body. How companies in the original zones would react was another matter.

By the time the group was close to Amity, Ahxenta had heard from

Captains Bluejohn and Holdspan. Both were keen to know more about the FMTE. Bluejohn had told the captain of the *Nyx Warrior*, whom he had met on Delta Iridium, and had sounded out the captains of the *Green Comet* and *Hexameter*, whose ships he had passed en route to the Web. Melly Goodsocks had also been in touch. The work done on the *Emerald* at Keystone Kell had caused no more than a trickle of interest there, and she was well on the way to Starfall.

The news that the convoy was on the bypass to Amity had travelled, for the *Adamant* and *Sparillia* were holding position off beacon. The *Kel'Moth* was hailed in a hollow courtesy call, to warn of unstable local gravity currents and sporadic signals that might imply alien activity, but as the ships had been scanned since before the node switch, and the two ISA vessels had increased their attempts and were striving to deep scan, Thal did not buy it. He voiced disbelief and insisted they desist. Swilf made the usual claims that the ISA, as a protecting power, had every right. Thal cut him off mid-sentence and ordered a direct transfer to the bypass for Kirtish as arranged.

The *Arianrhod's* holo-grid was fully engaged, and as the five changed course as one to comply, her chief tactical officer let out a warning cry.

"Captain! We have a blip on the bypass! It's a cloaked ship, huge, and she's heading this way!"

The much enhanced holo had shifted to show a signal that indicated a large ship on approach. Moments later, it was obvious that Thal had taken steps to deal with potential trouble, for the ship decloaked and her call-sign clearly indicated her origin.

"It's the *Kel'Torc*!" Azular called. "She's coming about."

"Just as well," Apnis hissed. "Those two are about to jump on after us! What's the excuse? We're here to see you safe home?"

"Like hell," Ahxenta replied grimly.

Thal was on the link directly to confirm the *Kel'Torc* as their escort, to protect their rear. The convoy would not stop at Kirtish, but given their loading, cut to Starfall as rapidly as possible. They would not run silent, as too many now knew of them.

"Bet it doesn't stop the ISA and its flies on the wall from asking," Apnis grumbled to the captain as the link was cut.

The first mate was right, for coming up on Selky three days later, comms called that the base had called for their IDs.

"That place has grown since last we saw it, and still has a string of transports on the ground," Azular reported. "And the *Elucida* and the *Crusader* in orbit. With the *Adamant* and the *Sparillia* at our backs, they'll think they have us surrounded."

"*Crusader* online with a request for our ID and our business in this sector, Captain!" Bellfish called.

"Us, specifically?"

"Aye, ma'am; it's a directed link."

"They can read our new call-sign, and with their buddy boats at our backs, they damn well know who we are and where we're headed," the captain fumed. "Put me on to Captain Flute so I can shout at him."

Flute was ready for the call but not for the scorching tongue-lashing that hit his ears before he could speak. He had just begun his demand for an apology when Ahxenta ordered the link cut.

"Another stain on our record," the first mate grunted. "I bet we've a file to ourselves at ISA HQ, in its sinners and rebels databank."

"We keep all our scanners and probes on those tricksters," was the response. "Flute's fast reaching the top of my irritating persons list."

"He'll never outstrip Myrtleberry," Apnis smiled. "I'm *so* in need of civilisation; compared to this, Starfall's a haven of tranquillity."

"Hardly," the captain disagreed. "But we'll have a quick cargo drop, resupply, and exit there, as I've things to attend to. I'll need at least one meet with Thal and his people, but then we're for Freskat."

"Now that *is* civilisation," the first mate nodded.

"And shore leave," whispered Box in a voice meant to be heard.

"Roger that, Mr Box," Apnis said, agreeing with him for once.

"We'll have time," the captain promised. "But we've still four days to Starfall and a tail that's trying to wind us up like a prop."

* * *

By the time Starfall was achieved, the *Adamant* and *Sparillia* had gone. The two had seen the group as far as Canna, and with nary a word had cut off on a line that indicated Minch Fettin. In Ahxenta's opinion, it was a blind. That route could put them on course for ISA's Kellybar One station, at the edge of the ISP-run sector of Kappa, but could equally take them to Wester 287 and Zeta or further into Mu.

The first cargoes unloaded were Thal's new shuttles, leaving the one for *Arianrhod*. Resupply was scheduled to go ahead in tandem with the discharge of the other loads, the spare crystals and gem-grade jurillium being the principal. The captain left the work to her first mate; she had other business, the first being a visit to the *Emerald*. Now that call-sign integration was done, she was fully under the FMTE flag.

Ahxenta found that Goodsocks had had to fend off a well-meaning series of queries from ships that included those of TA-linked merchant lines, as the TA had sent an advisory of its actions against specific PSS vessels to all the ships under its flag. *Emerald* had also been hailed by the *Snow Quartz* near Stook, and had met the *Tektite* at Wester 287. Both PSS captains had been supportive and had asked to be kept up to date. Goodsocks had not mentioned her new link to the FMTE but had warned them of the breached UV-III.

"Word will get round in time," Ahxenta said in a follow-up briefing. "But as we now have a batch of code-decode shards to hand on as we get the chance, the fleet might be able to keep the gossips down and halt the leak of data about our business that's getting into the wrong ears. *Why* they want to keep tabs on us is another matter. Hell, we had enough unwanted attention from lackeys of the aliens for the part we played in the war, particularly at Mellifly. And now the so-called forces of law and order are doing the same, as some of them are playing both sides against the middle as far as their own low doings are concerned, and we keep finding out about it and passing it on."

"But the ISA and the TA now know we belong to a zone Psi trades body, and because of Alliance and Psi treaties either set or in progress, they won't want to close too many doors to ships that fly that flag. It won't help trade relations, and it'll tarnish the TA's already half-rusty reputation into the bargain," Lindell pointed out.

"Don't count on it," the captain warned. "The TA has long arms and tentacles in plenty of pies. It'll find ways to hinder us. Though not for long: several of our disillusioned PSS colleagues are interested in joining a group that doesn't put us in the firing line every time there's a whiff of hostile trouble. Captain Bluejohn's met one or two that are openly hinting at a revolt if things don't change."

"But the FMTE would have to be recognised in the mapped zones, *and* have a presence," Apnis argued.

"That might be closer than you think," Ahxenta grinned. "But I've a meet later, at Thal's base. Azular, you're with me, as the new comms units will be part of it. We need to know how well they perform when the ships with them are distant from each other, but for now, those and the enhanced shards are for analysis and continuous testing. You'll liaise with Kinnitix, Nyvallish, Zel and the other science officers after we've discussed their merits and glitches, while I carry on in the talks. Yellowfork will be there, as *Emerald* needs to be up to speed once we bring them in for the whole fleet, if that's found to be the way to go."

"Aye, ma'am," he answered, a little downcast.

The captain could guess why but forbore to comment. She intended to complete her current shipboard duties and other matters that would take her off ship speedily. She felt that her people had been away from their usual haunts for too long, and everyone needed a break, herself not least. She hoped that the talks that Thal had called with the captains of the Starfall ships in port would finalise Starfall issues. A private chat after the main event, that would comprise only her, Thal and Kerrix, had been scheduled in as the last matter on the agenda.

Ahxenta decided to fly the new shuttle. She had tried the sim, and as a skilled pilot could operate it well, but it was no substitute for actual flight. Azular's presence was valuable as he was used to the *Xanna* and the new craft was based on similar but superior tech. The crew that had brought her up to the captain's rigorous standards had named her the *Gremlin*, as they had found a few irritating bugs in adapting her.

A silence bar for ops marked the trip to Thal's HQ. Ahxenta, aware of Azular's mood and his sigh as the craft docked, thought it best to clear the air before disembarking.

"You'll have to get used to leave taking. You've been lucky thus far, and with the new comms and our ties to Starfall, you'll have plenty of opportunity to catch up with Captain Kerrix. You're not the only one aboard *Arianrhod* with long distance relationship issues, you know."

"I know, ma'am," he laughed. "I apologise. Xanna told me the same not long ago. I think she sees more clearly than I do much of the time."

"*I* don't," was the brief reply, as the captain shut down and waited for the bay to pressurise. "But she has some of the nous you lack. Talk to Parri Millit, that's what he's there for. You'll get used to it. We've all had to adjust to life shipboard when there are other things we'd rather be doing. Let's move it. You can pilot her on return."

"Aye ma'am; thank you ma'am."

They found their escorts in the bay. The captain secured her shuttle, nodded at the salute, and followed the two. They had walking to do, as the briefing room was near the labs where the scientists would work. Ahxenta and Azular joined the group already in; the captains of all the PSS Starfall vessels and their science officers had been invited, as had the captains of the *Amber Flash* and *Lucent*. Goodsocks was there with Yellowfork, both interested in their first sight of Thal's HQ. The final trio, from the *Moonstone*, were on the way.

Coffee was offered just as the last three arrived. Discussion of the code-decode devices and the add on modules was dealt with quickly, as it was obvious that Thal wanted things moving. The main topic once the scientists had left was the position of the PSS ships that had thrown in their lots with the FMTE, and their likelihood of staying afloat in the TA-dominated markets of zones Alpha to Mu.

Ahxenta had come prepared: she had had Lindell draw up a list of the largest free and friendly ports in those zones, organised by their odds of trading with non-TA members. The consensus was that trade would be tight at first but would not suffer in the longer term.

It was possible that the TA would close the bypass routes it held to be its own to the barred ships, but as fleets not tied to the TA that were registered with local powers could use the routes, albeit at a cost, and ISA and other fleet defence ships had free passage, the issue would be likely to increase current unrest. The wide-ranging TA routes crossed zones Alpha to Mu to link the main trading centres in the most direct ways, but there were other bypasses; those used by Starfall were among the most extensive, but local routes were free to use as they brought in trade and other services to the planetary authorities that ran them.

The Starfall fleet had traded in and beyond Psi for some time, and would be little affected. As far as *Arianrhod* was concerned, travel in the mapped zones would not be a problem as she had access to Starfall routes, and as part of the FMTE, she had the right to trade in zone Psi. As a new private carrier on the scene, and with no fleet, she would be hindered at first by being an unknown quantity, and the same applied to the *Emerald* in what was unknown territory to her.

With the distribution of Ahxenta's list and a promise of nav-charts updates that would take in Starfall and local bypasses, suspected hostile bases, and bypasses or active worm-pockets, the talks were wound up and most of those present released to collect their science officers and return to their ships. Azular, Kinnitix, Nyvallish and Zel were told to carry on with their tasks whilst their senior officers were in the private talk that Thal had scheduled in as the last matter on the agenda.

Thal and Kerrix were obviously in the know about the matters to be discussed, Ahxenta realised, as she was invited to more coffee. And part of the reason she was there was because one at least of the issues raised was personal to her. She was surprised, however, when Thal told her they were waiting for someone else to join the group. That other appeared in a few minutes. It was Admiral Posettix.

25: FAREWELLS

The return to *Arianrhod* was made in the same silence that had marked the outward trip. Azular had plenty to say, but was bid to leave it until next day, when the senior officers could hear. The captain was pensive. What she had heard had given her food for thought, and part of it she was loath to share, even with her close associates. Apnis and Cottontail were there, keen to hear their views on the shuttle and the talks, despite the late hour. Ahxenta's short replies warned them to back off, and as an anxious first mate attended the duo out of the bay, the chief called her team to check over and shut down the craft prior to storage.

"It's late, so mess time for you two, a seat and a hot drink," advised Apnis. "I see you brought gear back with you, Azular."

"Yes, Commander. I'll put it in my lab for now and we can discuss it tomorrow. I take it we'll be here another day or so, Captain?"

"Two days at most, but business can wait for the briefing. I've more to talk over with Captain Thal and others – from the ship," she sighed. "I'll stop to change, and see you in the mess. You too, Azular. It won't be long, I need sack time. So do you two, it's been a long day."

The mess was quiet when the three met. The captain began quickly, as most of what she had to say would not be part of the staff briefing. The first related to the reason the *Serenity* had held on at Starfall, and the regular trips to the planet below. Thal's continuing salvage ops had dug up pieces left over from occupation by the hostiles that had once controlled the base. It seemed that the aliens had used the planet as a holding station for their malign schemes, and more remains, including Norvallan and Telziltic had been retrieved.

The Norvallan link affected the *Serenity*, but the admiral was drawn in for a highly personal reason. Years before, his son had worked in a science facility on Telzilt, and had been taken, with four colleagues, on a raid on his lab. The assailants were thought to be raiders until the all-out hostile attack on Telzilt soon after implied that the raid had been a prelude to invasion. Kerrix had known for a long time; it was why the *Serenity* had stayed at Alto Finglas. She persuaded Posettix to open his heart to Thal, and that had propelled *him* to increase the digging. The latest remains brought up had been sieved out. Nothing that could relate to the admiral had been found – except a small metal insignia bearing the crest of the institute for which his son had worked.

That prompted hard thinking, and Thal had had an idea. Many of the people that had escaped the aliens and been drawn into his group came from diverse planets, including those in Psi. With his vast setup, he could know only a fraction of those under his authority, but he had promised the admiral that he would trawl through what was possible of his fleet's records, to see what could be traced of Norvallan victims that *had* made it out. It would be a long job with no guarantees, but it had given Posettix a new hope that his son might still be alive, and *that* had been the reason he had quit his fleet to join Starfall.

"I'm happy that the admiral might find answers, but why did they bring you in, Cinnabar?" Apnis wanted to know. "Yes, you have links to the issue, but all this is pretty personal to Posettix, and I'm surprised he agreed to extend the list of those who know about it."

"Were there other pieces found, ma'am?" Azular asked gently.

She smiled sadly. "You haven't lost your touch. Yes. You know they found traces of the *Wing Skipper* a while back, in the hull fabric of one of the crashed hostiles? And Freski and Berzic tissue was found by the ISA labs on Alto Finglas, in that creature from the escaped transport out of Sella? Thal's people found more remains, but not attached to an actual body – in very old storage facilities, they think…"

"Oh hell, Cinnabar, no…" Apnis breathed.

"Oh hell, yes. Levettiza still had what she'd dug up of Freski fleet records, and she was able to get access to similar from the Berzic fleet. She's now got DNA signatures for more of those lost aboard the *Wing Skipper.* So it's certain the ship was taken by hostiles and the crew used. But how many? The storage records are being sifted out and analysed, but that's given Thal a problem, because there are people out there that have lost their own, and his results might provide answers for *them.* But how far do you go? Only a few people from the *Wing Skipper* have thus far been identified by the records he has, so did some escape?"

"You mean some of the *Wing Skipper's* crew, amongst others, might still be alive?" the first mate asked. "They'd be a good age by this time, but it's possible…" She sounded doubtful.

"Not if they were kept in cryo suspension for later use," interrupted Azular. "Remember Furze? And Skota, for that matter."

"Hell, I hadn't thought of that!"

"Thal has," the captain said. "He's still searching for clues to the seven kids missing of those stolen from Kelf. But that's it for tonight. I've personal calls to make before I turn in, so no more."

"If you need us, we're here for you, Cinnabar," the first mate said softly, as Azular nodded alongside.

"I know that. Thanks, both. I'll see you in the morning," she said as she rose heavily and set off.

"That's one heck of a load to bear," Apnis said to the science officer as she watched the retreating back in concern. "And I suppose Captain Kerrix has similar. How many more?"

"Too many," he said sadly. "Good night, Commander."

As Apnis sat on, she wondered what the morning would bring. That the captain had much more on her mind, she was sure.

Eight hundred hours brought the staff briefing. Azular was called on to explain what had come out of what he and his fellows had been able to do with the gear they had. He had brought back a case of their work: inserts for the new comms units that would up code complexity, make the network nigh-on impossible to crack, and render each unit unique. They were for test in the units in situ on the three ships, and if effective, Thal planned to fit his PSS ships with them and his non-PSS ships with a similar system. Metriklon's code-decode shards had been deemed a useful short-term fix, but assessment would continue.

The captain's sum-up began with her and Azular's view of the use of the new shuttle, and then a synopsis of trade issues. Thal's pledged nav-charts of hyperspace and other routes, and hostile risk, would have to be merged with theirs and the holo-grid, she told Gliss, but he and Azular could start by adding in Lindell's data on friendly and free ports. Their resupply was done and the materials for their contact on Freskat stored in small cases in a shielded inner hold. As delivery of the Starfall loads had left their huge outer bays free, she had agreed with Thal that *Arianrhod* and *Emerald* would take on cargo for Twilight. The shipment was ready, it would start loading at ten hundred and would take five hours. The admin would come in alongside, which meant that Lindell's next task was dealing with it. He could also begin to scout for trade, but within the limits they were now under. *Arianrhod* and *Emerald* were due to depart at twelve hundred the next day for Twilight.

"Whew! Short and sweet, Cap," Apnis remarked after the others had left. "The loading teams know what's coming their way?"

"Yes; I left the details with Chief Hardbake last night, and the bays are ready. It's not big stuff, supplies mostly. I don't have a full manifest, but every pod will be checked before it's brought in, and it'll be under surveillance. Azular can set Greffy on it; *he'll* be sorting the holo, as it'll have to be ready before we leave. Goodsocks is doing the same. We've no stops between here and Twilight, so a long haul; but as Thal's ships are patrolling the bypass, it should be a clear run."

"Roger that. Boy, do I need shore leave. I'll be glad to see Freskat and real sunshine. It's late summer in the main settlement, isn't it?"

"It is. I'll have a lot to do on surface, and Zillah will want a meet. The latest on us and Starfall will be out by the time we get in, and the whole PSS fleet will have heard by now. But I'd like to see Zillah; she won't hold back, and we'll get more sense out of her than the ISA and TA united. But for now, all speed with loading, and then prepping for the trip. I estimate twelve to fourteen days. Hardbake's seen the pod specs and wants to split them between the two outermost bays."

"Makes sense," agreed the first mate. "If we *do* meet trouble and get hit, it spreads the risk. The only base of Thal's we pass is Sunrise, but we'll pass spots like Flint Wolf and Kelfennig, and there must be jump points on the way. There are nodes by Pollens Sentry and Wemm, but Wemm's the only inhabited planet. That's a lot of empty space."

"True; but we'll have the *Emerald* alongside, and Melly Goodsocks can be depended on in a fight."

The bridge stations were already in action as the pods, attached to grapples, were heading in. Their track could be seen on a fly-out of the holo, and Greffy was scanning them on approach. The loading teams were on standby, the captain was assured, as the duty officer gave up the command chair. She and Apnis took their places.

* * *

Starfall base was long gone and *Arianrhod* and her sister ship were over two days into the bypass and about to skirt Sunrise when a blip on the grid indicated a fast ship closing with them. *Arianrhod* and *Emerald* were running shielded, but Ahxenta immediately called for weapons on line and an alert to Goodsocks. The orders were just given when Bellfish called that they were being hailed. Gliss and Azular had already set long distance scanners in a directional beam on the incoming ship.

"I have Captain Green of the *SS Glenblaze*, Captain!"

"Confirm ship as the *SS Glenblaze*," Azular added loudly.

"Tell *Emerald* to hold, Bellfish; and get Captain Green on visual,"

The *Glenblaze* had been sent out from Sunrise by base commander Captain Mint, to escort the ships as far as Pollens Sentry, Captain Neela Green stated. A scout had detected two small hostiles less than a day before, off the bypass and close to the empty Chelda system, half way between Pollens and Sunrise. The third planet had been a hideout in the past but was believed to have been abandoned years before.

"The commander of our scout reckons the two blips were small," Green said. "Possibly his opposite numbers: hostile scouts to check if

Chelda Three could be reclaimed, and have a good look round the local area – which means our bypass. He called it in and it'll be added to our list of possible trouble spots. Meanwhile, I'll ride with you and make a sweep of the system on the way – if you've no objections, of course."

"None at all; you're welcome, Captain. And we'll add our scanning power to yours," Ahxenta told her. "Lock in the alert to our grid, Mr Gliss. Notify the *Emerald*, Mr Bellfish."

With an agreed course set and Goodsocks informed, the ships flew on. It was three days to Chelda and much could happen. As it was, all that did was that the grid update came in from Starfall, with news that one of its ships en route to Arrissia from Heligon had identified a large hostile interceptor on a line to Kelfennig, and possibly the bypass. Thal had no ship free to check, but had sent word to Heligon and Arrissia, and on an open channel, from which the ISA would hear.

As far as the ships could tell, nothing had jumped onto the bypass at their backs, but Ahxenta had her seniors on duty and the ship at alert as the Chelda system came into range. She had agreed with Green on passing scans, so as not to endanger *Arianrhod* or *Emerald* by slowing. With every array on line, the three came to closest approach. All were aware that a base station might be at the far side of any planet, or be cloaked and invisible. Nothing registered, and they continued to scan as the system receded. Ahxenta was about to call stand down when the comms officer let out a yell.

"A distress, ma'am, PSS channel! Off the bypass in normal space!"

"What's a PSS doing in normal space outside zone borders?" Apnis asked, tightening her restraints as the red alert rang out and Bellfish called that the *Emerald* and the *Glenblaze* had both caught the distress.

"She'd been on this bypass," Ahxenta replied grimly. "Or it's a trap. Either way, we need more data. Hot them up, Earbleat! Slow to jump-off speed, helm, but be ready to resume on my mark! Ready *Loki* and the decoy! Updates, all stations!"

"Three ships, Captain!" Gliss responded loudly. "Sending to grid!"

"Confirmed!" Azular added. "Two definitely hostile in outline, large interceptors, I'd estimate... the third reads as a PSS!"

Ahxenta ordered a link to her flanking ships to tell them she was going in. Both agreed to follow: they had logged similar. As the three made ready to jump off in attack formation, Bellfish called again.

"Got a call-sign! It's the *PSS Nyx Warrior*! Repeat, the *Nyx Warrior*! Sending data to *Emerald* and *Glenblaze*!"

The three burst out to take up positions around the trio, angling to cover escape. The aliens were scarred and well-armed, with chameleon-cloaked hulls. The *Warrior* was holding on, but had taken heavy fire.

"Dox, all speed to that blip off the *Warrior's* port. Increase starboard shields! Earbleat, the second she's in your sights, hit her with all you've got!" Ahxenta ordered in a loud, angry voice, as *Arianrhod* spun under Dox's swift handling.

"Blip's closing on *Warrior*, deploying slicers!" Gliss cried. "No: she's marked us! Changing course to take us on! She's let loose with phase cannon and torpedoes!"

"Launch deflecting drones in her face!" bellowed the captain as the ship shuddered to a glancing missile hit and Dox pulled her out of the path of incoming fire whilst maintaining her angle of attack.

Earbleat's loud directives to her crews were rewarded by the searing bursts of flame of several direct hits, and their enemy erupted into an expanding ball of splinters.

"Get us out of this debris!" Ahxenta yelled as the thwack of metal striking *Arianrhod's* hull reverberated around them. "What's the status of the *Warrior*? I can't see her in all this flak."

"She's in one piece ma'am," Azular reported loudly. "Position on grid. *Glenblaze* and *Emerald* have got the second hostile on the run, but there's a lot of fast moving wreckage."

"Maintain red alert and keep distance scanners on line. Comms, get me the *Warrior*. Dox, get us close enough to let our tractors get a grip and haul her out of that flak field – she can't manoeuvre."

"*Glenblaze* and *Emerald* have taken out their target," Gliss told her, as Bellfish called that he had made a link to the *Nyx Warrior*.

Holdspan's bridge was chaotic, the thuds of impacting debris on his hull echoing over external comms, but he seemed unhurt. His ship had taken a beating, but once he had his engines back on line, she should be able to make the bypass, he told Ahxenta. *Her* first concern was to get them all safe, and she ordered her engineers to deploy tractors to pull the *Warrior* out of the danger zone and into a patch of clear space. The *Glenblaze* and the *Emerald* were already coming about.

"Those ships were poorly manned, Captain," Azular reported. "By cyber hostiles, I'd guess, as I read trace zukivianite and a deal of other recognisably hostile materials, but little organic matter."

With the three intact ships assisting, the *Warrior* was soon clear. No other craft were detected on the path to the bypass, but the *Glenblaze* had warned Starfall. Holdspan could not tell from which direction the hostiles had come. The *Warrior* had detected activity in the unmapped sector off the bypass, but read it as coming from a listening post ahead of Chelda. They were almost on it when an interceptor, its hull signals shifting, jumped in to strike. As weapons use in hyperspace was risky, Holdspan ordered his ship off at the node, only to find another homing in. With no option but to engage, he had sent the distress.

Damage assessment complete, the *Warrior's* captain was relieved to report that he could carry on. He had lost an auxiliary engine and had serious shielding and array damage, but his casualty list was short. He had been to Arrissia Five and was on his way to Nyx and had chosen the Starfall bypass as it was more rapid and direct than any other, and as a PSS, he had access. He had got Thal's alert on the sighting of a large interceptor, which had driven him to run cloaked, but even his top-notch sensors had not caught its signal.

"It could be that the two blips off Chelda spied by that scout from Sunrise picked up the *Warrior* and reported it to their base, but as she was cloaked, it's not likely," Ahxenta posited. "It's more likely that she was watched at Arrissia and seen to head this way instead of the route she'd normally have taken, and a hostile spy reported it back – hence the ship sent in, with the other at its back. But why?"

"To keep people away from Chelda, if they *are* trying to re-establish a presence there," Green said. "But hostile spies at Arrissia? That's not good. I'll report it to my people. But we'd best get back on the bypass. There can't be much on Chelda now, as we'd have seen a lot more action, but it's a long way from here to Twilight."

With accord reached, the four ships formed up and made the jump at the local node. Links passing between the *Glenblaze* and her base had prompted an increase in patrols by Thal, and the news that a ship had been diverted by Captain Ver to escort them. The *SS Firestar*, now at an unnamed settlement on Delta edge, would meet them by Pollens Sentry in forty hours, and carry on with them to Twilight Station.

* * *

The light cruiser *SS Firestar*, Captain Torri Slate in command, met them as agreed. They had had no upset nor hint of any craft on the bypass bar themselves, but all wanted to make quickly to Twilight. As Slate would give no details on the unnamed settlement from which he had come, Azular, always curious, had used his spare time to enquire. There was a system marked on the holo-grid that had one habitable planet within two days of their rendezvous point, right on the edge of Delta and in an empty area, which he took as a likely candidate. He had thus contacted Captain Kerrix for details, and had found himself in as close as they had come to serious argument. She had abruptly warned him off, and on that basis he had inferred it was a secret Starfall base.

He later told the captain, and to his chagrin, found her on Kerrix' side. As Slate had been so reticent, Ahxenta had suspected it might be a refuge for the vulnerable of Thal's people, and those caring for them. She recalled the chat with Thal after the attack at Starfall, when Kerrix risked her life in her small fighter to protect a section of Starfall's inner ring. The children from Furze were there, as there had been nowhere then safer to transfer them. Azular was warned to let the matter be.

The rest of the trip to Twilight was quiet, but everyone remained at alert. The vast swathe of space with no known habited worlds and little mapped data could hide surprises. Base commander Captain Kismulin Ver greeted them and agreed to carry out minimal repairs on the *Nyx Warrior*. *Arianrhod* and *Emerald* would stop only to drop their cargoes, Ahxenta ruled, as she was keen to reach Freskat. The *Glenblaze* and the *Firestar* had urgent duties and left soon after arrival. The base was busy, but Ver had gear ready to catch the cargo pods as they were released.

"Four hours and we'll be on the road to sunshine!" Box enthused to his mate. "First stop on Freskat, the *Bowsprit* and a jar of ale!"

"First stop on Freskat, the *Halcyon* and a hot tub," Dox corrected. "And we're not at the top of the leave rota, we'll have to take our turn."

"Whatever. And then the *Bowsprit?*" he added hopefully.

"And then the *Bowsprit*," she agreed.

Apnis nodded at the captain. "Seems a good idea. Ver runs a tight ship. She's got three heavy cruisers in orbit, listening posts and upped outer defences on the way in, and marker buoys further out."

"And there's a short local bypass to Aoria Six: handy for best quality weapons supplies and other useful items. I'll have to remember that. It makes things easier for Nat; he could stop off on the way home. Which reminds me, I need to have a chat with him before we leave – he asked. But we won't stop at Aoria this bout. I've a lot to do on Freskat."

The first mate looked across shrewdly, but said nothing. There was an issue taxing the captain, and it related to what had been going on over the last weeks. Ahxenta read the look.

"I want this show on the road, so you'll have to wait 'til Freskat. It'll take two days. Quiet days, I hope."

The captain's hope was realised, and two days later *Arianrhod* and *Emerald* made berth around the sixth planet. Ahxenta had no need to contact Zillah, for as soon as the ship had registered, a comm came in from her. The battlecruiser *ISAS Merrin Free* was in orbit and a watch was ordered on *her* lest she attempt a scan, but nothing was detected.

"They wouldn't dare," Apnis said as the two looked over their tasks. "Zillah wants an early meet, so she's first? Then the PSS registry office, to confirm our change of details in person?"

"Yes. Half the traders here know we're no longer TA. I had Lindell check for deals, and there were queries. Once we're set, I'll head to my buddy's place for a chat; the cargo for him can wait. He has stuff ready that *Emerald* can take on, once Lindell finds a market for it."

"He will: there must be plenty places keen for quality comms gear. That's maybe one thing Zillah wants to discuss. You plan to stay down for a time?" Apnis asked quietly. "You're entitled to leave and you sure as hell need it. I'm surprised the doc hasn't ordered you off."

"She has," Ahxenta admitted ruefully. "It'll keep. As all's quiet, start shore leave. Our people are desperate for sun, fun or whatever, and they all know Freskat like the backs of their hands."

"Roger that, Cap. We'll have Azular with us for the meets?"

"We will. He's been playing with comms modules and fancy fixes for the decoy long enough. And he's been tinkering with the *Gremlin*; he sees that as a new toy that could do with a few updates."

"And he uses that as an excuse to contact Captain Kerrix," the first mate added, smirking. "We taking her down for our meets?"

"We are. We'll all have to get used to piloting her, and it's as good a time as any to get flight time in. And it will give all the nosy vultures we'll deal with something else to talk about."

"I bet; the cams of the ISA office near Freskat fleet HQ will be twitching when we heave to."

"Can it, Commander, and get on with those leave rotas."

* * *

The main settlement of Freskat was as sunny and welcoming as always, Apnis observed, as she brought the shuttle in on a wide arc, scanning for her target. She swiftly found the earmarked landing bay outside the Freskat home fleet's HQ and set the *Gremlin* down as softly as a bubble.

"Nice landing, Tallica," Ahxenta approved. "You handle her well."

"Thanks, Cap. Those sims have paid off," she said as she shut down her systems and made an external security sweep before allowing her colleagues to undo their straps and move.

The *Gremlin* secured, the captain, Apnis and Azular stepped out to look across the large open precinct to the area beyond.

"That's new since last we were in," Ahxenta noted, pointing to an eatery outside the barrier. "We can try it when we're done with Zillah. It's close to the PSS registry office and we can leave the shuttle here."

"Good idea, Cap. A shuttle like ours won't have been seen before, so a bay next door to Freskat fleet HQ should be as safe as anywhere."

"There *are* secure cams on her," Azular stated, nodding at a cluster of eternally roving automated eyes, their output surely monitored from the gate office. "But I doubt they'd scan. Our insignia's visible and we're expected. And she's so shielded they'd not get through her."

"The Freskat Navy might not, but ISA HQ's in that fancy block next door, and I bet their cams have perked up," Apnis said mordantly.

"Let's move," the captain ordered, leading them to the gate office, through which they had to pass before being allowed entry. After a query and search, their credentials were sent in and they waited a guide to escort them into the HQ. Within minutes they were with Zillah.

She rose to greet them and bade them sit; her aide Tealdun, now a captain, was there. As expected, *Arianrhod's* forced removal from the TA, its purported reasons, and her joining a zone Psi trades body, had reached Zillah's ears, and she was curious. Ahxenta told her most of the tale: with the ISA next door, the admiral had its version, and had been sceptical. The captain also told her of the danger the *Nyx Warrior* had met near Chelda, but said only that the *Glenblaze* was a Starfall ship on the way to her own base. She then asked why the *Merrin Free* was in orbit, but the admiral was in the dark. The ISA ship had come in three days before, some crew had visited the local office, but that was it. The admiral's other news was pertinent. The reason the ISA had given for sanctions against *Arianrhod*, *Emerald* and Thal's PSS ships was that they were a destabilising influence within the TA, and their recent actions ran contrary to the TA code of conduct.

"I don't think we were given a copy of that code," Apnis remarked derisively. "I didn't know it had one."

The admiral clicked her tongue at the interjection, but continued. Her next key concern was the supply of protected crystal comms array wafers for her fleet's ships. The captain assured her that she could have as many as she needed. Given the hiatus on ISA orders, there would be units to spare, and quickly. Zillah's direct reaction was to call her senior procurement officer and get him onto filling the shortfall, and having Greskitty Comms gear up for their insertion into useable units. That done, she continued to her next item of interest.

She had spoken to associates in the planetary authority on free port status. They knew that *Arianrhod*, registered locally, was free to use the port for trade, but it would be closed to her non-TA sister ships. Zillah knew the matter had been raised in committee, and as free port status would not preclude TA-aligned ships from using Freskat, she could see no problem, even with the ISA presence there. Freskat had always been a minor ISP member, and its standing was the same under the ISA. A decision was due in days, but there *would* be talks with the ISA. How much those would impact on the result Zillah did not know.

With promises to keep in touch over the issues debated, the meeting was ended and the three set off to the shuttle. They had been permitted to leave her in situ until their business was done, but Ahxenta wanted to check that she had not been tampered with. That done, they headed towards the diner that the captain had noticed earlier.

An assistant led them to their chosen table at the rear, with a good view of the door and a wall at its back. "Interesting," said Ahxenta as she sat and flicked the menu-pad to make her selection and punch in the details. "You have to pay in advance or you don't get the goods."

"Before you know the quality and value of the stuff they serve up?" the first mate queried. "That's one way of not leaving a tip. What do you do if the food's *not* good? Ask to speak to the management and throw the plates at them if they don't cooperate?"

"That's one way of not being allowed back in, Commander," Azular pointed out. "But as the place is busy, I'd imagine the food *is* edible."

"Zip it," Ahxenta said, setting her jammer. "You two order, I'll set privacy. The table shielding's good, so that's a point in their favour."

In spite of the privacy shield, the three spoke of general things while they waited for their food, as they were aware that they were the object of many eyes. There were other uniforms in sight, personnel from fleet and ISA premises they guessed, and a sprinkling of civilians. Once their orders had materialised, the captain turned to the two.

"Now, what do you think to Zillah's take on the authority's chance of agreeing to free port status?"

"You'd know more than we would on that, Cap," Apnis said slowly. "But I thought she seemed confident that it would be positive."

"I agree," Azular nodded. "Freskat would lose little and probably gain much. How much sway *does* the ISA have out here?"

"It had little when it was the ISP," Ahxenta said. "But with trouble in the Star Desert and Psi as part of the family, that may have changed."

"With a direct route to Twilight, so Starfall on the doorstep, I bet it has. But in which way?" the first mate asked. "Though Freskat won't welcome any tightening of an ISA noose around its neck. It's planetary authority has always been a free spirit."

"We'll see; but eat up. I want to visit the PSS registry office soonish, as I have those other matters in hand," Ahxenta said firmly.

The registry office was a small concern on Freskat, it being a distant planet on the edge of zone Lambda, but the staff followed the fortunes of its ships and those on other PSS registries. The TA had advised it of the revoked flags of *Arianrhod* and *Emerald*, and it had learned about the others via PSS registry system links. That two Freskat-registered ships now belonged to another trade body was news, but the FMTE identity holo and call-sign marker were accepted and the data merged into the registry database.

"That'll give all their offices from Alpha through Mu a lot to talk about from here on in," Apnis smiled as they left the building. "Thal will have had to do the same for his on Kirtish. What's next, Cap? You have a visit scheduled in, a long one," she added delicately.

"I do; I'll fill you both in later, but for now you're for home. There'll be several of our shuttles up and down, so I'll hitch a ride as and when. I'll maybe need *you* at least Azular, down here later on, to talk tech, but I'll let you know. You can pilot the *Gremlin* to our contact's workshop Tallica, and drop me. I left my kit aboard."

The *Gremlin* was as they had left her, and they boarded quickly. With a short link to the gate office, the first mate took her up. Minutes later, they had made the fringe of the small, quiet suburb and set down in a berth close to the site. Ahxenta shouldered her kitbag and made her way out, her progress to the workshop followed by the other two.

"Have you any idea of what the Cap's up to?" Apnis asked as she began to power up. "She brought down a part of the load we have for him, so he can check the quality, she said, but there's a lot more to it."

He shook his head. "I don't know, Commander, but it's causing her concern. I'm sure we won't be the last to know."

"I know. Let's get home. We both have things to do. You planning shore leave on Freskat?"

"No ma'am. I'd rather save it until I have a use for it."

"Greffy too: *he's* refused on Merry's account. They haven't had time out lately, with all that's happened. Where's the *Moonstone* now?"

"She was to leave Starfall, but Xanna won't tell me her route. The galaxy's still full of ears, and until they're plugged, it's best to be wary."

The first mate found a message marked urgent and confidential for the captain when she made the bridge. She headed to the office to deal with it. It was from Captain Kerrix, with a tag saying that it had come from Ambassador Posettix. The Norvallan authorities had refused to heed her cautions and had agreed a treaty of unity with the ISA, as had its colonies Valla Key and Valla Port, and another two Psi worlds. The Union of Federated Systems, under whose banner most systems in Psi came, had refused to join in any alliance, trade or otherwise, until many issues were resolved, although the UFS would continue to recognise the ISA as a friendly power and would welcome its ships.

What it would mean for PSS and other fleets Apnis had no idea, but she did not plan to trouble Ahxenta with it, and simply confirmed receipt. The ISA had not broadcast the news, but the first mate figured it soon would: it publicised its triumphs, and that would be classed as notable, and maybe serve as a warning that with the Alliance larger, criminal groups might find even more watchful eyes on them.

It was late when the captain requested a shuttle. As many crew were already enjoying furlough, the first mate sent Azular down in the *Xanna* rather than use one on surface. She was small, with camouflage systems that would baffle inquisitive eyes. She was also fast, and Apnis was in hopes of a private chat once Ahxenta was back aboard.

The captain was tired, Apnis realised on meeting her in the docking bay, but after a trip to her office to look over updates and make private links, she asked that Apnis, Azular and Flintlock join her in the mess. All three were waiting when she came in. She collected her food, joined them, and immediately set privacy.

"Hard day, Cap," Apnis greeted her.

"And then some. And harder days to come. We'll be here for twelve at least. As will the *Emerald*. I've spoken to Melly *and* Captain Thal, as they're part of the equation, and they're on board. More pieces need to be put in place, but once that's done, things can be set in motion."

"You've got us going, Cinnabar," Flintlock cut in. "What's to do?"

"Removals," she said sourly. "There's been trouble over the comms arrays for a while: my buddy and his sub, Ruri, who's now his junior partner, have had attempted break-ins at the workshop. Nothing taken, it's shielded and there's a secure store elsewhere, but it's known about. And the goods are becoming popular, though we seem to have lost the ISA market. But his materials supply source has probably been worked out: us, the *Emerald* and the *Kel'Torc*."

"That's bad. So he's moving to a new site?" Apnis queried.

"He and his wife are, in a way," Ahxenta said enigmatically. "We've decided that a small-scale operation here is still viable, as there are local markets, like Zillah's comms suppliers and Coronis on Delta Iridium."

"By *here* you mean Freskat, ma'am," Azular deduced. "They'll move off planet but some work will still be done here?"

She nodded. "They've agreed to try for a year, as things can be set up almost right away. Jon, my contact, reckons that his partner's quite capable of running the site here, if there's support in place. Which there will be: I have Captain Thal's assurance."

"Thal!" exclaimed Apnis. "Now you've lost me."

"Remember our castaways from Furze? The parent of one trained as a crystal cutter-setter on Xerophyte, and has since worked on ships' comms on Sunrise. His wife's a security officer on the *Kel'Seth*. They want a safe place to raise their son, and Freskat fits the bill. He'll work with Ruri on wafers and small contracts, and his partner will deal with security and accounting."

"And your buddy and his wife are heading for where?"

Ahxenta paused for a second. "Letik," she said.

"Zone Psi! That'll be some trip, and into new territory! They won't even speak the language. And they've agreed?" the first mate asked.

"They have. *Emerald* will be their ride. We all had a long talk. I gave them advance warning: they've known since we were at Starfall, as I sent them a link via Twilight. They've had time to think. Jon's spoken to Ruri about taking over here small scale, as the manager at first, as it depends on the long-term outlook on Letik. He's okay about it, and is looking forward to it, in fact," the captain smiled ruefully.

"But what'll he *do* on Letik?" Flintlock asked. "It's a big deal to set up a new business in a place you've never heard of, with no contacts."

"He has a job at Metriklon to step into, everything's ready for them to make a start, and his wife's a nurse-tech, so needed in the expanded hospital. The family from Sunrise will take on their home here."

"The *Emerald's* set up for passengers and she can trade freely in Psi, as she's now FMTE," Azular said. "Does she have business there?"

"She does, partly passenger-related, but it's not your concern. I'm bringing the senior crew in on some of this, as they'll need to be aware when things start to happen, but only the bare minimum. I'll organise a briefing tomorrow, but for now, eat up all, and scoot."

The other two did, but the first mate requested a private word once the food had gone; she had sensed another reason behind the scheme. "Trouble over the comms arrays," she said. "How much, Cinnabar?"

Ahxenta snorted. "You don't miss much. A lot. And so has his wife. On top of attempts on the workshop *and* the house, they've both been threatened by unknowns, and *Arianrhod's* name has come into it."

"How long ago did you find out, Cinnabar? This isn't recent."

"No. Jon took a chance and called me at Telzilt. I don't know if the perps have linked them to the ship, or to me, but I'm not risking it, or them. I want them away, and Letik is as far as I can send them. They're a savvy pair and will make a go of it anywhere they settle."

"That I believe. If he has any of your talents, he'll certainly make it. Any ideas on the perps?"

"Not yet, but I've plenty enemies, so no lack of choices. It *could* be hostile-related. But no word of this to ours. Melly Goodsocks is aware there's been threats to him and his, but that's all."

"One thing I've never asked, Cinnabar, and you don't have to tell me… why is your buddy not called Ahxenta? I realise his safety has a lot to do with it, but I take it that was your brother's family name?"

"I had a rep by the time he was in college, and as he was due call-up for military service, he dropped it for his other name: his mother's. She was Lamellan. He's been Jon Skervok ever since."

* * *

The next days were busy with the transfer of goods between ships and surface. The *Merrin Free* had left, but the captain was still cautious. She took time out to be with her kin, tell them of Letik, provide them with essentials and ensure that business handover ran to plan. Azular was busy with Ruri, discussing technical issues and setting up a new secure storage facility for gems and parts. The young man had a home a short way from the workshop, and was looking forward to meeting his new help and office cum security backup. The couple were coming in on a Starfall ship and were already on the way.

Lindell had been able to drum up deals from companies that knew and were unworried over of the change of trade association. He was as well-known as the ship, and had talked to almost every local rep. There was a batch of bespoke parts from Fleete Corp of Freskat, an old client, ready to uplift, that was for another known firm, Rhomb Systems of Delta Iridium, who dealt in engineered goods, and a cargo of medical stores for a supply firm in Limekiln.

"There *are* other deals out there," the supercargo told the captain. "But even if the client's base is a free port, some reps are antsy about upsetting the TA, as Freskat's not."

"*That* may be about to change. I've had word from Admiral Zillah: the planetary authority's looked into it, tried to raise some points with TA HQ, and got stroppy comeback – and a memo that's allegedly been circulated to all TA-aligned ports that attempts to pull out of current contracts would result in immediate sanctions. Rather than putting the frighteners on the authority, all it's done is put its back up, and it's now in consultation with its opposite numbers on Lamella and Limekiln to see what change free port status makes. Bellfish keeps an eye on local nets: I'll have him send you relevant items. And talk to Helly Pinkhorn: she may have news, as she's as savvy a super as you."

"Must be something about the good teaching she had when she was aboard *Arianrhod*," he grinned in reply.

"I believe you. But I need to move; the *Kel'Seth's* on her way in, and I'll be heading over to meet Mr Keerin and Lieutenant Bindle and their boy, Victor. The child should remember me from when he was aboard. They'll be brought here, and Azular and I will take them down later in the *Xanna* – she can be cloaked to resemble a local runabout, which shouldn't raise eyebrows."

"Why the cloak and dagger?" Lindell asked.

"There's need. I don't know what they'll have with them, but things are being put in place on the surface, so they should settle in quickly."

She was interrupted by word that Captain Holdspan was on line, and turfed Lindell out of his office, grumbling that the call had better be short. She was done in fifteen minutes. The *Nyx Warrior* was at her home port, she mentioned in passing, but the news would keep until a briefing that she would call later in the day, to apprise her officers of Zillah's news, as the new information was relevant.

The flight to the *Kel'Seth* was easy. Victor recognised the tall captain as the one who had led the rescue party on Furze and seen them safe on the way to Starfall. The halt aboard *Arianrhod* gave the parents time to express their gratitude, but the captain's priority was getting them settled into their new home. She planned to bring her people up to her ship in two days, from where they would transfer to the *Emerald*.

The return trip ran to time, and as Ahxenta sat with a coffee before her scheduled staff update, she reflected on the rapid events of the past weeks. She was interrupted by comms with another personal link.

"I'm more popular that a bloody pay rise!" she groused as she made ready to receive the call from Captain Bluejohn.

Apnis was first to arrive in the briefing room as soon as the keep out had been switched off. "Hell of a day," Cinnabar," she greeted her. "Azular's with the *Xanna*. He's still not keen to let anyone but himself tie her down. Keerin and family settled in all right?"

"Yup. They'll be shown the home layout tonight and the workshop tomorrow. Victor will go to the local junior school, the one I went to," she added. "They're a decent pair. They've been set up with IDs that give Marridan as their home port; it's far enough from here and where Keerin's from. As that's where the hostiles started their war a couple of years ago, there shouldn't be questions over what they've been doing in the interim. But here's Axellina; the others won't be far behind."

Once the personnel had gathered, they were bidden to grab a drink and sit. "This'll be short," the captain promised. "It's late and we've all plenty to do. Our route once we ship out you know: Limekiln with the medical stores, then Delta with the Fleete Corp gear. After that, it'll be the Web, if nothing else comes in. *Emerald* ships out a day ahead of us, and she's for Letik with what she's taken on. She'll stop for resupply at Starfall and Thal's promised escort as often as he can en route. He has ships heading out that way and he'll organise his schedules to keep tabs on her. *Emerald* has business in Psi, and then she'll head back to Alpha, unless something else comes in to alter that."

Ahxenta began on free port status for Freskat, which looked to be further forward. The TA's actions had caused other ructions, especially in far-flung centres that had little or no TA presence. Nat Holdspan had called to let her know that Nyx and Aoria Six in zone Lambda had protested over the latest TA memo, and were on the verge of declaring themselves free ports. A similar action had been taken by Arrissia Five, on the edge of Theta, according to Grey Bluejohn.

"And as of now," Ahxenta smiled, glancing at the timepiece, "The *Obsidian Sky* and the *Nyx Warrior* are aligned to the Free-Market Trades Exchange, and have told the mightily arrogant Trades Alliance where to stick its insignia and its rules."

The table sat stunned for a moment, until Azular asked the obvious. "But how can they join the FMTE without a rep anywhere in Alpha through Mu? Doesn't alliance require a personal visit and exchange of details to get the registered call-sign marker for hull plating and the identity holo for communits and other ID units?"

"The FMTE isn't the TA. I registered the *Emerald* at Telzilt without her being there. But data *can* be sent over a secure link, and UV-III hardware with the plug-in code-decode bit is secure. The Telzilt office knows of the PSS fleet, as Thal's used the port for years and has history there. He vouched for Holdspan and Bluejohn. The FMTE plans to expand into our zones, as it's keen to have more of its registered ships trading here, so if the TA persists in denying rights to its bypasses for specific ships, they'll find other routes – Starfall's are the obvious ones – and will find new trades associations to look after their interests."

"I'd like to be a spy cam on the TA HQ council's wall when it finds out about this, Cap," Apnis declared. "But the TA can't keep us from its bypasses – we can jump on at spots not controlled by nodes, though it takes energy. But unless we were cloaked, we'd be detected as soon as we passed a node; and the TA could bring criminal charges against us, I guess," she added. "That's how it works."

"Not our problem. Grey and Nat will pass on the news over secure nets. The TA registration office now knows it's lost two more, but as we, the *Obsidian*, the *Warrior* and the Starfall fleet are tagged as pests, the TA upper ranks will maybe think they're better off without us."

"Not if the rest of the fleet follow," Cottontail put in. "You can bet a few will, if TA tactics include intimidation. Join our band and follow our rules or nobody'll employ you, you won't be able to use our routes or trade in our ports. Once the aligned ports find business falling off, they'll shout, especially about the fees they have to cough up for trade they're not getting. But what's the *Emerald* doing in Psi, Cap, after she drops off the gear and her passengers at Letik?"

"That's *her* affair. She won't stop long, and she's heading back here. You know what you're doing. If your people need gear, run your lists by Tallica, but that's for tomorrow. Dismissed. Tallica, you stay."

"What didn't you tell them, Cap?" the first mate asked as the door closed on the last officer.

"I've had a highly private and confidential despatch from the office of Ms Sigma Dishell, senior TA exec for the sector of Alpha that takes in Merkat Three. She's in charge of the Web TA office. She deplores the current situation, and as the TA's the only valid trades body in the Web for the PSS fleet, she's insinuated that it's only a matter of time before the Port Authority will rule that we have no right to trade there and it'll refuse us permission to transfer cargo."

"She can't do that!"

"Damn straight she can't. She didn't say it outright, but I guess that she thinks she'll be able to convince the PA to block us. She won't, of course – most PA personnel on the ground think the TA is a pain in the butt. She also hints that if we promise to behave and be good boys and girls, the current TA ban we're under may be lifted."

"Won't do it any good; we've already left the TA *and* have better trade cover. I hope you told her to go pee up a rope," Apnis growled.

"Not yet, but it's on my list. I broke the non-copy code on it and copied her highly private and confidential note, via our legal rep, to the Merkat planetary authority, its Central Advisory Council for the Web, the Port Authority, and to the ISA and TA HQs on Alto Finglas, asking for their views on it; politely of course, given we do not belong to the TA. I've also sent a copy to every ship in the PSS fleet, and to Zillah."

"You're going to be *so* popular, Cinnabar," the first mate snickered. "Ms Dishell obviously doesn't know you well enough."

"She doesn't know me at all. But I haven't started yet. In my reply, I'll tell her all that, and that I intend to take legal action against both the TA and her personally. That should take the wind out of her sails."

"So we'd best be on the lookout for rocks being thrown at us," Apnis warned with a laugh.

26: CHANGING TIMES

Two days later, *Arianrhod's* bridge crew watched the *Emerald* pull out of Freskat orbit on a heading for Twilight Station and then Starfall. She would have company part-way: the *Nyx Warrior*, still at her home port, was for Arrissia. She would catch her at Molly One, and travel with her to Sunrise Exit. Nat Holdspan was testing the water: he was to drop his current cargo at Arrissia and pick up another, already agreed by the related parties, for the TA-aligned Vellis Prime. Holdspan was positive, as Arrissia was already shaking off the chains binding it to the TA, and if he was refused consent to offload, he could pass his cargo to a local carrier at Prime's nearby neutral colony, Vellis Minor. He would lose revenue in the exchange, but he figured it worthwhile.

Ahxenta had made her farewells, and she sighed as she watched the receding ship. Things were moving fast and change was often a painful experience. The council had united in agreeing that Freskat become a free port; the tipping point was the TA's attempt to impose sanctions. As a body with no local presence and no legal right to interfere in any planet's governance, the action had been deemed dishonourable as well as illegal and had been widely condemned. The councils on Aoria and Nyx had followed suit, and declared their worlds free ports. As Aoria's colony of Molly One had never been allied to the TA, it meant that all the major settlements in the once ISP and now ISA-run sector of zone Lambda were now free ports. The press agencies in every charted zone were having high times with the resulting furore.

The fallout from the circulation of the confidential TA memo from Dishell had that body spitting quarks; it had distanced itself from the action of its executive, but an attempt to vilify the actions of *Arianrhod's* captain collapsed when the news that she was no longer linked to the TA became widely known. That had brought a bonus in that the name of the Free-Market Trades Exchange had been picked up and enquiries were being made about it. As the alliance of the ISA with Norvalla and its colonies had been broadcast to fanfare and self-congratulation, the ISA was sitting back from involvement, but Ahxenta had had queries from various bodies and individuals. She had blocked most of them, but *Arianrhod's* location at Freskat was now public.

The captain pulled her boards across to check that all her cargo was aboard. The only task left before next day's exit was the return of crew from shore. The shuttle was due at sixteen hundred. She sighed again.

"Cap?" the first mate questioned.

"We leave tonight, once we're shipshape," she told her. "Loads are tied down, admin's in order and PA clearance is a formality. Too many know we're here and some will guess our route. We can get to Limekiln via Umbel, Lamella and Stella Marina via local bypasses. It'll keep us off the TA bypass and away from big traffic, and won't take much longer. Delta's a straight run by a local, though we'll have to pay for its use once we make port. It's the Web after that, unless Lindell finds a cargo. He's trying his contacts on Delta. We're known there and there's always trade in zone Delta."

"Roger that. It's one of the most densely-populated zones. We can get as far as Quartic Cross without crossing the TA, but we might have to choose our route carefully from then on."

"I've been looking at it." The captain grinned wickedly. "There's a way through if we come off at Quartic and head for Alto Finglas."

Apnis began to laugh. "I like it," she said. "I like it a lot."

The change of plan was followed; by twenty two hundred, *Arianrhod* was passing the Ginseng Nebula and on the Starfall bypass that linked Twilight to Gemstone. The ship was part-laden and made good speed. By four days out she had passed Lamella. News had followed her from two trusted allies. The *Green Comet* had let go a load at ISA Silverglass holding station, and her captain had been called into the office and grilled on her plans in relation to TA affiliation. The livid Sarie Jikelleli had bawled out the reps for invading her privacy, and on being warned that cutting TA ties could result in loss of future ISA contracts, she told the reps where to stick their future contracts, and added that she would alert the PSS fleet to their position and send a complaint to the ISA, as it was none of its or their concern who her trading body was. She had executed her threat, but told Ahxenta that the reps had been edgy, as if they had been coerced. And as Jikelleli had recorded the interview, there could be no retraction on the ISA's part. ISA HQ had not replied to her complaint. A link from the *Firedrake*'s Pa Ma'Lappis soon after had more: *he* had found out from a friend on the marketing staff of the Web that some local firms had had visits from TA officials, who had hinted that using non-TA affiliated ships as carriers would be frowned on. Word had spread to almost every rep in the place.

Ahxenta mulled over the news. Stella Marina, on a TA bypass node at the edge of Gamma and Lambda zones, was a key cross-point and

TA-affiliated, but having had been Non-Treaty Alliance pre-ISA, it was open to all. However, she ordered a switch to a local node for Limekiln, where she planned to resupply. *Arianrhod* made orbit eleven days out of Freskat. As Limekiln PA had asked for a short update on events, the captain took the call in her office, leaving Apnis and Lindell to deal with cargo transfer and fee handover.

"Four of them," she said to her first mate later, as, freight delivered, payment made and a pod of stores brought in, *Arianrhod* was prepping for departure. "I don't know what they thought I was going to say. They wanted info on the FMTA, so that they'd recognise its ships. The news that all the Starfall ships had been booted out of the TA has gone round, and as the PA's dealt with one or two, it was nervous that the change in trade guild would cause upset, or that local firms would find it hard to get compensation for any damages."

"And you told them not to worry, that they'd be compensated more quickly and with less quibbling," Apnis smirked.

"Just so. With luck, they'll pass it on to their trading partners; that'll make it easier for the FMTA to be accepted in these parts, once it's set up. But we're for Delta Iridium. We shouldn't have to argue over cargo delivery or pick up there, *if* Lindell has found any cargo to pick up."

"Roger that, Cap."

"That's our clearance," Ahxenta noted as she replied to the civilities of Limekiln's Port Control. "Here we go, people. Engines set, Chief? Take us out nice and slow helm; estimated time to bypass?"

"Forty nine minutes, ma'am," Dox replied.

"Roger that. Safe speed to Delta. The crossing will take four days give or take, depending on the hyperspace currents, and they're usually stable on this stretch. Nothing looks like trouble on the grid. We won't cloak, but we'll be at alert. Unless *that's* trouble," she grated as comms called a private link for her from the *Moonstone*. "Awkward timing; I'll take it in my office. Keep us on course, Tallica. I hope this isn't long."

The comm was short, for the captain was back in fifteen minutes. "A data stream's coming in from the *Moonstone*, Mr Bellfish. Send it to science and tactical — it's for the grid, and not items that self-updating nav-charts can pick up. It's a new chart for outer Psi, and added charts that cover zones beyond that. It includes pointers to available markets for us, operational hyperspace routes and areas to be avoided. There's still problems out that way, and hostiles have been active," she said to Apnis in a lower voice. "Not anywhere near Telzilt or Letik, thanks be. *Moonstone's* sending the data to the *Emerald*. I'll make sure it's copied to the *Obsidian* and the *Warrior*, as they both have the add-on data we got at Starfall, courtesy of Captain Thal."

Apnis and Azular cast furtive eyes on the captain as activity stepped up whilst the data transferred. The task was done by the time the node to the bypass was gained, and once the bumps had subsided, the bridge crew sat back to savour an even tenor of ride.

"Nothing more's appeared anywhere near our route," the first mate noted, eyeing the shifting holo. "And zip from Lindell on possible new contracts at Delta. Another hour and we'll be off duty. You planning a staff briefing on the next stage to Delta, Cap?"

The captain was well aware of the thought behind the question and looked at her. "No, unless news comes in that needs one. But we'll have a look at the new nav records after this shift."

Once the next duty crew were in place, Ahxenta ordered Apnis and Azular into her office, and then sent a call to her chief medic. Neither of the former expected the nav-data to dominate the conversation.

"Help yourselves to a drink and sit," the captain told them. "You've got the new data, Azular? I want you to extract the substance into a file that I can send to the *Obsidian* and the *Warrior*. I've not been told that I can pass it on, but as they have what Thal gave us and will be trading out that way, they'll need it. Tomorrow will do, you'll have time, unless anything untoward comes up. But I'm not expecting trouble."

"What else did Captain Kerrix have to say, Cinnabar?" the first mate began. "You didn't drag us in here to talk navigation."

"As you both damn well know. I saw you looking. Yes, she did have other data, but we'll wait for the doc. I suspect the *Moonstone's* at Telzilt: there's digging going on in areas once occupied by hostiles, after they'd forced the owners out, or forced them into slave labour."

"Oh hell! What have they found?" Apnis asked anxiously.

"Bio-records – and other stuff. Here's Axellina now," she added at the discreet buzz at the outer door. "Grab a mug and sit, Doc."

Ahxenta brought the chief medic up to date on the data Kerrix sent. "I want you to cross-check the bio-records with our databanks to see if you can locate an origin on the traces, or relate them to anything we hold. Part of the material dug up at Telzilt isn't local, and Mettix thinks it's from our zones; he knows one piece is Marridani. But his records don't have the depth ours do, and we might be able to shine a light on what's been found. Starfall's got the same," she added to forestall the question she could see on Azular's lips. "But it looks like the hostiles ranged all over, and some victims were transported vast distances."

"Surely Commander Levettiza…" the science officer began.

"*Her* contact list's drying up and she doesn't want to risk info like this crossing space unless it's guaranteed secure. And yes, there's more. Obviously Admiral Posettix has an interest. From what they've found – and I'm damn sure Thal's on his way to join them – there *was* an active underground of people that escaped the hostiles. And at least one band has set up an outfit like Starfall. Remember, Azular, after we met Levettiza in the Web as Vettarista, we met her in the *Subspace* and came across Tommy Buntle with the nasty hostile plant, Flatt?"

"I recall," he replied. "Captain Thal turned up and removed Flatt at gunpoint. We figured Ms Vettarista then for an ISP Intelligence agent with a remit covering hostile incursion and alien issues, which brought in Captain Thal and his people, and Captain Kerrix."

"Her opinion was that victims who *had* managed to get free or had been freed had joined together for mutual defence and the need for normality, as they'd lost everything, including their identities – though you later figured, and it's been confirmed, that alien alteration induces subtle changes, and lets those interfered with recognise others in the same position. She worked out that there had to be several large groups of diverse origins, not just Thal's, with different agendas, and in various places. And the hostile range was and is huge."

"There's another fleet like Starfall?" Apnis cut in.

The captain shook her head. "Not as far as they know: Starfall's a huge outfit. But there *was* a freedom force on Telzilt, and it had a few off-world bases that ran ships. And it probably wasn't the only one: a lot of worlds were ravaged or taken over in Psi and beyond, more than in our neck of the galaxy, it seems."

"Thal wants to make contact, in case some of his missing people are out there?" the first mate posited. "Is it likely?"

"The admiral," Azular said quietly. "If he's been given hope that his son may be alive, it's more likely that he'd be in a Telziltic-run group. Even if he and his team mates had been taken elsewhere, it makes sense that he would try to make his way home. The only evidence found at Starfall *was* the insignia of his laboratory, and neither it or anything else had organic traces that could be linked to the admiral. As a deliberately-targeted scientist, his son would not have been used as a tissue bank. But is there anything else, ma'am?"

The captain grimaced. "Thal, as a victim that freed himself, still has a strong ability to identify others that have been victims of alien abuse. You'll remember that one of the alterations he had done by Norvallan surgeons – Mettix was one, I think – was a visual insert that let him scan others for the metallic implants the hostiles used to control their lackeys; *and* it also boosted his inherent sensitivity to people altered like himself. He wanted it to dig out the last of the spies he was sure were still in his group and causing him and his grief. We never did hear more of the success of that, but as he can sense them, it stands to reason that he'd be able to pick up on ex-victims that have made it out and not shown themselves. And they'll be able to sense him, to a lesser extent."

"He's hoping to find other groups and link up with them?" asked Flintlock incredulously. "It seems like a long shot to me."

"Probably. But one of Kerrix' people, Nyvallish, had a hunch about a guy digging in some ruins that he and she visited. She gave him leave to probe, and he found that the man was one of a group that had made it out, escaped off-world, and joined another band. The new lot were out for revenge, which wasn't to the taste of this guy, so he and a few like minds got out and set up on their own. They've now a niche as a legit scavenger op, searching and digging up stuff to sell as a living; but they're hunting for their own on the side, thus their presence at the dig. And they've contacts in similar ex-rebel groups. Now Telzilt and other targets are getting back on track, the groups are coming together. But the main obstacle is trust. How do you know that the person or gang you've met up with is genuine? And if it is, what is its agenda, and can you be sure that there's no alien plant? What is it, Azular?"

"Starfall is a trade fleet. Why is it using precious time and resources like the *Kel'Moth* and the *Moonstone* on this? It could be left to others."

"They've trade at Telzilt; and Captain Kerrix told me that they'd be on the move soon, as they had more cargo to take on and deliveries to make. They'll be well away by the time the *Emerald* makes it in."

"Is there anything more?" Azular persisted.

"I suspect so, but I don't know. I felt she was holding back, but it might be personal, so don't push when you contact her or you'll get a flea in your ear. But I'm for the mess, if you'd care to join me."

All three did, but the captain would not be drawn on anything else that had come up in the link from the *Moonstone*.

* * *

The huge port of Delta Iridium Colony welcomed the *Arianrhod* in and assigned her a berth close to her customer's orbital transfer point, and close to the *PSS Urania*. Captain Mikbeam had called Ahxenta two days before, and finding that she was for his home port, had asked her for a private meeting, as he was heading in from Iris Three. She arranged to see him the day after her arrival, in the *Blue Ripple* bar in Idrissa, a main town and trade hub for visiting ships. Mikbeam would have his first mate and supercargo with him, from which Ahxenta guessed that talks would involve trade under the FMTE. She included Lindell in her party, as he had meetings in the Idrissan business quarter later.

The load for Rhomb delivered, the captain spent the rest of the day on her schedule whilst her cargo teams were priming *Arianrhod's* holds, as Lindell was optimistic about the reps he was to meet. He knew them of old and was certain he could reassure them of *Arianrhod's* fitness for service under her new flag. Ahxenta herself had shed a few cares: the *Emerald* had reached Starfall and was taking on more cargo for Telzilt, and an escort, the *SS Firestorm*, which was also carrying a payload.

Cobalt Mikbeam, his first mate Kitt Parlen and his super, Kerriven Wiljet were in the *Blue Ripple* at breakfast when the captain, Apnis and Lindell arrived next morning. Ahxenta had been right: Mikbeam was another PSS captain so put out by TA intrigues that he was considering changing allegiance. Having had heard of the *Obsidian Sky* and the Nyx *Warrior*, he was optimistic, but he wanted more information than could be got over comms.

Ahxenta told him the whole, from when the TA had rescinded its flag until her ship had been ratified under her new trades association. As *Arianrhod* had let go a cargo and was trading in Delta, it was obvious that the lack of the TA flag had not affected her there. Ahxenta also advised Mikbeam of the change to free port status of Freskat, Nyx and Aoria, and offered the list Lindell had drawn up of the ports potentially open to PSS and other non-TA fleets from Alpha to Mu in order of ease of trading. The trade routes she did not, but as some of Starfall's were in common use and other local routes connected main centres to one another, it was possible to reach every sector in charted space. She continued with the conditions for and means of entry into the FMTE.

Mikbeam and his team were taking in the information when a buzz at Ahxenta's communit brought a holo-note from Bellfish to tell her that Sigma Dishell had been stripped of her post as head of the Merkat TA office, though she had not been discharged from the TA itself.

"Probably been sent for retraining on how to code non-copy codes on highly private and confidential despatches so that PSS captains can't break them and tell the galaxy," Apnis chuckled. "Bet there wasn't an apology to the PA for overstepping a mark in telling it who can and can't trade in the Web. Did she reply to your get lost note telling her what you'd done and threatening her and the TA with legal action?"

"No. Neither did the TA, though I took the precaution of checking my reply with our legal rep to make sure nobody could sue me for any of it, and getting him to send it out over an official net."

Mikbeam laughed quietly, accepted the port data, and called on his supercargo to talk trading with Lindell. In his view, the TA's mounting efforts to increase pressure and thus control over the fleets under its flag was being resented by merchant lines as well as private starships.

"Think we have more recruits for the FMTE?" Tallica Apnis asked her captain to the back view of the three from the *Urania* after the talks.

"We already have. Grey was on before we came down. He met Sarie Jikelleli at Fyvie Minor, and she's planning to join: she asked for details. The *Green Comet's* from Burr Two but uses the Web as her base, so she should have no problem."

"We're turning into recruiting agents for the Trades Exchange," the first mate laughed. "You off to meet your contacts now, Lindell?"

"Aye ma'am," he replied, stowing his gear. "We know Ceres Corp, we can head out quickly, they get a fast delivery. It's grain for Bistra, a new crop strain; we know the clients *there*, and Bistra's out of the way *and* neutral. The other rep I've to see is Coronis, but as her client's on Berzic, so firmly TA-linked, I don't know if she'll risk it. I'll see."

"Good luck. Tallica and I'll head up to the ship, as we've a lot to do before we leave. I'll send a shuttle for you when you're ready."

"Quick turnaround," Apnis observed on the way to their berth. "A lot of comms came in for you the other day," she added. "Anything that calls for a briefing?"

"As in you want to know what they were about," the captain smiled. "No, zip that I'd bother the crew with, but I'll fill you in at the shuttle."

Three of the calls had been from PSS captains and were about the changes of trades flag of the *Obsidian* and the *Warrior*, as that news had gone round, and possible damage to *Arianrhod's* trading status. Ahxenta had spoken generally of how the change had not affected her badly, and may have benefited the ship in terms of new trade links in Psi and beyond, citing the cracking of the UV-III by parties unknown as the reason for lack of in-depth detail.

"They all knew about the UV-III," she told Apnis as she powered up for lift off. "And I'd a strap line from ISA HQ about the Dishell affair, criticising my copying a personal link to it, and everybody else, but basically saying that trade was the TA's affair and it had no position on the question. And I'd a memo from the Merkat PA chief saying that the Web as a trade centre would always be open to *Arianrhod* whatever flag we flew, and he hoped to welcome us back in soon. It will be soon; if we get the Bistra deal, the Web will be our next stop after that, unless the Berzic contract is on. The Coronis reps know us, but they'll have to consider their clients' views, which may not be in our favour. But as more and more of the PSS fleet are questioning the TA's string-pulling, and now other shipping lines are getting jittery, something will have to give. And it may be sooner than they think."

"Cap?"

"I heard from Murmur Fleetskup, of all people. The *Tallulah's* in the Web and up to spec. He reckoned he'd a secure link, as his chief tactical officer had set it up. I took that with a grain of salt, but she and Spickle were at his back, so it may've been okay. He warned me that he'd been cornered by a Merkat TA rep, asking his views on the benefits of the TA as his flag, and hinting about problems that might affect those that decided to desert its cosy nest. Spickle was with him, so I doubt he was tied into a knot he couldn't get out of. The *Firedrake* was in, so he spoke to Pa Ma'Lappis, but Pa hadn't been waylaid at that point."

"Huh! Pa wouldn't take that sort of coercion and he'd set their ears on fire. It sounds like the TA's getting it's pants in a twist. But is Wekki Munnet to be trusted?" the first mate queried. "I know Azular felt she was okay, but is she still in the pay of ISA Intelligence?"

"I can't answer that, Tallica. But Juke Spickle's turning out to be no fool, so he'll have checked into her past; and though he wouldn't have got through the cover she used to get the job on the *Tallulah*, he'll have poked around and dug up enough to convince him she's bona fide. But we're nearly home, so enough for now."

"But you'll tell me the rest later?"

"Don't push me, Commander."

Apnis had to wait until the duties of the day were done. Lindell had returned with both deals in hand, meaning a round of admin, part fee exchange, and clearances. The huge grain shipment could then start to load early next day, with the small comms load shuttling up alongside. *Arianrhod* would ship out the day after.

"Ceres is moving the pods into orbit, so our team can start scans as soon as they're in range, but I don't expect glitches," the captain told the first mate on the way to the mess. "It strikes Lindell that even TA-tied ports are coming to resent the impositions being forced on them. The standard galactic year the TA gave until its full review of the PSS contract is pending, but there was a heap of add-on restrictions; what a port contract is like I don't know, but if the same's happening there, I can see why the PAs are getting nettled."

Ahxenta continued on the same tack until the two were seated at a side table away from curious eyes and ears. The captain sighed wearily.

"I don't know what to make of it," she began. "I had another link, high security and coded to blazes, from Captain Kerrix. The *Moonstone's* on the move. Kirtish is her first stop. She wanted to know our itinerary as she wants a personal meet with me, for a reason she says she won't spill, no matter how secure the channel. She reckons the Web, as she knows the *Emerald's* heading there with what she's picking up at Telzilt, after her trip to Letik, and the *Moonstone* has a couple of cargoes to bring in that will have to be there before *Emerald* gets in."

"What?" the first mate asked, puzzled. "Why?"

"That'll be made clearer later," was the reply with a wry grin. "Sorry, Tallica, but there are several pieces up in the air and I can't say more. But this other thing bothers me. I get the oddest feeling it's personal."

"To do with what the scavengers dug up on Telzilt from the alien occupation?" Apnis asked uneasily. "The doc got the bio-records from Kerrix, to check against our data for planetary origins or links or other gen, as Mettix figured some of the material was from our sectors. Did she get anything? You've said zip about it."

"Nothing positive; Marridani traces, but Mettix knew that, as the *Moonstone's* chief engineer is Marridani. Axellina got other DNA traces, but they only pointed to potential origins, not specifics. And they cover virtually every zone from Alpha through Mu. But Kerrix said that Thal *had* been able to contact four ex-victims of the hostiles. They're with a small band working out of Telzilt. They broke free and ran rebel ships during the occupation and war, guerrilla forces to strike at the enemy. Like his lot, they're turning to trade to make a living and get back to a normal life. She was cagy on what else came out, and I don't know if it's linked to that."

"But being as sharp as you are, you've picked up on something."

"Not so sharp," Ahxenta grimaced. "But I'll *not* bring Azular in, as he might prod her for more and she'll bite his head off. She damn near bit mine off when *I* tried. But I won't speculate; and neither will you."

"Cinnabar, I know you, and you will. Don't let it eat at you. You need an ear, I'm here. And I suggest you bring the doc in, she knows so much already. Have you talked to Parri Millit?"

"No I haven't and no I won't." She laughed harshly. "I told Azular to talk to Parri over *his* troubles. Maybe I should take my own advice. But no; if it was something she could have passed on, she would. But I let her know we *would* end up in the Web, probably before her."

"Way before her I should think. It's a straight run to Bistra via Ingle from here – three and a half days tops. A day and a half to offload and then we're for Berzic, unless something else comes up. You still reckon on a way through from Quartic by buzzing Alto Finglas?"

"I do; I've checked the latest our holo has got and the rogue worm-pocket by Furze still has an ISA alert tag, as has that alien holding area at that edge of the Drapes: *it's* marked as a nav hazard. There's nothing to say that the ISA's got a ship at either of them, but given our run-in with the *Steadfast* last time we hit Furze, and the fact she'd been in wait for us and Reddish knew we'd come in from Bistra, people will know we're here now and where we're going. I've had Box running nav sims, so he has more than one route plotted. He and Dox can work out the fine details as we go and change them as needed. Problem is, if we *are* on somebody's sensors, Quartic is the obvious place to catch us."

"The hostiles had a holding area at the Crimson Drapes. What route did they use to get in and out? It wouldn't have been a known bypass, so was it that worm-pocket that Azular worked out was recent?"

"And we sent the ISA its details, hence the alert," Ahxenta added. "No, the holding area must've been age-old, for why did they use it?"

"Or reuse it," Apnis argued. "There was maybe an old path into the area that they stopped using for some reason or other; maybe Thal and his lot had found it and mined it, or something."

"Interesting idea. I'll get Azular onto it, we've time before I have to decide." The captain's eyes narrowed as she pondered. "We could have our payload aboard and battened down by twenty two hundred. I feel the need to hurry, and I can't think why; but I won't ignore the hunch. As soon as we're shipshape, we move out."

"And then full safe speed to Bistra. We'll be heavy, but we'll be up to spec. I'll make sure all our departments have what they need. And I'd best check that *Loki* and the decoy are ready to run."

"They will be, but I need Azular now. We're going to be busy."

* * *

Busy was understatement, but forty-eight hours later, *Arianrhod* was on the bypass. Azular, Box and Dox had worked jointly, and with update input from tactical and comms and calls to Captains Kerrix and Thal, had plotted a route beyond Bistra that avoided Quartic Cross. It meant a longer hyperspace trip, it used an ex-hostile bypass that few of Thal's people had taken and needed a non-node jump into hyperspace, which would cost power. The captain had spoken to Thal over the plan: she was far from happy, as it would put her ship in danger. Thal was also anxious, but if the way proved feasible, it would help his ships. He had thus re-routed one of his fleet, the *SS Mevaena*, to Iridis. She would take the bypass from there to an agreed spot to meet *Arianrhod*, and run with her from there as far as Altina.

Apnis, the projected route on her board, was likewise nervous. "The reason *this* bypass isn't on Starfall's list is that it's disjointed, the hyper currents are wild, Thal's people think hostiles still use it, and it crosses a lot of empty, poorly-mapped space. We'd have to come off the Bistra to Iridis route in the middle of nowhere, and find a jump-on point that doesn't land in a cross-current; we'd then cut through the main trade route from Quartic to the Web between Furze and that rogue worm-pocket near it, and if we make it past *that*, we'd have to set for a node by Altina and jump off, at a spot we don't know, and in the area where hostiles have been logged."

"And join the Alto Finglas to Berzic local, which runs to a point on the Merkat route that's beyond the TA's control," the captain finished. "The *Mevaena's* a mid-range cruiser from Gemstone, so Thal's risking her. He wouldn't do it if he thought we'd miscarry, though that node is damn close to the third planet of the Altina system. But we'll be light, as we'd have shed the Bistra load. That's our chosen road, but it's fluid, and if there's news that changes things, I'll reconsider. I had a call from Nat Holdspan: he'd to pass his Vellis Prime load to a local ship at Vellis Minor, as the Prime authorities refused to let him bring it in. He tailed the local to talk to his Prime clients and call in at the PA. The PA reps were okay, but would say zip about the TA's edict. But *we* were named as being at Delta and heading for Bistra with a cargo. *That* came from a TA contact, but they'd say no more. It spooked Nat, so he filled the reps' ears with hooey and made as if he was for Vellisa. He's not, he's for Selliden via Vrackin, but it's got me edgy. It looks as if the TA and its minions are passing on details about us and our business."

"So we muddy the waters," the first mate said. "I can't imagine the TA or the ISA would deliberately hurt us, but if our business ends up in unfriendly ears, we could be in trouble."

"Exactly. We stay alert and assume we're a target. I have a link for Captain Radex of the *Mevaena*, but I won't contact him yet. But once out of Bistra, we rig for silent running and we cloak."

"Roger that, Cap," Apnis agreed as she cleared her board.

The remaining hours were quiet. The Bistra clients, happy with early delivery, unloaded at speed. All the data from comms nets and Starfall's listening posts was positive, and little new had surfaced by the time *Arianrhod* was ready to leave port. The captain had made sure that the word going round the PA office was that she was heading for Quartic Cross and the main four-way trade crossing.

"As soon as we pass the last beacon, helm, set for silent running," Ahxenta directed, as all ready, the ship swung free of her orbital berth.

"Affirmative, ma'am," Dox replied, and bringing *Arianrhod* into her assigned line, she set her nose towards free space and the shortest route to the local bypass for Quartic Cross.

"Reckon there will still be eyes on us, Cap?" the first mate asked.

"I do. Bistra's remote, but it's popular for grain and food supplies. We still read good to go for the Iridis bypass; once on we batten down and run at full safe speed. The rendezvous point's agreed, but we don't contact the *Mevaena* until then. Radex knows we'll be cloaked."

Hours turned to days, with only a hint of distant hyperspace traffic. No comms were sent, as it would now be obvious that *Arianrhod* had not made Quartic. It might be assumed that she had come off and back on either before or after the cross node, but the captain was wary. As the contact point was made, she ordered the cloak cut and a link made to the Starfall ship. Azular had pinpointed a signal on long-distance scanners that told of a ship hanging off the bypass.

A palpable sigh of relief ran round the bridge when Bellfish called Captain Radex of the *Mevaena* on the comm. He had arrived two hours before and had marked time by scanning likely jump-on points on the nearby risky bypass with all the means he had. His science officers had found a locus for safe entry, and he sent the coordinates for *Arianrhod's* science and tactical stations to verify the readings.

"I'm not surprised this isn't a used hyper route," Greffy stated. "It's got high fluxes in mass energy density a couple of clicks off the path that would read as a micro worm-pocket or gravity well to regular scanners. We'd best run with shields up and the crew webbed in tight."

Azular agreed, and the captain gave the ship-wide alert for the jump. With the *Mevaena* off her bows, Dox swung *Arianrhod* into the optimal position for entry. The ship, hit by a swell as the hyperspace barrier was breached, was then caught in an energy wash that caused her seams to strain. Dox held her for the ten minutes of a jolting, pounding ride, with the crew pinned in their seats by increasing gravity. As the stress levelled off, an even course was achieved.

"Nice going helm; how's the *Mevaena*, Gliss?" Ahxenta demanded.

"Holding her own, ma'am," the tactical officer reported. "She's off our starboard and matching course and speed."

"Thanks be," Apnis said feelingly, as with the ache across her chest falling off, she relaxed her webbing and glanced at the holo, which had settled into its normal shifting starfield pattern. "I reckon three to four days to Altina, but a lot depends on what we meet on the way."

"We're scanning for currents and other anomalies, Commander, in three hundred sixty degree sweeps," Azular assured her. "And with our enhanced holo, we should be able to map them in. If we don't have to fight against the fluxes, we should make good progress."

To give the lie to his words, there was a sudden judder and the crew was thrown sideways as the ship slewed.

"Cross current, ma'am!" Dox called. "Compensating."

"Hell, I'm not surprised this isn't a popular route, Cap!" exclaimed the first mate. "That damn well hurt! I'll need to get my ribs strapped."

"You'll have to get in line," she was told crisply. "Flintlock's logged casualties already. But as hostile ships run mostly with cyber crews, it shouldn't affect them overmuch."

"Good for them; but it might help us," Apnis said, wincing. "They won't expect we puny mortals to be stealing rides on their highways."

"Nice idea, but I'm not putting credit on it. As soon as we're stable, you're for medbay. Bellfish, check how the *Mevaena's* coping."

The Starfall ship had also taken casualties but was running on spec. Distance scans had shown no traffic, but craft could jump in along the way. The *Mevaena* had no cloak, but it was agreed that *Arianrhod* would deploy hers, as it would provide advantage in the event of interception.

** * **

The exhausting road to Altina had almost run its course, the exit node had been detected, and the captain was thinking on whether to decloak, as the energy drain was telling. "We'll keep the cloak up until we're off the bypass and have checked local subspace," she told Apnis. "We've had no news of hitches, but there's been trouble here in the past, we've sensed blips that might be ships on this bypass, and the node's way too close to the third planet for my liking. Gliss, keep tactical eyes and ears on what's off-node. You too, Azular. Earbleat, hold a tight beam and be ready to act if we spot anything. Bellfish, get me Captain Radex."

Radex held with her precautions. His long-range sensors had picked up bugs en route that may have been nothing, but the Starfall captain, like most of his kind, was innately suspicious. The two agreed that the *Mevaena* would drop out first, and set for the nearby node that would take her onto the local route linking Alto Finglas to Berzic. As Radex was for Minti, he had planned to head there via Alto Finglas.

"Right," Ahxenta called as the link cut. "Let's leave this highway to hell. Slow to jump-off speed helm, and ready us to follow the *Mevaena*; give her plenty head start and come off to her starboard. Do *not* drop the cloak until I give the word. Any advanced gear out there will detect our traces, but we should be a surprise to the usual run of space scum, if any are in wait. Chief, shields at max, and everyone stay tight: we're still riding these damn hyper waves. Azular, keep tabs on the *Mevaena*."

The cruiser speared off the bypass, her image on the holo wavering as she made the jump. Dox kept her course, holding back to give the other vessel ample leeway. As Azular called that the *Mevaena* was clear, the helmswoman sent the *Arianrhod* into an upward arc to come out in a clear patch of space with a good outlook, well to the right side of the Starfall ship's projected position.

As *Arianrhod* cleared the node, impelled by a quirky surge of energy, Gliss and Azular called out in chorus. Their scanners had detected two signals moving at speed towards their position. Bellfish cried a warning from the *Mevaena* that she had picked up two blips heading in from the direction of the third planet of the Altina system.

"Red alert! Battlestations!" Ahxenta called. "Dox, keep the cloak up. Gunnery crews stand by, I want every weapon we have ready to run. Chief, shields tight, ready to use those engines! Gliss, Azular, get a confirmation on what we're up against."

"Confirm two vessels, Captain!" Gliss called loudly as he honed the display of the bridge holo. "Cloak's hindering scans, but we have two big ships; readings suggest battlecruiser types, but I don't get anything that implies hostile configuration… that's odd…"

"They're reading as ISA, Captain!" Azular yelled. "They're swerving to come in either side of the *Mevaena,* but if they *are* ISA and new, they must've read us. They're heavily shielded but they must be targeting."

"Then we give them two targets! Drop the cloak, Dox. Earbleat, fix targeting eyes on the one nearest us," Ahxenta ordered, her eyes raking the holo. "What are they playing at? Get me the *Mevaena,* comms."

"We're reading them," Radex confirmed. "They've locked targeting eyes on me but haven't attempted a link. I'm not opening one. What have you got?" he added to one of his stations.

"I have their call-signs: they read as the battlecruiser *ISAS Defender* and the destroyer *ISAS Iris Quartz,* sir," a voice called back.

"What! Azular, confirm!" Ahxenta called to her science officer.

"Confirmed, Captain. Reading as *Defender* and *Iris Quartz.* We've had the *Iris Quartz* in our sights, and she's had us in hers. She's not hiding her spec or call-sign, and a bogus ship would not read so precisely. *And* she's changing position to come in off our bows," he warned.

"She knows us too well. Face her out, Dox; keep targeting eyes on her, Earbleat, but don't lose sight of the *Defender.* One shot from either and you *will* respond in kind. Stand by Captain Radex, but keep on line, and keep shields up and weapons hot. Cut the noise but maintain red alert. Comms, get me the *Iris Quartz!* What in blazes is she playing at?"

"Hide and seek?" Apnis remarked. "She must know it's us."

"I have the *Iris Quartz.* Captain Morgen Gulley for you, ma'am."

"Captain Gulley; we meet again," Ahxenta hailed him icily. "Care to tell me why you hot-footed it out of the Altina system to greet me with your targeting eyes and your weapons trained on my ship?"

"We had no idea who was coming off that hidden bypass," Gulley retorted. "I'd like to know how you knew it, what you and that Starfall ship were doing on it, where you came from and where you're going."

"I bet you do. My business is not your concern, and the routes I use to carry it out are also not your concern. And I'm justified, given the interest the ISA is taking in me and mine," she replied. "Do you plan to detain me, shoot me down or follow me? If so, please tell me so that I can take action. You realise that I *will* file another protest with the ISA if my ship or the *Mevaena* is accosted, impeded, or tracked in any way? And you're still targeting my ship. What do you mean by it?"

"You have not answered my questions…"

"And I don't intend to. We've been here before, Captain. I intend to leave Altina space, and if you or the *Defender* attempt to stop me, I *will* respond with deadly force. Is that clear?"

"You can't threaten me, Captain Ahxenta."

"I think you just did, Cap," Apnis muttered.

"Is that clear?" the captain repeated.

"*Defender* is coming about, Captain! She's arming!" Gliss warned.

"Commander Earbleat, target the *Defender* and prepare to fire on my mark!" Ahxenta spat.

"Targeting, aye!"

"Stand by!" Gulley snapped and cut comms.

"Captain Radex, I suggest you prepare to act if either of them is so stupid as to open fire; Ahxenta out."

As the link was cut, Gliss let out a loud expletive. "*Defender's* loosed a warning shot across our bows!"

"Earbleat, prepare to fire! One more shot and reply in kind. Helm, come about to get forr'ad torpedoes in range! Comms, send a distress all channels that we are under attack by the ISA battleship *Defender*!"

As seat restraints tightened further and Dox sent the *Arianrhod* into a tight arc to cut across the path of the *Iris Quartz* and come up on the *Defender* without putting the Starfall ship in danger, Bellfish called out that Gulley was on line.

"He's saying they'll stand down, Cap!"

"Too bad! His ship isn't the one that fired on mine; stay on course!"

"*Mevaena's* heading in to assist! And a ship's coming in off the main bypass!" Gliss warned. "One of ours: the *Green Comet*, ma'am!"

"*Defender's* powering down weapons but is still targeting, Captain," Azular added loudly.

"Hold for now, Earbleat, but maintain firing readiness. Bellfish, cut the distress and get me the captain of that ISA boat; record every iota and be ready to send it to the *Mevaena* and the *Comet*."

There was a slight delay before an arrogant face appeared in the holo. "I am Captain Ellast Skurrity; who might you be?"

"I'm Captain Cinnabar Ahxenta of the *PSS Arianrhod*, as you damn well know. Why did you fire on my ship without provocation?"

"I had provocation. You and that unknown cruiser jumped off a covert bypass that we believe to be hostile; *we* have the remit to keep space safe and that node sits close to a local route."

"That unknown cruiser, *as you know*, is Starfall. And that's no excuse: you and the *Iris Quartz* were in wait for us and *you* gave us a damn good once-over before you came about to attack. Your scans told you exactly who I was. I repeat, why did you attack without provocation?"

Skurrity would only repeat that as an ISA patrol vessel, he had every right; and his warning shot had not harmed the *Arianrhod*.

"What were you were warning me of?" Ahxenta asked frostily.

"That I would act if you obstructed me or refused to comply with directions from an ISA ship carrying out its duty," he told her.

"I did not obstruct you in any way, nor am I bound to comply with your directions, Captain. I *will* report your interception of me to your fleet HQ, to my trade body and my fleet, and to my legal advisor. I plan to leave Altina space now. I consider your targeting of *Arianrhod* as aggression, and if you fire another shot at me, I *will* defend my ship."

Ahxenta cut off his string of invective mid-sentence and ordered a link to the *Green Comet*, which had come up on *Arianrhod's* flank. In a few words, she brought Jikelleli up to date and called in Radex. He had decided to escort *Arianrhod*, as he was sure that the ISA ships would try to track him. He could make his end point via Silshoon. As Jikelleli was for the Web, she would take the same line.

"Captain Gulley for you, ma'am!" Bellfish cut in.

"I wondered when he'd be back," Ahxenta grunted. "Stay on line, both of you; let's see what he has to say."

Gulley reiterated that he and the *Defender* would stand down, but he still wanted to know how Ahxenta knew of the bypass, where her ship and the *Mevaena* had come from and their next heading.

"We've had this out before, Captain. You have no right to waylay me nor to enquire into my business, and *certainly* no right to fire on a civilian ship without provocation. I'm reporting this incident as soon as you're off my comm. I bid you good day. Ahxenta out."

"Where *does* the ISA recruit its personnel? Assholes United?"

"Can it, Tallica. We run with targeting eyes and weapons on line, and every shield and scanner active. Either of those two try to follow,

I want to know. Keep our comms tight, Bellfish. As soon as we're on the way, I'll send that protest, with a copy of Skurrity's comm."

The three ships set for Berzic and made the jump-on point shortly afterwards. As far as they could tell they had no tail, but none of the captains would take it as read.

"Lucky for us the *Comet* was switching at the Altina node and caught our signal. And good to know she's now FMTE. But how *did* the ISA find out about the bypass?" Apnis wanted to know.

"They'll still have science ships nosing around the Crimson Drapes and Furze," the captain said. "Given the currents on that damn bypass, they'd have picked up some sign and made a guess. And since we didn't show at Quartic, some quick wit figured a likely line that took in Bistra. But we're reading clear, so I'll send the protest to the ISA HQ *and* fleet. I bet Radex has told Starfall that the ISA's found the bypass; I'll check, as I need to talk to him. And to Sarie over her new flag."

The captain had no need to contact ISA fleet HQ, for the distress had caused fallout. She was frosty and brief with Admiral Best, cut the link and sent her protest in the directions she had planned. Comms had come from Goodsocks and Holdspan and she passed the latest to them. The *Emerald* was leaving Telzilt with her cargo, and the *Firestorm* as escort. The *Warrior* had left Selliden for the Web. She had met the *Hexameter* and the *Quarkstorm*, whose captains had been watching trade issues closely and wanted more on alternatives to the TA. Captain Sari Jikelleli had been quizzed on her change of allegiance, and it was likely that the *Tektite* and the *Firedrake* would soon also shed the TA flag.

"Why does the ISA keep setting Best on you, Cap?" Apnis asked. "Is he an info-sent that can't take no for an answer?"

"You could be right," the captain agreed. "Remember Burnet of the ISA office on Delta? ISA planting info-sents in key places? Enough of him. Sarie will stop at Berzic with us, as the admin and drop should only take half a day tops, and we'll head for the Web together."

"If the Berzic Port Authority will let us hand it over."

"That's covered," Ahxenta smiled. "The *Mevaena* is Starfall but not PSS, and Captain Radex will take on the pod and drop it at the client's orbital station if the PA won't let us do it, *if* the client agrees. Lindell's checking it. Fee transfer's not an issue, and there shouldn't be quibbles in Berzic space, as the transfer will be between two non-TA ships."

"Once the TA works out *that* loophole, there'll be ructions. Nat had to shift the *Warrior's* Vellis Prime cargo to another carrier but said that the PA reps were okay when he spoke to them. You planning to have a word with the Berzic PA office?" Apnis asked.

"No; I want to make the Web top speed. It's a free port, and I need to know which of our usual clients will deal with us. Lindell's sending out feelers. We'll be in port a while as our people need a break, so shore leave is a priority. We still have injured from the passage to Altina, but medbay's coping. And we'll need a full resupply and partial refit."

"Roger that. Nothing odd on the grid thus far, and it's a short hop to Berzic; and from there, we're not on a TA trade route. The crew will be glad to see the Web. So will I, it's been a helluva spell and a whole new world for our people. Can we expect to field flak at Merkat, Cap?"

"We'd better not," the captain said darkly. "Any harassment of my crew and I'll have the authorities by the ears. But we'd all best be sharp for Berzic. This will be a test of local reaction, and how much sway the TA has over trading. With ports like Freskat, Nyx and Aoria declaring free status, every main centre in the ISP-majority sector of Lambda is now out of TA control. And barring non-TA carriers from its bypasses won't help: it bawled for the use of Starfall's, and now they're known to many, we don't need the TA's."

When they made Berzic, the test that the captain had predicted was short. The client, mindful of a technical hitch in delivery by *Arianrhod*, had sounded out the Port Authority in advance. That body, having had the rough edge of an arrogant TA rep's tongue, had reacted by allowing the *Arianrhod* and the *Mevaena* to dock by the client's orbital transfer station and advised that the cargo pod be passed via the Starfall ship's tractors to the grapples. Port fees, clearances, and client cargo checks were quickly dealt with and the three ships given leave to depart. Berzic was added as a friendly port to Lindell's list an hour later.

27: GHOST OF THE PAST

The Web's outer grids glowed a greeting as the *Arianrhod* and the *Green Comet* closed. The *Mevaena* had left at Silshoon, and as the PSS ships came up on the first beacons, the routine scan beams of Web defences slid over their hulls in an icy caress.

Ahxenta sighed in satisfaction. "Take us in nice and slow, helm, and send out our call-sign. On speaker, comms… *PSS Arianrhod* to Merkat Three Port Control: request permission to dock."

"We have you on screen, *Arianrhod*. Welcome back to Merkat Three Free Port. Stand by docking instructions."

"Docking instructions in, ma'am; awaiting clearance," Dox called.

"That's us," Apnis noted. "And fast; must be glad to see us. *Comet's* heading in too, so she's cleared; we need to make sure she has the UV-III fix. And I see the *Warrior's* berthed this side, so Nat's made it."

"Take us in and lock us down, Ms Dox," the captain instructed.

The frame of docking struts moved to encircle *Arianrhod's* hull and the locking cross-pieces slipped into place, each turning red to confirm a grip. Dox steadily reduced power to bring the ship to station-keeping.

"Boards show green, Captain: docking complete."

"Roger that. I'll head to the harbour office once we're to rights and pay our fees, Tallica. There'll be things they want to hear. And I've had a call from the PA, so it's after facts. And I want to sniff out the mood Web-side before ours go down."

"*Half Moon*," Apnis hinted. "Best place."

The captain cocked an eye at her first mate. "You've convinced me. We'll take Azular, as his talents are useful. And Lindell's for marketing. But I'd best see what that Authority link's about," she groaned, rising.

"Merkat's PA chief," she said on return. "He wanted details on our new trading union, as he hopes to have more of its ships using the Web in the future. I pointed out that he'd two others in already – the *Warrior* and the *Comet* – and I asked why he hadn't spoken to Nat."

"He reckons you're the info-point on the FMTE," Apnis smirked.

"Seems like. I gave him the basics and the link, and told him to ask directly. He probed for the names of other ships that have joined up. He got the *Emerald's*, but he can work out the rest himself. If you contact Kit Biernop, see what you can find out from him."

"I'll do that once we're down; his people keep close eyes on their comms, and I bet there'll be a few of them with us in their sights."

"Them and others," the captain grimaced. "*Warrior* sent a courtesy salute, but that was all, so I guess Nat's Web-side."

The four set off later on. The stop at the harbour office was brief, as the staff were too much in awe of Ahxenta to make small talk. The captain left her shuttle and Lindell at marketing, and carried on with Apnis and Azular to the *Half Moon in a Puddle*, where Ally was surprised to see his favourite patrons in so soon, but hailed them heartily.

"We saw you dock. *Arianrhod* looks trim; no TA logos in sight."

"Tell me what people are saying about it," the captain invited.

"I'd heard that the TA had withdrawn its flag from you, the *Emerald* and the Starfall PSS ships, but it was temporary, and as soon as you'd toed some line or other, you'd get it back. I didn't reckon you or that Captain Thal could be pushed into toeing any line," Ally grinned.

"Toeing what line?" Apnis asked.

He shrugged. "Nobody could say. Some guessed you'd teed off TA bigwigs, or the ISA, after the faceoff here, when Captain Kerrix cooked that ISA captain's scanner and a colonel interfered. But that was a while back. *And* you've been out of circulation for a bit; people said you'd left our zones for the new one, Psi. But then a rumour starts that other PSS ships had been seen without TA logos – the *Obsidian* and the *Nyx Warrior*. And I've seen that new Trades Exchange ID holo," Ally said. "Captain Holdspan was in earlier and it was on his wrist unit; he says its marker has been merged into his ship's call-sign ID. I guess the PA here has no problem with ships that fly under that trade flag?"

"No," the captain said swiftly. "Why should it? Many other shipping lines and independents trade in the Web, what's one more?"

"When the new one's being set up as a rival to the TA, I'd imagine fur's going to fly sooner or later," was the sagacious rejoinder.

"Tell me more," Ahxenta pressed.

Ally had little else than gossip, but there was ample of it, and much of it about staff changes in the Merkat TA. But the general feeling was that it was time that officious bodies like the TA were stirred, and more competition was a good thing. Those in the Web not directly involved were merely biding their time and laughing up their sleeves. The three made soon after for a quiet table, watched by two pairs of curious eyes.

"That chat lasted a while, mate," Malty observed to his friend. "But as *Arianrhod* hasn't been in the Web for an age and she's not TA now, I suppose they had a lot to chat about."

"Ally was doing most of it," Jurry noted. "Bet it *was* about the TA: its reps are wetting their pants, wondering who'll be next out the door. If more Privates tell the TA to stick its flag where the sun don't shine, and its other tied shipping lines follow, its profits will drop big time. And howling over trade routes won't help. I hear the new Mu double bypass has so many private subscribers that the TA and the ISA can't call the shots on costs or usage. And as it's near zone Psi at Kollaskin edge, there's a ruckus over the ins and outs of strange fleets and ships: who knows what's a legit trader or not?"

"Not our problem," Malty replied lazily. "Here's another rebel back in: Captain Holdspan and his first mate. Aye, they've seen them. That'll be another cosy chat. We'd best stick around and see what we can pick up that might profit us later. I'll get us a couple of pots."

Ahxenta smiled wryly. "Nat and Sol Treskitt back again," she said, waving over. "But it looks like it should be okay for our people to head down. No undercurrents of anything in here, Azular?"

"Nothing other than curiosity, ma'am, but Captain Holdspan may have more information," he replied.

"You got your talk with Biernop set?" she went on to Apnis.

"Aye, Cap; I'll meet him in an hour in the *Pink Kettle*. Here's Nat."

Holdspan had left his supercargo to handle details with Redship, he told them. Their reps were wary, but not averse to making deals if their clients were happy, although their largest client was proving to be the stickiest. Redship had a load for ISA Silverglass and the latter's buyers had baulked at the *Warrior* as carrier, but the only ships large enough in port were his, *Arianrhod* and *Green Comet*, all FMTE. The alternatives were to wait for another bulk carrier or split the load. And *that* would cost more, the contracts would be trickier and it would be riskier.

"There were no big carriers listed as due, last I looked. Not that we Privates tend to call in advance," he smiled. "My super will keep me updated, but we've couple of contracts on the table, not huge, and local – Vreskota Two and Velish, both free ports – that will take us out the day after tomorrow. Are you stopping long, Captain?"

"My people need shore leave, so I won't take on urgent contracts," she told him candidly. "And then they'd have to be in sectors close by, as I need to be here when the *Moonstone* and the *Emerald* haul in, though they're not due for a while. Are your crew finding trouble port-side?"

Holdspan shook his head. None of his had reported being accosted, although he and his first mate had had to deal with harbour office and Dockers' Guild staff. He had heard of the sly TA visits to local firms to warn them off non-TA affiliated ships, and had asked. Most of those cornered had been irked and had complained to TA HQ.

"Its complaints department must be working overtime, just like the ISA's," Apnis chuckled. "Tell us about your trade at Vellis Prime, Nat, and the PA reps' attitudes there," she urged.

The *Warrior's* captain outlined what was said, and asked about the latest on fixes to the UV-III. Ahxenta was telling him about the success of the Metriklon comms modules when a link from Lindell interrupted. She was needed in marketing on a business matter. As it was near time for Apnis to set off for her tryst, the five broke off the chat.

"Lindell was to meet with Redship," Ahxenta said on the way down. "Looks like Nat got in first, but if the cargoes are urgent they wouldn't suit us. He'd meets with Silversnow and Ottolyx as well, but they major in small-scale gear and use short-haul carriers for local clients."

The supercargo had found a deal through a contact in Ottolyx that brought in Redship. Ottolyx micro-parts were being fitted into a batch of Redship mining gear for Beta Zegonia 68c; the load would be ready in four days and the chartered shipper had defaulted. Beta Zegonia was in Alpha and less than a day from Merkat; the deal was profitable and would mean a bonus. As Lindell gave the details, Ahxenta considered.

"I want to know more about it, but we *can* fit it in and turnaround would be quick. The shore leave rotas can be worked around it. You'd best head off to your get-together with Biernop, Tallica. I'll meet you back here when you're done. The Redship talks shouldn't take more than an hour and a half tops. Let's go, Lindell, Azular."

The time stretched, but accord was reached. Although in Coalition space, Beta Zegonia was independent, *Arianrhod* was known there and the captain had dealt with Redship for years. Apnis, back from the *Pink Kettle*, told them that the change of flags of the PSS ships was the hot topic. The FMTE was touted as a new kid on the block that might give the TA a run for its credit, but some cynics were predicting losses for those rash enough to cut the TA cord. But no-one was totally opposed to dealing with such renegades in Biernop's neck of the woods.

"So back aboard for us," the captain told her officers. "We've a lot to do before we ship out. And I have links to make."

The result of the links Ahxenta passed on in a senior staff briefing. The *Moonstone* was on her way and would be in before *Arianrhod* left for Beta Zegonia; the *Emerald* was running about ten days behind her.

The first mate was puzzled and stopped behind as the others filed out. "What's with the *Moonstone's* speed, Cap? You told Nat Holdspan only a few hours ago that she'd be a while."

"Like all Starfall's ships, she knows ways in and out that we don't.

And she's the fastest ship we know. Azular's no wiser – I spoke to him before the briefing. Part of it's the cargo she's carrying, but that's not the whole story. I don't like it, but I'm sure I'll find out what in hell's going on when she makes it in."

* * *

The *Moonstone* made Merkat the day before *Arianrhod* was due out, and Ahxenta was surprised by an urgent link from Kerrix, who was keen to release her load before their meeting. As she would be Web-side for *that*, she would like to meet up with the captain in marketing after it. Ahxenta agreed: she knew what the *Moonstone* carried.

"Cap?" Apnis queried.

"She's brought part of the gear to equip an office suite that's spoken for, on green four of inner two, off main marketing. And she's brought in two guards to set it up and make sure nothing happens to it."

"An office suite? For what?" the first mate demanded.

"A zone Alpha division of the Free-Market Trades Exchange," said Ahxenta with relish. "I don't think the Web Residency Office realises what it's in for, and the captain will need to be there to smooth things over and exert authority – the lease is binding."

"TA will be pissed," Apnis said flippantly. "It's offices and meeting rooms are level five. Captain Kerrix will smooth things over with the RO? I'd like to be there to see that. But it'll need staff to run it, *and* people who know what's going on Web-side and are familiar with trade in *our* settled zones. I can't imagine there'll be a rush of applicants for any jobs going, so where are they coming from?"

"Psi and Starfall: Thal's people are from all over and have various skills. And the FMTE people on Telzilt have worked under duress for years; they'll cope," Ahxenta grinned.

"But they've still to get here and get going. How do they plan to do that?" Apnis asked narrowly, as the captain's grin widened. "They're coming in on the *Emerald*, aren't they?"

"They are, with the rest of the office equipment. Thal's people have started to ship Metriklon comms units, but the *Moonstone's* also carrying enhanced code-decode shards to pass on to our own. I'm picking up a case of them when I meet Captain Kerrix later. She'll give some to the *Comet* on the QT, and to the *Warrior*, when Nat gets back in."

"If they work as they're supposed to, it'll mean the UV-III will be secure for a bit," the first mate agreed. "You going down alone for the meet with Kerrix?" she added in almost a whisper. "We're shipshape here, and loading's on target. Our people know what to do."

"Is that a hint that you want to come?" Ahxenta asked as quietly.

Apnis looked serious. "Yup."

"You may as well. Azular's asked, as he wants to see Captain Kerrix before we leave. I don't know how long she'll be with the RO, but the gear won't take long to ship over and she'll have her people on it. I'm taking the *Gremlin* down: it's time the Web had a look at her."

Ahxenta was as good as her word, and two hours later she and her officers were seated in a private marketing booth. Half an hour after that, a limping Kerrix appeared, a guard at her heels. She dismissed her with the order to return to Commander Inks.

"Xanna, what happened?" Azular demanded in concern as she slid in alongside him, hauling a kit bag after her.

"Certain parties object to the new offices we're setting up, maybe," she replied. "My security got the perps; it didn't occur to them that I'd have guards at back of my guards. They were distance shots and meant to scare us, I think, or the gunmen were lousy shots. One of my guards took a leg graze. In any case, my people got them and they'll hold them until they find out. Jesse's got it in hand. The Residency people were upset, as it was outside their main office. Web security's involved, but mine have first dibs," she said tersely.

"You suspected something would happen?" Ahxenta asked.

"My security chief did; *she* insisted on the extra guards. Our contact here who'd brokered the premises rental reported undue interest from strangers not known to the Residency Office; not nasty, but insistent."

"TA?" Apnis asked.

"I'm making no assumptions," Kerrix replied tartly. "For now."

"But have you been treated in medbay?" Azular cut in.

"Yes. Jesse insisted, as it may help the case we'll bring. It's fine, it'll heal. But that's not why I'm here. I booked a room over by," she said to Ahxenta, opening her bag. "Code-decode shards. You want to check them while the captain and I talk?" she added to Azular.

"Yes ma'am," he replied mechanically.

His eyes followed the two as they made off to a nearby door. It shut after them, and the occupancy light lit. Astute as always, he dug up his info-pad and began a rapid scrutiny. "That room's booked out for the rest of the day," he said to Apnis, his eyes troubled.

"Going to be a long talk, then," she sighed. "Want a coffee?"

Behind the closed door, Ahxenta had drawn out a scanner-jammer to sweep the room and the woman opposite. She then folded her arms. "Want to tell me what this is about?" she began abruptly.

"Please sit, Captain," Kerrix said mildly as she removed an info-pad and a tube from her bag. After setting up the pad, she pulled the tube apart to reveal two glass cups and an integral flask.

"I'm not going to like it, am I?" Ahxenta persisted, watching as she poured two drinks.

Kerrix shrugged. "To be honest, Captain, I don't know. Sit…" she gestured to a seat and slid a glass across. "You knew I visited a dig at a site used during the alien occupation when I was on Telzilt?"

"You sent me bio-data; we found nothing definite in it. What else did you find that concerns me and mine?"

"We found a digger who'd been part of a covert rebel group of ex-victims that ran strike actions during the occupation, and later in the war, with the ships and weapons they'd stolen…"

"You mentioned him. And that Captain Thal had picked up on a few working out of Telzilt and trying get back to what they had."

"He could tell us a little of what it was like: people put in cryo-tubes and woken later for slave labour or alteration as pawns, or worse. I'm not going into details. He and Captain Thal's links pointed us to others, victims brought in from distance for use," she said bitterly, raising her eyes to Ahxenta's face. "But made it out," she added, turning her info-pad so that her companion could see it. "That was one," she said softly.

Ahxenta scrutinised the portrait closely. It was an older woman with a defiant smile on her time-ravaged face. She wore an armoured jacket. There was a vague familiarity about her, the captain felt.

"Who?" she asked.

"Her name was Commander Kelva Ocean," Kerrix said gently.

Ahxenta felt a jolt zip up her spine as her mouth dropped open, a soundless *what* on her lips. She stared at her counterpart and then back at the image, sceptical but trying to take it in. "Was?" she croaked.

"She's known as Captain Kel Ocean. She runs a carrier out of Rom Betra, a colony of Rom Litra. She was an arms runner during and after the Telzilt occupation. She escaped from a hostile holding area a hyper-jump from Letik, near the Strell Nebula. You'll find out more on here," Kerrix said, holding out a data shard.

Ahxenta took the shard, looked again at the face on the screen and then at the woman beside her. "What's on it?"

"A message to you. Private – I don't know what it says."

"She knows about me, then?"

Kerrix nodded. "I told her. I recognised the name," she explained as she took a sip of her drink. "I figured you wouldn't mind. Do you?"

"Depends on what you told her," was the harsh retort.

"Not a lot. Only that you're the toughest person I know, one of the smartest, and that you scare the hell out of me. And that I look on you as a friend. I hope *that* wasn't a step too far?"

Ahxenta let go the shard and leant back, taking stock. "We've had our differences, but I guess I can see past them… friend," she said bluntly, raising her glass to take a sip, her eyes still on Kerrix.

"I'll leave you to the shard, but I'll take my info-pad. This room's booked until close of play tonight, so take all the time you need. You want me to tell Azular and Commander Apnis to wait?" she asked.

"Tell them to make for the *Half Moon*: I'll see them there later," the captain said slowly. "What's your plan for now?"

"I've things to do. I'll need to see what my people have found," she said wearily, emptying her glass as she stood. "Keep the flask; I've got more like it at home," she added, pointing with a thumb.

Ahxenta's mind was whirring but another thought intruded. "One thing: what did you find at that Telzilt dig that rattled *you* big time?"

Kerrix halted, startled. "Damn you," she said softly, raising her eyes to avoid the keen glance. "No. It's not your concern. I will not put my burdens on anyone else," she told her harshly. "I need to go."

"You damn don't," Ahxenta said, rising to her feet. "When *will* you learn to ask for help? And don't turn your back on me when I'm talking to you," she added, grasping both Kerrix' arms to halt her progress.

The woman stood rigid as the rough voice continued above her. "Well? What was it you found, or found out? I don't bite, you know."

"Yes you do."

"Tell me," she insisted softly. "What did you find?"

"My mother's body."

Ahxenta closed her eyes, releasing her hold. "Bloody hell."

"What was left of it. Mettix confirmed it," she said tonelessly. "In a cryo-tube. They'd removed bits of it, including an unborn child. I can appreciate Thal's burning hatred of them." She let out a hissing breath. "I'm dealing with it. Merry's a first-rate ship's counsellor."

"There's nothing I can say. But – tell Azular. He needs to know."

"You have that shard to deal with. There's a link attached. Captain Kel *would* like to hear from you."

"You're changing the subject… Captain Kel?"

"Her people call her that, from the old Telziltic *Kel'Nem*. It means *strong in heart*. She's a tonic," Kerrix turned with a sad smile. "I'd like to see her again. She calls you Cinna."

"Nobody else had better."

"Nobody else would dare – Cinnabar."

"You live dangerously," the captain growled.

"So I'm told. I *do* have to go. Look at your message," she advised.

"I'm shipping out tomorrow. I'll only be gone a couple of days and I can do without Azular for the trip. No argument," she cut the instant rebuff. "He wanted to see you anyway."

"Why are you interfering?"

Ahxenta looked at her quizzically. "What in blazes are *you* doing in giving me this?" she shot back, picking up the shard.

"You got me. As always. And it works both ways. If *you* need to talk or know more, link me. I *will* see you before you leave."

"I'll take that as a promise... Xanna."

With a startled look and an affirmative nod, Kerrix turned to leave. She looked all out, Ahxenta thought as she watched the door seal. She looked at the data shard in her tightly-clasped hand, swore softly and slid into her chair to slot it into the table-top reader.

In the main hall, Azular stood as soon as he saw the door open, but waited until she came over. "Xanna. Where's the captain?"

"She'll be a while. She asked me to tell you and Commander Apnis to head to the *Half Moon* and she'll see you there. And I'll see you there shortly. I've things to see to. Later," she insisted as he tried to speak.

With a quick farewell to both, she turned and walked stiffly off to a nearby comm booth, Azular's eyes following her.

"Let's go," Apnis announced. "It's getting towards close of normal business hours and I don't know about you, but I need food, preferably before the dinner rush at the *Half Moon*."

Azular picked up his gear, frowning, and set off in the wake of the first mate, with a last glance at the comm booth and its lone occupant.

The *Half Moon* was gearing up for the expected influx of diners, but was not yet busy, Ally told the two when they made the bar. They gave their orders and looked about. A handful of their own crewmen were there, several from the *Green Comet* and a few other regular drinkers.

"No-one from the *Moonstone*," Azular observed quietly.

"She's not long in; and Captain Kerrix would have wanted to scout out the lie of the land before she'd sanction shore leave, I imagine," Apnis said. "Wise, given what's happened."

"What's happened, Commander?" Ally enquired curiously, slapping two small mugs on the counter.

"Trouble," was the short answer. "Anything new in here, Ally?"

He shook his head. "Nothing since last you were in, Commander. Though two loudmouths standing here made snide remarks about the shuttle that came out of *Arianrhod* over an hour ago; your ride?"

"What two loudmouths?" Apnis demanded.

"TA reps," the barman said smugly. "One reckoned it was alien and said you'd maybe got it from Starfall, or as you'd been in zone Psi, you could've got it there. I asked how he knew and he told me to butt out. They didn't stay. *Your* guys over there had heard them."

"Engineering crew," Azular said mildly. "They would object."

"Any of ours would," the first mate said. "Let's find a table before our rations turn up. You got secure-cam pics of those reps, Ally?"

"I'll get them to you pronto," he promised.

Ally handed over a copy of the record when he brought their meals. Neither knew the faces, and Apnis stored the data on her wrist comm for later scrutiny. No-one disturbed them as they ate. An hour elapsed before a stir around them alerted them to the advent of their captain. Ahxenta placed her order at the bar and headed over.

"No Captain Kerrix? She said she'd see me before I left."

"No anyone," her first mate told her. "How are *you*, Cap?"

"I'll do," she said shortly. "But before she gets in: I've told her that you're not on our next trip out, so you'd best reserve a place here," she told Azular. "You can come up with us to get your gear, and take your own shuttle down before we ship out."

His eyes shot wide. "Captain?"

"You heard." She shook her head at Apnis' probing glance. "Leave it. Captain Kerrix will tell you what you need to know, Azular. I hope," she added. "What's new here? Ally said he'd passed data to you?"

The first mate gave her the details, whilst the science officer's gaze raked the *Half Moon*. Most of the eyes on them flicked away, but he sensed no undue interest. As the captain's meal arrived, Ally was quick to pop up behind the bar to attend to the newly-arrived Kerrix.

Two pairs of eyes in a dark corner booth took in the sight. "Bet *she* makes for them," Malty said. "She's limping. Had a scrap, you think?"

Jurry peered into the gloom. "It *was* her style when she worked here, and we've seen it since. Dr Azular doesn't look lit up with joy, he looks worried. Maybe he thinks he's bitten off more than he can chew, but as he's *Arianrhod*, I doubt it. She's heading in."

The privacy shield rippled as the captain breached it. Azular relieved her of her cup and helped her sit, watched by the two. Both sighed as the screen intensified, to veil their view and cut their snooping capacity.

Kerrix was greeted cordially. She intended to head back to her ship. Her people had got little from the two they had caught. Levettiza and Merkat security had sat in on the interviews. Checks pulled up that they had come in three days before from Sevolb, where they were wanted for felonies. As they were silent on motive and outside complicity, Inks had pushed for two counts of attempted murder and warned that he would bring a civil case if the prosecution service refused to pursue it. That, he hoped, might induce cooperation. He had left them to stew, and he and their people were now back aboard.

"How do you plan to ship up?" Azular asked anxiously.

She smiled faintly. "My shuttle's on green four. I can get from here to there. But if I did need backup, those two sitting at the door are the guardians of the FMTE office. They're not in uniform, but believe me, they're armed and dangerous."

That brought up the FMTE, and Kerrix told them that the premises were being fitted with enough kit to begin work as soon as the *Emerald* arrived with the remaining gear and the staff. The Web's business net was on board with publicity, and ships now part of the FMTE would be notified. The *Moonstone* would remain Web-side until the new set-up was complete.

Ahxenta did not miss the gleam in her science officer's eyes, and as Kerrix rose to leave, she indicated with a nod that he accompany her. "I'll catch up with you at the *Gremlin*. And I'll see *you* when we get back into the Web," she said to Kerrix. "Look after yourself – Xanna."

The *Moonstone's* captain smiled. "I wish you and yours a safe and a pleasant trip, and I'll see you when you do get back – Cinnabar."

Azular and Apnis exchanged amazed glances, but said nothing. The Berzic took Kerrix' kitbag from her and slung it over his shoulder. He shepherded her past the nearby tables, waving to Ally as they left.

"You going to tell me what that was about, Cinnabar?" the first mate asked. "And what's with leaving Azular here?"

"Not in here. It's been a long day and I've several things to do when I get back aboard. Finish up and I'll settle our tabs."

The two found Azular at the *Gremlin's* bay, his wife having shooed him off once they had reached her shuttle. Ahxenta had her first mate take the helm, as she wanted to speak to the duty officer. The three set for the bridge as soon as they reached *Arianrhod*, where the captain ran through her updates, talked to comms, and then told Apnis to organise the last crew pick-ups. Her next task was a chat to Azular in her office. He planned to take the *Xanna* down in the morning.

"What's going on with the Cap?" an anxious voice murmured in the first mate's ear. "What happened at the meet with Captain Kerrix?"

"I don't know what went on or what's up, Crizz, and I'm not about to ask. She'll tell me when she's ready," was the quiet reply. "Azular's heading down tomorrow and he'll stay in the Web while we're out, so the *Xanna* will have to be prepped."

"What? I'd noticed there'd been a lot of coming and going from the

Moonstone, but we've had zip over comms about it."

"There was an incident," Apnis sighed. "Two idiots let go shots that hit Captain Kerrix and one of her guards; not serious, they're okay," she added, aware that ears about her were staining to hear. "There *will* be legal impacts, and we'll hear more later. But here's the Cap now. We all set for the start at ten hundred hours?"

The chief engineer confirmed that *Arianrhod* would be ready to go, and slid back to her post. She was not there long: she was given the conn when Ahxenta called the first mate into her office.

Apnis shook her head but smiled slightly at Cottontail as she retook her chair almost an hour later. "Do you have that long-distance link set up for the captain yet, comms?" she called over.

It was almost complete and should hold, the first mate was assured, despite the large number of secure relays necessary. "That's it set now, ma'am. Patching through."

"Keep a tight rein, Gallus, and listen out for Web-side and incoming comms. Greffy, keep a beat on the security side of that link."

Curious glances were traded around the bridge, but no-one spoke. The chief engineer's report that the *Xanna* was readied was met with a nod, and Apnis sat on, hand on fist, as the minutes passed.

An hour and a half had gone before the office door slid aside. The link had been cut for twenty minutes, but the first mate, guessing that the captain needed personal time, had made sure that nothing had been sent in. She had delayed the start of the next watch, but once Ahxenta took her chair, she gave the order. In the stir, Apnis placed a hand on the captain's arm and smiled, relieved at the calm look. The duty officer reported in and, handover compete, the two stepped off the bridge.

"I'm here if you need to talk, Cinnabar," Apnis murmured once they were safely in the transport tube. "Want a nightcap?"

"I do," Ahxenta responded. "And you want answers."

The first mate only laughed as they headed down to the busy mess where, ten minutes later, she and the captain claimed a quiet table.

* * *

At ten hundred hours next day, *Arianrhod,* cleared to leave, released her docking ties and set for Beta Zegonia 68c. Azular had left two hours earlier and Apnis, troubled by the part-story she had heard the night before, had held back her usual breakfast badinage. There had been no word from the *Moonstone*, but Captain Jikelleli had let them know that she had been asked to ship the Redship cargo for ISA Silverglass, as the stock was needed and no other carrier was available.

"Sarie's agreed; she's no other big deal in train and it'll test the water for ISA loads," Ahxenta said to her first mate. "But having to use an FMTE ship will stick in its craw and will tee off its TA chums. And I heard from Melly Goodsocks that *Emerald's* on track and will make the Web two days after we get back from Beta Zegonia. Our route's clear, no reports of any trouble, and we're expected."

"We're sticking to the direct route?"

"We are; it's a short trip, there's no point in making it difficult. Our armoury's up to scratch, Earbleat has *Loki* on line and Greffy's got the decoy ready. And we have our enhanced hull protection."

"There's been no mention of alien activity for a bit," Apnis agreed. "But that doesn't mean there won't be."

"Too true. I called Nat Holdspan: the route to Vreskota was clear, and he figures the same to Velish. Maybe the last hiding the aliens took was enough to stall them, and with Myrtleberry and her fleet in empty space off Alpha, the sectors we're heading into may be safer."

"Huh! I wouldn't bet on that. Are we sure she made out that way?"

"Starfall's a good guide to what she's at, and that's the last *I* heard. Steady as she goes, Dox; we don't want to give any watching eyes the impression that we're in a hurry."

"Steady as she goes, ma'am; estimate sixty minutes to bypass entry."

"Roger that," Ahxenta said automatically.

Hours rolled by, until the steady progress was broken by entry into Beta Zegonian orbit, when *Arianrhod's* new flag raised polite interest in the planetary authority. The clients were ready and cargo drop began.

The ship spent most of the day unloading, but Ahxenta had no wish to linger and gave the order to come about as soon as the fee was paid and approval to leave granted. She remained on watch until the bypass for the return had been made, and just at the end of her stint, a call for her from Captain Kerrix came in. She chose to take it in her office.

The first mate waited until her return to the bridge. "News, Cap?"

Ahxenta's face was grave, but she had an amused glint in her eye. "A result from the enquiry into the RO shooting. The two caught were so scared by Jesse Inks' threats of attempted murder charges that they spilled a name. You have the conn, Mr Snow; let's go, Commander."

Apnis laughed quietly as the transport tube door closed. "And who did they finger for giving them the orders?"

"Nobody that anybody'd heard of. Levettiza dug deep and the signs pointed to a dimwit in the Web's TA office. The new senior TA exec for Alpha is trying to shore up the TA's slipping influence by barking at Dishell's former minions to work harder or else. So the accused did, but she seems to have a similar style to Dishell. Her brief had been to scare Residency reps off settling the FMTE premises deal. The clowns in custody weren't as good as they claimed, and how she recruited them without alerting her office isn't known. Or what else she had up her sleeve. More mayhem, according to the pair in the cells."

"So by shooting Kerrix and her guard, the TA's more or less shot itself in the foot," Apnis observed.

"*Captain* Kerrix," Ahxenta corrected. "But the suspect may've been set up, and the TA office knows more than it's admitting, though it *has* been quick to distance itself and denounce the action. The Web's news channel's picked it up, and now word's out."

"Fireworks, then. Anything else?"

"*Comet's* loading the cargo for Silverglass, so we may pass her on the way in. And another FMTE-flagged PSS has come in. The *Firestorm*."

"*Dexel* Thal's ship? But she's a heavy cruiser!" Apnis exploded.

"Now she's a well-armed carrier. She's for Nexus, but she's in the Web to resupply – and to show an FMTE presence, I suspect."

"Whew! And we've only been out for a couple of days! I'm looking forward to getting back to see what else has changed."

* * *

That the Web's outer bays were busier than before *Arianrhod* had left was the first thing her first mate noted when the ship made berth. The *Firestorm*, *Tallulah*, *Snow Quartz,* and *Obsidian Sky* were in, as were ships of other lines, but the most unexpected sight was the *ISAS Trueheart*.

"We last saw *her* at Wester, when we and the *Moonstone* brought the *Crusader* in," Apnis said tartly. "Captain Kerrix will be vexed: that ship tried to scan hers after she declined to answer leading questions from the nosy Captain Drevell. But what's an ISA battlecruiser doing in the Web, apart from eyeing up the rest of us?"

"It's a free port," the captain shrugged. "She's not been in long, or we'd have heard. I'll find out in the harbour office. But the *Moonstone's* jammers are active, by the look of things. Send out the usual courtesies to our sister ships, Mr Bellfish…"

She was interrupted by a link from Bluejohn. Drevell had called him to demand facts about the *Obsidian's* trade flag and the other ships that flew under it, particularly the *Arianrhod* and the *Moonstone*.

"He was on a fishing expedition, Cinnabar, to find out how many of ours are FMTE and how many are liable to ditch the TA for it. The *Trueheart's* been in for four hours and no shuttle's gone out of her. But she's surface-scanned what she could of the ships around her."

Bluejohn had called the PSS captains in the Web, including Dexel Thal, all of whose ships had been fitted with code-decode parts. The

Obsidian was in for trade talks and resupply, and her captain, having got the gist from Captain Kerrix, wanted to be at the opening of the FMTE centre, but his next task was to warn the other PSS captains of Drevell.

"I'd like to know where Azular is," Ahxenta said to Apnis once the link was cut. "And I want a word with Xanna Kerrix. It's well within business hours, so Lindell can see what's to do in marketing. We'll take the *Gremlin* and ours due furlough can use one of the bigger shuttles."

"Roger that, Cap. We've not been out long, but a lot's happened. And there'll be a lot more before this stopover's done."

Apnis was correct, and after visiting the harbour office, the two left their supercargo and made for the *Half Moon*. After greeting Ally, the next familiar face at the bar was Murmur Fleetskup. He was with his exec, having left Spickle aboard to deal with the *Trueheart*. The *Tallulah*, trading at Zidexall, had been in the right spot to pick up a load for the Web, but Fleetskup's current interest was the new trades body: his first mate had probed and felt that its benefits topped those of the TA. He was given few details. Ahxenta had no mind to be a mouthpiece.

They were still talking when Azular walked in minus his wife, who was in marketing. He had spent time in the *Moonstone's* labs, he replied to Apnis, where he had met Dr Nedja Grylke, the *Firestorm's* senior SO, and a Letik native. They, Kinnitix and Nyvallish had been refining link systems for the FMTE. The opening was set for five days hence.

"Tight," Ahxenta remarked. "But wise, I think."

"There may be a queue at the door when it opens," Ally remarked. "It's been a hot topic in here, due to the gunplay. And it's been on Web news channels. I think Captain Kerrix was waylaid by reporters."

"She was," Azular growled. "And by Dettis Banyotty, the new TA head; *he* asked her into his office for a chat. She told him to get lost."

Fleetskup was called away by his supercargo just as the *Moonstone's* captain joined them. Ahxenta quickly claimed a word, telling the others to find a table. She waited until Ally had discreetly moved off.

"You didn't tell me she'd named her ship for me."

"No; I thought it would be best coming from her. You mean a lot to her; at least I felt that. Was she still the person you remembered?"

"Yes and no; you can't fill in years in an hour. How are you?"

"Changing the subject," Kerrix grinned faintly. "I'll do. I don't want to think about it. I told him. And warned him not to bring it up." She cocked an eyebrow at the distant table. "Not that it'll stop him. Do you plan to meet up with Captain Kel? Or is it none of my business?"

"It isn't… but I will. At some point. We'd best get over to them."

The two rejoined Apnis and Azular and sat on, to catch up with the latest from the Web and plan for the *Emerald's* arrival. Azular, due on board his own ship, accompanied his colleagues back to the *Gremlin*.

* * *

The next two days passed swiftly. Ahxenta, keen to have deals in place, spent time Web-side. She took Azular, as she wanted to discuss things with him that she had no notion to share elsewhere, chiefly Kerrix. *She* had been deeply shaken by events on Telzilt, but had been supported by friends aboard ship, the captain heard. Other trials had taken a toll: her kin had again tried to grab her ex-property, using the *Moonstone* as a trading chip. Admiral Posettix had ended it by warning the Protector of Valla Key that if he nullified the contract, Xanna Kerrix' first act as a citizen would be to contest his title on the bases of primacy and rank.

"That shut him up," Azular smiled. "He'd already had a notice from the Telzilt embassy on Norvalla about harassing one of its citizens."

"Norvalla and two of its colonies are ISA, but few other Psi systems are signed up," the captain said. "If petty squabbling like that can bring in embassies, I'm not surprised. But back to the table for us, and then to the ship: *Emerald's* due in at twelve hundred."

The PSS was timely. Her crew were glad to be back in the Web, and after civilities, Goodsocks agreed to meet Ahxenta and Kerrix in the harbour office promptly, before the *Emerald* began cargo discharge.

A little later and back aboard her ship, Ahxenta called for the holo-grid down full, with all scanners in action that could lawfully be used and eyes on the *Trueheart*, *Emerald* and *Moonstone*. Gliss reported that all three were returning the compliment by scanning *Arianrhod*.

"What in..." Apnis whistled. "What's *that* heading to the *Emerald* from the *Moonstone*?"

"*That's* an armoured shuttle. With the *Trueheart's* scans and the RO trouble, Captain Kerrix offered to ferry the *Emerald's* load to inner two in *that*, or send fighter escort. She's got security aboard, and I bet she's along for the ride. Keep our scanners on that shuttle all the way, Gliss."

"Aye ma'am – though I can't read much through her hull."

"Neither can I," Azular added. "And I've never seen it before."

"She still keeps secrets, then," Apnis grinned wickedly.

"And there's more than one," the captain said. "It's well-armed, by what I can read. It's constructed like a Starfall escape craft..."

"It could ride hyperspace currents?" the first mate asked in surprise.

"I'm sure it could. Drevell will be mighty curious. I bet some of his are hiding round the corner at the FMTE office suite – there *have* been a couple of sorties, and I've noticed ISA uniforms about."

"We're not going down, then?"

"No, Commander Apnis, we are not. There'll be plenty down there as it is," Ahxenta replied briskly. "Melly Goodsocks will keep us up to speed and as the office personnel are heading down too, it'll be busy."

The shuttle made the *Emerald*, only to exit after a rapid turnaround, on track for inner four. A report shortly after let Ahxenta know that she had landed in one piece, and the gear had been transferred safely. Unloading and set-up would take two days; the opening of the FMTE zone Alpha HQ would take place on the third. That aside, *Arianrhod's* crew were busy. Contracts had to be bid for and there was competition, with the *Warrior* back in and the *Tallulah*, *Snow Quartz* and *Obsidian Sky* still in port. The *Firestorm* had left for Nexus, and a memo from Jikelleli reported that the *Green Comet*, almost at Silverglass, had met no trouble.

"Looks like the hostiles are hiding, or *have* been decked by the ISA," Apnis sniffed as she read a report that had filtered in on the third day. "Either way, it means a clear run to Delta. We'll be loaded and set day after tomorrow. What was the link from Captain Kerrix about, Cap?"

"The charges against the two that shot her; they've admitted serious bodily harm, but denied attempted murder. The TA op's admitted *her* part and the TA's playing the outrage card: it's threatening to sack her. But the local press is having a blast," the captain replied.

"Can't be many left in the TA office now," Box said to Dox as he set in new nav-data. "And a jailbird won't help its rep or its trade."

"She's not been sentenced," Dox pointed out. "She may not end up in jail – she may be given payback community service."

"The TA might take her back on that basis: it wouldn't cost it and she knows the ropes."

"Don't be a fool: ropes like that will hang it out to dry."

Apnis grinned over at Ahxenta. "Ready for the FMTE party?"

"We'll have to meet the staff, so it may as well be now. I hope it's quiet. Security's tight and the press is limited, but I don't have a list of who's invited. I imagine reps from FMTE ships, plus local interests."

"Including the TA?" the first mate smirked.

"We'd better go and find out."

The captain had agreed to Azular's request to take the *Xanna* down, if she could take the helm. She had long wanted to try his shuttle, and as having a craft that only one pilot could fly was a waste of resources, had ruled that others be trained. He was reluctant but resigned, and as the small shuttle landed safely, he had to appreciate her skill.

"Nice handling, Cap," Apnis agreed as the three stepped out. "You staying in marketing, Azular, or coming to watch from a distance?"

He grimaced. "I'll watch the opening, but I'll see you both later. Bix

Holt of the *Warrior* wants a word on the updated code-decode shard; he's tested it and is happy but knows it's short-term. He's hinted at a new system, so I'd like consent to tell him about the new units, ma'am. I've discussed their ops with Commanders Kinnitix, Nyvallish and Zel and we agree they're the way forward. Holt will be discreet, I'm sure."

Ahxenta mused. "Okay, but on the QT and he won't discuss it with anyone but his captain. In fact, I'll tell Nat Holdspan if I get the chance: we can trust him."

"He's heading over," Apnis indicated. "So he's left his shuttle here. And Treskitt and Holt are with him. No sign of anyone else we know."

The six found a few familiar faces at the FMTE office. After milling around, those invited in for the main event made their way forward to meet the senior rep. The last invited guests were the two command officers of the *Moonstone*, who had raced in at speed.

"Business aboard," Kerrix gasped in response to Ahxenta's enquiry. "Tell you later – it concerns you."

The opening was brief, the clipped tones of the director's translator echoing oddly as the guests were steered inside for drinks and nibbles. The outer office was a marvel of simplicity and the officers found that by using their wrist unit ID holos, they could call up their ship's record.

"Can't get a list of the PSS ships that have signed up," Bluejohn said at Ahxenta's elbow. "But all those in port must be here. I hadn't realised the *Snow Quartz* was FMTE," he added, waving to her captain.

"They're calling us into the inner sanctum, Cap," Ginger Stone cut in. "But not the press or the rest: the director will talk to them."

The inner office had several doors off and was as smart as the outer. The officers were given a list of the amenities available from their new Trades body, and invited to ask questions. As Ahxenta had heard it all on Telzilt, she cornered Kerrix for a quiet word. Apnis, watching from her post, saw surprise give way to a shrug and a rueful smile. The talk seemed to centre on what the *Moonstone's* captain was showing on a small info-pad. Apnis turned to find a chuckling Inks behind her.

"What's so funny, Jesse?" she asked.

"I've just had words with the records officer," he told her, nodding to a nearby desk. "This place has been open for less than an hour and it's got its first admission request: the *PSS Tallulah*."

28: NAMING DAYS

The captain and first mate met up with Azular a little later in marketing. He had talked to Holt and was ready to listen to what had come out of the party. Ahxenta had had a few words with all her opposite numbers, and on reflection had told them of the comms units, as their consensus was that most of the PSS fleet would follow them in joining the FMTE; the cut-off for review of the current TA contract was close and its rigid directives were not likely to improve. The FMTE director had issued a note that two new offices would open: Freskat in Lambda and Kirtish in Mu. As both were free ports in isolated sectors, the trade advantages were obvious. The press had jumped on it and the fallout would come soon. The captain left the rest of her update for a senior staff briefing, and called one soon after they were back aboard.

One reason she had alluded to the comms units was that Thal had begun to fit his PSS ships with those he had brought in, she told her officers. Captain Kerrix had told her that the Letik company had been contracted to produce more, with Starfall as broker for zones Alpha to Mu. In other news, the Selky-Kilda bypass was active, and transport ran both ways: a Norvallan carrier had been seen by a probe of Thal's taking on a load at Selky, implying that trade between Norvalla and Mu's ISA-linked independents was ongoing. Word had gone to Telzilt, relations between which and Norvalla were still sour.

The latest PSS to join the Exchange, the *Snow Quartz*, would refit in the Web: the Dockers' Guild was on board to start call-sign integration. The Guild, Port Authority and Merkat Central Advisory Council had sent reps to the opening and the mood had been positive. Banyotty of the TA had been invited as a courtesy but had withdrawn early, peeved.

"He tried to follow us into the inner office and security wouldn't let him in," said Apnis. "Members only. But I sent a quick link to my chum Kit Biernop before *this* meet, Cap: the Guild's bringing in more of the needful for FMTE call-sign integration into hull plates, so the Web will be a centre for that, if demand takes off."

"*When* demand takes off," the captain amended. "Melly Goodsocks told me she'd been hailed by the *Nova Stella* and the *Zephyr* on the way in: Captains Fleete and Kilmaur are both keen to drop the TA badge before contract shake-up starts, and they won't be the only ones. Once news of the Web office gets out, there'll be a rash of requests. *Tallulah's* got hers in. I haven't spoken to her captain, but I'm sure we'll hear the tale before we leave. Talking of which, if you need extra gear, get a list to Commander Apnis pronto, all. I want each pod of the Redship load deep-scanned before we bring it in, so it'll take most of tomorrow to ship up. There's no next job for us after Delta Iridium, but Lindell, you have tenders to bid for. I need to see Melly: she's for Freskat with Letik crystals she got at Telzilt. I'll head Web-side early, as I've other meets; you'll handle loading, Commander Earbleat. Any questions?"

There were few, and the captain dealt with them quickly, obviously wanting done. She looked at Flintlock, Apnis and Azular, who had held back as the others filed out. "What?" she asked.

The trio wanted private words and she could guess the topics. They knew what had been found on Telzilt, her link to Kel Ocean, and of another on the way back from Beta Zegonia. Flintlock's main concern was the captain's health; the other two wanted to know more of the second call and what had not been said in the briefing. Ahxenta was forthright: she was fine and would see the doctor later; her comm was private and not their present concern; and as for other news…

"The *Moonstone* is for Selliden via Veil, but if other fluid plans come off, she'll head to Delta for a pickup." The captain raised her hand to quell questions. "She's leaving a marker on Veil Three for the lost crew from the *Kel'Tarn's* shuttle. *Obsidian's* got a cargo for Cygilla, but Grey's heard it's open to non-TA carriers: he'll let us know. Nat Holdspan's heading to Nyx via Berzic and Stella Viridis."

"Come on, Cap, what else?" Apnis urged. "What did Captain Kerrix show you on that info-pad? It wasn't a technical spec."

Ahxenta smiled. "The newest crew member of the *Moonstone*."

"What? She's taking on crew?"

"Hardly," was the reply, as she pulled up an image on her info-pad. "Cinnabar Xanna Olanta-Nyvallish: her father asked Captain Kerrix to ask my permission to name his new daughter after me."

"Bloody hell! I take it they'll be dropped at the nearest Starfall safe base?" Apnis exclaimed, as Azular raised his brows in surprise.

"The captain's leaving it to them; they know the hazards of the PSS trade. She doesn't want to lose her senior SO, but she's not overly keen to risk a child on board. Though Starfall ships have of necessity been multi-generational in the past."

"I'll bet. But why you, Cinnabar?" the doctor asked.

"Gratitude for our rescue of the shuttle crew at Veil. And Xanna after the captain: she took Olanta on as crew. But you lot can shift, if there's nothing else. I have comms to take and make."

* * *

The *Half Moon in a Puddle* was busy early next day when Ahxenta walked in with Apnis. The ship had been left in her second mate's hands and loading was under way. The *Emerald*, *Warrior*, *Snow Quartz* and *Tallulah* were still in port, and as the latter had had the TA crest erased from her outer bay floors and repair bots were busy on her hull, the captain was surprised to see Fleetskup. Indicating his supercargo, Skillet, at his back, he told her he had reps to see. Lieutenant Buntle was at his desk: Spickle had him working on crew matters.

"Good for him," Apnis retorted, amused at Skillet's sly grin.

"We're here for a business meet over breakfast," Ahxenta put in, before he could suggest a joint table. "We're due out soon," she added, to avoid a later tryst. "But tell me about your new flag."

By what he let slip, it appeared that Spickle had induced him to join the FMTE, and after links home to Milkit Major to take advice from *Tallulah's* major shareholder, he had given the go-ahead. Spickle was no slouch, and had begun alterations almost immediately.

Apnis grinned at his back view as he set off, after saluting the newly-arrived Melly Goodsocks. "Wouldn't join up without his Ma's say-so, then," she said. "Tallulah Fleetskup has horse sense."

Breakfast and talks on the *Emerald's* next mission complete, the two made their way out. The captain dismissed her mate, who was meeting Kit Biernop. They met three hours later for the trip back aboard.

"What gives, Cinnabar?" Apnis asked as she piloted the shuttle into its bay. "You're quiet. And you said zip about those comms last night."

"Plates in the air. I dropped into the FMTE office: there've been a lot of enquiries from Privates and shipping lines, the director said. And from a couple of TA-aligned ports. The ripples from news reports are spreading like wildfire. Drevell's first officer was there, for info. He got the usual gloss. He knew me, and had the cheek to ask after *my* plans."

"You told him to go fly, I take it?"

"More or less; he wasn't open about what the *Trueheart's* doing here, where she's headed, or what the ISA's at beyond Alpha. He was pissed I knew so much. Anything from Biernop?"

"Not much, but because of the publicity, the Guild's gearing up for more call-sign hull-plate integration, ID add-on and logo removal," she chuckled. "Guild ops are contrary at the best of times, and TA hassle makes them worse. I saw Fleetskup again. He's picked up a deal to take him out in three days. What about your other meets?" she hinted.

"Clearing up a point or two with the PA, and telling Nat Holdspan where he can source Metriklon comms units. Thal's agreed: I spoke to *him* last night. As Nat's for Nyx, he can stop by Twilight to get them."

"The UV-III will soon be history for the PSS fleet, then?"

"I guess most of ours will switch when the tech's obtainable. Once PSS registry offices are clued-up, they'll likely advise the new system. But we'd best see how Earbleat's got on with loading."

"Efficiently," Apnis snorted. "She's taking her new pips seriously."

"I'd noticed. We'll be ready to leave on time – unless that's trouble," she added, as a request for the captain to the bridge met her ears.

A link on the transport tube told her that there was something on grid. Earbleat was amused, and moments later, Ahxenta could see why. A spanking new ship was settling into a berth next to the *Trueheart*. It bore ISA insignia, and Ahxenta instantly recognised the spec.

"What the... Azular, what's she reading as?"

"The *ISAS Skelterrix*, ma'am: a Norvallan heavy cruiser geared for scientific exploration. A ship of the *Skelfinnix* class."

"Of all the sneaky... so the *Trueheart* was waiting for *her*," breathed Apnis. "No wonder Drevell's mate would say zip. If they're headed for Myrtleberry, it'll turn her little fleet into an invasion force."

"Maybe. Gliss, Azular, keep eyes and ears on her, as she'll have top-notch scan-ware. Azular, send the spec of that ship to the *Emerald*, *Nyx Warrior*, *Snow Quartz* and *Tallulah*. I'll send it to the fleet when I get a chance. We're off as soon as we're loaded and locked. *She* must have used a few back doors to get here; via Alto Finglas, I suppose."

It took hours to finish cargo stowage and lockdown, but the captain wanted away from the Web's prying eyes, and gave the departure order as soon as possible. With Port Control's adieu echoing over the bridge, *Arianrhod* made for the bypass, her route set via Bezel to Pixel Point rather than the usual via Silshoon to Delta. It would take longer, with local bypasses to Iridis and then a flyby of the Triple Pinks.

They had gained the node when a comm from Captain Jikelleli told them that she had met a muted reception at Silverglass, but no overt hostility. As she was still clearing cargo, Ahxenta returned the link to send the *Skelterrix* data and ask that she enquire of the ship's ISA status at the office. Azular, curious, checked the ISA press office, as it had lauded the Norvallan alliance. He found nothing, but Bellfish, his eyes on local nets, reported that the Web's media people were digging. The Berzic bid the comms officer set up a relay system to bring in what he could from Psi channels: now that Psi was on their charts, with some worlds allied to the ISA, they should be able to access the latest.

Arianrhod sped on and hours later, as she was crossing into Delta at the Snoot beacon, Jikelleli linked in to say that the ISA reps had refused to discuss the *Skelterrix* or any Norvallan matters. Ahxenta, off duty, had taken the call and told Jikelleli that the less-restrained Norvallans had aired many allied projects. The *Skelterrix'* mission was not one, but other joint ventures were listed.

Although the bypass was quiet, *Arianrhod* ran silent: some stretches were hard to navigate and others hid dangers. Four days later saw them at the Sevolb beacon, on the edge of the Crimson Drapes. The system's third planet, Sevolb, was settled, and other ships were in the area. The *PSS Karillion* was one; she had come from her home port of Delta and Captain Flintlock assured Ahxenta that his route had been clear.

"I can see why Dr Flintlock seldom wants to see her brother," Box whispered to Dox after the captain's half hour chat and brusque cut-off of her opposite number. "He never shuts up."

"*You* can talk," she said curtly. "Keep your eyes on your boards and the grid. It's a tricky cross to the Iridis bypass; the currents are lively close to the Drapes. It's why the *Karillion* came up via Needle Beacon."

"Aye, ma'am. Hope we get shore leave on Delta," he remarked.

Apnis smiled. "*Karillion's* for the Web to change her flag then, Cap. Word's sure got out. You didn't mention the new comms system."

"If I had he'd still be talking," Ahxenta commented wryly. "As it is, I want the bridge crew on a break before we come up on Pixel. I'm not aiming to stop en route to Delta, as we can take on supplies there."

"There's a good flea market on Iridis," Box mentioned airily.

"It's a flea in your ear you'll get if we miss anything on the bypass," Dox warned. "Besides, there's one in Delta's main settlement."

The captain ignored the pair as she checked boards and called time out. She was about to head off the bridge when a link came in. Telling Apnis that she would see her in the mess, she stepped into her office.

"*Moonstone* must be at Selliden by now," the first mate muttered to Azular on the way out. "What was her job there, do you know?"

"Cargo drop," he informed her. "Of what, I don't know."

He had nothing on her business, but given her speed, he was certain their paths would cross at Delta Iridium. He and Apnis sat together in the mess. It was a full hour before the captain joined them and she was pensive, refusing to discuss most of what had come in, saying only that it related to their next stop. She had heard, however, that the *Skelterrix* had left the Web with the *Trueheart*, their heading unknown.

* * *

Despite tricky piloting at the Pixel-Iridis node, the crossover was calm and with no hitches. *Arianrhod* swung by the Triple Pinks and Elf One to make Delta Iridium to a cordial welcome in under five days. She was the only PSS in, although other carriers sat in the orbital docks. After registering with the PA, the captain left Apnis to supervise cargo drop whilst she and Lindell set off to meet clients and talk contracts.

"Cap's still twitchy over something," the first mate confided to the chief medic during a quick break. "Has she said anything to you?"

"Nary a thing; and I've noticed. Any news in I should know about?"

Apnis shook her head. "*Obsidian* had no problem at Cygilla, *Comet's* on her way back to the Web. The *Moonstone's* on track and will be here in three days. There's been a few fleet links: about a third have signed on with the FMTE, and more will. I know the Cap had a chat to Vexin Thal; she didn't tell me the topic, but she didn't look upset. And I think she's had another call from Captain Ocean, but she keeps it close. You, me and Azular are still the only ones that know about *her*, but that's it. Cap hasn't spoken to Parri Millit, as far as I know."

"Good. I'm heading down tomorrow for a meet with an old friend in Delta med school's teaching hospital, and as she and Lindell will be down to talk deals, I'll see if I can have a word on the QT."

"Roger that. I'll catch her when she gets in; we'll need to talk over our next contacts anyhow. I know she wants to visit Freskat to see how things are, but it depends on what's on the table with our clients here."

The captain and her supercargo returned to the ship several hours later to find that over half their cargo had been offloaded. Their teams were working at full tilt and would carry on through local night.

"The Rhomb reps are keen to get the gear in, as they need it in place for ongoing work," the first mate explained to her. "You and Lindell have any luck with the reps you met?"

Ahxenta stretched in her chair to ease the tension. "Two potential deals thus far, but I want to wait until other pieces are in place. I'll give you the details once we're off shift. We can take the long road to the mess: I need a walk, as I've sat at tables talking for hours."

The key details Apnis heard on an extended stroll through the lower decks. As well as Ceres Corp, who had a load for Lamella Four, Preens Medical had a small cargo of medical supplies for Hespera Two. The captain had also had a chat to old clients Coronis Comms, who wanted shielded crystal comms arrays to their own spec. She was sure that Ruri and his aide could create them, but preferred to speak to the two direct, as the Coronis contract was classified. Any long-term deal would have to be agreed between Ruri and Coronis, but that was for the future.

"So Hespera, Lamella and then Freskat, if everything falls out?"

"It would be useful to have a cargo for Freskat," Ahxenta answered. "Lindell and his team are trying to track one down, and he'll carry on with that tomorrow. I've to see Coronis again first thing, but then I'll be back aboard: there's a ship due in that I need to be here to greet."

"*Moonstone's* still just over two days away," Apnis observed softly.

"It's not the *Moonstone* – though she's putting on a spurt to get in as fast as she can, as it relates to her."

"And you're not going to tell me," the first mate smiled crookedly. "I may as well tell you: the doc and I are worried about you, Cinnabar, and she's planning to waylay you tomorrow for a private chat, as she's heading down to see an old mate at the hospital."

The captain halted mid-stride. "Tallica… what the hell. Let's hit the mess, grab our chow and talk. And then I'll see the doc. And Azular."

* * *

The captain was in her chair at sixteen hundred next day, Delta time, her first mate beside her. A shuttle had been prepped for flight. Azular was at his post scanning local space. The news that Lindell was on his way hardly raised a nod, and Apnis dealt with essentials. The tension was felt by the bridge crew; even the normally chatty Box only frowned in perplexity and mouthed a query at his partner.

Azular cut the hush. "Two ships on approach, ma'am, one Starfall, one Telziltic; the latter matches the spec the *Moonstone* sent. They have approval to come in. I have the call-signs. The Starfall ship's the *Lucent*. The other's the *SS Cinnabar*, out of Rom Betra in zone Psi."

"Thal sent a battlecruiser as escort," Apnis muttered, as the officers on deck traded surprised glances. "Delta PA's eyes will be on her."

"The *Lucent's* to take on supplies and then head to Gemstone," was the equally quiet reply, but the first mate noted that the captain's eyes were glued to the image that Azular had pulled in.

The *Cinnabar* was a small, battered, formidably-armed carrier with a range of hull arrays that included scanners and jammers. She had been directed to an inner bay whilst her escort made for a berth close to the PSS. As soon as the ships were at station-keeping, the captain ordered courtesy calls sent, and sat back to wait.

"I have a Captain Kel Ocean of the *SS Cinnabar* for you, ma'am," the comms officer called huskily several minutes later.

"On grid."

"On grid," Bellfish echoed.

"Captain Ocean." The captain could see the sidelong glances of her crewmen, but ignored them. "Good to see you again, ma'am."

"And you, Captain." A smile creased the rugged face. "That's quite a ship, Cinna: I'd like to see more of her. For now, I have your cargo."

Ahxenta mirrored the smile. "I'll shuttle over at your convenience to collect. I take it the *Moonstone* knows of your safe arrival?"

"She does. And you're welcome aboard my ship when you're ready. The goods are set to transfer."

The captain nodded and told her that she would be with her shortly. Leaving the conn to Apnis, she called for her shuttle to be ready to exit and left the bridge. The first mate sat back, sighing. Azular set scanners to follow the craft, and had barely readied the holo when Bellfish called that Captain Jame of the *Lucent* was on comm.

Ahxenta spent four hours on board the *Cinnabar*. Her first duty on return was to unload the cargo of two crates of Metriklon comms units that she planned to trade at cost to PSS ships that wanted them, and a case of gem-grade meta-jurillium slips and fine crystals for her Freskat contact. Lindell met her to take charge of the goods and update her on his mission. Apnis was at his back; she wanted to speak to the captain.

"Snow has the conn," she replied to the probing look, once Lindell had gone. "We're quiet, and it's time we were off duty. *Lucent's* headed out: I expect Captain Jame contacted the *Cinnabar*?"

"She did," Ahxenta said. "Her primary mission *was* escort, as this is the first time here for the *Cinnabar*, though her captain knows it."

"I expect she does. You didn't bring her across?"

"Tomorrow. We've had enough for one day," the captain sighed.

"Where's she headed next?" Apnis wanted to know as the two set off out of the bay. "Not Freskat, I assume?"

"No; she'll wait for the *Moonstone* as she has cargo for her. And then she's for Starfall and Telzilt."

The first mate scented overtones. "What kind of cargo?"

"Wait and see. But I need to look over the deal Lindell's found with Flenkaff Alloys for that load for Greskitty Comms. It's not big, but it'll do. *Emerald's* almost at Freskat with the crystals she took on at Letik, and she's got finished goods to collect for Starfall."

"It's going to be busy once we do get there," the first mate told her. "Bellfish picked up a buzz on a Lambda-wide net that there's an FMTE office going to open there in thirty days, Freskat time. It'll be near the PSS registry, so not far from Zillah's HQ – and the ISA's base."

"I'd figured. One of the team in the Merkat office said that gear was being sent to Freskat and Kirtish, and the staff would be close behind. That'll soon hit the nets and there'll be a fuss. The TA's kept a lid on part of what went on Web-side over the shots at the *Moonstone's* people, but questions are still being asked."

"Like how to ditch the TA," chuckled Apnis. "I heard that the Skelp Line deserted and signed on with the Exchange. Kymexa Vento *is* out on a limb at Gamma edge, so I guess they get damn all; Veximer Prime must be the closest TA office and it's half a zone away. Dox got it from kin on Stella Viridis," she explained.

"The Skelp's a small line as merchants go, but it'll hurt the TA," the captain noted. "I'm surprised it didn't opt for independent status."

"Affordable insurance," was the astute reply. "Few groups will take on a shipping line unless it coughs up a fortune in cover fees."

"Good point. But I'm for Lindell's office. I'll see you later."

"And tell me how you got on aboard the *Cinnabar*?"

"Don't push it, Commander," Ahxenta warned, smiling even so.

* * *

The captain's visit was returned next day at twelve hundred. Kel Ocean shuttled over for a long tour: used as she was to the lines of a *Vanguard* class ship, aspects of the *Arianrhod* were novel. Those of the crew who met her were taken by her quiet authority and extensive knowledge. The news that the *Moonstone* was now less than a day away recalled her to her own ship, and with regret, Ahxenta bid her goodbye.

The chief medic was waiting at the exit to the shuttle bay. "You all right, Cinnabar? You look a tad down in the mouth."

"Thank you for your concern, but I don't need cosseted, Doctor."

"Oh, don't come over the cool captain with me, Cinnabar Ahxenta! We've known each other too long. We'll head along to mine for a spot of medicinal spirit, and you'll tell me what's biting you. And how I can help. The crew don't need a grouch in command."

"You're sailing close to the wind," the captain warned as she trailed the CMO into a transport tube.

"It's not the first time and won't be the last. You need shore leave. We all need shore leave," she amended. "Time out at Freskat. Yes, I've talked to Tallica and I know we're for there. You're worried about what you've got your crew into: a change of flag, half the ports in the galaxy closed to us, trade taking us to the edge of nowhere. And your buddy on Freskat: bad times, so the Letik move. That's a half-finished tale. And now a blast from the past you could've done without. *She's* causing you worry, isn't she? The missed time you'll never make up, links to griefs you thought you'd mastered."

"Did you major in psychoanalysis at med school?"

"Cut it," Flintlock ordered. "Medbay's quiet, so my office, now."

Ahxenta spent an hour with her CMO and another pacing the decks of her ship before signing off. By next day, her world was back in sync.

She felt in control of herself and, loading of the Greskitty cargo over, she prepared to hail the *Moonstone*. The latter had scarcely made berth when a shuttle headed out to the *Cinnabar*. It was heavily armoured and armed, Azular noted.

The captain nodded. "Taking no chances, though Delta's a secure port. The captain's gone with it, as here's Inks on the comm."

Inks had called to pass on the latest Psi news, got from links there. The *Skelterrix* and *Trueheart* were en route to join Myrtleberry at Alpha edge and the group would possibly split and continue as two units, one exploring beyond Alpha and the other beyond Beta. More Norvallan ships would bear ISA logos, and the ISA had set up offices on Norvalla and Valla Key. There was a prison ship being built, and Norvalla's Lixt listening post had been rebranded as ISA. In contrast, Telzilt and its allies were digging in and refusing to be tied to the ISA by more than trade and data exchange. Ambassador Posettix was part of the process, and was creating waves over lack of openness.

The *Moonstone* would set out the next day for Starfall, but Inks, on Kerrix' behalf, invited Ahxenta, Apnis and Azular aboard to talk trade and tech issues, and to meet their new senior science officer. Captain Ocean and her first mate would also be there. Ahxenta agreed, cut the link civilly and looked at her first mate.

"Captain Kerrix will miss Nyvallish: he's a first-rate scientist as well as a good officer. But he and his will be safer on a permanent base."

"Starfall?" Apnis questioned.

"As a start; they may have other plans. She's only met her new SSO once, but Nyvallish rates him. As for her other passenger, I don't know how that will pan out. But we're off at twenty hundred, as all our pieces are in place. That'll get us to Hespera in four days and inside our client's business hours. It'll be a short stop; two days to Lamella, one day there, and then Freskat. I'll sanction shore leave, as I've a lot to do and people to see, Zillah included. Lindell can scout for contracts. I'd like to be on hand when the new FMTE office opens. I don't know if there will be more of the fleet in: *Emerald's* shipped out and no-one else is close, as far as I've heard. The *Warrior* will have made Nyx, but she's likely out again. I'll check secure channels before we head to the *Moonstone*."

Ahxenta found the relays quiet, she told Apnis on her return. The *Warrior*, new comms modules in place, had left Nyx for Stella Triplet. The *Tallulah* had had a tranquil trip to Zidexall and the *Green Comet* and *Obsidian* were in Epsilon. Bluejohn had met Captain Unity Rusk of the *Starwheel* at Vrackin: she was for the Web, to sign on with the FMTE.

"Grey brought her up to date and handed on the UV-III fix. The

Starwheel's out of Vrackin Twelve. I don't know Rusk well, but Grey's first mate reckons she's not easy to convince about anything, so if she's on board, a lot more will follow. But let's get ready to move."

The two met up with Azular in the *Gremlin's* bay. They spent three hours on the *Moonstone*, and all were pensive on the way home. Ahxenta called a short briefing, as she felt that her senior staff should be filled in over some aspects; and she wanted her senior scientist's opinion on his opposite number – and *his* new aide.

"Lieutenant Lymnik is not as skilled as Commander Nyvallish," was Azular's view. "*He* was exceptional, which is why he was originally with the *Kel'Moth*. Lymnik is up on the new comms and as a weapons expert, he'll benefit his ship. But the *Moonstone's* other new science officer is brilliant in his field: he's a biomedical specialist," he told his crewmates.

"Lymnik?" Flintlock cut in. "He's the one we picked off Veil?"

The captain confirmed as Earbleat interrupted to ask why two new science officers were needed.

"Not *needed*, as such," Ahxenta said. "But the other's been aboard a ship, he wanted similar, and was keen to stay with the *Moonstone*, though he'd be more useful in the Starfall labs. Captain Ocean brought him in; she tracked him down at Bexix, a rough station out beyond *her* base of Rom Betra. He was part of the crew of a small local trader."

"If he's *so* smart, what was he doing on a trader?" Earbleat queried.

"Working," Azular interjected shortly.

"He and his colleagues were seized by hostiles on Telzilt as a skilled workforce. A resistance unit got them out before they were inactivated for spiking hostile ops. He joined a ship that ran supplies, weapons and data between resistance posts during the occupation. But that's not the point," the captain stated. "His name's Dr Perti Posettix."

"Bloody hell!" Earbleat exclaimed.

"Exactly," Ahxenta continued. "And he's probably not the only one that may have survived relatively whole. But he has extensive expertise in hostile med and other tech, which makes him very useful; and a lot of knowledge about hostile ops during and after *his* war."

"Like where and how the hostiles kept and used people for their own ends, at least around Telzilt?" the CMO asked astutely.

"Yes. Thal and his people are still looking for clues to their seven missing kids. There's been nothing thus far that could link to them."

"Desperation," Flintlock sighed. "I feel for them. Anything else?"

"We've cargo to collect at Freskat. One of Thal's ships is hauling it in. High-grade meta-jurillium for Alto Finglas," Ahxenta grinned.

"You what?"

"The Kilda deposits are not high enough quality for ISA ships' hulls and there's a mining issue; the Kirtish source is small, and the miners say *their* clients have priority. We're getting stuff from Letik Aggregates, as they won't trade with Norvallan firms because of the Telzilt trouble. The ISA shipyard is screaming for good material for hulls *and* comms. It won't deal with a Starfall ship, but it's agreed to us as carriers."

"So the ISA's still scared of Starfall," Earbleat surmised. "Fools."

"The ISA has to come round," Azular told her. "Our fleet's among the main carriers of big loads, and if more of Thal's ships are registered as PSS, Starfall will be a key player."

"That's enough," Ahxenta cut in. "We're done. The details will be with you shortly, Lindell. We'll have packaged sheets of hull plate and pods of gem-grade alloy. The ISA's got its own crystal supply, but there are plenty other yards that'll want the latest comms gear for their ships, now that news of the high-spec stuff is out. That'll mean good business for zone Psi suppliers, and the fleets that trade out that way."

All the officers bar Flintlock filed out. "What's next for Captain Ocean, Cinnabar?" she asked once the door had closed over.

"Starfall, and then Telzilt."

"That's not what I meant and you know it. Personally."

The captain sighed. "Back to her trading, but I sense she has things in mind. She's for Rom Betra after Telzilt: her ship needs total refit."

"This deal with Admiral Posettix' son: how did she know where or how to start looking? Captain Kerrix, I suppose."

"Yes. Kel has contacts; and she now knows about Thal's losses, but I doubt she'll find much else. But I have a ship to prep for departure."

* * *

The trip to Hespera was peaceful and cargo drop quick. The *Moonstone* and the *Cinnabar* had left Delta, but Ahxenta heard no more until they had released their cargo at Lamella and left port, when a link from Thal told her that both were well en route. Other news was sparse, but she learnt that as PSS ships met at isolated ports, the benefits of the FMTE had induced more vessels to sign on. The statistics had so alarmed the TA that it had sent out a list of revisions to its existing contract and asked the Privates for their views and suggestions.

"Too little too late," the captain observed to her first mate. "Word's spread; and many of the fleet have the UV fix and want the new comms system. One or two have even contacted Thal."

"That'll be a new experience for him: popularity," Apnis laughed. "Any more on the Exchange office on Freskat?"

"Units have been brought from Limekiln, interior gear from Telzilt, and the build's nearly done. There's been no hitch on the ground, but as it's close to Zillah's HQ it's not surprising. Lindell's heard that Freski firms are not fazed, as Freskat's now a free port. The *Kel'Torc's* got our goods for Alto Finglas; she'll be in ten days or so after us. I'll see Zillah as soon as possible, and my other contacts after that. Our people can start shore leave once our freight's with Greskitty."

"Yippee!" Box burbled jubilantly to his mate. "Shore leave!"

"Keep your eyes on your boards; we're not there yet," warned Dox.

The two were among the first down once port *was* made and cargo delivered. The captain, first mate and senior science officer were close behind, for a meeting with Admiral Zillah. She had questions on events involving Ahxenta and her associates, as little had trickled through. Her ISA neighbours were of little help, despite Freskat's membership of its Council. And she had news: Tressbow, a minor local shipping line, was now FMTE. It's directors had switched after disputes with the TA over fee and route restrictions, imposed after Freskat had declared itself a free port. In other news, two hostile-type craft had been logged close to Byxt, an empty system in the Star Desert, by an ISA patrol. The local ISA office had passed it on, as it was close enough to raise worry, and the Freski Navy would be needed if trouble came of it.

The admiral could also tell them more of the tasks of the craft near the Outer Reaches. The *Peerless*, with the *Skelterrix*, *Trueheart* and *Mirk Arrow* at her back, was skirting Alpha on the way to Theta zone; the *Repulse*, *Advance* and *Matchless* were heading for Beta. The captain felt Azular stir restlessly alongside, and guessing why, she asked once the trio had left Zillah's office to cross to their shuttle.

"Nexus Station's in uncharted space between Alpha and Theta. The ISA knows roughly where it is, as it *was* once a hostile base. Myrtleberry has a science ship, a battlecruiser, and a deep-range destroyer. Why?"

"I figured Nexus," Ahxenta agreed. "I'll link Thal as soon as we get back. For now, we'll head to the PSS Registry to get the latest and then try the new Exchange agency; it's not open, but some staff are in."

"Your buddy's old place?" Apnis murmured.

"That's for after close of business. Ruri and his people know I'll be in with bits for them and a potential business deal to discuss. Azular and I will take the *Xanna* down."

They found the Registry busy, as every linked office had had queries over turmoil in the TA. With contract revision due and the TA missive on changes out, PSS owners were arguing their positions. One rumour hinted that the TA was opening up to non-PSS independents and small private shipping lines that had been snubbed previously.

"If we were still part of it we'd be rubbing elbows with the Treskk," Apnis snickered. "Or other dubious parties like raider packs, maybe."

"Stow it," Ahxenta advised. "Let's see what's what next door."

The FMTE office was located on an open patch near the Registry. The three were guided in by the entry team, to find domestic facilities in place and the ops system in final prep. The key part of the latter was linkage to the other Exchange offices galaxy-wide, due online in hours. Freskat's shipbuilding and repair facilities were on board to supply call-sign integration, and the last office staff were due in the next day.

"Efficient, and nice to meet civility," Apnis noted on the way back to the shuttle. "Hope it lasts: the Merkat TA reps were never friendly."

"Your impressions, Azular?" the captain asked.

"They're confident and secure, even though they're outsiders. The site's protected by high-spec measures despite the place having been set up so quickly; and from what I saw of the comms pickups, they've had enquiries already, though they're not open for business yet."

The captain piloted and as soon as she made the ship, she headed to her office to contact Thal. He was unavailable, but she left her news with Seer. Nothing new had surfaced for her, so she began to prepare for her visit to Ruri's workshop.

Ahxenta and Azular left the *Xanna* in the local transport bay. They wore casual dress and carried the goods in backpacks. Ruri and Keerin were busy when they arrived. The captain was pleased to be told that they had had no incursions since her last visit. Having handed on the meta-jurillium and crystals, she left Azular and Keerin to examine them and discuss the work, while she and Ruri made for the office to talk over the Coronis deal for bespoke comms arrays, after which Ahxenta was surprised that the young man asked that his aide be called in. As a comms expert, Keerin was central to the work, and Ruri trusted him and his partner implicitly he told her.

Two hours later, with all complete, Ahxenta and Azular left for the shuttle. The Berzic was optimistic when asked for his views on Keerin. The man was able, clever, familiar with advanced comms, and being Starfall, highly cautious. The captain was satisfied.

"They get the deal and it'll keep them in business for a while. And as the *Emerald* and Thal's ships will be in and out, one of them can be called on for transport. I take it you won't want shore leave?"

"No ma'am, I'll wait for Merkat. I assume we're for there after Alto Finglas, unless Mr Lindell finds us a contract to take us elsewhere?"

"That's where the *Moonstone's* heading next is it?" Ahxenta smiled.

"Possibly; Captain Kerrix won't say, but she has her own agenda."

"I'll bet. Most of the Starfall fleet do. We'll have the opening of the Exchange office before the *Kel'Torc* gets in, as they've kindly invited us to be there. Wonder who's bringing in the rest of the staff?"

"Starfall," was the short reply.

* * *

The inauguration of the FMTE office had come and gone, the last of *Arianrhod's* crew were back aboard, and the captain sat in her command chair awaiting the arrival of the *PSS Kel'Torc*. Her supercargo had found two contracts that took them towards Alto Finglas. It would mean a stop at Limekiln Central on the way out to drop one load and pick up another. Lindell was scouting for more trade along their route.

"That's the freight from Fleete Corp tied down, Cap," the first mate reported after a check of her boards. "Was it worth the chinwagging?"

"Barely," was the reply. "Many of that clan are chattier than Maris. At least Turret says the essential and that's it. The Fleete crates will be caught by Orea Mining's grapples, and our Form-tech pick up will be waiting at the same transfer point. It's not huge, so it should be a quick job. And drop at Berry won't take but half a day, local time. Lindell's checking with his contacts here and beyond, and it looks like even TA ports won't turn us away if it means trade."

"The TA won't sink, but it looks like it'll be slimmer and fitter after the ruckus around it has died down," Apnis observed.

"Serves it right," Ahxenta replied as the comms officer called that he had Captain Turret of the *PSS Kel'Torc* on line.

The Starfall ship was an hour away and on schedule. The transfer of the huge stacks of hull plate would be made by tractor and grapples after the pods had been sent across. It needed complex handling and *Arianrhod* would have to leave her berth and make for a higher orbit. The port authorities were aware and had raised no objections.

"Busy time ahead for us, then," the first mate said ruefully. "Just as well all your business on planet's done and dusted."

The captain's goodbyes had been said after two more visits to the workshop and approval of the Coronis deal. She had called her nephew to report and had heard cheering news. The young couple were settled on Letik and enjoying work. Of her other contact out that way she had heard little. A link to Kel Ocean many days before had told her only that the *Cinnabar* was somewhere in Psi, with a Starfall ship as escort.

It took six hours of hard graft to transfer the loads for Alto Finglas, and at the end the captain decreed a halt of two more before *Arianrhod* left. The *Kel'Torc* had set off for Lamella as soon as she had done and was well away by the time Ahxenta gave the order to move out.

"She's for Stella Marina after that, so we may cross on the bypass, as we're heavy in the beam and she has a quick stop," the captain told her first mate as the ship speared off towards the local node.

"It's surprising you got that much out of Turret. And we're using the Twilight to Gemstone route as far as the main trade bypass?"

"We are; it's safer than local routes. And as Thal knows about the *Repulse's* convoy, he'll have *his* ships on it, and all the way to Zenith and Nexus. It must be stretching him, but from what he's hinted, he has plans to add to his fleet. His Telzilt network seems to be growing."

"How does he keep tabs on it all?" Apnis wanted to know.

"Trusted aides at all his bases; his office hub at Starfall is huge and we've only seen a part. He's driven by his past and he still has burdens we can only guess at. As have his people. They won't be taken again."

"Too deep for me," Apnis sighed. "I wish him luck."

As the captain had deduced, the *Arianrhod* found the *Kel'Torc* on her tail three days out from Freskat on the main trade route. The two ships continued to Stella Marina, where the Starfall ship peeled off, her line implying she was making deep into zone Gamma. *Arianrhod* carried on alone, her long-range scanners active and her cloak up.

They were less than ten hours from their target when the shriek of the red alert cut the air and a call for the captain to the bridge rang out. Ahxenta had just left her quarters and was on the way to the mess. She began to run, hauling up her communit to demand the cause.

"Two blips heading in at speed!" the duty officer responded. "Off our stern and closing!"

She made the bridge with Apnis and Earbleat on her heels. Azular was in post and every station was gearing up for action. The holo-grid was full down and locked in on the local patch of space, battlestations had been called, shields were up and weapons on line. The hull arrays were bringing in details of two ships of different specs, one positively hostile. Ahxenta took her command chair, webbing in tight.

"Ready *Loki*, Earbleat! All weapons set! Decoy on standby and run those engines hot, Chief! Azular...?"

"I can't get readings on the rear ship! The closer blip has massive weapons capacity and limpet drone pockets! It matches the ship that hit the *Warrior*! Science arrays confirm same spec!"

"Damn! We're heavy and this is no place to fight from. Comms, distress, all channels! Dox, ready to jump at high speed! All power to engines; up our aft shielding, Chief! All stations set for jump... jump!"

Arianrhod's hull creaked and gravity generators whined at the force needed to jump. The starfield spun as Dox sent the ship into an arc to sustain a defensible position as she hit free space. Earbleat's voice rang out over all that she had the hostile in her sights. The other had *not* jumped. Ahxenta had no time to think, for the huge ship was closing.

"We can't outrun her, ma'am!" Dox called as she fought the helm.

"Then we turn and engage! Bring us about, helm! Tactical, pinpoint her main weapons arrays and comms! Earbleat…"

"On it! Team one, set those forr'ad torpedo emplacements! Team two, hit anything your targeting eyes can lock onto and make it count!"

"She's got us in her sights!" Gliss called as a bolt flashed the hull to score the plating. "Confirm weapons as phase cannon, torpedoes, and slicers! She's loosing those damned drones!"

"Micro-sensor units sending out blocking signals! Extending, but I need them targeted, they're spreading!" Azular bawled over the racket.

"Tallica, man auxiliaries and take them out! Earbleat, keep up that fire. Tactical, where the hell is that second beast?" the captain yelled as the ship shuddered to the thwacks of multiple hits.

"No sign, ma'am! She hasn't jumped off the bypass – but I've got two more blips coming up fast on the same line *and* a ship jumping off the bypass from Gamma!"

The captain felt her webbing constrict as Dox sent the ship into a sliding spiral to avoid incoming streams of photon fire, and the second mate's powerful voice queried the release of *Loki*.

"Not yet! Status of drones?"

"Killing them, Cap! They can't seem to get lock-on!"

"Wide-spread missile salvo incoming! Team two, launch deflecting drones!" Earbleat screamed, as the powerful thud of a direct impact shook *Arianrhod's* hull. "All gunnery crews, keep on target!"

"Ship from Gamma's the *Nyx Warrior*!" Bellfish hollered, his hand at his ear to cut the external noise.

The huge black-hulled ship wheeled in a mighty arc to come in off *Arianrhod's* starboard, every weapon spewing fire. The outclassed alien turned in a wide curve for the bypass, but the *Warrior's* fire had bit and it missed the jump, careening off in a cartwheel of flame and flak.

"Stand down red alert, but make sure you get every last one of those drones!" Ahxenta sang out. "All stations, damage reports. Get me the *Warrior*, comms… Am I glad to see you, Nat. Thanks for the assist."

"Pleasure, Captain. *That* beast seemed familiar."

Ahxenta confirmed that the blip matched the deadly ship, disguised as the *ISPS Revenge*, that the *Warrior* had faced at Silverglass. Holdspan offered support, and after a status check and the news that the last drone had been taken out, she accepted escort to Limekiln. The *Warrior* was for Delta, Holdspan told her as the two ships made ready. He had come via Stella Triplet, Veximer and Stella Beacon, planning to enter Lambda by Stella Cross. Given the two signals on their line that Gliss had noted, the possibility that other hostiles were on the bypass was troubling, but an alert to the Limekiln authorities produced nothing.

Holdspan held his curiosity as to how *Arianrhod* had dealt with the limpet drones until they made Limekiln. Ahxenta had chosen cargo release before ordering repairs, and drop was barely done when a link from the *Warrior* was called. She took it in her office and was gone a while, as other links had come in. She was seething when she emerged.

"Nat wanted a heads up?" Apnis queried.

"He did, and I gave him the bare minimum about the micro-sensor system. He wants more, he'll have to get it from Starfall, but as he and Thal are now acquainted, I don't think he'll have a problem."

"And what else? You had a couple of comms and you look narked."

"I did and I am. *Obsidian* caught our distress en route this way from Quartic to Stella Marina, but too far out to help. She'll pass Limekiln in a few hours. She logged a blip hauling off the bypass with two others on its tail and firing shots across its bows, between the Limekiln and Torch Crux nodes. But the two in pursuit were ISA destroyers: the *ISAS Steadfast* and the *ISAS Stalwart*. They jumped off after it."

"What! *Those* were the blips on the same line that *we* picked up?"

"Looks like; there were no other close signals. Nat confirms he got no others, and Grey had none on his route."

"They must have registered our distress!" the first mate exploded.

"And ignored it to chase down that blip. I'll be having words at Alto Finglas when we get there with that damn ISA cargo," Ahxenta said grimly. "I've sent in a query, so the ISA knows we and the *Warrior* took the other ship out and are here to tell the tale."

"The ISA must know the hostile was carrying limpet drones, and as we've not been breached, it'll want to know how we did it."

"I bet. Grey will drop his load at Stella Marina, head back this way and ride with us as far as Berry; we'll make for Alto Finglas after that. Form-tech's not fretting the delay here and the units are compact, so loading will be quick once our bay's up to spec. Nat's off in an hour, but he'll query the failure of the ISA ships to respond to our distress."

"And have his ears bent, I'll bet," Apnis remarked.

"He can handle it. But *I* have more comms to make."

The *Obsidian Sky* hit Limekiln five days later. Her repairs complete and cargo loaded, Ahxenta welcomed Bluejohn aboard for a closed session. An hour later, the ships were readied for joint departure. Ahxenta said only that she would call a briefing en route to Berry, but *at* Berry, the *Obsidian* would hold for them, and the two would continue together to Opalite and thus to Alto Finglas.

The briefing was held two hours into the flight, and Apnis was first through the door. "Azular's heard from Kerrix, hasn't he?"

"He did, two days ago: she wouldn't say where she was or what she was doing, but she *did* say to tell me to avoid the Twilight to Gemstone bypass, as there's been hostile and ISA action on and off it from Beta through Lambda. He's had Bellfish keep his ears to every net and he and Greffy have been going over our array data. He'll update us."

Once her officers were settled, Ahxenta set the holo to local sectors, and lit up their flight path. She began with Azular's alert from Kerrix, and then switched to her talk to Bluejohn.

"We're not the only ship that's had ISA trouble. Grey Bluejohn met the *Quarkstorm* at Stella Marina. She'd come in on the local hyper-route from Stella Triplet, after a run-in with the *ISAS Merrin Free* a dot off the Twilight to Gemstone. The *Merrin's* captain hailed her to demand why she was so close to a bypass claimed by Starfall. Captain Peakfrost blew him off, but he warned her to keep off it, and wouldn't say why. She protested to ISA HQ, but all she got was a strap line that the ship was on ISA duty and had every right to question her, *and* a warning not to mention it. She didn't put it on the UV-III, figuring ISA ears, but told Grey and asked him to pass it on privately. But Adhara Peakfrost had met the *Urania* at Stella Triplet earlier, and Captain Mikbeam told her that he'd logged the *Moonstone* going all out on the bypass as he was leaving Veximer, and Inks had linked to warn him to watch his back, as hostiles had been seen off Coral and Facet. There'd been no alert, but Mikbeam met no trouble on the main route to Triplet. So, it reads as if hostiles *and* the ISA are active around the Starfall bypass."

"Reads as if?" the first mate queried. "What else, Cap?"

"*We* were hit on the trade bypass. Bellfish trawled the local nets and found that Lamella's Umbel Station was buzzed by two blips that cut across to it from Kolly Blue," she replied, nodding at the senior comms officer. "Other stories mention sightings of alien and ISA ships around that bit of Lambda and into Gamma, so I called Zillah. She was close, but did say that the ISA's reported upped hostile activity and thinks it's spreading from the Star Desert; the ISA didn't mop up all the outlaws from Bell, Blox or Peden maybe, or they have other dens. But the view is they're homing in on the Starfall bypass, maybe as it's an old one of theirs and they've an agenda. It doesn't explain our incident or why those ISA ships went after that other blip, but Myrtleberry's navy *has* been diverted to Fivepoint in case of trouble, Zillah told me."

"Did you warn Captain Thal, ma'am?" Azular asked abruptly.

"I did. Why? What have you picked up?"

"You recall our trip with the *Mevaena?* The bypass we used connects Lartzeg Trine to Lemon: that's near Mellifly *and* Gemstone. Thal thinks aliens still use it, though his people avoid it. *That* bypass may have been the heading of the two ships that caught us up en route to Limekiln. The ISA knows of it, given our trouble, but perhaps not its extent."

"Then hostiles *are* targeting Thal at his other bases?"

"Or making for an old base? Cox 455 is still listed as query risky in nav-data, and there are others. Greffy and I reanalysed the data we got on the ship that kept on the bypass. It wasn't a design we hold; it was smaller and had a range of hull arrays, most of which we couldn't read. As far as we could make out, it had a fluid hull, possibly to ride hyper-currents or shift in response to threats such as weapons."

"What do you mean *fluid?*" the captain demanded.

"We believe it can physically alter, change shape – morph."

"What in… that tech's been around for eons, but not for something the size and complexity of a ship," Cottontail breathed. "If *that's* what it is, no wonder the ISA's interested. But that doesn't explain the upped activity. Do we know if other ships of that spec are about?"

"The ISA wouldn't report it, and I've not heard of similar, even as a theory," Azular told her. "I'd like to contact Captain Thal and see if his people have. Did you pick up any rumour of it, Lieutenant?"

"Not a thing," Bellfish replied.

"It's not a problem now, but if there *are* new alien boats out there more capable of harm than the usual, it might become one," Ahxenta said shortly. "What is, is possible hazard on *this* trip. I take it there's been no word of that ship, or if those ISA destroyers did take it out?"

"Nothing, ma'am," Bellfish told her as Azular shook his head.

"The *Obsidian* spotted the ship leaving the bypass between Limekiln and Torch Crux and being fired on. I *would* like the data that her sensors got," the Berzic said. "Or we may find out more at Alto Finglas?"

"Ha! You'll be lucky!" Apnis snorted.

"If it *was* a new design, Captain, the larger ship may have been its escort, saw us as a threat and took us on, in effect giving the ISA ships time to come up on the mystery ship and attack it," he postulated.

"We'll both talk to Grey and Thal. We send news of the hit on us and an alert on the blip to our fleet, but *not* the data. I'll ride the ISA people over it. They'll have got the readings you did, or more. But back to posts: it's a haul to Berry, and we'll be at amber all the way."

The captain next called Bluejohn. He sent her the data his stations had got at once, but it gave Azular less than he already had. The link to Thal, on the *Kel'Moth*, took time. He was sharply attentive over the odd ship, but cut quickly to the attack on *Arianrhod*. *His* latest was that Nexus had sent out ships on the basis that the ISA convoy or hostiles were homing in. His other bases were at alert, but thus far had caught nothing. He *did* agree to the wisdom of alerting the PSS fleet, even if it meant risking links to those still on the original UV-III. They were few, but if ISA ears were listening, it would give them a jolt.

Ahxenta sat back after closing, and sighed. "We can't do more. Thal *was* interested in that blip, but he was more worried about the hostile. If the Star Desert *is* a focal point for renewed alien activity, it might spill across to Delta, and a lot of sectors there are settled."

"And thus more heavily patrolled," Azular put in.

"Good point. Zero we can do. Back to the bridge."

The remaining time to Berry was broken only by the hum of distant traffic on the intra-zone bypass. Lindell had been hunting trade, and by the time orbit was made, a contract had been agreed to ship a batch of Berry plant pharmaceuticals to Merkat. After a rapid about-turn, the two vessels set for Opalite to drop *Obsidian's* cargo. The orbital facility was busy with local craft. Ahxenta used the day it took to offload to take on extra arms. It would be a long twenty two hours to Alto Finglas and she wanted nothing lacking that might benefit her ship.

Her downtime the captain spent in private links, as the usual space chatter was noticeably limited. Azular was fretting, she knew, at lack of contact with the *Moonstone*. She had tried to raise Captain Ocean several times, and although the links went through, she had no success.

"It's as if nobody wants to talk to anybody," she grumbled to Apnis. "I even had Axellina call Captain Flintlock: *Karillion's* at Settle but she's heading home to Delta Iridium. Race Flintlock reckons there's an odd vibe about the place that's making a lot of people jittery."

"Settle? Coalition's main shipyard, though most of the boats will be ISA I guess, as they were building advanced explorers before they were hit during the last big run-in with hostile scum."

"Yes; *Karillion* was hauling hull plate. But the yard was fine with her flag, even with Settle's strong TA presence. Race figured it was frantic for supplies. One rep said she'd had hints to avoid FMTE ships, but trade is trade. Rumour says the Coalition is arguing the ISA framework, as the ISP part of it is calling the shots too often, the Norvallan link being an example. But if the hostiles are taking advantage of the upset, the ISA will have to pull together."

"Politics," the first mate declared.

"Which impacts us," the captain reminded her. "We're targets."

"That's for sure," Apnis groaned. "They'll tell us zip at Alto Finglas, but with the *Obsidian* with us, they won't make too many waves."

"Don't count on it," Ahxenta said darkly.

* * *

The trip to the ISA HQ was quiet and the welcome from Port Control icy as the vessels hove in. Their assigned berths were distant from the yard transfer point, and once docked, *Arianrhod* was asked to stand by for the grapple drones that would take on the bound hull plate sheets. The pods of gem-grade alloy would be picked up once the sheets had been unpacked and thoroughly checked.

"It's so we can't see what fleet ships are in, or under construction," Box grumbled to his mate. "As if we care."

"As if," Apnis agreed. "They're peeved *Obsidian's* with us, but they can say zip, given our run-in and the neglect of two ISA ships to answer our distress. How long until fleet calls wanting our data on the blip we and the *Warrior* took out, and how we avoided its nasty limpet drones?"

"I'll be calling it first," the captain told her. "You hold the conn and keep all our eyes on that lot. Azular, you're with me."

The two were in the bridge office for an hour. Ahxenta was irritated but resigned. The aloof aide she spoke to made her hold, and then put Admiral Trestle on. She reacted to *his* defence that the ISA ships were chasing down a serious threat that was not her concern by asking why two were needed against a smaller, though novel, vessel.

"*That* made him sit up," she said to Apnis. "It told him that we'd read it; and he knew that we and the *Warrior* had got the other without being shot full of holes. He pushed on what we'd got on the unknown, but he couldn't take the moral high ground, with complaints from the *Warrior* and the *Obsidian* on the ISA refusal to answer our distress, and because he knew we'd alerted the PSS fleet, meaning that the ISA *has* cracked the UV-III. But from what he *didn't* say, the unknown got away: he was too keen to get what we'd got. And as we'd outfoxed those limpet drones, he figures we have tech the ISA doesn't."

"He's right. But what if the ISA pay office refuses to hand over our fees unless we spill?" the first mate asked.

"We get our legal rep in, and make sure the entire mapped galaxy knows about it," Ahxenta said firmly. "There's no excuse, the cargo was checked at every step, and as it came from Letik, the ISA would be in hot water if it maligned the source. It wouldn't get more, for one. But as we'll still have the gem-grade alloy, we make sure we have the first part of the fee before we hand the pods over. But here are those grapples, so let's get the show on the road."

With all her and the *Obsidian's* scanners on the transfer, *Arianrhod's* load was safely handed on, and the wait until checks were carried out began. The captain had planned to use the time on other matters, and had just passed on the details of her talk with Trestle to Bluejohn when comms called over to say that Fleet Admiral Best wanted a word.

"Trestle wasn't tough enough," she said tartly. "I'd be grateful if you'd keep *Obsidian's* sensors on us, in case his minions try anything, Grey, and I'll see what he wants to shout about. Azular…"

The talk was short. Ahxenta, back on her bridge, called Bluejohn. "He wanted the data we got on the alien ship that's slipped through ISA fingers; and to know how we'd dodged the drones of the one that came after us. You caught the attempted scans of my hull, Grey?"

"I did. And that you blocked them."

"And him. He doesn't get no way in hell, and none of your damn business. I cut him off as soon as the scans started, and sent a protest to his HQ, with the tag that it'll be copied to our fleet and every news net in creation if I don't get answers. Your take on him, Azular?"

"He's changed: I'm certain he now has info-sent capability, but the alteration's been as effective as Mr Horn's, maybe," was the dry reply. "He was furious when you taxed him with ISA's cracking the UV-III."

"Info-sents in key sites," Apnis put in. "We've heard that before. It's a wonder they keep at it; all it does is piss people off."

"Stow it," the captain said. "But until we get our fees for the hull plate, we don't release the pods. I'll keep you updated, Grey."

"The pay office is sending it in now," the first mate noted, tapping her board. "Maybe there *is* somebody with sense around here."

Lindell verified receipt directly, and Ahxenta ordered release of the next load. The seamless transfer led her to suspect that the process had been expedited. The cargo was rated valid, the second fee received, and clearance to leave Alto Finglas granted.

"They want us gone, Cap," Apnis remarked.

"Not without answers. Resend my protest to fleet HQ, Bellfish, tagged urgent – and copy it to the ISA Council."

Time crept by, broken by an enquiry from Port Control asking why the ships had not left. The captain enlightened it, but thirty minutes had gone before Admiral Trestle called to request a private link.

"Private my boot; get *Obsidian* back on, comms, and then patch him in," Ahxenta growled. "This is as private as it gets, Admiral. Go on."

The captain dismissed Trestle's token excuse of crucial security for the scans, and thwarted a steely request for *Arianrhod's* data by asking for his views on the rise in hostile and ISA activity, citing the buzzing of Umbel Station and the sightings of ISA and alien ships in Lambda and Gamma zones reported on local nets. She tartly offered him that data when he cast doubts on its authenticity.

"Stalemate," Apnis remarked as the link was cut from the ISA side. "But now they know that we know they've decoded the UV-III. You sending it out as confirmed over the UV-III, Cap?"

"Once we're out of here," Ahxenta replied. "But you're right: we'll get no more here. Make ready to leave Alto Finglas space," she ordered her teams. "You set, Grey?"

"Roger that, Cinnabar. I'll be glad to see the back of this place."

The two ships were speedily on the way to the bypass, their line fixed by the authorities to avoid most of the work ongoing at the ISA base. Both captains had agreed to maintain amber alert all the way.

* * *

The Web's outer lattices lit the night as the *Arianrhod* and *Obsidian* came into range. Allotted adjoining berths, the two were soon secure. It was busy, as four of their sister ships, all with FMTE call-signs, were in. Ahxenta's first concern was business, and she left her first mate to deal with cargo while she paid the usual visit to the harbour office. Captain Bluejohn had beaten her to it, and once that was done, they set off for inner two and their usual haunt of the *Half Moon in a Puddle.*

"A few Privates in," Ally greeted them as he set up their drinks. "It's been hectic since you left, ma'am, but no bust-ups. Staff from that new Trades place on level four drop in. They're getting the hang of things, though they still use translators. You having food, ma'am, sir?"

"I can't, I have things to see to," Ahxenta replied. "But that's Jury Djassi and his mate waving us over. We'd best go and pass the time," she said to Bluejohn. "I noticed the *Equinox* had changed her flag."

"As has the *Pearl Shield*, the *Tektite* and the *Zephyr*," he laughed. "The local TA reps are probably still reeling from shock."

Djassi and Tynissel hailed them cheerily. The captain had read the alerts sent out by *Arianrhod*. The ISA breach of the UV-III he knew of via Captain Jikelleli. News of the Metriklon comms units had also been passing on the quiet, and Djassi knew several captains keen for them, himself included. Ahxenta increased privacy and told him that she had units that she would trade at cost, but *that* was to be kept under wraps.

"We'll be here a while, as my people need a break," she informed him. "Have your supercargo contact mine."

He agreed at once and the talk turned to other matters, the last alien incursions, and ISA involvement. A short time later, Ahxenta took her leave: she had matters aboard ship to attend to.

As her shuttle docked, the captain noted that their cargo had been delivered and the first mate had begun the minor repairs always needed after a stint in space. Busy bots skittered over *Arianrhod's* pink hide and she could see the glow of systems testing. But she was surprised to find Apnis on the far side of the bay door when she made her way out.

"What gives, Tallica? You don't normally meet me at the bay."

"Needed the walk from the bridge. And a chat. About Azular."

"What's he done now?" the captain demanded.

"Nothing off beam that I know about. But a message came through for him from Captain Kerrix that's obviously upset him: he was tight-lipped. He's on the bridge, but he's off duty shortly."

Ahxenta nodded. "I'll catch him. But first I have to see Lindell: we have a taker for two comms modules. And Azular will have to be there to talk over the nitty gritty with Djassi's comms and science officers."

Apnis nodded. "*Equinox*? Good. But I hope *he's* not had bad news."

"Roger that."

The captain called the science officer into her office to talk comms units and meetings. Azular being Azular knew that the first mate had spoken to her, and after trade had been dealt with, he brought up the *Moonstone*. She had been sent to Nexus via Gemstone, as there had been fly-by incursions at both bases. Base ships had been deterrent enough and the intruders had been chased off, but Starfall listening posts had picked up undue activity at the Delta side of the Star Desert and across Lambda. Thal's contacts had warned of similar by his bypass through Gamma, and he was worried that a strike at one or more of his bases was imminent. He did not have the ships to counter a large offensive.

"Why the *Moonstone*?" Ahxenta wanted to know.

"She's the most advanced of his fleet," Azular sighed. "And as the *Skelterrix* is ISA, I expect Captain Thal reckons it'll take one Norvallan ship to outwit another. The ISA *is* taking an unjustified interest in Thal and his people, so he can't trust it. But Xanna still won't say what her mission is, which is why I guess she won't link me directly."

"Because you're pushy *and* you can read her," the captain told him.

"No doubt," he admitted. "But I *had* asked about the strange blip in my last link to her *and* sent the spec, and she made no mention of it at all. I don't like it; it's not like her."

"I'd imagine she has a lot on her plate, but I agree, it's curious. But this ship is biting at you. Why?"

"It's design and its mission; there's only been one seen, it's not been recorded anywhere else as far I know, and it's still loose. And we don't know the extent of its weaponry. But it's a stealth ship, that much is clear. Where did it come from, who built it, how and why?"

"It was escorted by a definite hostile," the captain recalled.

"Or it was in pursuit of the hostile that caught us," Azular said. "Or it had nothing to do with the hostile: its carrying on when the alien left the bypass suggests that's more likely. I've gone over the data again: it's sparse, but nothing suggests hostile tech. The ISA ships probably logged both and caught a spec of the tailing one. *That* was a mystery to prompt pursuit, despite the lead hostile, whose spec they *must* have on record. They may have called it in and been ordered to contact or to capture the odd ship, or take it down if it struck back. When the hostile shot off the bypass, the ISA ships knew it had a target, and once they picked up our distress, they knew who it was."

"And didn't care," the captain added shortly. "We keep our eyes and ears open, but there's nothing we can do. Your next job is the meet tomorrow aboard the *Equinox*. We'll take the *Gremlin*. The news of the comms units will get into the ears of the other PSS captains here, I bet, so we'll have more to do. But as of now, you're off duty. Hop it."

Ahxenta sat on for a while, musing on what she had heard, before she made for the mess, where she had arranged to meet her first mate.

"What's eating him?" Apnis greeted the captain as she took a seat. "He came in to get his rations and he's sat by himself over there."

"He knows I'll be speaking to you about him."

The captain gave the gist of the exchange, and her mate sat deep in thought for a minute. "It strikes me that Captain Kerrix is ducking the subject because she knows what that ship is," she shrugged. "You said that Thal had been quick to express interest in it and then dropped it to ask after our hit. Was he doing the same?"

"You may have a point," Ahxenta said pensively. "But that doesn't tell us where it's from, or how or why it was built. We'd have picked up something if it was created at Starfall. I must go over the log of that link Azular and I had to Thal; now I think of it, Thal said he'd not seen another ship of that design, not that he hadn't seen *it* before."

The captain was curious enough to return to her office to call up the link; she called both Apnis and Azular in after it and all three went through it. The upshot was that as it did not immediately affect them, they could take the matter no further.

* * *

The captain of the *Equinox* welcomed Ahxenta's party aboard. As she had inferred, word of the new comms system had reached the captains of the *Pearl Shield*, *Tektite* and *Zephyr*, and all had enquired. In Lindell's opinion, had they charged what people were willing to pay, *Arianrhod* could have made a substantial profit on the trade.

A few days and trades later, and with all the PSS vessels in port now equipped with the new units, Ahxenta used the excuse of the need for more stock to contact Thal to ask if he had heard more of the mystery ship. He was as snippy and wary as always.

"Why do you wish to know?"

She was as blunt and voiced her view that he and his knew more of it that they were saying. She also let him know that Azular was of the opinion that the ship was not hostile.

"He didn't deny or confirm," she told Apnis and Azular. "But he's worried over his own. In spite of the lack of news on the nets, there's been more action in Gamma that's spilt over into Beta. I called Zillah: the ISA's on alert in her backyard, as it's damn close to the Star Desert; and she says that ISA Fleet HQ's upped its alert status. And I spoke to Ruri. He's had orders for high-grade comms arrays from Greskitty, and everybody there's leery."

"It's general," Azular put in. "The *Marjenna's* in, and I ran into my friend Zelujmar. He said they'd met ISA patrols at Vreskota and Orriga Two that were not keen to talk about what they were doing. It's making the locals at that edge of Alpha jumpy."

"As if there's a big bang waiting to go off," the first mate said. "I'll contact Kit Biernop to see if he's heard anything on his turf. Dock-rats are always one of the first to find out about things."

"Do that," the captain told her. "We're meant to be on leave, but we'll all be Web-side shortly, as Lindell has meets set up. It's time we were out in the space lanes again. I've a business to run."

* * *

Ahxenta, Lindell and Azular were on the way to Redship, having left Apnis to meet her friend. They had just found their reps when the wail of a siren hit the air from every direction. Multiple expletives followed as everyone turned. The huge emergency holos fitted in salient places throughout the Web had dropped down. An urgent face was speaking from the one closest, the words being relayed in text below.

"What in blazes!" the captain exclaimed as she read.

"Telling the locals not to panic," Apnis panted as she ran up, Kit Biernop at her back. "That's just what this'll do."

"I'll have to get back to my HQ," Biernop said.

"We're for the ship," Ahxenta told her team. "Talks are off," she advised the reps, who were rooted to the floor and staring at the screen. "Let's go; half the people in here will be scrambling for their shuttles."

The four raced for the bay, along with others. In ten minutes they were aboard the *Gadfly*. Ahxenta, at the helm, ordered Earbleat to track their progress, as she knew that the rush could result in trouble.

Half an hour later saw them safely aboard. Earbleat had ordered an amber alert, all arrays on line and a search of every comms channel.

"Wonder what sparked it?" the first mate demanded on the run to the bridge. "They don't call a general alert and everybody not resident to pack up and head home for nothing."

"It's never happened before while I've been here," the captain said.

Earbleat greeted them grimly. "Lockdown: Web's gearing for attack and the ISA's sent out an all-channel crisis bulletin. A massive fleet's exploded out of the Helix Cluster worm-pocket. It's confirmed hostile, and every ISA, allied and merchant fleet's been called up. It's split into two wings and one's heading this way. Gliss is tracking it." She nodded at the fully-extended holo-grid.

"Bloody hell!" Apnis breathed as she and the captain webbed in and Azular took his station by Greffy. "It's on track for Pilt 24."

"It won't stop there," Ahxenta predicted. "And we're next in line. Where's the other wing heading, Earbleat?"

"The ISA reckons Fivepoint. I alerted Captain Dun in case Nexus is the target, but she knew. *She* wants to know where the other end of the Helix pocket exits: a worm-pocket, a patch of mass-energy density, a gravity well... or what may still be *in* hyperspace between exits."

That had occurred to Azular, who was hunting databases. "Crimson Drapes. By Furze *and* near Alto Finglas. And where else? That worm-pocket at Greel, close to Starfall? Or the hostile-altered pocket at Sox: maybe that's what they've been at. As for gravity wells: Jete and Swan Two are closest to the Helix, but there must be plenty we don't know."

"Thal will know the score; get me a link to him, comms."

The leader of Starfall was well aware of the danger, as were all his station commanders, though he judged a route from the Helix to Greel unlikely, as no hostile intrusion there had been obvious to his probes.

Ahxenta was direct. "If the Web or local outposts *are* targets, we'll be needed here for defence. If not and we can get through to Nexus, you can count on us as support. Keep me updated."

"Roger that. Thank you, Captain. Thal out."

"Call to arms," Apnis grated, as Bellfish reported an urgent link from Merkat's Advisory Council. "FMTE or no, we're being called in."

"We don't have a choice if whatever's out there *is* headed here," the captain said harshly. "Web defences are limited and Merkat Three's planetary defence grid and fleet won't hold for long. I hope Zillah's news that Myrtleberry was diverted to Fivepoint *was* accurate."

The link *was* a request for every ship in port to be ready if and when called on. Ahxenta ordered a *will comply* sent and then studied the holo. Small craft leaving the inner bays in droves would hamper the larger vessels that had registered support. Port Control had called a state of emergency and given departure timescales, based on the speed of the approaching hazard, which was still on a direct line.

"There must be ISA ships out there and closer to that fleet than we are," Apnis muttered. "If *that's* accurate, they're going at some speed. I reckon less than a day on the local bypass to hit the Web once they make Pilt. No numbers yet."

"*If* they hit the Web," the morose voice of Box cut in. "They might head straight on at Merkat for Linza, Skoon and Silshoon, then Furze. There might be another fleet heading *to* Furze from Altina," he added.

"Prophet of doom," the first mate said. "If they did, ISA HQ would have noticed; it's upped patrols around its own space."

"Altina's off that bypass *we* used to avoid Quartic and close to Alto Finglas, but there's a worm-pocket at Bissy on the same line, and light years from anywhere. Bet nobody's stopped *there* for a look," Box said.

Apnis shook her head resignedly. "We're in trouble, whatever."

Over the next hours, the Web emptied of small craft; some flew to the planet below, others to nearby systems. The *Quarkstorm* rode in to join the six Privates in port; all were strategically placed in the outmost belt. As the alien fleet had kept line and speed, it was reckoned that most were auto ships primed with explosive. ISA listening posts in every charted zone, alert to other incursions, had recorded none.

* * *

The warning when it came was terse. "Multiple blips! Jumped off the bypass and heading straight for us!" Gliss yelled, his tactical sensors at full stretch. "They'll come in at this side if they maintain course."

"Cut the racket!" the captain called as Port Control's alarm sang.

"Planetary defence grid's gearing up," Larai called.

"Battlestations!" Ahxenta ordered. "As soon as they're in range, get their specs. Comms, set the links to our fleet ships."

"Skyrtek over again, except we're the sitting ducks," snapped Apnis, tightening her webbing as pulsing red light bathed the bridge and each station signalled ready. "Hope they're okay at Fivepoint."

ISA Fleet Command had chosen the remote post where five zones met as the most strategic locus to halt the first enemy wing. The fleet there, boosted by local ships, was under attack. Gliss sent his data to the holo, homing in to check the position and strength of the Web's defensive force. The nearby systems Kelpin and Skoon, and the ISA's Linza Base, had sent ships to add to those in port. They were few.

"*Remia Cross* and *Tenacity* are moving to positions either side of outer beacon array four," Gliss sang out, and as two ISA ships swept by, Bellfish called that Captain Mocryst of the former was on line.

"To tell us who's in charge," Apnis grimaced.

The ISA captain realised that she stood little chance of directing the Privates, but requested that they stood ready to protect the main sector of outer belt nine at the point of most likely assault, whilst she and the *Tenacity* would provide flanking fire. The remaining ships would hold as a second protective line. The planetary defence net and fleet were already on board to provide additional cover.

"Agreed," Ahxenta said. "But I won't sit still to let them close in."

As Mocryst confirmed and cut the link, Ahxenta faced her six fellow PSS captains, all of whom were on line. "A lot depends on what they'll do when they get here. If those blips *are* travelling bombs, they might break and attack at any angle the second we're in their sights. We need their specs to anticipate their tactics."

"A cloaked probe?" Azular suggested loudly.

"Bet he has one in his pocket," Apnis muttered as Ahxenta looked askance at her senior science officer and then back at the holo. "Forty minutes tops till they're on us," the first mate added softly.

"Do it!" the captain hissed irritably. "Buckle up, all!"

"Seems we've been told what to do," Bluejohn sniffed. "You took point at Skyrtek, Cinnabar, and you're still the most qualified to outface these scum. You up for it?"

"Will do," she assented as Azular called his probe en route and Gliss reported that the hostile line and angle of approach were constant.

Ahxenta glanced at the countdown to firing range set up by tactical. She would not discount a speed increase, she told her colleagues as she set her attack line. "We ready for advance. Link your guidance systems and follow us out, but keep distance. Helm, ready strut release and take us out on mark four by nine to holding point six two by eight. *Obsidian* and *Quarkstorm*, take port and starboard abeam; *Equinox* and *Zephyr*, cover our midline astern; *Pearl Shield* and *Tektite*, flank *Equinox* and *Zephyr*. On my mark… Mark!"

The ships slipped their traces and advanced to form a fighting wing, *Arianrhod* at point. Moving as one, the group set for the holding point, every ship at battle readiness. *Arianrhod's* tactical holo, filling the forr'ad bridge section, shifted to give the positions of the defenders – and the hostile taskforce, now a distinct wedge, on approach.

"Comms, keep links to ours open, and maintain lines to *Remia Cross* and all Web and Merkat defences. What have you got, Azular?"

"Probe almost at optimum; it *will* be picked up once it starts a scan, but I'll get their specs… twelve discrete blips! Most are destroyers, an old design. Refining data… Zukivianite-rich hulls; they've seen action as overall shielding's patchy – and absent on underside towards stern! No life signs thus far, but I get *huge* explosive capacity! Capturing data! Sending to grid… Mr Bellfish, get this out to all ships! Keep distance!"

"We've seen *that* design before, Cinnabar!" Bluejohn exclaimed. "So have you, Adhara, Jury!"

"Relics from Skyrtek," Djassi said grimly. "Repurposed as bombs."

"They got my probe!" Azular's voice was strident.

"Speed increasing, homing in… diverging into two wings!" Gliss called. "One's set for Merkat!"

"Get me *Remia Cross*! Ahxenta to Mocryst: I'm taking the wing on direct approach; request you mark the other. All ships, spread out and set for distance fire! We go in fast, but don't let them close in!"

"They've marked us! Incoming!" warned tactical as the acceleration pushed the crew into their seats. "Damn! convoy splitting, central and flanking! They want to cut through and past us!"

"Then we break and attack!" thundered Ahxenta as *Arianrhod's* hull plates rattled to deadly discharge. "*Equinox*, *Quarkstorm*, *Tektite*, set for beacon array nine and engage at will; *Zephyr*, *Pearl Shield*, take that blip on line for beacon twelve. *Obsidian*, you're with me for those incoming in a direct line. All ships break on my mark… mark!"

Dox instantly sent the ship into an upward spiral and spun down to mark the hostiles that Earbleat had set up in her sights. The weapons chief was barking orders to her gunnery crews and had called that she had prepped *Loki* to go on the captain's mark. A storm of fire burst against *Arianrhod's* hull as she sheared off to avoid a barrage of torpedo fire. Ahxenta held on grimly as she took in the grid.

"Helm, come about to one six mark two! Launch deflecting drones, wide spread! Earbleat, target that aft underside plate and send in long-range torpedoes! Dox, ready us to cut off at speed!"

Incoming fire rattled their shields as Earbleat let go a massive salvo, and then shrieked at Dox to get them out of range. The crew clung on as *Arianrhod* speared up and away, but the tail of a burst caught her and she slewed, her momentum throwing her into a clear patch of space.

"Hull breach!" Cottontail screamed. "Seal off the whole damn bay!" she bawled down her comm link. "The hell with the shuttles!"

The weapons chief was raging as she tied herself back in. "She's still alive! Request we send *Loki* in to finish her!"

Ahxenta, red-eyed with fury, took in the blazing hostile off her far side as Dox pulled *Arianrhod* back to an even keel. "No! Helm, get her in range of our aft torpedoes! Concentrated fire right down her throat!"

"Down her throat, aye! …Torpedoes away!" Earbleat roared.

"Where in hell's *Obsidian*?"

"It was her target exploding that caught us," Azular replied loudly as their adversary burst into stardust. "She's port of us and closing."

"*Zephyr* and *Pearl Shield* calling for aid!" Gliss interrupted. "Another blip's heading in to engage!"

"Helm, turn us about and get us to beacon twelve!"

The *Arianrhod* and the *Obsidian Sky* bore through an expanding flak field to make the locus where the smaller vessels were fending off two huge hostiles whilst trying to keep safe distance. One of the targets was afire, but set on a deliberate line past the beacon. Ahxenta, judging her position and that of the *Obsidian*, ordered Bluejohn in to assist the two and set her sights on the alien. With few long-range missiles left, she had no option but to order Earbleat to send *Loki* in and make it count. She could not risk the hostile making the outer reaches of the Web.

Guided unerringly, the projectile ate up the gap to its target. *Loki's* circular gun port, its beams focussing as a single deadly burst, shot a hole through the hostile's hull and screamed through it like a banshee. Earbleat, cursing, fired the self-destruct that sent her craft to oblivion. The outburst of light and fire lit the space off the Web's outer belt like an inferno, to fizzle into vast drifts of flak as the flames died.

"Got it, then," grated Apnis at the captain's side. "Where the hell *is* everybody? It looks like the day of reckoning out there."

"At least the Web seems to be intact from this angle," was the weary reply. "All stations, report in."

The worst damage for engineering was the hull breach. The shuttles in the wrecked bay were past repair, and three of Cottontail's crew had taken serious hurt. Similar was echoed across the ship. The casualty list was lengthening, Ahxenta noted bleakly. As reports came in, she took stock of her fellow vessels and made quick calls to their captains. Every ship had suffered damage, but their targets had been taken out. It was with surprise that she was hailed by another PSS. The *Kel'Torc*, heading past Kelpin, had been ordered in to assist and had fought with ISA and local ships over Merkat. After a rapid refit, her next mission would take her to Nexus, which had not been targeted, she told Ahxenta: the main hostile wing's sights had been set on Fivepoint, and as far as she knew, the outcome had been positive for the defending forces, as Captain Thal had sent in some of his ships.

"So the ISA and their petty chums owe him – and us," Apnis noted. "I see Merkat's got clean-up squads out already, though it'll take ages to clear the mess, even with help from the neighbours."

"Unless the local scavengers get wind of it," Box said. "So what else went down while our hands were full?"

That was a question on many lips, but the captain's priority was her own ship and crew. She was spared a call to Mocryst, as the captain of the *ISAS Remia Cross* linked in to tell the PSS vessels that the order had come in to stand down. She and the *Tenacity*, both minimally damaged, were heading to Alto Finglas: there had been a minor scrap at the ISA's HQ with a small fleet that had jumped off at Altina. The standing force at the base had dealt with it and were now dealing with the result. There had been no other incursions, as far as she knew.

"Bet the ISA will be combing the debris for usable bits and pieces," Box piped up brightly, as the captain acknowledged the news and the thanks that the ISA captain sparingly tendered, and cut the link.

She stretched. "We'll have to find a berth, as we'll be stuck here for the duration. All of us," she added as she gestured at the holo. "Contact Port Control, Bellfish, and request we be assigned a repair bay."

* * *

It was hours down the line before the captain could leave her post. The PSS vessels had been assigned premier repair bays, as had the other ships that had fought for the safety of Merkat. Although not expecting free refits, Ahxenta and her fellow captains hoped for favourable rates. Thanks to their actions, Merkat Three had been little damaged and the Web itself was practically unscathed.

"I'm for medbay to see our people," she told her first mate. "Here's the doc's list of essentials; if you get that sent out before you go off, it would be good. Her team are hard-pressed, but I don't know where we'd find a spare medic. I've heard zip of the result at Fivepoint, or how Thal and his people got on. And I've endless links to make."

"Not before you take a break," Apnis said firmly. "I'll give all our supply lists a once-over and send them out, and then I'll come and find you in medbay, and haul you by the ears if I have to."

"I'd like to see you try," was the grinning rejoinder.

Ahxenta found medbay in a state of orderly chaos, with Ma'Lappis as duty medic. Her report was succinct: she had sent Flintlock off for two hours rest, but the CMO was in her office; Oak was operating with nurse-tech Kelp as assist; and she had drafted in Parri Millet and every unhurt emergency aider aboard. She had five critical, eight serious and fifteen less acute cases; the latter would be let loose soon. The captain made her rounds, deeply conscious of the cost to her people.

"They'll be all the better for having seen you, Cap," a quiet voice at her elbow said as she made her way out.

"You're supposed to be off duty," she told Flintlock.

"I'm back. We all need a break, but it's not going to happen. Maybe we should get a holo-doc, like the *Moonstone*?"

"No way," Ahxenta said shortly. "Tallica and I are for the mess, and you're coming with us. I'll tell Ma'Lappis. No argument."

The mess was quiet, as most of the crew still fit were on repair and clean-up duties. The exhausted chief engineer hauled over for a coffee and a chat, her face still streaked with sweat, her fatigues looking like she had slept in them. She was shaking her head.

"We'll need new shuttles, Cinnabar; we'll not get scrap value for the two we lost. And the bay needs a total refit: grapples, tractors, consoles, inner plating... *And* the arrays on the outer hull. Azular's griping that one of his was hit. But if I must have Merkat dock-rats on my decks, I want security there as well," she said militantly.

"You'll get it," the captain assured her. "Our insurers are on the case, and the FMTE is aware. In fact, the local office contacted me."

"Top marks, then," Apnis approved. "Catch the TA doing that."

"The list's getting longer," Cottontail grated. "I sent you the bare minimum, as I'd other things on my plate. I'll have the update as soon as maybe. Gem's in medbay still, but reckons he'll be let out shortly, so he can handle it. This will be a long job."

"Don't I know it," groaned Ahxenta. "But we've seen worse before – after Kifferbuck, for one. We'll come through it."

"Naturally we will: we're the *Arianrhod*," the first mate smiled. "Any news from the rest of the PSS fleet out there, or our other buddies?"

"I've a stack of comms, but none tagged urgent. That's my next job," the captain sighed as she picked up her mug.

"Here he comes, and his look could sour milk," observed the chief MO as the senior science officer trundled over. "Hasn't been able to link to the *Moonstone*, then."

She was correct. In fact, Bellfish had been unable to link to any of Thal's fleet bar the *Kel'Torc*, Azular told them, but he had contacted his friend Zelujmar to get his story. The *Marjenna* had taken damage and would need repair locally before heading home, but an associate of her captain had told them more of Alto Finglas. Box had been partly right: a band of seven hostiles, tracked from Bissy onto the covert Lemon to Lartzeg Trine bypass by ISA listening posts, had jumped off at Altina to target the ISA's HQ. If they had assumed that the base had been left with few defences because of other attacks, they were mistaken: they had been cut to pieces.

"Listening posts that take in Bissy?" Ahxenta remarked. "That'll be news for Thal, if ever I can speak to him."

Once at her desk, the captain dealt with her inward comms. Many were from PSS captains in the zones beyond Alpha, but one came from her nephew, news of the strikes having made Letik. Another was from Zillah: there were three ISA warships in orbit around Freskat that had come from the Star Desert, having seen action in taking out two hostile bases that had been used to refit derelict hostile vessels. The latter had probably been in situ since before Skyrtek, the admiral surmised. From other news gleaned from ISA and elsewhere, most of the ships used in the attacks at the Web, Fivepoint and Alto Finglas had been remnants of the original hostile fleet. Minor clashes at Hervesta and Salt Three had been handled locally, but no others had been reported. From that, and scraps from her own contacts, Ahxenta inferred that Thal's people had not been the main targets, but doubts remained.

As she sat back and ruminated, there was a buzz at her door. She stretched her aching muscles and ordered the door open. It was Azular, who did not wait for permission to speak.

"The *Moonstone's* at Vreskota Two," he said. "She's with that novel ship with the fluid hull that we logged near Limekiln. And the *Peerless*, *Skelterrix* and *Trueheart* have left Fivepoint at high speed."

30: CHANGED DAYS

The *Half Moon in a Puddle* was hectic when Ahxenta and Apnis stepped in, Bluejohn and Stone behind. Ten days had gone since *Arianrhod* had settled into one of the best repair bays of outer nine, and she would be there for twenty more. Every head in the place turned, eyes approving. A faint murmur ran around the tables, and after a fractional pause, a handclap, followed by cheers, began.

"What in the name…" Ahxenta murmured.

"We're popular," Apnis noted. "Will all our people get this?"

Ally was at the bar, four frothing mugs ready. "We saw your shuttle leave *Arianrhod*, Captain," he addressed Ahxenta. "Welcome back. And you, Captain Bluejohn, Commander Apnis, Commander Stone. These are on the house. And so is every other one you have today."

"Why?" Tallica Apnis wanted to know.

"Because of what you did. You and the other Privates could've run and left us to that horde of alien scum, but you didn't. And we saw the mess of your ships when you got back, so you paid a heavy price. We're all grateful."

The four acknowledged the drinks and the cheers and turned back to their host. He wanted to know why the *Remia Cross* and *Tenacity* had left so rapidly, as not one of their people had come into his bar.

"Last time the ISA was in here when we were, Captain Kerrix fried a scanner that one of their officers was using to spy on us; Goldcriss of the *Matchless*, wasn't it?" Apnis snorted. "Myrtleberry was put out. They'll be back. Fur will fly once the *Moonstone* gets in, and Myrtleberry will be mightily peeved that her fancy taskforce was outfoxed."

"You what?" Ginger Stone exclaimed.

"Not here," the captain of the *Arianrhod* said. "We'll sit over there." she pointed to a wall table with a good all-round view. "We'll order at the menu-pad, Ally. You both eating here, Grey?"

"We will," he responded. "We need a break and the food in here is as good as it gets in the Web."

Ally, gratified, promised that their orders would be there as soon as chef could make them. Once at the table, Bluejohn waited only until the privacy screen settled, jammers were set and food was ordered.

"What's this about the *Moonstone* and that ISA taskforce?"

"*Moonstone* hauled into Vreskota ten days ago with that unidentified blip you picked up dropping out of the bypass between Limekiln and Torch Crux – the one with two ISA ships firing on it."

"You what!" Stone cut in. "*With* it?"

Ahxenta nodded. "It's not hostile: what it *is* I don't know, but Thal's got a stake it in. It was on a Starfall mission and on that route instead of the Twilight to Gemstone, as there'd been trouble on and near there, as we know: the *Moonstone* ran into part of it, as she'd been on a similar mission in Gamma. The ship sensed a hostile ahead and slowed to keep back, but then realised it had the ISA ships on its tail. The hostile either wasn't aware of it, or it had logged *us* and we were a priority. As it was uncrewed, its coding maybe kicked in, and it jumped after us."

"The unknown *did* get away from the ISA ships, then," Bluejohn said. "But why did they try to take it down if it wasn't hostile?"

"It was new tech, so they wanted it. They fired shots across its bows as it wouldn't respond to hails. It got away, but it was seen at Fivepoint. It was one of the ships Thal sent in, as he figured Nexus would be next if the hostiles beat off the ISA and the locals. Myrtleberry's quartet had been ordered in, and *they'd* heard of the blip. I don't know all the details, but I expect she tried her heavy-handed tactics on Thal's crews, so the blip made off with the *Moonstone* as escort – for Vreskota."

"You don't know all the details, Cinnabar," Bluejohn echoed as the privacy screen rippled to the entry of a waiter with their orders. "You seem to know most of them."

He waited until the screen had reformed before pressing for more. The tip had come from Lieutenant Zelujmar. The *Marjenna's* crew were calling home daily for news of the Vreskot ships that had seen action at Fivepoint, and the arrival of the *Moonstone* and her companion had raised curiosity. Both were in for repair, and knowing Azular's links to Captain Kerrix, Zelujmar had enquired, and alerted his friend. Azular's first reaction had been a fruitless attempt to raise the *Moonstone*. He had tried for two days. From other sources, he and Ahxenta had pieced out events. The *Peerless*, *Skelterrix* and *Trueheart* had followed in the wake of all the Starfall ships to Nexus, where they found the *Kel'Moth* and four heavy cruisers, but no sign of the *Moonstone* or the mystery ship. Thal had been tight-lipped over both.

"Standoff," Ahxenta said. "Myrtleberry couldn't risk a breach with him, given the help he'd given at Fivepoint, much less try to take him on at his own base. But that high-tech Norvallan science ship caught the *Moonstone's* ion trail, knew she *had* been there, and had a fair idea of her heading. It pointed to Marridan."

"I thought you said she'd made for Vreskota," Bluejohn broke in.

"Captain Kerrix isn't a fool: she laid a false trail. Word will have got to Myrtleberry by now, and she'll probably track her down; but it seems that the mystery ship is one of Thal's, or working with him or for him. And it's probably occurred to the ISA's upper strata that if they'd held off and asked nicely, Thal may have told them some of what they want to know. Now they've no chance," Ahxenta said tartly.

"No way would Thal pass on new tech, Cap," disagreed Apnis. "But Azular's not been able to find out more about the new ship, even if he did finally get a link to Captain Kerrix."

"She's wary; *I* called her and she wouldn't tell me about it. And the yards at Vreskota can't read much, she's too well-shielded, despite the hurt she took to her hull. Jedinlok of the *Marjenna's* mighty curious."

"*I'd* like a close look at her," Bluejohn admitted.

"You and me both, Cap," Stone agreed.

"You'll have a chance," Ahxenta told them. "They're heading here: secure as Vreskota is, it's no match for the Web. What they'll be *doing* when they get here, I don't know. Starfall's prolonging the mystery, for reasons best known to Thal. And I've no idea what their missions were. Azular couldn't persuade Captain Kerrix to spill."

"At least he's found his smile again," her first mate said. "They may be bringing in cargo: Vreskota and its colonies are agricultural, and it's a free port, always has been. So, no TA. But I wonder what happened to the *Mirk Arrow*. Lost in transit?"

She was interrupted by a shuffle and then the rising crescendo of a handclap. It heralded the entry of the veteran Captain Kurrin Tilius of the *Pearl Shield*, with the *Tektite's* Teal and Zoa Buckle in tow.

"Turning into an expensive day for Ally," observed Ahxenta as she watched the three being greeted and drinks poured.

Two topers sitting well back in a booth at the far end were equally observant. "Haven't see a credit slip cross a palm yet," Jurry sniffed. "I bet they haven't set up tabs either. What's happened to Dowris, or has she been left in charge of the *Pearl's* repairs?"

"Tilius has a limp and a hand-brace, so maybe," Malty replied. "But the Buckle twins got off with nary a scratch, from what I can see."

"Young and fit," was the morose reply. "Just like us, once."

The three spied their peers and made for the adjacent table. His first mate was improving, Tilius replied to Apnis. He had been in marketing to rearrange the *Pearl's* last contract. The others nodded: all had had to face rescheduling and contract loss, as well as repairs that insurers were classing as war damage and thus not insurable. At least the FMTE had intervened to demand justice, Teal Buckle noted bitterly. He had been able to call on family support, and the *Firedrake* was due in soon to take on the cargo he should have loaded several days before.

"Good news for Flish Ma'Lappis," Tallica Apnis said to her captain. "She'll get to see Flick and her father. And our chief engineer wants to visit the *Tektite* to see her son," she told Captain Buckle.

"Any time," he answered. "Though he's busy: two of our engineers took bad hits and main engineering's still a wrecker's paradise."

"Likewise," Ahxenta groaned. "Guild hasn't certified our breach as fit yet; Crizz'll have to hold fire until that's done."

"And we're two shuttles down, we're having trouble finding stores, and our medbay's just coping," Apnis added. "But we're all in the same fix: our chief medic says *Quarkstorm's* as bad. *Her* CMO had to send three of their worst hurt to the Web medbay; we were spared that."

"What's the racket at the holo?" Commander Zoa Buckle asked.

"Can't be the *Moonstone*," Apnis muttered. "She's not due for three or four days; or at least that's what we were told."

A trill at Ahxenta's wrist comm alerted her to news. She slipped her earpiece in and tabbed quickly to receive. Her reaction was explosive.

"What! Have you warned Captain Kerrix and Captain Thal?"

The reply reassured her. "Do *not* respond. Any of them tries a scan, you jam and send a protest. I'm on my way. Let's go, Tallica."

"Cinnabar, what in blazes is going on?" Bluejohn demanded.

"The *Matchless*, *Repulse* and *Advance* are on approach. Goldcriss has called in, asking for me. Last *I* heard, the *Matchless* and her mates were skirting the edge of Beta. They may have been recalled because of the action at Fivepoint, but I wouldn't put credit on it."

"Trying to find the mystery ship," Apnis hazarded. "They think the Web's a good bet, as they know the *Moonstone's* with it. They'll know already they're not here, but they know *we* are."

"Mystery ship?" Tilius asked. "The one you sent the alert on?"

"That's the one. Grey will update you… *on the QT*," she added in an urgent whisper as she collected her gear. "I'll settle later," she called to Ally on the way out, as she and her first mate set off at a fast pace.

"What was that all about, Jurry?" Malty demanded, startled. "Let's go see what they're all staring at over the bar. Or we could ask *them*."

"Not if you value your skin," his chum replied.

Their shuttle was close enough to reach easily, although by the time Ahxenta and Apnis reached *Arianrhod*, the three ISA ships had docked. Goldcriss had not tried to link again, but the second mate had every scanner at her disposal ready to use on the huge explorer-destroyer.

"Zip about her or her cronies on any ISA or other news feed. And not a mark on *her*," Earbleat said tersely as she quit the command chair. "Captain Goldcriss wanted to speak to whoever was in command in your absence, Cap. I didn't oblige."

"Roger that. She'll know I'm here now, as I'm damn sure she'll have tracked *Arianrhod Six* back up. And she'll be eyeing us up."

"Good call, Cap," drawled Apnis as the comms officer called that the *Matchless* was online and asking for her.

The captain sat down heavily. "Set all arrays to jam and scan if she tries anything, Gliss, Azular: her hull's chameleon, and her response plate and other gear may have been polished since last we saw her, as she's had contact with the *Skelterrix*. Get a visual, Bellfish."

"I bet we still have better gear that they do, and it rankles," muttered Apnis, as the sour face of Captain Kresta Goldcriss filled the grid.

The ISA captain asked for an update on the action since the *Remia Cross* and *Tenacity* had left. It was a spurious excuse, Ahxenta knew.

"I'm not an info-point. What do you really want to know?"

Goldcriss' eyes glanced to the side, where a profile of *Arianrhod* was obviously in her sights. "You've taken severe damage, but survived. As you did recently, when you were hit by an alien battleship with highly destructive limpet drones, so high-spec that they almost destroyed the *PSS Nyx Warrior*, some time before. How did you do it?"

"If the *Steadfast* and *Stalwart* had answered our distress, they'd have found out," was the waspish retort. "As it is, my hull and my tech are not your business, as I've told you before, Captain. Anything else?"

Goldcriss was angry but remained calm as she alluded to Ahxenta's Starfall allies. As the captain had expected, the ISA officer wanted all she could get on the *Moonstone's* location. Goldcriss also reckoned that Ahxenta knew more than she was telling about the alien but seemingly friendly mystery ship. Ahxenta was short. The *Moonstone* was a Starfall ship and as the ISA had links to Captain Thal, who *had* supported it at Fivepoint and elsewhere, she advised Goldcriss to contact him.

"Why do they keep it up, Cap?" Apnis asked as the captain of the *Matchless* linked off. "And I see they still have surface-scanners pointed at us. Best watch out they don't send out covert probes."

"Azular's got it covered," Ahxenta said grimly. "They do, we blast them and warn the whole Web about it."

"And send a protest to ISA HQ. We've not done it for a while, and we don't want them getting withdrawal symptoms."

"Stow it. But I won't risk talking directly to Kerrix about this, even with our new comms gear; I'll call Thal and he can do it."

"And the other PSS ships here: she might try it on them, though they know less than we do," the first mate advised.

* * *

The three ISA ships were still in the Web four days later. The captain, first mate and Lindell were in marketing, but with her ship well below par, Ahxenta knew her chances of landing a contract were nil. The Redship cargo she had been in talks over before the attack had been taken on by the *Cresset,* and she was already out. No other Privates had come in, but the *Nyx Warrior* was due and Nat Holdspan had linked days before to ask if the ships under repair needed items he could bring in on his way in from Berzic.

"That other Redship payload for Skoon is a good deal, but it needs moved quickly; we're in no fit state, nor are the other Privates here," the captain sighed as she flicked through her info-pad. "*Warrior* could take it on if Nat's got no other plans."

"We could suggest it to the reps. Nat's a good man," Apnis said. "You gave him the latest, I take it, when he called?"

"He knows what's here and why," replied Ahxenta. "He'll have our med-cradle in his hold and the stores Axellina wanted, so I'll hear from him when he docks. Back to base for us: the *Moonstone* and that other ship are still heading in, hell knows why. You can give the Redship reps the heads-up on the *Warrior* once we're aboard, Lindell."

The three made good time and the captain and first mate were in place well before the scheduled arrival of the two vessels. The first one to reach the Web was, however, the *Nyx Warrior.*

"Nat must have put a spurt on," Apnis said in surprise. "That'll be another PSS if those ISA ships start anything. Wonder if the *Matchless* knows what's riding in from the other direction?"

"Goldcriss will have been briefed," the captain said. "Nat will want to release his load and head down to the harbour office, but he'll have to be quick. None of our other ships have shuttles out."

She had hardly spoken when Bellfish announced Captain Holdspan on the comm. He would bring their shipment over on a shuttle on his way to the harbour office, if it was convenient, he told her. She agreed, and within an hour she was in the bay to receive it. Formalities were brief, and the young captain soon on his way again.

"He gave us the gear at cost," the captain told her mate. "Said it was in his way, as he'd kit to collect at Medi-Tech for Merkat. And yes, he put on speed to make it in before the *Moonstone.* He'd no trouble all the way from Delta Iridium, and he came in via Istrel Statice."

"Direct route, then," Apnis stated. "And I see unloading's begun. Sol Treskitt must be on it. Nat runs a tight ship."

Scarcely half an hour later, a comm told of the impending arrival of the two expected ships: they had jumped off the local node and would be in the Web in fifty minutes. Ahxenta ordered the news sent to the other PSS captains and sat back to wait.

"They're on approach," Azular warned half an hour later, picking out the shapes in the fully-extended bridge holo in a light ring.

"All stations, keep your eyes on them – and on the ISA ships," the captain directed. "Can we get any details on the unknown?"

"The PA *will* allow them to dock, I take it?" Apnis asked anxiously as they watched the two ships coming closer.

"I can't see why not. The *Moonstone's* known, she's a PSS, and she's carrying cargo, according to Thal."

"I read the *Moonstone*!" Azular called. "Her jammers are on line but her shields are down. I can't get a bead on the unknown; I suspect the PA won't allow her to dock without an ID. They're holding station off the outer beacon... What in the... she's dropped her hull camouflage! She's reading as a PSS!" he exclaimed.

"You what?" the captain demanded.

Azular gaped at his readings and then at the holo. He pulled up and enlarged the image of the ship. No bridge officer had seen such a shape before. She was a sleek, pale grey rhomboid, her hide flecked in silver, her midline bright violet. A layer of sparkly haze implied shielding and hid the extent and form of her hull arrays, which melted into her body as soft undulations across the surface. Gliss cried out that the *Matchless* had begun a scan, but even as he called, a ray shot out from the hull of the stranger towards the ISA vessel.

"I think she's neutralising the scan beams before they hit her hull," Azular said. "Definitely reading her as a PSS." He sounded shocked.

"Have we got a call-sign and name for her?" the first mate asked.

"Yes." The Berzic officer turned full round to face the command chair. "She's FMTE. The *PSS Cinnabar II.*"

"You *what*!" Ahxenta was stunned. "Any more?" she croaked.

"No ma'am; checking registers." He turned back to his post. "She's listed by the Telzilt FMTE and was registered as a PSS at Kirtish, under the Starfall banner."

"This gets weirder by the minute," Apnis whistled. "They're coming in: they've evidently been granted entry."

The docking procedures took an hour, as the berth assigned to the *Cinnabar II* had to adapt to a novel design. The *Moonstone* was at station-keeping sooner, and as her final struts moved into place, the watchers could see her outer cargo bays glowing as they prepared to open to the grapples that were already heading in for her cargo.

"Big stuff," the captain observed to her first mate. "Looks like silo pods, so maybe Vreskot grain."

"She wants done in a hurry. How long 'til a shuttle heads out to the harbour office? And what's Goldcriss at? She'll have something to say over that – whatever – that blocked her scans."

Ahxenta had other matters in mind, and as the grapples neared the *Moonstone's* hull, her eyes were drawn to her partner vessel. "That's her at station-keeping. Bellfish, send courtesy calls to the *Moonstone* and the *Cinnabar II*. Starfall," she mused. "But where was she built, and why? And who's in command?"

"Bet *you* can guess," Apnis said shrewdly but softly. "But how?"

"We might be about to find out," was the reply as Bellfish called that the *PSS Cinnabar II* was online requesting to speak to the captain.

"On grid, Lieutenant."

Ahxenta's eyes softened as the familiar features appeared. "Captain Ocean. It's been a while, ma'am. I see you have a new ride."

"Captain Ahxenta," Ocean said formally. "I do. The details I'll keep until we meet in person; soon, I hope. I have a cargo for you," she told her. "We can talk about that later too. I'm for the harbour office, and am heading there now, if I can keep those ISA eyes off my property."

"Good luck with that," Ahxenta smiled. "Cargo for me?"

Ocean smiled. "A shuttle; I hear you're two down. I've six aboard. They were for Nexus, but I didn't drop them, for various reasons."

"I know: the *Peerless*, *Skelterrix* and *Trueheart* were three," the captain replied. "Your ship's in good trim?"

"I had some of the damage I took at Fivepoint repaired at Vreskota, but she needs more. I'll get that done here. My repair drones are already patching minor scuffs on my hull – though I doubt even your scanners can pick that up."

A glance at Azular told Ahxenta that he was having trouble, and she grinned in response. "I'll let you settle in and link you later, Kelly."

"Roger that, Cinna. Ocean out."

"Whoa! A long story there; and she's giving us a shuttle? On whose say-so?" demanded Apnis. "What now?"

It was Captain Kerrix, also with little that could be said on an open link, but she had new micro-sensor units that might prove useful for *Arianrhod's* hull arrays. Before ISA's interest in the failed limpet-drone attack near Limekiln, her scientists had been working on the *Moonstone's* units, and had come up with an entirely new design as a replacement. It had proved effective in lab-scale trials.

Ahxenta looked quizzically at her opposite number, but agreed, and, her curiosity piqued, asked about the mission that had taken her across Lambda, Gamma and Beta zones, and her tie to Captain Ocean's ship.

The response was a shake of the head. "Later," she promised. "I've cargo to shift. And a delivery for you. A new shuttle." She linked off with a wink and a mischievous grin.

"Don't say a word, Commander Apnis."

* * *

Thirty six hours later, the captain shuttled down to inner two with her first mate and Azular. She had separate meetings with Captains Ocean and Kerrix. Marketing was chosen as the venue. *Arianrhod* had already received her new shuttles, both based on the *Gremlin's* design and from Starfall. She had found out from Ocean that the idea had been Kerrix,' and sanctioned by Thal. They had been destined for Nexus, along with the covert cargo that the two ships carried.

Ahxenta was not over-emotional, but her first sight of Kelva Ocean caused tears to well. "It's been a while," she said, giving her a hug and standing back to take in her uniform. "Come into the briefing room and tell me what you've been up to, that you've been avoiding me."

Azular and Apnis made themselves scarce, the former to seek out his partner, who was due shortly. The first mate had been introduced to Commander Oksev Torlist, Captain Ocean's first mate, and hoped to find out more about his ship as she showed him about the local area; he hailed from Rom Litra and zone Alpha was new to him.

Ahxenta was already on the topic of the *Cinnabar II*. Her design had been initiated years before by hostiles active in zone Psi, chiefly around Telzilt, Ocean told her. Such ships were wanted as large carriers for the human-like aliens rising to dominate the command structure. Lacking expertise, the hostiles had abducted a team of scientists and engineers from a Telzilt lab to refine and perfect the design. They had misjudged both the superior intellect and the obstinacy of the team – a team led by the Norvallan Dr Perti Posettix.

"They'd hidden the plans and all the data on the work to date, and destroyed everything in their lab and workshop – and remotely blown up the test ship being built to the new design – by the time they were caught. They were due for termination but were got out by a resistance unit. But the team had the data and some of them decided to carry on, to build a ship to fight the hostiles. It's been going on in secret during and since the war, but with limited materials, expertise and labour, only

489

one was built. I'd been assisting off and on, so I knew her ops. She'd become a bit of a redundancy, so I put in a bid for her, and got her."

"And named her for me," Ahxenta said. "There's another thing I'd like to know: you must have known *Arianrhod* was ahead of that hostile on the bypass to Limekiln…"

"Believe me, I did, Cinna. We'd logged the *Arianrhod*, but given the cargo I was carrying, I couldn't jump off to help, or even risk answering your distress. I'd a choice to make that I didn't want to, but I knew what was right, and I did it."

"What were you carrying?" the captain asked intently.

Kel Ocean smiled sadly. "A group of Starfall's children, and their carers – and others."

"What! Why? To where?"

"To a site it was hoped was safe. Starfall's no place for kids, and its base at the edge of Delta had drawn attention. The *Moonstone* had some too. We took separate paths, as she'd a diversion to Sheel Four with a few of them. On the way back to Reddik Well, she logged hostiles off Coral; and other reports were coming in that meant trouble. Starfall was put on alert and I made for Nexus via Linza and Jurassa. I passed the kids over to one of Captain Dun's fleet ships…"

"Via *Linza*? An ISA base?"

"Would you have expected that?"

"Knowing you, yes," Ahxenta smiled. "They're safe, the kids?"

"They're safe. And here I am. And you're wondering why Starfall rather than totally independent."

The captain of the *Arianrhod* could only nod.

"I've been on my own, flying by the seat of my pants for too long, Cinna. I *and* my crew need something to belong too. We're all victims. The groups in Psi are too disparate, with agendas that don't run parallel to mine. Not that Thal's does, fully; but he's a good man, he looks after his own, he's got more guts than most and he doesn't give up; stubborn as hell, in fact. And I don't belong in Psi. I want to see familiar places. Oh, I know it'll never even remotely be the same, but there it is. You've done well, Cinna. You're like your father, you know: tough as an old boot, and shrewd, but with a soft side under the prickles."

"Thanks."

"The sarcasm you get from your mother: *she'd* a sharp tongue."

"Thanks again."

"Welcome. That's one of the reasons I named my ship for you; she's unique and stroppy, just like you," Kel Ocean smiled.

"You're getting soppy in your old age, Kelly."

"And you're not? I know what happened after the *Wing Skipper* was lost; and after Rede and Jo were killed. You took on their son, provided for him, made your own way. And now you've two ships to your name. I've met the *Emerald's* captain – a good asset there. And when I'm gone, you'll have more: I'm leaving the *Cinnabar II* to you. I know you'll take care of her and her crew…"

"You're *what?*" Ahxenta was thunderstruck. "A *Starfall* ship? Why? And what in blazes will I do with a Starfall ship?"

"You'll cope, Cinna. And because I look on you as family. I thought I'd no-one after the *Wing Skipper*, and never would; and now I've found you. You'll have the *Cinnabar* as well: she's under overhaul at Starfall, and I'll register her as a PSS. Don't let it bother you for now: I've no intention of hanging up my uniform just yet. But let's see where our first mates are. And you've a meet with Captain Kerrix. She's a puzzle."

"She's a pain in the butt," was the dry rejoinder. "But as she's tied to my senior science officer, I'm stuck with her."

"Guess who's docked," Apnis greeted the two as they emerged.

"Not Myrtleberry?" Ahxenta demanded.

"No, thank hell. But the *PSS Tallulah's* now in orbit, shiny as a new pin, and no doubt looking to trade, as a shuttle came out of her. Azular and Captain Kerrix are over there. He looks like he's struck gold."

"I've other business, so I'll leave you to it," Captain Ocean declared. "You're with me, Oksev. I'll see you again shortly, Cinna."

"Count on it, Kelly."

Apnis watched the two walk off. "Torlist told me that the *Cinnabar* is refitting as a Starfall carrier. And the paint and call-sign jobs on our new shuttles are done. Earbleat's pleased. So's Goldwash, as he can get his guys back to their real jobs: riding shotgun on dock-rats is no fun. And half the crew want shore leave. When do *we* hit the *Half Moon?*"

"When I'm done with Captain Kerrix. I want to shout at her about a couple of things."

"The new hull micro-sensor units and what else?"

"Later."

"I'm hearing that a lot lately. Are you all right, Cinnabar?"

"Yes I am, Tallica. Been a bit of a ride, but yes," she smiled.

"Did you tell Captain Ocean that you plan to name one of our new shuttles the *Kelva?*" Apnis persisted.

"No; it'll be a surprise. But here's Kerrix… Xanna," she greeted her opposite number. "Ready for a chat?"

That chat took slightly longer than the one-to-one with Kel Ocean, but both women looked cheerful when they finally reappeared. Azular had been going over the plans for the new design of micro-sensor units with Apnis. They had been developed by Ter Kinnitix, Perti Posettix and Cor Lymnik, with long-range input from engineers at Metriklon, and he was looking forward to receiving a small batch.

"Juke Spickle was in with the *Tallulah's* supercargo, but he didn't say a lot," the first mate told them. "Fleetskup and Buntle are elsewhere: *Half Moon*, I bet. One of *your* crew's been by, Captain," she smirked at Kerrix. "Admiral Posettix. His uniform's not one I've seen before: all pips and stat bars. Do you call him admiral?" she asked curiously.

"Amongst other things. It dawned on us that a PSS *admiral* might be a way to scupper the ISA captains that think they're superior to the likes of us. And Norvallans *do* seem to figure a lot more in ISA circles."

Apnis grinned wickedly. "Interesting. It strikes me that someone else has enough clout to be called admiral: Captain Vexin Thal."

"Can I be there when you suggest it?" Kerrix responded.

"It *would* differentiate him from his brother, now that the *Firestorm's* a PSS. As is half the Starfall fleet," Apnis added. "Is there still deadlock at Nexus?" she continued in a low voice, looking at both.

"We discussed it," Ahxenta replied. "Myrtleberry and her band are heading this way: they met the *Mirk Arrow* at Fivepoint, whatever *she'd* been at. But there's no reason to assume they're for the Web."

"I'd say there were plenty reasons to assume that, Cap. How many of our fleet are in? Twelve with the *Tallulah*? She, the *Warrior,* and the *Moonstone* are the only ones fit, but the *Firedrake's* due. With those three ISA boats here still, place'll be busier than Cygilla Prime Resort-Dorm at peak party season," she grumbled.

"Myrtleberry has better things to do," the captain replied. "Get back to her HQ and shake up her fleet, Admiral Best for one: *he* ordered the *Steadfast* and *Stalwart* to fire on Captain Ocean's ship and take it out if it didn't respond to hails. Thal found out from a contact and faced her with it at Nexus. Naturally he wouldn't tell who told *him*, and that's got her furious, figuring she's got a leak in her own backyard."

"More than one, I bet," said Apnis, as the four turned to leave.

Admiral Posettix and Jesse Inks were at the *Half Moon's* bar. Several ISA people had been in, Ally told them after greetings. The *Cinnabar II* was the hottest topic: no-one had seen a ship like her and rumour was rife. And she had been linked to the *Arianrhod*, Ally hinted delicately. Ahxenta gave him a quizzical stare.

"Only that your crew knew more than most, and *she's* Starfall," he said hastily, pouring drinks. "She lent a hand at Fivepoint, Commander Inks said. But now these ISA guys are here and asking questions about her. And why there are a lot of Privates in."

"There are a lot of cargoes to shift," Apnis said airily. "And as many of the Privates in dock were damaged defending the Web, they're not fit. And the FMTE – our trades body – has an office here."

The two pairs of eyes in a dark corner booth that had been looking closely at the group by the bar now flitted to the door of the *Half Moon*.

"What d'you reckon to those two, Jurry?" Malty said. "I don't know the faces, but they're wearing PSS uniforms. One's a captain, but I can't make out her badge from here, though they both look to be veterans. Like the guy in the flashy PSS uniform, whatever he's meant to be; but I swear I've seen his face before. *Where?*" he demanded squinting.

Jurry chewed it over. "I've got it! *He's* the guy that arrested Captain Kerrix last year, isn't he? But why are they now best buddies?"

"You *could* ask, but I don't recommend it. We'll find out…"

Ahxenta, spying Ocean and Torlist, hailed them. Introductions to Ally over, she led the group to a table away from Fleetskup and Buntle. Privacy set, the talk began with a caution from Ocean: she and her first mate, while visiting the FMTE office, had been waylaid by Tranger of the *Advance*, quizzed, and a bid made to scan the captain. The FMTE staff had intervened and sent a protest to ISA HQ.

"That'll do little, Kelly," Ahxenta told her. "The ISA thinks it's got policing rights in every sector of the mapped galaxy, and most of its fleet captains exercise them when they feel like it."

"Maybe they get brownie points," Apnis said facetiously.

She was interrupted by the buzz of incoming links to Ahxenta and Kerrix. Both captains took them by earpiece.

"I guess we got the same message," the *Moonstone's* captain said.

They had: the *Peerless*, *Skelterrix*, *Trueheart* and *Mirk Arrow* had come off the local node and were on a line to the Web; and shuttles had left from the inner belts to the *Matchless* and the *Advance* and were docking. *Arianrhod's* first mate excused herself with the promise that she would be back directly. She was gone only minutes.

"Kit Biernop," she said briefly. "Dockers' Guild has *not* been alerted by the PA to stand by for incoming, though that's no guarantee they won't ask to berth. He'll alert me if that changes."

The next news came from the *Cinnabar II*: all three ISA ships in port were heating engines, a sign of intention to depart, but the wary Ocean warned her duty officer that the *Skelterrix* might come close enough to attempt interference.

"Back aboard for us," Kerrix ordered her people. "If she tries, I'll set the admiral on her. He knows her captain: Nilkillid, isn't it?"

"It is," Posettix agreed. "A hard liner, but an honest one."

Word had spread and there was a general exodus as PSS crews were recalled. Ahxenta, Apnis and Azular reached their ride, to a note from Earbleat that the *Nyx Warrior* would hold until the situation resolved. It took them twenty minutes to reach the ship, by which time the four new arrivals had made the Web and were standing off. Ahxenta raced for her bridge, the other two behind.

"*Matchless*, *Repulse* and *Advance* are prepping to leave," Earbleat said as she vacated the command chair. "*Firedrake's* on the way in. Tactical and science are keeping tabs, but nobody's tried anything yet."

"Myrtleberry not said hello?" the first mate asked.

"No, ma'am, nor anyone else. But *Cinnabar II*, *Moonstone* and *Kel'Torc* have increased jamming."

"Sending a message," the captain surmised. "But what's that on grid? It's not the *Firedrake*."

Azular smiled over from his station. "It's the *PSS Firestorm*, ma'am."

"That'll be our Metriklon units from Starfall – Thal *did* promise."

"He was quick off the mark," Apnis commented. "But those three *are* readying to move out. Given up on us, then."

"Looks like. Or trouble at home," said Ahxenta.

"There will be, once Myrtleberry gets in."

The bridge crew followed the action as the three huge ISA ships cut struts and made for free space, to join the group off station. An hour later and the flotilla was gone, its line implying ISA HQ. None of the ships had attempted contact with or interference of the PSS ships. The *Nyx Warrior* was the next out, just as the *Firestorm* arrived. As Ahxenta had surmised, *she* carried the promised stock of comms units.

"Busy times," the first mate noted as a new dot on the grid heralded the *Firedrake*. "She won't stop long: a pick-up of the *Tektite's* load."

The next hours were taken up with cargo transfer amid ongoing repairs to ship's structure. The *Firestorm* had also brought arms stores for the *Kel'Torc*, some of which Ahxenta was able to claim, and Earbleat was quick to bag the huge Starfall cargo pod as soon as it arrived in the outer bay, to make a start on a replacement for *Loki*.

"All we need now is Azular to ask for time off ship to see his other half," Apnis told the captain as they ran over schedules.

"He'll see her when he ships over to pick up the new micro-sensor units. And then he'll be busy with Crizz on their fitting, once those repair crews are off my hull. Ma'Lappis will want to see Flick and her father, but they can come over with their SSO and comms officer to get the specifics on the new comms units – Pa's sent a note about it."

"Word's getting out; and now Starfall's part of the PSS family, Thal will be the main source, and he's no slouch at arranging things. How long until the entire fleet has them, Cap?"

"Not long; Starfall ships cross every galactic zone and they can deal with distribution. No captain yet has refused them. The ISA will know we've got a fix for the UV-III, as it'll be intercepting zip comms. And then there's the clean-up after this last spell of alien action, including its own backyard. Another reason for recalling its ships."

"The Alliance will never totally stop the aliens," Apnis reckoned. "From here on in, it'll be busy scouting for likely hidey holes to prevent future surprise attacks, which should keep it off our backs."

"Give it time," the captain replied ironically.

* * *

The shiny new shuttle *Kelva* settled into her berth on level four of inner two. The captain was at the helm: this was her first foray in the craft, but the controls were similar to the *Gremlin's* and she had no problem piloting. The *Arianrhod* was almost herself again, and Lindell had set up a contract session. She had her first mate and senior science officer with her. Azular wanted a quick meeting, for the *Moonstone* was due out in twelve hours and this was a final chance to see his wife before she left for Starfall. Ahxenta had said her goodbyes to Captain Ocean: the *Cinnabar II* had left two days before on an unspecified mission that the captain strongly suspected was related to Vexin Thal's continual quest for his missing people. Several PSS ships had come and gone, and the vast port of Merkat was slowly returning to its usual busy buzz.

Apnis was still chuckling over news from Admiral Zillah of shake-ups at the ISA's head office on Alto Finglas. Two senior staff had been dismissed and locked up, and many had been reassigned. One of the latter was Admiral Best. *He* had been appointed as Fleet Advisor to the expanded Interstellar Systems Alliance, and was on his way to a plush new office in Lixtalla, the main city of the First Continent of Norvalla.

"Our reps are waiting for us," Lindell stated as he came up, having seen them the second they made marketing. "Standard heavy gear for Selliden, and we have first dibs, but I saw the *Nyx Warrior's* supercargo with one of Redship's other reps, so she got in fast."

"I'll say: *Warrior* docked only an hour ago," the captain said.

The talks were as swift as the senior science officer had hoped, and with one solid deal under her belt, Ahxenta was content to make for the *Half Moon*, halting only to alert her ship to the cargo spoken for and order her loading teams to begin on prepping the bays.

Ally spotted them as they came through the door. "Haven't see you in a while, Captain," he greeted her, fishing up a fistful of mugs.

"Put those on my tab, Ally," the voice of Grey Bluejohn called from further along the bar. "Talks go okay, Cinnabar?"

"They did. Nice to be back to near-normal," she greeted him, her eyes lighting. "*Obsidian* must be about ready to move out."

Bluejohn nodded. "We are. I'll be locked down by sixteen hundred and we'll be out soon after. Shouldn't take us more than ten days; we may be back this way, but it depends on what trade we can pick up."

"Quite a few Privates are set to move out," Ally cut in. "*Quarkstorm's* on her way and *Tallulah* won't be far behind, Commander Spickle said, when he and the captain were in earlier. Don't see much of Mr Buntle these days," he added, grinning. "Tied to his desk, apparently."

"How's Juke Spickle managing that? Restraint cords?" Apnis asked.

"He's certainly found his feet," the *Obsidian's* captain laughed. "And here's the team from the *Moonstone*. They were set to argue with the TA over the attack on Captain Kerrix at the Residency, Jesse Inks told me. The employee implicated was charged, but got off with a slap on the wrist: supervisory order, but free to return to work."

"That'll help the TA's rep," Ahxenta said cynically, saluting the new arrivals. "Best find a seat: every eye in here's turned this way."

"It's that uniform," Apnis murmured in her ear, cocking an eye at Admiral Posettix, who had come in with Kerrix, Inks and Levettiza.

Azular's eyes had lit up, and he called Ally for more ale. He quickly captured a place at his partner's side as the group made for a large table. The *Moonstone* was for Starfall, but trade would bring her back to the Web, she told him. As for the TA, Dettis Banyotty had been arrogantly unapologetic. The reckoning was on its way: Captain Thal's ongoing battle with the TA and the ISA over their blatant attempts to misuse Starfall bypasses had led him to consult the FMTE and other agencies, and with Admiral Posettix on legal issues, he had registered many of the bypasses his fleet used with the Exchange, as free trade routes for all shipping. That body had agreed to maintain and support the new resources for the general good. The upshot would be a greater toehold in the original mapped zones for the FMTE, and probably drastically curtail the use of TA-run routes.

"So how many on the PSS register are now with the FMTE instead of the TA?" Apnis asked the table at large.

"All of them," Levettiza replied. "I got it from someone who was trying to prise details out of *me* about our affiliation." She nodded at her captain. "They got zip. The TA's wetting itself."

"Here's to free trade then, Cap," her first mate said to Ahxenta.

"That'll be the day, Tallica. Nothing's free but trouble, and you can bet there's still plenty out there with *Arianrhod's* name attached."

In the deepest depths of the *Half Moon*, two pairs of eyes were taking in the haze around the distant table.

"It's good to see things getting back on an even keel round here, Jurry," Malty observed to his drinking partner, indicating the group beyond. "But the changes! The Trades Alliance has been told to go hang by half its registered ships and there's an admiral in the PSS fleet!"

"You're right there, Malty: Captain Ahxenta's hand shields are out of sight, and there's nary a body on the deck with an imprint of her left hook in their jaw. The Web will never be the same again."

FINIS

ABOUT THE AUTHOR

SANDI CAYLESS is the author of the *Pirates' Web* books: *Arianrhod*; and *Arianrhod's War*; the Mars-based *Sub Martis* series: *Dome Lowell*; *Dome Beagle*; and, *Starship*; and the novella: *The Ghost of Glow-Worm Alpha*. Her poem, *Ghost Walkers*, is included in: *Futuredaze: An Anthology of YA Science Fiction*.

www.submartis.com

www.sunskerrypress.com